Carlos Rubio

Forgotten Objects

Editions Dedicaces

FORGOTTEN OBJECTS

OTHER WORKS BY CARLOS RUBIO:

- Caleidoscopio
- Saga (Finalista, Letras de Oro 1993)
- Secret Memories/Recuerdos secretos
- Quadrivium (Premio Internacional de Novela Nuevo León, 1989)
- Orpheus' Blues
- Orisha
- Hubris
- American Triptych (The Neophyte/Bullwhip/California Fever)
- Dead Time/Tiempo muerto (Foreword's Magazine Book
 of the Year Award 2004)

Published by:
 Editions Dedicaces LLC
 12759 NE Whitaker Way, Suite D833
 Portland, Oregon, 97230
 www.dedicaces.us

Library of Congress Cataloging-in-Publication Data
 Rubio, Carlos
 Forgotten Objects / by Carlos Rubio.
 p. cm.
 ISBN-13: 978-1-77076-417-0 (alk. paper)
 ISBN-10: 1-77076-417-8 (alk. paper)

Carlos Rubio

Forgotten Objects

I would like to express my
gratitude to Jorge Finlay for his
patience and invaluable suggestions.

About the Author

A native of Cuba, Carlos Rubio came to the United States in 1961 and finished high school in Wilmington, Delaware. He holds a BA degree from Concord College and a MA degree from West Virginia University.

A bilingual novelist, in Spanish he has written *Caleidoscopio*, *Saga*, *Orisha* and *Hubris*. In 1989 his novel *Quadrivium* received the Nuevo León International Prize for Novels. In English he is the author of *Orpheus' Blues*, *Secret Memories* and *American Triptych*, a trilogy of satirical novels. In 2004 his novel *Dead Time* received Foreword's Magazine Book of the Year Award. He recently finished writing a memoir entitled *Dancing with Ghosts*.

To Marisa, who
never ceases to amaze me.

Book One: Italy

I

No one was surprised when Anna d'Amio agreed to marry Harold Wilson, a man many years her senior and not particularly good looking. Sole heir to a fortune whose origins could be traced to the steel mills around Pittsburgh, his wealth and social connections still made him, in the eyes of many, a great catch.

The unexpected announcement was received with dismay among his friends and acquaintances. He was, after all, a wealthy and influential industrialist who moved in the highest circles of society; she was a stranger whose fortune — or rather, her late husband's fortune — was nothing but a remote memory from a distant Caribbean island. Her only assets were her physical beauty, now clearly beginning to decline, and an innate charm that men found irresistible due in part to her indefinable accent whenever she spoke English. Ann d'Amio, they all agreed, was a social climber. Deep down, however, she knew that Harold's fortune had not played a role in her decision to marry him. How his friends felt about her was completely irrelevant. In many ways, Harold was no different from Giacomo or Ramón, her previous husbands. She had given each his due — as she was fully prepared to do with Harold — socially, emotionally and sexually — but without ever crossing that indelible line that had been traced so early in her life, a line that clearly separated her from the rest of the world. Whether this attitude had been learned or inherited made no difference; Anna could not remember a time in her life when this demarcation had not been present.

Having been born just after World War I and growing up under Mussolini's rule, she had developed a sharp awareness of her place in the world and the inescapable fact that ultimately she was responsible for herself.

She lived then, with her mother Francesca and older brother Guido, in a small house in a rundown section of Naples. Somehow, it seemed that there was never enough food; their next meal was always an uncertain proposition underscored by growing rumors of an impending war. At that time in her life, Anna was too young to comprehend or even care about the political situation, since it was all beyond the scope of her immediate reality.

Francesca, a slender woman now showing signs of premature aging, did the best she could to care for her children. She made sure that their clothes, although well-worn and mended, were always clean. Early every morning, after a meager breakfast, she would walk them to school and then go into the city to work as an apprentice in a seamstress shop. Sometimes she took in laundry in order to earn a little extra money. Even though life was hard, Anna remembered her mother singing arias from the most popular operas as she tirelessly scrubbed the piles of laundry in a cement sink inside a small courtyard or cooked dinner for the family. This was one of the few occasions that Anna remembered her mother smiling; inexplicably, the music rescued her, if only momentarily, from the life of drudgery and hardships that she was living. Through it all, however, she never complained.

"One day all this will be a memory," Francesca would often tell her children during their simple meals. "You can go as far as you like, be anything you like. Just don't allow life to distract you from your goals." Perhaps this was a subtle allusion to the disappointments she had endured in her own life. As a young woman she had dreamed of a bright operatic career, of a triumphant debut in La Scala. In her case, because of her gifted voice and willingness to work, such a dream had been not only justified, but well within her reach.

It did not take long for her parents — opera lovers themselves — to recognize the potential in young Francesca. Encouraged by friends and relatives, they enrolled their daughter in the oldest bel canto school in the city. Many of the singers that appeared with regularity in the San Carlo Theater had had their humble start there, under the watchful and stern tutelage of signore Frondizi, a confirmed bachelor who had devoted his life, with the aid of a widowed sister, to the vocal development of aspiring singers. Every year he sent his most promising pupils to auditions that resembled, because of their convoluted rules and baroque procedures, clandestine enclaves whose ultimate purpose was the election of a new pontiff.

The judges, usually a coterie of middle-aged men whose infallible ears never failed to detect incipient stars, sat impassively in an ample chamber whose windows were partially occluded by thick and musty drapes. After a few rounds of espresso abundantly laced with anisette, they got down to business. The de facto leader of the group would ring a small silver bell, signaling that they were ready for the first audition.

Led by an austere looking woman dressed in black, the candidate was escorted into the chamber. The semicircle of chairs faced the door, so the faces of the men were always enveloped in shadows. The young singer, on the other hand, as he or she faced the men, was bathed by the unavoidable light that came in through the windows. The committee was interested not just in a disembodied voice, but in the facial expressions and body language as well. Every detail was important, every nuance worthy of scrutiny.

After a period of brief questions, they allowed the aspirant to intone the operatic section of his or her choice — usually an aria—while they listened attentively and studied every gesture. Throughout the performance the group never gave any signs of either approval or dislike, but maintained Sphinx-like expressions on their faces. Once concluded, they simply thanked the singer and excused him from the chamber. It was then that, invoking the esoteric rules of the ancient canons, they would comment on the merits and weaknesses of what they had just heard. Usually they were in agreement if the candidate deserved a recommendation to one of the operatic companies. Such a recommendation, obviously, was an assurance that a position on stage would be secured. Those students whose performance had not made the necessary impact, would receive through their teachers an envelope containing the succinct message: 'Find another career.' There were no appeals; a subsequent attempt the following year was not permitted.

The parade of aspirants, underscored by the bell and expertly ruled by the austere looking woman, continued uninterruptedly for most of the morning. Everyone was kept in the dark; the news, either good or bad, would be delivered through their bel canto instructors.

Eventually, young Francesca found herself alone in the waiting room, surrounded by a sundry collection of antiques, old paintings and busts of famous musicians who stared at her with their blind eyes. Through the closed door she had heard every performance and mentally had given each a grade. She could tell, with a fair degree of certainty, who would be recommended and who would not; she had recognized all the signs. Signore Frondizi had taught her well.

The muffled sound of the silver bell reached her through the door. A few moments later the same waxen looking woman appeared; her eyes, Francesca noticed, were as lifeless as the expression on her face. If she ever had any dreams, they had surely died long ago.

"It is your turn," she said to Francesca with a voice completely devoid of emotion.

The chamber where the men sat, because of the high position of the sun at this hour, was inundated with light, but the shadows below the windows seemed denser.

"And what do you have for us today?" asked one of the men.

"With your permission," she said in a clear and decisive tone, "I would like to do an aria from *Carmen*."

At once a faint whispering emerged from the members of the committee. Although not a written rule, it was customary for the applicants to perform selections from Italian operas.

"Proceed," said the same voice after a few moments.

Francesca closed her eyes and took a deep breath. She began to sing *Les tringles des sistres tintaiment*. Her mezzosoprano voice filled the chamber, almost dispersing the semidarkness in which the group of men resided. There was purpose, clarity and complete assurance in her delivery, denoting a musical maturity usually not found at such early age. When she concluded the presentation, the men remained silent for a few moments, then one of them rang the silver bell. The same middle-aged attendant appeared, ready to escort Francesca out of the chamber.

"Wait outside, please," asked one of the men. This was un-usual; the students were always dismissed after their auditions.

After fifteen minutes of waiting in the next room, wondering why she had been asked to stay, the sound of the bell was heard again. The sour assistant materialized and for the second time led her into the performing chamber.

The assembled men had not moved from their chairs; the same voice as before addressed her again.

12

"We were most intrigued by your choice," he said, "Could you do something else from the same opera for us?"

Apparently, during their period of discussion, there had been dissenting voices; they now wanted to make sure that what they had heard was not a one off performance before recommending the student to one of the opera companies.

Although puzzled, young Francesca was no longer nervous. Carmen had always been one of her favorite operas and she was fully prepared to comply with the committee's request. Mentally she decided on *Habanera*, a lively and popular aria with a light melody.

Just as she had done the first time, she began her delivery with conviction and control and, most important, with a gusto that was contagious. Her love for the music showed with every note. Although she could not see the anonymous faces of the men in the chamber, she sensed that her performance was indeed hitting the mark. After the last note vanished in the musty air, there was sudden silence and then subdued whispering.

"Thank you," said the same voice, while ringing the silver bell, "You may go now." That was all; there had been no outward signs of how her encore performance had been received. The door to the waiting room opened, and she was escorted out by the attendant. All she could do now was wait.

The following afternoon, just as she had done for several years, she knocked on the door of signore Frondizi's academy. She did not intend to miss her lesson just because she had had a promising audition the day before.

Signore Frondizi himself answered the door. This, in itself, was unusual, since it was his sister who took care of the student traffic in the academy. Often a student had to sit in a waiting room for a few minutes while another pupil finished the lesson for the day or went over a difficult section of a libretto.

The ample smile on his face did not allow room for doubts as to the results of the audition. The students were never contacted directly. This communication, however, sometimes took as long as a week. Stepping aside, he invited his pupil to come in.

"Tell me about the audition," he asked, just wanting to hear the account from Francesca herself.

She recounted her visit, the long wait in the anteroom and how she had been asked to stay and then sing for a second time. All the while signore Frondizi shook his head affirmatively and smiled.

"So our plan worked," he said. "I knew that we were taking a chance, but I also knew that they could not help but be impressed by your performance. Besides, that bunch was in need of some fresh air anyway," he commented with a smile.

"I am glad it is over," said Francesca. "I tried to control my nerves, but it was most difficult. I heard all the other singers and some were quite good."

"That will never change," offered signore Frondizi. "In fact, the competition is going to get a lot tougher. Until now, you have been surrounded by students who aspire to be singers. In a matter of weeks, you will be asked to join a production, probably at the San Carlo. Once that happens, everyone around you will be a professional. You will be expected to acknowledge that fact and also to conduct yourself as such. What I am trying to say is that you will be challenged like never before."

"I understand," said Francesca in a voice that was almost a whisper.

"But now," said Signore Frondizi suddenly changing his tone of voice, "let's start with you lesson for today."

By the end of the month, signore Frondizi's words had become a reality. Francesca was asked to join one of the established opera companies in town. And just as her mentor had predicted, the work increased proportionally to the talent of the performers. Most were young, eager and unknown singers hungry to make a name for themselves in that often unstable but always exhilarating world. Eventually, if they got a lucky break, they would move onto the stage of the companies that toured the world. Despite their youth, their focus did not wane from the common goal of honing their craft to the best of their abilities.

Among the new talent was a young man by the name of Louis d'Amio. Although neither of them knew it yet, he was to play a pivotal role in Francesca's life. Of French descent, as his name clearly indicated, he had been raised in a family whose musical tradition reached back several generations. Louis had never questioned his path; his goals had been clearly defined since an early age. His rich but controlled baritone voice had caught the attention of several directors; his good looks and innate charm were just added bonuses to the package.

These attributes, along with his aforementioned willingness to work as long and as hard as necessary in the pursuit of a perfect performance, had earned him a leading role in an upcoming production of *The Marriage of Figaro*. Some dissenting voices in the company commented in private that he was still too green to tackle the role of Figaro, but the decision had already been made.Only time would tell if Louis could handle such an important part.

Francesca was cast in the role of Susanna, Figaro's future wife. Once again, the same anonymous voices concurred that she was too inexperienced to undertake such a major part, that it should be played by a more experienced performer.

On the first night, all doubts were completely dispelled and all objections abruptly silenced. Despite the obvious opening night jitters, once Louis and Francesca came on stage they were not playing a part, but in essence they became Figaro and Susanna. All the hours of practice, combined with their natural talents, were showcased on the stage. From the start the audience was mesmerized; they realized immediately that they were in the presence of an artistic combination that was not likely to be repeated any time soon.

When the curtain came down, there was a standing ovation. Moments later, it rose again and the members of the cast, beginning with the minor roles, appeared again. When Louis and Francesca came out, the round of applause intensified.

With each passing performance, the accolades — both from opera aficionados as well as serious critics — became more profuse. It seemed as if every night they infused their roles not just with their masterful execution and delivery of the music, but also with the attraction that the characters felt for each other.

Almost overnight they became local celebrities. As a means of publicizing the theater, and simultaneously furthering their careers, they often appeared in public together. In the mind of the public they were Figaro and Susanna, not Louis and Francesca. Invariably, small crowds gathered to shake their hands, introduce their children or ask for an autograph.

Perhaps it was inevitable that the Art they portrayed on stage should be reflected in their personal lives. They were both young, good looking and possessed a zest for life. They also spent much of their time together, both off and on stage. What had started out as a scripted romance, soon turned into a real one. The intensity of their passion competed favorably with that of the characters that had brought them together. On or off stage, they could not get enough of each other.

Towards the end of the season, the exuberance of youth triumphed over common sense: they decided to marry. Louis was barely twenty-one; Francesca was in her late teens. They were aware that if they made their plans public, they would encounter instant opposition from family and friends. Everyone expected them to refine their craft and continue in an upward trajectory in that often unstable but most fulfilling operatic world. Not to do so would amount to squander their God given talents.

Soon after their decision was made, while sharing a bottle of robust wine punctuated by passionate kisses, they concluded that the only way to carry out their plan was to elope. Once their marriage was consummated, all opposition would be a moot point. Their plan could have easily been conceived by any of the composers whose works they so skillfully portrayed on stage.

They chose a Sunday, when most people stayed in bed recuperating from a late-night of dancing, visiting friends or just plain debauchery. Concealed by the predawn darkness, they met in front of a familiar café — now closed — and sped away in an automobile that Louis had borrowed from a friend.

Three days later, holding hands and more in love than ever, they knocked on the sacristy door of the local church. They explained to the priest what had taken place and their desire to legitimize their union before the eyes of God.

The old priest had seen it all before: the constant holding of hands, the furtive glances, the tender whispers. Yes, there was no way they could be dissuaded from their goal. And besides, they had already gone too far; better to sanction the union than have them sneak around in order to be together.

Not wanting to waste any time, lest they changed their minds, the crafty priest organized an impromptu ceremony. The cook was

16

summoned from the refectory; the old maid in charge of the cleaning put aside momentarily her broom. They served as witnesses to the nuptials.

When Louis and Francesca reappeared — now as husband and wife — most people were delighted. They still saw them as Figaro and Susanna, and not as two very young and inexperienced people facing all the uncertainties that life always brings. Francesca's parents, realizing that there was nothing they could do, just hugged her and wished her the best when she came home to pick up her things.

Life continued as before, except that now Louis and Francesca shared a minuscule apartment a few blocks from the San Carlo. They had each other and they had their art. They were happy.

It was during the middle of the second season, while rehearsing for a production of *Madame Butterfly*, that Francesca suddenly collapsed on a nearby recamier. Smelling salts were used to bring her around, but the paleness of her complexion and the weakness of her voice left no doubt that there was something not quite right. Everyone thought it had to do with the stress of a new production and the long hours of rehearsal.

The following day, after a thorough examination at a doctor's office, the physician delivered his findings.

"There is absolutely nothing wrong with you; fainting spells are sometimes common with women who are expecting."

This was a possibility that neither she nor Louis had considered. They were so wrapped up in each other that their love prevented them from seeing beyond just the two of them, so the unexpected news was almost a shock. After the new reality began to sink in, they agreed that nothing would have to change, that their feelings for each other could remain intact, even if they had to channel their time and attention away from each other.

For several months life continued as before, but soon there came a point when Francesca could no longer fit into the operatic costumes. As the pregnancy progressed, she felt less and less attractive; she no longer could move as gracefully as before. It was agreed that she would stay at home until the time of the delivery. She could keep up by studying the librettos of upcoming productions and by helping Louis with his own parts; after the baby was born, she could resume her artistic life. At least, that was what she told herself.

With the arrival of a baby boy—whom they named Guido—she soon realized that caring for an infant consumed all her time and energy. Louis tried to help as much as possible, but he was usually busy with rehearsals or performances. Francesca's return to the theater, for one reason or another, was always postponed until 'A more convenient time' came along. That time, of course, never seemed to arrive. Her days were filled with feedings, diaper changes, and the rest of the domestic chores that combined into an endless and exasperating drudgery. Even her husband was becoming a stranger; they now lived in parallel, but separate worlds.

Just when she thought that things could not get any worse, the unthinkable happened. The fainting spells and the morning sickness returned. At first she told herself that she was just tired, that a good night sleep would take care of it, but when the monthly cycle did not come, she could not lie to herself anymore. Her operatic dreams were quickly slipping away.

Louis, on the other hand, welcomed the news. He came from a large family and assumed that one day he would be the head of one too. At this point in his career, he was landing the better roles and beginning to make some money, so finances were not really a concern. He was glad and proud to become a father again.

After the birth of Anna, a healthy baby girl, Francesca did her best to seem cheerful and happy—just as society of that day expected of a young Italian mother—but privately she fought off bouts of depression. Several times a week she took Guido and Anna to a nearby park, where other mothers congregated to enjoy the mild Neapolitan weather and watch the children play.

Sitting on the benches, they would exchange bits of gossip, comment on a recent recipe, or talk about their husbands' career and their children's progress. Seldom did the other women express any personal ambitions of plans for their own futures; their self-sacrificing lives were led through their families, especially their children. This fact did not escape Francesca's attention; from the beginning, she made a concerted effort to conceal her own intentions of returning to the theater and resuming an artistic career whenever her children became of school age.

In an attempt to keep her dream alive, she would practice arias from different operas whenever she was performing those endless household tasks that had become her immediate reality. She would also try to help Louis with his own parts, but he seldom wanted to sing when he was home. He doted on his children, especially on young Anna. Francesca had no reason to complain; she had a devoted husband and a beautiful family. But deep down there was the persistent echo of dissatisfaction; a silent yearning to fulfill an incomplete dream that she had nurtured since she was a child and to which she had devoted countless hours of practice and hard work.

The life of the d'Amio family proceeded at a normal pace; Guido was already in third grade and Ana was about to enter first. Louis continued to strengthen his reputation in the theater with every new role he undertook. Some opera critics, carried away in a typically Italian prose given to exaggeration, proclaimed him to be as popular as Enrico Caruso.

As the children became older, Francesca anticipated her long-awaited return to the theater. Her bouts of depression disappeared and her mood became almost jovial. Louis was delighted, and he had already spoken to don Alberto, the manager of the San Carlo, about his wife's return. What they were not prepared for, what never crossed their minds was something so unexpected that it took the entire town by surprise and shook it to its foundation.

The company was staging a production of *Aida*. The tickets for the first performance had been sold out weeks in advance. Opening night, Louis, in the role of Radames, delivered such powerful and commanding performance that even his most loyal admirers had to admit that he had gone beyond himself. It was, they commented, as if he had suddenly and mysteriously tapped into a secret and inexhaustible source of new energy and talent. Night after night, when everyone thought he could not surpass the previous night's performance, he would leave the audience in awe once again with the rich, deep modulations of his voice and fresh and subtle nuances to the role. Soon it became an impossible task to get tickets to any of his performances; the newspaper reporters, having exhausted their repertoire of laudatory adjectives, were now having difficulties—not wanting to repeat what had already been said—describing his absolute command of the stage.

But with every masterful performance, with every feature in the local newspapers praising his voice, Francesca's own career faded even more, to the point of being completely eclipsed by his success. Even the other mothers at the park gradually stopped referring to her by her given name and instead they just called her Louis' wife.

Towards the end of that stellar season, and to celebrate the current success and the many more to come, an elaborate party was organized by don Alberto. In attendance would be the entire cast, the producers as well as the most illustrious citizens of the town. Not even the smallest details of this lavish affair had been overlooked, from the entertainment to the food—which would be catered by a local restaurant famous for its international cuisine—to the sitting arrangements during the banquet. Even the mayor would be present.

This affair would not only celebrate the success of the operatic season that had just ended, but also an event directly related to the d'Amio household: Louis' first recordings, entitled Immortal Arias, would be released that week. It had taken months of negotiations in order to raise the necessary capital, rehearsals at all sorts of odd hours, and countless sessions at the recording studio. Even a professional portrait of Louis was commissioned to grace the cover of the album. It was indeed cause for celebration. Now even those opera fans who could not come to the theater would be able to enjoy his performances in the comfort of their homes. During the off season, Louis planned to promote the recordings personally in order to supplement his income and solidify his reputation.

As the appointed evening approached, Francesca's mood became lighter, as if a heavy burden were gradually being removed from her shoulders, or a heavy fog that had enveloped her for so long were finally dissipating. The soirée would afford her an opportunity to renew the connection with the operatic world and to return—if only for one evening—to the kind of life where she truly belonged and stop being an extension of her husband. Conscious that first impressions were most important, she went shopping for a bolt of fabric and had a dress of her own design made by one the other mothers she had met in the park. The latter's skill as a seamstress allowed her to earn some extra money while simultaneously caring for her young twin boys. Francesca also bought some new shoes to match her new outfit; that small shop she often frequented would become, years later, the now world famous Ferragamo factory.

On the appointed day, she had her hair done by a neighbor and arranged for a friend to take care of the children. That evening not only did she look like her former self, but more important, she felt that the clock had turned back and she was about to embark on a new and more fulfilling phase of their life. Truly, she looked absolutely radiant.

When she arrived at the party, holding on to Louis's arm, she was fully conscious that all eyes were on her. Undoubtedly many of the women in attendance felt a tinge of envy mixed with jealousy. After all, she was married to Louis d'Amio, the most sought after singer; she was the mother of his children; they were both young and beautiful people with a future full of possibilities.

A crew of waiters unobtrusively, yet efficiently made their way amongst the attendees, quietly dispensing glasses of champagne. As the evening progressed the mild effects of the drinks began to manifest themselves. The demeanor of the guests became looser, their mood more jovial, their laughter louder than before. By then Louis and Francesca had gone their separate ways, mingling with the crowd. Of course, everyone wanted to talk to Louis, ask him about his operatic career and the roles he wanted to play in the next season.

Francesca, also a current celebrity if only by association, had met previously some of the more influential people in the town; she was also renewing some old acquaintances from her former opera days. They asked her about her immediate plans and if she intended to return to the theater. Francesca was thrilled not only that they remembered her, but also that they should be interested in her career.

The unexpected sound of a small bell interrupted the lively conversations; it was time for dinner. The places had been carefully arranged in order of rank. At the head of the massive table sat the mayor of the town; next in proximity were the directors of the San Carlo Theater, the members of the cast and the other guests.

Seated next to Louis and Francesca was don Alberto, who years earlier had cast—against everyone's advice—Francesca and Louis in the leading roles in the production of *The Marriage of Figaro*. Indirectly he was responsible for their having met and the subsequent turn of events.

Through Louis he had kept up with her life—he prided himself in being abreast of all significant events in the lives of his cast—and throughout the dinner, rather than talking about her children, he steered the conversation towards her plans for her own future. Years of experience had taught him that performers, especially talented ones, could not stay away indefinitely from the theater. It was in their blood, so everything else, no matter how important in the eyes of others, was always secondary.

Throughout the meal, and propelled by generous amounts of wine, he spoke with a tone of satisfaction of the season that had just concluded—the most successful in the history of the San Carlo—and of the plans he had for the immediate future. Without being direct, he hinted at the possibility of Francesca starring opposite Louis in the opening production—*Madame Butterfly*—of the coming season. He also suggested, in vague terms, that now that the children were in school, there was no reason why she should not resume her career, since she would be free to come to rehearsals during the day.

All this periphrastic enticing, of course, was not necessary; it was all that Francesca had thought about for a long time. It was a yearning that could only be appeased with the fulfillment of her true destiny. At this point in the evening, she felt, everything was returning to its proper order, when she and Louis were together on and off stage and their lives revolved around their art. She agreed with everything he suggested, and confessed that she had been counting the days until a return to the theater became feasible. Her husband supported her decision, so the only thing left to do was work out the particular details.

"Then it is all settled," concluded don Alberto with a smile. "Come to the theater next week and we can talk some more about it."

Francesca could hardly believe it; in a matter of days she would be on track again, pursuing that elusive dream and accompanied by her husband.

Around midnight the first guests began to leave; Louis was still surrounded by a group of middle-aged men and their wives. They were probably discussing the upcoming season—never a moment too soon—and Francesca deduced that they were members of the board of directors and local patrons of the arts. She also knew that whenever her husband started discussing his favorite operas, because of his strong opinions and undisputed knowledge of the subject, the conversation could go on for hours.

A neighbor was looking after her children, but she had told her to expect her a little after midnight. Not wanting to drag Louis away from what could be important business, she asked don Alberto, who was about to leave with his wife, if they could drop her off. He was glad to do so—it was on his way—and they could talk some more in the car about her future plans. She quickly informed Louis, kissed him lightly on the cheek and stepped outside, where the car was parked by the curb. During the ride they commented some more about the possibilities for the upcoming operatic season and how to best reintroduce Francesca before the eyes of the public.

She found her next-door neighbor in the living room, dozing off with a magazine while the radio played softly in the background. Guido and Anna had been asleep for hours; there was really nothing worth mentioning about the evening.

After thanking her and saying good night, she went to the back of the house to check on the children. They were sleeping soundly, just as her neighbor had said. As she began to get ready for bed, Francesca kept hoping that Louis would come in. She was eager, despite the late hour, to discuss with him the events of the evening and her visit to the theater that coming week. Purposely she prolonged the tedious ritual that she performed every night: removing her makeup, brushing her teeth and hair, and getting into her nightgown. Eventually she got into bed, still waiting for her husband. She picked up a book, intending to read until his arrival; she heard the living room clock strike two o'clock and then, still holding the book, quickly drifted into sleep.

The loud and abrupt knocking on the front door, like a sudden barrage of gunfire, brought her back to reality. At first, she did not know what was happening, but immediately realized the urgency of the call. Quickly putting on the robe she kept by the bed, she almost ran to the living room and opened the door.

Two uniformed policemen were standing on the other side of the threshold, their somber faces auguring unwelcome news. They asked if she was the wife of Louis d'Amio. When she said yes, they asked to come inside.

They did not sit down—a further sign that their visit was not a social call—and then removed their hats.

"There has been a terrible accident," said the older one. As if to underscore the seriousness of his words, the clock struck five.

At this point Francesca knew instinctively that their visit was directly linked to her husband's prolonged absence. He had never stayed out all night before. She wanted to know, but at the same time she was afraid to ask, so she just stood there, frozen between uncertainty and fear. Apparently the older policeman had done this before—surely one of the least pleasant aspects of his job—so he delivered the news clearly and with few words.

"I am afraid your husband is dead," he said in a somber tone.

Francesca felt a sudden rush of blood to her head, as if a loud and endless train were going through her brain. The word 'Dead' carried the impact of a sledgehammer, knocking the wind out of her. She felt faint, as if all life were being abruptly drained from her body.

She must have shown outward signs of her spell, because the younger policeman helped her to one of the living room chairs. She sat there, holding her hands and looking down, not fully aware yet of the immensity of the news. She was in a state of shock.

After that everything became a blur. She remembered her next door neighbor returning; the children awakening; the clock relentlessly striking the hours and someone bringing her coffee from her own kitchen. It was as if her brain, perhaps trying to protect itself from the pain, had severed the connection to reality and only allowed mere forms without substance or meaning to register.

Don Alberto came at midmorning, to offer his condolences and assured her that he would personally see to all the funeral arrangements. She shook his hand and thanked him, but those actions were performed mechanically; her mind allowed the body to move, but not to feel. Had anyone been able to look into her eyes they would have realized at once that the Francesca that they knew had retreated to a distant and most inaccessible place.

Although customary in southern Italy for the wakes to be held at home, given Louis d'Amio's popularity and the size of the house, this would not have been feasible. It was decided—a rather logical alternative—that the most befitting place for the gathering would be at the San Carlo Theater. Louis' life had centered around opera; not even death could change that fact.

The stage was hurriedly cleared of all operatic props that remained from the last performance, and the coffin, resting on discreet trestles that rose about two feet from the ground, was placed in its center. To one side, almost shrouded in darkness, a couch meant for the widow and her children. On the other, exuding an unidentifiable mixture of fragrances, were the profuse flower arrangements—their baroque designs a stark contrast with the simplicity of the coffin—sent by friends, fans, and even strangers. Long before the appointed time, a long line of mourners formed outside the theater. Louis d'Amio's performances never disappointed; this last one would not be an exception.

The uninterrupted procession lasted the entire night; people came from the most remote places to pay their respects, fully cognizant that the loss went beyond the operatic world. In the background, rather than silence, the sound system played uninterruptedly Immortal Arias. The cruel irony that the deceased would sing at his own funeral was not completely lost on Francesca and the attending crowd.

The mourners entered the theater through its right doors, signed a book that would later be delivered to the widow, and slowly made their way down the aisle until they reached the steps that led to the stage. At this point they paused, waiting patiently for the stage to clear so they could have their turn to speak briefly to the family sitting on the couch. After that task was completed, they moved over to view the deceased lying in the open casket and then exited the stage using the steps on the left side.

In life, Louis d'Amio's performances never fell short; this last one, everyone agreed, was his best. It had been don Alberto's intention, since the burial was scheduled for nine the following day, to close the theater around two in the morning. But when that time arrived the line outside, if nothing else, had grown longer. The crowd, he knew, would have rioted had he tried to send them home; he shrugged and resigned himself to allow the mourners into the theater until the last one had paid his respects to Louis and his widow. The children, of course, had fallen asleep before midnight, so Francesca sent them home with her next-door neighbor. It was the sensible thing to do, since they would have to be up early for the funeral.

The doors of the San Carlo did not close at all that night. The new day surprised the last mourners leaving the building and meeting those who had gone home and returned for the funeral; the music had played uninterruptedly all night. Through a back door of the stage, the coffin was loaded onto a hearse and taken to the church. By the time Francesca and the children arrived, a crowd had gathered in front of the portico. Inside the building, there was not even standing room. Father Rego, the local priest and opera fan himself, cognizant that the church would be packed, had been working feverishly on the homily to be delivered during the requiem mass. Since dawn he had been burning incense; he had also replaced the half consumed candles flanking the main altar with new ones.

Mass started promptly at eight o'clock. Father Rego knew that time was of the essence, since the sun would soon be too hot and the cemetery was almost two miles away. The ceremony proceeded flawlessly; during the short, but fact filled and packed with praise homily, he exalted the qualities of the deceased as a citizen, as a family man and as an artist while pointing at the casket below the altar. He even hinted that God, momentarily jealous of the mortals who were enjoying Louis' voice, had called him to His bosom so he would eternally sing for Him in heaven. Some of the older attendees shook their heads in agreement. In conclusion, he warned everyone present, while morosely resting his hand on the casket, not to second guess the will of God, that it was futile for any man to try to understand the divine plan.

At this point, Francesca stood from the pew where she had been sitting and led the children to the open casket. First Guido, and then Anna, kissed their father lightly on the forehead. Francesca followed suit, but held back her tears, showing an emotional restraint that perhaps dated back to an Etruscan tradition.

After a final blessing, they exited the church. The temperature had already risen a few degrees; the somber hearse was silently waiting. Some of the flower arrangements were hurriedly placed on its roof; later they would cover the grave. Francesca and the children would follow in a black sedan, while the general public would walk slowly behind the cars the two miles to the burial site.

It was a clear, perfect day, more befitting for a country outing than an unexpected funeral. The southern Italian sun, still forgiving at that early hour, clearly showed the way to Louis d'Amio's final resting place. As the cortege meandered through the narrow streets, women dressed in black and with rosaries in hand made the sign of the cross; men instinctively stopped whatever they were doing and removed their hats as a sign of respect.

People whose houses were on the way came out to watch the funeral go by. Others, for whatever reason, silently joined the cortege; maybe they had briefly met Louis, or perhaps the subdued and dark seduction of the funeral procession on that sunny morning was too strong to resist.

By the time they reached the cemetery the crowd had grown to such proportions that it was impossible for everyone to watch as the casket was lowered into the ground and the elaborate marble lid of the grave was laboriously slid into place by the cemetery workers. The flower arrangements that rested on top of the hearse were hurriedly placed around the grave; the temperature had climbed steadily, and now that the burial was concluded, everyone — including Francesca and the children — wanted to return home.

The same black sedan that had taken them to the cemetery returned them to their house. Francesca never found out whose car it was or who had arranged for its use. Tomassina, her neighbor, was waiting for them; on the kitchen table she had arranged some food that her other neighbors had prepared, but the last thing Francesca wanted to do at that moment was eat. At this point she just wanted to be alone with her children.

"If you need anything just ask," the old woman said before leaving.

Francesca nodded. Those were words that people said, because deep down they knew that there was nothing they could say or do to make the situation better. No one had the power to undo what was already done, to turn the clock back a few days to a time when her husband and the father of her children was still alive. Guido and Anna, after having some food, retired to their rooms.

Now that she was alone in the house, surrounded by the endless silence, for the first time Francesca felt the unbearable weight of her solitude compounded by the awesome responsibility of two small children. It was the harsh realization that her life had forever changed that triggered the torrent of emotions she had so successfully repressed during the wake, the funeral, and the burial. She started sobbing uncontrollably, holding her face in her hands and whispering her husband's name. Eventually, emotionally spent, she fell asleep.

The knocking on the door—minutes or hours later, she didn't know—brought her out of her slumber. It was don Alberto, still wearing the same dark suit he had worn to the funeral.

"I do not mean to intrude," he said softly, "but I wanted to deliver this to you as soon as possible." In his hand he had Louis' recordings, Immortal Arias. "I thought you and your children would like to have it."

"Yes, thank you," she said, "It was kind of you to bring it."

"It was the least I could do; if you need anything, don't hesitate to call," he said while simultaneously squeezing her hand softly as a sign of support. Then he was gone.

Always the same words, Francesca thought. Words that reflected total impotence before the finality of death, words that allowed people to overcome the awkwardness of an unavoidable situation.

The children, curious about the knocking on the door, had come into the living room. At this point there was no need for an explanation; Francesca showed them the album, took the record out of its sleeve and placed it on the turntable of the ancient gramophone. Suddenly Louis' rich voice filled every corner of the room. At that moment, sitting on the couch while holding her two children, Francesca felt a sense of warmth and security that only the certainty of Louis' unconditional love and devotion to his family could convey. He was present, if not in the flesh, in spirit.

But Louis's sudden death, besides the obvious impact on his family, also brought with it a sense of loss, confusion—and in some cases even fear—to the town. Now that the funeral was over, everyone had more time to consider the particulars of his untimely end. The police had not released the results of their investigation. This lack of official conclusions only gave rise to a series of rampant and, at times, wild rumors about the unfortunate events.

It was a fact that Louis was the most successful performer in the opera company. It was also a known fact that his first recordings, an event anxiously awaited by everyone, would soon be released. Since Louis had no known enemies, many people conjectured that his tragic death had been motivated by money. Some suggested that he had refused to sign an exclusive but usurious contract with the consortium that was bankrolling his debut album; anticipating the success of his career, they had decided to secure an exclusive contract for all future recordings. In view of his outrage at the mere suggestion of selling out, the consortium decided to send him a message that would persuade him to accept the contract. What they had not foreseen was that Louis, not unlike one of the heroic and fateful roles he portrayed on stage, would not bend. According to the rumors he had fought off his aggressors until the end. These were, of course unsubstantiated conjectures without any foundation, idle talk that made people feel a little more secure in the thought that, as part of an amorphous crowd, they would never be targeted.

Others, given more to the dramatic, conjectured that the tragic events had been the result of a secret love affair gone awry. They even put forth the theory that the jealous husband, and perpetrator of that crime of passion, was already in police custody, awaiting transfer to another jurisdiction where he could receive a fair trial without the influence of Louis' popularity.

Nothing, of course, could have been further from the truth. Louis d'Amio had only had two loves in his life: his family and his music. He was completely devoted to both.

Ultimately, when the police report was released, the truth of the matter was rather disappointing in comparison to the rumors that had been concocted for an entire month. He had not been targeted because of his popularity or because of his social status. He had just been the random victim of an attempted hold up. The perpetrators — two young drifters who didn't even know who Louis was — were already in jail. They had been apprehended while trying to pawn an engraved Breguet pocket watch — an earlier present from Francesca — they had taken from their victim.If he had not resisted, they declared during the interrogation, they would not have had to stab him to death.

For an entire week their unshaven faces were plastered all over the front pages of the newspapers, along with all the details of the investigation. Being a topic of local interest, the story would boost circulation. Even the police chief himself visited Francesca to deliver in person the news of their arrest, and to assure her that they would receive the harshest punishment allowed by the law. She thanked him for his diligence, but nothing could change the reality that Louis was never coming back.

Guido and Ana had returned to school. Francesca realized that it was imperative for the children to resume a life with a certain degree of normalcy. During the evenings she helped with their homework or played games—just as their father had done—and afterwards they listened to different operas. She always took the time to explain the convoluted plots to the children, since they were often performed in a language other than Italian. It was a love that she wanted to keep alive. Some evenings they listened to

Immortal Arias. On those occasions they did not speak, but tried to assimilate every note, every nuance of Louis' voice that reached out to them, like an intangible caress, from an unknown and remote place. But no matter how hard she tried to keep intact their previous life, Louis' absence was much too deep to be filled. Furthermore, their economic reality was quickly sinking in. Don Alberto would drop in from time to time and leave an unmarked envelope with varying amounts of money, but this would not go on indefinitely. He no longer spoke of Francesca returning to the theater. Old Tomassina often knocked on her door with a loaf of freshly baked bread, some linguini or anything else that she thought Francesca and the children might like.

As the months went by, paying the rent as well as meeting other expenses became increasingly difficult. Without the steady income that her late husband had provided, their meager savings were quickly being depleted; it also seemed that as the children became older they needed more things. Forced by her circumstances, she decided that a move to a cheaper place was in order and that it was time for her to start working.

As she often did, Francesca called on don Alberto for advice. "It just so happens," he said after listening to her with a pensive look, "that I own a small house that just became vacant. It is not in the best neighborhood of Naples, but if you are interested you and the children can live in it as long as you like."

"I am most grateful," she said and as a sign of her gratitude kissed his hand.

"Then it is all settled; I will stop by tomorrow and we can take a look."

The house, just as don Alberto had said, was a far cry from what she and the children had become accustomed to. The house itself, despite its size and age, did not bother her as much as its location. The neighborhood was mostly inhabited by lower-class working people, but also by some characters of dubious reputations whom she suspected of having ties to the *camorra*, the Neapolitan equivalent of the Sicilian mafia. She just would have to keep a closer eye on the children, she thought.

On the day of the move, Tomassina came over to say good-bye. She was the one person whose company and help Francesca would surely miss. Don Alberto had hired a truck and a small crew of young men who quickly loaded her possessions and transported them to their new home. She and the children followed behind in his car. She realized that not only was she leaving behind the house where she had shared so much with Louis and the children, the neighborhood where friendships had been forged, but also all her plans for a future in the world of opera.

As they approached their new dwelling, the streets became narrower and less tidy; the buildings more run down and in obvious need of paint or general upkeep. All the while, she kept talking to the children, telling them of the new friends they would make and all the new things they would see. When they finally stopped in front of their new house, a line from Dante's Inferno came into her mind. `Abandon all hope, ye who enter here.´

II

The focus of Francesca's life, especially after their move to their new house, became her children. She made sure that they never missed school, always wore clean clothes and took them to church on Sundays. She hoped that life would be a little kinder to them and that it would spare them the unexpected and unfortunate turns of fate that had besieged her.

Guido, now almost eighteen, had opted for a technical school and according to his teachers possessed a natural talent for mechanical devices, especially in the automotive field. This talent had landed him a part time job in a nearby shop, and most of the money he made went to pay for family expenses. He was also interested in soccer and followed fervently the exploits of his favorite teams through magazines and radio broadcasts. And, of course, as a healthy Italian male, he was passionate about the opposite sex.

But just as any other boy growing up under Mussolini's regime, he had been taught in school that the great days of modern Italy started in 1922 with the March on Rome. Further, it was common to teach the children that Il Duce was the only man capable of leading Italy back to greatness.

Guido also joined one of the youth movements that met after school. First he entered The Sons of the She Wolf, and proudly displayed the black shirt that identified the group. At age eight he moved up to the Balilla, which incorporated in their outfits — besides the black shirt — a black cap, shorts, and gray socks. By the time he turned fourteen, he easily made the transition into the Avanguardista, who substituted the shorts worn by the Balilla for knickerbockers. Besides receiving fascist instruction, the boys were also taught that fighting was a natural extension of the male lifestyle. Members of the Balilla had to remember the following: 'I believe in Rome, the Eternal, the mother of my country... I believe in the genius of Mussolini... and in the resurrection of the empire.'

33

The glory of the Roman Empire was always present in what the children did and learned. Francesca had
tried to temper these tendencies as much as possible with Christian values; Guido always attended mass with his mother and sister, but Francesca suspected that he did it because he was the only male in the family and not necessarily out of religious convictions.

Anna, two years younger and more reserved, although not an introvert, was more careful with her words. Her thoughts were her own and she seldom shared them with anyone. Unlike her brother, who had many friends, there was no one who could be considered close; her acquaintances were mostly other school girls from her class, but none could claim to know Anna well.

Beside her school work, she often helped Francesca with the laundry she took in to make a little extra money. During the evenings, while Guido was out, they would sit in the tiny living room and listen to operas that Francesca played in the old and tired gramophone. Although still too young to know, Anna sensed that there was something missing in her life, an ineffable piece that would complete her. Looking at her own mother, she just knew that there had to be something more, something that would make all the work and drudgery of everyday living bearable and worthwhile. Whatever that was, exactly, she didn't know.

As it often happens in life, the answers that we seek are found in the most unlikely places, and at times when they are least expected. It was no secret in the neighborhood that Francesca was the widow of Louis d'Amio; it was also a well-known fact that she possessed a musical talent of her own, which she often displayed while doing the laundry in a cement sink in an open-air courtyard.

One of her acquaintances, signora Sofia Alberti—also a widow—had high hopes for her young son Paolo in the operatic world. Cognizant that Francesca had performed at the San Carlo and was friends with don Alberto, the manager, she invited her to come to her house and listen to young Paolo one Saturday afternoon. This request was not an unusual one; it was not the first time that hopeful parents asked her to listen to their children, hoping to impress Francesca and somehow open a door into the world of opera through her tenuous connections. More often than not, the purported talent only existed in the minds of the relatives. Although this became apparent from the beginning, Francesca would sit politely through the performance with such composure that her thoughts and impressions were never revealed. Afterwards, while everyone awaited her verdict, she would sip a cup of espresso or a small glass of Amareto while thinking of a way of letting everyone down easy with noncommittal words.

"Make sure to practice every day," she would say, "The voice must be like a fine-tuned instrument." With these words she kept alive both her friendships and the hopes of the aspiring singers. After all, everyone in Naples wanted to be in opera.

She did not expect Paolo, signora Alberti's young son, to be any different, but the canons of friendship—especially with another widow—compelled her to listen to the boy, although it was an unappealing prospect. To make the visit a little more palatable, as she had done before, she asked Anna to accompany her. It would give her an opportunity to leave the house and socialize. She was at that most radiant, yet vulnerable age when mothers had to keep a watchful eye and a tight rein on their daughters; young men, especially exuberant Neapolitans, were always on the prowl.

The thought of asking Guido to accompany her never crossed her mind. Obviously, he would never have considered accompanying his mother on such a visit; he was more interested in auto mechanics and had never shown, despite his upbringing in a musical household, the least interest in the arts.

Anna accepted her mother's invitation more out of boredom than anything else. She had sat previously through those singing exhibitions and had never enjoyed them; she kept comparing the feeble voices to the strong and commanding one of her father that had been forever captured in the grooves of Immortal Arias.

Signora Alberti's house was not far; Anna and her mother made their way skilfully through the maze of narrow streets flanked by minuscule sidewalks that led to the bay. Even though the ocean was out of sight, occluded by the buildings, its presence floated in the air.

The young men who worked at the different shops or traveled the streets at that hour did not bother to disguise their admiring glances as the two women walked by. Just as she had been taught, Anna looked straight ahead, ignoring their piercing eyes and praising comments, as if they were but incorporeal and impermanent apparitions without substance. They stopped in front of a small house with a white façade and windows guarded by wrought iron gratings. Below the windows and under the bright sunlight, the colorful content of ample flower boxes contrasted sharply with the white background as it cascaded joyously over their edge. As Francesca was about to knock, the door opened. Undoubtedly signora Alberti had been anxiously awaiting their arrival.

"*Benvenuti*," she said with a smile and signaled the visitors to sit down.The small living room was decorated with some baroque style furniture that young Anna thought was somewhat overdone. She preferred, as did the younger generations, a more simple, direct and modern design. The walls were covered with cheap reproductions of works of art—Anna recognized a Last Supper and a detail from the ceiling of the Sistine Chapel—and photographs of people she assumed were family members, both living and deceased. The largest and most prominent one, over the sofa, showed a middle-aged man wearing a suit and a faint smile that could have been interpreted as one of mild amusement or quiet resignation. There was also an assortment of small cut-glass vases with fresh flowers under a portrait of the Virgin Mary. Anna noticed that she had a pious look on her face, as if silently and eternally dismayed at the endless array of human frailties she was destined to witness and endure.

"I will be right back," signora Alberti said and without waiting for a response, disappeared towards the back of the house. Anna and her mother did not say anything, but limited themselves to inspecting the pictures, knick-knacks and other items that signora Alberti displayed in her minute living room.

A few minutes later she returned with a metal tray replete with an assortment of pastries and three cups of espresso. She smiled and asked the visitors to help themselves. As they drank the coffee and ate the sweets, Anna could not help but wonder about the whereabouts of the young man whose voice signora Alberti praised so highly. For some unknown reason, there were no pictures of Paolo in the living room. The deep silence in the house suggested that the widow was its only occupant; further, she had only brought out three cups on the tray.

"Paolo will come out shortly," she said before Anna could find an answer to her conjectures. "He is shy, just like his father was," she explained as she looked at the photograph of the gentleman with the faint smile.

"I don't allow him to drink coffee; in the long run it might have an adverse effect on his voice," she explained without being asked. It was at this point that Anna began to suspect that signora Alberti wanted to control every aspect of her son's life.

The two widows made small talk, sipped their coffee and savored the pastries. They talked, of course, about their families, how fast the children were growing up—at that point signora Alberti turned to Anna and commented on the fact that she was no longer a little girl—and about the uncertainties of the political situation in Italy. Throughout the exchange Anna remained silent; she listened and slowly drank the cup of espresso.

Eventually signora Alberti's comments focused on Paolo and the bright future that awaited him. She hoped that in the near future they might move from Naples to Rome, where there were more opportunities and a chance of exposure to a foreign audience receptive to upcoming talent. It was as if she were building up momentum before finally introducing her son to the visitors.

"But enough talk about Paolo; I think it is time for you to meet him. I will be right back," she said and then stood up, retrieved the tray with the empty cups and plates from the center table and disappeared towards the back of the house.

Anna and her mother looked at each other silently, both secretly hoping that the visit would be over as soon as possible and they could return to their daily routines. As a rule these visits dragged on after the young man or woman sang; the parents always wanted to discuss the possibilities of turning incipient talent into a full-fledged professional career. This time, however, they were both in for an unexpected surprise.

Just as quietly as she had left, signora Alberti returned to the living room. With her was a lean boy with blond hair and very fair complexion. He did not look at the visitors, but straight down at the floor, as if he were embarrassed because of an unexplained infraction.

On the day when Paolo was born, everyone thought that Sofia Alberti had brought an angel into the world. The boy's light complexion, clear blue eyes and blond hair immediately evoked those images usually found depicted on the inner cupolas of European cathedrals. Some of the neighborhood's women surreptitiously looked for a pair of wings, conclusive and irrefutable evidence that the boy's birth was a divine manifestation.

"Paolo is shy," signora Alberti explained again. "But he is a good singer, and that is what matters," she added with a smile. "Today he is going to do for us one of his favorite pieces, a religious one in praise of the Virgin Mary." As she was introducing her son's performance, she opened a small rococo console that hid a record player, turned it on and placed the arm on the record that was already resting on the turntable. It was obvious that those sessions—no doubt under the stern direction and control of signora Alberti—took place with regularity.

As the music began to emerge from the console, a dramatic metamorphosis took place in Paolo. He stood straight, towering over his mother, and faced the image of the Virgin hanging on the wall. His chest became fuller; he lifted his arms, as if giving praise or readying them for an imminent battle. Then, the sound of his voice. How could anyone so young possess such a gift? Even with his back turned to the visitors he immediately transported them from the small living room, elevated them to a plane that was a step above the mundane and closer to the divine. The sweet modulations, buttressed by the undeniable passion with which the words were being uttered, literally transformed the song into a vehicle that easily carried the listeners beyond their physical selves and into their most spiritual realms.

Anna had stopped breathing, visibly affected by the modulations of Paolo's voice. Although somewhat surprised at the incredible sound, she had come prepared to hear the young man sing. What caught her completely off guard was what happened next. As the last notes of the song dissolved into the musty air of the living room, giving way to a deep silence, Paolo turned around and looked straight at her, momentarily ignoring the two older women in the room. It was a deep, piercing look that had a way of melting away any resistance and making one feel utterly transparent. Anna could swear that he touched—caressed?—her with his eyes. Throughout the rest of her life, she would still remember this first time she felt enveloped by his unforgettable eyes, the purest and clearest blue eyes she had ever seen. From the beginning she was mesmerized by Paolo's gaze. Whether her mother and signora Alberti had noticed anything, she didn't know.

"Magnificent, just magnificent," she heard her mother say. By then Paolo had become once again the shy, prepubescent young man that had come into the room a few minutes earlier. The seat of his power and self-confidence resided in his voice.

"Thank you Paolo," said signora Alberti. The tone of her voice, however, was one of dismissal rather than gratitude for the beautiful song he had just delivered.

"*Scusi*," he said in a soft tone and disappeared into the back of the house. Signora Alberti turned towards Francesca, waiting for her comments.

"You should be proud of you son," she finally said, "He has a most beautiful voice and a most controlled delivery. I must confess that when you asked me to come I did not expect to find such talent."

"I understand," said signora Alberti with a smile. "Mothers tend to exaggerate about their children; it is only natural. That is why I wanted you to visit and see for yourself. After all, you are a professional and your ears cannot be fooled."

"You are most kind, signora," answered Francesca, "but those days are now behind me." There was no bitterness in her voice, just acceptance of her current situation. "Now I only think about my children, as it should be."

"Of course," agreed signora Alberti, "We all want what is best for our children. By the way, Paolo will be singing tomorrow in church; perhaps I will see you there."

"Yes, I would like to come," said Anna unexpectedly, even though the comment had clearly been directed at her mother. The two older women looked at each other, a little surprised, but did not say anything.

"Does Paolo have any plans for the future?" asked Francesca, genuinely interested in the boy's career.

"I have already secured a manager for him;" explained signora Alberti, "he thinks that Paolo can make the transition from singing in church to the opera theater. He has even arranged for Paolo to perform at private functions during the past few months. With his contacts and Paolo's voice there should be no problems whatsoever. I am hoping that before long he will be performing at the San Carlo."

The fact did not escape Anna that signora Alberti had not stated what Paolo wanted, but what she wanted for him. Sure, it was a nice dream, to sing at the San Carlo, but what Paolo himself wanted was still unclear. His talent was evident, but how that talent should be developed and utilized should ultimately be his decision and not his mother's. Everybody should follow his own dreams. At that moment, without realizing it, Anna began to nurture a tinge of resentment for signora Alberti and her controlling attitude toward her son. Perhaps, as signora Alberti herself had stated, she only had Paolo's best interest at heart, but Anna suspected there were also ulterior motives.

"I see that you are thinking ahead," Francesca said as she stood up, signaling that the visit was over. "Just make sure that he keeps practicing and listening to other singers; there is always something else to be learned."

"I hope to see you in church tomorrow," said signora Alberti.

"We will try," answered Francesca. "Say good-bye to Paolo from us, and thank him for the beautiful song."

On the way back to their house, Anna noticed that her mother seemed preoccupied, perhaps a little somber. These were the obvious signs that something was on her mind. Anna also knew that it was pointless to ask her mother; whenever she was ready to talk, she would do so.

"Paolo has a beautiful voice, doesn't he?" said Anna, stating the obvious, and trying to make small talk.

"Yes, he does," agreed Francesca and then let out a sigh, but said nothing more.

It was not until later the same day, when supper was finished and the two women were alone in the kitchen doing the dishes—Guido had already left to see his friends—that Francesca let her daughter know what was bothering her.

"I have to speak to signora Alberti," she said suddenly, with an almost vehement tone in her voice.

"You just saw her," Anna pointed out, "What could be so urgent?"

"It is about Paolo..." here she made a pause, maybe not knowing just how to say what she had to.

"What about him?" asked Anna. "He is very talented and I am sure he has a great future as a singer."

"That is precisely it; I am not so sure about that future that signora Alberti is so convinced will happen."

"Please explain," said Anna, a little annoyed at her mother's evasiveness.

"You are aware that the human voice is not unlike an instrument; it requires constant care and training. Unlike a musical instrument, however, which is created in a certain way, the human voice undergoes certain natural changes throughout its life. The most pronounced, of course, is during late puberty. Paolo's voice will soon change drastically; it is as if the most accomplished musician were being handed a different and unfamiliar instrument overnight. More often than not, what emerges is a completely different sound, one that is seldom as melodious as the previous one. I am afraid that when that happens, Paolo's career will be over."

"What about all the practice and training?" asked Anna.

"As I said, he will be dealing with a brand new voice, so whatever he has done in the past will not mean anything."

"Could he train his new voice?" asked Anna.

"Anything is possible," answered Francesca, "but his new voice may not be worth training. And even if it is, it would take him years. One way or another, his musical career will be over soon."

"What do you think signora Alberti will say? All she thinks about is Paolo's singing."

"I don't know," said Francesca, "but I feel a responsibility to tell her. She is his mother, so she should know," she concluded.

"I agree," said Anna, "but I hope she does not take it too hard."

"We'll ask her to visit and have some coffee tomorrow, after mass," said Francesca, "I think we will be able to talk more freely here, and the sooner the better."

It was settled. The two women returned to their kitchen chores and to the privacy of their thoughts. Francesca's concern was for the dream of a better life that signora Alberti had founded on her son's voice; Anna, on the other hand, was only thinking about Paolo and how the changing of his voice might impact his future. Even though she and Paolo had never exchanged a single word, she felt an indefinable bond, a quiet affinity that went beyond the realm of oral communication. She had never felt like that about anyone. Paolo was clearly different from the young men who lived in the neighborhood and who often roamed the streets in search of anything that might prove a source of excitement, whether it be an impromptu game of dice, a weekly soccer match, or the easily attainable favors of young women whose morals left much to be desired.

The following morning, Anna woke up earlier than usual. She had the vague feeling that she had been having strange dreams all night, but could not remember any of the details. From her bed she heard her mother in the kitchen, preparing breakfast, so she got up to help her.

Francesca always got up earlier, even on Sundays, because she knew it would take a while to get Guido out of bed. She insisted, no matter how late he came in the night before, that he eat breakfast with the family and then go to Sunday mass. Not that she was particularly a religious woman—as were many of her neighbors—but she believed that certain family bonds should be preserved at all costs. Every Sunday morning Francesca knocked on her son's door, just to make sure he knew that breakfast would be ready soon. She had no complaints about Guido; he studied, worked and contributed to the household expenses without being asked. She understood that, as a growing young man, he needed other male friends who shared his interests. The fact that he lived with two women did not make matters any easier.

From the kitchen Francesca and Anna heard a door opening and a few moments later Guido stepped into the room. Even though he was fully dressed in a Sunday attire —the jacket was a little tight at the armpits, so he did not button it any more—the expression on his face gave away the fact that he was not completely awake yet.

He sat at the table straight across from his sister after muttering the customary 'Buon giorno.' Francesca knew that it was pointless talking to him until he had some coffee and his brain began to come back to life. She placed a cup of freshly brewed espresso in front of him. Guido reached for the sugar bowl on the center of the table, got a spoonful and then stirred the coffee vigorously, provoking a tinkling sound as the spoon hit the inner surface of the cup.

By that time, his mother had also placed on the table a generous dish filled with cannoli, which Anna approached with unabashed delight. It was a traditional Sunday treat that Francesca took pride in making before going to church.

Guido was showing signs of life; he smiled as he sipped his coffee and reached for one of Francesca's homemade pastries. Before long, the tray was empty; after a second cup of coffee, they were ready to go.

The Santa Chiara Church was not far from their house, and the early coolness of the Neapolitan mornings always made the walk an enjoyable one. Along the way they usually encountered neighbors and acquaintances on their way to mass or coming in the opposite direction if they had attended an earlier service. They kept looking to see if they could spot signora Alberti and her son, but were unsuccessful. In all probability they had left their house earlier, since Paolo would be singing during the service.

As usual, father Benito was greeting the worshippers in front of the church. His appearance did not suggest any age in particular, but he had been in the parish as far back as anyone could remember. No one recalled either a time when he was not in a good mood or had missed a Sunday service. He had baptized, married or buried at least one member of the attending families, so more than the local priest he was considered a family friend. He was also, as were most Neapolitans, an opera buff.

His most noticeable facial feature was his nose. It was not quite straight, but turned to the left. Many people were aware of the fact that during his youth he had worked on the docks unloading cargo and that, given his physical strength and agility, had soon begun to take part in the clandestine and often brutal — but always profitable — fist fights that were regularly staged in empty warehouses. These were not free for all fights, but rather encounters strictly controlled by the *camorra* — the local mafia. Fighters and their opponents were carefully chosen and groomed, thus insuring a growing attendance and the heaviest betting. If a fighter was deemed good enough, he always caught the eye of a manager and stopped being a free agent. This carried the advantage of not having to negotiate for himself; even if he had to give up a percentage of his take to the manager, it always resulted in a higher pay off.

Benito had made a reputation for himself as a ruthless fighter who usually knocked out his opponents during the first ten minutes of the contest. He was a rising star in that dark and never acknowledged world; he was also making more money from fighting than from his regular day job as a stevedore. By this time, he had already acquired a handler; he was fighting less but bringing in more money, since he was now facing more experienced opponents and the outcome of the bouts brought in a much heftier purse. Before long his name had become well known in that substratum of society.

Everything came to a head one fateful November evening. He had already defeated all the local fighters, so a special match was arranged. He would be facing one of the most ferocious men from Sicily. Everyone understood that since there were huge sums of money riding on the outcome of the contest, anything was allowed.There was only one goal: winning. A month before the fight, Benito's handler appeared at his door early one evening.

"Don't report for work tomorrow," he told him. "Your only concern now is the fight ahead of us." It was not a request, but a thinly disguised command. All handlers expected their fighters to obey them blindly.

"If I don't show up I'll lose my job," Benito said softly.

"Just do as I say," answered the handler, "Everything has been arranged. Tomorrow you start training." He then turned around and started to walk out, but at the last moment he stopped. "One more thing," he added, "I don't want you seeing any women during the training. They are nothing but a distraction and they drain your energy."

This was a common belief among handlers and trainers. The reason he had brought it up was because Benito, taking advantage of his reputation as a fighter, never missed the opportunity to bed the women who constantly flocked to him.

This time the handler, because of the high stakes, was not about to allow Benito the luxury of making his own choices. He returned early the next morning, accompanied by a trainer, to pick him up. They sped away in a black sedan, leaving behind a thin cloud of dust.

For an entire month they kept Benito isolated from the outside world; from the moment he awoke until the time he went to bed, they controlled every minute of his waking hours. His days were filled with endless sessions of calisthenics, shadow boxing, punching bag training and sparring with other fighters especially hired for that purpose.

His diet was also carefully regulated. Rich in proteins and fresh vegetables, but low in carbohydrates, it was meant to give him the necessary stamina he would doubtlessly need on the day of the fight. By the end of the month, he was in the best physical shape of his life; his every need had been met. Except, of course, having any sort of contact with females. This extended period of abstinence, both handlers and trainers believed, made the fighters meaner, gave them the necessary edge to beat their opponents.

On the outside, talk about the fight had been growing by the day. This had the dual effect of encouraging people to attend and to bet more than usual. Even those parties who were not necessarily interested in pugilistic bouts, were eager to place their illegal wagers through the representatives of the *camorra*. It was a win win situation. Or so it seemed.

The fight, as always, was to be held at one of the empty warehouses in the waterfront. The exact location was shrouded in secrecy until the very day of the event. This prevented potential disruptions—and hence loss of income—by either the police or rival gangs.

Benito was ready, both physically and mentally. He was tired of the isolation and of having his every move controlled. He wanted to go back to his previous life and have some fun, even if he did not make as much money.

On the day of the fight there was no training, just a series of callisthenic exercises meant to keep him limber. His lunch was lighter than usual and dinner nonexistent. It was better to keep the fighters on an empty stomach, so blood flow would not be diverted from the muscles toward the digestive process.

During the ride back to Naples he sat in the back, between his handler and his trainer. They kept whispering last words of advice, but by that point he was beyond retaining them. His brain was racing too fast in anticipation of what was about to happen.

The warehouse where the encounter was to take place was indistinct from the rest. From the outside it looked unoccupied, or even abandoned. The only sign of life was the two men, both dressed in black, that stood on either side of the huge door. As the cars approached, once the identity of the occupants had been confirmed, they opened the enormous gate and the vehicle would disappear in the hangar like immensity. For an instant, the men were encased in the abrupt projections of the headlights and resembled dark angels engaged in a mysterious and sinister task.

Soon thereafter the warehouse was filled with cars; this was a night that everyone would remember. In an inner chamber, a makeshift ring had been set up. It was surrounded by concentric circles of folding chairs, meant for those in attendance, but in all probability they would not be used much. Once the fight got underway everyone would be on their feet, cheering for their favorite fighter and trying not to miss a single punch. Past experience had taught everyone that anything was possible during these clandestine encounters.

The inner chamber was also full; mostly with men in dark suits whose protruding breast bulges and furtive looks left no doubt that they belonged in the lower strata of society. They gesticulated effusively, sometimes greeted each other with contrived smiles or just placed bets on the outcome of the fight. Many smoked cigars. They were there for one purpose and one purpose alone.

On a wooden table that had been hastily set up in a corner of the room a middle-aged man mixed and dispensed drinks—they were included in the exorbitant price of admission—from an assortment of bottles. Some of the patrons availed themselves of this service, but most simply smoked nervously, placed their bets carefully or paced impatiently.

At exactly ten o'clock, a short man wearing a dark suit and a vest suddenly materialized in the cone of light that encased the improvised ring. At this time, everyone present halted whatever they were doing and moved closer.

"I would like to welcome everyone tonight," he said without any preambles."I am sure this will be a memorable evening that will exceed our expectations. With us tonight we have two of the most promising young fighters in recent times." The solemn tone of his voice made it sound as if everything were legal and sanctioned by the national boxing federation, and not a clandestine brawl with no holds barred and whose only purpose was to win, not matter what means had to be employed or the injuries incurred by the opponent.

The announcer first introduced the challenger, a burly Sicilian who had carved a reputation by beating everyone in his village and subsequently other fighters from nearby towns. Because of his unconventional and unpolished—albeit successful—ways and

46

brutal attacks, combined with a most impressive physique and legendary endurance, he was aptly named The Boulder. So far he had not found a worthy opponent. A subdued wave of applause rose from the crowd. Those who had not yet placed their bets quickly surveyed the fighter before making up their minds. It was a tossup; there was no favorite, since both men were so far undefeated.

Cognizant that the crowd was growing restless, the announcer quickly introduced Benito. There was no need for words; everyone knew his record and most had seen him fight before. His style brought to mind the words elegant and fluid. As he stepped into the ring, an enthusiastic round of applause filled the chamber. It was obvious that he enjoyed the favor of the crowd. They all hoped that the bets they had placed on him would multiply their money many times over.

At this point each contender was in his designated corner. As a matter of formality, the announcer made his way to the middle of the ring and repeated out loud the rules that everyone knew.

"This bout is one of endurance," he explained unnecessarily. "There will be a brief pause every five minutes; the fight will end when one of the contenders is unable to continue. A bell will signal the beginning and the end of the match."

Silence.

The sound of a small bell, as if summoning a distinguished group of guests to a succulent dinner, filled the chamber. Even at that early stage of the fight everyone was already on their feet.

The two contenders came out of their respective corners slowly, until they met in the center of the improvised ring. At first they moved cautiously, throwing an occasional punch that was easily blocked or avoided by the opponent; the men were simply studying each other, trying to discover a weakness they could exploit in the adversary's style.

From the onset, everyone realized how different the fighters were. The Boulder adopted a rock-solid stance from which he delivered devastating punches; he was as firmly grounded as the rock of Gibraltar. Benito, on the other hand, had a more fluid, mercurial style that evoked the swiftness and unpredictability of a hummingbird in flight. It also became apparent that neither man was about to yield an inch of ground to the other; each had the confidence of a champion that had never tasted defeat.

For the first quarter of an hour they struggled, trying unsuccessfully to land a blow that would ring the other to his knees. At this point Benito began to realize that he had never met a contender like this before. The Boulder, on the other hand, also knew right away that he needed to neutralize as soon as possible such a relentless attacker. The audience was mesmerized; it was readily apparent that both men were in top physical condition and confident in their abilities.

Unexpectedly, the small bell sounded again, calling for the first recess in the fight. The announcer stepped into the ring, just to make sure that each fighter returned to his assigned corner.

The handlers quickly wiped the sweat off their faces—as of yet without any traces of blood—and produced bottles of iced water to replenish the fluids lost during the first stage of the fight. While the restorative session took place, they also whispered words of advice as to how to proceed when the bout resumed.

The bell sounded; the fighters, now refreshed, returned to the center of the ring. One thing Benito had learned during the first stage was that no single blow, no matter how powerful, would bring down The Boulder. This would be a long and arduous task, where he would need to wear down his opponent and then deliver the coup de grace that would finish him off. While blocking or avoiding The Boulder's probing, Benito had noticed that as he delivered his crushing right-hand blows, he lowered his left for just a fraction of a second. This was the opening he had been looking for; he would concentrate on the body and forego completely the hope of landing a knockout punch.

Benito danced around The Boulder with the grace and agility of a gazelle in a Serengetti field of grass. His opponent delivered his blows, but only found empty air. Then Benito, as the brief opening appeared, began to exert pressure by systematically landing punches on the hairy chest and tight stomach. At first, despite the crushing power behind them, the blows seemed not to have any effect. It was, indeed, as if he were hitting a mountain. This approach, of course, had to be carried out with the outmost care and speed. The Boulder was not just going to receive the punishment without dishing out retaliatory blows. So far, Benito's speed and footwork had worked in his favor; he had managed to land some significant punches without being hit by his opponent.

The indifferent bell sounded again, signaling the three-minute recess in the combat. The pugilists returned to their respective corners. The Boulder was showing signs of fatigue and frustration; it was impossible to fight an opponent who seemed to be as swift and erratic in his approach as a hummingbird.

Once again the minute bell summoned the gladiators to the combat. Benito continued with the same relentless attack, trying with every blow to wear down his opponent. The Boulder, on the other hand, knew that he could not hold out indefinitely against the merciless punishment; somehow he had to connect a punch that would bring his opponent down as if hit by lightning. With every attack he blocked, or every blow he tried to deliver, he felt his arms getting heavier, as if the muscles were systematically being filled with lead. But he wasn't finished yet; he kept looking for the opportunity to deliver that one good punch that would end the fight. He hoped that Benito would become overconfident and in a moment of carelessness let his guard down.

As the bell was about to ring again, the very situation that The Boulder had been so anxiously awaiting, developed. While Benito delivered a hammering right to the stomach, he himself dropped his guard for just a fraction of a second, but long enough for The Boulder to connect that fatal blow. It caught Benito square on the nose—inside his head he heard the cartilages popping as they shattered—and the impact landed him on his back.

The crowd let out a roar.

Benito's face was completely covered in blood; the tissues were beginning to swell. For an instant everyone though the bout was over, but at that moment the merciful sound of the bell filled the chamber again. Benito's handler rushed him to his corner, placed a towel over the face and made him lean back in order to stop the bleeding.

"It's over," he whispered, "We can ask for a rematch in a few months."

Benito shook his head negatively; he had not trained so hard, come this far to quit now. He would give the crowd a performance they would never forget.

"Your nose is broken," insisted the handler, "if you get back in there, The Boulder will go straight for your face."

"I hope so," Benito said as the sound of the bell summoned the fighters again. Everyone expected to see the towel tossed into the middle of the ring, signifying surrender, so they were simultaneously surprised and thrilled when Benito answered the call.

Corroborating the handler's predictions, The Boulder—perhaps enraged because he thought the contest was over—concentrated his attacks on Benito's face. But the very fact that he was trying to land high punches with his right, combined with his propensity to momentarily drop his left during the instant of delivery, made him vulnerable. His energies spent, trying to fend off Benito's relentless barrage during the first half hour, began to manifest itself in the slowness of his movements. This, of course, further compounded his vulnerability. Neither pugilist could last much longer.

It was during one of these attacks that Benito, spotting the opening through the blood that covered his face, delivered the fatal blow that caught The Boulder right on the solar plexus. It was—some of the spectators later recalled—as if a mountain that everyone thought indestructible would suddenly crumble and begin to disintegrate.

The Boulder stumbled for a few seconds; his arms were lowered, no longer offering a threat or a defensive shield. Then he collapsed. His body showed irregular spasms, perhaps reflecting a severe arrhythmia brought about by the brutal blow to the chest.

Benito, although still standing, was also in bad shape. Besides the broken nose that kept bleeding profusely, his eyes were beginning to swell shut. It was obvious that both men were in need of immediate medical attention. His handler, with the aid of some of the spectators, placed them in his car and rushed them to the nearest hospital. The Boulder was still unconscious; Benito was in a haze induced by the pain.

The doctor on duty was appalled at the condition of the men. After all their wounds were cleaned and disinfected, they were placed in one of the hospital rooms. The Boulder had not regained consciousness, but his condition had been stabilized. Benito, although swollen and unrecognizable, was aware of everything around him.

A week passed. The same doctor, who had admitted him on the night of the fight, came into the room one sunny morning.

"You are almost ready to go home," he told Benito. "But before you go, I would like to fix your broken nose."

"What about him?" asked Benito, pointing to The Boulder on the next bed and ignoring the doctor's comment.

"He will have to stay; we don't know how long it will be until he wakes up. Maybe he never will. In the meantime he will require constant care."

Benito pondered for just a moment.

"Forget about the nose; I will leave that money so you can take care of him. It's the least I can do."

"As you wish," said the doctor, "Then you are free to go." He understood it was a matter of priorities.

After his discharge, Benito did not bother going back to his job at the docks, but walked directly to the seminary and asked to be admitted. His broken nose was a reminder, every time he looked in the mirror, that he had almost killed a man for no good reason at all.

Because of his reputation around Naples as an ex-boxer, his superiors decided to assign him to a local parish, where he would have the most influence, especially among young people. From clandestine fighter to catholic priest. The Lord did work, indeed, in mysterious ways.

As father Benito saw Francesca and her children approaching the church, he smiled amply and opened his arms as a sign of welcome. Years earlier, he had seen her perform next to Louis at the San Carlo Theater and since that time he had kept up with her career and the unfortunate events that had led to her present situation.

He welcomed Francesca with a hug and then, turning to her children, commented on how tall Guido had gotten and how beautiful Anna had become. Somehow, he had memorized the names of the children that attended the church—no small feat, since families were usually large—when they had been baptized and when their first communions or confirmations were coming up. Everybody knew that they could count on father Benito for anything, and stories abounded as to how he had helped many families not just with their spiritual development, but also when they needed help meeting their financial obligations.

The sound of the bells announced that it was almost time for the mass. The small crowd that had congregated on the portico of the church slowly began to make its way into the temple. They would have to settle for the less desirable pews in the back, since the early comers and those who walked right in without lingering to make small talk always took the better seats, close to the raised pulpit with its baroque carvings, or next to the baptismal fountain sculpted from Carrara marble. Some families even occupied entire pews every single week; their names might as well have been engraved on the wooden surface, since everyone respected their tacit claim. Before long, father Benito appeared at the altar, dressed in his ecclesiastic garb, and began the mass. Everyone knew what to do; the liturgy went back centuries, and it would no doubt go on unchanged after they were dead and gone.

After the homily—it usually dealt with making the right choices in life—while father Benito was readying the altar for the consecration of the host, Paolo appeared. He was dressed in white, furthering his resemblance to an angel. He stood silently next to the altar, waiting for the music to begin. When the first notes of the organ were heard, he looked up, closed his eyes and began to sing. This was, indeed, the highlight of the mass; he managed to transport everyone present with his voice to a higher plane, to suspend momentarily the mundane cares that kept them from achieving a glimpse of the divine. Yes, he was an angel.

When the hymn concluded, father Benito was ready for the consecration. Paolo's performance invariably awoke in the congregation a yearning for the ineffable that could only be satisfied by partaking of the flesh and blood of Jesus that the priest was about to offer them.

They slowly made their way to the altar, pious looks on their faces and hearts filled with resolutions of becoming better Christians. At the end of the mass, father Benito delivered a final blessing and exited the church followed by the altar boys. He greeted the parishioners warmly and wished them a happy Sunday. His sincere smile and broken nose had become his trademark.

Signora Alberti and Paolo exited the church followed by Francesca, Guido and Anna.

"I want to tell you how much we enjoyed Paolo's singing," said Francesca to signora Alberti once they were outside. "He has a priceless gift."

"You are most kind," she replied.

"We would like to invite you for coffee, if you have the time." Then, to make sure signora Alberti would accept the invitation, she added "I would like to talk to you some more about Paolo's career."

"That would be nice," she said, maybe a little surprised at the invitation. "Is one hour suitable for you?"

"That is fine," answered Francesca, "It will give us time to change and get things ready. We will see you then."

"What will you tell signora Alberti?" Anna asked her mother on the way back to their house.

"The truth," she answered, "Just the simple truth. She came to me for an honest opinion about Paolo's voice and career, so she deserves nothing less."

"She will not like it," said Anna. "It seems that her entire life revolves around Paolo's future."

"I know, but I can't change the facts," concluded Francesca. "Not to tell her would be more cruel."

Guido, on the other hand, had stayed out of the conversation. He was only vaguely aware of Paolo Alberti's talent and was more interested in looking at the young women who, in their Sunday's best, were exiting the church after the mass. It was his custom to change clothes and go out to meet his friends.

Back in their house Francesca and Anna, alone in the kitchen, began to make the preparations for signora Alberti's visit. They took out and washed the Sevres porcelain cups—the set had been bought by Louis d'Amio himself after he and Francesca had married—that were only used during special occasions, and prepared the tray on which the coffee would be served.

Since they were having company, they did not bother to change their clothes. It was nice to have an afternoon off from daily chores and just relax in the company of friends.

Anna, in order to pass the time as they tidied up the living room, placed Immortal Arias on the turntable and turned on the machine. Her father's powerful voice reached out at her from behind a curtain of faint static. Listening to him always made her feel better, as if his voice were a reassurance that even though he was not physically present, his spirit was constantly watching over her. She only wished that he could have been around longer.

The two women went about their task silently, each immersed in her own thoughts, memories and emotions that Louis' voice invariably evoked. When the recording was over, Francesca came closer to her daughter and hugged her silently.

"I miss him too," she said with tears in her eyes. There was no need to say anything else. Each one acknowledged the void that he had left, as they both acknowledged the fact that it would never be filled.

Before long there was a knock on the door. Anna opened it and, punctual as ever, found signora Alberti. Paolo, however, was nowhere to be found.

"Come in; my mother is waiting for you," she said, and then, not being able to help herself, "But where is Paolo?"

"He had things to do at home;" explained signora Alberti, "It is just as well; I don't think he should hear what your mother has to say. Good or bad, it would take his concentration away from his singing," she explained as they walked into the modest living room.

Francesca welcomed the visitor and asked her to sit down. Anna, in the meantime, disappeared into the kitchen to prepare the coffee and pastries.

"I am glad that you could come," Francesca began. "Ever since the visit to your house and Paolo's beautiful song, I have been wanting to talk to you."

"You said then that he had talent," said signora Alberti, thinking perhaps that this visit had to do with Francesca's connection to the San Carlo opera house and a possible opportunity for her son.

"His talent is undeniable, but I am concerned about something else that may impede the progress of his career. That is why I wanted to speak with you, to make you aware of it. I believe that as his mother you would want to know."

"Go on, please," urged signora Alberti.

"Paolo is at a very critical age; before long his voice will break. No one knows what it will sound like, but one thing is certain, it will be nothing like the voice he has now. I am afraid that once that happens all his hopes for an operatic career will be shattered."

"I understand," said signora Alberti, "and I thank you for your concern. I know you have Paolo's best interests at heart."

"You do not seem to be very concerned; is he aware of the situation?" asked Francesca.

"We have never discussed it," she said. "There is no need."

54

"How so?" asked Francesca with genuine curiosity.

"I mentioned before that I was looking for someone to manage Paolo's career; signore Giacomo Pace has agreed. He says that Paolo has a great future in opera."

Giacomo Pace was well known in the operatic world. A middle-aged, balding man who was always looking for that big break that would consolidate his professional reputation and reinforce his already solid financial standing. For the most part, so far he had only been able to manage third-rate singers who could hardly command top billing and draw the crowds necessary to establish stellar careers.

"I still don't understand how that can stop what is inevitable; his voice will change," Francesca added vehemently.

Signora Alberti made a pause, as if trying to find the words that would make everything clear.

At that precise moment Anna came in from the kitchen holding the tray with the freshly brewed espresso and some pastries. She placed everything on the center table and sat down. The two women made a pause in their conversation, sipped their coffee and ate the pastries.

"Signore Pace and I have been planning Paolo's career; he told me the same thing that you just did, but I offered a solution," explained signora Alberti as she sipped on the coffee again.

"What kind of solution?" inquired Francesca.

"Have you ever heard of Alessandro Moreschi?" She pronounced the name softly, almost with reverence.

Francesca's hand stopped in mid air, still holding the steaming cup of espresso. Her mouth was half open with disbelief.

"You can't be serious," she finally said.

"Nothing is more important than Paolo's career," she added. "Besides, the list is endless: Moreschi, Farinelli, Porporino, Bernachi... do I need to go on? They all led successful lives."

Anna, in the meantime, was taking in the exchange between her mother and the visitor. She had noticed that Francesca's face had gone pale when the name of Moreschi had been mentioned, but she had no idea why.

"And how does Paolo feel about this plan?" asked Francesca.

"Paolo will go along with whatever I say, especially if I am backed by signore Pace. He wants to have a career in opera; I will go to any length to make that happen. Besides," added signora

Alberti after a pause, "this is nothing new; it has been going on for centuries. Even the church has condoned it. The important thing is that Paolo will have a bright future doing what he was meant to do: sing."

"I hope you are right," said Francesca, "but if you ask me, the price is too high to pay."

There was nothing more to be said; suddenly the atmosphere had become tense, as if an impending discharge of electricity were on the verge of striking the occupants of the small living room. Francesca had voiced her concern about Paolo's imminent change of voice; signora Alberti had been quite clear about what she intended to do about it. One thing was certain; she would not let anything or anyone stand in the way of her goal of making her son an opera star.

"Thank you for the coffee and the hospitality," she said while standing up. "I must go home and check on Paolo."

"Thank you for coming," answered Francesca. "Please give our regards to your son; tell him we missed him."

"I will," she said on the way out, "and I hope both of you come to visit again to hear Paolo sing."

After closing the door, Francesca collapsed on the sofa, still trying to assimilate the full impact of the revelation. She could not believe that signora Alberti would go through with what she considered to be an almost demented plan.

Anna, in turn, had remained silent during the conversation, but had easily detected the change of mood as it progressed. She knew her mother and the tone of her voice, although controlled, had shifted from cordial to almost hostile.

"Who is Alessandro Moreschi?" she finally asked Francesca.

"Alessandro Moreschi was a soprano opera singer who died recently," she explained, but without offering further details.

"So what was so special about him? You turned pale and your hand shook when signora Alberti mentioned his name."

"Not special, but different," clarified Francesca. "As a boy he was subjected to an operation that prevented his voice from changing; he was turned into a *castrato*. At the height of his career the range of his voice went three octaves beyond the reach of other male sopranos."

"Is that what signora Alberti intends to do to Paolo?" asked Anna with a tone of disbelief.

"I am afraid so," answered Francesca. "The sad thing is," she continued, "that I believe that she is not truly acting on his best behalf, but based on an opportunity to better her economic conditions."

"But isn't this against the law?" protested Anna in a vehement tone, "After all we are not living in the dark ages; this is the twentieth century!"

"Of course it is against the law," explained Francesca, but unscrupulous individuals who will perform this operation can always be found. Greed is a most powerful motivation."

"But there must be something we can do," protested Anna. "That is barbaric. Maybe we can go to the police."

Francesca smiled faintly, amused at her daughter's passion and naiveté.

"Alessandro Moreschi was not a unique case," she explained. "This practice has been going on for centuries, especially here in Italy. In fact, during the Baroque era the works of Vivaldi, Bach and Handel contained parts written specifically for the *castrati*. Furthermore, even though at first the Vatican was ambivalent towards this practice, eventually Pope Clement VIII authorized the practice of castration, but only *ad gloriam Dei*: for the glory of God. I am both sad and appalled that signora Alberti has even considered such a course of action," added Francesca after a brief pause. "We can only pray that she will change her mind."

"I just think it is wrong," retorted Anna with a tone of frustration.

"I could not agree with you more," said Francesca, "but there is nothing we can do about it."

There was nothing more to be said. Francesca started to clear the tray and the empty cups of coffee from the living room. No matter how humble a house, she always maintained, there was no reason for messiness. Once she was done in the living room, she took everything into the kitchen, so she could wash it right away.

Anna, on the other hand, stayed in the living room. She turned on the old gramophone and placed Immortal Arias on the turntable. Somehow her father's voice had the ability to soothe her, to infuse her with confidence and clarity of purpose. By the time the record was over, she had conceived her plan. Now it was just a matter of waiting for the right moment to implement its execution.

In subsequent nights, unable to fall asleep and listening to those distant yet distinct sounds that were always present beyond midnight, she marveled at the decision she had made. She realized that it was a desperate plan, but she saw no other alternative. She also thought of Paolo, completely oblivious to his mother's machinations, and the future that awaited him. Why she felt as strongly as she did was still a mystery.

One thing was clear; she had never felt about anyone the way she felt about Paolo. Surrounded by the darkness and the distant sounds, she would finally fall asleep, thinking of his blue eyes looking at her.

Signora Alberti, as did most Italian widows, led a very structured life. Besides going to church on Sundays and to her job as a bookkeeper during the week, she spent the rest of her time supervising her son's activities. Although she considered Paolo's school work important, she had always viewed it as secondary, for she knew that ultimately he would pursue a musical career. She took him to choir rehearsal on Wednesday nights and to voice lessons on Monday nights. He was only left alone on Friday nights, when she attended the weekly novena led by father Benito at the Santa Chiara Church.

Anna knew of these activities—after all, signora Alberti and Francesca were sort of friends—so it was not difficult for her to figure out the few hours when Paolo was alone. The most propitious time—perhaps the only time—was on Friday nights. Her own mother also attended the novena, so she would be able to carry out her plan unfettered by her presence. But even after figuring all the details, she still had a nagging question in her mind: would she have the courage to pull it off? After all, her plan involved taking a course of action that went against all the precepts she had been taught as far back as she could remember; if discovered, her life would practically be ruined.

The days until Friday seemed slower and longer, as if the individual hours had been drenched in heavy molasses that impeded their flow towards the natural completion of the days. She busied herself with her school work, helped her mother in the kitchen and even gave her a hand with the laundry that Francesca took in to earn a little extra money. When Friday finally came around, the tension had built to an almost unbearable level. Again, it was not the decision, but the uncertainty of her resolve to carry

58

it out what made her nervous. Her mother, as usual, made small talk and after a light supper began to get ready for the novena. Her brother Guido, as he did every Friday night, would go out with his friends.

To calm her nerves Anna went into the living room, opened an art book, turned on the old gramophone and placed Immortal Arias on the turntable. She closed her eyes and tried to ease her breathing while she listened to the music.

The first one to leave the house was Guido; he would meet with his friends and would not return until after midnight. About fifteen minutes later Francesca stepped into the living room and informed her that she was going to church for the novena. This was completely unnecessary, since she had been doing it for almost two years, but somehow she felt compelled to let her daughter know of her whereabouts, just in case. The novenas, besides their obvious religious aspect, also had a social component. The women always gathered after the service to exchange a bit of harmless gossip, a favorite recipe, or the latest news to come out of Rome or the Vatican.

At last Anna was alone. She did not, however, leave right after her mother, but waited for the needle to reach the final grooves of the record, for the last notes delivered from beyond the grave by her father to softly dissolve in the dimly lit room. She returned the record, with careful and respectful hands, to its protective sleeve, placed it with the others beside the gramophone and then left the house. Despite the mollifying effect that her father's voice always had on her, she felt her heart beating faster with every step that brought her closer to Paolo's house. Being a Friday evening, the streets were more populated than during the week, but she did not notice. The wild beating of her heart echoed her hurried steps towards that improbable mission she had conceived. Eventually she found herself in front of signora Alberti's house. For a moment she hesitated; this was, indeed, the most momentous and consequential decision she had ever made in her entire life.

Once she knocked on the door, all reservations were gone. What few doubts she may have had about her plan were immediately dispelled when she saw Paolo standing in the threshold. Somehow he seemed taller than before, his eyes bluer and more piercing. Maybe this was directly attributable to his proximity;

they had never been this close and now he was looking directly at her. He seemed surprised, maybe even a little puzzled to see Anna.

"My mother is not home," he said softly, hinting that she should return at a later time.

"I know," answered Anna, "but I did not come to see her." By this time she had already made her way into the small living room. Her boldness not only surprised Paolo, but Anna herself. She knew that she could not linger by the doorway, lest she be recognized by a passerby, so she slipped into the house as soon as possible. From the back wall of the living room she detected what seemed a look of reproach on the face of the late signore Alberti's photograph.

"I know your mother is in church," she said, "What are you doing, all by yourself?"

"I wasn't singing, if that's what you mean," he answered softly, without looking directly at her.

"Were you doing school work?" Anna persisted.

"No, I was arranging my postcard collection. Friday evenings is one of the few times in the week when I have time for myself," he explained. "My mother schedules every moment of my life," he added, as if it were an afterthought.

"I would like to see your collection very much," said Anna.

"It is in my bedroom; I will bring it out," said Paolo.

"That's not necessary; just show it to me," said Anna softly placing a hand on his right arm.

Paolo did not object; he led Anna to the back of the house, where his room was located. Just as he had said, spread on the bed, an assortment of post cards could be seen.

"They are mostly from Italy," he explained as he picked up a post card showing the ruins of Pompeii. "But I have some from other countries too. Sometimes I wonder what it would be like to visit those faraway places."

Anna had sat on the bed and started to pick up some of the post cards, feigning an interest that she did not feel. She had not forgotten the purpose of her visit.

"What about this one?" she asked innocently while tugging on Paolo's arm. He sat down next to her on the bed and looked at the post card she was holding.

"That's the island of Capri," he explained.

She put her arm casually around his shoulders and leaned forward, pretending to get closer to the post card that Paolo was holding. Then she placed her other hand wantonly on his thigh and began to caress him softly.

Once again she marveled at her own boldness, but at the same time she realized this was no time for introspection. She could tell that Paolo was completely disconcerted; he had not tried to pull away, but he had not made a move either. Anna attributed this not to lack of desire, but lack of experience. The irregular rhythm of his respiration told her that whatever she was doing was having an effect and that Paolo did not find it completely unpleasant. She closed her eyes and thought that what she was doing would deliver Paolo from a fate worse than death, for what could be worse than to live without ever knowing love?

Their complete inexperience did not prevent them from finding the appropriate path; soon they were locked in a tight, passionate embrace. The initial kisses—soft and timid—soon turned into passionate ones whose ultimate goal was at once to possess and be possessed by the other. That first taste of physical love for both of them was like the taste of a forbidden fruit whose nectar sent them into a state of absolute euphoria, while simultaneously—rather than satiating that uncontrollable yearning—made them desire the other even more.

Paolo's postcard collection was now randomly strewn on the floor, along with the clothes they had instinctively discarded in the heat of their growing passion. Anna's hand did not have any difficulty in finding the most sensitive, yet hardened component of his form. She stroked him softly, again marveling at her lack of restraint and indescribable joy of the moment.

Eventually she found herself on her back, with Paolo on top of her. He had, indeed, the physique of an angel. Nature was taking its course; before long they achieved a common rhythm, punctuated by occasional moans and smiles of sheer pleasure. Their youthful vigor made up what they lacked in experience. At the common moment of release, she felt his body tensing momentarily and his back arching. Then the two bodies lay flaccid on the bed, momentarily spent and gasping for air. They did not think of separating, but stayed in the same position—still one being—and softly caressed each other, this time at a more leisurely pace and with infinite tenderness.

Suddenly Anna thought of the time. She had no idea how long she had been with Paolo and the last thing she wanted was for signora Alberti to come home from the novena and find her there.

"I have to go," she said softly and gently pushed Paolo off her. She started to dress hurriedly, picking up her randomly scattered clothes. All the while Paolo stayed on the bed, simultaneously transfixed by the sight of her beautiful, youthful body and in awe of what had just taken place. After a few minutes he also got off the bed, got dressed and walked Anna to the front door. Before leaving, they shared one last, passionate kiss that conveyed everything that words never could.

The walk home was as quick and furtive, but in reverse, as the one she had made earlier. She stepped into the house and let out a sigh of relief when the reigning silence confirmed that her mother was still in church. She remembered that the women who attended the novena always lingered after the services in order to share the latest news about their families or some exciting piece of gossip they had picked up at the local market.

Anna went into the kitchen and, despite the late hour, made some coffee. She took the steaming cup to the living room and placed it on a side table; her hands were shaking, despite the fact that she had made it home safely. While the coffee cooled off a bit, she placed Immortal Arias on the old record player and then sat down, trying to assimilate all that had happened in that short interval of time. Without a doubt, she had attained her original objective: now that Paolo had experienced physical love, he would never submit to a procedure that would emasculate him and remove any possibility of future intimacy with a woman. She had taken his innocence and the possibility of a brilliant musical career. In exchange she had surrendered her virginity. Had it been a fair trade? Only time would tell. Italian society—or maybe it was just men—placed a high value on maidenhood at the time of marriage. Any doubt cast about the virtue of a bride could be disastrous. It was not uncommon for men to return their new wives to her parents if on the wedding night he felt he was dealing with 'damaged goods.' Whether it had been a good move on her part, Anna realized, could be debated, but she was glad that her plan had proceeded as planned. If necessary, she would do it again. One thing was certain: there was no going back now; the person who had left the house earlier that evening no longer existed, just as the innocent boy who sang in church had surely vanished.

She sipped the hot coffee, closed her eyes and listened to Louis d'Amio's voice. She always felt that her father was singing just for her, that his infinite love was being delivered with every note that enveloped her, the notes that often times made her cry with his passionate delivery and the insurmountable chasm of his absence. She missed him.

The sound of the door opening brought her back to the present moment. She knew it was her mother coming back from the novena. Suddenly Anna felt a rush of emotions overtaking her; she feared that her mother would hear the uncontrollable beating of her heart and read on her face all that had happened during her short absence. She took a deep breath and tried to look calm.

"How was church?" she said as her mother stepped into the small living room, trying to make the tone of her voice a normal as possible.

"The same," answered Francesca as she placed her purse on a side table. "But it is always nice to leave the house for a while and see other people," she added.

"That is true," agreed Anna, "Especially when someone works as hard as you do."

"We do what we must," answered Francesca with a faint smile. As far back as she could remember, Anna had never heard her mother complain about the long hours and the burden of raising two children without the benefits—financial and emotional—of a husband. Anna also suspected that her mother, although still a relatively young woman, would never marry again. After all, who could measure up to Louis d'Amio? These were some of the many reasons Anna loved her mother and why she was so close to her. What had taken place at Paolo's house, obviously, she could not share with anyone, especially Francesca. For the first time she felt an invisible, yet most tangible wall rising between them.

"I think I will turn in for the night," announced Francesca. "Tomorrow will be a long day." She was referring to the extra work she had been doing for years every Saturday since the children were small. It was during these long days, surrounded by piles of clothes to be washed, that Anna and her mother had had their most meaningful conversations. This particular instance, for the first time, she knew it would be different. What she had done would have to be kept secret from her mother—from the rest of the world, for that matter—for it went against every precept she had ever been taught. Yet, she was not sorry. She had acted in the only way that was available to save Paolo from a terrible fate. Everything in her own life would go on as before.

"Good night," said Anna as she kissed her mother on the cheek. Suddenly she felt tired herself, not so much a physical exhaustion, but an emotional one. The tension that had been building up during the past few days as the time to carry out her plan approached, was finally catching up with her. She must have been more tired that she thought, for the following morning she realized that she had not heard her brother Guido come in the night before.

Despite her careful planning, Anna could never have guessed the unforeseen consequences that the short, but intense time she had spent with Paolo would trigger. She had intended all along to awaken a sleeping Eros in a boy that was entering the threshold of manhood; that goal, without a doubt, had been accomplished. He would never submit to the perverse procedure that signora Alberti had planned for him; of that she was certain. Now that her purpose had been met, everything could go on as before; no one would find out who was responsible for the abrupt change in Paolo's attitude when he rebelled against his mother's wishes.

Yet, despite herself, she felt an inner restlessness, a secret yearning that at first she refused to acknowledge, but that after a few days surfaced with the force of an erupting volcano: she wanted to see Paolo again. In her mind she relived time and again the moments of complete ecstasy that they had shared, shrouded in the secrecy of his room, while Francesca and signora Alberti attended father Benito's novena. It was a demented idea, she concluded. No matter how she felt, she could still control her own actions. Besides, she had no idea how Paolo felt about her. Life should go on as before; time would take care of the rest.

For the next two weeks Anna busied herself more than ever with her school work and helping her mother with the household chores. She even asked her brother about his work in the automotive shop, and patiently listened to him as he tried to explain the mysteries and complexities of an internal combustion engine. In short, she purposely sought the physical and mental exhaustion that would allow her to sleep at night and prevent her mind from wandering and try to recapture the secret communion — spiritual and carnal — she had shared with Paolo.

It all seemed to be working; her mother welcomed the help without any questions, her grades were better than ever and Guido was more than happy that his little sister had taken an interest in what he was doing. But as it often happens in life, seemingly insignificant and unforeseen events have a way of altering the course of lives in unpredictable and unfathomable ways.

One Sunday morning, as Francesca, Anna and Guido were leaving the church; they ran into signora Alberti and Paolo. Francesca, of course, stopped to talk to signora Alberti; Guido was busy with his friends. For a moment Anna was startled; she did not know what to say or where to look. But this time it was not up to her; it was Paolo who, overcoming his shyness, made his way through the crowd to where she was standing. Suddenly he was facing her, looking at her with those deep, beautiful blues eyes of his. Anna did not know what to say. Neither one had the right words—if they existed at all—but Paolo reached into his pocket and handed Anna a post card depicting the ruins of Pompeii. She recognized it at once; simultaneously she felt the onrush of memories being triggered by that image. Then he was gone, lost in the crowd that gesticulated wildly under the soft morning sun, making his way back to where signora Alberti and Francesca were still talking.

Anna realized that it must have taken a tremendous effort for Paolo to approach her, especially in public. His motivation had had to overcome his innate timidity. It was obvious that he wanted to see her again; maybe he had been trying to make some sense—as she had—of what had taken place several weeks earlier and the torrent of new and overwhelming emotions that no doubt the encounter had awakened. The post card had been a tacit, yet explicit invitation. Of one thing Anna was certain: signora Alberti had not yet unveiled her plans to Paolo. That revelation would have to come soon, before his voice broke and her plan to direct her son's musical career—his life—was no longer viable.

Anna joined Francesca and Guido; no one had noticed the brief exchange between her and Paolo. On the way back to the house Guido kept talking to her about an engine he and his friends were building; by now he had gotten used to his sister listening to his exploits at the automotive shop. Anna pretended to be listening and from time to time she nodded or uttered monosyllabic words of approval or understanding. Her mind, of course, was in a different place—a chaotic labyrinth—and contemplating other possibilities. She did not know what to do, and the worst was the knowledge that she could not ask for anyone's help in making a decision.

As Friday approached, just as before, she tried to convince herself that the easiest and most sensible thing was to do nothing, to stay away from Paolo and allow life to proceed at its own pace without any disruptions or surprises. She was in awe at how life — her school work, her chores at home — was seemingly unchanged, but how everything, at least from that new perspective, was radically different.

Taking shallow breaths in her bed and unable to sleep at night, she listened to the distant sounds that came from the streets, closed her eyes tightly and evoked vividly Paolo's beautiful features, the gaze of his deep blue eyes and the gentle touch of his hands.

By the time Friday came around she had made up her mind. Just as she had done previously, she waited for her mother to go off to church. Fifteen minutes later, she left the house, walking hurriedly and looking down at the cobblestones, lest anyone would recognize her and stop her to make idle conversation, or worse, tell her mother that they had seen her on the street. When she reached Paolo's house, her heart was pounding with such force that Anna thought that certainly it could be heard by anyone who was close by. Before she could knock on the door, it opened by itself. It was evident that Paolo had been watching the street from one of the windows; he was as anxious to see her as she was to see him.

Once inside and out of view, they did not speak, but became locked in a long, passionate embrace and an ardent kiss that seemed to last an eternity. Anna realized then that the Eros she had awakened was bigger and stronger than both of them, not unlike a hunger that listened to no reason and whose only and ultimate goal was to be with the other until the longing was completely satiated. She didn't know how long that would take; she didn't care. The only reality at the moment was to be with Paolo, the only thing that mattered was the unbridled urgency of his hands caressing every part of her body. Without breaking the embrace, they made their way to his bedroom. Anna was truly surprised, given Paolo's innate shyness, when he started to unbutton her blouse and to run his hands on her bare skin. Without preambles, they freed themselves of the confinement imposed by their clothes and sighed with pure delight as their bodies made contact.

Anna received him without reservations, with the exuberance and passion that can only be found in youth; she rejoiced in his presence and allowed her feelings to flow unrestrained. This time Paolo was more sure of himself; he took more time exploring Anna's body and purposely lingered on those parts that caused her to emit moans of pleasure or sighs of ecstasy whenever his hands or his mouth caressed them. He was learning fast—albeit instinctively—that the ultimate joy that a man could experience was the joining with that female who was the subject of one's affection. The moment of release came sooner than they would have wanted; at that point they lacked the control that only comes with experience. For a while they lay together, attempting to make contact with every inch of the other's body, breathing closely and still caressing each other.

Then Anna, as she had done weeks before, jumped out of bed and dressed quickly. At the door Paolo gave her a last passionate kiss as she furtively disappeared into the night, praying that her mother would not have returned from her weekly novena. That night, lying awake in her bed, she recalled the events of the evening. Her feelings for Paolo were becoming stronger, and despite the absurdity of the situation, she could not conceive her life without him. A hundred times she told herself that he was merely a boy, that she was still attending school, that the possibilities of an open relationship were nil. Reason dictated that she should stop seeing him, that with time they would both get over it and life would resume its normal course. Yet, she kept thinking of his blue eyes, his perfect complexion, the softness of his hands and the urgency of his lovemaking. They were at an impasse.

During Sunday mass, when he sang, Paolo's voice displayed a brio that had not been there before; his eyes gleamed with a new light as he lifted his head toward the figures on the main altar and delivered the prescribed hymns with absolute conviction. It was as if he had found and tapped into a new and inexhaustible source of energy and inspiration. Everyone, of course, attributed the change to a deepening religious experience and inner commitment to his appointed destiny. Just as on the day he was born, many thought they were in the presence of an angel, for surely no mere mortal could be capable of producing such melodic sounds that inspired even the most recalcitrant parishioners to embrace the faith.

Signora Alberti could not have been more pleased; she envisioned the future singing engagements that would bring her son — and her, of course — national fame and abundant wealth.

But Anna knew that Paolo's enthusiasm emanated from that illicit relationship they had maintained for almost two months. He had tapped into a source of inspiration that had sustained men from the beginning of time and in turn had given rise to the most exquisite and creative artistic expressions throughout history. On the other hand, besides the boundless joy they found in each other's company, an element of fear was always present. Although they had both purposely avoided the subject, lest their intimate moments be clouded, they were both aware of the dire consequences if their clandestine affair were to be discovered.

Another concern—one that Anna had not shared this with Paolo—was that soon signora Alberti would have to break the news to her son about the surgical procedure that would halt his masculine development. She knew that Paolo would never submit to such operation, but what would happen then was anybody's guess. All these conjectures, as it turned out, were in vain; the hand of fate was soon to precipitate a series of events that would drastically change their lives.

One Friday evening, indistinct from the rest, Anna and Paolo were in the privacy of his bedroom making passionate love. In the heat of their passion, they did not hear the front door opening as signora Alberti came home from the novena. Father Benito had been called to administer the sacrament of last rites to a parishioner who was on his dying bed, so the novena had been cancelled for that evening. To make matters worse, signora Alberti was not alone; Francesca was with her. In view of the cancellation of the church service, she had asked her friend to join her for coffee at her house. Francesca had accepted because it was on the way home and because she still hoped to dissuade signora Alberti of the plans she had for Paolo.

From the bedroom the couple heard signora Alberti calling her son's name, and then the approaching steps. Assuming he was in the bedroom, perhaps organizing his post card collection or studying, she opened the door and walked in.

Her return had been so unexpected and swift that Anna and Paolo had only had time to break their embrace and leap out of his bed, but their clothes were still strewn on the floor. There had been no time to get dressed. Signora Alberti, upon finding the naked couple, knew immediately what had taken place. She stood in the threshold, one hand over her open mouth and the other clutching her heart.

"Why, God, why?" she screamed at the top of her lungs. It was not a plea for an answer, but a lamentation of the fate that had befallen her.

By that time, upon hearing her friend scream, Francesca had run to see what was the matter and was now also in Paolo's bedroom. At first she turned white, and after a few moments of silence her face became flush with a mixture of rage and shame. She approached Anna with slow, deliberate movements and stood in front of her. She looked at her daughter up and down, as if trying to convince herself that she was not having a nightmare. Then, with swift and unexpected motion, she slapped her forcefully.

"Get dressed," she told her daughter with a fury she could barely contain; "We will settle this at home."

Signora Alberti, in the meantime, had collapsed on a chair and was weeping softly; all her dreams, like a mirage in the desert, had evaporated in a matter of seconds.

Anna and Francesca left the house without saying a word; there were no words that could undo what had taken place or rectify the damage that had been done. Anna walked behind her mother, with her head down, trying to contain the tears that kept streaming down her cheeks. But they were not tears of remorse for the pain she had inflicted on her mother, or the shame she had brought upon the family, but rather tears of sorrow at the thought that she might never see Paolo again.

III

After that fateful night when she and Paolo were discovered in his bedroom, Anna remained at home indefinitely. It was just as well; the consequences of her actions were now beginning to be felt. For the first time in his life, Paolo had fought with his mother, and after a heated argument, he had left the house in the middle of the night. In her frantic search for the boy, Sofia Alberti did not hesitate to tell anyone who would listen how her young and innocent son had been led astray by Anna. As far as everyone was concerned, she was no better than a whore, a common *puttana* who was out only for a good time. Of course, every time the story was told, it acquired more graphic details as it was embellished with every new version. Anna's reputation was ruined; from this point on no man would look at her with honorable intentions.

The tense situation was also taking its toll on Francesca. As if she did not have enough making ends meet to provide a decent life and a future for her children, now she also had to bear this cross. Although on more than one occasion she asked herself what terrible infraction she had committed for God to punish her so terribly, her faith did not falter. Sheltered in the privacy and darkness of her room she clutched a rosary and tirelessly intoned the monotonous recitations while tears streamed down her face. The answer to her prayers—further proof that the designs of God are unfathomable—arrived a month later in the form of a most unexpected visitor.

Francesca had returned from her job, eaten a quick dinner and was in the process of cleaning up the kitchen. Anna, as usual since the night she and Paolo were discovered, was secluded in her bedroom; Guido was out with his friends from the shop. The unanticipated knock on the door made her stop in midair what she was doing. For a moment she thought it was a random noise from the street, but after a few seconds the firm knocking was repeated. She was not expecting anyone, so there was no way she could even begin to guess who would be calling at that hour. She dried her hands on the apron she was wearing and went to open the door.

"*Buona sera*," said the man standing in the threshold.

At first Francesca did not recognize him, and then she thought that her eyes were deceiving her. It was none other than Giacomo Pace, manager of third-rate performers and signora Alberti's accomplice in the task of shaping Paolo's musical career. Maybe she had sent him on a nefarious errand to extract revenge for derailing her son's future.

"May I come in?" he asked. His polite, unctuous manner gave no clue as to the purpose of his unannounced visit. After a few moments Francesca stood aside and Giacomo Pace stepped into her modest living room. She noticed that he was wearing the same suit that he had whenever she had seen him in previous occasions at the San Carlo Theater.

"How may I help you," asked Francesca, still without a clue as to the manager's visit. She wanted it to be quick so she could get back to her chores in the kitchen.

"I have a proposal for you," he said. "But let's sit down so you can hear me out."

Francesca sat down in her usual chair, under Louis' photograph, locked her hands on her lap and waited. Across from her, Giacomo Pace made himself comfortable in one of the secondhand chairs that someone had given her when the family had moved in years before. He sat up straight and looked at Francesca directly in the face. She could almost see the small cogwheelsturning is his head, as he readied to disclose what had brought him there that night.

"Let me be direct and to the point," he uttered. "I want to marry your daughter."

Francesca started to say something, but Giacomo Pace raised his hand before she could articulate her thoughts.

"Please hear me out before you give me an answer," he said. "I am aware, as everyone else is, of the events that took place recently. I will not place the blame on anyone; what is done is done. The fact remains, however, that signora Alberti's son no longer has a career. In fact, no one knows of his whereabouts. As a consequence, Anna" — this was the first time he spoke her name — "has lost that which is most prized by our culture." Francesca realized at once that he was speaking of Anna's virginity, that priceless gift which a bride offered her husband on their wedding night, but he was using vague terminology in order not to shock or to offend, lest his proposal be rejected. "No sane young man," he continued, "now or in the future, would approach her with a serious proposal of marriage. And the worst part of this situation, in my opinion, is the shame that has been cast on the entire family."

Francesca knew that everything Giacomo Pace had said was true. At work she had observed the other women gossiping, as they always did. Except this time they stopped talking whenever she was within ear reach of the group. Even at church she soon realized that the very group of women with whom she conversed every week after mass were reticent to speak to her for more than a few minutes and they always made excuses for having to leave. Perhaps they feared that if they stayed too long the dark cloud that Francesca seem to carry with her would spread over their own families and bring them shame by association. They considered her situation, even though it had not been of her own doing, something like a plague. Better not to get too close to the carrier, just in case.

And to make matters worse, two nights before Guido had returned home with a black eye and a torn shirt. Although he refused to give any explanations as to what had happened, Francesca knew instinctively that he had gotten into a fight over a comment that someone must have made about his younger sister. This type of behavior, she knew, went against her son's easy going demeanor.

"And why would you want to marry Anna?" asked Francesca in a skeptical tone. "Are you not bothered what people will say, especially behind your back?"

It was a fair question, and one that Giacomo Pace was prepared to answer. As a businessman, he was always looking for opportunities, financial and otherwise. During the past few months he had spent a lot of time and energy laying the groundwork for Paolo's future career. Now that this project had taken a turn for the worse, his attention had turned to Anna. He had reached an age when most men had married and started families, an age when men needed a woman to take care of those details that were involved in running a household.

It was common knowledge that he had always lived with his mother. As an only child, and later as an adult, he enjoyed the undivided attention and care that the old woman bestowed upon him. As she aged, he hired a maid who would take care of the household chores and ease her burden. Towards the end, when she was confined to a wheel chair and eventually to her bed, he would sit with her to keep her company and up to date of what was happening in the world by reading aloud *Il Correo d'ela Sera*, her favorite newspaper. Most of the time she dozed off while her son dutifully read to her, first the international and then the local news. One afternoon she did not wake up; her passing had been as peaceful and serene as her life, guided into the next life by her son's soothing voice. Father Benito was notified and he applied the holy oils post mortem while intoning a prayer entrusting her soul to the Lord.

Although Giacomo was not particularly religious, his mother was; he wanted to follow her wishes until the very end. In life, as long as she was able, Giacomo took her to church every Sunday and sometimes to other religious gatherings. After a funeral mass, she was buried next to her husband. Giacomo Pace had the satisfaction of having been an exemplary son until the very end, but he now recognized that it was time to marry.

As far as Anna was concerned, of course, he had no illusions about love—both the age difference and the unusual circumstances made the possibility nonexistent—but he would settle for female company and maybe in time the welcome touch of a tender hand. What people said did not worry him; he had more important things to think about. In Giacomo Pace's mind, it all made perfect sense. If he could not have Paolo, he would settle for Anna.

"In my line of business, signora d'Amio, one does not worry about what other people think. Let them say what they will; I am not concerned in the least. I do promise you," he continued, "that if you accede to my proposal, your daughter will be well taken care of and she will have a kind and devoted husband. I can offer no more."

Because of her former association with the San Carlo, Francesca was well aware of Giacomo Pace's lack of scruples when it came to business matters and to his loyalty to his mother. Somehow he seemed to be able to compartmentalize the two personas, keeping them completely separate and independent from each other. This knowledge gave her the confidence to conjecture that as far as family relations were concerned, especially the devotion he had shown his late mother, Giacomo Pace was a trustworthy prospect. He would make any woman a good and loyal husband. Of course, she realized that Anna was not just any woman, but an inexperienced teenager with her head full of romantic notions that in no way corresponded to the reality of the world. First she would reason with her daughter, Francesca decided. If that did not work, she would have to use other methods. It was an honorable solution to a most shameful episode.

Although Francesca had already concluded that marrying Giacomo Pace was the best—the only—logical course of action that would break the emotional impasse and deliver her daughter from a most precarious situation, she did now want to seem too anxious. Men, she had learned, did not like things to be too easy; they wanted to feel a sense of triumph and accomplishment, even with the smallest of endeavors.

"I cannot speak for my daughter, signore Pace," she said, "But I promise you that I will speak with her and relay your proposal."

"I understand," he answered softly, "If you like, I can return in a week. We can talk some more at that time," he added in an understanding tone that sounded like that of patient businessman rather than that of an ardent lover. This was, Francesca realized, just as he had said: a symbiotic proposal that would meet the needs of both parties involved.

"That will be fine," she said. "I will see you then."

Giacomo Pace stood up, bowed slightly and left the house. It had been a most unusual visit, but one that had the potential of changing the dynamics of the entire family. Francesca sat down again, trying to decide how she would announce the proposal to Anna. Although she knew her daughter well, it was impossible to foretell her reaction. Love always made people unpredictable. Maybe Anna would even try to run away from home, like Paolo had done, rather than enter into a loveless marriage to a man whom she had never met and who was old enough to be her father.

After giving it some thought, Francesca decided that there was no point in sugar coating the situation. Just as Giacomo Pace had done with her, she would simply relay the proposal to Anna in a direct and straightforward manner. It would be then up to her to accept it or reject it. Given her present state of mind, there was no point in trying to second-guess her reaction.

Family dinners had changed, from occasions where Francesca and her children spoke openly about everything and exchanged opinions, to somber events where the only sound was that of the silverware on the plates. Even Guido, as talkative and expansive as he was, simply looked down and ate his food mechanically; he still could not bear looking at his sister or watch the expression of anguish on his mother's face. Once he finished he would simply excuse himself and go out to see his friends. The door would close softly behind him and he would not return until past midnight.

"We have to talk," said Francesca to her daughter one evening that week, while cleaning the dishes and after Guido had left the house. Anna did not say anything, but Francesca knew that she was listening.

"I will get right to the heart of the matter; there is no point in beating around the bush. A man came to see me yesterday to ask for your hand in marriage. He is financially stable and I believe that he will be a good husband. He owns a nice house overlooking the bay and you will live there. He also has a villa in Ischia. Considering the situation, I think you are lucky to have someone interested in you."

Anna did not say anything immediately, but it was obvious, by the expression on her face, that she was as surprised as Francesca had been upon hearing Giacomo Pace's proposal.

"Who is he?" she asked.

"His name is Giacomo Pace; he manages a number of actors and singers." Anna, of course, had no idea of who he was. First of all, she was too young, and she had never moved in those circles.

For a few moments Anna did not say anything, but by the concentration reflected on her face it was evident that she was considering all the alternatives and possibilities, not unlike a chess player trying to undo the damage caused by a careless move.

"When do I meet him?" she finally asked without showing any emotion in her voice.

"In a few days," answered Francesca. "He is coming back to hear your answer."

"That will be fine," she said in a matter of fact tone and then returned to her room.

Although both women were counting the hours until Giacomo Pace's return, neither one mentioned the impending visit. It was as if they had entered into a pact of silence that purposely forbade the discussion of that uncomfortable topic. Francesca had been surprised by her daughter's aplomb after she relayed Giacomo Pace's proposal. She had expected a highly charged emotional scene, in which Anna would have sworn her eternal love to Paolo and an adamant refusal to marry someone whom she had not even met. Anna, she concluded, was maturing at a fast rate and now realized that every decision, big or small, often carried with it unexpected consequences that had to be accepted, whether they were to one's liking or not. It was called growing up; she had tried to shelter her children from that reality, but eventually it was inevitable.

As the appointed day approached, Francesca tried unsuccessfully to detect in her daughter's demeanor a sign of nervousness, apprehension or even regret. Anna stayed in her room in the evenings and during the day, when Francesca went to work; she cleaned the house and cooked the meals. This she did without being asked or showing signs that this behavior was a small way of atoning for the shame she had brought upon the family.

Finally, the day of Giacomo Pace's return arrived. Just as he had done the previous week, he knocked on Francesca's door with the punctuality of an Englishman. From the first moment it was clear that he considered this a most important visit; he was dressed in a sober gray suit, white shirt that had been carefully starched and ironed, and a silk tie of discreet colors. Even his shoes had been polished to a degree that seemed to defy the laws of physics. In his left hand he was carrying a dozen red roses. Despite his age and experience, he showed all the nervousness and apprehension of a young man calling on a love interest for the first time.

"*Buona sera*," he said politely and offered a faint smile.

"*Avanti*, signore Pace," said Francesca inviting him to come into the living room.

The first thing that he noticed as he came into the room was that Anna was not there. This could be a bad sign, he thought. Maybe after considering his proposal she had decided to turn it down and had sent her mother to relay the message. As he walked in front of the mirror that hung over the faded couch, he realized that he was sweating.

"Would you like some coffee?" asked Francesca. "Anna will join us in a few minutes," she added after realizing that the visitor must have thought it strange that she was not present.

"Yes, that would be nice," he answered, not wanting to offend in any way the hospitality he was being shown.

"*Scusi*," said Francesca as she made her way to the kitchen.

Giacomo Pace, still holding the flowers in his hand, suddenly found himself alone in the tiny living room, surrounded by the fading photographs of people he did not know, by the pieces of secondhand furniture whose style had been fashionable decades before, and by a stack of old magazines that had accumulated in several anachronistic strata in a wicker basket that rested next to the sofa. He would always remember that experience—despite the fact that it only lasted a few minutes—as one of the most endless in his life. In his mind, even the time when he negotiated a contract for thirty six straight hours, would pale in comparison to the unbearable intensity of those uncertain minutes of waiting in signora d'Amio's living room. He contemplated the audacity of his previous visit, his outrageous proposal and immediately began to doubt his own good judgment. For an instant he toyed with the idea of letting himself out quietly so he would not have to face Anna's rejection, its subsequent feeling of secret shame, and the blanket of despondency that was sure to follow.

Before he could finish his conjectures, Anna appeared in the living room holding a tray. She placed it on the center table, next to Guido's Popular Mechanics magazines. She was lovelier and younger than he remembered. Suddenly he felt diminished in her presence—the idea of a middle-aged man proposing marriage to an adolescent seemed absurd—and once again his heart sank in anticipation of her impending rejection.

"These are for you," he said while standing up and offering the red roses to Anna. Although he wanted to be calm, his voice betrayed a tinge of the anguish he had experienced a few minutes before.

"*Grazie*," she said and smiled at him, secure in the knowledge that from the start she had the upper hand, and placed the flowers in an empty vase. "How do you take your coffee, signore Pace?" she asked in a casual tone.

"Black will be fine," he answered her "and please, call me Giacomo."

He kept looking at the door that led to the kitchen, thinking that Francesca would come into the living room at any moment, but she had disappeared, leaving him and Anna alone in the living room to discuss his earlier proposal.

"Do you know the purpose of my visit?" he said after sipping his coffee.

"Yes," answered Anna while pouring herself a cup, adding some sugar and stirring it thoroughly, "My mother said that you wanted to marry me."

Giacomo Pace was startled, not at the fact that she knew the reason for his visit, but at the tone of her voice. She sounded calm and unemotional, as if she were about to barter some goods at the local market and needed to keep her wits about her in order to make the most advantageous deal.

"And may I ask why?" asked Anna in the same business like tone of voice, "You do not know me." From the first moment she was trying to establish a position of advantage in her relation to her suitor.

"I know enough," he said, but immediately realized that his comment could be interpreted as a reference Anna's clandestine encounters with Paolo. "What I mean is that I know enough about your family. I knew your late father since he came to Italy; I have also known your mother since she sang the first time at the San Carlo."

"That does not answer my question," insisted Anna, "just because you know my family is not sufficient reason to marry me."

"Of course," said Giacomo Pace, "but it is a deciding factor. My mother died recently; up to this point my personal life revolved around her care. Now that she is gone, I think the time has come for me to marry. I just hope it is not too late. There is also the matter of taxation." He was referring to the exorbitant penalty that Mussolini's regime, as an incentive for men to marry, had imposed on bachelors.

"Yes, that makes more sense," Anna agreed.

"I am financially secure and my future wife will not have to concern herself about making ends meet by taking on a job, as so many women have to do these days." He had stopped short of mentioning Francesca by name, but Anna understood perfectly what he meant. He was playing his hand correctly, expounding on the assets that he possessed and bypassing his shortcomings, mainly a youth that had already come and gone.

"Then you would expect your wife to devote herself to you," Anna clarified.

"Yes, it would be just the two of us," added Giacomo Pace, "and she would want for nothing. I don't think it would be such a bad life." Without saying so, he had clearly implied that he was not interested in having children, and that he was prepared, as he had done with his late mother, to devote all his time and resources to his wife.

"No, it would not," said Anna after a brief pause. Giacomo Pace did not notice, but she was talking to herself rather than agreeing with him. After a few moments, she came out of her momentary reverie, looked directly at him and smiled. "Giacomo," she said using his name for the first time, "I accept your proposal."

"Anna," said Giacomo overcome with emotion and surprise, "I promise you that I will be a good husband, that I will care and provide for you to the best of my ability. When would you want the wedding to take place?" he asked, making sure to secure a definite date for her commitment. Experience had taught him that people often said things that they did not mean or changed their minds at the last minute. But this time he had no cause for alarm; Anna was just as anxious as he was — although for different reasons — to resolve the situation.

"As soon as possible," she said and smiled again.

"Then I will take care of everything; tomorrow morning I will speak to father Benito and see how soon he can perform the ceremony."

"That is wonderful," said Anna, "Let me know as soon as you know something."

"I will be back tomorrow," said Giacomo as he stood up. "Now you can give the good news to your mother; don't worry about anything."

Anna followed him. Just before leaving the house, he turned around. For a moment Anna feared that he would try to kiss her, but he simply shook both her hands.

"I look forward to seeing you again, Anna," he said and then quickly disappeared into the street.

Later that evening, when Anna told Francesca all the details of Giacomo's visit, she realized that they had spoken of everything about a future life together. Everything, except love.

Good to his word, Giacomo Pace reappeared the following evening. Just as the day before, he was impeccably groomed and sported a fresh carnation on the left lapel of his suit. He was holding a gift wrapped box in his right hand.

"This is for you," he said to Anna, who had answered the door herself, while extending the gift. By that time Francesca had also come into the living room.

"*Grazie*," she said while receiving the box from Giacomo, who was now standing in the middle of the living room.

"Well, open it," Francesca urged her daughter, conscious that whenever men brought women presents they liked for them to be opened right away, in order to receive an exaggerated thank you for their thoughtfulness, even if the gift was not exactly right.

Following her mother's instructions, Anna tore the colorful wrapping paper and exposed a metal box with a bas-relief lid depicting an Alpine scene.

"They are chocolates from Switzerland," explained Giacomo. "I just thought you might like them."

"Thank you Giacomo," said Anna. Then, showing an unexpected sign of boldness, she leaned towards him and kissed him lightly on the cheek. It was evident that he was not used to receiving such demonstrations of affection, for his face turned red with embarrassment.

"Sit down, signore Pace," said Francesca, attempting to make the visitor more at ease. After all, they would soon become family.

"I have some good news," said Giacomo with an excitement in his voice that he could not contain. "Yesterday, after I left here, I went directly to see father Benito. He said that he can perform the ceremony as soon as we are ready, but that he requires a few more details; I could not provide them until I spoke with Anna," he said looking in her direction.

"What sort of details?" asked Anna, beating her mother to the question. It was obvious that she wanted to make all the decisions about her life from this point on.

"He wants to know if a nuptial mass is desired and he also needs a definite date so he can put it on the calendar and announce the banns of marriage to the congregation. Of course, I told him I would have to consult with Anna and that I would give him an answer this week."

Father Benito's request was routine. Banns of marriage had to be announced for three consecutive Sundays, just in case someone in the community knew of a reason why the wedding should not take place. As for the date, this was a flexible item that could be placed anywhere within the ecclesiastical calendar.

"That gives us about a month," said Francesca. "Not much time to plan a wedding."

"There is nothing to plan," said Anna, again taking charge, "I would like to have a simple ceremony, without a mass, and only family members in attendance."

Francesca looked at Giacomo Pace, as if trying to find support for her plans of a more elaborate affair and perhaps a small reception afterwards, but looking at Anna he simply said, "Whatever Anna wants is fine with me." It was evident from the beginning that he wanted to please her, even if it meant antagonizing his future mother in law. Besides, those considerations were of little importance to most men, and Giacomo was not an exception.

"At least let me make you a dress," protested Francesca, invoking her undisputed skills as a seamstress.

"That is fine," agreed Anna. Then, turning to Giacomo, "Tell father Benito that a month from now will be fine; I just wish it could be sooner."

"Then it is all settled," Giacomo concluded, "I will take care of everything. And with your permission," he said to Francesca, "I would like to visit Anna, under your supervision, several times a week. There is much that we have to discuss."

"Of course; we will be available whenever you want to come," she said. "I realize that a month is not a lot of time."

"I have something for you," Francesca told her daughter after Giacomo had left, "Now that you are getting married, I think it will be useful to you; I just wish I could give you more." From a nearby cabinet she produced a hardcover notebook and handed it to Anna."These are the recipes that I have collected over the years; the ones that have a star next to their names were your father's favorites." For a moment Anna was startled. She knew that the notebook, with its handwritten recipes, was one of Francesca's most prized possessions.

"Are you sure?" she asked.

"Take it," answered Francesca with a decisive tone in her voice. "After today you will need it more than I do." There was nothing more to be said. Anna embraced her mother, acknowledging how much that gesture meant to her. "Now we have a wedding to plan, and we don't have much time."

Francesca's words were no exaggeration. Father Benito insisted on speaking to the bride and groom several times before the ceremony. During these sessions he imparted to the couple the church's teaching of how a Christian marriage should function. Unquestionably he had heard, as had everyone else, of Anna's clandestine liaison with Paolo, but prudently never mentioned it, just as he never mentioned the difference in age between the prospective bride and groom. He simply saw the upcoming wedding as a priceless opportunity to convey what he thought was a much needed premarital instruction that would buttress the relationship against the hardships they were surely to face in the future.

Giacomo, of course, still had his obligations with his clients, so there were times when he had to be away on business, but he always made sure to attend the meetings with father Benito.

Francesca had worked feverishly in the evenings trying to finish Anna's wedding dress. Oftentimes Guido would find her still awake, when he came in past midnight, still working at her sewing machine. He would urge his mother to go to bed, reminding her that she had to get up early the next day to go to work. He had not said much when he learned that his younger sister was to be married, but his silence let everyone know that he was still not convinced that it was the best solution to her predicament. For some unknown reason he did not seem to like Giacomo Pace; whenever he came to the house to visit Anna, he made sure to avoid him at all costs. The situation was beyond his control, but he did not have to pretend to like him.

Eventually, the day of the wedding arrived. Just as Anna had requested, the ceremony would be a simple one, without a mass and all the fanfare and celebration that usually comes along with Italian nuptials.

Giacomo had arranged for a car to pick up the bride and her family and bring them to the church. Since early that morning

Francesca had spent her time making sure that her daughter's appearance, despite the fact that very few people would attend the ceremony, was as it should be for such a special day. After all, a woman did not get married on a regular basis. She had finished the dress the day before and she made Anna try it on several times, just to make absolutely sure that the fitting was correct. Most of the time, however, had been spent on her hair and makeup. As young as she was, Anna had little experience, especially with the latter, so her mother had to guide her every step of the way.

Early that afternoon, after a luxurious shampoo, Francesca dried Anna's hair, combed it patiently and with the aid of bobby pins, rollers and other sundry beauty aids, arranged it into an elegant style that accented Anna's features and somehow made her look older, more mature. As she carried out this task, she could not help remember how she had done the same thing every morning before her young daughter went to school. Thinking of those days, now gone forever, her eyes became misty, but she held back the tears, not wanting Anna to see her cry. As for the makeup, she started with the eyebrows, and worked her way down to the lips, highlighting eyelashes and overall enhancing Anna's better features while simultaneously concealing those on which nature had not bestowed perfection.

By the time they came out of the bedroom, Anna looked radiant. Guido was waiting for them, silently flipping the pages of one of his automotive magazines. When he saw his sister he put the magazine down and stood up. He was in awe of her beauty. For the occasion, he was dressed in a dark suit, white shirt and black shoes. The attire had once belonged to his late father. No alterations had been necessary; he had grown into it as naturally as he bore the original owner's name. It was only right that he should be wearing it, for the responsibility of giving away the bride had befallen upon him. Anna herself had made the request, so it was impossible for Guido to decline. Even though he had not changed his mind about the wedding, part of him felt flattered, for he knew that he was literally filling the shoes of Louis d'Amio, a man whose presence was felt in that house on a daily basis.

"Just one more thing before we go," said Anna while going over to the old record player.

"The car will be here any minute," said her mother. "Everybody will be waiting." By 'everybody,' of course, she meant Giacomo Pace and father Benito.

"It won't take long," Anna said as she placed Immortal Arias on the turntable and turned on the machine. As usual, Louis d'Amio's powerful voice overcame the shortcomings of the mechanical device, completely overpowering he faint static that was created by the scratches on the record. No one spoke, but simply listened to the powerful voice that evoked in each one of them very private feelings and secret memories that they would carry with them until the end of their days.

Just before six o'clock, the unmistakable sound of a car stopping in front of the house was heard. Guido came out first, to confirm that it was indeed the car that had been sent by Giacomo. He did not have to ask; it was a black sedan, very shiny and with a spacious back seat. Not a vehicle that was used for every day occasions. He alerted his mother and sister and they came out of the house. By that time the chauffeur had stepped out of the car and was holding the back door open, so the two women did not have to linger in front of the house. Guido chose to ride in the front, to give his mother and sister more room. Besides, he always thought that men should either drive or ride in the front.

Outside the house, a group of children had gathered. They were not accustomed to seeing such automobiles go through their neighborhood, let alone stop and park in front of one of the houses. As soon as they saw Anna in her wedding dress they began to giggle and make comments to each other. By then their mothers, usually busy inside with other chores, had come out to see what the fuss was all about. Even though they had known Francesca and her family for years, they had no clue about the wedding, since they seldom attended church and had not heard the banns of marriage. Anna had been adamant about the size of the ceremony and keeping the news under wraps. She was much aware that had she made it known, it would have been fodder for the constant gossiping that went on among the women. As the car sped away, followed by the children, each of the occupants experienced in a private way a feeling of relief.

Francesca now realized that when she returned home that evening, for the first time Anna would not be there; she would be a married woman, with all the responsibilities that came along with it. She wished that her daughter could have stayed home a little longer, hold on to that phase of life that, despite their poverty, she knew it was the most precious, simply because of her youth. Once Anna came out of the church, Francesca realized, her dreams would slowly begin to die.

Guido, sitting next to the driver and looking straight ahead, did not betray any emotions, but deep inside he was glad that everything was coming to a conclusion. Sure, he did not think the marriage to Giacomo Pace was such a good idea, but despite this belief, he could not see any other way to salvage his sister's reputation, short of her entering a convent. He was tired of defending her, with words and fists, in front of his friends whenever someone had a little too much to drink and made a comment concerning her clandestine relationship with Paolo.

As for Anna, she did not feel much of anything, except for the peace of mind brought about by the resolution of a difficult situation. She had made a decision and was fully prepared to live with the consequences, just as she had made the decision to go to Paolo's house that first night. What was done was done and there was no sense in lamenting it; no one had the power to change the past, so it was best to try to shape the present. She realized that this decision was not just a good solution for her, but for her family as well. Although she did not love Giacomo, she found him agreeable enough. During the weeks when he had come to visit, and the times they had attended father Benito's talks, he had always been kind and polite. That was good enough for her. Anna was also aware that even though Giacomo was not rich, he was financially comfortable, so that in itself would free her from all the drudgery of keeping a job as well as the other menial tasks that common housewives had to endure on a daily basis. Maybe she could even help him with his business.

As usual, Father Benito was standing in front of the Santa Chiara Church, waiting for the bride and her family. His imposing figure, dressed in the black cassock and set against the baroque façade, for an instant suggested something a little sinister. The priest raised his arm unnecessarily, signaling the car to park in front of the main door. As the car stopped, he walked over and opened the back door.

86

"*Bella, molto bella,*" he exclaimed as Anna emerged from the car followed by Francesca. By then Guido had come around and was standing next to his mother and sister. He shook father Benito's hand, but refrained from making any comments. He wanted everything to be over as quickly as possible.

The inside of the church had been beautifully decorated with fresh flowers. This was the only concession that Anna had made to Giacomo, who originally had wanted to invite his friends and acquaintances from the San Carlo Theater, have a choir sing during the ceremony and hold a small reception afterwards. But at the end, yielding to her wishes, the wedding would be strictly a family affair.

Father Benito led Anna and her party to a side chapel, suggested that they say a prayer and then disappeared through a side door that led to the sacristy. He reappeared a few minutes later in front of the main altar, now dressed in a more formal ecclesiastical garb and ready to commence the ceremony. Giacomo Pace stood in front of him. He wore a dark suit, a sober gray tie and patent leather shoes that reflected the trembling light of the candles whenever he moved his feet.

A few minutes later Anna, led by her brother, reached the altar. Giacomo could not take his eyes off her; the wedding gown, the new hair style and the soft light of the candles miraculously transformed her from the often awkward adolescent he had visited during the past weeks into a most desirable woman. He told himself that he was indeed fortunate that she should have accepted his marriage proposal.

Father Benito started the ceremony with the customary invocation. He told the nonexistent congregation the purpose of the gathering and asked who would be giving Anna away in marriage. Guido, still with a serious look, escorted his sister to where father Benito and Giacomo were standing. After placing his sister next to the groom, Guido stepped back. At that crucial moment he realized more than even that he was standing in the place that should have been occupied by Louis d'Amio. Even though the memories he had of his father were vague and diffuse, as if they had originated in a distant dream and not in reality, it did not diminish the feeling of responsibility that he had felt for the first time a few days earlier and had achieved its culmination as he led his sister to the altar. For an instant he thought that Louis d'Amio would have been able to find a viable alternative, that if he were alive Anna would not have to marry Giacomo Pace.

Now that the couple was standing in front of him, Father Benito did not lose any time. Fully aware of the unusual circumstances behind the wedding, he was just as anxious to see its conclusion as the couple itself was. He read the prescribed prayers and asked Giacomo and Anna to repeat the wedding vows. They did so willingly, but everyone—especially Guido—could tell by Anna's lack of enthusiasm that her heart was not truly in it. These were mere words that had to be spoken out loud and in front of witnesses to comply with a formality that would transform her into Giacomo Pace's wife.

Francesca, once the ceremony got underway, was no longer able to contain her emotions; she cried openly, remembering that not so long ago Anna was but a mere child, and that from this day on she would not return home with her family.

Father Benito concluded the ritual with a blessing for the new couple; he reminded them once more that happiness in matrimonial life could only be found in the ability to compromise and putting one's spouse first. Fully cognizant of the unforeseen difficulties that marriage implied, these were the same admonitions he gave every couple during those meetings when he tried to impart a sense of reality to what was to come after the wedding. Anna and Giacomo, now man and wife, walked slowly out of the church. She looked straight ahead and her hand rested on his arm. Francesca and Guido followed the couple; she was still shedding some tears and he had the same somber expression he had worn through the entire ceremony. In a very personal way, each realized that from that point onward, Anna was no longer a part of the family, that everything had changed.

Outside the church, unbeknownst to the bride, a photographer was waiting. He often did work for Giacomo Pace when the latter wanted to build up a portfolio for one of his clients, so he was more than happy to take some pictures of the newlywed couple.

As soon as they emerged from the church, he readied his equipment, so he could capture on film as much as he could of the event. At first Anna looked a little surprised, but then realized that it meant a lot to Giacomo. She did not show any objections to the photographer, who was now in front of them, and had begun giving them directions about how he wanted them to pose. She even made an effort to smile; after all, this was supposed to be one of the most significant days of her life.

The same limousine that had brought them to the church was still waiting. Giacomo and Anna would use it to leave the church; Francesca and Guido would take a taxi back to their house. Giacomo, with his usual efficiency of a good businessman, had foreseen everything.

After the round of pictures was over, Anna hugged and kissed Francesca and Guido good-bye. It had been decided that the couple would drive first to Giacomo's house, on the hills overlooking the bay, where they could change clothes and then go out to enjoy a quiet dinner.

Despite his earlier desire to invite his friends to the ceremony and have an intimate reception afterwards, Giacomo had acquiesced to Anna's wishes—except for the flowers and the photographer—for a completely private ceremony. Even from that early phase Anna felt that it was a good beginning, that it established a pattern that most likely would continue throughout their married life.

When the car pulled away from the church, Anna saw her mother bringing a handkerchief to her eyes while Guido put his arm around her. But that image was quickly replaced by new and unfamiliar ones. As they left the center of the city and began the climb towards the surrounding hills, the fresh air coming in through the open windows seemed cleaner, less oppressive than the one that Anna had been breathing for so many years. Perhaps it was all her imagination, but it did not really matter, for she surely felt that in a number of ways, many of which she could not fully identify yet, from that day on her life had changed for the better.

Even though they were now husband and wife, Giacomo did not sit too close to her in the back seat of the car. To mollify his obvious nervousness, he simply pointed out the landmarks that they passed on the way to his house, adding idle comments about each.

Anna listened to them and from time to time nodded in agreement, but in reality her mind was racing in anticipation of the events that would soon take place, more specifically, that first night with Giacomo. He was her husband, and as such had every right to expect her full favors on their wedding night. The idea of rejecting him did not enter her mind; she sensed that how the night unfolded would determine the future of their relationship. So far he had proven to be attentive and willing to make her happy; this was something she did not want to jeopardize.

Giacomo Pace's house appeared abruptly after the car negotiated a sharp bend on the road. Although it could not be called a mansion, it was a sizable structure — more than a bachelor needed — whose white façade and ample double doors of carved wood extended a silent welcome to the occasional visitors. There was a stone path, flanked by carefully pruned rose bushes, leading to the portico. The well-kept appearance of the house immediately appealed to Anna, who had always possessed a sense of order and tidiness, even as a child. "I love the roses," she said as they exited the car. She stopped and stooped down to smell one, holding it carefully in her hand so as not to damage it or prick herself with the thorns. With the other hand she kept the train of her gown from dragging unnecessarily on the ground.

"Those were my mother's passion," Giacomo explained. "She would come out early in the morning and work in her little garden for hours, even though she knew I could have hired someone to do the work. She said that the pruning, weeding and overall care of the flowers brought her a sense of peace. At the end of the week she would cut some of the more beautiful ones, make an arrangement and place them in a vase, by the main door."

"I think I understand," Anna said. "If you find something you like to do, then it is not really work. It brings purpose into one's life."

"Yes, I suppose you are right," agreed Giacomo, who had walked ahead of Anna on the stone path and had taken a key ring out of his pocket. He opened the double door and stepped aside so Anna could come in.

If Anna had been impressed with the rose garden and the exterior of the house, the ample living room was beyond her expectations. The furniture looked new and the room had been tastefully decorated with works of art, from delicate porcelain vases—all empty—tapestries that showed bucolic scenes, and paintings that Anna's untrained eye could not decide whether they were genuine or skillful reproductions. A cut-glass chandelier hung from the ceiling, flooding the room in a light abundant in playful refractions.

"All this was my mother's domain," Giacomo explained, noting her amazement at the contents of the room. Once more it dawned on Anna the depth of Giacomo's devotion to his mother. He had tried, until the end, to be as good a son as possible. Part of her felt a tinge of remorse at the knowledge that now his feelings would be focused on her and that she would never be able to reciprocate them to the same degree. Sure, she was already fond of him, but he would never be able to fill that indefinable void that she had always felt as far back as she could remember, a void that had only been filled completely—if only momentarily—during the hours she had shared with Paolo.

The rest of the house, although not as impressive as the living room, was spacious, airy, and well lit. The main bedroom, especially, with its double windows that opened onto the side of the garden, was particularly welcoming. Surrounded by the rose bushes a small patio looked upon the Bay of Naples below. A beautiful and secluded spot for sharing a cup of espresso, a glass of wine and intimate conversation. How different, Anna thought immediately, from the crowded streets of the city below and the cramped quarters of her former house.

"You can change here," Giacomo said, "I had all your clothes brought from your mother's house. I will wait for you in the living room." As Giacomo left the room, Anna thought that the tone of his voice had been almost like that of an adult addressing a child, rather than a man speaking to his wife.

It did not take Anna but a few minutes to shed the wedding gown that Francesca had so painstakingly and lovingly made for her. She placed it on the double bed and then put on her Sunday dress. She realized suddenly that she was in the bedroom that she would share with Giacomo, with her husband. That was the bed they would share in a matter of hours and every night from that day on. She tried not to think about it, to concentrate on something else, anything else.

Although she did not know where they were going for dinner, Anna was certain that Giacomo would want to impress her, especially on that first night as husband and wife. On a mirror above the dresser she checked her hair and touched up her makeup. This last task was done awkwardly, since she had learned of its use recently and most of the time dispensed with it.

All along, she had been correct about Giacomo's desire for that night to be memorable. He was waiting for her in the living room—he had changed into one of the business suits that he usually wore—standing by one of the empty flower vases that were so prevalent in the room, not unlike a schoolboy before his first date. Apparently his nervousness had not waned since leaving the church, so she tried to put him at ease with a smile, then extended her hand and placed it on his arm.

"I am ready," she said.

"The car is waiting," he explained, and then, almost as an afterthought, "You look beautiful." Anna realized that he was at a loss of words in her presence, especially now that the reality that they were married and undertaking a life together was beginning to take hold.

They traversed the stone walk—Anna held on to his arm—to where the car was parked. The driver, still behind the wheel, was reading a newspaper whose headlines announced the unstable political situation and the possibility of an impending war. Giacomo opened one of the rear doors for Anna, and then sat next to her.

"We are going to the Vesuvius," Giacomo instructed the driver. The latter folded the newspaper to the page he had been reading, placed it on the seat next to him and started the car. They drove down the hills, in the direction of the city below. The restaurant was only fifteen minutes away, but the time seemed longer to the couple in the back. Although legally husband and wife, they had not yet shared that intimacy that turns two separate individuals into a couple. Giacomo, just as he had done after they left the church, made small talk about the different places they passed; Anna corresponded by showing an exaggerated interest in what he was saying. What really was on their minds, however, was the inevitability of their first night together, although their concerns were of a different nature. Anna worried about being able to surrender herself to a much older man whom she did not love. Even though she was now Giacomo's wife, part of her considered this capitulation a betrayal to Paolo.

Giacomo, being much older, realized the importance of that first encounter, since it would set the tone for the type of physical relationship the couple would enjoy—or endure—in the future. During their short courtship he had made every effort to win over

Anna's affection and respect, but deep down he had realized that he would never possess her heart. By the time the wedding date had come, he had succeeded in creating a certain bond between them. But would that bond be strong enough to survive the wedding night? That was the question that plagued him.

The Vesuvius Restaurant, arguably one of the most exclusive in Naples, had been alerted earlier in the week to reserve one of the best tables for the couple. As soon as they arrived, a member of the staff efficiently guided them to an interior courtyard, replete with flowers in bloom and isolated from the rest of the establishment. Its advantageous location, away from the rest of the patrons and the foot traffic, extended the diners an air of intimacy that they would not have been able to enjoy had their table been located in a different part of the restaurant.

Anna smiled, obviously pleased with the surroundings and the obvious topnotch service. She had never been to a place like this before. Giacomo, noticing her reaction and wanting to enhance the mood, ordered a bottle of champagne. It arrived shortly, in a silver bucket and encased in crushed ice. The same waiter who had led them to the secluded courtyard, after acquiring Giacomo's permission, uncorked the bottle; its popping sound resembled that of a subdued firecracker during one of the many festivities that the city observed on a yearly basis. After the waiter poured the first glass, Giacomo raised it, looked into Anna's eyes and made a toast.

"To our future," he said.

"Yes, to the future," she answered him while they tapped their glasses lightly. As she drank the champagne, maybe a little too fast, the new and strange sensation overcame her, for she started to laugh.

"Sip it, slowly," said Giacomo. "One must take time to enjoy the best things in life; they should never be rushed." Anna did as he suggested, and by the expression on her face he had no doubt as to the pleasurable sensations generated by the champagne.

"You are right," she said, "It must be sipped in order to be appreciated."

It was an auspicious beginning. They made small talk and drank some more. By the time their dinner was served—Giacomo had ordered lobster thermidore for both of them, one of the specialties of the house, before their arrival—the bottle was almost empty and their mood was lighter, almost buoyant. Towards the end of the meal, it was almost as if they had done this before and this was just one more occasion in a string of many. Above their heads, in the enclosure of the small courtyard, a million stars resembled diamonds tossed randomly on black velvet. The fragrance of the flowers permeated the entire atmosphere, transforming the setting into one worthy of a fairy tale.

So satisfying had been the meal that they decided to dispense with dessert. In order to counteract the effects of the champagne — the bottle was now empty — Giacomo ordered coffee for both of them. If only momentarily, they had both forgotten the earlier tension and nervousness. For a while they made small talk, about the house, about the garden that had belonged to Giacomo's mother, about all those insignificant things, which are immediately forgotten but serve the purpose of delaying more serious or pressing topics.

Eventually, the evening came to a conclusion. Giacomo signaled the waiter for the bill and they prepared to leave. The car was still waiting outside; the chauffeur stood by the car, smoking patiently. He opened the rear door for the couple and then sat behind the wheel. There was no need for instructions; he knew the couple was returning home. After that final trip his day would be over.

The journey back was no different from the previous one, except that Giacomo did not comment on the landmarks they passed, but asked Anna about the particulars of the meal and if it had been to her satisfaction. Again, it was idle talk meant to mask the underlying nervousness.

When they arrived, Giacomo exited the car, opened the door for Anna and then dismissed the chauffeur. The car disappeared on its way back to the city and they were left alone in the garden, which was only illuminated by the soft light of the new moon and the stars. In the distance below they could see the shimmering lights of the bay. Anna instinctively put her hand on Giacomo's arm, and they traversed the path that led to the house. At that hour, she noticed, the smell of the roses was more intense than it had been during the day. Or maybe it was just her imagination, magnifying all sensory stimuli before they reached her brain.

In the semidarkness Giacomo produced his key ring and with apparent familiarity inserted one in the lock; with a soft click it yielded and the door was open.

"We are home," he said.

"Yes," answered Anna, not knowing what else to say at that crucial moment.

"Would you like something from the kitchen?" asked Giacomo, aware that Anna was still not familiar with the house.

"No, I am ready for bed," she said as she started to walk to the room where she had changed earlier. "But first I want to brush my hair and change."

"Of course," he said, "the bathroom is this way."

She followed Giacomo down the hall, but as she was about to go into the bathroom, he stopped her gently with his hand.

"Anna," he said looking at her.

"Yes, what is it?" she answered him with a tone of curiosity.

"About tonight... we don't have to..." there was a slight trembling in his voice, "I understand that this is not the most typical situation... if you need more time..." This last phrase contained a question mark. Once again he was making sure not to pressure Anna into a situation for which she was not yet ready.

"I think you worry too much," she answered him, trying to put him at ease. "Everything will look different in the morning; I will join you in a few minutes."

From the start Anna had made up her mind that she would not put off the consummation of the marriage. She felt that if she and Giacomo ever hoped to achieve a semblance of normalcy as a married couple, that first night was the first step. There was no getting around it, so in her mind postponing it, no matter what her feelings were, made no sense at all.

The bedroom was illuminated by a small side lamp that cast a yellowish circle of light of decreasing intensity. Before getting undressed, Giacomo turned it off; the artificial light was replaced by the faint light of the moon and stars that came in through the window, mixed with the fragrance from the garden. In the semi-darkness he shed his clothes and got in bed.

A few minutes later Anna came into the bedroom. As she walked in front of the window Giacomo noticed that she had changed into a light nightgown. One again he marveled—as he had done so many times in the past month—at her beauty and her youth. A few moments later she was next to him in bed, enveloping him in the soft fragrance that her body seemed to exude. At that instant Giacomo felt that he was the luckiest man on earth.

"You are wonderful," he whispered in the darkness.

"Shh..," she quieted him, and reached out to him, taking the initiative on that first and decisive night. What followed was unexpected for both of them. Anna, accustomed to the unrestrained and passionate lovemaking with Paolo, was not expecting the tender, delicate touch of a middle-aged man—not unlike someone handling a priceless Sevres porcelain that could shatter at any moment.

Giacomo, on the other hand, was both relieved and pleased thatAnna was encouraging his advances. At the crucial moment he did not allow the weight of his body to rest on hers, but rather rested on his elbows, as if fearful of crushing her. Under the soft light of the moon they swayed slowly, achieving a common rhythm that inevitably led to a climax. At the moment of release, Giacomo's body became tense, as if undergoing a mild   electroshock, then it became flaccid. Simultaneously, a soft sound escaped from his mouth, like an involuntary whimper that echoed or mimicked his mild ejaculation. Afterwards, he lay next to Anna, holding her close while she stroked his back with a monotonous caress.

For Anna, the experience had been neither painful nor altogether unpleasant; it simply left her with a vague feeling of dissatisfaction mixed with mild indifference. The earth had not shaken, as it had with Paolo. In fact, that act, seemingly so intimate and personal, had barely made a dent in her consciousness.

The stress of the day suddenly manifested itself as they drifted into sleep. The last thought in Anna's mind, before sinking in the temporary darkness, was that the most difficult part of the deal she had made with Giacomo was now behind her.

IV

Just as Anna had hoped, life settled into a comfortable and predictable pattern. Giacomo did not go to work until the afternoon, so they could sleep late in the mornings, eat breakfast on the small terrace behind the garden and have time to read the paper and discuss those trivial things that often occupy married couples: the decoration of a room; that evening's dinner menu; the possibility of getting away on vacation. Even though Giacomo represented many clients, and dinner parties or soirées would have benefited his business, Anna was not keen to the idea of having guests. Giacomo, as expected, did not pressure her; he hoped that as time went by her aversion to visitors would wane and that eventually guests would be welcome in their home.

After a late lunch, he would go to his office and meet with the artists that he represented. He also attended many of the performances in the local theaters, always trying to spot new talent that he could add to his list of clients while they were still in the early stages of their careers. He had learned that even though the profits were usually slim at first, as their talents developed and their names became better known, the money began to flow more freely.

To fill the hours during Giacomo's absence, Anna resumed her interrupted studies. Rather than returning to school — that possibility never entered her mind — he started to make ample use of the study, where the tall and wide bookshelves held, besides all the classics of literature, the thick volumes of an unabridged encyclopedia. She asked him why he had so many books, since he was a businessman and not a scholar. He explained to Anna that he had read every day to his late mother, until her death. As the years accumulated, so did the books, since she would not part with them. This was yet another indication, Anna concluded, of Giacomo's sense of commitment.

She made sure to balance her studies between the arts and the sciences, and found her self-imposed curriculum not entirely unpleasant or boring; she was in complete command and welcomed the opportunity to explore those subjects that aroused her natural curiosity. The hours went by quickly, and she was always surprised when she heard Giacomo coming back from his office; to her it seemed that he had left a few minutes before.

Although from the very beginning Giacomo had made sure not to place demands on his young wife, he welcomed her interest in his library for several reasons. First of all, he knew that one had to be occupied, to have a goal that would fill the days. Since his cook and housekeeper had freed Anna from household chores, it was a wonderful opportunity to cultivate her mind. His second reason was that he was much aware that besides a vast difference of age, they were also separated by a wide cultural gap. Even though he did not hold any university degrees, that did not mean that he was without culture. He had traveled extensively, read voraciously—both for himself and his mother—and had been exposed to the arts for decades. He felt that the more Anna learned, the closer they would become, since that schism would narrow with every passing day.

He was always glad to return home, for he found Anna eager to discuss with him what she had been learning or reading that day. Because of her unbridled enthusiasm, he often thought that she was like a child discovering things for the first time, then realized that in many respects she was indeed still a child.

Their intimate life had also acquired a pattern. Most of the time, after a late dinner punctuated with glasses of robust wine, they would retire to the bedroom and after undressing, Giacomo would rest his head on Anna's breast and talk about his day, about the people he had met, while she stroked softly the back of his neck. Eventually they would fall asleep.

On those nights when he wanted more than mere caresses and whispers, she received him without regrets, just as she had done on their wedding night, accepting his touch and gentle lovemaking until he climaxed and went to sleep in her arms. Anna often asked herself if he approached her out of desire or simply because he felt that she expected it of him and that it was one of his duties as a husband. But in the end, she concluded, it did not matter; they were both making the best of the situation they had entered of their own free will.

Sundays were always special.

Even after his mother's death Giacomo had continued attending a midmorning mass, maybe out of habit or as a way of remembering and honoring her. But now, rather than going alone, he and Anna would drive in his old Alfa to Francesca's house, pick her up and then go to the church. Guido had stopped going to mass altogether, so it was just the three of them. Those who did not know them must have thought that Giacomo and Francesca were husband and wife and Anna was their daughter. Of course, those were few and far between; everyone knew the circumstances that had led to such a union, but no one spoke of it openly. They greeted the group as if nothing had happened, but once in the privacy of their homes they would verbalize what they did not dare to say in public. They all decried the absence of Paolo and his wonderful voice, and sympathized with Sofia Alberti for having lost her son, whose whereabouts were still unknown since his abrupt departure from home.

Francesca, Anna and Giacomo took it all in stride. The marriage had been performed at that very church, so they felt there was no need to hide or feel shame. After mass, they drove back to Giacomo's house and had lunch in the small courtyard surrounded by the garden. Francesca was pleased to see that Giacomo, good to his word, was making every effort to make her daughter as happy as possible. Sure, it was obvious that there was no fire between them, but at least she had a solid foundation on which to build a future.

Even though the conversation during those weekly lunches was light, usually revolving around family matters, local gossip or Giacomo's latest clients, there were some issues that weighted heavily on everyone's mind and that could hardly be ignored by anyone living in Italy at the time. One Sunday, sitting on the small terrace and overlooking the bay below, Giacomo announced that it was rumored and feared that the civil war that had broken out in Spain might spread to the rest of Europe.

At first Anna did not quite understand how that affected their lives in Naples — usually peaceful under the tight rule of Il Duce — but then Giacomo explained to her, with the patience of a teacher, the precarious state and volatile situation of Italian politics. Mussolini had invaded and conquered Ethiopia, and more recently he had proclaimed the Rome Berlin Axis, aligning himself with the Third Reich. He feared, Giacomo continued, that sooner or later Italy would be drawn into a war; all the facts pointed in that direction. Even though they were far from Rome, they were still part of the same country and the repercussions would be far and wide, affecting every citizen.

"What can we do?" Anna asked with a worried look on her face. The severity of the situation was beginning to dawn on her.

"For the moment, nothing," answered Giacomo. "We will try to live as normally as possible and stay out of Fascist politics as long as we can; all we can do is handle the situation on a daily basis."

From that day on, Anna developed an almost insatiable interest in politics. She read the newspaper and discussed the news with Giacomo every evening, aware that his experience and astuteness were invaluable tools in sorting out the wheat from the chaff and in navigating the mercurial and tortuous labyrinth of Italian politics. She also developed a hunger for history, for she realized that knowledge of the past would give her a vantage point from which to survey the present and anticipate the future.

"Always remember," Giacomo told her on more than one occasion, "that the press is completely controlled by the government, so they print only the official version. If you want to know what is important to the people in power," he continued, "read their official newspaper." At this point Giacomo held up that day's issue of one of the official dailies. "Just read between the lines; whatever they say it is, think of its opposite and most likely you will be closer to the truth."

Anna listened quietly, digesting every word. She realized that Giacomo did not speak lightly. He was also very prudent with his words—as were most people—outside the house, so she felt flattered that he trusted her so much that he would divulge his views to her so openly.

Life continued on a more or less regular basis. They were far from the politics of Rome and everyone could have thought that life was normal, except for the news about the conflict in Spain and the occupation of Ethiopia. Not wanting to unduly alarm Francesca, the couple continued to invite her for lunch every Sunday after mass. During those occasions, both Anna and Giacomo avoided talking about politics. Since her marriage to

Giacomo, Anna had noticed a gradual decline in her mother's spirits. She could not pinpoint it because it was not something external and definite, but rather a change of mood from the jovial woman she remembered, always smiling and often singing arias when she worked. Now she seemed somber and always preoccupied; smiling was a thing of the past. If she spoke, it was about church affairs or her job as a seamstress, nothing more. Even though Francesca never did mention it, Anna suspected that if she gave her mother the news of a pregnancy, the prospects of becoming a grandmother would restore her good mood. But this was, in Anna's mind, an absurd idea. She had no intentions of bringing any children into a world that offered no certainties except the imminent prospects for war. It had also been part of the tacit agreement she had made with Giacomo while they were settling on the nature of the relationship. Furthermore, she saw on a daily basis the countless women who were expecting, gladly complying with Il Duce's exhortation to procreate that he had promulgated in his Battle of the Births in 1927. Even as a child, in Anna's eyes there was something grotesque, almost to the point of being obscene, in the fact that the government just considered women mere baby making machines, rewarding them with all sorts of incentives for them to meet the five children established goal. She had witnessed many young and beautiful brides turn into middle-aged matrons right before her eyes once they joined the birthing marathon.

One thing was certain: she intended to keep alive the relationship with her mother; the short time she had been away from her home—now enjoying a much easier life—had opened her eyes to all the sacrifices that Francesca had made for her and her brother. She and Guido were all she had, and she did not intend to let her down. That was the main reason for the Sunday lunches; they meant more to Francesca than they did to her.

"The situation is getting worse," Giacomo told Anna one sunny morning while holding up a copy of *il Mattino*, the largest Neapolitan daily. Anna looked at him with a look of curiosity mixed with fear. "As you know, Mussolini had sent support and 'volunteers' to Franco. What he was not counting on was the Garibaldi Brigade, completely made up of Italians who oppose his rule. Mussolini's men inSpain were defeated by the Republican side at the battle of Guadalajara. It has come to this," Giacomo lamented, "Italians killing Italians! We have no business in Spanish affairs."

"Maybe things will improve from now on," said Anna, not really convinced, but trying to offer some words of solace to Giacomo.

"May God hear you," he said, "but I still believe that this country is headed for war."

As usual, Giacomo was correct in his assessment of the situation. Mussolini left the League of Nations after it imposed economic sanctions on Italy for the invasion of Abyssinia, and in 1938 he played a crucial role in the Munich agreement. Secretly, Giacomo knew that Il Duce would not stop, that his egocentric personality would not allow him to see all the pitfalls in the road ahead. He had seen it many times before in the theater. Opera singers, under the impression that their talent was greater than what everyone believed, disregarded the advice of their managers, until they found themselves at the point of no return with a career that could not be salvaged.

Not wanting to alarm Anna, Giacomo toned down his discussions of European politics; he wanted to enjoy whatever time was left with her. He concentrated more on her studies and made it a point to cut short his business hours in order to return home to her and struggled to create an environment devoid of the harsh and unpredictable reality of the outside world. He wanted nothing to change, to come home to Anna every day, to have their discussions in his library or in the garden overlooking the bay surrounded by the fragrance of his late mother's roses, to listen to opera in the evenings and make soft love to her at night. In short, he wanted time to stand still.

Giacomo finally knew that the tipping point had been reached when Mussolini officially joined Germany by signing the Pact of Steel in May of 1939; this pact committed both countries to support the other if one of them became involved in a war. Given Hitler's hunger for domination, this pact clearly tied Italy to the Fuhrer's whims. It was just a matter of time; all the pieces for a disaster were now in place. Just as a precaution, he got passports for himself and for Anna. He also liquidated many of his assets and kept the proceeds—all in cash— hidden in a suitcase.

In the spring of 1940 Giacomo, still trying not to alarm Anna, proposed that they should spend some time in the villa that he owned in the island of Ischia. Although he seldom used the property because of the demands on his time in Naples, he had decided to keep it because it had always been one of his mother's favorite spots. He still remembered fondly the holidays they had spent there and how the slower pace of the island, the clean beaches, pinewoods, and the salubrious visits to the hot springs at Formello always seemed to invigorate her. It was during her lengthy stays in Ischia that she acquired her passion for gardening. Presently the villa was under the supervision of a caretaker and his son; Giacomo sent them a monthly stipend so they would take care of the place and keep everything in running order.

One night, over a quiet dinner at the Vesuvius, Giacomo casually proposed the trip, and was pleasantly surprised when she did not object to the move. In fact, rather than thinking of any obstacles, because of her youthful exuberance she welcomed the opportunity to stay on an island whose beauty was legendary. Despite the fact that both Capri and Ischia were just an hour away on a ferry, she had never visited either place. Right away she wanted to know everything about Ischia and about the villa, so she made Giacomo tell her in detail about the times he had spent there.Upon hearing of all the pleasant memories that Giacomo still had of the place, she was curious as to why he had never returned.

"It would not have been the same without Mother," he answered her. "As you know, she was mostly bed ridden during the last few years of her life, so traveling was very difficult, if not impossible. After her death I did not think much about it; I just kept sending the money to the caretakers. Nothing changes much over there; I am sure we will find everything just the way I remember it."

"I hope so," said Anna with an enthusiasm she could hardly contain, "I want to see exactly what you saw during your visits."

"You will; I promise you," he told her and kissed her lightly on the cheek.

That night, as Giacomo made love to Anna in the darkness of their bedroom, surrounded by the sound of the crickets and the fragrance that emanated from the rose garden, he had the impression that Anna was particularly tender with him, as if she wanted to play simultaneously the role of wife and mother, thus filling the emptiness that he carried inside after his mother's death. Before drifting into sleep, he concluded that a move to the island was the right thing to do if his current life with Anna, based on the tenuous peace that the country enjoyed, was to continue. Somehow he felt that the more distance he could place between them and Rome, the safer they would be.

The week that followed was somewhat hectic. Anna was deciding what to take to the island, while Giacomo met with his clients and assured them that he would be gone only for a short period of time and that he would return weekly on the ferry.

Francesca received the news with mixed feelings. She was now used to the Sunday mass at Santa Chiara Church and the subsequent lunches with Anna and Giacomo. During the three years that had transpired since the wedding, she had learned that her son in law—the term always sounded odd to her ears, since she was younger than he was—was a kind man who had made good on his promise to care for Anna and try to make her as happy as he could. Granted, she could plainly see that still there was a lack of passion in Anna's eyes whenever he was present or when his name was mentioned, but that did not preclude her from being contented with her present situation. He had come along at the right moment, and for that she would be eternally grateful. On the other hand, she did not look forward to her daughter's absence, even if the distance was not so great, but after speaking privately with Giacomo, she had to agree that his reasoning, as usual, was sound.

"I made you a promise to look after Anna," he told Francesca, "I intend to keep it."

So, in the end, she accepted the turn of events the same way she had accepted Anna's marriage three years earlier. Although she did not necessarily like all of it, she realized that it was the best thing to do for her daughter.

That last Sunday before the departure for Ischia, Giacomo had the cook prepare an especially lavish meal that would mark the occasion. By the time he returned from mass with Anna and Francesca, the table had been set with an exquisite tablecloth and that expensive china and silverware that only made an appearance during very special occasions. These were not just valuable pieces, but heirlooms that he had inherited from his mother. Giacomo had also taken the precaution of securing several bottles of fine Bordeaux. He expertly uncorked the first and poured the wine proudly into one of the Baccarat glasses. He took a sip, and after nodding approvingly, filled the others for Anna and Francesca.

During the course of the meal he was at his most jovial, telling stories about his stays in Ischia, how he had acquired the villa and how beautiful and serene it was.

Towards the end of the afternoon the other bottle of wine had been consumed. By that time Anna, Giacomo and Francesca gradually became more pensive; the reality of impending change was finally making itself felt. In a few short hours Anna and Giacomo would leave everything behind; Francesca would return to her empty house and dreary job. Even Sunday mass would not be the same.

"We need some music," said Anna while standing up and disappearing into the living room, where the old record player sat on a side table. Giacomo and Francesca joined her, but without saying a word.

A few moments later the unmistakable voice of Louis d'Amio, easily breaking through the faint static engendered by the minute scratches on the record, filled the room, and beyond, making the crystal in the dining room cupboards resonate. As the Immortal Arias were delivered, their emotional impact, compounded by the uncertain situation and magnified by the alcohol, caused both Anna and Francesca to loosen their grip on the pent up emotions they carried. They did not speak, but wept softly and freely, thinking of how different life would have been if Louis were alive. The years had not managed to erase his memory or lessen the devotion that both women felt for him. Even Giacomo, as used to as he was to exercising full control, found it difficult not to join them, since he had been present during the memorable opening night when Louis and Francesca played the leading roles in The Marriage of Figaro. Because of his work, he often ran into Louis at the San Carlo or in other functions where the operatic world converged. He had also been present at Louis' funeral. Although they had never become friends, he was a man whom he both admired as a rising singer and as a man who was devoted to his family. So he sat in the living room with Anna and Francesca, wisely respecting their tears, until the record was over and the last notes dissolved in the air.

Giacomo took a handkerchief out of his pocket, hesitated for a moment—vacillating whether to offer it to his wife or to his mother in law. Finally he handed it to Anna, who dried her tears and then offered it to Francesca.

"Forgive us," said Anna as she squeezed Giacomo's hand.

"No need for apologies," he said. "We are all under constant stress." After a brief pause, he added: "He was a good man and a great singer; it is only right that you should miss him."

"You have a long day ahead tomorrow; I am sure you still have things to do," said Francesca. "I think it is time for me to go home."

"We will be back soon," offered Anna.

"Yes, I am sure you will," answered Francesca, but her voice betrayed an underlying tone of doubt. She was aware, just as Giacomo was, of the worsening political situation in Italy and in the rest of Europe.

The return trip to Francesca's house was quiet, even somber. Night was approaching, and the sky over the bay was slowly turning from blue to a deep indigo that suddenly and without warning would turn completely dark. When they arrived, Giacomo exited the car and opened the back door for Francesca. Without any words, Anna hugged her mother and repeated what she had said earlier: "We will be back soon." This time, however, Francesca did not answer with reassuring words. Without knowing why or how, she felt the certainty that this would be the last time she would see her daughter.

The ferry trip from the port of Naples to the harbor on the island of Ischia took less than an hour. For Anna, it was one of those events in her life that she would never forget. First of all, she had never been out of the city of Naples; second, she had never been on a boat of any sort. As she and Giacomo walked on the plank that joined the ferry to the dock, a momentary shifting of the hull, caused by the soft waves, made her instinctively hold on to his arm in order not to fall.

Once on board, they sat on the wooden benches that covered the deck. It was a clear day, and from that vantage point Anna could easily see all the surrounding hills and the houses that populated them. She tried to locate her own house, but the distance was too great and the hills just appeared as a giant jigsaw puzzle whose pieces had been scattered randomly without much thought. She wondered how long it would be before they returned and immediately realized how much she had gotten used to her orderly life, with a husband that was old enough to be her father and in a house that always seemed too large for just two people.

The sound of a siren was heard; the plank was removed and the moorings were untied. The diesel engines, suddenly awakened by the hand of the helmsman, began to propel the vessel slowly across the bay. As the speed increased, so did the soft breeze that swept the open deck of the ferry. The passengers, to make themselves heard, talked loudly. They also laughed and shared some cheese or fresh fruit. In the distance, becoming smaller by the minute, sounds fading to a faint whisper, Naples eventually disappeared.

Within the hour, the island of Ischia, like a bright jewel in the sunlight, came into view. Since the turn of the century it had become a favorite resort of Neapolitan middle classes for their summer vacations, but only a handful owned villas that they could use year around.

Soon the shoreline became sharper, and the ferry slowed down noticeably. It had been an uneventful crossing, like the many hundreds that took place every year. Even before docking, many of the travelers stood up, as if that action could somehow shorten the time they needed to reach the harbor and set foot on the island. No one thought it strange; it was just one of the many idiosyncrasies that Italians exhibited on a regular basis. As they were docking, Anna noticed a church and pointed it out to Giacomo.

"Yes," he said, "It is the Church of Santa Maria di Porto Salvo; it was built by Ferdinand the Bourbon." Anna was both impressed and surprised that he should know these details, since Giacomo was not particularly a religious man.

"How do you know that?" she asked.

"I told you that my mother and I used to spend long vacations in Ischia; I always came to mass with her on Sundays, so it was inevitable that I should learn something about the history of this parish."

"Maybe we can come next Sunday," suggested Anna.

"If you wish," he answered. "But if it is churches you want to see, then you must visit San Nicola. It is on the hills and not very accessible, but worth the visit."

Giacomo's comments were cut short by the slight bump of the ferry against the dock, and the opening of the narrow gate that allowed the passengers to exit into the harbor; they joined them in the slow procession that made its way to the shore and eventually dissolved into the recesses of the island. At the end of the dock a group of men awaited the passengers; they hired themselves to carry luggage that was either too heavy or excessive for the visitors. As they were walking on the wooden plank that joined the ferryboat to the dock, Anna again lost her footing momentarily and instinctively held on to Giacomo's arm to keep from losing her balance.

As soon as they were on firm land, Giacomo signaled one of the young men who were standing next to carts pulled by horses. After an exchange that lasted a few minutes, the young man walked to the end of the dock, grabbed the heavy suitcases and placed them on the bed of the cart. He then climbed on the bench like driving seat and held the reins firmly. Giacomo helped Anna up and then sat next to her.

"I hope you don't mind the ride," Giacomo said to Anna, "Things here in Ischia are a little more primitive than they are in Naples. Besides, it is difficult to walk with all these suitcases."

"No, not at all," she answered him, and meant it. "Is it very far?"

"No," answered Giacomo, "Villa de'Bagni is a short distance from here. You will like it there, I am sure."

Under the supervision of the young driver, the cart slowly made its way on Via Roma, away from the harbor and the crowd that was still gathered around the dock, waiting for friends or relatives or simply giving themselves a few minutes to get their bearings. On either side of the street there were small shops and a few restaurants that usually catered to the faithful on their way to or from church. As they advanced, the small businesses gave way to private residences of humble appearance, where children interrupted their playing and stared with curiosity as they rode by. Their stares were often accompanied by the loud barking of dogs.

After about twenty minutes of riding on the narrow and irregular road, a small cluster of houses, nestled in a small cove, abruptly appeared.

"Just as I remember it," exclaimed Giacomo. "It is the third one from the end."

"I know," Anna answered him.

"How could you?" he asked with curiosity. "You have never been here."

"The garden," she explained. "You told me that your mother spent hours cultivating her flowers, just as she did in Naples."

The salient feature about the third villa, just as Anna had pointed out, was the exuberant flower garden that surrounded it. As they came closer, she realized that it was not just a random or eclectic proliferation, but one that had been carefully planned and executed.The abundant flora, but especially the roses, surrounded the structure in layers of colors and fragrances, reminiscent of the houses that were often depicted in children's books. A narrow path led to the front door.

The driver stopped the cart, got off and retrieved the suitcases from the wooden bed of the vehicle. After receiving a more than ample amount for his efforts, he drove off. Giacomo picked up one of the suitcases and with his free hand reached into his pocket to retrieve a key. "I hope you like it," he said to Anna with a smile.

"I already do," she answered him, as she lifted one of the smaller suitcases and followed Giacomo on the narrow path that led to the front door. On the porch there were some white wicker chairs arranged around a small table of the same material. Giacomo placed the key in the lock and turned it; the door yielded readily, as if welcoming him after a long absence. They found themselves in a small living room whose furniture had been covered with sheets or large pieces of linen to shield them from the dust. Lowering the suitcase with a slow motion, Giacomo slowly began to uncover the furniture.

"Nothing has changed," he said, not necessarily speaking to Anna, but making a comment to himself. "I remember when Mother and I bought this furniture," he added while running his fingers along the back of a sofa. For an instant Giacomo felt as if he had stepped into a still photograph taken long ago of a place he had thought forgotten. A place, however, that offered him the safety and stability that his current situation lacked.

Suddenly he snapped out of his memories and turned to Anna. "We will have to clean up the place; no one has lived here for quite a while. The caretaker keeps up the grounds, but that is all."

"Just leave it to me," said Anna enthusiastically, "I am sure we can bring it up to par in no time at all."

Since the day of the wedding, despite her initial lack of experience, Anna had slowly become quite proficient in running a household. Even though she had hired help since the beginning, she enjoyed doing all the household chores—from cooking to cleaning—that she had always seen her mother perform when she lived at home. She did not consider them a burden, but rather an important part of being an efficient wife.

The small kitchen and two bedrooms were as undisturbed as the living room. Everything was in order, but the thin and uniform layer of dust proclaimed that the house had been empty for some time.

"I will get the rest of the suitcases," said Giacomo as he walked out in the direction of the small garden in front of the bungalow, and returned after making several trips. "All the suitcases are in the bedroom now; we can unpack later. We have nothing to eat so we will have to go out."

"Is there anything nearby?" asked Anna.

"Here at Villa de'Bagni is mostly small houses, but farther down the road is Spiaggia dei Pescatori. Just a small village, mind you, but I am sure we can find a seaside cafe that will serve us something. The first few seasons that we spent here in Ischia, Mother and I used to walk there often. She liked it because it was remote and very rustic; the village does not even have electricity and the mail only comes once a week."

"That sounds wonderful," said Anna.

"Don't be so quick to pass judgment," said Giacomo with a smile. "You may not like all the walking and the food will not be what you are used to eating at the Vesuvius." He made the comment because he knew that Anna would welcome the long walk along the shore and would also love the home cooked meal that they were certain to find in the fishing village. Her enthusiasm for anything new would infuse—it always did—him with the energy that had dissipated with his years. It would also remove him further from the forthcoming hardships that Mussolini's policies were sure to bring all Italians. Every moment with Anna was precious, and he was most aware of it.

The walk along the shore to Spiaggia dei Pescatori was not as long or as difficult as Giacomo had suggested. Just a small exaggeration on his part, to challenge Anna. With the late afternoon, a soft breeze that came from the ocean brought with it the smell of salt water. From time to time, as they progressed on their walk, the whiff of an open fire, mixed with the aroma of fish cooking, would intrude in the fresh afternoon air.

After a while, the deserted coastline gave way to a random assortment of humble houses that became progressively closer, until they were barely a few feet from each other. Barefooted children were everywhere, and in the distance fishing boats either approached the coast or moved away from it. It was, indeed, a fishermen's village.

"Do you know where we are going?" Anna finally asked.

"Just a little bit farther," answered Giacomo as they passed a small pier where some children were playing and others were fishing. A large round building with a conical roof, partly anchored in the water and built on solid beams, became visible. It was devoid of any signs to identify its purpose. As they came closer, Anna realized that its walls were open, allowing the breeze to circulate freely. Inside there were wooden tables—their scarred surfaces did not enjoy the benefits of tablecloths—and wooden chairs. In the center of the structure, right below a chimneystack, there was a rustic grill whose fire was propelled by glowing charcoal and was surrounded by a circular counter. Several people sat around the grill; others sat at the bare tables, eating and drinking, while two waiters made sure that the orders were served immediately.

"This is it," announced Giacomo as they went in and sat down. "I told you it was not the Vesuvius, but I guarantee you will have the best fish this side of heaven. The catch is brought directly here from the ocean, so it you can be assured that your dinner is always fresh."

"I have never seen a place like this," said Anna with excitement in her voice. "It is certainly not the Vesuvius, with all its frills, but everything is more authentic."

"Precisely," agreed Giacomo. "The only thing that matters here is the quality of the food. Everything else is secondary. The prices are a lot better too," he added with a wink.

One of the waiters appeared, greeted them with a smile and then proceeded to tell them what was available that day. Unlike the Vesuvius, there was no printed menu or fancy descriptions of the available dishes. They opted for the catch of the day, and while the dinner was being prepared on the grill, Giacomo ordered a bottle of wine of an unknown vintage that was produced and consumed locally. A few minutes later, the waiter returned with the bottle and the glasses—certainly not the expensive Baccarat that they often employed—and Giacomo uncorked the bottle, poured some into his glass, tasted it, and then served Anna.

"Let's make a toast," Anna said while raising her glass.

"And what are we toasting?" he asked, always eager to know what was on her mind.

"To the beauty and peace of Ischia, and to our luck for being here to enjoy it," she said without hesitation.

"To Ischia it is," echoed Giacomo. "May its beauty and peace last forever," he concluded as he gently tapped his raised glass against Anna's.

The meal arrived as they were on the second glass of wine. The soft sound of the ocean, the gentle breeze and the aroma emanating from the grill made for a perfect setting. The fading siren of a departing ferryboat, combined with the distant sound of a song coming from one of the boats returning to the pier provided a haunting, even melancholic backdrop.

Anna saw the beauty of the moment and lost herself in it, with the complete abandon that only the license of youth allows. Her mind did not harbor even the remotest possibility that it could be otherwise. Life itself spread out in front of her, like an endless road she was eager to explore at her own leisure. Giacomo also enjoyed the moment in the company of his young wife, but his enjoyment was tempered by maturity and somewhat dampened by the certainty that all experiences—especially the most beautiful ones—were the most fragile and always ephemeral; it could all end without warning, not unlike the trembling flame of a candle snuffed out by an impatient and capricious hand. He had managed to distance himself and Anna—at least momentarily—from the turmoil of Italian politics, but the same apprehension that had made him undertake the trip had not disappeared, but simply subsided a little. He smiled at Anna, grateful that he could at least share the moment through her eyes and filtered by the innocence of her youth.

After the meal, which they both agreed was one of the best they ever had, they slowly walked back to the villa holding hands. The sun was beginning to set and the colors of the beach were now different, as if the entire landscape had been redone in a different hue. At that hour the beauty of the scenery was almost intoxicating, and when they arrived the sun had almost disappeared. It had been a long and busy day, but one that they would both remember as one of the most peaceful and beautiful of their married life. They felt content, removed from an unsettling world they had managed to put aside for an entire day.

"Let me turn on some lights," said Giacomo as they came into the small living room. On a side table there was a kerosene lamp; he expertly removed the glass shield, adjusted the length of the wicker, lit it and put it back on the table. It was obvious that he had had a lot of previous experience.

"There is no electricity, but we do have running water," he explained.

"Good," she said. "Tomorrow we can go to the market and stock the kitchen; we should have a special dinner."

"Of course," he agreed, thinking that every dinner, every day without war was special, but most of all giving thanks for every day he managed to share with Anna.

"I will go change now," she said taking a nightgown out of a suitcase and making her way to the bathroom.

While Anna was preparing for the night, Giacomo went into the bedroom, opened an armoire and retrieved a set of clean sheets. By the time she joined him, he had finished making the bed.

"I would have helped you," she said.

"I know," he answered her, "but we are both tired and for the moment I am the only one who knows where everything is. Don't fall asleep on me, I will be back in a second," he said and then disappeared into the bathroom.

When he returned, just a few minutes later, Anna had her eyes closed, but he knew that she was not asleep. Since that first night he had learned to read the rhythm of her breathing. Sometimes he liked to watch her sleep under the pale moon that came in through the window and guess what she was dreaming. Looking after her had given him a sense of purpose and a renewed lease on happiness.

As he got into bed she drew instinctively towards him, placing an arm on his chest. He reciprocated by stroking her hair and caressing her face. There were no words exchanged; at this point they were beyond that. Their relationship had evolved from an initial one of justified apprehension into one of mutual caring; each had been exemplary in honoring the agreement into which they had entered years before. Even though passion had not been part of the equation, they had both learned to accept and embrace gladly what the other had to offer.

After the busy day, they had no trouble drifting into sleep, holding each other closely, as they did every night, further proof that each drew strength and comfort from the other. In the darkness Giacomo's age, his reputation as a less than scrupulous promoter, and Anna's past transgressions in Paolo's bedroom, were magically erased. They were transformed simply into two human beings, who recognized their frailties and their need for each other, at a point in time that offered less than a certain or bright future.

The Church of Santa Maria di Porto Salvo, as it had done every Sunday for countless generations, welcomed the influx of eager worshippers. The priest, now approaching his seventieth birthday, had been assigned to the diocese of Ischia fresh out of the seminary, before many of the local residents were even born. Unquestionably, he had seen many changes—even in a place as stable as the island—during his tenure there. Keeping true to his Christian beliefs, he welcomed everyone into the church. His homilies, without falling into the realm of politics, always exhorted the faithful to look beyond the immediate and place their attention on more lofty and lasting goals.

Since her first Sunday in Ischia, Anna had not missed a single mass. It was a habit acquired over a lifetime. She enjoyed watching the people and listening to the clever sermons that were delivered by the old priest every Sunday. She preferred the midmorning service, so she could sleep a little later. After getting up she prepared breakfast, put on one of her best dresses and took a leisurely walk with Giacomo to the church. After the service, rather than returning home, they went to the Piazza Antica Reggia, where they had lunch at one of the local restaurants. In the afternoon they usually went to the movie house or to a play being performed by an itinerant troupe. Sunday evenings, back in the villa, they prepared a light supper and retired early.

Weekdays were just as leisurely as Sundays, but in a different way. Anna had developed, to Giacomo's delight, an interest in horticulture and spent most of her mornings working in the garden, pruning, weeding and making sure that the plants had an optimum access to the abundant sunlight. During the afternoon, after lunch, they went for walks along the beach. Anna always liked this because as they explored the hidden paths of the island Giacomo would tell her stories of his childhood and how he had walked the same deserted courses then and how little everything had changed. After returning from those walks, they would go in the kitchen and Giacomo would help her prepare dinner.

The evenings were devoted to Anna's continuing education, since it was a goal both wanted to pursue. One of the trunks they had brought from Naples contained those books that every educated person must read—from Dante's Divine Comedy to the works of Shakespeare—and they discussed them by the light of kerosene lanterns in the small living room of the villa. Anna was a good reader and had a keen eye for details, a quality that Giacomo admired, since it was that very same quality that had allowed him to succeed in his line of work. Inside that artificial bubble they had created, the topic of Italian politics was carefully avoided, as if by ignoring it altogether they could place themselves beyond its reach, or somehow the deteriorating external situation would magically disappear.

Once a week, in order to keep his business contacts current and to check on the house, Giacomo would take the ferry back to Naples. Without fail he would return the following day, always carrying more books in his suitcase and wearing a somber expression on his face. He also served as a courier between Anna and her mother, bringing back and forth the letters that the women wrote regularly. By then the Italian mail service had become spotty and unreliable. The one item that he never brought with him was the newspapers. The grim news that they contained would have surely disrupted the idyllic and fragile world that he had constructed in Ischia, where time had ceased to exist and the clangor of distant wars was but a faint, almost inaudible echo lacking the necessary force to enter their lives. It was best to keep the outside world at a safe distance.

But no matter how much he tried to isolate himself and Anna from the turmoil that prevailed in the rest of Europe, Giacomo could not prevent the events that he had foreseen so clearly. On June 10th, 1940, Italy entered the war. Mussolini feared that Germany would get all the spoils, so on June 17th, the date the French sought surrender terms from Germany; he ordered the invasion of southern France. The news did not take long to reach Ischia. Although most people had not been personally touched by the conflict, many had relatives and friends in other parts of the country. That Sunday morning, without making any specific reference to the politics behind the war or impugning guilt on anyone, the local priest prayed for peace in the world, a sentiment that was echoed by the entire congregation. Everyone hoped that the war would end quickly, and that the remoteness of their island would isolate them from the violence that seemed to spread with every passing day.

Giacomo Pace had no such hopes. Somehow, he felt that this was just the beginning, that Mussolini would not stop there. As he had been doing for months, he tried to conceal his true beliefs about the situation from Anna. They continued their reading sessions in the small villa, punctuated by frequent outings to the shore or leisurely walks to the nearby villages. Anna also spent quite a bit of time in the garden, taking care of the flowers and other plants. There would have been no point, Giacomo felt, in worrying her with things over which neither one of them had any control. He still traveled to Naples once a week, delivered Anna's and Francesca's letters, and tried to keep his business afloat. This was proving to be rather difficult; many artists had either fled the country or stopped performing altogether. The public was in no mood to attend opera performances with other more pressing and urgent matters at hand.

When September came around, and the news that Italy had invaded Egypt became known, Giacomo knew for certain that everyone's life had taken a turn for the worse. A month later, Italian troops entered Greek soil. Even in the remotest villages of Ischia the people gathered around old radios, eager for some news, but they were not what they had hoped for. The seriousness of the situation could not be underestimated.

One evening, after one of their study sessions, Anna suddenly turned to Giacomo and made a comment which was, in reality, a request.

"My mother should be with us," she said, "I don't think it is safe anymore in Naples."

"I have to agree with you," said Giacomo, always eager to put Anna at ease. "I will bring her with me this week; she can stay with us until this turmoil is over."

"Thank you," said Anna with relief and kissed him on the cheek, unsuspecting that her husband and mother would soon disappear completely from her life.

On October 31st, 1940, as he did every week, Giacomo took the ferry from Ischia to Naples. Before leaving the villa he reassured Anna that he would be back with Francesca the following day. If there was one thing she had learned about her husband during their short years of marriage, was that his word was as good as gold. Secure in the knowledge that soon her mother would be staying with them, Anna went about readying the second bedroom. After she finished, she went in the kitchen and started preparing a special meal to welcome her and celebrate the reunion. That night, she slept better than she had in weeks.

The following day at midmorning, not being able to contain her excitement at the prospect of seeing her mother again, she walked to the port to wait for the ferry. As she approached the dock, she was surprised to see a larger than usual crowd. They were mostly young women with children and older women with scarves covering their heads and rosaries in hand. What alerted Anna that something was not quite right was not what the people were saying, but rather what they were not. There was a tense silence — most unusual for a group of Italians — that immediately betrayed the anguish of an anxious wait. They thought of husbands, fathers, sons and friends who by all accounts should have arrived by now. Making her way through the crowd, she reached the end of the pier.

"What is happening?" she finally had the courage to ask one of the strangers.

"Naples was bombed," answered the old woman in a soft voice that almost broke into a sigh. "It is all over the radio; they targeted the harbor."

Anna raised a hand to her mouth in shock, not believing what she was hearing. For a moment everything seemed to be taking place in slow motion, except the beating of her heart. She saw the old woman's mouth opening again, trying to tell her something that she could not grasp because the words traveled so slowly that it took them forever to reach her. Eventually the sounds became words that held an ominous message.

"There are no more news; we are all waiting for the ferry and hoping for the best," she said and then made the sign of the cross.

The rest of the morning was spent in a futile wait. From time to time a loud whisper would emerge from the fringes of the throng, as if some news had arrived, but it was soon subdued and the silence blanketed the crowd once again. By one o'clock it was clear to everyone that the ferry would not arrive that day. As the crowd began to disperse, rather than returning to their homes, they instinctively marched into the Church of Santa Maria di Porto Salvo. The priest was already at the pulpit, and by the somber look on his face Anna knew that the news he had could not be good.

Since her arrival in Ischia, Anna had been attending that church with Giacomo every Sunday, so she felt comfortable and secure within its walls. She had also become accustomed to the old priest who had spent his life tending to the spiritual needs of the inhabitants of the island. He knew why they were there, as he also knew who was missing and why. So that afternoon, conscious of what the congregation needed to hear, he told them of the infinite power of God, of the miracles that could be realized through prayer. At the end of his sermon he made a special invocation for the safe return of all who were absent and gave a special blessing to all those present.

The following morning, and for an entire week thereafter, Anna waited at the dock. Just as the first day, no one present spoke; they just stood there, looking into the line of the horizon hoping to discover a faint plume of smoke that would announce that the vessel was coming. Every afternoon she returned to the villa filled with the disappointment of a futile wait, yet already thinking of the next day and telling herself that certainly the ferry would arrive then.

A month passed without any change. According to the news on the radio, the bombing of Naples had intensified; the British were fearful that the Axis might gain control of the eastern Mediterranean, and they had put forth every effort to prevent that from happening.

Anna did not know what to do; in fact, there was nothing that she could do. Another three weeks went by. As an act of faith, on Christmas Eve she decided to visit the Church of San Nicola, on top of Mount Epomeo—the highest point in Ischia—and offer special prayers for the safety of Giacomo and Francesca. The journey was, in every respect, an act of desperation. She had never been there, and the road that led to the church was nothing but a narrow path on the side of the mountain, but deep down she felt that by offering this sacrifice it would prove how sincere she was and this way receive a divine answer to her constant prayers.

The following day she rose at dawn, walked to the small plaza in the center of the village and contracted one of the young men with a horse drawn cart to take her to the base of the mountain. The rest she would do on her own. During that slow journey she prayed and concentrated on the task ahead. Around midmorning they arrived at the spot where the path leading to the church was located. She thanked the driver, paid him and looked up. At that hour of the morning the top of Epomeo was immersed in clouds, adding to the mystery and allure of the climb. Some *ciucciari* — mule owners — waited for potential clients they could carry to the top of the mountain. Anna was not interested; if this journey was to have any significance, it would have to imply a sacrifice on her part. That morning she had had the common sense to wear a pair of sturdy, yet comfortable shoes that would facilitate the ascent.

Although Mount Epomeo was less than one thousand meters in altitude, the steepness of the climb, combined with the irregular surface, made it a most challenging task. Paradoxically, this was exactly what Anna had hoped for.

The first half hour was spent in a cautious climb, getting herself used to the twisting path and sudden crevices on its surface that had been created over the years by the summer rains. From time to time she was forced to stop and catch her breath. An hour later, she knew that she was close to the top because she could no longer see the base of the mountain as she entered that zone that was covered by the clouds. This was the most difficult part, not only because of the increased steepness, but also because visibility had decreased. All the while she thought of Giacomo and Francesca and tried to hold back her tears.

Suddenly and without warning, as she emerged from the mist, there was sunshine. Below she had an unobstructed view of the Gulf of Naples and the entire island. For a moment she felt dizzy from exertion and simultaneously elated that she had completed the climb. Instinctively she looked at the sea below, searching for the ferry that made its way from Naples on a daily basis, but she only saw the line of the horizon and a few fishermen's boats closer to the shoreline.

On the opposite direction, looking away from the sea, rose the Church of San Nicola. It was not at all what Anna was expecting. Rather than a traditional building erected on a plateau, the church had been carved into the light green tufa rock that was part of the geological formation of the island. The splendid façade, without giving way to the baroque excesses found on the mainland, welcomed the visitors with its understated elegance. As Anna transposed the threshold, she realized that from the outside it was impossible to ascertain the magnitude of the beautiful church.

Completely deserted at that hour of the day, her steps echoed as she approached the main altar. Votive candles provided a subtle, almost mystical light that was underscored by the faint smell of incense. Surrounded by the images of the saints and immersed in the deep silence of the temple, Anna fell on her knees, closed her eyes and prayed as she had never done before, asking God for the safety of those she loved and for a sense of direction in her life. As she immersed herself into her own thoughts, images of her life flashed on the inside of her eyelids: early memories of Louis d'Amio and his unmistakable voice; playing in a park with Guido; helping Francesca in the kitchen; her father's funeral; moving to a smaller house; a new school; visiting Paolo's house for the first time; her outrage at signora Alberti's plans for her son; her desperate plan to save him; everyone's outrage at their discovery; Paolo's disappearance; Giacomo's proposal of marriage; the house overlooking the bay; the move to Ischia. All the while, she kept asking God to put everything back together the way it was just a short time ago, when things seemed a lot more clear and she had the support of Giacomo and Francesca.

The Lord, as He often does, answered her prayers, but in a most oblique and unexpected manner. From the rear of the church she heard a muffled sound, as if someone, not wanting to disrupt the silence, were trying to suppress a cough. Still on her knees she turned around, searching for the source of the sound. At first, because of the lack of light, she saw nothing, but as her eyes surveyed the back pews, she discerned a kneeling figure completely dressed in white. As the figure stood up she realized it was a man who was now approaching the main altar. For a few minutes he stood before the cross, saying a silent prayer. As he turned around, he became aware of Anna, who was still kneeling in one of the front pews and shrouded in semidarkness.

"I did not mean to startle you, or interrupt your prayers," he apologized in a subdued voice. "This is a most holy place, and I came to say good-bye to my mother. Mothers are always special," he added. "My name is Mr. Ioso."

"I also came to pray for my mother," answered Anna, "Somehow I sense that there is a special significance to our meeting in the same remote place and for the same specific purpose."

"I agree," said Mr. Ioso, sitting next to Anna. "But let's start at the beginning. You must be asking yourself what coincidences, what previous events have led us to such a vital encounter. My father, as you can tell by my name, was Greek. For generations the Ioso family had devoted itself to the delicate but demanding creation of bas-relief designs on metal plaques. These plaques both celebrated and immortalized with their images a sumptuous wedding, the baptism of a first born, or the exequies of an exemplary citizen. Wealthier clients, of course, requested the most noble and durable metals, such as gold and silver. Others, less affluent but no less worthy of our unique art, chose bronze or copper to perpetuate their family events.

"My father, although he never attended school beyond the third grade, knew the work of the philosophers and the Greek theater with a familiarity that bewildered everyone he met. His mother, my paternal grandmother, during the tedious hours of metallurgical preparation by a forge, laborious engraving with rustic tools or polishing with soft suede, would read aloud while the different tasks were being carried out in the shop. In the mornings she always chose selections from the philosophers; in the afternoons, after a lunch that consisted of bread, olives, cheese and wine that they fermented themselves in wooden casks, she offered them a work by Sophocles, Euripides or Aristophanes. She was also very fond of Hellenistic epigrams.[1]

"Some time ago, due to recent events and the threat of German troops to the entire European continent, my father's family, after a meal too elaborate to lack a special significance, held a midnight meeting to discuss the events that were on everyone's mind. They decided to go into the hills; the following night they disappeared through the Turkish border. I was, of course, prepared to join them when my father, with the firm gesture of a patriarch of the Greek Orthodox Church, informed me that I would have to accompany my mother to the island of Lesbos. From there we would secure clandestine passage in a Swedish freighter that would bring us to the Italian island of Ischia."

At this point Mr. Ioso made a pause, perhaps trying to organize his thoughts or maybe restrain his emotions.

"It was, in reality, a very logical decision on my father's part. Although Italian, culturally this island had always been ours. It was later named Aenaria by the Romans; the name is derived from the Latin *aenum*, which means bronze or metal in general. This fact confirms the flourishing metallurgical activity that was introduced by our ancestors centuries ago. Furthermore, even today one can see on the hills of Mezzavia the ruins of the first forges where the ancient Greeks processed bronze, iron and, of course, gold and silver. The name Epomeo, the very place where we are standing, comes from the ancient Greek and it means 'look around.'

"By then the name Ioso had become synonymous with art in the entire Mediterranean basin, and that reputation preceded us. With the help of some countrymen and the meager resources that my mother and I had, I opened a modest metallurgical shop. Little by little, as my artistic work became better known on this island, the number and importance of the commissioned works increased. Although we were not getting rich, the steady work gave us enough to live with dignity."

Once again Mr. Ioso made a pause in his story. This time he looked towards the main altar, as if requesting guidance from an ever-present yet invisible presence.

"What happened then?" asked Anna, genuinely interested in Mr. Ioso's tale.

---

[1] For a definitive study of Hellenistic epigrams, consult Poetic Garlands, by Professor Kathryn J. Gutzwiller, University of California Press, 1998.

"My mother's health was declining. Although we had every-thing necessary for our corporal sustenance, the distance from the Greek coasts, the sudden suppression of the unique sound of our language and our music, but especially my father's absence, slowly undermined her spirit and created a void in her soul. Seated in an old chair upholstered with flowery material and looking towards the sea, she waited for news from my father. Perhaps she strength-ened him with her thoughts or silently sent him the necessary courage to overcome those difficult moments. So busy was I with the work in the shop that I failed to notice her inexorable spiritual decline.

"One afternoon, like any other, I left the premises in order to deliver a gold plaque whose manufacture had taken me an entire month. It depicted, in all its bas-relief splendor—the inconsolable disciples; the reclined central figure; the limp hand; the lethal cup carelessly dropped on the floor of the cell—Socrates' last moments after drinking the hemlock. It would proudly crown the main wall of the incipient library."

Once again Mr. Ioso made a pause. This time he loosened his tie, as if to facilitate the flow of blood through the carotids and revive his memories.

"And then?" asked Anna. "What happened when you returned?"

"Upon my return I knew immediately, without even having to come in, that something nefarious had taken place. As I crossed the threshold, I was welcomed by a rarified atmosphere and a silence that was too deep, as if I were in a vacuum chamber. It all augured an immediate tragedy.

"On the aforementioned chair I found my lifeless mother. I felt, at that instant, as if an unexpected colony of African termites were gnawing relentlessly at the base of my skull, until they managed to seize with ease the recesses of my medulla oblongata. On the floor, next to my mother, I collapsed.

"Some time later, on my work bench and surrounded by awls, chisels and pieces of suede, I came to. I was surrounded by familiar faces and nervous voices who solicitously looked after me. Kind hands—I never found out whose—held cold compresses on my burning forehead.

"After the exequies, which were celebrated with all the extensive liturgy demanded by the Greek Orthodox Church, I returned to the shop. I immediately covered all the mirrors with pieces of black cloth and placed a funeral wreath over the threshold. This way everyone who came through the door was forced to acknowledge the great loss that our house had suffered.

"Three days later, as usual, I found my mother sitting in the same chair, looking at the sea. So forceful was her will, so deep her love for life, that she had managed to survive even death. Nothing had changed. I continued with my work in the shop; she continued waiting for my father.

"One sunny morning, like every morning here in Ischia, I left to deliver an ornate rococo jewel box with elaborate engravings that would grace the toilet table of a wealthy lady. During my absence the maid, in her zest for cleanliness and order, uncovered all the mirrors that I had so patiently shielded from the light. That night, as usual, my mother's ghost wandered through the hallways, awaiting the call of sleep that often came after midnight. As she walked in front of one of the mirrors, she became aware that her image did not return a reflection. It was at that moment that she realized that death had already come."

One more time Mr. Ioso produced the handkerchief and removed the thin film of perspiration from his face and neck. It was apparent that it was difficult for him to evoke such personal and painful memories. Although Anna did not want to appear rude, her curiosity made her urge the stranger to go on.

"Did you continue with your work?" she asked.

"Not at all," answered Mr. Ioso. "Since that cruel day I lost all my decorative powers. The metal sheets turned into hideous and amorphous creations at the mere touch of my hand; the engraving tools slipped out of my trembling fingers; the polishing suede, so obedient in the past, openly rebelled against the dictates of my will. I realized then that it was my mother, and not I, the true master and governess of that ancient art," concluded Mr. Ioso. "I came here today, as I already explained, to say good-bye to my mother for the last time. She is buried in the small cemetery next to this church."

"What will you do now?" asked Anna.

"As you can suppose, my situation is intolerable. Since I am unable to work, I have liquidated everything of value and will be leaving Ischia in three days."

"But there is a war going on," said Anna, pointing out the obvious.

"I am not just leaving Ischia, but the European continent as well," explained Mr. Ioso. "I am seeking a new beginning on another island, on the other side of the world. Its name is Cuba."

"It sounds distant and exotic," commented Anna, not knowing exactly what to say.

"You are correct on both counts. Just as surely as my mother guided my hands in life, she will guide my destiny in death. Of that I am certain."

"I wish I could be as confident as you are about a bright future," said Anna, struggling to control her emotions. "I have no one anymore"

"Then allow me to suggest something. There is room in the Danish freighter for one more person; gather what you can and leave Italy. You too can start a new life in a new land. Today we both came to the shrine of San Nicola looking for guidance. I suspect that you knew all along that there is no longer a life for you here; you just needed corroboration so you could then move forward, just as I am about to do," he concluded. Anna was about to protest at the suggestion, but Mr. Ioso's raised hand stopped her before she could utter any words.

"There is no need to decide at this moment. I will wait for you at the pier; the ship leaves at dawn. But just in case I don't see you again, I would like to give you something as a token of this most fortuitous encounter. That way you will always remember this day."

As he said this, Mr. Ioso reached into his coat pocket and retrieved what appeared to be a small, flat packet wrapped in white linen. He opened it slowly, allowing the light of the candles to shine on its surface. Before Anna's eyes was a silver plaque with a detailed bas relief depiction of San Nicola.

"I want you to have this; it was the last piece I completed before my mother died. When I left the shop this morning, although I knew there was no reason for me to bring it with me, a mysterious force compelled me do so. I now understand why," he said and handed the silver plaque to Anna.

"I don't know what to say," she whispered in the silence of the church.

"There is nothing to say," added Mr. Ioso, "Accept it as a sign of good fortune. You must remember that even though we may not see them, there are forces that watch over us and guide our steps on this earth."

"Thank you," she said while accepting the gift, "I will always treasure it."

"Now I must go; I hope to see you again in three days," he said softly before exiting the church.

Sitting in the semi darkness of the empty church, for an instant Anna doubted that the strange meeting had taken place, but the silver plaque in her hand was undeniable evidence. She looked at the crucified figure above the main altar and then closed her eyes, praying and asking for strength. She did not know how long she stayed at the church, nor had any recollection of the descent, but when she found herself at the base of the mountain, it was almost dusk.

The following two days were spent in a state of indecision. Anna still went to the pier every morning, hoping that the ferry from Naples would come. The news from the mainland was not good; the bombing had intensified. Ischia was now completely cut off from the rest of Italy.

On the eve of the third day she finally accepted the fact that Mr.Ioso was right. Before packing her suitcase, she went over to the old hand crank gramophone and placed Immortal Arias on the turntable. Louis d'Amio's voice filled the room, imparting his daughter a sense of calm. As she collected her most prized belongings, she replayed the record. Eventually, it also joined the rest of the objects in the suitcase. All that was left to do was wait for the arrival of the new day...

Even though the sun had not risen yet, she recognized the tall silhouette standing on the pier next to the plank that led to the main deck of the ship.

"I knew you would come," he said, "It is impossible to escape one's destiny."

"I almost didn't," said Anna.

"Just think of the new world that awaits you," said Mr. Ioso as he picked up Anna's suitcase and helped her walk on deck. She noticed that all the lights had been turned off in the freighter, although there was apparent activity on board. The sound of wenches raising the anchor and the hands untying the rigging suddenly broke the silence before dawn. Then it was the potent rumbling of the diesel engines coming to life and the slight swaying of the ship as they got under way. Once again Anna noticed that they had sailed in complete darkness, for all the lights were still off.

About an hour later, the sky became lighter and eventually the sun rose. In the distance, bathed in the soft morning light, Anna saw the disappearing Italian coastline.

At that moment, she wondered if she would ever see it again.

Book Two: Cuba

V

The days and nights of the crossing, although uneventful, proved to be eye-opening for Anna. Huddled in the bowels of the Danish freighter were people of different nationalities, all hoping to escape the war and find a more stable future. Some were alone; others had their families with them.

Since Anna did not know anyone on board, she spent most of her time in the company of Mr. Ioso, the mysterious Greek whom she had met Christmas day at the Church of San Nicola on top of Mount Epomeo. He spoke mostly about his family, about his Greek traditions, about the war in Europe and the uncertain future in a new land, but especially about the devotion he had for his late mother. Anna reciprocated by telling him about how she presumed that both her husband and mother had died during the recent bombing of Naples. They found solace by sharing their grief; the burden of their sorrow became a little lighter because they had found in each other a sympathetic listener.

One evening, while eating one of the simple meals that were the usual fare aboard the freighter, they found themselves at the same table with a man whom they had often seen on board. By his clothes and the way he moved they realized immediately that he was not European, a fact that was further corroborated by his accent. He introduced himself as Oppiano Licario, a citizen of Cuba. Later they were to find out that he had been traveling throughout Europe when the war broke out, and that he had also studied numismatics and Ninivite art at Harvard University.

This casual meeting, as insignificant as it appeared at the time, was to prove most fortuitous in Anna's life. In fact, it supported Mr. Ioso's own assertions about these 'Unknown and invisible forces that guide our destinies.' Oppiano Licario inquired as to what plans she had after her arrival in Cuba. Anna, of course, had not formulated anything concrete; she just wanted to start a new life away from the mindless destruction of war.

"Perhaps I can offer you some guidance once we land," he told her. "Just think of what you would like to do; our country is going through a rather prosperous time, so opportunities abound in every endeavor."

What Oppiano Licario said was true. Paradoxically, the political instability in Europe had brought about an unexpected largess to the Cuban economy. The price of sugar, its main export, had risen in the world market. This bountiful time was colorfully referred to by Cubans as 'The era of the fat cows.'

"Thank you, you are very kind," said Anna, but not really convinced that the offer of help would amount to anything. She was just one of many immigrants who had lost all stability in life and wanted to build a future elsewhere. As to what that future had in store for her, she had no idea.

A few days later, emerging softly from the morning mist, the Cuban coastline became visible. A tall structure—like a medieval fortress—towered over the bay. During the crossing Anna would invariably wake up at dawn, go on deck and search for land. Now that it had finally materialized, she felt her heart racing with anticipation and apprehension. As the coast became closer she thought of Ischia, except that on this island the sun seemed to be harsher, less forgiving. Instinctively she raised her right hand to her face to protect her eyes from the light.

Suddenly she realized that she was no longer alone on deck; in a brief time people who had been asleep just minutes before crowded around her to get a first look at the coastline. Now bathed in the bright light of the Cuban sun, Anna suddenly noticed that the journey had taken a visible toll on the passengers: many of the men were unshaven, the hair was unkempt and their clothes were wrinkled and smelly. The women were no better, showing circles around their eyes and looks of uncertainty mixed with fear. Mothers held their children tightly, as if fearing that if they let go for just a second they would disappear. The comments that reached her ears were delivered in different languages, most of which she did not understand.

Abruptly, the hoarse sound of a siren filled the air and the freighter began to slow down. The crew — mostly below deck — busied themselves in preparation for the docking. At this point the feverish activity in the port was clearly visible; this vessel was just one of many that would be arriving that day.

The captain had also appeared on deck. As he walked through the group of passengers he instructed them, in several languages, to gather their belongings because they were about to land. For many of the passengers this reminder had been unnecessary; they usually kept their modest possessions with them at all times, and the few that had a suitcase—as in the case of Anna—did not take long to retrieve it in order to take their place in the line that would lead them to their new futures. They clutched passports or other documents that, not unlike magic passwords, would open the mysterious doors of this new land.

Once the engines were turned off, the freighter reached the dock under its own momentum. The crew hands skillfully cast the rigging, which was received below by the dock workers. Once the vessel was securely tied and its anchor lowered, a narrow plank was extended so the passengers could disembark. The captain, who was still on deck, tried to maintain a modicum of order that would control the excitement of the passengers after spending those days in the high seas inhabiting the rustic quarters below deck. As the line of passengers slowly left the ship, once again Anna became aware that despite the different languages that were being spoken, the tone of the voices reflected the same unanimous feelings of excitement.

The dock ended at a wooden structure with ample windows shielded with screens, another precaution against the oppressive tropical heat. As the group marched into the building, they were led by a uniformed official to a central chamber whose inner circumference was furnished with bare wooden benches. It was obviously a waiting room where the incoming foreign passengers were to stay until they were summoned by the Cuban immigration officers. Already sitting on one of the benches she spotted Mr. Ioso, the Greek responsible for her presence there. Apparently he had been one of the first to leave the ship. She walked over to where he was, hoping he would have some recent information.

"Good morning," he said, while offering Anna a place to sit.

"Good morning," she answered him with a faint smile. "It is hard to believe that we are finally here. So what happens now?"

"Now we wait," he said. "We will be called by the officials and asked about the reasons for our presence in this country. In our case, the best reason we can offer is the ongoing war in Europe."

"Will that be enough?" asked Anna with true concern in her voice.

"Then depends," answered Mr. Ioso. "Cubans can be rather volatile, so it is up to the person who is conducting the interview." Then, after a brief pause, "It is really a roll of the dice."

"We have come this far; we have left everything behind. There is no way we can return now," commented Anna.

"Have confidence in the hand of fate," offered Mr. Ioso, "There are invisible forces that guide our lives," he added, repeating what he had told Anna during their first meeting at the Church of San Nicola.

"I hope you are right," she said without much conviction, and suddenly fell silent, contemplating what was in store for her.

The number of passengers in the waiting area, as they were called, began to diminish visibly. Anna did not understand the system employed by the erratic Cubans; maybe their method for interviewing the influx of immigrants was just random. Before long, her own name was called. She stood up and took her suitcase.

"Good luck," said Mr. Ioso as he also stood up. "I hope we meet again."

"Good luck to you too," said Anna, "And thank you for everything." She added before following the uniformed officer through one of the doors to the offices where the interviews were conducted

The small office was ordinary in every way. In a back corner a file cabinet, whose different drawers corresponded to a range of letters in the alphabet, also served as an improvised pedestal for the small oscillating fan that constantly circulated the already warm morning air. On the wall behind the central desk, hung a Cuban flag and a photograph of a man wearing a suit and tie. Anna assumed it was the president of the country, but she did not know his name.

The ruler of such domain was a balding, middle-aged man with thick glasses and a drab bow tie. He signaled Anna to sit down in one of the chairs in front of his desk, then lit up a cigarette and leisurely exhaled the smoke through his nostrils. It was quickly dispersed in the stuffy atmosphere by the force of the oscillating fan.

134

Leaning back in his chair, he asked Anna for her documents and inquired as to the reason for her visit to Cuba. She handed him her passport and explained, in broken Spanish, that she had had to leave Italy because of the war. Both her husband and mother had died during a recent bombing of the city of Naples.

The official opened the passport and compared the photograph to the person that was sitting across from him, and then proceeded to verify the dates, to ascertain that it was in force. All the while he shook his head affirmatively, denoting that so far everything was in order. Suddenly there was a severe frown.

"Where is the visa?" he asked, still flipping through the section of the passport where the official seal of the Cuban embassy would have been found.

"There was no time to reach the embassy," explained Anna, "I was isolated in the island of Ischia."

"Be that as it may," explained the functionary, "I cannot approve your entry into the country without a proper visa. You will have to wait out there again, until my superiors decide what to do," he said in a tone that allowed no room for further discussion while returning the passport to Anna. "Just wait for your name to be called."

Anna could think of nothing else to say, so she put the passport back in her purse, picked up her suitcase, returned to the waiting area and sat on one of the wooden benches. Instinctively she looked around to see if she could locate Mr. Ioso, but he was nowhere to be found. She realized that she was alone in a country that was completely new to her. And what was worse, she could not return to Italy. She thought of Giacomo; certainly he would know what to do in such a predicament. Suddenly she felt an overwhelming desire to cry, like an irresistible tide that would vanquish everything in its wake and cleanse all the tension and apprehension she had held in check since Giacomo's disappearance. Burying her face in her hands she began to weep softly and inconsolably, allowing all her feelings of frustration and anguish to manifest themselves in the steady stream of tears that she was no longer capable of holding back.

"Is there anything wrong?" came a voice from above. For an instant she thought that Mr. Ioso had returned, but when she lifted her face she did not recognize the man standing in front of her and offering her a linen handkerchief.

"Everything is wrong," Anna managed to mutter, momentarily controlling her sobbing and drying her tears with the handkerchief she had accepted from the stranger. She noticed that it exuded a mild and unique fragrance.

Now somewhat more composed, she looked at the man again. He wore a white suit, an equally white shirt and a discreet silk tie of soft hues.

"We met briefly one evening during the crossing," he explained. "I am Oppiano Licario, at your service," he added as he sat down next to Anna.

She recounted what had happened during her interview with the customs officer, and how her immigration status was most uncertain because her passport lacked a Cuban visa. The eagerness of her voice, verging on incoherence, denoted that she saw in the stranger one last hope to exit the labyrinth where she was currently trapped.

"War has an uncanny way of disrupting everything," said Licario, but the comment was more of a thought that he had expressed out loud and not directed at Anna. "Excuse me for a few minutes," he said after a moment, "I will be right back."

Anna watched him disappear through one of the doors that led to the exterior of the building. She could not imagine what he intended to do, but a short time later he returned.

"Get ready to leave," he said.

"I do not understand; my passport does not have a visa," she repeated. Before Oppiano Licario could explain, the same officer who had interviewed her earlier came out of his office into the waiting area. In his hand he had what appeared to be official documents. He walked directly to where Anna was sitting and handed her the papers bearing recent seals and signatures. One of them was a card with Oppiano Licario's signature as her reference in Cuba.

"You are free to go;" he said in a voice devoid of emotion, "everything is in order." Within seconds he disappeared back in his office. Anna looked at Oppiano Licario with awe, for he had been directly responsible for what had just happened.

"I just made a phone call to expedite things a little," he explained. "I am not without influence in this city. Besides, you are a guest in our country; the least we can do is show a little courtesy."

"I don't know how to repay you," Anna said, "I don't know what I would have done if you had not come along."

"Do you know where you are going now?" asked Oppiano Licario, disregarding her previous comment. "Since I know the city, I can take you there."

"No," said Anna, "I don't know anyone; I left Italy without much planning; the war came upon us suddenly."

"In that case," said Oppiano Licario, "join me and my sister, Ynaca Eco, for lunch. It is a sort of celebration, since I have been traveling and have not seen her for a few months. I just spoke to her on the telephone and she is preparing everything. We can talk about your options during the meal; I am sure that things will become more clear then."

"I would not want to impose; you already have done so much for me," Anna said.

"It is no imposition," retorted Licario. "I am sure that once you learn your way around you will enjoy our city," he said while picking up Anna's suitcase.

They left the building and walked towards the busy street, away from the port. The sun was already high in the sky, so Anna had to squint instinctively to protect her eyes from the glare. Even though Cuba and Ischia were islands, she realized from the beginning, that the climates were different; this was not the mild, usually pleasant weather she was used to, but one that was more severe and oppressive.

Once on the sidewalk, Oppiano Licario walked toward one of the parked cars that waited by the docks to transport the arriving passengers into the city. The driver, who was reading a newspaper behind the wheel, came out of the car, opened the trunk and placed Anna's and Oppiano Licario's suitcases in it.

"Where to?" he asked as he sat behind the wheel again.

"Espada 615," answered Licario while opening the back door for Anna.

"Are we far from your house?" asked Anna.

"Not at all; just enjoy the view of this new city that you have made your own," suggested Licario.

As they left the docks the car traveled on a wide avenue along the shore. There were people promenading and hawkers pushing their assorted goods. Some children sat on the low wall that faced the ocean. Later Anna would learn that this avenue that ran along the bay was the most famous in Havana, and it was called the Malecón.

"Cubans come here all the time," explained Licario. "It is cool, especially in the evenings, and we like the breeze that comes in from the ocean. Most likely you will also run into someone you know, so it is also a meeting place of sorts."

Anna thought that it was fortunate to have such a beautiful place to enjoy, but even more fortunate that it was so far removed from the conflicts of war, with the death, destruction and instability that it always carried with it. She also understood—one of Giacomo's lessons—that these forces were invariably fueled by men's ambitions and that they would always be present.

About ten minutes later, the driver made a ninety-degree turn, away from the ocean, and into the city proper. Eventually the wide avenues, lined with trees and ample sidewalks, gave way to narrow streets and buildings whose façades evoked a bygone era. The car had slowed down noticeably, and eventually stopped in front of an austere looking building.

"Here we are," announced the driver, and then he exited the car, walked to the rear and opened the trunk in order to retrieve the suitcases. Oppiano Licario and Anna were now standing on the sidewalk, but before they could get the suitcases, a young man came out of the building.

"Welcome back, señor Licario," he said and grabbed the suitcases while the taxi driver was being paid.

"Thank you," answered Licario, "It is always good to be home."

They followed the young man into the building and down a short corridor. In front of the last door the young man put down the suitcases. By then it had become obvious to Anna that he was a doorman of sort. Licario reached into his pocket and gave the young man a handful of coins.

"Thank you, señor Licario," he said with a smile, "And welcome home again," he added before returning to his post.

Oppiano Licario reached into his pocket again, this time searching for a key, but before he could retrieve it the door opened. In the threshold there was a slender young woman with black hair and green eyes. Without words she smiled and embraced Licario with obvious affection.

"And who is this with you?" she asked after a moment while looking at Anna.

"This is Anna d'Amio, a guest in our country," said Licario making the introductions. And then, looking at Anna, "This is my sister Ynaca Eco." The two women embraced briefly and then they all stepped into the house. Immediately Anna noticed the smell of something cooking, but she could not identify the aroma.

"Your brother helped me after we docked; the authorities said that my passport was not in order, but he managed to straighten everything out," explained Anna.

"I am not the least surprised," said Ynaca Eco. "He always appears at the least expected places, but at the most opportune moment."

"I agree," said Anna. "I don't know what I would have done without his help."

"It was nothing," interrupted Oppiano, perhaps a little embarrassed. Then, changing the subject abruptly while looking at his watch, "How long until lunch?"

"Lunch is ready," answered Ynaca Eco. "We can go into the dining room whenever you like."

It had been a long and trying morning, but now that Anna's momentary difficulties with her passport had been resolved and Oppiano was home after an absence, their appetite made itself known.

The dining room table, although relatively small by Cuban standards, had been immaculately set for two, so Ynaca Eco quickly set another place for Anna. On the white linen tablecloth, accompanying the silverware, a set of china of obvious quality was present. In the center of the table, larger dishes of the same set held the food whose aroma had welcomed Anna a few minutes before.

"This is a special occasion," explained Ynaca Eco. "It is not every day that my brother returns home from Europe. Having no news for the past month and being aware of the political situation did not make matters easy. You can imagine," she said looking at Anna, "how happy and relieved I felt early this morning when I received his phone call from the port, telling me that he was back in Havana."

"There is nothing worse than uncertainty," agreed Anna, thinking about the fate of Giacomo and Francesca and how she would never know what became of them.

Ynaca Eco started serving the food on the individual plates, taking care of Oppiano first, who sat at the head of the table, then Anna and lastly herself.

"This is a simple, yet delicious Cuban meal. I am sure that Oppiano did not have anything like this while he was traveling in Europe," said Ynaca Eco, smiling and looking at her brother.

"You are correct," answered Oppiano, who was already busy consuming and enjoying the home cooked lunch.

"The basic fare of the Cuban diet," explained Ynaca Eco, "is white rice with black beans. This is usually accompanied by meat, chicken or fish and some vegetables. The recipe for the chicken fricassee I have prepared today," she continued, "is also popular here in Cuba, but I have modified it by adding sesame seeds, a handful of cloves and a small amount of clear honey from the province of Pinar del Río. I believe it enhances the overall flavor of the dish without overwhelming the palate of the guests."

The explanations about the meal, although interesting, were not really necessary. By the expressions that showed on Oppiano's face, along the rolling of his eyes every time he took a bite, it was evident that the meal was a success. Anna, at first a little cautious, did not take long to start eating with the same gusto as her hosts.

"Cuban cuisine," added Oppiano, "incorporates the elements inherited from Spain, but it adds all the native elements found on the island. What emerges is a unique combination that surpasses both components to become unique, as it challenges and flatters the palate simultaneously."

As the meal progressed, Anna felt more relaxed in the company of the Licarios, and could not help but think of her brother Guido, and how they had never enjoyed the closeness that these brother and sister had. She found their conversation stimulating, and before long found herself discussing freely her days in Ischia with Giacomo, the unforeseen events that had brought her to Cuba, and how she needed to find a sense of direction for her life.

"Maybe we can be of assistance," said Ynaca Eco while getting ready to serve dessert. It was a pudding covered with caramel and whose ingredients, while cooking over a slow fire had been saturated with cinnamon sticks. The recipe had been in the Licario family for several generations, and it had been passed down, hand written in yellowing notebooks, by the ruling matriarchs.

140

"You already have been most kind," offered Anna while receiving a dessert plate that Ynaca Eco extended to her.

"Excuse me for a moment," interjected Oppiano unexpectedly while standing from his privileged position at the head of the table, and disappeared into the next room. Both Anna and Ynaca Eco were puzzled as to what he was doing, but the reason for his absence soon became apparent.

At first there was the sound the brief static evoked by the needle at the beginning of a record. Then, without warning, the powerful voice of Louis d'Amio completely filled the air. The two women at the table had finished their desserts and were silent; Oppiano sat down again at the head of the table and leaned back in his chair.

As the music progressed, the different moods were reflected on the face of Ynaca Eco; it was evident that she was familiar with the arias, but this appreciation was strictly an aesthetic one. Anna, on the other hand and despite the fact that she had closed her eyes, was unable to hold back the tears that came down her cheeks in a steady stream. During every stage of her life she had found solace and strength in her father's voice, so meeting him on the other side of the world, in the unlikely setting of a Cuban house, brought to a head all the emotions of an entire life. It was as if Louis, reaching from beyond the grave, were telling her that everything would work out, that she was in the company of good people who would help her find her way in this new land.

"It was not my intention to upset you," said Oppiano after the record was over. "When you told me your name, I knew that I had heard it before, but I could not quite pinpoint the circumstance. It was not until a few moments ago that I realized that I'd seen it on one of my favorite records. Rather than asking you if there was a connection, I opted for this less direct, but more insightful way of finding out."

"He was my father," said Anna while drying her tears with her napkin. "He died a tragic and senseless death when I was still very young; at that moment he was at the height of his musical career," she explained. Then, after a brief pause, "Everybody loved him."

"That explains," said Oppiano, "why I could not find any more of his recordings. After hearing Immortal Arias for the first time, I knew without a doubt that your father's name had a secure place in the operatic world."

"That very recording is the only thing I have left of him," said Anna softly.

"We should not look upon this occasion as a sad one," said Oppiano, "but as a source of wonder. Life is a web of indeterminate situations, each coincidence is something that wants to speak at our side. That indeterminate situation, the daughter of Louis d'Damio sitting at our table eating her first Cuban meal in our company, takes on a form. I have to interpret it, because it will not be repeated in my lifetime.

"Oppiano is correct," interjected Ynaca Eco, "We should interpret this coincidence as an omen, as a sign that points the way not just in your future, but in ours as well. The fact that we have been listening to your father for years and that you should end up in our house after coinciding with Oppiano in the bowels of a Danish freighter cannot be ignored. We are bound to help you find your way on this island, where everything is new to you, but familiar to us," she said while getting up from the table. "Now, let's have some coffee and talk about your options for the future."

"Ynaca Eco is right," added Oppiano. "We will help you find a sense of direction; there are many opportunities in this country. As you have probably heard, there is a rapid economic expansion going on. The war has paralyzed sugar production in many areas of Europe and Asia, making it possible for further growth of Cuba's sugar industry. The deterioration of international trade has given this country an extraordinary amount of foreign exchange."

Before Ynaca Eco reappeared in the dining room, the aroma of coffee brewing preceded her. She returned a few minutes later, holding a tray with three steaming demitasse cups and a sugar bowl that matched the china set. She placed the tray on the table and sat down again.

"We have our coffee beans ground and delivered," she explained after filling the cups and placing one in front of Anna and another in front of Oppiano. "That way both the flavor and aroma are retained until the last moment, so none of the qualities are lost. When it is brewed they materialize on the palate of coffee drinkers."

"That reminds me of my stay at Harvard, when I was studying Ninivite art," interjected Oppiano. "The coffee that people drink in the United States, compared to ours, is nothing more than tepid water that lacks flavor and character. It is served in large cups, and to make matters worse, they dilute it further with milk or cream, thereby eliminating any trace of the original coffee flavor. Fortunately for me, there was a small Italian restaurant near the university, so I went there whenever I wanted to drink real coffee."

"You are correct," agreed Anna. "My late husband and I would sit for hours in our small garden overlooking the bay of Naples. We drank coffee and talked about many things; sometimes we just enjoyed the view, but the coffee was always present," she said after sipping her cup. "This is the same as we used to drink in Italy," she commented after a few moments.

"The coffee that is consumed in Mediterranean countries," offered Oppiano, "is something learned from the Arab world. In fact, the word coffee is derived from the Arab *qahwa*, a truncation of *qahhwal albun*, or wine of the bean. Since Islam prohibits the use of alcohol, coffee became its favorite substitute. It was introduced to Europe through the city of Venice, and from there its use spread. Cuba, as a former colony of Spain, adopted the same custom."

"But enough about coffee," said Ynaca Eco, aware of her brother's ability to converse extensively on any subject, no matter how seemingly insignificant or obscure. "Do you have any plans at all?" she asked, looking at Anna.

"No," confessed Anna, "All I wanted to do was get away from the war and have a fresh start. I could not think much beyond that."

"That is understandable," agreed Ynaca Eco. "I think the first order of business should be to find a place of your own. Then you can think about what you want to do here in Cuba."

"Is there a hotel nearby?" asked Anna. "I could stay there for a few days until I move into my own place." She paused for a moment and then added, "My husband left me some money, so I am not completely destitute."

"I suggest," said Oppiano, "that you stop at a bank first and deposit whatever money you have. That will provide a foundation for your new life."

"It is a good idea," agreed Anna. "But once again I find myself in a position where I must ask for your guidance."

"Do not trouble yourself," Oppiano assured her. "Ynaca Eco and I are more than glad to help you in any way we can."

"He is right," added Ynaca Eco. "We can take care of these things as soon as I clear the table and wash the dishes."

"At least let me help you," said Anna. "It is the least I can do."

As the two women started to clean up, Oppiano returned to the living room. Once again he played Immortal Arias, this time as an affirmation of the tacit pact of friendship that had been forged between the Licario and the d'Amio family during that memorable morning.

By the time the record had concluded, the two women emerged from the kitchen and joined Oppiano in the living room. Within minutes the three walked out into the hallway and through the door that led to the street. The young man in charge of the elevator was nowhere to be seen. Oppiano expertly flagged down a taxi and instructed the driver where to go after placing Anna's suitcase in the trunk.

"The hotel is not far," he explained, "but this time of day the temperature is too high to walk."

The taxi made its way out of the narrow confines of Espada Street and into the wider and more traveled sections of Havana. From time to time a whiff of ocean air would find its way into the car, evoking in Anna memories of her own city of Naples. Eventually they reached the Paseo del Prado, one of the busiest avenues of the city. The taxi stopped in front of a building whose sign proudly bore the name Hotel Sevilla. Oppiano paid the driver and retrieved the suitcase.

"This is one of the most centric hotels in the city," he explained. "You will be within walking distance of anything you may need."

As they walked into the lobby, the man behind the reception desk greeted Oppiano with an obvious sign of familiarity.

"The lady needs a room," Oppiano said to the clerk after shaking hands with him. "We don't know yet how long she will be staying," he added.

"No problem, señor Licario," said the man while ringing a desk bell that summoned one of the uniformed young men that handled the luggage. "Room five eleven," he told the young man, who picked up Anna's suitcase and walked across the lobby to the elevator.

The ride to the fifth floor did not take long; the doors of the elevator opened onto a long hallway. They followed the bellboy to Anna's room. The latter opened the door, placed the suitcase out of the way and left the key on the dresser. As he was leaving, Oppiano gave him a tip.

"This side of the building," explained Oppiano as he moved across the room, "has a series of balconies that face the Paseo del Prado. You will have a view of the city below, including the Capitol and farther out, the ocean." He then opened the double doors to the balcony, allowing the afternoon light and the soft breeze to come into the room.

"What a wonderful view," exclaimed Anna as she stepped into the balcony and looked at the street below, and beyond. "I had heard many things about this city, but I had never imagined it to be this beautiful."

"You will have the opportunity to see many other things," said Ynaca Eco, "Havana has something for everybody."

"That is true," agreed Oppiano, "but we must hurry before the banks close," he said while looking at his watch and walking toward the door.

The two women followed him and soon they were in the lobby of the hotel again. Oppiano waved good bye to the clerk and stepped out onto the busy street.

"The bank is not far," he said. "As I mentioned before, everything you need until you find suitable housing is relatively close to the Hotel Sevilla."

Oppiano, as usual, was correct. The bank was located less than a ten-minute walk from the hotel. On the way they passed coffee shops, where Cubans gathered to talk about sports or politics, consume the strong brew in cups that almost resembled thimbles and which were served with accompanying glasses of iced water.

As soon as they stepped into the bank, a middle-aged man wearing a suit despite the warm temperature stood up and walked over to greet Oppiano. It was becoming obvious to Anna that her host was well known in the city.

"Don't be surprised," said Ynaca Eco, "my brother has acquaintances everywhere. There is something about him; some call it an underlying air of confidence born of a secret knowledge that draws people without their realizing it. As time passes you will feel it too."

"I already have," said Anna. "This morning, after we docked and I had the problem with the immigration officer, my head was in a state of turmoil and complete confusion. As soon as your brother appeared, inexplicably, everything became calm and clear. Somehow I felt that he possessed an ancient and secret wisdom

145

that placed him above the situation, a knowledge that allowed him to see clarity in chaos and instinctively seek the correct course of action."

Oppiano and the man in the suit signaled Anna and Ynaca Eco to come closer. After a brief introduction, they sat around the banker's desk. From a drawer he produced the appropriate documents and handed them to Anna, along with a fountain pen from an elaborate marble holder that rested on his desk.

"Rest assured," he said, "that our institution is capable of handling all your financial needs. Not only do we have offices here in the capital, but branches in every province of the republic." Then he added, as if to further reassure her about the solidity of the bank, "Our mutual friend Oppiano Licario also does business with us."

"My late husband left me a sizeable amount of money," said Anna while handing the papers to the banker, "so I would like to establish and account from which I can draw funds from time to time. Fortunately, he had the foresight of exchanging the Italian lira into American dollars, which he felt were a more stable currency and less susceptible to fluctuations brought about by the uncertain political situation in Europe."

"He was correct," agreed the banker while accepting a hefty manila envelope that Anna had retrieved from her purse. Using a letter opener, he neatly cut it open and placed the stack of high denomination bills on the desk. With the efficiency that his profession demanded, he counted the money and wrote down the amount on a piece of paper, which he handed to Anna.

"Yes, the amount is correct," she said after looking at it.

"In that case," said the banker, "I will open the account and give you a receipt." Then, after a moment, he added, "Carrying so much cash is never a good idea, but I understand that there are times when there is no other choice."

"I kept it with me at all times," Anna said while accepting the receipt.

"We are done here," said the banker. "If you need anything at all do not hesitate to contact us," he added while shaking Anna's hand and assuring Oppiano and Ynaca Eco that their friend's money was in good hands.

"It is relief not to be carrying all that money," commented Anna as they left the bank. "I don't know what I would have done if it had been lost or stolen."

"What you must consider now," said Oppiano, "is what you want to do. At least you have a financial base, and as we discussed at lunch, there are many new opportunities here in Cuba," he suggested as they started to walk back to the hotel.

"I agree," added Ynaca Eco, "The sooner you get on with your life the better it will be."

"I will give it some thought," said Anna, "But I need a little time to sort things out."

"Understandable," said Oppiano, "Remember that we are here to help you in any way we can."

"Thank you again," answered Anna, "for everything."

By then they found themselves again in front of the Hotel Sevilla. Above the trees that lined the street the afternoon sun was beginning to decline, following its inexorable parabola that would eventually lead into night, cooler temperatures and the inevitable crowds that emerged after dinner for an evening stroll.

"If you have no plans for dinner," continued Oppiano, "we would like you to join us. We can talk some more then about your plans."

"That would be wonderful," exclaimed Anna, "But you already have done so much for me."

"It will also give us an opportunity to talk about your father," answered Oppiano. "Is eight o'clock acceptable?"

"That is fine," answered Anna, "I will wait for you in the lobby." "Until this evening then," said Oppiano.

Anna stayed in front of the hotel until she saw them disappear into the city as they turned a corner; then she stepped into the hotel and took the elevator to the fifth floor.

In the room only silence welcomed her; the double doors that opened onto the balcony and the Avenida del Prado below were still open. With a pensive look on her face she went out to the balcony and tried to take in the entirety of the view: the colonial architecture; the tree lined avenue; the people below who hurriedly came and went to unknown destinations, but each one with a purpose, a goal; the cupola of the capitol. And beyond it all, ever present, the ocean.

Looking at the view below, Anna realized that everything was new to her. It was as if she had just been born into a different world that welcomed her with an endless myriad of uncertainties, opportunities and an infinite number of yet to come experiences. She also realized her incredible good fortune of having run into Oppiano and Ynaca Eco Licario. At that moment she thought of Mr. Ioso and what he had told her at the Church of San Nicola about his belief in invisible forces that guide the destinies of mortals. This day, in particular, seemed to fully corroborate those words, those beliefs. After all, what were the odds that Oppiano Licario would also be a passenger in the Danish freighter and that he would be the one to help her when she needed it most? Further, how many people on his island would have heard the name of Louis d'Amio and have his Immortal Arias in their musical collection? Were these events but temporal coordinates destined to converge, at this particular moment, in the city of Havana at the beginning of 1941? There was no way to be certain, but everything pointed in that direction; all one could do was to accept the immediate reality and explore the upcoming days as they offered their vague promises.

Contemplating her new and uncertain future, Anna wondered how Giacomo would proceed had he had been here with her. She silently thanked him for having had the foresight to get the passports and to exchange the Italian currency into dollars. At least she had arrived with a sizable amount of money that offered her a great deal of financial security and the chance to start a new life.

She returned from the balcony into the room and placed her suitcase on the bed. She had only been able to bring the most essential items, but she felt the need to start arranging them into neat little categories. The suitcase, in reality, was no different from her life. She had left Italy with the bare essentials, and those needed to be organized as well if she was going to make any headway in this new country.

In a mahogany armoire, by the side of the bed, she placed her dresses, skirts and blouses. Her more intimate garments, including a pair of silk stockings her mother had given her for one of her birthdays, were neatly put away in an adjacent drawer. Finally, the two extra pairs of shoes that she had been able to fit into the suitcase were placed on the bottom shelf.

At this point, the only item left in the suitcase was a large metal box whose top showed a bas-relief depiction of a bucolic scene. Even though she knew what was in the box, and that its contents did not need to be removed and stored elsewhere, she opened it anyway. The largest item was the album Immortal Arias. She took it out slowly, almost with reverence, and looked at the handsome face of Louis d'Amio that appeared on its cover. Just holding the recordings and looking at his picture somehow always made her feel closer to him; it gave her the reassurance that even though he was not physically present he was with her, extending his guidance and protection even beyond the grave. Next to the album, in a velvet-lined case which she also took out of the box, was the gold Breguet pocket watch that the police had returned to Francesca after Louis' death. At this instant, sitting in an anonymous hotel room in Havana, Anna desperately needed to establish a connection that would bring her closer to him. Taking the watch out of the case, she placed it in the palm of her hand and slowly ran her fingers on its engraved surface; her father's hand, no doubt, had done the same thing many times. This inanimate object now went beyond its intended purpose to become a conduit between the living and the dead, thus extending and strengthening a bond that reached across generations and turned temporal limitations into nothing but meaningless and artificial measurements conceived by men.

From a faded envelope, next to the watch case, she retrieved a post card showing the ruins of Pompeii. Every time she looked at it, evoking the passionate episodes with Paolo, she had to smile. Why couldn't love always be like this, spontaneous and unpredictable, like an erupting volcano whose force nothing could contain? Thinking of his uncertain fate, and the fact that she did not even know if he was dead of alive turned her incipient smile into an expression of deep sadness. After a moment she returned the post card to its envelope and turned her attention to a framed medium sized photograph. It showed a young woman in a wedding gown in front of a church. Next to her stood a much older man. On either side of them, a middle-aged woman and a young man.

Looking at the photograph, across the ocean and across almost four years of experiences, Anna hardly recognized herself. She saw a naive teenager who at that time believed that she possessed the answer to any contingency that life might throw at her. How little did that person know that in life there are always unpredictable and powerful forces that change destinies, no matter how strong or clever the person may be. That knowledge, acquired only through experience, was clearly reflected—she realized now—on the faces of Giacomo and Francesca: the wrinkles; the slightly drooping corners of the mouth; the brightness and arrogance of youth gone from their eyes, substituted by one of vigilance and caution trying to anticipate the next move in that unfathomable chess board called life. At this point Anna had to put the picture down to wipe the tears that had suddenly materialized and were streaming down her cheeks. Thinking that life was not fair, she had learned, was an exercise in futility. No matter what, the only option was to pick up the pieces and go on the best one could.

Searching for a momentary source of strength, she reached into the box once again and retrieved the silver plaque with the bas-relief image of San Nicola. As she held it, Anna had to think of that Christmas day she had received it from Mr. Ioso, the mysterious Greek who had appeared out of nowhere at the top of Mount Epomeo. Had their meeting been a mere coincidence or, as he himself had stated, something that had always been meant to be, one more preordained event in the endless and enigmatic confluences of time which ruled life itself? Anna could not be certain, but Mr. Ioso certainly believed in such forces. There was no denying though, that had it not been for him, she would not have left Ischia, come to Cuba and met the Licarios. Her very presence in this hotel room in Havana was but the latest link in an endless chain of events that reached back and joined her to other lives completely unknown to her.

Somewhat more composed and in control of her emotions, she neatly arranged the items in the metal box and placed it in the bottom drawer of the armoire. Looking at her watch, she realized that soon Oppiano Licario and his sister would be back for her. It had been a most trying day, full of unexpected events. Before going out for the evening, she decided to take a bath and change, a most appealing prospect after spending so many days in the confined and uncomfortable quarters of the freighter.

The tiled bathroom in her room offered the luxury of an ample tub, clean towels and perfumed soap. She filled the tub a third of the way, and after undressing she stepped into the water. As she sat quietly and the tensions began to dissolve, Anna realized how emotionally spent she really was. She closed her eyes and thanked the forces of destiny for having brought her to this particular moment, to this particular place, but most of all for those new friends who, because of her father's voice, were not complete strangers. Then, giving way to her emotional exhaustion, she thought of nothing, but just enjoyed the warmth of the water at a sensory level, until the feeling of tightness in her body slowly gave way to the one of relaxation that usually precedes sleep.

She did not know exactly how long she stayed in the bathtub, or if she actually dozed off, but by the time she dried herself off and consulted her watch, she realized that it was almost time to meet Oppiano and Ynaca Eco in the lobby. From the armoire she chose one of the dresses that she had earlier taken from her suitcase, put it on and then proceeded to brush her hair and apply a small amount of lipstick and rouge. The mirror returned the image of a young, beautiful woman getting ready to go out for the evening. Because of Anna's light complexion, black hair and hazel eyes — all these features enhanced by the immaculate dress she was wearing — she could have easily passed for the daughter of an upper-class Cuban family, and not of a woman who had just arrived on the island without any sense of direction or connections in the city. Before leaving the room, she picked up her purse and looked at herself once again in the mirror.

The hallway leading to the elevator was deserted. Rather than using the mechanical device, she opted to take the adjacent stairs that also led to the lobby; within minutes she was at ground level. Herarrival coincided with that of Oppiano Licario and Ynaca Eco, and after the usual greetings, they walked out of the hotel.

Anna noticed that Oppiano had changed into a light suit, white shirt and tie, items more in tune with the Cuban weather, since even January was mild in Cuba. He had also shaven. No doubt he also wanted to erase as quickly as possible the memories of the cramped journey aboard the freighter. Ynaca Eco had also changed her more informal morning attire and now wore a dress that showed delicate prints on a light blue background.

"Let's walk for a while before dinner," said Oppiano, "I am sure you will enjoy some of the sights of Havana," then, followed by the two women, stepped out of the hotel and started to walk down the Paseo del Prado, in the direction of the sea.

The wide boulevard, with its tree covered center promenade and elaborate mosaic work, was now busy with the evening crowd.

On either side—one coming from, the other going toward the sea—busy automobiles and busses left in their wake the sound of their engines and the unmistakable smell of exhaust fumes that were eventually dispersed into the evening air by the soft breeze that came in from the ocean.

They walked at a leisurely pace, taking in the sights, sounds and smells of the city. Eventually they reached the end of the Prado; the Morro Castle, overlooking the bay, came into view.

"This fortification was built by the Spaniards during colonial times," explained Oppiano Licario, "to guard the city against invaders. It was not uncommon for Caribbean cities to be threatened by pirates," he continued, "so these fortifications can be found in other cities as well, such as San Juan in Puerto Rico and Cartagena in Colombia."

"Even the English occupied Havana for a short time in the eighteenth century," added Ynaca Eco, "so the city has a very colorful history."

"I see that I have a lot to learn," answered Anna, truly interested in the historical details the Licarios were giving her.

"We are now walking on the Malecón, the avenue that runs along the sea for about seven kilometers," said Oppiano, "We came through here this morning, on the way from the east side of the port, where the ships dock and also where they have the immigration offices."

This last comment was not necessary; Anna had immediately recognized the familiar landscape. At this time of the day many people either walked on the Malecón or enjoyed the cool breeze that came in from the ocean by sitting on a low wall that separated the sidewalk from the water. There were also vendors offering ice cream, roasted peanuts, Italian ice and other items to eat out of their portable carts. Before long they came upon a massive stone structure whose architecture clearly indicated it was centuries old.

"This structure is called La Chorrera," explained Oppiano once again, "a fortress built by the Spaniards in 1645. If you look farther, away from the ocean and toward the city, you can clearly see that we are standing at the estuary of the Almendares River, which traverses Havana from south to north."

"Yes, I can even tell, by the smell, that there is fresh water nearby," said Anna.

At that precise moment, an explosion was heard in the distance.

"Do not be alarmed," said Ynaca Eco to Anna. "Since 1774, at exactly nine o'clock, a cannon is fired from the fortress of La Cabaña to announce that the gates of the city are officially closed. Of course, it is now just a symbolic act, one that is performed to preserve tradition."

"That is precisely what I was waiting for," interjected Oppiano. "We can now go to dinner, and I know exactly the right place."

Since they could go no farther on the Malecón, they started to walk back. Anna noticed that the crowds had intensified, and that there were many more people sitting on the wall. Some were facing the ocean; others faced the wide sidewalk to look at the passersby. After walking for about twenty minutes, Oppiano stopped abruptly.

"We have to cross the street," he said. Anna looked in the opposite direction and saw a square that undoubtedly also dated to colonial times. "That is the Plaza de Armas," explained Oppiano. "We are now in the section known as Old Havana."

As if to corroborate Licario's explanation, after they made their way across the Plaza de Armas and into the city, leaving behind the wide throughway of the Malecón, the streets immediately became narrower. Their surface, rather than showing the smooth surface of contemporary asphalt, displayed a more irregular one made up of cobblestones. Modern day automobiles, thought Anna, would have difficulty negotiating the tight turns on these streets that had clearly been designed during an era when horse drawn carriages were the norm. Affixed to one of the stone corners of a building, just below the preponderance of balconies, Anna managed to read a small sign that announced the name of the street: Empedrado.

In the middle of the block, where one would least expect it, a narrow door seemed to welcome the visitors. They followed Oppiano into the small, inconspicuous restaurant and sat down at a vacant table. Within the cramped quarters and running the length of the back wall, there was also a bar. Some patrons were busy with their drinks; others were in the process of ordering. The bartender listened attentively to their requests, as if he were a priest hearing a vital confession.

Within minutes a young man approached their table, and after a moment greeted Oppiano with a look of recognition.

"We will have the *ajiaco*," he said, not even bothering to receive the menus that the young man was about to offer them.

"This is a most typical Cuban dish," said Ynaca Eco looking at Anna, "One that embodies part of our Spanish, Indian and African heritage; it is also one of the most popular in our country."

"I am most grateful to both of you; from the first moment you have made me feel at home. It is as if I had known both of you for many years."

"At lunch you mentioned an interest in cooking," said Oppiano, "that is why we came here tonight. This is not, as you can plainly see, the fanciest or most expensive restaurant in Havana, but one that is famous for its authentic cuisine. As you spend more time in Cuba you will realize that our dishes borrow and adapt recipes from other places."

The same young man who had taken the order earlier suddenly reappeared, carrying an ample tray that contained three individual plates. He placed the plates in front of the guests, along with some silverware, napkins, a small basket with bread and a pitcher of water.

"Enjoy the meal," he said before returning to the kitchen.

"I hope you are hungry," said Ynaca Eco to Anna, "I think you will find this a most interesting dish."

"*Ajiaco* is a culinary reflection of Cuban culture," interjected Oppiano, "It is a mixture of available vegetables, sometimes combined with chicken or meat, seasoned with whatever spices are at hand and cooked over a slow fire. The result is a dish with a unique taste, but one that incorporates native as well as foreign elements. As I said, not unlike Cuban culture itself," he concluded and turned his attention to the plate in front of him.

As the meal progressed, the conversation first centered around the food, about Cuban cuisine and its differences from the more traditional European approach to the gastronomical art. Oppiano, of course, offered all sorts of obscure and interesting historical details about how each country had developed its own national dishes.

The Licarios also wanted to know more about the circumstances that had brought Anna to the island, and to the dreadful fate that had befallen the d'Amio family after Louis' untimely death.

154

"I already mentioned that as an opera lover," said Oppiano, "I found it strange that your father had not made more recordings. I even hoped that he would tour the Americas, as Enrico Caruso did at the turn of the century, so I would have the privilege to hear his voice in person. I suspected that it somehow had to do with lack of funds, but I never imagined that he had died so unexpectedly."

"Our family never recovered," explained Anna. "We managed to survive, but things were never the same. I think that my mother always felt, as a singer herself, that fate had cheated her out of a destiny that she imagined with my father by her side."

Inevitably, they came back to the topic of Anna's future and her need to begin her new life in Cuba. It was Oppiano, showing his usual acumen, who offered a most obvious and logical suggestion.

"As we were discussing a short time ago," he said, "most of the immigration to this island has been from Spain, and to a lesser degree, from China. The reception center where we were this morning is called Tricornia;" explained Oppiano, "it was built by the orders of General Wood in 1900, when the United States occupied Cuba after the Spanish American War. It was fashioned after the one built on Ellis Island, in New York, to handle the immigrants coming into that country." Here Oppiano made a pause to have a sip of water. "The influence of these groups on Cuban culture is evident everywhere. The one group of immigrants, however, that has not had a significant impact because of their small numbers, unlike in the United States, is the Italians. One of the ways in which I perceive this vacuum is in the lack of Italian restaurants in the city. Because of this obvious need, and given your passion for cooking, it only seems logical that you would open such an establishment. I am certain that once its doors open and the word gets around, it will do a brisk business."

"But I have no experience running a restaurant," said Anna. "The cooking is no problem; it is just the business part makes me hesitant."

"You have said the key word," retorted Oppiano, "Business. All businesses, whether they are restaurants, clothing stores or sugar-cane mills, have one thing in common: they need to make a profit. In order to accomplish this, they calculate the expenditures and their revenues. If these calculations are done correctly, they end up with a positive cash flow."

"You make it sound so simple," said Anna.

"If my brother says it is possible," interjected Ynaca Eco, "then I believe it. At least give it some thought; nothing has to be decided tonight."

"It is a most appealing possibility," agreed Anna with a tone of excitement, "and must do something with my life."

On the way back to the hotel they continued talking about the viability of the project, beginning with its possible location, permits required in order to open a business, interior decor, and the necessary staff to run such a place. Although to Anna it seemed like a daunting enterprise, one whose attainment would have many requirements, Oppiano seemed to have a logical solution for each of the possible hurdles. With his usual lucidity, he explained the process in a logical manner, almost making it sound easy.

"Just sleep on it," he said as they found themselves in front of Anna's hotel, "We can discuss it again, if you wish, in a few days."

"I will certainly consider it," said Anna. "And again, I want to thank both of you for your kindness. I don't know what I would have done if you had not helped me at the port."

"Everything was meant to be," answered Oppiano. "Good night."

Anna saw them turn the same corner and disappear into the city. She realized, after coming into the lobby of the hotel, that it was past midnight. Suddenly she felt tired, as if the entire weight of the day had been suddenly placed on her shoulders.

As she had done earlier that evening, she took the stairs to her room. Just as before, the hallway leading to her door was deserted. Once inside, she placed her purse on the dresser and went out on the balcony. The sounds and the lights of the city below offered a welcoming, yet mysterious concert that Anna imagined as a sort of greeting. At that moment, she realized that her future, a future that had yet to unfold, was now irrevocably linked to this new land to which she had no ties, where she had no family or friends. But she also realized her good fortune at having met the Licarios, who seemed eager to help her find her way. She thought of her father and how his voice had unexpectedly reached across distance and time during lunch, auguring a bright future.

By the time she got into bed, all the events of the day, all the wondrous opportunities that lay ahead, and all the uncertainties quickly dissolved into the soft mist of sleep.

VI

Oppiano Licario's words proved to be prophetic. Just a few months after that first dinner in the old section of Havana, Anna's restaurant opened its doors. It was called, appropriately enough, Pompeya—Spanish for Pompeii.

He had also been correct in his assessment about the need for such a place in Havana, but Anna had to admit that without his guidance—especially making her way through the labyrinth of red tape—it would have been almost an insurmountable task had she undertaken it alone.

Given her lack of knowledge about the city, that first week in Cuba she called upon the Licarios to let them know that she had decided to follow their suggestion about opening an Italian restaurant. They were both pleased and offered to help her in any way they could.

The first order of business had been to find a suitable locale. Being a new business that had yet to establish a name for itself, it was imperative that it be located in a busy thoroughfare in order to attract customers and ensure its success. For an entire month they searched the city, but without much luck. The old section of Havana was not even considered, since it was sort of out of the way and not the best location for a new venture.

It was just by coincidence that one afternoon, on her way back to the hotel after a stroll on the Prado, that Anna spotted a sign on the window of a restaurant—The Flower of Galicia—that she had passed many times before. In fact, she had eaten there several times since her arrival in Havana; it served the usual fare of Cuban dishes along with the more popular Spanish recipes. The sign succinctly stated that the business would be closing within a month. She found this to be rather surprising; the restaurant was on the Prado—an ideal location—and seemed to have a steady clientele. Without hesitation she went inside and asked one of the waiters if the owner was in the premises. The young man simply pointed to a narrow hallway beyond the dining area. Making her way through the maze of tables, Anna reached a small office at the end of the hall. An elderly man was sitting behind a desk going over some papers that Anna interpreted as recent orders and invoices for the business. The expression on his face denoted an even-tempered, affable individual who had reached a stage in his life when everything had finally come into perspective.

"May I help you?" he asked, somewhat startled to see her standing in the threshold.

"Forgive the intrusion," she said, "My name is Anna d'Amio; I came to inquire as to the reason why the restaurant is closing. Business appears to be good."

"That is part of the problem," answered the man with a soft smile on his face.

"I do not understand," said Anna.

"My name is Antonio Gamboa. Please, sit down," he said pointing to a chair in a corner of the small office and putting away the papers he had been studying a few moments before. "You do not understand because you are young."

"What does age have to do with anything?" asked Anna with a puzzled look on her face.

"Let me explain," he said. "Many years ago, at the turn of the century, I came to Cuba from Spain. I had only the clothes on my back, but I had big dreams and the energy to make them come to fruition. I was only twenty years old. Through lots of hard work, frugal living and a measure of good luck I managed to open this business and make a very good living. I now find myself in a fortunate position that I no longer need to work, so I intend to sell the restaurant, along with the upstairs apartment, and return to Spain."

"Why not stay here?" asked Anna.

"I have asked myself that question," he answered. "Yes, I do own other properties in this country, so I could retire here if I wanted to, but as the years accumulate I find myself thinking more and more about that region of Spain I left so long ago."

"It must be very beautiful, if you miss it so much," said Anna.

"When I left Galicia as a young man I only looked toward the future, and my thoughts were about making money; back then I believed I had all the time in the world. Now that most of my years are behind me, and despite all the wealth I have accumulated, my thoughts are of a simple life, one that is free from the pressures of the business world. I yearn to wake up and see the soft mist that comes in from the Atlantic Ocean and wraps itself around the emerald green mountains, and the warm sunlight that dissipates the clouds by midmorning. I long to hear the distant voices of the fishermen, traveling over the water as they come in for the day. As I said, I plan to return to what I left so many years ago. I realize that to many this may not sound like such a big dream, but that is what I wish to do, spend my last years surrounded by all I had to give up as a young man because of economic hardships. Believe me, money is not everything; it has taken me a lifetime to learn that."

"I understand," said Anna, "The place where one grows up, no matter where it is, will always have a special significance; I have not been in this country very long myself, and everything is new and strange." By then Anna's command of Spanish had improved dramatically, but her undeniable accent betrayed the fact that she was not a native Cuban, so her explanation to Antonio Gamboa was completely unnecessary.

"But you did not come to talk about the plans of an old man," said señor Gamboa suddenly, "You expressed an interest in the restaurant. Are there any questions I can answer?"

"I have a million questions," said Anna. "First of all, of course, how much you are asking for your business. I would also like to know how soon you would like to sell it."

"I do not believe we have the time to answer all your questions now. Could you possibly come back tonight?" asked señor Gamboa. "Besides, I would like to fill you in on the operation of the business, and that will take some time. It would be impossible for anyone to make a decision just based on the price and how soon I want to sell."

"Is eight o'clock acceptable?" asked Anna.

"That is fine," he answered. "And by the way, you should plan to have dinner here tonight, on the house."

"That is most kind," she said, "But I would like to bring some Cuban friends who have been helping me with this endeavor."

"I will be expecting you," said señor Gamboa, "I am sure we will be able to address all your concerns, and others that you have not considered."

Anna was in a buoyant mood as she left the restaurant. As soon as she arrived at her hotel, she placed a telephone call to the Licarios. Surprisingly enough, given their erratic schedule, the phone was picked up after the first ring and she heard Oppiano's familiar voice. She hurriedly explained to him about the events of the afternoon, and asked if he and Ynaca Eco could join her for dinner that evening, since she considered their opinion indispensable and wanted them to participate in every aspect of the transaction.

"We can stop by your hotel," he said, then asked the name of the restaurant. What surprised Anna the most, after telling Oppiano that she was referring to The Flower of Galicia, was finding out that Oppiano had known Antonio Gamboa for years, and that from time to time he would dine at his restaurant. This fact made Anna feel even more confident about the possible venture she was about to undertake.

At seven thirty, after consulting her watch for the tenth time, she left her room and walked down to the lobby. Her arrival coincided with that of the Licarios, who were just coming in. At that particular hour the heat of the afternoon had not quite dissipated yet, so the streets were not as crowded as they usually became later on in the evening, when Cubans came out in droves to walk on the Prado with their friends, or take a leisurely stroll along the Malecón in order to enjoy the cool ocean breeze.

"Señor Gamboa said that he wanted to return to Spain," commented Anna as they walked to the restaurant, "That is the reason why he is selling his business."

"This does not surprise me at all," said Oppiano. "Many Spanish immigrants arrived in Cuba with nothing to their name and they have managed to amass huge fortunes. In the back of their minds, however, there was always the idea of returning home, of recapturing that ineffable and elusive time in their lives when they were young. Antonio Gamboa's decision, I am certain, has been triggered by the recent events in Spain; they have just gone through a civil war, and he wants to make sure that he does not run out of time, as was the case with so many of his countrymen."

"What about his family here?" asked Anna.

"He never did marry," answer Oppiano, "But devoted all his time and energies to his business ventures. What little family he has left is in the village of Baiona. He realizes that he is in a race against time, one he cannot possibly win, but one in which he must compete."

"He feels that time is running out for him," offered Ynaca Eco, "that is why the urgency of his actions. He must return to Baiona, the coastal town he left so long ago, even if it is as an old man."

"There is a poem called *An Obscure Meadow Lures Me*, written by José Lezama Lima, one of our young poets," added Oppiano with a somber voice, "that I believe sums up his situation:

An obscure meadow lures me,
her fast, closefitting lawns
revolve in me, sleep in my balcony.
They rule her beaches, her indefinite
alabaster dome recreates itself.

On the waters of a mirror,
the voice cut short crossing a hundred paths,
my memory prepares surprise:
fellow dew in the sky, dew, sudden flash.

Without hearing I'm called:
I slowly enter the meadow,
proudly consumed in the labyrinth.

Illustrious remains:
a hundred heads, bugles, a thousand shows
baring their sky, their silent sunflower.

Strange the surprise in that sky
where unwilling footfalls turn
and voices swell in its pregnant center.

An obscure meadow goes by.

Between the two, wind or thin paper,
the wind, the wounded wind of this death,
this magic death, one and dismissed.

A bird, another bird, no longer trembles.

"Antonio Gamboa intends to return to Spain and reclaim the totality of what he left behind as a young man," he concluded.

"Yes," said Anna, "I understand now why everything that used to be so important has lost its appeal; the economic pressures of his youth have been removed, so he can return to the land he would have never left had circumstances been different."

This last comment by Anna found them at the door of The Flower of Galicia. At that hour, being dinnertime, the restaurant was a lot more crowded than during Anna's first visit in the afternoon. Every table in the dining area seemed to be occupied; every waiter hurried through the maze, balancing trays on their frantic back and forth trips to the kitchen in order to fulfill the orders of the awaiting patrons. At that moment, thought Anna, this was a less than ideal time and place to discuss business, but she kept that impression to herself.

As soon as they came into the restaurant, one of the waiters disappeared through the small hallway that led to Antonio Gamboa's office. He had obviously been instructed to alert the owner whenever his guests arrived. Within minutes he appeared in the dining area and walked directly to where Anna and the Licarios were standing. At first, after realizing that Oppiano and Ynaca Eco were the friends that Anna had mentioned earlier, his face first showed surprise and then pleasure. He greeted Anna, and then the Licarios with an effusiveness that denoted a deeply rooted friendship.

"A coincidence?" he asked, addressing Oppiano.

"A confluence," he answered, "We simply follow the coordinates of our individual destinies."

After the greetings, Antonio Gamboa led the group to a smaller, private dining area at the back of the restaurant. The large table was covered with an immaculate white linen tablecloth and the silverware—Anna noticed that it was not the utilitarian type used at the restaurant, but made of silver—had been neatly arranged. She also noticed that there were wine glasses next to the plates. A young waiter, wearing black pants and a white shirt, waited silently in a corner.

Antonio Gamboa sat at the head of the table, Oppiano sat at the other end, and Anna and Ynaca Eco sat in the remaining chairs, across from each other. After a few moments, he signaled the waiter and ordered him to bring the meal.

162

While they waited, he inquired as to how Anna had met the Licarios, since it was, indeed, a most strange coincidence. It was Anna herself who relayed, with an abundance of details, the events that had taken place during her arrival at Tricornia several months before, and how Oppiano had come to her aid in that desperate moment of need, when she thought every door was closed.

"I am not surprised," commented Antonio Gamboa with a smile, perhaps suggesting that Licario had also helped him in the past.

The exchange was interrupted by the silent waiter carrying a tray with the food, which he placed on the center of the table. It was a large clay pot with *arroz con pollo* — rice and chicken — embellished with peas, pimentos, saffron and other condiments. By then Anna knew that this was not an everyday dish, but one that was usually prepared during family reunions and special occasions. The waiter had also placed on the table a bottle of wine. It was Ynaca Eco who expertly proceeded to pour the wine into the glasses that had been set by the dinner plates.

Antonio Gamboa made a toast to the future and then served the food himself, making sure that there was more than enough on each plate, while assuring his guests that there was plenty more in the kitchen, should they want a second serving.

As expected, there was the initial small talk — a logical preamble to the more substantial topic that had brought them together — in which one asked about family, work, and other sundry activities. Antonio Gamboa talked enthusiastically about the beauty of that region of Spain he had left as a young man, and how much he was looking forward to seeing it again. Anna, in turn, offered some details about the events that had brought her to Cuba, and how she hoped to put her life together in this new country. She made no mention of the restaurant and her intention of buying it from señor Gamboa. There was no point in rushing things; the meal would be enjoyed without any mention of business. That would come later.

The silent waiter reappeared in the small dining room from time to time, unobtrusively filling glasses of water or efficiently removing empty plates and dishes from the table. By then the bottle of wine was empty. After everyone had finished, Antonio Gamboa instructed him to bring desert. The waiter reappeared a few moments later, carrying a tray with a *flan*—a typical Spanish desert made with eggs, milk and sugar covered with a caramel coating—and some small plates and spoons. He once again served the guests, starting with Anna and Ynaca Eco, Oppiano and finally himself.

"The key to this dessert," he said, "is to allow the caramel to burn slightly, so the bitter taste can then contrast with the sweetness of the sugar and eggs on the palate." By the expression on everyone's face as they tasted the dessert, it was evident that the cook had prepared it to perfection. To conclude the meal, the waiter appeared with another tray, containing demitasse cups of strong black coffee. Sugar would be added according to the individual taste of each of the guests.

It was at this point that Antonio Gamboa himself steered the conversation towards the topic of business, but rather than talking about the asking price for the restaurant, he began praising the virtues and skills of this staff, starting with the chef and ending with the waiters. At first Anna did not understand what this had to do with the purchase of the business, but it became apparent soon enough that one of the preconditions for the sale would be the assurance that the men would not lose their jobs. This was an aspect of the transaction that Anna had not considered, but it really made no sense to let the staff go. They knew the place and she would need them anyway.

After telling señor Gamboa that she agreed with him, Anna inquired about the other expenses and the profits that remained after everything had been paid. At this point Antonio Gamboa gave her exact figures and suggested that she should consult, at her convenience, the books where everything was recorded.

"I could come back tomorrow," Anna said, "and we can go over the figures with more time."

"That sounds like a good idea," he agreed, "Join me for lunch and we can discuss the smaller details. I am sure you have a million questions."

Eventually they got around to the price of the business. Antonio Gamboa reiterated that his intention was to return to Spain as soon as possible, so he was not looking to make a huge profit. After he mentioned the amount, Anna looked at Oppiano, since she had no idea about what was reasonable and what was not. He nodded in agreement and Anna said that the price was acceptable. At this point Antonio Gamboa called the waiter and gave him some instructions. The latter reappeared a few minutes later with a bottle of champagne in an ice bucket and some glasses on a tray.

"This calls for a celebration," he said while he expertly uncorked the bottle.

"I agree," answered Oppiano Licario. "Tonight marks a new beginning for both of you." After filling the glasses, they raised them and brought them together with a crystalline sound.

"May each of you," said Ynaca Eco addressing Anna and Antonio Gamboa, "no matter where you are, find that which you are looking for."

It did not take long for the bottle to be consumed. Now that business matters were behind, the mood had become more relaxed. During the following weeks the small details could be worked out.

At the end of the evening, Anna expressed how excited she was to return the following day to go over the details concerning the restaurant. She also wanted to meet the staff and assure them that just because the business was changing hands they had no need to concern themselves about the security of their jobs. They agreed that late afternoon would be best, when the restaurant was getting ready for the evening crowd.

On the way back to the hotel, Anna mentioned to the Licarios that the following morning she intended to visit the bank and then a lawyer, just to make sure that the transaction would take place smoothly. She was not surprised when Oppiano suggested a law firm that was near the bank and that was equipped to handle all the necessary paper work involved in the purchase of the restaurant.

"I will keep both of you informed as to the progress of this deal," Anna said to Oppiano and Ynaca Eco when they arrived at the door of the Seville. "It is the least I can do."

"Feel free to call on us if you need anything," said Oppiano. "Good night."

Once again she watched them disappear into the city, in the direction of Espada 615. Anna knew that the excitement would keep her up that night. Before this evening the idea of opening a restaurant had been a vague possibility, a dream without substance. Suddenly everything had changed. The place had been found; she had spoken with the owner and a tentative agreement had been reached.

By the time she stepped into her room and got into bed, the awesome myriad of possibilities that opened before her also became a reality. In the darkness she began to consider a new name; she imagined the menu. Would there be a specialty of the house? And what about the decor? What would be the cost of a complete renovation? Was it even necessary? Considering all these alternatives, and with the sounds of the city coming in through the open balcony, she drifted into sleep.

The sounds of the city, coming in through the open balcony, slowly made their way into Anna's consciousness, opening a breach to the memories of the events of the previous day. She quickly got out of bed, took a shower, got dressed and walked down to the hotel cafeteria. Being in a hurry that morning, she only had some black coffee and hot buttered toast. The anticipation of the new venture was foremost on her mind. After finishing her breakfast, she stepped out onto the street and walked hurriedly towards the bank.

The same middle-aged gentleman who had helped her with her funds after her arrival in Havana greeted her as he saw her coming in. Once they were in his office, she explained to him the purpose of her visit.

With the efficiency that his career demanded, he took out his fountain pen and began to write down the details that Anna was providing him on a sheet of paper crowned with the bank's letterhead. At the top, in big numbers, he wrote down the price of the property and below it, in smaller letters, its location. The rest of the page was quickly filled with the projected income, expenditures for salaries and expenses, taxes, business license and other sundry items. After finishing, he leaned back on his chair and looked up at the ceiling, as if he were processing all the information contained on the piece of paper.

"I do not foresee any problems," he finally said. "This business is a solid enterprise and you have a substantial amount of money available. Of course, I must present this to the bank officers, but it is just a formality. You can tell señor Gamboa that the money will be available in a few days."

It had been that simple. From the bank she walked directly to the law firm that Oppiano Licario had suggested the night before. Much to her surprise, when Anna told the secretary her name, she was told that one of the lawyers had been expecting her and was immediately led into his office. A tall, balding man wearing thick glasses and a three-piece suit — Anna thought it was much too warm for the climate in Havana — was sitting behind a desk covered with documents and letters. She also noticed that resting on a file cabinet there was a large oscillating fan that created an artificial oasis in the midst of the warm enclosure.

"Señor Licario called and said that you would be coming by," he said, "How may I help you?"

Anna quickly explained the particulars about the purchase of the restaurant, its location and her earlier visit to the bank. From time to time, in order to clarify a point or to obtain further information, the lawyer would interject a specific question or ask Anna to elaborate on a certain point.

"Everything seems to be in order," he said eventually. "All we need is to set up a date when you and señor Gamboa come in and sign the appropriate documents. Once that is accomplished and the transfer of funds is completed, the restaurant will be in your possession."

"I have to meet with señor Gamboa later on today," said Anna. "I will inform him that everything is ready and then we can set up the date."

"Excellent," said the lawyer, "In the meantime I will start preparing the documents. It is really a straight forward transaction," he added, "nothing out of the ordinary."

"Very well then," said Anna "I will give you a call as soon as we agree on a date."

"By the way," said the lawyer as Anna was preparing to leave his office, "I am familiar with The Flower of Galicia; my family and I dine there from time to time. I believe it to be a sound enterprise."

"Thank you, I believe so too," said Anna before leaving the office.

The transition from the coolness and soft light of the lawyer's office into the heat of the midday sun was so abrupt that Anna had to stop for a moment to allow her eyes to adapt to the sudden brightness. Her watch told her that it was almost lunchtime, and that señor Gamboa would be waiting for her at the restaurant. She was eager to let him know that everything was in order at the bank, and that the lawyer was in the process of preparing the deed to transfer the ownership of the business.

When she reached the Prado, in order to protect herself from the relentless Cuban sun, she walked under the trees that lined the wide avenue that led to the sea. At that hour people were getting off work to take the two-hour break for lunch. Some returned home; others, constrained by time or distance, opted for the restaurants that abounded throughout the city. Many of these workers, she was sure, would make up the bulk of the business at The Flower of Galicia.

She saw Antonio Gamboa through the plate-glass window even before entering the restaurant. He was busy directing the waiters, showing customers to vacant tables and occasionally receiving money at the cash register. Wearing just black pants and a short-sleeved white shirt, he could have easily passed for one of the workers at the restaurant.

When he saw Anna he put down the pitcher of water he was holding and signaled her to follow him to the same secluded dining area they had used the night before. One of the smaller tables was set for two. Before sitting down he signaled one of the waiters, who immediately disappeared in the direction of the kitchen. Within minutes he was back, holding a tray with two plates.

"Welcome back," he said, "Our lunch today is the special of the day; I hope you don't mind."

"Not at all," answered Anna, "this will give me a better idea what the customers want."

"I have been thinking a lot about the conversation we had during dinner last night," said Antonio Gamboa as he took his first bite.

"It has been on my mind as well," answered Anna, "It is a new beginning for each of us, just as Oppiano said."

"An auspicious beginning, I hope," he added.

"No doubt about it," Anna assured him. "I spoke with the bank officer this morning and everything is ready. I also managed to see a lawyer and he is in the process of preparing the documents. All he needs now is a date when we go to his office and make everything official."

168

"That is excellent," said Antonio Gamboa with an obvious look of satisfaction on his face. Throughout the meal he told Anna about the specific details of operating the restaurant, such as suppliers, delivery dates and a myriad of other facts that combined to make the business a successful one. At the conclusion of the meal, Anna felt that she was indeed lucky to be taking over such a solid business. Throughout the years Antonio Gamboa had done all the work and put together all the loose ends. Now it was all up to her.

"I want you to meet the staff," he said. "They already know that there is a prospective buyer for the restaurant, and I think that meeting you will make the transition easier for everyone."

"I agree," said Anna, "Since we are going to be working together every day, the sooner we get acquainted the better."

"Let's meet the chef," he said and led Anna from the dining area to the back of the establishment, where the kitchen was located. As they walked in, a tall man in his mid thirties was in the process of mincing some onions while simultaneously telling one of his assistants about the dishes for that evening's menu. As he saw Antonio Gamboa and Anna he stopped what he was doing and put the knife down on the counter.

"Sergio, I want you to meet Anna d'Amio," said Antonio Gamboa, "She will be the new owner of the restaurant very soon."

"Sergio Osorio, at your service," he said. Then, after a pause, "Señor Gamboa tells me that you come from Italy."

"Yes," answered Anna, "from the city of Naples, in the south."

"I have always wanted to visit your country," added Sergio, "Not only because of its culture but because I hear that Italians take cooking very seriously."

"You are quite right," answered Anna with a smile, at that moment thinking of her mother and the many times she had dined at the Vesuvius with Giacomo. "But I am afraid that at this particular time Italians are concerned with other matters."

"The war will end," interjected Antonio Gamboa, "just as it ended in Spain two years ago. Then life will resume its normal course."

"Let's hope so," said Anna, but without much conviction in her voice. Even if the war were to end that very day, she knew, the damage had already been done. No one could put back the shattered lives or bring back the dead; it was as simple as that. "My mother loved to cook," said Anna addressing Sergio again. "She gave me a book of her favorite recipes. Perhaps you would like to look at it some time."

"Yes, I would love that," he said with a smile, "Señor Gamboa can tell you that cooking is my passion, although I find myself limited sometimes."

"We have to offer what people want," said Antonio Gamboa. "That is one of the keys of having a successful business."

"We will talk again soon Sergio," said Anna, "Now I have to meet the rest of the staff."

"It was a pleasure," he said as he picked up the knife again and returned to his half minced onions.

The rest of the afternoon was spent meeting the other employees and going over some of the ledgers that Antonio Gamboa kept in his office. In one of the books he had written down all the expenses associated with the restaurant, and in a second one the names, addresses and telephone numbers of everyone who had any type of connection to the restaurant, from the people who supplied the food and drink to those who did the laundry. Below each name, he also had had the foresight to write down alternate suppliers, just to make sure that his daily routine would not be disrupted by circumstances beyond his control. No wonder his restaurant was so successful.

"When we first met you mentioned an upstairs apartment," said Anna, "Is it vacant or occupied at the moment?"

"The last tenants moved out two months ago. I had intended to rent it again, but I decided to wait. No sense in having new tenants if I am going back to Spain. Besides, it is just a small apartment that is part of the restaurant."

"If you don't mind, I would like to see it," asked Anna, "I think it is about time I moved out of the hotel."

"Of course," answered Antonio Gamboa as he opened the top drawer of his desk and reached for a ring of keys. "In your case it would be ideal, if you don't mind the small size. Living upstairs would allow you to keep track of everything that goes on in the restaurant. Come with me," he said and led Anna out of the building and onto the sidewalk.

Next to the entrance of the restaurant, almost unnoticeable, there was a narrow wooden door devoid of numbers. Antonio Gamboa placed a key in the lock and opened it. A square landing led to a steep stairway; in order to reassure the visitors or the tenants, a wooden banister had been attached to the wall.

Anna followed him to a second landing on top of the stairs, then he stopped in front of the apartment door and opened it with another key from his ring. They found themselves in a small and vacant living room with bare white walls; two windows, now bare of curtains, in the front of the building faced the Prado.

"It is not much," he said pointing to the back of the apartment. "There is a small bedroom, a kitchen and a bathroom."

Anna walked around the different rooms without making any comments, inspecting everything thoroughly and considering the different possibilities of future living arrangements.

"This is perfect," she finally said. "All I need is a place to sleep, and I could take my meals downstairs."

"Yes, I suppose you could," agreed Antonio Gamboa. "In that case, I am glad I did not take any new tenants."

"Just one more question," said Anna, "When can I move in?"

"Feel free to bring your things any time you want to," he answered her, "I see no reason why you should pay a hotel bill if this apartment is available. Besides, as soon as we sign the papers it will be yours anyway," he added while taking the keys out of the metal ring and handing them to Anna.

"Thank you señor Gamboa," Anna said as they approached the stairs, "I will start looking for some furniture right away."

"I will call the lawyer today," he said once they were at street level again. "I am anxious to tie all the loose ends here in Cuba."

"He is expecting your call," Anna reassured him, echoing what she had said earlier. "And tell Sergio that it was a pleasure to meet him and that I look forward to discussing some new recipes with him."

"He will be glad to hear that," said Antonio Gamboa. "We will talk again soon."

"Good-bye, and thank you again," said Anna before starting back to the hotel.

After that particular meeting things moved at a rather brisk pace. Antonio Gamboa contacted the lawyer, and before long the date to finalize the transaction arrived. Anna, in the meantime, purchased some furniture and moved out of the Seville Hotel and into the apartment above The Flower of Galicia. She took advantage of the proximity to become more acquainted with the day to day operation of the restaurant and the flow of customers. Antonio Gamboa was thrilled that she had taken such genuine interest in the inner workings of the business.

Most of her time, however, was spent in the kitchen. Anna found that she and Sergio Osorio shared the same love of cooking, that they believed that every dish was special and that it deserved the time and care of whoever was preparing it. Often in the afternoons, between the lunch and dinner crowds, when traffic was slower, they would explore the recipes that Francesca had so laboriously recorded on the notebook she had given Anna on the day of her wedding to Giacomo. His almost unlimited enthusiasm upon discovering those recipes reminded Anna of a wide-eyed child on Christmas morning when confronted with an assortment of brand-new toys.

"We should put this on the menu," he would say pointing to a specific page. "And this one too," he would add as soon as Anna translated the ingredients and procedures for him. She would simply place a small check mark at the top of the page, to remind her later of Sergio's choices. It was obviously impossible to incorporate every recipe into the menu, but this would facilitate the process of narrowing it down when the time came.

A week later Anna found herself back at the lawyer's office in the company of Antonio Gamboa. Nothing had changed; the desk was still covered with papers and the oscillating fan continued its losing battle against the Cuban heat. After the usual courtesies, the lawyer reached into a file cabinet and produced a folder tied with a thin red ribbon.

"Everything is in order," he said, "The documents are ready to be signed. The originals will be filed with the city and each of you will have notarized copies. Do you have any questions?"

Anna and Antonio Gamboa shook their heads negatively. It was all a very routine transaction. Once the documents were signed, Anna would receive the deed to the restaurant and Antonio Gamboa a certified check from the bank.

Anna was the first to sign the documents. With this gesture of youthful exuberance, she was commencing a new chapter of her life in a new country. Antonio Gamboa was slower in accepting the fountain pen that Anna offered him; he took a moment to adjust his glasses and looked at the papers one more time. Once his signature was placed on the appropriate lines, there would be no

turning back; his life in Cuba would end and his return to Spain —
an event he had longed for his entire adult life — would be
underway. His signature would complete an inexorable cycle from
which there was no retreat. At that moment, Anna recalled the
poem, *An Obscure Meadow Lures Me*, that Oppiano Licario had
recited one day as they walked toward The Flower of Galicia. For
him this was the first step into that dark meadow mentioned in the
poem. Finally, with a decisive gesture, he placed his signature on
the documents. He then turned to Anna, shook her hand and
offered his congratulations.

"I know the business is in good hands," he said, "but I will miss
it."

"Do not worry señor Gamboa," offered Anna, "I will take care
of your restaurant; there will be no changes in the staff, as we
agreed."

The lawyer, as efficient as ever, filed the signed documents and
handed Anna and Antonio Gamboa their copies. "I think our
business here is concluded," he said while standing up, signaling
that he probably had an appointment with another client. "Good
luck to both of you."

Once outside, Anna and Antonio Gamboa said good-bye one
more time. She stood on the sidewalk and watched him walk away
in the opposite direction of The Flower of Galicia, until he disappeared into the city. He was going to meet his destiny, and Anna
knew they would never see each other again.

Now that she was the rightful owner of the restaurant, she could
carry out some of the plans she had conceived since the initial
meeting, when she first inquired about the sale of the business. She
had looked around the city and corroborated that Oppiano Licario
was correct in his assessment: there were no Italian restaurants in
Havana. She intended to correct that, while filling a niche that was
needed in the city. The first thing she wanted to do was to remodel
the dining area, upgrade the kitchen and change the name. So as
not to confuse the regular customers and to attract new ones, she
also planned to take out a series of advertisements in the *Diario de
la Marina*, the most prestigious newspaper in Havana. Aware that
many of the patrons would still demand the usual Cuban and
Spanish dishes, she intended to keep those on the menu as well.

The new name of the restaurant would be—she had decided
from the beginning, Pompeya—Spanish for Pompeii. But more

significant was the fact that the mural she commissioned to be painted on the back wall, depicting the ruins of the ancient city, was to be a large replica of the post card she kept in the metal box. The amplified reproduction attested to the fact that she had not forgotten the passion she and Paolo had shared—not unlike an erupting volcano whose burning lava would sweep away everything in its path—that although presently dormant, could erupt again when one least expected it.

The changes to The Flower of Galicia were completed within one month after Anna assumed ownership. Besides the change of name and the refurbishing of the dining room and kitchen, she also replaced the tables and chairs. New menus, proudly bearing the new name and the additional dishes, were soon to be printed. To make the public aware of opening night, just as she had intended, she took out a large ad in the newspaper.

While in preparation for this special night, she had met repeatedly with Sergio and discussed the Italian dishes that should be offered on a regular basis. They both agreed that it would be virtually impossible to offer every dish; further, they also agreed that they should concentrate on those dishes that came from southern Italy. Being well versed on the subject, Anna offered Sergio an impromptu lesson about the origin of some of those dishes.

"Although Italian cuisine is famous worldwide," she said with obvious pride, "what people know most is southern Italian cooking. This region is made up of Lazio, Abruzzo, Molizse, Campania, Basilicata, Calabria, Sicily and Sardinia." At this point Anna felt that she was back in grade school, reciting from memory the different southern regions of the country. "This is home to the *cucina povera*, or peasant cooking. Most of the ingredients are sunriped vegetables and fruits, wheat for pasta and local cheeses. Very basic, but also very delicious."

"I am sure we can find all the ingredients here," said Sergio. "Everything must be as authentic as possible."

"I agree," said Anna, "That is what will make this restaurant unique."

It did not take them long to decide which dishes should be permanent on the menu, and which should be rotated on a regular basis so as not to offer the public the same recipes. The more popular Cuban and Spanish dishes, as they had agreed before, should always be available. As this conversation progressed, Anna wrote everything on a notebook. The next morning she delivered the information herself to the shop where the menus were to be printed. On the front and in full color, the same picture of the ruins of Pompeii was prominently displayed.

Eventually that crucial night arrived. Both Oppiano and Ynaca Eco Licario were well aware of the date. Since they had been instrumental in Anna's decision to undertake this venture, they had followed closely the progress leading to that special night and made sure to arrive early in the evening. Anna greeted them effusively, led them to one of the more advantageous tables, and gave them the newly printed menus.

In anticipation of the event, Anna had hardly slept the night before, wondering if all her efforts would come to fruition. By early evening, a larger than usual crowd began to arrive at the restaurant. They were mostly middleclass Cubans eager to sample a new and exotic cuisine that offered their palates a temporary respite from the usual Cuban, Spanish or Chinese restaurants so prevalent in the city. By then it was apparent that the radio and newspaper ads she had taken out had indeed paid off.

Besides the huge mural of the ruins of Pompeii and the new furniture, the renovation of the dining area also included the clever and discreet incorporation of speakers that could deliver music to the diners. At exactly eight o'clock—by then the restaurant was already full and a line of waiting customers had formed outside — Anna placed her copy of Immortal Arias on the turntable that an astute craftsman had concealed inside a carved wooden cabinet. It was only befitting that this should be the first record played at the opening of the new venture. Not only would she be honoring her father's memory, but also be asking symbolically for his blessing. A few moments later, the incomparable voice of Louis d'Amio filled the dining area. She saw a look of approval on Oppiano Licario's face; he also understood, better than anyone sitting there that evening, the great significance that the music carried with it. Then everything became a blur through tears of joy, longing and pain as Anna suddenly realized how far she had come,
but also how much she had left behind—not just materially but emotionally — in order to reach her present position.

That brief interlude of introspection was quickly replaced by the ever-increasing number of patrons that arrived at the Pompeii.

She greeted them personally, and assured them that they would be seated as soon as a table became available. The waiters, all dressed in black pants and starched white shirts, went about their business, efficiently bringing the orders to the tables, filling empty glasses, or retrieving the empty plates of those patrons who had finished their meals.

From the kitchen the aroma of tomatoes, basil and mozzarella cheese made its way into the dining area every time one of the waiters opened its double doors to bring an order to one of the tables. As anticipated by Anna and Sergio, most of the patrons dining at the Pompeii on that opening night had opted for the typical Italian dishes that were featured on the menu and that would soon become the trademark of the restaurant. Many of them, as they left the premises, took the time to congratulate Anna and to assure her that they would return soon to sample different offerings of the house. Everything augured a rotund success for this new venture in the Cuban capital.

From that day on, there was not a single night when the Pompeii was not filled to capacity during dining hours. So busy had the restaurant become, that before long it was suggested that the public make reservations, lest they be forced to wait an indeterminate amount of time for a table. Despite this success, Anna made sure to keep the prices at a moderate level and not take advantage of the overnight popularity of the new venture.

"Customers always recognize a good value," was one of the dictums of Antonio Gamboa. It was one of the cornerstones on which he had built his financial empire. Guided by that principle, Anna made sure that at the Pompeii the patrons were provided with a pleasant atmosphere, unequaled service, continuous Italian music and, most important, an authentic Italian meal at a reasonable price.

To enhance the traffic during the lunch hour, and at Sergio's suggestion, they started offering pizza with an assortment of toppings. A novelty at that time in Havana, the trend caught on, especially among those busy individuals who were reluctant to return home for lunch and needed something quick to eat. The smaller, more intimate dining room was made available to those customers who wanted more privacy while celebrating an anniversary, birthday or any other special occasion. The Pompeii had something for everybody and for every pocketbook.

176

Anna's life became a whirlwind of menus, delivery schedules, employees' payrolls and all the other sundry responsibilities that come with running a successful business. Although this frantic schedule left little time for leisure, it also had the effect of making her focus on everything except her own life and all she had had to endure and give up to finally achieve this degree of success. But this busy, yet predictable pattern was about to end, not through her own doing, but through a seemingly innocent and common occurrence.

It was carnival time. Despite the news of the war in Europe, and propelled by their economic prosperity, Cubans celebrated the event with elaborate floats that rolled slowly on the wide expanses of the Malecón while onlookers stood on the sidewalks. Organized dance groups called *comparsas* displayed their expertise in front of judges and the general population usually followed behind, trying to emulate what the dancers had mastered through many hours of practice. After hours, private parties that lasted until dawn were organized. This contagious festive air was reflected in the attitudes of the population, for they danced, ate and drank more than usual. Hotels and restaurants experienced a surge in the number of clients, due to the influx of visitors from other parts of the island. Business was good.

One night, a young couple came into the Pompeii. Although this was nothing out of the ordinary, Anna sensed immediately that there was something special about them. He was tall, slender and wore a perfectly tailored suit. She was also thin, had light brown hair and green eyes, and wore a beautiful dress that had probably not been purchased in Havana. By the way they looked at each other it was obvious that they were very much in love. What caught Anna's eye—something that no one else would have noticed—was the way they moved, exuding with every step an air of elegance and sophistication. That ineffable quality immediately brought memories of her life in Europe, of the exclusive soirées that brought together the most refined people after the performances at the San Carlo Theater.

One of the waiters efficiently led them to a vacant table, handed them the menus and returned a few minutes later to see if they had decided what to order. Apparently they had already made up their minds, for they told the waiter immediately. The latter wrote quickly on his pad and retreated to the kitchen.

From the back of the restaurant Anna watched them engage in a lively conversation that was punctuated, from time to time, by spontaneous laughter. All the while, she also noticed, they held hands. When the food arrived — spaghetti with tomatoes and basil accompanied by freshly baked bread and a bottle of red wine — they raised their glasses in a discreet toast and started to eat. Intermittently they made approving gestures that Anna assumed were elicited by the food.

At the end of the meal, the same waiter approached the table to bring the cups of espresso the couple had ordered and to remove the empty dishes. The man sitting at the table asked him something; he nodded affirmatively and left the table again. This time, however, the waiter did not go to the kitchen, but approached Anna.

"The gentleman sitting at that table," then he pointed in their direction, "said he would like to meet you."

"Did he say why?" asked Anna.

"No," answered the waiter, "He just asked if you would join them.."

During the months that the Pompeii had been in operation, Anna had never received such a request. As a rule, if the patrons had comments, they would tell her on the way out. She sensed that this was different. As she approached the table where the couple was sitting, the man stood up.

"Allow me to introduce myself," he said while extending his hand, "My name is Herminio Aguado, and this is my wife Adriana."

"And how may I help you?" asked Anna.

"We just wanted to congratulate you on your restaurant and the authenticity of its food," he answered her in Italian, switching languages without warning and with absolute ease. "I have spent time in your country, and my wife Adriana is from Venice."

For a moment Anna was stunned; up to this point she had not met anyone else from Italy during her stay in Havana, so this was a complete surprise.

"Please, sit down," asked Herminio Aguado.

After the initial shock was over, Anna's silence was suddenly broken, like a dam that abruptly gives way to a silent but relentless pressure, and she started to speak without pauses. Unable to contain her curiosity, she began to ask all sorts of questions of the couple: How had they met? What did they do in Cuba? What did they think of the war going on in Europe? The mere fact that she could formulate these questions in her own language made a tremendous difference, as if by using her mother tongue she could somehow transcend a huge distance and be closer momentarily to her homeland.

"We met in Venice," said Adriana, speaking for the first time, also in Italian.

"I had just finished my degree in architecture, here at the University of Havana," added Herminio "and my father sent me to Italy as a graduation present. He felt that I should experience, first-hand, centuries of architecture before beginning my career. Little did I suspect at the time that I would find the most beautiful of all creations," he said with a smile and looked at Adriana.

"Once we met we both knew instantly," she corroborated, "After that day we became inseparable and spent most of our time exploring Venice and attending cultural events. Eventually we married; it was inevitable. Afterwards we decided it was time to return to Cuba, so Herminio could start his career."

"What a wonderful story," said Anna, "It almost sounds like a fairy tale."

"Not everything is perfect," said Adriana, "Sometimes we miss Italian food; that is the reason we came here tonight, in the hope of finding authentic cuisine. We were not disappointed."

"Well, I hope you return often," said Anna enthusiastically. "We can even prepare something not listed on the menu if you let us know when you are coming."

"Unfortunately, we only come to Havana once a month," interrupted Herminio, "This time we came to watch the floats and dancers and to participate in the general festivities of carnival. Since I have to visit the city on business often, Adriana and I always take advantage of those times to go to the theater, concerts and any other events that may be available. We also try to find new places to eat, so you can imagine our surprise when we found out about your restaurant."

"Well, I hope to see you whenever you are in the city," said Anna. "My offer stands, if you let me know in advance, we can prepare any Italian dish, even those not on the menu."

"Do you have any plans for tomorrow night?" asked Adriana.

"My life revolves around this restaurant," said Anna, "From the time I wake up until the time I go to bed I am doing something related to the business. But to answer your question, no, I do not have anything in particular planned."

"In that case," retorted Adriana, "why don't you join us? We are going to a concert of Vivaldi's music, featuring The Four Seasons; it has always been one of our favorite pieces. As you know, he was also from Venice."

"Well..." said Anna, considering the offer and what she would do about the restaurant. "I suppose I could get away for a few hours."

"Good," said Adriana, "We will come by at eight o'clock, have dinner and then go to the concert. It will do you good to have a night out."

"I agree," said Herminio, "There is more to life than work, especially when one is as young as you are."

At that moment Anna had to think of Antonio Gamboa, how he had devoted his entire life to building a fortune and in the end he had sold everything just to go back to the same small village he had left long ago. Sure, he had made a lot of money, but his time was running out; in many respects life had passed him by. On the day she signed the documents that made her owner of the restaurant, she told herself that she would not allow the same fate to befall her, that she would enjoy her life—her youth—as much as possible. That resolution, however, had been gradually forgotten once she became involved in every aspect of her new venture. It seemed that there were not enough hours in the day to attend to all the details of her new enterprise. In the rare occasions when she had some free time, she was usually so tired that she preferred to stay in her apartment, above the restaurant, and rest. Without realizing it, at twenty-three years of age she had assumed the role formerly occupied by Antonio Gamboa.

The unexpected appearance of Herminio and Adriana Aguado had served as a stark and sudden reminder that her life was becoming out of balance. In contrast, here was a couple who was apparently successful in their chosen professions, yet always made time for each other and for those cultural activities that nourished their minds and their spirit. No wonder they exuded an air of vitality and even youth. But most of all the fact that they were deeply in love could not be hidden. It showed not only in their furtive glances, when they thought no one else was looking at them, but in the brief and frequent—yet meaningful—physical contact they shared: the holding of a hand; the tenuous caress of a bare arm; the unconscious brushing of a shoulder. It was as if each body reclaimed contact with the other in order to both proclaim and corroborate a hidden undercurrent of deep feelings.

"I am sure I will enjoy myself," said Anna, "I have not been out since I bought this place."

"So much the better," added Herminio as they walked out of the restaurant, "We will see you then tomorrow night."

During the next twenty-four hours Anna thought of nothing else but the return of Herminio and Adriana Aguado. Without a doubt, they were the most interesting people she had met so far, with the exception of Oppiano and Ynaca Eco Licario, during her stay in Havana. Just the fact that Adriana was also Italian and that she could converse in that language with the couple was one of the obvious things that had impressed her. But it went beyond the realm of language. Herminio and Adriana offered a link, a virtual passport of sorts through which she could freely access her culture and all that was familiar. Being an architect, having lived in Italy and being married to Adriana gave Herminio a most advantageous perspective and understanding of that culture. Later Anna was to find out that the couple had also traveled extensively throughout Europe. All these things had bestowed them that air of subdued sophistication that she had noticed that first night they came into the restaurant. From the first moment she had felt completely at ease with the couple. The fact that they were somewhat older and already well established, also inspired in her an underlying feeling of confidence.

Just as they had promised, Herminio and Adriana returned to the Pompeii the following evening. Because of the rather formal atmosphere of the concert they would be attending, she was wearing an elaborate dress—Anna suspected from the house of a French couturier—and he had on an immaculately tailored suit with matching silk tie and handkerchief that protruded discreetly from his lapel pocket. Anna herself, in view of the special occasion, had changed into her best dress. Although adequate, she instantly realized that it was no match for what Adriana was wearing.

That morning Anna had instructed Sergio to prepare, in order to honor her guests, a new recipe from her mother's cookbook: bucatini all'amatriciana. If the dish met with their approval, she was considering making it part of the regular menu.

After greeting the couple she led them to the more private dining area at the back of the restaurant. She had personally set the table earlier, making sure that every detail—from the embroidered tablecloth to a central vase with fresh flowers—met her exacting standards. After they sat down a waiter brought a bottle of red wine to the table. Herminio poured the wine and then raised his glass to make a toast.

"To new friendships," he said.

"To new friendships," echoed the two women as the three brought their glasses together. The sound created by the glasses coming together seemed to augur an auspicious beginning.

Not surprisingly, the conversation centered around the great music that had been created by Italian composers throughout the centuries, and how that musical tradition, especially opera, had influenced the rest of the world.

Before long, the food arrived. This was a crucial moment, for Anna knew that the true opinion was not to be found in the words spoken by her guests, but in those almost imperceptible facial gestures that truly conveyed their verdict about the meal. To her delight they soon manifested that the dish met with their approval.

"The food is excellent," commented Adriana. "You are lucky to have such a skilled chef in your employ."

"I will pass on the compliment," Anna said. "Sergio has a passion for cooking; it shows in everything he does in the kitchen, with every new dish he tries out."

"Just make sure that he is not lured away by another restaurant," warned Herminio. "As his skills increase he will become more valuable and his craft more marketable."

"I have thought about that," answered Anna. "Since I took over ownership of the restaurant I have raised his salary and given him more say in what goes on in the kitchen and the restaurant in general. I think he knows that he is a valued employee."

"We should be going soon," said Herminio after consulting his watch. "We do not want to be late if we want to get good seats."

Anna signaled the waiter and a few minutes later, without having to order, three cups of espresso were brought to the table.They drank with gusto, concluding a memorable meal.

"We will not be having another meal like this one for a while," commented Adriana. "Tomorrow we leave Havana and go back home."

"Just promise me that you will call again during your next visit," said Anna."

"We certainly will," answered Herminio. "Now, we really have to get going," he said while standing up and putting down the empty cup of espresso.

As they walked out of the Pompeii onto Avenida del Prado, Herminio signaled a taxi that was parked on the curb. The driver, a middle-aged man holding a cigar between his teeth, nodded to let him know that he was available for service and not waiting for another fare.

Herminio opened one of the back doors for Anna and Adriana, then he sat in the front, next to the driver and told him where they were going. This was probably unnecessary, for he must have guessed it from the way they were dressed. The ride from the restaurant to the Teatro Nacional did not take long. Along the way they noticed that the sidewalks were more crowded than usual due to the festivities of carnival. Vendors hawked their wares to passersby, trying to catch their attention and bring about a quick sale.

The eclectic façade of the Teatro Nacional, with its massive columns that culminated in Corinthian capitals, was an evident and irrefutable proof of that secret yearning that most newly consti-tuted republics aspire to become the equals of their former European masters. At that hour of the evening the building, due to the number of music lovers already gathered there, gave an impression of inaccessibility. On either side of the main door, identical ticket booths welcomed the patrons. The attendants sat behind twin iron grates, received the money placed before them on a marble slab, and quickly returned the change along with the numbered tickets. Those seats closer to the stage or on the balconies commanded the highest prices.

Herminio Aguado left the two women momentarily, ap-proached one of the booths and returned a few minutes later. They walked to the main entrance of the theater, where an usher collected the tickets in front of a thick vermilion curtain and gave the public general directions where their seats were located.

"Upstairs, to the right," he said politely after receiving the tickets and looking at the printed information. Herminio had bought tickets to one of the private boxes in the balcony. Anna did not say anything, but this confirmed once more her suspicions about her new friends' wealth. They were in a position to enjoy the best things life had to offer.

"This is very generous of you," she said. "It is the first time I have attended a concert and sat in the balcony."

What Anna was saying was true. Having been brought up in a household that revolved around music, the opera and the symphony had always been some of her favorite activities. During the years she had shared with Giacomo Pace, they had often attended concerts; Giacomo considered this activity part of Anna's education, but they had always sat with the general public. After a while Anna realized that the seats that he secured were gifts from his friends in show business. From him she had learned that *Le quattro stagioni*, as The Four Seasons was called in Italian, was a set of four violin concertos, that it was Vivaldi's best-known work and that it was, overall, one of the most popular pieces of Baroque music.

"I find a private box less confining," explained Herminio, "The privacy allows us to enjoy the music to its full extent."

As they reached the balcony level, another usher led them to the assigned box. Immediately Anna realized that Herminio Aguado was correct; they would not be as confined as if they were sitting in one of the chairs below — no matter how comfortable — surrounded by a sea of people. She also noticed that the seats they would be using were much wider and plusher than the ones below. For a moment she wondered about the difference in price of the tickets, but at that moment the lights started to dim, in order to alert those attendees still in the lobby that the performance would start momentarily. Down below the orchestra was already in place, instruments ready, its members dressed in impeccable dark suits and white shirts.

At the appointed time, the conductor came on stage, and stood on a small platform in front of the orchestra. The whispers below, along with the lights, gradually died down, until there was nothing but darkness and silence, except for the lights that focused on the musicians. Then, the notes of the first movement filled the concert hall, immediately voiding the external reality and taking the public on an unforgettable journey. Those who were not familiar with the composition were surprised and delighted with its intricacies and ability to convey the difference of the seasons with music; those who had experienced it before exulted in anticipation of their favorite passages. Summer evoked a thunderstorm in its final movement, while Winter, peppered with silvery staccato notes from the high strings, called to mind icy rain.

The quality of the musicians, as well as the well-attended performance, attested to a growing middle class that was emerging in Cuban society. Anna thought that Giacomo would have approved. It also became apparent to her that Herminio and Adriana were quite at home, that they took advantage of their visits to the capital in order to meet those cultural needs that probably went unfulfilled in the town where they lived.

At the conclusion of the concert, a unanimous round of applause filled the theater. The lights came on and the crowd started to march out of the building onto the streets. It was still early, at least by Cuban standards, so Herminio suggested that they should go to a cafe and have a something to eat or drink. Such places abounded in the city, especially near the theater, so rather than looking for a particular establishment, they just followed the crowd that left the building, until they came upon a well-lit corner establishment that was of their liking. They sat at a table close to the sidewalk, and within minutes a waiter came to take their order. They settled for some coffee and guava pastries, and while they waited for the food to arrive, they made comments about the concert, about the work of Vivaldi and how far cultural events were advancing in the Cuban capital.

"We have nothing like this in the town where we live," offered Adriana.

"But we have each other," answered Herminio in his flawless Italian while gazing upon his wife adoringly.

"Don't mind him," said Adriana, "He has always been an incurable romantic. I knew it the first time we met in Venice; my suspicions were confirmed when he bought me a glass rose in one of the shops in Murano. Truth be told, we live away from the capital because of his architectural firm."

After the coffee and pastries arrived, the lively conversation continued. Adriana and Herminio talked about their meeting in Venice, and how they knew from the start they were destined to spend their lives together. As they talked about days past—all the while holding hands and looking at each other—Anna realized that they were like pieces of a puzzle that fit perfectly together, and for a fleeting instant she wondered if she would ever find that sort of intimacy with anyone. Sure, she had been married to Giacomo for a number of years, but that was quite different from what Herminio and Adriana shared. Giacomo had been a kind, stabilizing influence in her life, almost like a father who watched over her, but the passion had been absent from the start. Then, of course, there was Paolo. Her short but intense relationship, if it could be called that, had its foundation on the irresistible attraction they felt for each other. In time, Anna thought, it might have developed into what Herminio and Adriana had. They were indeed a most fortunate couple, she concluded.

The conversation had been so engrossing, the company so pleasant that when Anna looked at her watch she realized that it was past two in the morning.

"I have to go;" she said with and apologetic tone, "I must get up early tomorrow," she explained.

"We understand," said Herminio while signaling the waiter.

"The check," he said, "and could you flag a taxi for our friend?"

"Yes sir," said the young man and then left to comply with the request.

"Thank you for an unforgettable evening," said Anna. "I hope to see you again when you come back to Havana."

"We will," answered Herminio as they stood up and got ready to leave.

By the time the three of them made it out of the cafe, the taxi that Herminio had requested was already waiting. Anna disappeared into the back seat and gave the driver directions to the Pompeii. Before turning a corner, she looked back. Herminio and Adriana were holding hands and kissing unabashedly, as if they were newlyweds or lovers that had been reunited after being apart for a long time.

After that unforgettable evening with Herminio and Adriana Aguado, Anna kept hoping that they would return to Havana soon. She became aware of how much she missed good company with

186

whom to share the cultural offerings of the city, but she also realized that she missed even more the sound of her own language. The evening she had shared with them had been sort of a revelation; the couple spoke Italian fluently, were well traveled and knowledgeable about European culture. For the first time since her arrival in Cuba, she had felt at home. It was a feeling that she missed and wanted to recapture.

Every evening, especially on weekends, she kept looking at the front door, hoping that the couple would materialize out of thin air, just as they had done during their first visit to the Pompeii. As the months passed, the hope of their return began to fade, and she became more engrossed in the ever-growing business. One morning, while sitting in her office and sorting out the mail — it was usually bills, and other sundry items related to the restaurant — a letter immediately caught her attention. The envelope stood out, for it was not plain paper, but resembled real parchment and the name and address had not been typed, but handwritten. It was an elegant, clear writing whose characters conveyed a sure hand. The back of the envelope was sealed with red wax and it bore the letter A.

Putting aside the stack of bills, she opened the envelope with an ivory opener she kept in the top drawer. Inside, matching the parchment-like material of the envelope, she found a letter from Adriana. She asked Anna to excuse them for their prolonged absence from the capital, then went on to explain that Herminio had been extremely busy with the completion of an architectural project. He had just finished designing a house for one of the most prominent tobacco producers in the region, and to celebrate the conclusion of such an important project, they were having a party at their house. They would like for her to attend and be their guest.

At first Anna was surprised, then flattered that they would have thought of her. Then, the realization that she would have to be away from the restaurant for a few days dawned on her. She had no idea how long the trip would take, or how she would get there, just in case she decided to go. Undeniably, the prospect of seeing Herminio and Adriana Aguado again was most appealing; she vividly remembered that evening when they had gone to a concert of Vivaldi's music and how truly blissful she had felt in their company. Leaning back in her chair she read the letter again, and then left her office in the direction of the kitchen. She found Sergio, busy as ever, preparing the lunch menu for the day.

"How far is the city of Pinar del Río?" she asked him, without giving any explanations as to why she wanted to know.

"Roughly about one hundred eighty kilometers west of Havana," he said without hesitation, "I have a cousin who lives there."

"Is it a difficult journey?" she asked.

"It used to be," answered Sergio, "But now that the central highway is open, it is not too bad. That highway, by the way, was one of the main projects completed under president Gerardo Machado. At first he was a good president," added Sergio, "but then he turned into a dictator, so we kicked him out of office. They used to call him a tropical Mussolini."

Anna ignored this last comment; she just wanted to know how to get to that distant city. "How does one get there?"

"All depends," answered Sergio.

"What do you mean?" Anna retorted.

"The most economical way is to take a bus; it takes longer because it stops in different towns along the way to pick up and let out passengers. The other is to go in a private car; once the drivers have enough passengers they leave Havana and don't stop until they get to Pinar del Río. I think it is worth the extra money. They usually leave early every day; they are not far from here."

"Thank you Sergio, as usual you have been most helpful."

"My pleasure," he said and then turned his attention again to the dishes he was cooking.

Anna returned to her office and read the letter once again. By then she had already decided to accept the invitation; Sergio could look after the restaurant and she knew it would do her well to get away for a few days. From the top drawer of her desk she took out a sheet of paper and an envelope, but before she could start drafting a response, she changed her mind. A letter would take too long.

After putting the paper and the envelope back in the drawer, she left the restaurant and walked directly to the telegraph office.

VII

A week later, after carefully reviewing with Sergio all that needed to be attended to during her absence, Anna got into the back seat of the car that would take her to meet Herminio and Adriana Aguado in the city of Pinar del Río.

"Everything will be fine," Sergio reassured her, "It is not as if you are going away for a year."

Of course, he was right. She would only be gone for a few days and he was more than capable of running the restaurant without her. She told herself, as she had done in the past, that if she did not get away from time to time from the all absorbing influence of the business, eventually she would turn into another Antonio Gamboa. That was the last thing she wanted for herself, so she decided that she would enjoy the journey and the visit as much as possible.

The driver of the car, a young man with red hair and a scar on his cheek, slowly made his way out of the city. In the front seat, next to him, sat a much older man; he read the paper and did not seem very interested in what was going on around him. In the back seat, next to Anna, a middle-aged lady held tightly a handbag with floral prints and looked out the window.

As they left behind the more congested city streets and reached the open highway, the crowded urban architecture slowly gave way to open expanses of virgin green spotted by an occasional cluster of houses or small businesses.

After an hour of traveling, they passed a sign on the side of the road welcoming them to the province of Pinar del Río. Through the open windows the soft breeze carried with it a myriad of smells that mixed in an eclectic and random combination: roasting coffee; fresh fruits; cigar smoke. The others, although not altogether unpleasant, Anna could not identify, especially one in particular that brought to mind something excessively sweet, almost to the point of being repugnant. The driver of the car seemed to have guessed her thoughts, or maybe he just wanted to start a conversation with the passengers, for he offered the unexpected explanation.

"We are near a sugar mill," he said, "The smell in the air is the sugarcane juice being boiled to turn it into molasses."

No one else in the car answered him; it was apparent that they all knew what it was. The older man in the front had dozed off, still holding the newspaper open to the sports page. The woman sitting next to Anna continued to be immersed in her own thoughts; her eyes were open, but her mind was obviously miles from there, maybe thinking about something urgent she had to do once the journey was over.

"Are there many sugar mills in this province?" asked Anna. The conversation, she hoped, would make the time go faster.

"The province of Pinar del Río is known for its tobacco, without a doubt the best in the world. Most of Cuba's sugar mills are east of Havana," he said with a knowledgeable tone. "The soil on this end of the island, along with its topography, is best suited for the cultivation of tobacco. Somehow this industry has made the inhabitants of the province different from the rest of Cubans."

"How so?" asked Anna, always eager to learn something new about Cuba.

"The cultivation and harvesting of tobacco is done individually, as opposed to the communal effort that is involved in the sugar-cane industry. As a result, the pinareños, as the natives of this province are called, are a lot more introverted than other Cubans. I suppose that years of solitude, spent in the silent care of the tobacco leaves, has taught them to delve deeper into their own inner and private worlds. If you look carefully, you can see it in their eyes. Even when they are talking to you directly, there is a certain underlying detachment, as if part of their being were somewhere else, a place that no one else can reach."

"That is quite interesting," commented Anna, not knowing if the driver was quite serious about his comments or if he was just making conversation to pass the time.

"I should know," continued the driver, "I was born in Havana, but my job as a driver takes me to every corner of the republic. Take the people from Oriente, the province at the other end of the island. They are nothing like the pinareños. Since the main crop in that province is sugar cane, whether in the fields or in the mills, they are forced to work within a group. Their lives are led outside

190

of themselves, so they are not often given to introspection. When they celebrate an occasion, they do it openly, including as many people as possible. Sometimes entire towns participate and the festivities are conducted in the streets."

Anna found the driver's observations, even though she could not corroborate their veracity, to be interesting. If nothing else, it made the monotony of the journey a bit more bearable, and the thought of striking a conversation with the other two passengers was too remote.

"Are there any other differences?" she asked with genuine curiosity.

"Of course," retorted the driver, encouraged by the fact that he had found someone who was interested in his words. "As you know, the national drink in this country is rum; our own Bacardí is known worldwide. Everybody drinks rum. This holds true for most Cubans, except for the pinareños. They have their own liquor, called Guayabita del Pinar. It is made from a dwarf variety of guava that only grows in this province. The drink is less potent, but a lot more aromatic than rum. I assure you that you will find a bottle in every house."

Anna noticed that the car had slowed down, and that the open highway eventually led them into a square where, at that time of the day, restaurants, cafes, and other businesses did the bulk of their business. Eventually, they stopped in front of a small restaurant.

"Are we in Pinar del Río?" asked Anna, somewhat surprised that the journey had not taken as much time as he had expected.

"Hardly," answered the driver. "This is the town of Artemisa; we are almost half way. We are stopping to stretch our legs and get something to eat. It is lunchtime," he added while looking at his watch.

The three passengers followed the driver into the small restaurant. The latter, rather than sitting at a table, chose to sit on a stool along a long counter. It was apparent that he knew the people who worked there, for the waiters and the man behind the counter greeted him with obvious familiarity.

Instead of ordering from a menu, Anna opted for one for the sandwiches that was permanently advertised on a plaque above the counter. The Cuban sandwich, as it was called, was prepared on a warm baguette and it contained ham, pork, Swiss cheese and sour pickles. It was a quick, popular and inexpensive fare among travelers who were just passing by and did not want to wait for a full course meal. Along with the sandwich, she also ordered a fresh glass of orange juice. It only took minutes for the sandwich to arrive, and while she ate it silently, she also had a chance to observe the activity in the restaurant. Most of the patrons, she concluded, were travelers on their way to another part of the island. They looked at their watches frequently, as if fearing that they would be left behind in a completely unfamiliar town. After a while, tired of looking at the customers, she started to ponder about the name of the town: Artemisa. She found it somewhat disconcerting that a town in a rural section of Cuba would be named after a Greek goddess, daughter of Zeus and sister of Apollo. But this was Cuba, and by then Anna had begun to realize that oftentimes things did not appear to have a logical explanation, or if they did, she could not fathom it. Unavoidably she had to recall her first encounter with Mr. Ioso in the Church of St. Nicola, and how he had expounded on the influence of Greek culture throughout the Mediterranean basin. Apparently, it went well beyond the Old World, reaching across the ocean and the centuries so this small rural town could bear the name of one of its goddesses. She also wondered why the name Artemisa had been chosen over that of Diana, its Roman equivalent.

Before she could formulate a hypothesis, her conjectures were interrupted by the driver, alerting the passengers that the trip was about to resume. They occupied their former places in the car, perhaps not wanting to upset an invisible equilibrium that had been established earlier in the journey. The lady next to Anna continued clutching her purse, but the older man in the front, now fully awake, put on his glasses, and returned to the sports section of the newspaper with renewed energy.

"We will not be stopping again, so I hope everyone had enough to eat," announced the driver. The comment was followed by a unanimous silence from the passengers, which meant an answer in the affirmative.

Before long they were on their way again, leaving behind the town and once again venturing into the open road. The landscape was in no way different from before: an occasional house with children playing in the yards; fruit stands along the highway under the shade of a ceiba tree; groups of men in work clothes returning to their jobs after lunch.

The driver, his energies replenished by the recent lunch, wanted to engage Anna in conversation again, for he pointed out a field along the highway. It was obvious that the tract of land had not had recent care of human hands; there was brush and vines growing along with the bushes that had been planted with careful symmetry as far as the eye could see.

"This used to be a coffee plantation, but it has not been cultivated for as long as I can remember," he said addressing Anna and now pointing to a stone fence with a wrought iron gate and a bell tower also made of stone. All the structures were overrun with vegetation and in an obvious state of abandonment.

"Where is the owner of the land?" she asked, again intrigued by the driver's comments.

"Dead," answered the driver, "He was Cornelious de Souchy, a German who came to Cuba many years ago, during the first half of the nineteenth century. Here he met Ursula Lambert, his Haitian lover; they came to this part of Cuba in order to establish this coffee plantation. Since slavery was still prevalent at the time they had to keep their relationship a secret."

"Did the plantation have a name?" asked Anna.

"They called it Angerona," answered the driver, "A rather strange name, if you ask me."

Once again Anna had to think of Mr. Ioso. Angerona was the Greek goddess of silence; her statues often depicted her with a finger raised to her lips. Maybe the name was linked to the secrecy that the owner and his black lover had to maintain about their illicit relationship during a time when such liaisons were strictly forbidden. For a moment Anna also considered, drawing on her previous experience with Paolo, how difficult it must have been for them to keep up pretenses so as not to reveal the feelings they had for each other. She also thought that it would make a good story for a novel or an opera.

"Was the business ever successful?" asked Anna, trying to find out more details about what she thought was a most interesting tale.

"At first it was," answered the driver. "Angerona was the highest yielding coffee plantation in the province of Pinar del Río, but then the Brazilians introduced their coffee into the world market and the Cuban plantations went bust. Coffee, of course, is still produced in this province, but at a much smaller scale that only meets domestic demand; we have not exported coffee for many years."

"If you don't mind my asking," said Anna, "How do you know all these things?"

"Madam," answered the driver with an obvious tone of pride in his voice, "Although I make my living by driving people to different places in Cuba, that does not preclude me from learning as much as I can. I like to think of myself as a student of history and a very interested observer of the human condition. During my time off, I try to read as much as I can. If you look around, you will realize that this country of ours is full of interesting people and interesting stories; I strive to absorb as much as I can every way I can, in order to broaden my understanding of the world that surrounds me."

"I think you ought to be commended," said Anna, "Learning is a process that should never stop, especially after one leaves school." These words echoed Giacomo Pace's belief. Even though Anna's formal education had been abruptly interrupted because of her marriage, he had made certain that she acquired a thorough understanding of world history, politics, art and literature. Being so much older and experienced than she was, one of the roles he had assumed during their years together had been one of teacher. Anna remembered fondly the many sessions and discussions, and how Giacomo had guided and nurtured her intellectual growth.

"So there is no more coffee for export in Cuba," Anna said, trying to get the conversation back on track.

"That's right," said the driver shaking his head affirmatively, "The two main crops are sugar cane and tobacco. I have often thought that Cuba is too dependent on those two products, but world demand, especially from the United States, makes it difficult to diversify. Everyone is riding this wave of prosperity without giving a thought to what might happen if the demand were to decrease, or even stop. But what do I know?" he said while momentarily letting go of the steering wheel and throwing his hands up in the air, "I am just a driver."

"You are aware of what is going on in your country," said Anna, "If all citizens were as informed, maybe the politicians would think twice about making hasty decisions that usually have

194

adverse repercussions for years to come." At this moment, Anna was once again repeating what she had learned from Giacomo during all those sessions, sitting in the garden overlooking the Bay of Naples, about the world of politics and the clandestine exchanges that took place behind closed doors.

As they rode westward on the central highway, they went through and left behind other small towns: Candelaria, San Cristóbal, Los Palacios and Consolación del Sur. Eventually, at the very end of the highway, they arrived in Pinar del Río.

"The western city of Pinar del Río," explained the driver, "capital of the province of the same name and founded in 1699, at first was nothing more than a conglomerate of houses that had grown into a small city, slowly and randomly, along the banks of the Guamá River. It still retains the slow pace and country friendliness that are absent in Havana."

Along the main street, Anna noticed, groups of people strolled leisurely, gathered at a kiosk to drink a cup of espresso, or simply enjoyed a cigar on a park bench while talking to friends or having their shoes shined.

As the driver maneuvered the different intersections, now approaching the center of the city, he honked and waed at pedestrians along the way from time to time.

"We are here," he finally said as he pulled in front of an impressive looking corner building showing neat rows of identical rocking chairs in its porch. Above the entrance, a sign with the name of the establishment was prominently displayed: Hotel Ricardo. The driver exited the car, opened the trunk and started to place the suitcases on the sidewalk.

"Don't forget," the driver reminded them, "I will be going back to Havana in three days, just in case you need me. The cars can be found right here in front of the hotel."

Before going into the building, Anna approached the driver. "Thank you for a pleasant journey and the interesting conversation," she said, "I hope I can drive back with you."

"You are welcome," he answered, "I am at your service."

The Hotel Ricardo, although having no official associations with the drivers, was the point where they picked up and dropped off their passengers. The relationship was a symbiotic one: the hotel allowed the cars to park in front of the building while the drivers delivered a steady stream of customers who opted to stay there because of the obvious convenience.

With suitcase in hand, Anna stepped into the building and approached the man at the reception. In her purse she had a paper with the Aguados address, which was supposedly not too far from the center of town. She intended to take a taxi or a bus, but before she could request any information from the clerk, she heard Herminio's familiar voice coming from the lobby of the hotel.

"Welcome to Pinar del Río; we hope you had a pleasant trip."

Herminio and Adriana Aguado had been waiting for her at the hotel. Although no such arrangements had been made—in her telegram she only told them the day of her arrival—as her hostesses they felt it would have been thoughtless not to meet their guest.

As usual, their attires were impeccable, but without the same degree of elegance as the ones Anna remembered they had worn in Havana. Herminio wore a light beige suit, white shirt, and a tie with matching pastel colors; Adriana sported a blue dress with a discreet floral embroidery—also blue, but of a darker hue—on the upper part of its front. As always, the couple exuded an air of subdued sophistication and success, perfectly suited for their station as professionals in this provincial town.

"I did not expect you to be here, but I am very happy to see you," said Anna with obvious delight in her voice. "I was just getting ready to ask the man at the desk directions to your house."

"We could not invite you and not meet you," answered Adriana in Italian, an unmistakable sign that she was also happy to see Anna. "How was the trip from Havana?"

"Not bad at all," she answered. "We stopped in Artemisa for lunch and the driver talked about the history of this region the entire time. I found out a lot of things I did not know; it was actually quite interesting."

"Then you know," interjected Herminio, also in Italian, "that this region of Cuba is known for its tobacco, and not for the cultivation of sugar cane."

"Yes," answered Anna, "the driver mentioned that the best tobacco in the world is grown here."

"He is correct," said Herminio. "The project I just completed was commissioned by one of the wealthiest men in this area; he owns a large tobacco plantation. That is what we are celebrating

196

tomorrow. If you are interested in tobacco, he can tell you all about it. His name is Ramón Contreras."

Herminio picked up Anna's suitcase and started walking out of the hotel to where his car—a shiny beige sedan—was parked.After placing the suitcase in the trunk, he opened the back door for Anna and then the front one for Adriana. They drove away from the center of town, went around the gazebo in Independence Park, and before long they were on a boulevard. One side was lined with almond trees, and on the other rose an eclectic variety that Anna failed to identify.

"There is one thing that intrigues me about Ramón," said Adriana. "What is that?" asked Herminio.

"The house that you designed for him is very large, as if meant for a family. Yet, he is a single man. Why would he want to live in such a place?"

"That, I don't know, but you can ask him yourself tomorrow night. When he came into my office a year ago, he had already decided what he wanted. All I had to do was design it for him. He is very happy with the results, and that is good enough for me."

"Perhaps he is thinking of the future," interjected Anna. "There comes a point in a every man's life when he wants to settle down and raise a family."

"Be that as it may," answered Herminio without taking his eyes off the road, "the point never came up during out conversations, but I suppose that is a real possibility."

As they drove away from the center of town, the main street became a two-lane highway and the houses more sparse. They passed the local cemetery, with its elaborate wrought iron gates and expanses of white marble that reflected mercilessly the afternoon sun, until one had to look away to find the protection of darker images that did not offend the sensitivity of the retinas and were not such a stark reminder of an inevitable fate.

About half a kilometer past the cemetery, Herminio slowed down and eventually turned onto a short lane flanked by euca-lyptus trees and which led to a medium sized house. As the car pulled up in front of the house, a spotted dog came out of the garden, barking loudly.

"Welcome to our home," said Adriana, "I think you are going to like it here."

By then Herminio had exited the car and was solicitously opening the doors for the women. They walked together into the house, while he stayed behind to retrieve Anna's suitcase. It was obvious that speaking their native language made both Anna and Adriana feel a little closer to home, to everything that made up Italian culture and that for different reasons they had left behind.

"Let me show you the house," said Adriana with obvious pride as she led her guest through the front door.

Although the Aguados' house could not be described as palatial, it did not lack any of the modern day conveniences. Its living room was tastefully decorated with traditional furniture and enhanced with imported pieces—paintings, vases, glass—that they had acquired during their travels in Europe.

The next room, in Anna's mind, defied classification. It was as least twice as large as the living room, but the fact that it was almost devoid of furniture made it seem even larger. The ample expanses of glass on the back wall—the retractable wooden slats had not been drawn—allowed the afternoon light to come in unchecked, easily chasing the shadows from every corner. Along the walls, bookcases reached the hand carved cornices, and although Anna could not see the titles of the books, she made a mental note to survey the collection at the earliest opportunity. Also housed in the ample bookcase a record player was evident. On the only wall devoid of books hung two canvases, one depicting a corner building with a neoclassical façade and whose prominent marquee immediately identified it as a theater. The name 'Milanés' stood out. That Spanish word, meaning 'From Milan,' once again made Anna think of the links that Cubans seemed to have to Europe. The other painting showed the contrast of light and shadow in an interior courtyard with Romanesque arches and a central fountain. Because of her previous experience studying art with Giacomo, she readily identified the classical influences and the mastery of the artist in capturing the play between the sunlight and shadows under the arches.

"Those are wonderful paintings," she could not help but comment.

"We think so," answered Herminio. "They were done by an upcoming local artist. We have them on exhibit here so all my clients will see them and perhaps become interested in one of them or in the artist's work."

"That is a great idea," said Anna. "So you are patrons of the arts as well."

"We just like to help talented and deserving people," answered Herminio, dismissing the comment.

In the center of the room, surrounded by a dozen chairs done in embossed leather, stood a massive rectangular table whose surface was protected by a sheet of clear glass with beveled edges. The carvings on the legs and its supporting bridge underneath, Anna observed, matched those of the cornices above.

"Here is where we conduct business," explained Herminio, "The room is large enough to accommodate a group of clients, if needed."

"And beyond that door," added Adriana pointing to the right, "we have bedrooms for our guests."

On the opposite side of the room, flanked by two bookcases, a wooden door stood out. Adriana walked over and opened it. Rather than leading into another room, it opened onto a short corridor whose walls had been paneled in light wood, and showed paintings on one side and an immense tapestry on the other. It led into a studio whose focus was an architect's table by a window that faced a rear garden—much more private than the one in front of the house—a central desk, and a record player on a stand with two matching chairs.

"Here is where Herminio and I spend most of our time, either working or just enjoying each other's company," explained Adriana, "Our bedroom is there," she added pointing in the direction of another wooden door.

As she saw the unusual layout of the house, Anna realized that this wing, separate from the rest of the dwelling, was yet another attempt by the couple to preserve their privacy, to create a very intimate space where anyone else's presence would be an intrusion. She also wondered why, if they were so much in love, they did not have any children, but immediately realized that in such a unique relationship there was only room for two. Children would be intruders who could add nothing, but surely disrupt the perfectly balanced dynamics of what they had.

"It is almost tea time," said Adriana looking at her watch, "another of those little rituals that my husband and I like to observe," she added while returning through the small corridor to the ample room with the bookcases and the massive central table.

"That is true," said Herminio, who had all the while remained behind the two women, "Although most Cubans only drink coffee, we believe that tea is a more cultured beverage, more suited to the lifestyle that Adriana and I maintain. We started drinking it every afternoon, years ago, in Paris; we have continued this custom throughout our marriage. Of course, we like coffee too, but we drink it mostly in the mornings or when our friends come to visit."

While explaining these preferences, Herminio opened a small door between two of the imposing bookcases—Anna asked herself why she had not noticed it before—and stepped outside. It led to a section of the garden behind the house that was covered by a medium sized pergola; the thick grapevines clinging to the wire structure shielded the wicker table and chairs below from the sun.

"We always take our tea in this garden, unless it is raining," said Adriana.

Once again, Anna had to think that every detail in the life of the couple was meant to enhance and deepen the relationship that they had, and for an instant wondered if she would ever find a mate as perfectly suited.

Following Herminio and Adriana's cue, she sat down in one of the white wicker chairs. A few minutes later, even though neither one of her hostesses had alerted anyone, an old woman appeared with a tray in her hands. It had a tea pot, several cups, and individual containers of milk, honey and lemon juice.

"Will there be anything else?" she asked.

"No, thank you Dolores," answered Adriana. Then, addressing Anna, "How do you take your tea?"

"Just a little honey," she said, but without much conviction in her voice.

Adriana poured the tea into the three cups, then added a spoonful of honey into one of them, which she handed to Anna. To the other two she added a dash of lemon juice and gave one to Herminio.

"Dolores has been cooking for us for years," she said to Anna while sipping her tea. "After her husband died we asked her come and live with us. She makes sure that the house runs smoothly."

"That was nice of you," said Anna after tasting the tea. "It was Herminio's idea," answered Adriana.

"She had no place to go," he explained. "Besides, she spent most of her time here anyway. It was the logical thing to do."

As the day progressed, Anna realized how lucky she had been that Herminio and Adriana Aguado had come into her restaurant months before, and even more lucky that they had taken a liking to her. The late afternoon, aided by the conversation and the tea, turned into evening. The sun had disappeared behind a huge ceiba tree, and the sky had imperceptibly given up its almost painful brightness to be replaced by a burst of orange that would soon give way to a deep purple on its way to absolute black. Under the moon and the bright stars, the nocturnal insects would then make their appearance, first with their unmistakable sounds and then with their insistent buzzing around any artificial source of light. But before this could take place, the ever vigilant Dolores appeared again under the pergola to announce that dinner was served.

They adjourned to the room with the massive table, which the servant had covered with the largest tablecloth that Anna had ever seen. The table had been set for three. After pulling back the chairs so the women could sit, Herminio sat at the head of the table, with Adriana to his right and Anna to his left. At this point Dolores started to serve the food—a chicken fricassee—with the same efficiency with which she seemed to do everything else.

"Ramón Contreras, as I mentioned earlier, is one of the wealthiest men in the province," said Herminio after taking the first mouthful. "His tobacco plantation has been in the family for generations. He also has a degree in agronomy from the University of Havana, so he knew all along that he was going to manage and eventually inherit the plantation. We have been there several times and it is a most impressive place."

"Herminio is right," said Adriana looking up from her plate. "I think one of the reasons he wanted that house built is because as a student he became accustomed to the conveniences of the city; he was very specific as to what he wanted."

"As I mentioned before," said Anna "the only reason I can think of is that he is thinking about getting married. Most men do after they reach a certain age."

"You will meet him tomorrow night," said Herminio. "Then you can draw your own conclusions, but don't be surprised if his reasons turn out to be something you had not considered."

Toward the end of dinner, Dolores appeared again, this time holding a tray with individual dessert dishes containing guava shells in syrup with a slice of cream cheese. It was a typical Cuban dessert that Anna had learned to like since her arrival on the island.

"Most Cubans have a sweet tooth," commented Adriana, "My husband is no exception."

"She knows me too well," said Herminio with a smile while taking the first mouthful of his dessert.

"The two of you are very fortunate to have found each other," said Anna, making a pause and then going back to her dessert. It was not so much the words, but the tone of her voice that conveyed the absolute sincerity with which she had made the spontaneous comment.

"We know," Herninio and Adriana answered simultaneously, as if they were a single entity and not two separate beings. Once again, Anna felt almost a tinge of jealousy; they had everything while she had nothing. But the feeling was a fleeting one, for Herminio stood up and walked over to the record player. A few moments later, the soft cadences of a classical piece filled the room.

Although Anna prided herself in her knowledge of music, she could not identify the composition. It was certainly the work of a European composer, she thought, but the music playing was completely new to her. Rather than asking her hostesses, she remained silent, listening attentively to see if she could find a clue.

"By the expression on your face," said Herminio with a smile on his face, "I see that you have not been able identify the composer."

"Certainly European," ventured Anna, "It is obvious by the maturity of the music."

"I thought you might say that," said Herminio, "but that is the work of a Cuban composer. His name was Ignacio Cervantes, and it is generally agreed that he was the best composer of 19th century Cuba."

"I am surprised that I never heard of him," said Anna.

"Many people haven't," answered Herminio. "He spent five years in Paris, where he became well known, and was friends with Liszt and Rossini. Everyone augured a brilliant career ahead of him."

"What happened?" asked Anna.

202

"Cuba happened," said Herminio with a sigh, "He could not bear to be away from this island. His friends advised him that if he returned it would be equivalent to professional suicide, that his career had to be pursued in Europe, where the opportunities were. As you may suspect, he did not listen. He returned and started touring the island, raising money for the cause of independence. He even wrote Maledetto, an opera that he left unfinished. Of course, his career as a world-class musician was over."

"That is a sad story," said Anna. "I mean, all that talent that could have been developed under the tutelage of European masters."

"As you spend more time in Cuba," answered Herminio, "you will come to realize that this is a country full of contradictions. I need to go no further than José Martí, our greatest patriot. Even though he was living in New York pursuing a career as a journalist and poet, he chose to return to Cuba and fight for its independence. If you read his journals you realize that he knew that he would soon die, but that did not stop him. Had he stayed in New York his impact on Spanish-American letters would have been greater than what it is and he probably would have lived to a ripe old age."

"Yes, I see what you mean," said Anna, "Apparently the lure of this island is too strong to resist." When Anna made this comment, she was not thinking of Ignacio Cervantes or José Martí, but of Herminio Aguado himself. He was a cultured man who had traveled extensively in Europe, who had experienced firsthand the depth and breadth of its culture, yet he had chosen to return to Cuba. It was a question she had not dared ask. Yes, this was indeed a land of contradictions and enigmas.

The rest of the evening was spent conversing about and listening to music. Anna realized that even though her hostesses lived away from Havana, they made it a point to have at their disposal the latest recordings that arrived in the island from Europe and the United States.

"Before we retire for the night," continued Herminio, "my wife and I have a surprise for you."

"A surprise?" asked Anna, not knowing what it could possibly be, or why.

"Yes," answered Adriana, "We are certain you will like it."

While she was saying this, Herminio took another record out of its protective sleeve and placed it on the turntable. A few moments later, the amplified sound of the needle scratching the grooves was heard. Then, Louis d'Amio's powerful voice filled the room without any difficulties with his masterful interpretation of Immortal Arias.

No one interrupted the performance with idle conversation; there was nothing that could be added. When the final aria was concluded, the abrupt silence was permeated by the monotonous and persistent sound of the crickets in the garden.

"How did you know?" Anna finally asked with an expression of awe on her face and coming out of the very private reverie that had been induced by her father's voice.

"That evening we went to the Vivaldi concert you mentioned that your father was an opera singer," explained Herminio. "So we looked in the usual shops in Havana for his records. Immortal Arias is the only one we could find."

"It is the only one he recorded," said Anna, trying to hold back the tears. "He died shortly thereafter."

"We are sorry," said Adriana, "It was not our intention to make you sad."

"His voice never makes me sad," explained Anna, "It always reminds me of how much he loved us. Thank you for playing it for me."

"The pleasure was ours," said Herminio, "You can be certain that now that we have discovered him, we will listen to his recordings often."

"He would like that," said Anna "All he ever wanted to do was sing and bring joy to people with his voice."

"It has been a long day for you," said Adriana suddenly, perhaps trying to dispel the pensive mood that had come over Anna, "Tomorrow will also be a busy one and you must be tired; let me show you to your room."

"Before we retire for the night," added Herminio, "Let me offer you a night cap," then he walked over to a small cabinet, opened one of its double doors and retrieved a clear round bottle whose surface showed symmetrical rows of diamonds and a label with the picture of a monkey. "This anisette liqueur is imported from Spain; it has been manufactured in the city of Baladona since 1867.There is nothing better," he said while pouring the clear liquid into three small glasses. He offered one to Anna and one to Adriana. "Let's toast to tomorrow," he said while raising the small glass and taking a sip. It was apparent that the couple often drank the liqueur, for Adriana also savored hers with obvious fruition. Although Anna was not a drinker, she did not want to appear rude. She took a cautious sip, and was pleasantly surprised at the sweet, aromatic taste of the liqueur. "Now we are ready for bed," said Herminio after everyone had finished their drink and looking at his wife. The room where Herminio had earlier taken Anna's suitcase was off the large central living room through a short hallway. Just as every other room in the house, it had ample windows that could be opened to allow the breeze to flow through, but equipped with wooden slats that afforded full or partial protection from the sun, depending upon the angle in which they were placed. In the center of the room stood a double bed with corner posts, and the mosquito net that covered it. Anna thought of a giant and delicate cocoon. There was also a dresser with an oval mirror matching the bed, and two nightstands.

"I think you will be quite comfortable here," said Adriana. "The bathroom is two doors down; at the moment we have no other guests, so it is all yours."

"Thank you so much for everything," said Anna, "Good night."

"Good night. We will see you in the morning," said Adriana before closing the door.

Anna heard their footsteps fading away, until there was only the ever-present sound of the crickets and other nocturnal insects coming in through the window. After opening her suitcase and retrieving the necessary toiletries and her nightgown, she disappeared into the bathroom. When she returned to the bedroom, she quickly slid through the opening in the mosquito net, got in bed and closed her eyes. It was time to end the day. The recent events paraded on the inside of her eyelids, as if they were being projected by an inner and invisible device. It had been an enlightening day, beginning with her journey from Havana and the strange tale of a forbidden love affair between Cornelious de Souchy and Ursula Lambert, the German and Haitian owners of Angerona, the coffee plantation named after the Greek goddess of silence.

Anna also realized that although she had spent time with Herminio and Adriana Aguado before, they were more complex than she thought at first. In Havana, they had moved with the ease and sophistication of city dwellers, their elegant, yet discreet attires perfectly suited for the upper social circles in which they moved. But in the more rural and less refined setting of Pinar del Río, they had managed to create their own private island, where culture and good taste reigned supreme and admission was not open to the general public, but by invitation only. She truly felt fortunate to have been invited into their home and to the party that was to take place the following day. Besides Ramón Contreras, the owner of the tobacco farm, she could only conjecture about the prominent guest list. As these thoughts shifted in her head, she drifted into sleep.

When Anna opened her eyes, for a fleeting moment she did not know where she was. The enclosure of the mosquito net, the high ceilings with the carved moldings and the unfamiliar sounds coming in through the window evoked the villa in Ischia. An errant beam of sunlight came into the room through the partially open blinds, was somewhat softened by the mosquito net, and came to rest next to her head. Then the distant sound of voices speaking Spanish made her realize where she was. Reaching through the opening in the mosquito net, she retrieved her watch from the might stand: ten o'clock. She had slept more than she had intended to. Perhaps it had been the journey of the previous day, or maybe the nightcap right before bed. In all probability a combination of all, including the fact that she had not taken a day off from the restaurant for the past month.

Leaving the bed hurriedly, she went into the bathroom, then she returned to the room a few minutes later, got dressed and proceeded to apply some make up and do her hair. The mirror on top of the dresser faithfully reproduced the image of a beautiful young woman preparing to face the day.

When she emerged from her bedroom, Herminio and Adriana Aguado were already sitting at the massive table in the central room. It was obvious that they had been up for a while, for the empty plates attested to the fact that they already had had breakfast. Herminio was reading the paper and savoring an extra cup of coffee, while Adriana was carefully buttering a piece of toast and also enjoying a second cup of coffee.

"Good morning," said Adriana, "Did you sleep well?"

"Perhaps too well," answered Anna, "I did not mean to sleep this long; I suppose I did not realize how tired I was."

"That is good," said Herminio while putting down the newspaper,

"That way you will be rested for tonight. Sit down please."

Anna sat to the left of Herminio, across from Adriana. Before she could say a word, just as silently and mysteriously as the previous day, Dolores appeared in the central room, holding a tray with fresh coffee, toast and a small bowl of fresh tropical fruits — papayas, mamey apples, bananas and pineapples — that had been neatly cut into individual pieces. Without a word, she placed the dishes in front of Anna and then left the room.

"Everything looks delicious," commented Anna. Suddenly she realized that she was hungry.

"We have some fruit trees on the property," explained Herminio, "The rest we buy locally, that way we are assured that everything is fresh. The bread is delivered to us every morning, directly from the bakery. Living here, as you can see, has some advantages over living in Havana." At this point, he looked at his watch and stood up. "You ladies will have to excuse me, but I must go to work. I will be home early, though."

Adriana stood up too and walked Herminio to the front door. There was a brief exchange and they kissed good-bye. From her seat at the table, Anna realized that the kiss had not been a mere formality, but one that lasted longer than necessary for a morning good-bye and was charged with passion.

Adriana returned to the room where Anna was sitting, occupied her place at the table, and took a sip of her coffee. Anna realized that this was the first time, since they had met, that she was alone with Adriana, who was older and more sophisticated. For a few moments neither one spoke, but concentrated on the coffee. Although she had no valid reason, Anna felt a little intimidated in her presence.

"Finish your breakfast and I will show you around," said Adriana, "Herminio will not be back until later, so there no sense staying here."

Anna did not say anything, but finished her coffee, stood up and started to follow Adriana, who by then had picked up her purse from a nearby side table. As they went out the door, Anna realized that the same beige sedan they had used the day before was parked in front of the house.

"Herminio usually walks to the end of the lane and rides into work with his partner," explained Adriana, "so we can use the car today," she said in a most natural tone. This did not seem to be an isolated event, but an everyday occurrence. To Anna, it was further proof that this couple was way ahead of their time, for women usually did not drive.

Adriana got behind the wheel and produced a set of keys from her pocketbook. She placed one in the ignition and started the car. Anna, sitting next to her in the front seat, had a perfect view to observe the expertise with which she controlled the car as she went through the ascending progression of gears.

They made their way onto the main highway, and by some of the familiar landmarks—especially the cemetery—Anna realized that they were going toward the center of town. Eventually they reached Independence Park—a group of people were gathered in the central gazebo—and continued down the main street. They passed the hotel where less than twenty-four hours before Anna had arrived from Havana. As they drove, Adriana made comments about the architecture of the different buildings, explaining their influences and how well or how poorly they harmonized with their surroundings.

"How do you know these things?" asked Anna, amazed at the detailed information.

"Have you forgotten that I am married to an architect?" she answered with a smile.

They drove aimlessly around the city for about an hour, until they reached a wide boulevard with a median divider where trees had been planted. The sidewalks were busy with people and Anna thought that it resembled the Prado in Havana, but in much smaller and modest scale.

"The inhabitants of this city call this place the Malecón, just as they do in Havana," explained Adriana.

"But there is no water," observed Anna.

"I know, but that does not seem to matter. It is a place to promenade and gather, so that seems to be enough for them."

Toward the end of the boulevard, the houses became more sparse, until there was nothing but an open and undeveloped field. At this point Adriana made a sharp turn and drove again towards the center of town, but in the opposite lane. Before reaching Independence Park, she turned onto the road that led to the central highway. Anna did not ask where they were going, but assumed correctly that Adriana would tell her. After traveling a few miles, she slowed down and turned into a lane that led to what appeared to be a country club.

"This is the Rumayor Club and Restaurant," said Adriana as she parked the car, "Perhaps the most exclusive in the entire province. Herminio and I come here often, not just for the food, but for the atmosphere as well. We like it because it is close enough to town, yet secluded at the same time."

The narrow path leading to the restaurant proper was flanked by long stalks of bamboo, and a small foot bridge joined the two banks of a creek. Some of the customers were sitting in a pavilion devoid of walls, while others preferred to eat in the more sheltered enclosure of the restaurant.

A uniformed man greeted them at the door, and by the expression on his face, Anna surmised that he had recognized Adriana from previous visits. He led them to a table by one of the open windows and handed them the menus that he had been carrying.

"The smoked chicken here is excellent," said Adriana, "They roast it and baste it with a combination of spices mixed with honey. It is served with rice and a fresh salad."

"So the chicken it is," agreed Anna putting down her menu.

The waiter, noticing that the women had closed their menus, approached them once again with an order pad in his hand.

"We will both have the chicken," said Adriana, "And two bottles of mineral water."

"Very well," he said while writing down the order and then retrieving the menus from the table.

The time at the restaurant — before and during lunch — was spent in small talk about the town, Herminio's architectural firm, the limited social life that a town the size of Pinar del Río had to offer, and the frequent trips to Havana that the couple made. With every passing minute, Anna realized even more how cultured and sophisticated her hostess was. She could not help but notice a solid gold brooch, depicting a gondola and gondolier, pinned on Adriana's blouse.

"Your brooch is lovely," she said while taking a closer look.

"It is one of my most prized possessions," answered Adriana, "Herminio gave it to me on the day we were engaged."

It was not until they were back in the car, driving back to the house, that Anna asked a question that had been on her mind all afternoon.

"Despite all the limitations of this province," she said to Adriana, "You choose to live in this city, rather than in Havana or any other capital in the world. You are obviously very happy. What keeps you here?"

"You overlook the obvious," answered Adriana after a few moments, but without taking her eyes off the road, "Love."

By the incessant activity going on that day in the Aguado household, it was apparent that something special would take place that evening. During the early afternoon, a van from a catering service had delivered a wide assortment of hors d'oeuvres and canapés; there had also been a delivery from a flower shop. Dolores seemed to be everywhere, making sure that everything was in its place, especially in the central room, where the gathering was to take place. For the occasion, she had covered the huge table with a fine linen tablecloth that sported lace edges from Bruges. The focal point of the table, however, was the bright floral arrangement that had been delivered to the house during the early afternoon. Its irrepressible exuberance of tropical colors contrasted sharply with the snowy whiteness of the tablecloth, creating an explosion of color that was impossible to ignore.

Around seven o'clock the guests began to arrive. Their presence was announced loudly by a barking dog as the cars approached the house, and then by the sound of the closing doors as they exited the vehicles. They were greeted at the door by Herminio himself and led into the central room, where Adriana and Anna were already waiting. They had both changed into somewhat more formal attires suited for the occasion; Herminio also had changed into a darker suit with a gray silk tie.

As the guests came into the room, either Adriana or Herminio would introduce them to Anna. They were mostly upper middle class who moved in the same social circles as the Aguados. After the introductions were over, they would mingle and greet   other acquaintances they had not seen for a while. By eight o'clock the room was almost crowded; everyone who had been invited seemed to be present, except for Ramón Contreras, the guest whose house they were celebrating.

"Don't be concerned," said Adriana to Anna, "He has a reputation for being punctual; he will show up right on time."

"I am not concerned," answered Anna, "I am just curious about him." As if echoing her words, the loud barking of the dog was heard once again. A few minutes later, there was a knock on the door.

It was Dolores this time, with her usual efficiency, who answered the call, for she knew that both Herminio and Adriana were occupied with the guests. Standing in the threshold and leisurely surveying the entire room, was a tall, muscular man wearing a white suit. His jet-black hair contrasted sharply with his light complexion; his features were strong and angular, as if they had been chiseled by a Renaissance sculptor and meant for a marble statue that would grace the courtyard of a wealthy patron of the arts or for the inner cupola of a basilica. His most salient feature, however, was the pale and cool blue hue of his eyes. Somehow they brought to mind the placid waters of a Nordic lake at dawn, when the first rays of the sun have barely begun to awaken the color from the darkness of the night. His looks, both men and women agreed, were unusual and striking.

"He is here," said Adriana.

"I know," answered Anna without knowing how she had arrived at that conclusion. Perhaps it was the way he moved, exuding an air of self-confidence that rested on his wealth and social standing. Or maybe it was not that at all, but an assuredness that emanated from his youth and good looks that almost reached the point of arrogance. At that moment he was aware that all eyes, especially those of the women, were upon him, committing to memory every one of his gestures, his words, the expression on his face as he reacted to the different people in the room. Ramón Contreras was, because of all these qualities, undoubtedly the most desirable bachelor in the city. As far as anyone knew, however, he had never been close to marriage. Sure, for years he had often been seen in the company of young, eligible young women at dances, private parties and other events, but those short-lived interludes —

to the dismay and disappointment of those women and their mothers — had never come to fruition. After a while, and for no apparent reason, he simply stopped calling. At this point, some believed that he would remain a bachelor. As he moved among the guests, smiling and greeting each with a smile, Anna had the fleeting thought that he was just too handsome to be a man. Eventually, he made his way to the spot where Adriana and Anna were standing.

"And who is the beautiful creature?" he asked Adriana, widening his smile and lowering his voice in order to enhance his air of self-confidence and obvious charm.

"You are incorrigible, Ramón," answered Adriana.

"I simply have an eye for beauty," he answered, not fazed at all by her comment.

"My name is Anna d'Amio," said Anna, extending her hand without waiting for Adriana to introduce her to the guest of honor.

"I am Ramón Contreras, at your service," he said while taking Anna's hand in his own, but rather than holding it briefly, as etiquette dictated, he bowed and kissed it lightly. Suddenly and unexpectedly, Anna found herself immersed in a most unique fragrance — enticing and intoxicating simultaneously — of his cologne. There was something strangely overpowering in the scent that momentarily clouded her judgment and weakened her will.

Anna felt a little uneasy at the unexpected gesture, and even more so at her reaction, but she stepped back and managed to keep her composure. The last thing she wanted was to appear intimidated by this man. "I have been told that your new house is quite beautiful," she said, shifting the conversation to a safer and more neutral topic.

"Yes, it is," said Ramón, "But in all fairness, all the credit goes to Herminio. When I first approached him about the project, a couple of years ago, all I had in my mind was a vague idea of what I wanted. After several meetings the project began to take shape; with every session he had a more detailed sketch, until the entire concept was finally on paper. From there he drew the plans and then the rest was up to the construction workers."

"It was not quite as simple as he makes it sound," interrupted Adriana, "It is hard to tell how many hours he and Herminio spent going over preliminary drawings and making changes."

"But now it is all finished," concluded Ramón with a smile, "And everyone who visits the house will want to know about the architect who designed it. Just think of the free publicity."

Adriana was about to make another comment, when her husband, from the center of the room and tapping lightly on a glass, commanded everyone's attention.

"I would like to thank all of you for coming out tonight," he said in a voice loud enough to reach every corner of the room, "We are here to celebrate the successful conclusion of a project for Ramón Contreras, one of the most prominent citizens of our province. It is at this time I would like for all of you to see what has taken so many hours of planning and execution."

At this point, Herminio walked to a corner of the room to a small table that had been set up that afternoon. Under a white piece of cloth, an irregular outline stood out. With a decisive motion, he removed its cover, exposing below an elaborate maquette of the house he had designed for Ramón Contreras. At once, the people gathered in the room rushed to the table to view the model, and as they examined the project, involuntary exclamations of awe and surprise were heard. Although everyone present knew about the new house, Ramón had kept everyone not directly associated with the work off his property, so this was the first glimpse the guests had of the project.

Once the initial surprise subsided, the group moved over to the central table, where Dolores was already busy at one end dispensing the plates of food that had been delivered by the catering service, while Adriana poured the champagne that had been kept in ice buckets throughout the afternoon. After leaving the table, a plate in one hand and a drink in the other, the guests started to mingle once again, taking advantage of the opportunity to catch up on the lives of friends or acquaintances they had not seen for a while. Eventually they returned to the table where the maquette was displayed, surveyed it more leisurely, and invariably gravitated towards Herminio or Ramón in order to ask specific questions about the new house.

After accepting a glass of champagne from Adriana, Anna moved slowly around the room. Some of the people there walked up to her and introduced themselves — as Cubans usually do — without any hesitation; to others she was introduced by either Adriana or Herminio. Throughout the evening, as the guests came and went, there was a succession of names usually followed by professions: Vicente Rodríguez, an engineer and Herminio's best friend; Dr. José Sotolongo, a local physician; Luis Alberto, a lawyer of great renown who did not seem to need a last name and who wore a sober suit, white shirt and a black bow tie. There was also a thin, young man with jet-black hair just wearing a simple white shirt and black slacks. He was simply introduced as Dionisio René, without the benefit of a last name. Later Anna would find out that he was the painter who had done the masterful canvases hanging on the wall.

As the evening progressed, the amorphous and eclectic group of guests began to cluster into little groups; they gravitated to those who had the same interests or professions and with whom they could converse more easily.

At this point, Anna found herself standing alone, so she walked over to the maquette of the new house. As she was examining it more closely, admiring Herminio's work, a sudden voice coming from behind startled her.

"Beautiful, isn't it?"

Without turning around she knew that Ramón Contreras was behind her. It was not so much that she had recognized his voice, but rather the unmistakable fragrance that he exuded had announced his presence. For a moment, just as before, she felt a little weak at the knees, as if the evaporations that had suddenly enveloped her were sapping her strength and clouding her reason.

"Yes, it is," she said mustering her inner strength as she turned around.

"How would you like to see it? In person, I mean," asked Ramón.

The invitation, Anna realized immediately, was most unusual. She had just met this man; they had only exchanged a few words before. She also knew through Herminio and Adriana that he was adamant about guarding his privacy.

"My intentions are completely honorable," he added after seeing the hesitation on Anna's face. "Tomorrow morning we are having a final walk through, before I move in. Being the architect, Herminio will accompany me, just to make absolutely sure everything is to everyone's satisfaction."

"And why would you want me there, señor Contreras?" asked Anna, purposely trying to establish an air of formality "We do not even know each other; I am sure there are other people who would love to see the house."

"Of course there are," answered Ramón, "But since the moment we met I sensed there was something special about you. Call it intuition, if you will. Just say yes; you will not regret it," he pleaded, getting a little closer to Anna and lowering his voice. "And please, call me Ramón."

"Very well Ramón, I accept," she said after a few moments. But it had not been the tone of his voice that had persuaded her to accept the invitation, but rather the intensity of his gaze when he had made it. Looking into those light blue eyes she had the fleeting sensation of being completely removed from the room and transported to a distant and inaccessible glacier whose rarified and icy atmosphere was saturated with the fragrance that always seemed to envelop Ramón and that had the strange ability to undermine her will.

"You will not be disappointed," he said while stepping back. "I have to meet Herminio here at noon; we will leave shortly thereafter. Now, if you will excuse me, I have to speak to our host. I will see you tomorrow". Then he was gone, leaving behind a tenuous trail of that unmistakable fragrance that Anna found so intoxicating.

As she watched him disappear with Herminio into the latter's office, she wondered how he knew that she would be there the following day. Apparently, he had made some previous inquiries as to where she was staying. Still holding her drink, Anna looked at the maquette and tried to visualize what it would be like walking inside the actual house, breathing the air within which would probably be saturated with Ramón's fragrance. After a few moments, she finished her glass of champagne and walked over to the table, where Adriana was still waiting on some of the guests. Somehow she needed to let her know of the unexpected invitation and ask her opinion. She renewed her drink and circulated among the other guests, making small talk, which almost always had to do with the project whose miniaturized model had been unveiled by Herminio. It was not until several hours later, after the last guest had gone, that she found herself alone with Adriana. She hurriedly recounted the brief exchange she had had with Ramón Contreras and his unexpected invitation to tour the new house.

Adriana listened attentively, taking in every word without making any comments. "Did he suggest or imply anything else?" she finally asked.

"No, nothing at all. Just the invitation," answered Anna, "But it was not his words," she clarified, "But the tone of his voice."

"Just a word of caution," said Adriana softly, as if she were afraid of being heard, "Be on guard. I know Ramón, and he never does anything without a reason. He usually ends up having his way."

"Thank you for letting me know Adriana, I will certainly keep it in mind," answered Anna. "Oh, yes, just one more thing," she said while raising her right hand to her forehead, "Do you know what is that strange cologne that Ramón wears? It is certainly over-powering."

"Cologne?" asked Adriana with a puzzled look on her face. "I don't think Ramón uses any cologne at all."

After a late breakfast with Herminio and Adriana, Anna tried to prepare herself mentally for her visit to Ramón Contreras' house. She told herself that she was making too much out of it. After all, she would be with the architect himself, just touring the premises. Yet, there was something vague gnawing at her, like a distant admonition from the back of her mind.

Throughout breakfast, the conversation gravitated to the gathering that had taken place the previous evening, and the different guests that had attended the soirée. It had certainly been an eclectic list, but they had all been unique in their own way; that was certain. Once again Anna was able to corroborate the fact that even though Herminio and Adriana lived in an environment far removed from the more culturally advantageous Havana, they still managed to surround themselves with the elite of Pinar del Río. In a way, she thought, they had the best of both worlds; they enjoyed the privacy and tranquility of a rural life, where Herminio could devote himself to his work, and several times a month, or whenever obligations permitted it, they spent time in Havana. The couple had also mentioned that they traveled abroad once a year.

Around eleven thirty there was the sound of distant barking and then a knock on the front door. From the central room Anna saw the perennial Dolores walk by in the direction of the living room. A few moments later she reappeared in the company of Ramón Contreras.

"*Buenos días*," he said, offering a wide smile that exposed his perfectly symmetrical teeth.

"Good morning Ramón," answered Herminio while getting up to meet his guest. "Would you join us for a cup of coffee?"

"Yes, thank you," he answered as he sat down next to Anna. Out of nowhere Dolores appeared, holding a tray with an extra cup and a fresh pot of coffee. Anna thought that because of the number of Herminio's clients coming to the house, she had learned to be prepared at all times.

"I have a feeling that today will be special," said Ramón while sipping his coffee. "I am also sure that Anna will be impressed with the house," he added after a few moments as he turned and looked at her.

Anna could not be sure if the previous comments had been unrelated or if Ramón had meant that the day would be special because she would like the house. Even if he had meant this, she still could not understand why her opinion would matter to him. It was his house anyway; the following day she would return to Havana and most likely never return.

"I am ready to go," said Ramón after finishing his coffee in a single gulp.

"Yes," agreed Herminio while standing up, "it is that time."

Parked in front of the house, next to Herminio's beige sedan, was a car that at once Anna identified as Ramón's. It was painted bone white, had only two doors and its sleek, modernistic look was enhanced by the chrome bumpers and a shining ornament prominently displayed on its hood. Hardly the type of machine that one would associate with a tobacco grower, since its limited interior space and low carriage made it a most impractical vehicle to traverse the expanses of his land or travel on unpaved roads that demanded more sturdy means of transport. Yet, in an odd way, the car suited Ramón perfectly. It seemed to be but a natural extension of himself, a tangible statement that proclaimed that even though he was a resident of this province, he was not like anyone else.

As they approached the parked vehicles, Ramón opened the passenger door for Anna. For a moment she hesitated; she had not given any thought as to how she would travel to visit the new house. Herminio and Adriana had already settled in their car, so it would have been rather awkward for her to walk past the open door and attempt to ride with them. If this had been a preconceived ploy by Ramón, she did not know, but it worked because after the initial pause she sat down in the passenger seat. He closed the door with a firm motion, went around the front of the car and sat behind the wheel.

"It will not take long," he said as he steered the car towards the highway. "Herminio and Adriana are right behind us," he commented. "After the visit you can return with them; I have some work to do later on this afternoon."

"I heard that you were wealthy, that you really didn't have to work," Anna said.

His unexpected laughter took her by surprise. Ramón shook his head, seemingly amused by her comment.

"A common misconception," he said in a more serious tone. "Sure, I inherited some property and I have been able to put together some profitable deals, but that does not exonerate me from the responsibility of looking after my assets. On the contrary, as my land holdings grow, so does the work. I must oversee personally every aspect of the business, and that consumes a lot of my time."

"Yes, I see what you mean. I also have a business, although not as impressive as yours; it takes most of my time," said Anna.

"Oh, yes, the restaurant. Herminio and Adriana were raving about it after their last visit to Havana. I told them that I would eat there during my next trip to the capital," he said.

"And what else did they say?" asked Anna, now truly curious.

"They also mentioned that you had come from Italy and that you enjoyed good music, but because of your restaurant you had not had time to make many friends or go out much," explained Ramón. Then, after a short pause, he added, "They also told me that you were very beautiful."

Although Anna was a little taken aback by this last comment, she tried not to show it. Ever since she had entered her teens, she had been aware of the men looking at her—sometimes they could not help but stare—because of her looks. It was something she had learned to live with, like someone who puts up with a mild but permanent ailment, but fully conscious that it is always present.

"What they said is true," she finally said, "About the restaurant and my lack of time, I mean."

"And the rest is quite obvious," concluded Ramón.

At this point, even though the windows in the car were partially open, Anna became aware once again of the strange scent that Ramón exuded. It seemed to permeate everything—especially in this small enclosure—impregnating whatever was within its reach. The thought of someone drowning in a sweet, flowery and intoxicating syrup came into her mind. In an effort to counteract the effects of the enervating fragrance, and searching for fresh air, she lowered her window completely, but it did not seem to help.

They rode in silence for a while, just watching the narrow road that led away from the city and into the less populated areas of the province. From time to time someone on horseback or just walking along the road would wave, but Anna could not tell whether they were just being friendly or the gesture was a sign of recognition. On either side of the highway, under the perpendicular midday sun, almost endless expanses of tobacco fields reached out to the horizon, occasionally interrupted by the royal palms that stood proud and tall, like exclamation marks that culminated in mush-rooming clusters of fronds that swayed softly against the cerulean Cuban sky. But what Anna found most disconcerting was the thin sheets of what appeared to be gauze, like an infinite mosquito net that had rested on wooden frames about six feet off the ground, covering all the tobacco plants.

"Why are the plants covered?" she asked Ramón.

"Growing tobacco is very demanding," he explained, "It is a delicate crop, one that requires constant care and attention. The coverings that you see serve to cut down the intensity of the sunlight while simultaneously allowing the rain to reach the plants. The soil, by the way, is also treated in a special way. Before the tobacco seeds are planted, along with the proper fertilizers, we add ground peanuts. That gives the leaves a silky, smooth texture that has no equal in the entire world," he concluded in a proud tone. "As you know, the rest of the island grows mostly sugar cane. That process is quite different, and certainly not as arduous. That crop needs no special care, it grows under a full sun, and once it is harvested and taken to the sugar mills, the barren fields are set on fire, to prepare them for the following season. The difference between the two crops is like night and day; tobacco requires constant care and special men who can provide it," he concluded.

At that moment, Anna had to recall the words of the driver who had brought her from Havana. He had said the same thing about the crop, about the men who tended it and how they were different from the rest of Cubans. Ramón's words corroborated what he had said.

"This is the area of San Luis and San Juan," continued Ramón, "the very heart of tobacco country. Those tall houses that you see, with thatched roofs, are where the leaves are hung to dry after they are cut from the plants. The process cannot be rushed, since the leaves have to dry naturally, in the air and out of the sun. They are strung together with a needle and a long piece of twine, then hung from the rafters. This phase of the process is usually done by women, since it is less physically demanding. After the leaves have dried, they are taken down and sorted out, according to size and what part of the plant they came from, and packed. Those bundles are the ones that are sent to the cigar factories, where the workers remove the veins from the leaves and roll the cigars."

"I never realized that the process was so complex," offered Anna. "I thought that a cigar was just a cigar."

"Don't let anyone around here hear you say that," admonished Ramón in a joking tone, "Tobacco is what defines this part of Cuba," then he laughed spontaneously.

Anna laughed with him, feeling for the first time since they had met that Ramón had done something without forethought or calculation.

"I will keep that in mind," she said, "I am sure you will let me know all there is to know about tobacco. I would not want to offend anyone," she added in a half joking tone.

From that moment on the atmosphere in the car became more relaxed; Anna felt that she did not have to keep her guard up at all times, that at least there was a side of Ramón with whom she could just be herself, without having to second guess if every word that he uttered, every gesture that he made was a front for a hidden agenda. The uneasiness that she had felt the night before was beginning to wane. The unusual fragrance, she also noticed, had also dissipated into the afternoon air, leaving behind just a trace.

A few kilometers farther Ramón slowed down and made a right hand turn into a wide, but unpaved lane. "We are here," he announced, "The house is behind that cluster of trees," he said while pointing with his forefinger.

As they reached the trees that Ramón had mentioned, the lane made an abrupt ninety-degree turn that culminated in a wide clearing. In its center, gleaming in the sunlight, stood the house. Even though Anna had examined carefully the maquette the previous evening, trying to capture every detail, she was not prepared for the impact that the actual structure would have on her. Despite the fact that she was familiar with classical architecture, upon beholding the house that Herminio had designed, the word majestic came into her mind. The two-story, white stucco dwelling had been constructed and positioned in such a way that it was integrated into its surroundings, creating the illusion that it was a natural part of the landscape and not a man-made object. Part of the second story served as a terrace, from which the lands beyond could be surveyed with more ease because of its height.

"Very impressive," said Anna as they exited the car and stood in front of the house, at the edge of a cobblestone path that led to the front door. Herminio and Adriana, who had kept up with Ramón's pace, joined them.

"Let's go in," said Ramón, leading the way. He opened the door with a key he had produced from his pocket and signaled the ladies to go ahead. Even though the house was of spacious dimensions, being devoid of any furnishings, gave the impression that it was even larger. As they walked through the different rooms and commented about various aspects of the dwelling, the walls, floor and ceiling returned a brief echo of their voices.

"The place will look a lot better after I have it furnished and decorated," added Ramón.

"Those areas are beyond my scope," said Herminio jokingly. "I believe my job here is finished."

"And what a nice job it is," added Adriana as the group emerged from a stairwell onto the second floor terrace Anna had seen upon their arrival. From that vantage point the covered tobacco fields, several tobacco storage houses for drying out the harvested leaves and a dirt path that crisscrossed the sheltered expanses of green were clearly visible.

"What a wonderful view," said Anna without being able to help herself. "Everything you said about this house, and more," she said addressing Ramón directly, "is true. I thought you might have been exaggerating." The excitement on her voice was reminiscent of that of a child when presented with an unexpected surprise.

"I am happy that you like it," said Ramón, "I am just sorry that it is not furnished at the moment. I also plan to buy some outdoor furniture, so I can get some of my work done up here on the terrace."

Everyone agreed that it was a good idea, since the location of the house, along with the high fronds of the trees sheltered it from the sun most of the day. There were also some suggestions and questions about the furnishings, and the decoration of the house. At this point Adriana and Anna reverted to their native Italian in a quick and spontaneous exchange where they expressed their opinions simultaneously and emphasized them with the gesticulations of their hands.

Herminio and Ramón looked at each other and then started to laugh at the unexpected outburst. Ramón, of course, did not understand a word, but the humor was not so much in what they said, but in the spontaneity and quickness of the exchange.

"Italians can get excited easily," commented Herminio, still smiling. "By the way, it is past lunch time and I am hungry," he added the non sequitur.

"Italians can also be clever," answered Adriana in Spanish. "I had the forethought to bring a picnic basket. I knew that neither of you would be thinking about anything else except the house."

"As usual, you are right," conceded Herminio and then gave his wife a kiss on the cheek.

"The perfect couple," commented Ramón in a half mocking tone, but everyone knew that it was true.

The group went downstairs and Herminio retrieved the wicker basket from the back seat of his car. It was well stocked with ham sandwiches, fresh fruit and a bottle of red wine. Adriana had even included some glasses and red and white-checkered napkins. Since they had no furniture, they opted to sit o n the exposed roots of a huge centenary ceiba tree that grew next to the house and whose fronds provided shade for the terrace. During the planning of the house Ramón had insisted that the tree should not be disturbed; this was not a strange request, since many Cubans held the belief that ceibas were sacred.

"And when do you return to Havana?" asked Ramón, sipping his wine and looking at Anna.

"Tomorrow, after breakfast," she answered. "I have a business too, remember?"

"Well," said Ramón, "I hope you come back soon, so you can see the house again after it has been furnished."

"I would like that, but I have no reason to return to Pinar del Río," she answered, "I only came this time because Herminio and Adriana invited me."

"You know that you are always welcome in our home," interjected Herminio.

"At any rate," concluded Ramón, "I would like to see you again."

Upon hearing this remark, Herminio and Adriana looked at each other, but did not say anything. It was obvious that Anna had awakened an interest in him, but this was nothing new. In the past he had courted other eligible young women, but in time his interest had waned and the potential relationship had fizzled.

"I think it is time to head back," said Herminio while looking at his watch. "We all have worked to do."

"I thank you all for coming," said Ramón as he stood up and dusted off the back of his pants. As he walked by Anna, once again she caught a whiff of that indefinable fragrance that seemed to envelop him.

After returning the glasses, empty bottle and napkins to the wicker basket, Herminio and Adriana started to walk back to their car. Anna followed them and took her usual place in the back seat. As they drove off, she saw Ramón, still standing in front of the house, waving good-bye, and she thought that most likely she would never see him again.

As she packed her small suitcase, Anna pondered about the significance of the past three days. Her friendship with the Aguados, especially with Adriana, had solidified after spending the day together and having lunch at the Rumayor. She had also met some of the more prominent citizens of the city of Pinar del Río. Then, of course, there was Ramón. She did not know quite what to make of him. Since the moment they met, he had shown an interest in her, something that puzzled Anna. With his good looks, unquestionable charm and abundant wealth, his advances would certainly be welcomed by the many available young women of the highest strata of society. Yet he had chosen to overlook all those eligible women when he asked her to join him and the Aguados during the tour of his new house. Ultimately, she concluded that Ramón was a capricious young man whose fancy had been struck momentarily by a young and beautiful Italian, but that his interest, especially after her return to Havana, would soon be replaced by another distraction. It really did not matter; she was ready to resume her life. That evening she would be back in the restaurant, busy with all the decisions that running a business implied.

Earlier that morning, during breakfast, she had thanked Herminio and Adriana for their hospitality. Since Herminio was going to his office, it was agreed that Adriana would drive Anna into town for her return trip to Havana. Before leaving, Anna insisted—although it was not necessary—in thanking Dolores for all she had done during her stay. The old woman simply smiled and offered a faint 'De nada.' As Adriana and Anna were preparing to leave, the sound of an approaching car coming up the lane caught their attention. The puzzled look on Adriana's face conveyed the fact that they were not expecting anyone, especially at that hour. Herminio was already at the office, so his clients would look for him there, and not at the house.

Enveloped in a cloud of dust, a familiar bone white coupé with a shiny hood ornament suddenly materialized and stopped right in front of Adriana's car, blocking its way. The tall, youthful driver emerged from behind the wheel and simply delivered a '*Buenos días*,' as if he had been expected.

"What are you doing here, Ramón?" Adriana's face showed surprise, but the tone of her voice also betrayed a little annoyance, since she knew that Anna had to be in the center of town at a certain hour if she was to find a ride back to Havana. "Anna has to leave and you are blocking the way."

"I know," said Ramón calmly, "That is precisely why I came. Did I forget to mention that I have some business in Havana myself? I figured that since I have to drive there anyway, Anna could come along and keep me company. I can take her anywhere she likes," he continued with a perennial smile on his face. "Actually, I think it will be fun; besides, my car is a lot faster and more comfortable than anything she could possibly find in town."

For a moment both Adriana and Anna were startled. Ramón's sudden appearance and unusual offer were most unexpected, but in a strange sort of way, it made absolute sense. It would keep Adriana from having to drive into the center of town; Anna would be spared looking for a car and a journey shared with complete strangers. She already knew Ramón and, as he himself had stated, they could keep each other company during the trip.

Despite all this, the tone of Adriana's voice betrayed the fact that she was not completely convinced, that Ramón's appearance was an unexpected nuisance that had derailed their plans. "It is up to Anna," she said, "But it is no trouble for me to drive her into town; there are plenty of cars there going to Havana."

"I apologize for not announcing my visit," said Ramón before Anna could give an answer, "But I appeal to your sense of reason. My offer is the most sensible alternative," he concluded and started to open the rear door of Adriana's car, where Anna had placed her suitcase just minutes before. As he walked by, once again Anna perceived the indefinable yet relentless fragrance of his cologne.

"Well..." said Anna, still trying to decide, "I suppose it is alright, since you are going that way." Then, looking at Adriana, "Thank you so much for everything; I hope we will see each other again soon." They embraced briefly and then Anna settled herself in the passenger's seat, next to Ramón.

As they left the lane that led to the house and reached the highway, Anna noticed that Ramón drove with the same unbridled enthusiasm as the day before, guiding the car expertly through the curves and shifting gears seamlessly whenever the situation required it, instinctively anticipating the needs of the powerful engine. As they reached the outskirts of town, he slowed down, but once out of the city and onto the central highway that led to the capital, he picked up the pace once again.

"You certainly like to drive this machine," said Anna, stating the obvious.

"You are right," agreed Ramón, "It is one of the few pleasures that I have in my life, since my work takes up most of my time. Whenever I am behind the wheel, in control of the car and in command of all the horsepower under the hood, it gives me a feeling of freedom and exhilaration that I certainly do not get when I am sitting at my desk. The speed also allows me to think more clearly, to discern the best way to proceed in my business dealings.

"You told me yesterday that being wealthy was sometimes a heavy burden," said Anna.

"The responsibility is with you twenty four hours a day, seven days a week. That is why allow myself these little pleasures, to convince myself that all the work is worthwhile," he answered while stepping harder on the accelerator, taking advantage of a straight and empty expanse on the road. "Besides," he added after a pause, "What good is money if you can't have a good time once in a while?"

The tired image of Antonio Gamboa going over the ledger books of his restaurant suddenly popped into Anna's head. He was the perfect example of what Ramón was talking about. She wondered how many times he had taken time off from work to do something utterly unproductive, but filled with joy.

"I agree with you completely," she said, "Work is important, but it is not the only thing in life."

"Then you won't mind if I call on you whenever I am in Havana," said Ramón, not wasting any time in laying the groundwork for future encounters with Anna.

"If you wish," she answered in a noncommittal tone. "You know that I work most of the time."

"But not all the time," he persisted. "I think that as you get to know me better you will realize that we share the same outlook on many things."

Anna could not imagine what those things could be, or how Ramón had arrived at that conclusion, so she opted not to answer this last comment. She still believed that once he returned to running his tobacco farm in Pinar del Río, he would forget all about her. After all, Ramón himself had said that he tried to fill his free time with distractions. Soon there would be something else that would capture his attention.

They rode in silence for a while, just watching the changing landscape on either side of the road. From time to time, they passed brightly painted makeshift fruit or vegetable stands that had been erected for the sole purpose of attracting the travelers that were coming from or were going to the capital. Ramón ignored them without any problems, leaving them behind in a blur of color that he skillfully controlled with his right foot.

226

"Are you hungry?" he asked, suddenly changing the course of the conversation and noticeably slowing down. Anna noticed that they were entering the town of Artemisa.

"We had an early breakfast," she answered, not giving a direct answer, but hinting that it was time to eat lunch.

"We can stop and get something light," said Ramón, "If we have a real lunch we will lose too much time." He was right, Cubans ate a very light breakfast — usually coffee and buttered toast — and then made lunch their largest meal of the day. Everything stopped at noon so people could return to their homes and devote the next two hours to the meal. Afterwards, adults returned to work and the children to school, for the afternoon session.

Apparently, Ramón was familiar with the town, for he maneuvered the car through the side streets until he arrived at a small restaurant. He parked in a nearby space, exited the car and opened the door for Anna.

"I always stop here whenever I am in Artemisa," he explained, "The food is good and the service is even better."

As soon as they came in, a young waiter greeted them, led them to an empty table, and gave them the menu. Ramón did not bother to look at it; being familiar with the place he already knew what he wanted.

"I will have whatever you are having," said Anna, placing her unopened menu on the table.

Ramón signaled the waiter, who was waiting nearby, and returned the menus. "Two *medianoche* sandwiches and two orange juices," he said. The waiter left immediately to deliver the order to the cook.

"That is a strange name for a sandwich," commented Anna.

"No, not really," answered Ramón. "As you know, the word *medianoche* means midnight. I think this sandwich became popular with theater and concert goers. Before returning home after a performance, which usually ended a little before midnight, they would stop at a restaurant to have something to eat, hence its name. I think it is rather appropriate. Of course, Cubans eat it for lunch as well, but the name has persisted. I like it because it is easy to prepare and it is very tasty."

As if to corroborate his words, the waiter reappeared with two plates and the glasses of juice. After placing everything on the table, he left. Ramón started on his meal right away, taking big bites out of his sandwich, which he alternated with sips from his juice. Anna was a little more cautious, so she took a small bite from the end of her *medianoche*.

"It is delicious," she commented, "What's in it?"

"First of all," said Ramón, "They use a special kind of bread, like a small baguette. Then they fill it with slices of ham, lean pork, Swiss cheese and sour pickles. Before serving it they put it in a hot press, just to toast the bread and melt the cheese inside. After it comes out of the press they cut it in half, so it will be more manageable. Not a bad sandwich, in my opinion," he concluded.

"Not at all," agreed Anna, now taking bigger bites. "We do not offer it at the Pompeii; as you know, we specialize mostly in Italian dishes."

It did not take long, just as Ramón had predicted, to finish their lunch. Still talking about the different dishes that Anna served at the Pompeii, they made their way back to the car and once again they were on the road to Havana. Just as before, Ramón drove with the same zest, braking while entering a curve, and downshifting as he exited so as not to lose speed and stay on top of the power band of the powerful engine.

The conversation during the trip centered mostly around Ramón's business. Anna was truly interested in the different stages of growing tobacco and he was more than glad to answer all her questions. She also found out that Ramón had no siblings, that he had become an orphan at an early age and that he had been raised by an aunt and her husband. The land had been in his family for generations, so it was only natural that he would learn the business from the time he was very young. After his twenty-third birthday, he returned from Havana with a degree in agronomy and assumed legal control of the business. This was, in reality, just a formality, for he had been making all the decisions for several years. He did not mention his parents much, and Anna, not wanting to cast a somber mood on the moment, did not ask. He also spoke freely of his childhood and early years growing up in Pinar del Río. By the fondness with which he spoke of the town and its people, it was evident how much he loved living and working there. Towards the end of the journey he also told some anecdotes that Anna found most amusing. As they arrived in

Havana, Anna secretly wished that the trip could have taken longer.

Because of the heavier traffic, the pace with which Ramón drove had slowed down considerably, but when they reached the Malecón, he drove as fast as traffic would allow and with all the windows down, to soak in the ocean breeze.

"This is my favorite place in Havana," Ramón said, "I miss the ocean sometimes while I am working in the fields."

"Have you ever considered moving?" she asked.

"That would be impossible," answered Ramón, "My business requires me to be there in person, but as I mentioned before, I manage to come to Havana at least twice a month. That is good enough for me."

"It appears that you have managed to find a balance that satisfies all your needs," said Anna.

"Well, not all my needs, but most of them," he answered cryptically as he turned into the Paseo del Prado and joined the slower traffic.

"My restaurant is three blocks up, on the right," explained Anna.

"I could take you home first, if you wish," offered Ramón.

"You are," she clarified, "I live in an apartment right above the Pompeii. It is rather convenient."

"Yes, I agree," said Ramón, "and it is a lot easier to keep an eye on the business when you are close."

In an open spot right in front of the restaurant—unusual at that hour—Ramón parked the car, walked around the front and opened the door for Anna, then reached into the back seat for her suitcase.

"Would you like to come in for something to eat or drink?" she offered. "It is on the house."

"Thank you, but I can't at the moment. I do have a business engagement, that is what brought me here," he said as he walked back to the car.

"Thank you for everything," she said, almost having to shout over the noise of the cars and the conversations of the passersby.

"Don't mention it," he shouted back. Then he started the engine and merged into the traffic. Still standing on the sidewalk, Anna saw his left arm protruding from the window and waving good-bye.

Then, with a quick pace and suitcase in hand, she walked into the Pompeii.

During the following month, Anna busied herself with the restaurant. Right after her return from Pinar del Río, she had written a thank you note to Herminio and Adriana Aguado for their invitation, telling them how much she had enjoyed the visit, but so far had not received a response. She had also mentioned to Sergio the possibility of incorporating the *medianoche* sandwich into the menu, a suggestion with which he agreed. As for Ramón, the thought had crossed her mind of writing him a thank you note as well, but she had no idea of how to get in touch with him, so she had to desist. Although he had openly told Anna that he would call on her, now that he had his new house—she conjectured—he would be busy furnishing and decorating the place and not have too much excess time for socializing. And even if he had, Anna believed that Ramón was so self-absorbed that he mostly thought about himself and his amusements. Her visit to Pinar del Río was becoming a distant memory. Several weeks later, on a Friday night, one of the waiters knocked on her office door.

"There is a man up front who is asking for you," he said, "He would not give his name, but said that he was a friend of yours and that you were expecting him."

Anna thanked the waiter and for a moment pondered who could possibly be calling in such a mysterious manner. She was certainly not expecting anyone, and as for her circle of friends in Havana, it was rather limited. She thought of Oppiano Licario, but immediately discarded the idea. He would not resort to such antics.

Closing the ledger book on her desk, she stepped out of her office and walked through the short hallway that led to the restaurant proper.Wearing a light suit, white shirt and striped tie, was Ramón. She also noticed that his hair had been carefully barbered, probably at one of the most exclusive salons in Havana. Everyone in the place was surreptitiously looking at him. His tall and slender figure, light complexion and blue eyes combined into a magnet that drew looks everywhere he went. He resembled, thought Anna as she walked into the dining area, a sophisticated movie star that one might see on the silver screen or between the

230

slick pages of a fashionable magazine. The last thing anyone would take him for was a tobacco farmer.

As she approached him he smiled and then, just as he had done the night they met for the first time, took her hand and kissed it lightly. This time, however, rather than releasing her hand immediately, he held it longer than necessary and took a step forward, diminishing the distance between them until she was once again enveloped in the emanations of that unmistakable fragrance that he seemed to exude. Anna felt the blood rushing to her head; she knew that she was blushing, but tried to maintain her self-control; the fact that everyone in the restaurant was looking at them did not make the task any easier. After what seemed an eternity, he released her hand and stepped back.

"You are looking well," he said. "How have you been?"

"Just fine, thank you," Anna replied, consciously trying to sound a little aloof. "So what brings you to Havana this time?" she asked.

"Business, as usual," he replied succinctly, "But I have another reason," he said somewhat mysteriously. "Is there a place where we can talk more privately?"

"Let's go into my office," said Anna. As she left the dining area, with Ramón a few steps behind her, she felt the curious glances of the patrons on her back.

"So what's on your mind?" she asked after sitting behind her desk and pointing to a nearby chair for Ramón.

"I need your help," he said.

"I do not understand," replied Anna. "What could you possibly need from me? You have everything."

"Not quite everything," answered Ramón. "Let me explain. One of the reasons I am in Havana is because I want to furnish and decorate the new house. After visiting the different stores, I have to confess that I am at a total loss. Would you consider helping me out with this? I realize that you are busy, but from time to time you must have some free time."

"But I am not a decorator," protested Anna.

"No, but you are a woman; you possess that innate quality that allows you to see what will work and what won't. Besides, I think it will be fun," he added with a smile.

Ramón was right, at least on the fun part. Anna had to admit that after getting past her first impression of him as a self-centered and spoiled young man, she had had a good time in his company, especially during their trip from Pinar del Río. As for the rest, even though she was not a professional decorator, she had enough experience to know what was tasteful and not gaudy. The last thing he wanted to do was to decorate the house ostentatiously; Anna preferred a style that proclaimed a subdued elegance and refined good taste, and not the flashy excesses so often found in the houses of the nouveau riche. Good taste could definitely not be bought, but acquired.

"I suppose I could find some time," she finally acquiesced after making a grimace that conveyed it was a sacrifice on her part. At this point she did not want to show Ramón that she enjoyed his company.

"You can come by tomorrow around nine o'clock," she said, "But now I have to get back to work."

"I will be here," said Ramón as he stood up, "And thank you in advance."

"You are welcome," answered Anna as he walked out of her office, leaving behind—as a reminder of his presence—a faint trace of his unique fragrance floating in the air.

At nine o'clock sharp the following morning Ramón pulled up in front of the Pompeii. One of the qualities that Anna would come to discover in the future was his insistence on punctuality. To that effect, he wore a solid gold Gruen Curvex watch imported from the United States. Just like his elegant Packard coupé, it was another extravagance that he could afford because of his wealth. On that sunny morning, Ramón had dispensed with his usual white suit and wore light slacks and a short-sleeved shirt with pale and discreet designs. As he exited his car, ready to walk into the Pompeii, Anna came out of the adjacent door that led to her upstairs apartment. Instinctively Ramón looked at his watch.

"Exactly on time," he said.

"I learned to be punctual as I was growing up," she said, "It is a good quality, especially when running a business."

"I could not agree more," said Ramón as he opened the passenger's door for Anna.

They took off with a slight squeal of the rear tires—further evidence of Ramón's eager foot—and soon they blended into the morning traffic of the Paseo del Prado. As they reached the corner,

Ramón made a U turn, away from the city and toward the Malecón.

"I thought we were going shopping," said Anna.

"We are," answered Ramón, "I just want to get some fresh air before I spend my day going from store to store."

The fresh ocean breeze, especially with all the windows down, soon filled the cabin. As the car entered the wide avenue that ran along the ocean, Ramón increased its speed.

"What a beautiful morning," he said That comment, Anna realized, was meant for himself and not for her. At the end of the Malecón stood a seventeenth century building—La Chorrera—that had been erected where the Almendares River joined the sea. Once again Ramón skillfully guided the car through the increasing morning traffic as he now drove toward the center of the city.

"I think it is best to park the car and walk to the different downtown stores, since they are so close," he suggested.

"I agree," said Anna, "Besides, we have all day. I left Sergio, my cook, in charge today."

"Good, very good," exclaimed Ramón, "I suspect that it will take us a while to pick out all the things I need for the house. I want everything to be special."

"I am sure it will be," agreed Anna, "The stores here in Havana stock everything, especially goods from the United States."

At that point Ramón had spotted an open space and skillfully guided the Packard into it. After turning off the engine and rolling up his window, he walked around to open the door for Anna. The center of Havana, especially at that hour, was busy with the pedestrian traffic, the cars, the street vendors competing for attention and the hoarse gasping of the occasional buses that left in their wake dark clouds of diesel exhaust that rose morosely between the tall buildings and eventually dissipated into the soft breeze that came in from the ocean. As soon as Ramón and Anna started to walk, they were intercepted by a lottery ticket vendor claiming that he had the winning number for that afternoon's drawing, and that they should not pass it up, but Ramón easily avoided him as they became part of the kinetic and colorful kaleidoscope that the street scene had become.

Anna, holding on to Ramón's arm, followed him through the maze of businesses, until they were in front of a large building whose façade showed ample showcase windows inhabited by mannequins sporting the latest fashions.

"This is *El Encanto*, the most exclusive department store in Cuba," explained Ramón as they walked through one of the glass double doors, "They have everything one could possibly want, maybe more."

"Everything looks expensive," commented Anna while looking around.

"It is," agreed Ramón, "But if you want top quality you have to pay for it."

The rest of the morning was spent visiting all the sections of the store, and discussing at length how the items that caught Ramón's eye would look in the house. From lamps, crystal vases, and bronze figurines to kitchen utensils they were all carefully examined. Those deemed worthy of the new house were purchased, while the majority remained on the shelves.

Anna was surprised at Ramón's good taste, and did only disagree with his selections on a couple of occasions, but had to admit to herself that it all came down to a personal preference, for what he had chosen would have worked as well. They undoubtedly gave the impression of being a young and affluent couple making the last preparations for a life together after a well-attended wedding in the city's cathedral.

"Let's take a break and have lunch," said Ramón, "The store has a cafeteria, so the clients don't need to leave the premises."

"That is convenient," said Anna.

"Not just convenient, but smart," he explained. "They provide that convenience in order to keep the customers here. This is nothing new," he added, "every department store in the United States is set up that way. It was just a matter of time until it made its way to Cuba." Then, after a brief pause, "Of course, there is nothing like this in Pinar del Río; we still have to go home or to a restaurant in order to eat lunch."

The spacious and functional cafeteria where Ramón had led Anna was clearly fashioned after its American counterparts. Unlike anything else in Cuba, its efficient self-serve style — customers placed the items they wanted on a tray and then paid the cashier — allowed for a quick meal devoid of the cumbersome delay had waiters been involved. Of course, the meals available consisted mostly of ready-made sandwiches wrapped in cellophane, hot soups and fresh drinks, quite different from the fare of a typical Cuban lunch.

"Americans value time above all things," commented Ramón while looking at his Curvex watch. "They figure that by maximizing efficiency their profit margin will increase. Of course, they are correct. We have much to learn from them in that respect," he concluded.

Throughout lunch, Ramón made a verbal inventory of the items they had found that morning, and of the ones they still needed to complete the list he had in mind. Anna realized then that everything on the list was of a decorative nature, and that the furniture itself was conspicuously absent. When she mentioned this fact to Ramón, he smiled broadly, as if he had been expecting her words.

"I was waiting to see when you would mention it to me," he said with a smile. "The answer is simple. Rather than buying all the bulky items in Havana and having them shipped, I am having them made for me at home. We have some excellent cabinet makers who can make anything you want. I gave them the designs last week and all the pieces should be ready in a month. That way I will have exactly what I need, and at the same time I will be saving some money."

"That is very clever," said Anna, "I would like to see the drawings."

"Of course," said Ramón, "But you realize that I do not have them with me. Besides, I would much prefer that you saw the finished product once it is delivered, that way you can give it your seal of approval."

"That means that I would have to go back to Pinar del Río," said Anna.

"I know," answered Ramón with a smile that left no doubts that he wanted her to return.

"It hardly seems like a good enough reason for me to go back," Anna retorted, "I am sure you must have many other people who would give you an opinion."

"Of course I do," agreed Ramón, "But they are not you; it is your opinion that I value the most, that is why I asked you to help me in the first place. Otherwise we would not be here today, looking for the other items for the house."

"I am flattered," said Anna, somewhat at a loss for words when confronted with Ramón's vehement and open admission that she was, indeed, special in his eyes.

"Just let me think about it," she said noncommittally, "You know how busy I am with the restaurant."

"That is all I can ask for," he said smiling and looking straight at Anna with his dancing blue eyes.

The rest of the afternoon was spent shopping in different high-end stores. Ramón seemed to have an insatiable appetite for glass figurines, small alabaster statues or wrought iron ornaments. Toward the end of the day Anna finally put her foot down, realizing that such an excess would detract rather than enhance the looks of the new house.

"That's enough Ramón," she said firmly, "You brought me along so I could give you an opinion, so I am telling you that you have bought more than enough."

"You are right," he agreed while putting down a cut-glass candle holder from Murano, "Thank you for pointing it out to me," he said and then took Anna's hand into his own.

Although she was somewhat surprised at this unexpected gesture, she did not withdraw her hand right away, but allowed it to remain in Ramón's tender grip long enough to feel both his strength and his warmth. At that moment, as he looked into her eyes, once again she felt enveloped in that tenuous fragrance that he exuded and that always had the ability to cloud her mind, as if she were just a little tipsy after inadvertently consuming one glass too many of imported champagne. Her perception of Ramón was changing drastically; she was discovering a side of him that had not been obvious to her before. Or maybe she had just let her guard down. One thing was certain, with every passing minute she spent in his company she liked him more.

"We should go," she finally said as she withdrew her hand, "It is getting late."

"Yes, you are right," he agreed, "I will drive you back to your apartment; I am sure that you still have things to do at the restaurant."

Just as he had done that morning, rather than taking a direct route to the Pompeii, Ramón avoided the late afternoon heavy traffic and before long he was driving with all the windows down and as fast as the traffic would allow him on the Malecón. The ocean breeze, intensified by the speed of the car, made Anna's hair dance, but she did not seem to mind.

"I never get tired of looking and smelling the ocean," said Ramón, repeating what he had told Anna before. "Sometimes, when I can't sleep at night, I just lay on my bed and pretend that I am aboard a ship on its way to a remote place, and that the ocean is just feet away, on the other side of the bulkhead."

"Does it help?" asked Anna.

"No, not really. The sounds and the smells of the countryside are too strong and too different to permit my imagination to succeed at such charades. I usually end up getting up and reading for a while, or going over the accountant's ledgers until dawn catches up with me. Then I just make some black coffee and start the day."

"Maybe you should take a trip," suggested Anna, "On a ship, I mean."

"I have thought about it from time to time," confessed Ramón, "but I would not want to do it by myself," he said while momentarily taking his eyes off the road and looking directly at Anna.

"It was just a thought," she said, not acknowledging his obvious allusion.

"I would be happy," Ramón continued, "if I could just be at sea with no land in sight. It would not have to be for a prolonged period of time, you understand, but just long enough to savor the experience of being completely surrounded by the ocean."

"That is not such an unreasonable goal," said Anna, "and I am sure you have the means to carry it out."

"If you are alluding to financial means, the answer is yes," he said while letting out a small sigh, "but I lack the time and, as I just said, the right person with whom to share the experience."

"Maybe you were born to be a sailor," said Anna jokingly, trying to make light of the situation.

"We are here," said Ramón as he parked the Packard in front of the Pompeii. "I want to thank you for the day," he said while looking straight at Anna, "I could not have done it without you."

"It was my pleasure Ramón," she answered while stepping out of the car onto the busy sidewalk, without waiting for him to come around and open the door for her.

"See you tomorrow?" he asked, but Anna instinctively understood that rather than a question it was plea.

"Sure, why not? How about nine o'clock?" she said as she disappeared into the restaurant.

In subsequent months, Ramón never failed to come to Havana at least twice a month. During his stays, which usually lasted several days, he invariably called upon Anna. At first he offered the feeble excuse that there were still some things that he needed for the new house, but soon he just showed up at the Pompeii in order to see her.

Those visits offered Anna a welcome respite from the interminable lists of chores to be performed at the restaurant, and she began to rely more on Sergio, who did not mind having the extra responsibility. On those occasions when Ramón failed to appear, Anna found herself falling into a state of despondency, for she had by then become accustomed to his presence and counted on his visits to get out of the restaurant and enjoy the cultural activities that the city had to offer. From the start she had known that Ramón's interest in her went beyond a mere friendship, but being aware of his fickle tendencies, she had held her emotions in check. As the months passed, however, she felt herself slowly being drawn to him, as if being caught in a slow, yet inexorable undercurrent from which there was no escape. Their time together was filled with many long drives in the Packard, usually along the coast, and by exchanges that with every passing day and as Anna's reticence waned, became freer and filled with intimate details about their personal lives. Before long, she became aware that all her free hours were being dedicated to Ramón; in short, they had become inseparable whenever he was in the city.

A large part of this attraction, Anna also realized, was their common affinity for music and art. Unlike most Cuban men, who mostly concerned themselves about sports — especially baseball — and the latest exploits of Hollywood starlets, from the beginning Ramón showed both a proclivity and understanding of the arts that soon endeared him to her even more.

One Saturday night he showed up at the restaurant, but would not tell Anna where they were going. He expertly made his way in the Packard through the maze of streets and traffic, until he arrived in front of a building with a neoclassical façade, which Anna recognized immediately as the Teatro Nacional. This was the very building she had visited two years before with Herminio and Adriana Aguado in order to attend a performance of Vivaldi's Four Seasons.

"What are we doing here?" she asked after Ramón parked the coupé about half a block away.

"I just thought I would surprise you, that's all," he answered while producing two tickets from his shirt pocket. "They are performing Swan Lake," he continued as they walked towards the entrance, "I think you told me that you knew the music but had never seen the ballet, so this is a perfect opportunity to remedy that situation."

"Oh, Ramón, you are wonderful!" exclaimed Anna, not able to contain her excitement, then she threw her arms around his neck and kissed him on the cheek.

After that day, it was a steady schedule of visits to art exhibits and other events, so propelled by their love of the arts, it was inevitable that they would be inexorably drawn to each other. The time they spent together was not limited to visiting theaters and museums. Ramón made sure to take Anna to some of the hottest night spots in Havana, where he taught her the steps to the mambo, the latest dance craze that was sweeping the island in those days. He even took her to a late-night jam session led by Cachao, the musician credited with the invention of that dance. But regardless of where they went or what they did, at the end of the evening and sitting in the Packard, they exchanged long kisses whose passion only increased as they found a corresponding ardor in each other. One evening, after they had left a dance club, Ramón drove to a secluded spot near the ocean and parked the car.

"I have something for you," he said as he reached into his pocket.

"For me?" asked Anna, somewhat surprised.

"Yes," said Ramón as he handed her a small cardboard box wrapped in pink paper.

Rather than tearing it, she opened it slowly, with infinite care, and then removed the small lid. Inside she found what appeared to be a silver medallion set in a Y shaped bracket and whose pivot allowed it to spin freely. Engraved on one side was the silhouette of a man, on the other, that of a woman. On the small handle, also engraved on the metal, the expression *'Through Love Two Become One'* was also visible. Anna held it up to the light of the full moon, not knowing exactly its significance.

"Let me," said Ramón taking her hand in his, and with a flickering motion of the thumb and forefinger, he set the medallion in motion. As it spun on its axis, the two figures appeared to kiss.

"It is lovely Ramón," she said and, just as the silhouettes on the medallion had done an instant before, they kissed passionately.

"Anna," he whispered softly, enveloping her in his unmistakable fragrance and holding her even closer, "Will you marry me?"

VIII

The nuptials took place in the San Rosendo Cathedral of Pinar del Río, and the ceremony was officiated by the bishop himself. The wrought iron fence surrounding the building was decorated in its entirety with white roses — another one of Ramón extravagances — and its double gate proudly displayed an elaborate and gigantic wreath that squandered its chromatic combinations under the mild November sun. The joyous sound of ringing bells, coming from the twin belfries presiding over the cathedral's neoclassical style, openly announced that this was a most special day.

Although the engagement and subsequent wedding date had been widely publicized in the social pages of the local newspapers, many of the young and eligible women of the city still believed that this was just another one of Ramón's passing whims that would never come to a conclusion. In reality, they all secretly hoped that they would be the one chosen to walk with him down the aisle of the church. At the altar and under the scrutiny of countless witnesses, they would solidify and give substance to the relationship after taking the marriage vows and receiving the blessings of the bishop. Many of these women and their families, even though they had not been invited to the wedding, came anyway, just to ascertain on a first-hand basis if Ramón would actually go through with the marriage. They stood outside the cathedral; not wanting to waste their time inside waiting for a ceremony that they believed would never take place.

A few minutes after two o'clock — the appointed time for the wedding — a familiar beige sedan pulled up in front of the cathedral. Herminio Aguado emerged from the driver's seat; Adriana had also exited the car and stood next to him. In the back seat, wearing her wedding gown and a veil, Anna stepped onto the sidewalk with their help.

At once, there was an involuntary gasp of awe coming from the crowd that had gathered by the gate. Although many brides had celebrated their nuptials there, Anna was arguably one of the most beautiful. At twenty-three, her light brown hair and fair complexion seemed to glow, reflecting the soft rays of the sun that, filtered by the veil, highlighted her attractive features. Or maybe the glow she irradiated was an inner one, completely independent of the sunlight and whose source was the deep happiness she felt at that particular moment. The wedding gown itself, although an external factor, also had to be taken into account, for it had a special way of enhancing Anna's slim and youthful figure, bestowing upon her an air of elegance and sophistication without being stuffy. She had found the material in an out of the way shop in the old section of Havana, and for several months she had gone repeatedly to see a seamstress and have fittings every step of the way. The elaborate bodice, decorated with intricate designs of minute pearls, had taken many hours to complete. The detachable train, although not as long as it was customary at the time, rather than detract, increased the overall harmony of the gown. No wonder the crowd had let out a gasp of admiration. Yet, among the young women, the feeling of underlying resentment persisted, not just because Ramón had not chosen one of them for his wife, but also because he had opted for a stranger who was also a foreigner.

As Anna walked slowly through the double gate of the cathedral and then disappeared through its massive carved doors, the women, knowing that Ramón had not yet arrived, exulted in anticipation of the disappointment and humiliation Anna would suffer as she waited in vain for the groom to show. If past performance was an indication, Ramón would change his mind at the last moment.

The bells in the twin belfries repeated their joyful beckoning, while those fortunate to have been invited continued to arrive and make their way into the cathedral in anticipation of what was to be one of the most memorable weddings in the city. Although the appointed time for the ceremony had already passed, no one became alarmed. An unwritten protocol dictated that these events should be delayed at least half an hour.

Anna had been ushered into a small waiting room at the back of the church; there she would wait with Oppiano Licario, who had agreed to give the bride away, and the rest of the wedding party. The only person missing was Ramón. Once he was standing by the altar, she would walk down the aisle to meet him and exchange the marriage vows. Adriana, who was one of the women waiting with her, looked at her watch nervously, but did not say anything. The thought had also crossed her mind that Ramón might get cold feet at the last minute and leave Anna standing at the altar. "He should be here momentarily," she said in order to reassure Anna, for both women were aware of Ramón's insistence on punctuality.

Outside the mood of the crowd, now certain that the groom would not show, had taken on a circus-like atmosphere. They laughed and told jokes about how lonely the bride would be, all by herself, that special night. Some of the women even hinted that Ramón would have a great time that night, probably drinking and carrying on with some of his female friends; others, looking at their watches, decided to wait a few more minutes and then go home.

At exactly three o'clock, an hour late, a bone white Packard pulled up in front of the cathedral. Ramón Contreras emerged from behind the wheel; the expression on his face was one of deep concern. But this was not what immediately caught the eye of the bystanders. His immaculate white suit and starched shirt, along with his hands, were soiled. Later they would learn that he had had a flat tire on the way to the church. Being by himself, he had changed it as quickly as possible and then had continued on his way, since there was no time to return home to clean up and change. He rushed through the double gate of the cathedral and then ran up to the front door, hoping that Anna and the wedding party would still be inside waiting for him. He was both relieved and grateful to see the guests still seated, quietly making small conversation and waiting for the ceremony to commence.

He walked slowly, under everyone's scrutiny, to the main altar, realizing fully that they were conjecturing about his lateness and his disheveled appearance. The bishop, fully dressed in his impressive ecclesiastical garments, was more than happy to see him appear.

Anna and her party had been immediately alerted of Ramón's arrival; they also let out a sigh of relief that corroborated their secret fears that he had changed his mind at the last possible moment, thus confirming his reputation as a fickle and spoiled young man. Adriana and Ynaca Eco gave a final inspection to Anna's gown, straightened her veil and placed in her hands a bouquet of fresh white orchids meant as an offering she would place at the feet of the Virgin Mary after the ceremony.

As Anna emerged from the waiting room at the back of the church, all eyes shifted from the groom to the bride. The contrast could not have been more dramatic. While he appeared unkempt and dirty, the adjectives that Anna evoked as the guests gazed upon her were radiant, beautiful, or even divine. Yes, everyone in attendance knew they were fortunate to have been invited, for without a doubt this would prove to be one of the more memorable weddings in recent times.

Anna walked down the aisle holding on to the arm of Oppiano Licario. Everyone scrutinized her face, looking for faint signs of anguish or despair caused by Ramón's failure to appear on time, or by the unexplained appearance of his clothes. But at that moment all they could find reflected on Anna's face was the joy of the moment, a serenity engendered by the knowledge that in a matter of minutes her life would be joined with that of Ramón Contreras, the most eligible bachelor in Pinar del Río and probably the most handsome as well. She felt, indeed, fortunate. They were both young, good looking and were ready to forge a bright future together in the years to come.

As they reached the altar, they stopped directly in front of the bishop, who then delivered the customary question. 'Who gives this woman away in marriage?' to which Licario answered 'I do.' As the ceremony proceeded, it was Ramón's turn to stand next to Anna for the exchange of the vows. At this point, from the back of the church an anonymous guest was heard crying involuntarily, so deeply had she been touched by the beauty and sanctity of the moment. After receiving a final blessing, now as man and wife, Anna placed the offering of orchids at the feet of the Virgin and then, holding on to Ramón's arm, walked out of the church. Without exception, everyone in attendance agreed that they made a perfect couple and augured a bright future together for them. After all, they had everything anyone could possible want.

Outside the cathedral, the photographer who had been hired for the event was already waiting. First he took some candid shots of the bride and groom, then of the entire wedding party. This, of course, was just a preamble to the real work, when he worked his magic and made everyone—especially the bride and groom—look their very best. Once the guests had exited the church and had dispersed into the street, he began to position the bride and groom—first by themselves and then surrounded by the wedding party—for different shots with the double doors of the cathedral as a background. Although Ramón's suit, now under the bright light of the late afternoon showed every wrinkle and every smudge, contrasting even more sharply with Anna's immaculate white gown, no one seemed to object. It was just a minor detail that would not detract from the festive mood of the day. At that moment Anna had to think of her wedding to Giacomo six years earlier, how she had refused to have any of his friends in attendance, and how she had posed reluctantly for the photographer in front of the Santa Chiara Church in Naples, but only as a minor concession to her husband on their wedding day. But now, standing in front of the San Rosendo cathedral in Pinar del Río, under the bright light of the Cuban sky, all those memories seemed faded and distant, as if those events had taken place in another life she had lived a hundred years before.

Once the photographer was satisfied that he had all the pictures he needed, the bride and groom walked to the Packard followed by the wedding party and other guests. They were on their way to the Rumayor Club, where the reception would be held. The lavish affair, of course, had been Ramón's idea. Not only did he want his friends there, but also those men with whom he did business, for he believed that being invited would strengthen his influence with them and increase his chances of favorable transactions in the future. The extravagant reception, Ramón reasoned, would also be the perfect setting to introduce his wife to his circle of friends and acquaintances.

They left the church under an intense shower of white rice that the well wishers threw from every direction, until they took refuge in the Packard and sped away, followed by their guests. Driving as skillfully as ever, Ramón left the city behind. As they turned off the main highway and turned onto the lane that led to the main pavilion of the Rumayor, Anna heard the music through the open window. A live orchestra had been hired for the occasion, and they had started to play for those guests who had arrived while the bride and groom were still having their picture taken.

As Ramón parked the car, Anna could not help but notice that the place was a lot more crowded than the time she had been there a year before with Adriana Aguado. She told herself immediately that Ramón Contreras did not get married every day, and she had learned that he did not do anything half way. Surely there would be many such surprises during their married life.

When the couple entered the main pavilion, arm in arm, there was a spontaneous burst of applause from the guests. The orchestra, acknowledging their arrival, stopped playing a popular song then in vogue and seamlessly made a transition into the wedding march. From that point and without pause they started to play The Blue Danube, perhaps the best-known waltz by Straus. Ramón took Anna into his arms and the couple started to dance; everyone had cleared the floor and they glided gracefully under the admiring gaze of everyone present. It was at this point that Anna became fully conscious that she was, indeed, now married to Ramón Contreras.

The year leading to this particular moment, however, had not been as smooth as the music and the gracefulness of the dancers on the floor suggested. After accepting Ramón's marriage proposal on that evening when he presented her with the spinning medallion, Anna began to realize that there were many details, legal, financial and personal, to be considered. In the solitude of her upstairs apartment, she placed Immortal Arias on the turntable and allowed the incomparable voice of Louis d'Amio to bring a sense of order into the chaotic whirlwind of loose ends that would have to be resolved before the wedding could take place.

First of all there was the matter of her status with the Cuban immigration officials. Still affixed to her Italian passport was the card proclaiming: Temporary Permit. At the bottom of the card was Oppiano Licario's signature as the Cuban citizen who had vouched for her during her stay on the island. Now that she intended to marry, her status would have to be formalized, either by becoming a permanent resident or applying for Cuban citizenship. She made a mental note to visit the same lawyer who had handled the purchase of the restaurant from Antonio Gamboa. Although it might take a little time, this matter could certainly be rectified. The fact that she was marrying a Cuban citizen — especially one as prominent as Ramón — would undoubtedly expedite matters.

Second, and probably more difficult, was the matter of the Pompeii. Since its opening, the restaurant had become one of the favorite spots of Havana's emerging middle class. They enjoyed the superb Italian cuisine, the attention to detail, and the top notch service. Closing down the business, in Anna's mind, was unthinkable. Too much planning, work and endless hours in the kitchen with Sergio had gone into its creation. Besides, the fate of all the employees had to be considered. They were counting on their jobs to support their families. Finding no immediate answer, she decided to discuss it with Ramón; maybe he could offer a viable solution to the problem.

The third matter to be attended to — not an unexpected hurdle — was the preparations for the wedding itself. Perhaps the main impediment was the fact that she lived and worked in Havana and the wedding would take place in Pinar del Río, over a hundred miles away. Ramón had assured her that he would handle the details concerning the church arrangements — he purposely failed to mention that the wedding would take place in the cathedral and that ceremony would be presided by the bishop himself — and those of the reception. They both agreed that the Rumayor Club would be an ideal setting, since it had the ability to accommodate a large number of guests and was located just a few miles outside the city. Its exclusivity also appealed to Ramón, who always insisted on having the best of everything.

On her end, Anna had to find a suitable gown and assemble a wedding party. Not wanting to purchase a ready-made dress, but have one made, placed an extra sense of urgency on the preparations; the wedding was just three months away. It was too bad, she thought, that Francesca was not there. Just as she had done when Anna married Giacomo, she would not have allowed anyone else to make a wedding gown for her daughter. This small problem was accidentally solved one Friday afternoon, when she mentioned to Sergio that she could not find anyone to make a dress for her.

"You are not looking in the right place," he told her while stirring one of his creations. "My cousin has a small shop in the old section of Havana. Go and see her and she will take care of whatever you need." It appeared that Sergio had cousins everywhere. The following afternoon, Anna took a taxi to the address that Sergio had given her. As they left the more modern sections of Havana, the driver made an abrupt turn at the Plaza de Armas. The streets suddenly became narrow, their surface more irregular, for they were no longer riding on smooth asphalt, but on the cobblestones that had been laid during colonial times.

The address that Sergio had written on a piece of paper corresponded to a rather nondescript doorway that lacked any sign that would indicate the existence of a business within. She paid the driver, and using the brass knocker in the shape of a clenched fist, Anna made her presence known. After a few minutes—for a moment Anna feared that there would be no one home—the door opened. A middle-aged woman, wearing a white dress and bedroom slippers appeared in the threshold. Anna introduced herself, and mentioned that Sergio had sent her. Upon hearing his name, the woman smiled and asked Anna to come in.

The ample room was filled with mannequins sporting dresses in different stages of completion. Anna explained that she was to be married in three months and she needed someone to make a wedding gown for her; she had brought some preliminary sketches of what she had in mind. At this point she reached into her pocketbook and handed the seamstress several sheets of paper. After adjusting her glasses, the woman nodded her head affirmatively and said that it could be done, but also explained—she pointed with a circular motion to the unfinished work in the room—that she had other obligations to meet. It was agreed then that Anna would return in a week, to discuss the design after she had a chance to examine it in detail, and to take some preliminary measurements. So for the next two months, every Friday afternoon, Anna made her way to the remote shop in the colonial section of Havana, to watch and participate in the gradual and arduous process involved in the creation of the gown she had conceived. Not only were cutting and fitting involved, but also the painstaking process of creating the intricate design that would grace the bodice of the gown with minute pearls that had to be affixed to the cloth one by one. Just a week before the wedding, at the beginning of November, the gown was finished. During that final fitting, when Anna saw herself reflected in the full length mirror that the seamstress kept on the premises, tears came to her eyes. Not only was the dress all that she had imagined, but at that moment, she realized how much she needed Francesca.

During these months, Anna had also visited the lawyer to make sure her legal status would not impede the progress of her plans. Of course, this was not the first immigration case that he had handled, and he assured Anna that her status would soon be that of a legal resident of the country. After all, she was marrying a Cuban citizen, her presence on the island had been sponsored by Oppiano Licario and she had a well-established business that employed people and paid taxes. In short, he concluded, it was a mere formality.

The matter of assembling a wedding party had not been that complicated. Since Ramón was handling the arrangements with the church and the reception, all that Anna needed were two maids of honor and a man who would give her away. Having so few close friends in Cuba made the choice an easy task. She would ask Adriana and Ynaca Eco to serve as maids and Oppiano could give her away. Once the decision was made, she contacted everyone involved. Upon hearing the news, they all congratulated Anna and agreed to participate in the ceremony.

The only matter that remained unresolved was that of the Pompeii. From the beginning Anna had made up her mind that she would not sell the restaurant, but running a business that required constant attention from Pinar del Río, over a hundred miles away, was impossible. During one of Ramón's frequent visits to Havana, she discussed all the possibilities with him, but in the end, no matter how hard they tried, they could not find a feasible solution.

In the middle of October, just a month before the wedding, Sergio came into Anna's office. By the expression on his face — Anna had learned to read all signs — she immediately sensed that he had come because something serious was on his mind. At that point, being as efficient and knowledgeable as he was, he seldom bothered her with the minor decisions that had to be made in the kitchen.

"I need to speak with you," he said, "Do you have a few minutes?"

"Of course. Sit down," Anna said pointing to a chair across from her desk, still without a clue as to what Sergio had in mind.

"In a month you will be getting married," he said, stating what everyone knew; in fact, he was one of the few people in Havana who had received an invitation to the wedding. "There is no way you can run the Pompeii from Pinar del Río, and I know you do not want to sell it." At this point he stopped, allowing his words to sink in.

"So what do you suggest I do?" asked Anna.

"You could make me a full partner in this venture," said Sergio decisively, "That way the restaurant will continue in good hands and you will not lose anything. You would simply be sharing the profits with me."

What Sergio suggested was, indeed, a most logical course of action. Anna could check in from time to time during her visits to Havana and she would still have part ownership of the business. The only reason that she had not considered this idea before was because she did not believe that Sergio had the initial capital investment in order to buy half of the restaurant. It was not until years later that she was to find out that Ramón was behind it all. He had lent Sergio the money to remove the last obstacle that stood in the way.

He must have guessed what was going on in her mind, for he immediately approached the subject of money. "I have been saving my money, so I am prepared to pay for my share of the business. I believe that this is a good solution that will work for both of us," he repeated what he had said just a few minutes before.

"What you propose is a most interesting solution; just give me a few days and I will have a definitive answer for you."

"Of course," he said while standing up, "but don't forget that the wedding is just around the corner. I don't want anything to change here at the Pompeii."

"I know," said Anna smiling, "We can talk again in few days."

That weekend, while riding with Ramón in the Packard along the Malecón, Anna told him about the proposal that Sergio had made. Ramón did not say anything right away, but kept his eyes on the road. For a few minutes the ocean breeze coming through the window played with his black hair, making it execute an unlikely dance.

"I suppose that would take care of our last worry," he finally said, "You would not have to sell the restaurant and you would be assured that it will continue to be run the way you want. The only drawback, of course, is that your profit margin will be cut in half."

"You know that for me the Pompeii has been a labor of love; besides, I will have Sergio's money." Anna did not mention that besides the profits from the restaurant, she still had left some of the money that she had brought from Italy three years before.

"You will also have my money," added Ramón with a smile. "I think you should go ahead and sell half the business to Sergio. It will give us an excuse to get away and come to Havana often, so you can keep an eye on things."

"I will take care of everything tomorrow," she said and threw her arms around Ramón's neck and kissed him on the cheek.

"You'll make me lose control of the car," he protested in a joking tone as he slowed down, "I you are not careful you will become a widow before you become a bride," he admonished her. They both laughed at Ramón's comment, for they foresaw many happy years together after the upcoming wedding.

Once back at her apartment above the Pompeii, Anna placed Immortal Arias on the turntable and, while looking at the Prado below and listening to Louis d'Amio's incomparable voice, she contemplated a bright future that was beginning to unfold: she was young, beautiful, owned her own business and was about to marry Ramón Contreras, a handsome and wealthy bachelor from the city of Pinar del Río. To expect more from life would certainly be an act of hubris. But that feeling of complete elation was also tinged by one of unrelenting remorse. She had managed to make a successful life for herself in this new land, but no matter how hard she tried, those beautiful images of an anticipated future as a married woman of means, were always marred by the horrific images of imminent death and destruction brought about by the war in Europe. Louis' voice, paradoxically, brought her closer to her fondest memories of a happy childhood and simultaneously to the stark and inescapable reality that her entire family had been suddenly and violently wiped out in a single day.

As usual, she told herself that there was nothing she could do, that the dreadful events precipitated by the war were beyond her control. It was not her fault that she had survived. She shifted her thoughts to the wedding, anticipating the day—as she had done so many times before—and tried to visualize every single detail.

That night, Anna slept better than she had in a long time; all the hurdles that separated her from her wedding day had been removed. All she had to do now was wait. The following morning, she told Sergio that she was ready to accept his offer. To say that he was elated would be an understatement, for all he had dreamed about during his youth was to be the owner of a restaurant. Within the week, they visited the lawyer's office and the preliminary documents were drawn. Anna also returned to the old section of Havana for a final fitting of her wedding gown.

As the date of the ceremony approached, despite the fact that everything of consequence had been resolved, Anna found herself becoming more nervous and impatient. Although she should have felt more at ease, logic did not prevail. She finally concluded that these were normal wedding jitters and that everything would disappear once she and Ramón were husband and wife.

The only detail that Anna had overlooked was how she would travel from Havana to Pinar del Río. Although it was easy enough to take a bus or ride in one of the many cars that made the daily trip, she did not look forward to the prospect. A week before the wedding, Oppiano and Ynaca Eco Licario came into the Pompeii. It was a casual visit; they wanted to see Anna and at the same time enjoy the superb Italian cuisine that the establishment had to offer. It was inevitable that Anna should join them, for they were the closest friends she had in the city and she could not forget how Oppiano had helped her during her arrival in Cuba. It was during this dinner that Ynaca Eco mentioned that they would be driving to Pinar del Río several days before the wedding. They wanted to take advantage of the opportunity and visit other places, the Valley of Viñales in particular, one of the most beautiful places in Cuba, since it was only a short distance from the city of Pinar del Río. They had already made reservations at the nearby San Vicente Hotel, famous for its sulfurous waters whose reputed curative powers were commonly acknowledged.

So it was agreed that Anna would ride with the Licarios to Pinar del Río, where she would stay with Herminio and Adriana Aguado until the day of her marriage to Ramón. Everything would fall right into place and no one had to be inconvenienced in any way, since the Licarios were traveling to that city anyway.

Just as they had planned, the three of them left Havana a few days before the wedding. Oppiano drove straight through, often making comments about the different towns along the way. Of course, he also commented on the former splendor of the Angerona coffee plantation and on the cruel fate that had befallen Cornelious Souchay and Ursula Lambert due to the intolerance so prevalent in Cuban society during their time. By his comments Anna deduced that Oppiano was quite familiar with the history of the island, but that his knowledge went beyond historical facts and that he interpreted correctly the dilemmas and tribulations of those individuals whose lives had now become — at least for most people — mere names lacking in depth and buried in dusty history books or moth ridden archives.

As they entered the city of Pinar del Río, besides providing some information about the early settlement and the tobacco industry, Oppiano also made the comment about taking back to Havana a few bottles of Guayabita, that aromatic and scarce liquor native to the province. Before long they passed Independence Park, with its majestic gazebo and statues of the founding fathers and heroes of the Cuban revolutionary war against Spain, and continued to the Aguado's house. Although Oppiano Licario had never been there, he did not have any problem finding the place with the directions provided by Anna.

The familiar beige sedan was parked in its usual spot in front of the house; the dog that guarded the place came out from the coolness of one of the flowerbeds, where he had been resting, and started to bark so as to alert the owners that some strangers had arrived. As they exited the car, Oppiano said something that Anna did not quite understand. The dog stopped barking and came to him, wagging his tail, as if he were friend he had not seen for a long time and had momentarily failed to recognize.

"They have a language of their own," explained Oppiano as he petted the dog and then opened the trunk of the car in order to remove Anna's suitcases. There was also a large box where Anna's wedding gown, after a final fitting, had been carefully stored.

"My brother has always had a way with animals," explained Ynaca Eco, "When we were children dogs and cats used to follow him everywhere."

"I am not surprised," commented Anna. By then, after knowing the Licarios for almost three years, she had learned that they were not like most Cubans she had met, that they were in possession of ancient and esoteric knowledge that bestowed upon them that air of practical wisdom that always seemed to surround them.

The door of the house opened and Adriana Aguado came out to greet them. Anna introduced them and Adriana invited them in for coffee, while explaining that her husband was at his office in town. Although the Aguados had never met the Licarios, because of Anna, they were aware that Oppiano was in the same Danish freighter that had brought her to Cuba and that he had vouched for her when they landed at Tricornia.

After bringing in the suitcases, they sat at the table in the huge room that Anna remembered so well; from out of nowhere, Dolores appeared holding a tray with freshly brewed coffee. Anna said hello and she smiled, then disappeared as silently as she had come. "Anna tells me that you helped her with Cuban immigration on the day of her arrival," said Adriana.

"It was nothing," answered Oppiano, dismissing the comment as if what he had done had not been important at all.

"It wasn't just that," insisted Anna, cognizant that the Licarios were in the habit of helping others without any ulterior motives, "If it hadn't been for Oppiano and Ynaca Eco I would not have opened the Pompeii. It was all their idea."

"We just offered some possibilities," explained Ynaca Eco, "Anna took the initiative; it was the least we could do."

"At any rate," concluded Anna, "I am glad they did; the Pompeii has been a great success."

At that point, the conversation turned towards the upcoming wedding. Adriana commented that Anna and Ramón had met in that very room, during a celebration for the completion of his new house, and how he had literally forced his way into Anna's life by offering to take her back to Havana a few days later. She also mentioned how efficient a businessman Ramón was, and how he had taken care of all the wedding preparations while Anna was in Havana.

The one topic that the Licarios carefully avoided during the visit, lest they cast a somber mood on the visit, was that of the war in Europe. Aware that Anna and Adriana came from Italy, they felt it best to keep the conversation on the light side, even though they were abreast of all the latest developments in the front. After a second cup of coffee, Oppiano looked at his watch and announced that it was time for them to leave, since the still had to drive to Viñales. Adriana and Anna walked them to their car, wished them a good trip and waited until the car disappeared. Then they returned to the house and continued their conversation about those last-minute details about the wedding. Anna had made a mental list of those details, and as she enumerated them to Adriana, the latter assured her that Ramón had taken care of it all. She reminded Anna that she was not the only one getting married, and that Ramón was rather fastidious about his reputation, so he wanted everything to be perfect. It all made sense, thought Anna; if there was one thing that she had learned about him during the past year was his insistence on small details.

Even though everything had been done, Anna could not help but feel a vague sense of nervousness, as if something vital had been overlooked and no matter how hard she tried that detail eluded her. She had certainly not felt like this before marrying Giacomo; her nervousness then was clearly attributable to the fact that she was an inexperienced seventeen-year old about to marry a man in his fifties.

Adriana, being older and more experienced, accurately diagnosed Anna's mood as a common case of wedding jitters. In order to distract her, she drove Anna to different places around Pinar del Río, including a tobacco factory, where the workers assembled the cigars by hand one at the time while listening to the official reader, a person whose job was to read aloud to the workers while they rolled the cigars. It made the time go faster and at the same time everyone became familiar with the great works of literature.

The night before the wedding, the Aguados invited Anna and Ramón for dinner. Dolores had prepared arroz con pollo, a favorite Cuban dish that besides rice and chicken also incorporated peas, red pimentos and other spices. Ramón, as usual, arrived right on time. He was carrying a bottle of Bordeaux imported from California, and apologized for not bringing a European wine. But no apologies were necessary for everyone was aware, although they did not voice it, of the precarious situation in France and Italy.

During the meal, Anna exhibited a particularly jovial mood. The nervousness of the past days had completely waned; she ate heartily and drank a generous portion of the wine that Ramón had brought with him, and by the end of the evening, over coffee and desert, she was laughing at some of the amusing stories being told by Ramón.

Around ten thirty Ramón looked at his solid gold Gruen and announced that he was ready to go home. He thanked the Aguados for the meal and the hospitality and then stood up. "Tomorrow is a big day," he said, "We should all be rested." The group walked him to the door, and before getting in the Packard he kissed Anna lightly on the lips. "Good night," he said and then he was gone.

Ramón's suggestion about being rested for the next day made absolute sense, so Anna also thanked the Aguados and retired to the room she had occupied during her previous visit to their house. She felt fortunate to have such good friends. Once in bed, with the lights out and the sounds of the nocturnal insects coming in through the window, she felt beyond the reach of nervousness and unfounded apprehension. Everything had been carefully planned, so there was no cause for concern. The morning would bring with it the start of her new life. With that certainty in her mind, she fell asleep.

The soft knocking the following morning brought her back to consciousness. From the other side of the door she heard Adriana's voice announcing that it was time for breakfast. Anna answered that she would be there momentarily and then got up. Ten minutes later, she came into the room where the Aguados took their meals. Dolores, because of the special day, had prepared a hearty breakfast that went well beyond the mere coffee, bread and fresh fruit. She had also prepared scrambled eggs, ham, and freshly squeezed orange juice. Anna realized that there would be no time for lunch that day—Cubans devoted two hours to that meal—due to the final preparations for her wedding. After saying good morning she sat down and served herself a generous portion of everything that Dolores had prepared. She was truly hungry, and Dolores' cooking made everything taste even better.

At the end of the meal, Herminio excused himself and retired to his study. He realized that the rest of the morning would be spent on Anna's hair, make up and dressing for the ceremony, so it was best for him to stay out of the way. The two women went to Anna's room, where her wedding gown had been hanging for the past two days. Adriana had with her a box with different creams, rouges and lipstick, as well as a wide assortment of combs and brushes. She had acquired these beauty products—she explained—during different visits to Paris with Herminio. Once again Anna felt most fortunate to have Adriana as a friend, especially in Pinar del Río, where there were no other Italians.

By one o'clock they were finished. After taking a final look in the mirror, Anna came out into the large room with the table and bookcases, and Adriana went to alert her husband that it was time to leave for the church. When Herminio came into the room he was visibly impressed, for he stopped for a moment to admire Anna in her wedding gown.

"You are one of the most beautiful brides I have ever seen," he said in Italian. Anna realized that these were not merely hollow words, but that he meant what he said. She also realized that he had not said the most beautiful bride, since that place would surely be occupied by Adriana.

"You are most kind," she answered and she also realized that she was blushing.

As they were about to leave, Dolores came into the room. She stood silently, admiring Anna's radiant beauty.

"Señor Contreras is a very lucky man," she said and then returned to the kitchen.During the trip to the church, Herminio and Adriana kept the windows in the car almost closed, lest the wind undo all the work involved in doing Anna's hair and veil. Although Herminio was not driving very fast, they knew that they would arrive at the church with time to spare. When they approached the building, Anna was surprised by the number of white roses that decorated the iron fence that surrounded the cathedral, and even more so at the gigantic wreath that graced its entrance. For an instant she thought that Ramón had gone overboard, but then she told herself that at this point nothing that he did should surprise her.

Outside the cathedral a throng had gathered. This was truly surprising to Anna; although she was well aware of Ramón's high social standing, she failed to understand why so many people who had not been invited to the wedding would want to stand outside the church. She also noticed that they were mostly young women.

At exactly five minutes after two, Anna exited the car and walked to the entrance escorted by Herminio and Adriana. A collective murmur rose from the crowd, acknowledging that they were in the presence of one of the most beautiful brides that had ever graced the San Rosendo Cathedral. In a small room at the back of the church Oppiano and Ynaca Eco Licario were already waiting; they greeted Anna effusively and commented on how beautiful she looked, but at that moment, always aware of Ramón's punctuality, she was more concerned with the start of the ceremony. She asked if he had arrived, but Oppiano informed her that he was not at the church yet.

Not wanting to unduly alarm Anna, Ynaca Eco and Adriana began a final inspection of the gown, starting with the soft folds of the veil and concluding with the flowing satin of the long train. While this was going on, Herminio and Oppiano kept a watchful eye for the groom.

By two thirty everyone in the wedding party was becoming concerned. Adriana kept looking at her watch, secretly thinking that Ramón had changed his mind. Everyone else made comments about the church, the flower arrangements, or Anna's beautiful wedding gown, but no one expressed a concern about Ramón's absence. It was as if by ignoring the problem it would magically disappear, and everything would be restored to what was meant to be its original outcome. The attending guests, simultaneously clueless and intrigued by the absence of the groom, conjectured openly as to the possible causes of the delay.

A few minutes before three o'clock, to everyone's relief, Ramón arrived at the church and hurriedly made its way to the front of the main altar, where the bishop had been waiting. The deplorable state of his clothes—wrinkled and soiled—further fueled the wild speculations as to what had detained him on such an important day.

But as Anna walked down the aisle escorted by Oppiano Licario, she did not think of Ramón's unexplained tardiness or the fact that his white suit was less than presentable. At that moment she felt beautiful, completely alive, and confident in a future based on the fact that in a few short minutes she would become the wife of Ramón Contreras.

Following the reception at the Rumayor Club, the new couple had decided to drive to Havana. The next morning they would be flying to Miami to spend their honeymoon at the beach. After changing their clothes they danced, ate, and accepted the congratulations and well wishes from all the guests in attendance. Eventually it was time to leave. As it was customary, they were showered — for the second time that day — with handfuls of rice as they made their way to the Packard. The grains of rice, in Anna's mind, symbolized all the joyful and plentiful days that lay ahead in the company of Ramón, a man who appeared to be devoted to her in every way.

The trip to Havana was an uneventful one. Being usually dry during the month of November and finding little traffic on the central highway at that hour, gave Ramón the opportunity to unleash the horses under the hood of the coupé. They did not stop to eat—they had had more than enough during the reception—so the trip was relatively a short one. They arrived in front of the Hotel Nacional—undoubtedly the best and most exclusive in Havana—a little after ten o'clock. After checking in, a bellboy took their suitcases and led then to a room on the fifth floor. Its ample balcony allowed the ocean breeze to come into the room, and its panoramic construction was clearly meant for the sole purpose of taking in its entirety the view of the bay below. In the distance Anna could see clearly the lights from the colony of Regla on the other side of the bay. Ramón could not have chosen a more perfect setting for their first night together, she thought. On a side table, resting in a silver bucket of crushed ice, the neck of a bottle of champagne was visible. He had thought of everything.

Although she had been married before, Anna was understandably nervous on that first night. She realized that every relationship was different, as every man is different, and that the first night with Ramón would set the tone of the days to come.

She felt his embrace from behind, and without breaking it, she turned around and put her arms around his neck. They kissed passionately for what seemed an eternity, then Ramón broke the embrace gently and started to open the bottle of champagne. After a few moments the cork, aided by the pressurized gasses inside, was ejected with a loud popping sound. A bubbly cascade materialized, but Anna was ready and she caught the liquid in the goblets she was holding. They laughed simultaneously and eagerly drank the champagne as they kissed again. They drank some more and talked about the events of the day, and how fortunate they both were to have found each other. Soon the bottle was empty; it was time for bed.

Anna went into the bathroom to change; when she came back into the room a few minutes later the lights were already out and Ramón was in bed. Through the open doors that led to the balcony the soft light of the November moon made everything in the room acquire a silvery tone. Once she got in bed the room seemed to spin slowly—perhaps she had drunk too much champagne too quickly—but then it seemed to settle down. In the semidarkness she felt Ramón moving closer to her, then his hand reaching out and caressing her hair. Before long she also felt his breath on her neck as he began to kiss her and to explore her body, timidly at first, but more boldly as Anna encouraged him with her own caresses. Their youthful exuberance could not be suppressed, so it did not take long for them to be locked in a passionate embrace in which their clothes, as scant as they were, became but an impediment to the culmination of their desire and were soon carelessly discarded. Years later, as Anna remembered that wedding night, what would stand out in her mind would not be the physical bond that would be forged that night, but Ramón's unique fragrance. It permeated everything almost to the point of saturation, creating the believable illusion that the room possessed an atmosphere of its own, completely isolated and independent from the rest of the world. At dawn, after a brief period of sleep, Anna felt Ramón's urgent call again. They made passionate love once more, continuing the slow yet pleasurable way of discovering ways of pleasing the other. That continuous exploration guided by Eros, they hoped, would last a lifetime. Once their passion was satisfied, they fell asleep again, only to be awakened abruptly by the sound of the alarm clock. It was time to get up, and get ready for the trip to the airport.

After a quick breakfast in the hotel dining room, they were on their way. It was a beautiful day, and the oppressive heat that was usually present had not materialized yet. Ramón took advantage of the light traffic, as he usually did, to propel the Packard at a high rate of speed on the open highway. Before long they reached the airport, and after parking the car and retrieving the suitcases from the trunk, they walked to the to the ticket counter in order to verify they travel arrangements and to check in their luggage. Ramón — as efficient as ever — had foreseen everything. They received their seating assignments and then made their way to the gate and into the plane. Since neither one had traveled by air before, they were both excited at the prospect and glad that they would be sharing the experience together.

The deep rumble of the engines was suddenly heard; a stewardess reminded the passengers to buckle their seatbelts. As the plane gained speed on the runway, Anna held on tightly to Ramón's hand. Then they were off the ground, circling the city as they gained altitude and the pilot chartered a course to the north. Through the window they recognized some of the more prominent buildings of the city, until they were occluded from view as the plane went through a thick bank of clouds. Then it was nothing but ocean below and the occasional cloud above. Since there were no visible landmarks, Anna had the impression that the plane was not moving, that somehow it was just suspended in midair. This impression, however, was short lived, for within minutes she felt an indescribable sensation in her stomach as the plane began its descent over the city of Miami. She looked at her watch and realized that they had crossed the strait of Florida in less than an hour.

Going through customs took a lot less time than she had anticipated. The officer checked the date of their passports to make sure they were not expired, compared the photographs to the actual faces before him and them stamped one of the pages with a rubber seal that showed the port of entry and the date. It was that simple. After retrieving their bags, they took a taxi to the hotel.

"Miami Beach is a separate city from Miami," explained Ramón, "they are joined by a series of bridges."

"That is very interesting," said Anna, but she was busy looking at the landscape. Being as used as she was to the colonial buildings of Havana, she realized immediately that the architecture was of recent construction, an obvious clue that the city had not been developed until much later.

Within minutes the taxi was speeding down Biscayne Boulevard, and then onto one of the bridges that connected the two cities. The ocean breeze came in through the open windows, bringing with it the smell of the nearby ocean. Eventually it came to a stop in front of a corner building that faced the ocean. Above the entrance the name Cardozo Hotel was prominently displayed.

"This hotel was built just a few years ago," explained Ramón as he paid the driver, "A friend of mine recommended it because it faces the ocean." Ramón was correct in his description. The Cardozo Hotel, along with many others built during the thirties and early forties, was located on the street appropriately named Ocean Drive. The guests had only to cross the street and they were right on the beach. There was a piano bar right in the lobby as well as an adjacent restaurant, thus providing the visitors with all the amenities necessary for a pleasant stay.

After checking in at the front desk, Anna and Ramón climbed one flight of stairs to their second story room. Anna was both surprised and pleased that, since it was located in the corner of the building, it resembled more a small apartment than a typical hotel room. The panoramic window offered them an unobstructed view of the ocean and the beach below. Once again Anna thought that Ramón had considered every detail in order to make this honeymoon an ideal one. It would be hard to imagine a more idyllic setting to start a life together.

"Let's go for a walk," she said, "I want to see everything."

"Of course," said Ramón, but before leaving the room he embraced Anna and kissed her passionately, a preamble to the unforgettable days and nights that were soon to follow.

After leaving the hotel they strolled aimlessly along Ocean Drive, just watching the people and admiring the art deco architecture that seemed to be springing up everywhere. They also wandered in and out of the small shops so prevalent on Collins Avenue; there Anna bought a straw hat, dark glasses and some Coppertone lotion that would protect her from the sun during their visits to the beach. Eventually, they went into a small restaurant and sat down for a quiet and intimate meal. At that moment, away from everything and protected by the cloak of anonymity, Anna felt truly happy. Ramón, too, seemed more relaxed, as if the world outside had ceased to intrude in his private life. She also noticed that he had left his Curvex watch at the hotel, a clear sign that he wanted to share these days with her unencumbered by an unemotional and relentless reminder of the passing of time.

On the way back to the hotel — dusk had turned into night — rather than using the sidewalk, they took off their shoes and walked along the shore hand in hand. From the darkness of the beach, they could see the brightly lit hotels, like a luminous necklace that graced the city. Below, the soft splashing of the waves and the feel of the wet sand on their feet made the experience seem more real. From time to time they stopped to kiss and caress each other; eventually, from the darkness of the beach they saw the sign above the entrance of the hotel; it was now illuminated by a bluish light whose source had been cleverly concealed. They noticed that the other hotels on either side of the Cardozo—the Netherland and the Carlisle—employed the same method of illumination, but with different color lights. It made the combination of façades more distinctive and readily identifiable at night, while imparting the entire strip of hotels along Ocean Drive a most unique appearance.

That first night in Miami Beach the couple retired early. In the privacy of their room, they turned off all the lights and opened the panoramic windows that faced the ocean. The same source of light that illuminated the hotel name painted the walls of the room a pale blue, turning everything the same soft hue. In the darkness once again Anna felt Ramón's warm breath and lips on her face, while his hands slowly caressed her body and gently undressed her, until all the impediments to their growing passion lay strewn on the bed. They made love slowly, cognizant that they had all the time in the world, that with every caress each learned more about the other and that this was just the beginning of their mutual exploration. After they finished, they kissed and then fell asleep in each other's arms. At dawn, as he had done the night before, Ramón woke her again with kisses and caresses that soon ignited their passion once again.

The next five days settled into a routine: they rose early, and after having breakfast at the hotel, they went to the beach. Afternoons were devoted to shopping and during the evenings they usually went to the movies or to one of the many clubs available. Anna was surprised that the mambo was also popular here, so she and Ramón had the opportunity to practice what they had learned in different Havana clubs during their courtship. Then it was back to the hotel, where they invariably made love with the open windows, under the soft illumination provided by the sign of the hotel.

Even though it was not Anna's intention to compare Ramón to the other men she had known, from the beginning she realized that their approach to lovemaking was completely different. Paolo, because of his youth and inexperience, had been impetuous and awkward; he had surrendered himself without hesitations during every encounter. This had been possible, Anna realized, because they were sharing a first love, and they were learning the way together. Giacomo's approach, on the other hand, had always been soft and tender, always guided by the knowledge that because of its fragility, love was a most precious commodity. Despite his age he also had shown a certain amount of insecurity, which Anna attributed to those countless years he had lived as a bachelor taking care of his mother. Then there was Ramón, always eager to please. It had not taken long for Anna to realize that his lovemaking was that of a man in full command of his virility: arduous, passionate and without insecurities of any kind.

During their beach outings, even though the November sun was not as strong as it would have been in earlier months, Anna wore the straw hat and dark glasses she had bought the first day. Before and after going in the water—which they both found a little cold—she applied a generous layer of Coppertone to her face and arms. Already conscious that one of her responsibilities as a wife was to look after Ramón, she also covered his face, shoulders and chest with the same protective cream in order to shield his fair complexion from the sun.

As they lay on identical beach towels next to each other, holding hands, Anna closed her eyes. As her thoughts drifted she considered her good fortune, but also how far she was from Italy, from everything and everyone she had ever loved. She kept telling herself that these days were precious, that soon they would be returning to Cuba and begin to settle into a comfortable routine of married life.

Those thoughts were soon dispelled as she felt Ramón's hand tugging gently, an unspoken signal that they should go swimming and then return to the hotel for a quick shower and lunch. The sun was directly overhead, so they took advantage of the warmth and went into the calm waters and embraced. Anna was still wearing her straw hat, but Ramón took it off and then kissed her. That afternoon, after returning to the hotel, they skipped lunch and made love and then fell asleep.

Their last night in Miami Beach was a Saturday, so they decided it should be a fun one. After inquiring at the desk about the different possibilities the city had to offer, they decided to go to one of the many clubs that had sprung up along Ocean Drive. For the occasion Anna put on a bright red dress and high heel shoes; Ramón wore a white suit and two-tone shoes. Because of their light complexion and their sophisticated demeanor, they could have easily passed for a wealthy couple from New England escaping the cold and taking a vacation in a more temperate climate.

The club, according to the directions they had received from the desk clerk, was within easy walking distance of the hotel. They strolled leisurely up Collins Avenue and before they could reach their destination, the sound of loud music told them they were getting closer.

Even though it was still early, a small crowd had gathered by the door. After paying the cover charge, they stepped into the club. The locale was rather small—Anna was used to the larger places in Havana where Ramón had taken her previously—and the tables were set close together, in order to maximize the number of patrons that could be accommodated. There was also a small dance floor and a live band on a platform about a foot off the ground. The numbers they played alternated between swing—the rage at that time—and the mambo. Anna found this surprising, but was told by Ramón that it was not uncommon for Cuban dances to find their way into the United States, especially southern Florida and New York.

Once a table was secured, Ramón ordered a bottle of champagne. He wanted this last night in Miami Beach to be a memorable one. Once the bottle arrived—encased in crushed ice to keep the liquid at a steady 39 degrees Fahrenheit—he took it out of the bucket, uncorked it, filled the two glasses that were still on tray and returned the bottle to its icy enclosure.

"To us," he said looking at Anna.

"To our happiness," she answered before clicking the glasses together.

They drank the champagne slowly, listened to the music, and watched the people on the dance floor. Since it was still early, the band was playing mostly slow numbers that would entice the patrons onto the dance floor. As the night progressed, the musicians imperceptibly altered their repertoire to include faster numbers. They knew that as alcohol was consumed things would heat up and the pent-up energy and inhibitions would have to find an outlet. It did not take them long to start playing a mambo, so Ramón and Anna took advantage of this opportunity to step onto the dance floor and show off the latest steps they had picked up during their visits to Havana night spots. Then there was a succession of fast numbers, mostly swing, that the band alternated with Latin numbers. Even though Ramón and Anna were not familiar with some of the dances, they managed to pick up the steps and by the end of the night, their movements were credible enough. All the while they kept smiling and laughing; everything — at least for a few hours — had been left behind.

By the time they returned to the Cardozo it was almost two in the morning. It had been a long and busy day, but they still mustered the energy to make love once again before falling asleep in each other's arms.

As the plane approached Havana on a descent trajectory, through the small window and occasionally occluded by fluffy banks of clouds, Anna saw the familiar skyline of the city. At the end of the bay she saw El Morro and the fortress of La Cabaña. Somehow she now thought of Havana as her city, even though she had only lived there for three years. Cuba had been good to her, she concluded. She was fortunate to have met Oppiano Licario, to have Adriana Aguado as a friend and to be married to Ramón. Unquestionably they were the pillars on which her life in Cuba rested. Those pillars, as solid and stable as Anna believed them to be, would eventually collapse one by one, leaving her as helpless and alone as she had been during her last days in Ischia. But these events would not take place until years later, so for the moment she basked in the certainty — engendered by that false sense of security and unsuspecting of what was to come — that everything in her future would bring nothing but happiness and good tidings. A new chapter was beginning; she was glad that this time she would not be alone. Although the prospects of leaving Havana were not entirely to her liking, she understood — and accepted — that Ramón's business required his constant attention, and that as his wife it was her duty to be by his side, no matter where he lived. They would visit the city often, so she could keep abreast of the Pompeii and at the same time take advantage of all the cultural events. She thought of Adriana Aguado, how she had left Italy to be with Herminio, and of the simple explanation she had given her during their first lunch at the Rumayor Restaurant: love. Nothing else really mattered, not if one could share the days with that one chosen person that would turn every hour into a unique, almost magical event. She and Ramón were off to a great start, and she planned to keep the flame alive, just as Adriana and Herminio had done for so many years.

After the plane landed and they retrived their suitcases, they walked over to where they had parked the Packard a few days earlier. Once the suitcases were in the trunk, Ramón started back to the city. They would spend the night at Anna's apartment above the Pompeii and drive back to Pinar del Río the following day. Anna had decided to keep the apartment, rather than renting it, so she and Ramón would have a place to stay whenever they visited the capital. Being above the restaurant, it would also be convenient so she could readily discuss business with Sergio during those visits.

It only took twenty minutes for Ramón—given his driving skills and his knowledge of the city—to reach the Pompeii. He parked the car and then went around to open the door for Anna. With suitcases in hand, they went up the stairs that led to the small apartment overlooking the Prado.

"I realize that it is not the Hotel Nacional, or your new house in Pinar del Río," said Anna.

"It is home and you are here with me," said Ramón while putting his arms around her and kissing her, "And that is enough for me; the rest is not important." At that moment Anna felt happier and more complete than she had ever felt. She could not think of anything that she wanted; every wish had been fulfilled.

Their last dinner in Havana, they decided, should be at the Pompeii, so they went downstairs and walked into the restaurant. Sergio Osorio was not surprised to see them, for he knew they were coming back that day. After greeting them, he led them into one of the smaller, but more private, dining areas. They asked for a bottle of wine and ordered without looking at the menu, since Anna knew the dishes that were available on a daily basis.

That dinner, somehow, was a bit more relaxed than the ones they had shared at the Nacional or the Cardozo. For the first time since their wedding, they were actually home, or at least in a place that Anna had considered her home for the past three years. At the end of the meal, Sergio brought to the table a tray with espresso, and they asked him to sit down They discussed the different aspects of the business—which was better by the day—and they agreed to meet again every time Anna and Ramón returned to Havana.

After dinner the couple took a stroll down the Prado and then walked along the ocean, on the wide avenue of the Malecón, for almost an hour. Anna remembered how much Ramón liked the ocean, so she indulged him, despite the cool November breeze that made her shiver. She did not mind, since Ramón kept his arm around her shoulders during their walk. On the way back to the apartment, they stopped at a small cafe and had some churros—the Spanish version of funnel cake—and hot chocolate. Around ten o'clock they returned to the apartment. Since they intended to leave early the next morning for Pinar del Río, the wanted to get a good night's rest. Once in bed, as he had done every night since the wedding, Ramón reached out for Anna. That night his lovemaking was more subdued, more tender, as if he wanted to take his time and make every kiss, every caress count. Eventually, when they were both satisfied, they fell asleep still holding each other, as they had done since their wedding night. The last thing she remembered was the fragrance that Ramón exuded permeating the entire room.

The following morning, after a quick breakfast in a nearby cafeteria—the Pompeii did not open until eleven—they were finally on their way. In many ways Anna still could not believe that she was leaving Havana to start a new life in a provincial capital, that she was married to Ramón, and that in a matter of hours she would be responsible for running a household. It all seemed to have happened so quickly, as if she were inside a dream and could wake up at any moment.

When they reached the town of Artemisa, Ramón stopped at the cafe where he had taken Anna after her first visit to the Aguados. They both ordered *medianoche* sandwiches and fresh juice, and in less than an hour were back on the road again. After his absence, although brief, Ramón was anxious to get back to work overseeing his tobacco farm and making all those other decisions pertaining to the business. Within an hour they reached the outskirts of Pinar del Río, so Ramón slowed down to a more reasonable speed. As they went through the town Anna recognized many of the landmarks that Adriana Aguado had pointed out to her during her first visit to the city. From time to time Ramón would beep and stick out his left arm out the car window to say hello to someone he knew. Yes, thought Anna, he was indeed one of the best-known residents of the province, and now, because she was his wife, she would be just as well known. Although this fact did not bother her, she wanted to be more than Ramón's wife. In Havana she had the Pompeii, but here she had no idea what she would do. The next time that she saw Adriana, she would ask her advice. No doubt she would have some suggestions for her. So immersed was she in her thoughts, that before she knew it they were on the lane that led to Ramón's

268

house. The huge ceiba tree reached eagerly into the blue Cuban sky, occluding the house from view from the main road.

Ramón parked the coupé in front of the house and walked around the car to open the door for Anna. "We are home," he said with a smile. It was obvious that it brought him a great deal of satisfaction to be back in Pinar del Río, not just because of his business, but because he truly loved everything in this province. Even though Ramón traveled often, Anna had learned during their courtship that he would never leave this part of Cuba. Despite his wealth, he could not be happy any place else in the world.

The house was exactly as Anna remembered it. As they walked towards the front door, Ramón put his arm around her shoulders. "This is your house; your presence makes it a home," he whispered into her ear as he placed the key in the lock and opened the door for her.

The furniture that Ramón had commissioned had been finished and delivered, so the house had taken on a different character from the empty place that Anna remembered. As they explored the different rooms she recognized, on the walls and the tables, the items she and Ramón had bought during their shopping spree in Havana.

"Feel free to rearrange anything you like," he said, cognizant of the fact that women always wanted to add their personal touch to any house.

"I like it Ramón," she said, throwing her arms around his neck and kissing him with excitement, "You really have done a fantastic job."

"Thank you for saying that," he answered, "but I am aware that it needs a feminine touch. I want this house to reflect who you are," he concluded.

"I am sure I will think of something," she said and smiled, hinting that she already had a few things in mind.

Eventually they came out to the second floor terrace; the unobstructed view of the tobacco fields with their thin coverings was both magnificent and odd.

"I don't know which I love more," Ramón said looking into the distance, "these fields or the sea. I always miss one when I am with the other. I suppose they represent different things in my life. Tobacco is my heritage, my roots, what defines me. For generations this crop has provided a livelihood for the Contreras family, but it really goes deeper than that. It has also provided a sense of purpose and pride; our tobacco is the best in the world, and that knowledge carries with it an immense satisfaction that goes beyond words. I would be lost without that certainty. The ocean, on the other hand, represents something infinite and unattainable, like the dreams and aspirations we all have, but something that must be always present if one is to struggle to exceed oneself. For me it is impossible to give up either one of them and still be true to myself. Am I making any sense?" he asked, looking directly at Anna.

"Very much so," she answered, "We all need an anchor to give us meaning, but we also need dreams that allow our imagination to grow, otherwise we would become stagnant and wither away," offered Anna.

"But you must be hungry," said Ramón suddenly, snapping out of his pensive and introspective mood. "Let's go to the kitchen and see what's in the refrigerator."

"I am sure I can prepare something," said Anna with a smile. "Don't forget that cooking is my specialty."

"Just one of them," commented Ramón with a smile. "I am also aware of your other talents," he said, making an obvious reference to their passionate lovemaking.In the kitchen Anna found some eggs and a few onions, so they had to settle for an omelet. She also found half a bottle of red wine. Ramón had not bothered to stock the pantry or the refrigerator, being as busy as he was with the preparations for the wedding and the honeymoon in Miami Beach.

Anna placed the plates and glasses on a small kitchen table and they sat down. Even though this was the simplest meal she had prepared in a long time, she still made sure that the table had a clean tablecloth and napkins. She also set the silverware with the same care she offered her customers at the Pompeii, for she was aware that a good meal went beyond the consumption of food, and that its presentation was just as important as the cooking itself.

"We need groceries," he said, "There are some excellent stores in town where you can find anything you want."

"I can see that there is a lot to do here," agreed Anna with a smile, "I will take care of it all tomorrow."

"I am sure you will," said Ramón, much aware that Anna was anxious to take command of the household and especially the kitchen. By the time they finished the omelet and the bottle of wine, it was almost dusk.

"Thank you for the meal," said Ramón, "It was delicious."

"It was all I could find in the kitchen," said Anna, "But you are welcome."

"I want to show you something," said Ramón while extending his hand.

"I thought we had already seen the entire house," said Anna.

"We have," answered Ramón, "It is not in the house, but outside," he explained, but without being specific.

Anna followed him out the front door; for a moment she thought he was going to get in the Packard, but Ramón walked past the car and then around to the back of the house. Parked under a rustic ramada, a Jeep was waiting. He helped Anna onto the passenger seat and then got behind the wheel. As soon as he turned the ignition key, the engine came to life. Anna noticed that the gear shifter was located on the floor, and not on the steering column.

"This is the vehicle I use to go on the fields," he explained, "The Packard was built to run on smooth surfaces that allow low ground clearance, so it would be completely useless here."

Despite the obvious difference in vehicles, Anna immediately became aware that Ramón guided the Jeep on the dirt roads with the same skill and precision as he did the coupé on the highway. With the top down and headlights on, they drove down a lane that led away from the house. As they drove deeper into the covered fields of tobacco, Anna understood why Ramón had often compared them to the ocean. Under the soft evening breeze, the white gauze overhead undulated softly, not unlike the foamy waves in a sea that was anchored to the ground.

"These are the fields that I survey on a regular basis," explained Ramón, "I make sure that the plants are getting the right amount of water, light and fertilizer."

"It sounds a little complicated," commented Anna, "How can you tell?"

"Experience," he answered without hesitation. "Sure, one learns a lot of theory on agronomy at the university, but it is not until one actually gets out and watches the crops on a daily basis that all that theory begins to make sense. The plants, believe it or not, give you very definite signals. It is my job to interpret those signals and eventually decide when the tobacco leaves will be harvested."

"You make it sound almost like a magical and esoteric process, and not a science," Anna said.

"That is not an inaccurate way of describing it," agreed Ramón. "I mentioned to you once how easy it is to grow sugar cane, since it requires very little attention. Tobacco demands constant care and monitoring. As I said, the plants tell you what they need, we just have to read the signs and be there to provide it for them," concluded Ramón as they approached a clearing in the fields. He expertly parked the Jeep next to what appeared to be a single room structure with a thatched roof, turned off the engine and signaled Anna to follow him.

There was no door per se, just a rectangular opening in one of the walls. In order to dispel the darkness, Ramón produced a flashlight and led the way. Once inside Anna realized that there were no walls inside the building.

"What is this place Ramón?" she asked.

"Just close your eyes and smell," he answered and turned off the flashlight.

Immersed in the unanimous darkness, Anna did as he requested. Immediately she became aware of a single and unique smell that permeated the entire enclosure.

"Tobacco?" she asked.

"What else?" answered Ramón as he turned the flashlight on again. "You did not recognize the smell at first because you have never been exposed to it, but any Cuban, especially those from this region can spot it a mile away. "Here is where we hang the leaves so they can dry naturally and out of the sun," he explained while pointing the flashlight above their heads. Hanging from the rafters, like huge botanical bats, were clusters of leaves that had been bound together with thin twine.

"So what is the next step?" asked Anna with genuine curiosity. "After the leaves have dried," said Ramón, "they are separated according to type, put into bales, and sold. Then they are taken to the tobacco factories, where the cigars are made by hand, one at a time."

"It sounds like a long and complicated process," commented Anna.

"I mentioned that tobacco leaves are sorted out by type; some are best for the outside layers of the cigar, while others go on the inside. After a while, you identify them just by looking at them. I promise that I will take you soon to one of the houses where the cigars are made; I think you will find the experience interesting. Besides, now that you are married to me people will expect you to have a certain amount of knowledge about this business."

"I am willing to learn," said Anna.

"I know that," said Ramón as he turned off the flashlight and brought Anna closer to him. They kissed for a long time, enveloped in the darkness, the aroma of the drying tobacco leaves and the sound of the nocturnal insects, thus reaffirming the emotional pact that had culminated in a wedding ceremony at the San Rosendo Cathedral.

"I will show you more tomorrow," finally said Ramón, turning on the flashlight again while leading Anna out of the storage house and towards the Jeep. As they began their journey back to the house, the light of the full moon gave the covered fields the appearance of fluffy clouds that had quietly settled on the ground for a temporary respite from their airy domain.

"I never tire of these fields," commented Ramón, "They have a character of their own, and no matter how well you think you know them, they always manage to surprise you."

By the vehemence of his words, once again Anna realized how much Ramón was a part of that region of Cuba. Tobacco was in his blood, to such an extent, she concluded, that he was as much a part of the landscape as the fields and the trees. At that moment she had to evoke the words of the nameless driver during her first visit to the province, and his theory that pinareños were different from the rest of Cubans, not as expansive and more introspective. She also concluded that it was not a conscious decision on their part, but that the land slowly shaped them into its own image.

"Are you sure we are going home?" asked Anna, suddenly realizing that the Jeep was moving in a direction opposite to where the house was.

"Eventually," answered Ramón, "These fields are crisscrossed by many lanes; I wanted you to experience them at night, under the moon and without the workers present. I have never shared this with anyone," he said, "but I wanted to share it with you, to give you an idea of what all this means to me."

"I think I am beginning to understand," answered Anna, delighted that Ramón had made her participant of his innermost feelings, revealing to her what he considered to be most important.

The headlights of the Jeep kept piercing the darkness as they traversed the tobacco fields; at that point Anna had lost all sense of direction, but Ramón could have found his way back even with his eyes closed. Eventually they emerged from the labyrinthine expanse and he parked the Jeep on the same spot behind the house.

"Thank you for sharing this with me," said Anna as she came into the house, "I know how much it all means to you."

"I just hope that you learn to love this land as much as I do," said Ramón, then took Anna into his arms and kissed her tenderly.

"I am sure that with time and your help I will," she answered.

"The important thing is that finally we are home," then, after a pause when he looked at his Curvex watch, "but it is getting late. I have an early day tomorrow; being away makes the work pile up."

With his arm still around Anna's shoulders, they walked towards the main bedroom. Through the open windows the unique smell of the fields, mixed with the distant cacophony of a thousand nocturnal insects, filled the chamber. They did not bother to turn on the lights, but undressed very slowly, as if the darkness somehow hampered their movements. Once in bed, the bodies found each other, to begin a carnal concert that eventually exploded in a crescendo of youthful passion.

The sounds coming from the kitchen made their way into Anna's consciousness. For a moment she thought that Ramón had left the bedroom without waking her, but then she realized that he was still in bed next to her, sound asleep. Suddenly alarmed, she shook him into wakefulness. "Ramón, there is somebody in the house!" she said placing her mouth next to his ear, so as not to be heard by whoever was in the kitchen.

"Yes, I know," he said, "Go back to sleep."

"What do you mean?" asked Anna, both intrigued and upset as his lack of concern.

"That's Flora; she is probably preparing breakfast," he said and then turned over.

"Flora? Who is Flora?" asked Anna and shook him again. This time Ramón opened his eyes and sat up in the bed.

"Flora is Flora," he answered.

"I don't understand," said Anna.

"Flora has been working for me for many years," he finally explained, now more awake. "Being as busy as I am with the business, I needed someone to make sure everything ran smoothly. After I built this new house I decided to bring her with me." Then, after a pause, "She will be a great help to you."

"And what exactly does Flora do?" asked Anna.

"Everything," answered Ramón. "When I took over the business she always made sure that I had a hot meal waiting for me and clean clothes to wear. She makes sure that the pantry is well stocked and sends out the laundry once a week. She also does errands for me, if necessary."

"What about me?" asked Anna with a tinge of jealousy in her voice she could not manage to conceal.

"You will run everything as you see fit," said Ramón with a reassuring tone, "Flora will help you; after all, I don't want you to spend all your time working," he added as he kissed Anna on the cheek. "Let's have breakfast so you can meet her."

Flora was nothing like Anna had expected. Her sudden pang of jealousy had stem from an irrational fear that Flora could somehow compete with her for Ramón's affection. She had imagined a young Cuban woman who had slowly worked her way into his life, just waiting for the right moment to make a move that would catapult her from her station as a servant to one of mistress and confidant. Anna was surprised to find in the kitchen a black woman of indeterminate age—by the strands of silver in her hair she guessed mid fifties—who went about her duties with an obvious familiarity while humming a monotonous tune. She wore a white dress and a necklace made of blue beads.

"Good morning Flora," said Ramón, "What do we have for breakfast today?"

"Good morning, señor Ramón," she answered with a wide smile that exposed her perfectly symmetrical white teeth and openly conveyed how glad she was to see him.

"I brought some bread and milk," she said, "I knew there would be nothing to eat, since you were away on your honeymoon." At this point she looked at Anna, acknowledging her presence for the first time.

"This is my wife Anna," said Ramón as they sat down.

"I am glad to meet you, señora," said Flora, pronouncing this last word slowly and taking in her image leisurely, as if wanting to engrave every detail of her features in her brain.

"It is nice to meet you," answered Anna, perhaps not noticing the servant's obvious curiosity.

"Cubans usually don't eat a large breakfast," explained Ramón, "Most of the time it is just bread and butter accompanied by hot milk with coffee and a little sugar. Sometimes a piece of fresh fruit will be included in the meal."

These explanations were completely unnecessary. By now Anna was aware of the eating habits of the population. It was an area of the culture that she had studied carefully, in order to tailor the offerings of the Pompeii to her growing clientele.

As they ate, Flora washed some dishes and then looked in the pantry and the refrigerator, apparently taking a mental inventory of what was needed. She went about her tasks quietly and unobtrusively, not wanting to disrupt the meal in progress. Once Ramón and Anna were finished, she removed the dishes from the table and placed them in the sink.

"And how was your trip, señor Ramón?" she suddenly asked.

"Fine, everything was fine, but I am happy to be back," he answered.

"I am also happy that you are back," she said, "Things are not the same around here without you."

"Don't worry," added Ramón, "I don't have any more plans to leave the country anytime soon. By the way, just let me know what we need and I will have it delivered," he added as he and Anna were leaving the kitchen.

Back on the terrace, overlooking the tobacco fields, Anna could no longer hold back her curiosity. "Tell me more about Flora," she asked Ramón.

"What else is there to tell?" retorted Ramón, "I already told you what she does."

"What I want to know is not what she does, but what she is," insisted Anna.

276

"It is difficult to explain," said Ramón. "She is more than a servant, but less than family. It is not unusual for Cubans to have someone who becomes part of the household and whose responsibilities go beyond just cooking and cleaning. You could say that she helped my mother raise me, so when my parents died she had been in our employ for many years. I did not see any sense in dismissing her, so I had her kept on the payroll. Even after I went away to the university she always made sure that everything ran properly and, in her own way, made sure there was a home to return to whenever I came back to Pinar del Río. I can't really think of a time in my life when Flora has not been around. In a way I am indebted to her, for she provided a sense of stability at a time in my life when it was most needed. As I said, she is more than a servant, but less than family."

"That is very interesting," said Anna, not knowing what else to say.

"I think you two will get along just fine," answered Ramón.

"I hope so," said Anna, not wanting to reveal to Ramón the apprehension she felt about her future relationship with Flora, who had been running the household and looking after Ramón for years. Anna knew that it was always hard to step aside and relinquish that position of authority without feeling resentment, even if the other woman was the man's legitimate wife and not a stranger who was usurping her privileges.

"I have a surprise for you," said Ramón, suddenly changing the subject. "I am taking you out to dinner tonight; if you like we can invite the Aguados."

"What a great idea," said Anna as she put her arms around Ramón's neck and kissed him. Now that she was in Pinar del Río to stay, she knew that it was important for her to acquire a sense of direction and purpose. The Aguados, especially Adriana, represented that stability and success that she hoped to achieve living with Ramón, so she welcomed the opportunity to see them again. The fact that Adriana was also Italian, despite the difference in age, had created from the beginning a special bond, and speaking their language made Anna feel even closer to her.

"Then it is settled," said Ramón. "I will give them a call and ask them if they are free for the evening."

The rest of the morning was spent unpacking and attending to the endless array of details involved in organizing a household.

Shortly before noon a delivery van pulled up in front of the house and two men brought a series of boxes into the kitchen. Apparently Ramón had called the grocery store from his home office after speaking with Flora, who had not left the kitchen since breakfast.

At exactly one o'clock—they were on the terrace, overlooking the tobacco fields—Ramón announced that it was time for lunch. Noticing Anna's surprise, he explained. "Lunch is always at one; I usually drive up from the fields to eat here and afterwards go into my office for a while to take care of correspondence and phone calls."

By the time they entered the dining room, the table had already been set and the food had been served. It was apparent that Flora was more than familiar with Ramón's habits and his insistence on punctuality. During lunch she stayed out of the way, yet close enough to fill an empty glass or to retrieve a plate that was no longer necessary. At the end of the meal, without being asked, she reappeared holding a tray with steaming cups of espresso coffee. No words had been exchanged; no requests had been made; she knew exactly what to do and when to do it. No wonder, thought Anna, Ramón relied on her for so many things.

"I have to go to the fields for a while this afternoon," announced Ramón after finishing his coffee. "Even though I was away, the work did not stop; I will not be long," he said and then kissed Anna lightly on the lips before leaving the house. She heard the door closing and after a few moments the rumble of the Jeep engine coming to life.

For a moment Anna thought about returning to the bedroom upstairs and perhaps reading for a while on the terrace. Earlier that day she had put away all her clothes and tidied up the place, so there was nothing else to do. At the last moment, she changed her mind and decided to go into the kitchen. She was aware, by the sounds coming from that room, that Flora was there, cleaning up after preparing lunch. Anna was not accustomed to having servants; she had always done her own work, and she did not intend to stop now.

As she stepped into the kitchen, by the expression on Flora's face, Anna realized at once that she was surprised to see her there. She stopped washing the dishes and fixed her eyes on her, but remained silent. Resting on a central table, the groceries that had been delivered that morning waited to be put away. Anna did not hesitate; she opened several cabinets and started to arrange the different items by their categories. When she was done, she walked over to the sink, where Flora was occupied with the dishes and still refusing to acknowledge her presence. Taking a clean cloth, she started to dry the plates that Flora was stacking neatly on a dish holder, and then put them away in a side cupboard. The old woman dried her hands slowly on her apron, turned to face Anna and while looking into her eyes finally said, "You will be good for señor Ramón."

It was almost inevitable that the two couples would end up at the Rumayor for dinner. They all liked the location and their specialty, smoked chicken, was legendary. Ramón and Anna arrived first, and a short time later the Aguados walked in. They greeted each other effusively and, being a special occasion, ordered some drinks.

The men, predictably, talked mostly about business and about the house that Herminio had designed for Ramón. The women — they switched from Spanish to Italian right away — concentrated on more personal items. First of all, Adriana wanted to know about the honeymoon in Miami Beach and Anna's impressions of the United States. She also asked about the new house and her new life in general.

Anna was more than happy to share all the details with Adriana, whom she considered her closest friend in Pinar del Río. In her presence she felt all reticence to share her thoughts disappear. She spoke freely about the days in Miami Beach, about the subsequent journey back, about the new house and most recently about her apprehensions of having Flora in the house.Adriana listened attentively and told Anna how happy she was that everything was working out so well. She also put her mind at ease about Flora, assuring her that it was common for Cubans to have someone work, or even live in the same house. After all, she had met Dolores, who had worked for the Aguados for many years.

That evening the two couples stayed at the restaurant for a long time, enjoying each other's company and even more conversation over coffee afterwards. Before returning home, they decided to get together for dinner on a regular basis. This was the beginning of a tradition that would last for many years, and that would cement the already strong connection between Anna and Adriana.

Life continued its inexorable course and Anna settled into her new life. Ramón would go into the fields early in the morning and return home for lunch. Anna always made sure that everything was ready for him; after he returned to work, she and Flora would share the kitchen chores and plan the menu for dinner. In the evenings, surrounded by the incessant sound of the insects, she and Ramón would sit on the terrace and he would tell her about his day. Then they would retire for the evening and make love, or just lie in bed caressing each other until they fell asleep. On weekends they went to the movies or attended other events that were offered in the city. Once a month they made the trek to Havana in the Packard. On those occasions they usually left early on Friday and returned late on Sunday. Ramón would meet with prospective buyers or conduct other business, and Anna would meet with Sergio to make sure everything was going well at the Pompeii. They also took advantage of the more sophisticated offerings of the city, especially those events—concerts, ballet; etc.—that would never reach the provincial city of Pinar del Río.

In all respects, although away from the capital, it was a good life. To fill her hours, Anna took up the study of English with a set of records and books that she had found in Havana. She spent her afternoons, while waiting for Ramón to return, practicing her pronunciation and learning new vocabulary and grammar. Sometimes they entertained at home or visited friends of Ramón's. Of course, their friendship with the Aguados was reinforced by the regular dinners they shared in the different restaurants in the city. Yet, there was something missing in Anna's life.

It was during one of these dinners, while the men were busy discussing politics, that Anna confessed to Adriana her growing lack of fulfillment with certain aspects of their current life. Although Ramón could not be better to her — he constantly showered her with extravagant gifts and took her places — somehow she felt that despite all her efforts to remain active, she was languishing without a real purpose in her life.

"Maybe you need something that will get you out of the house," said Adriana after a brief silence, "When I first moved here I felt the same way. Herminio was working and I had a lot of time on my hands, so I volunteered to work at the local art museum. It has been very fulfilling; besides, you are used to having responsibilities."

"That is true," agreed Anna, "But I do not know anything about art."

"That may very well be," retorted Adriana, "but you have other talents. After all, you own one of the most successful restaurants in Havana."

"You are not suggesting I open a restaurant!" said Anna in a tone of surprise.

"No, not at all," answered Adriana, "That would take up all of your time; but there is another alternative."

"What did you have in mind?" asked Anna leaning forward on her seat, now truly curious as to what Adriana was about to propose.

"Just recently a new school for girls opened its doors. It is called *La Escuela del Hogar*, or Home Economics School. The curriculum includes anything and everything that has to do with running a household efficiently, from creating a successful budget to preparing nutritious, yet economical meals. I believe that you would fit well in that setting."

"But I do not have any teaching credentials," protested Anna.

"What you have is better, for there is no substitute for experience. If you like, we can talk to the lady who founded the school," said Adriana with conviction.

"I did not realize that you knew her personally," said Anna, a little surprised at the discovery.

"Pinar del Río is not as large as Havana," explained Adriana, "After a while you get to know everybody, if not personally at least by reputation. The reason I know her is because she comes into the art museum frequently."

"Well," said Anna in a tone of voice that conveyed that she was still not quite convinced, "I suppose that it would not hurt to try. Where is this school located?"

"We have gone by it many times; it is close to Independence Park. I can come for you tomorrow morning and from there go to the school. In the meantime, I will call the principal," said Adriana.

"That is a great idea," said Anna, now somewhat more enthusiastic.

"Then it is settled," said Adriana, "I will come tomorrow morning and we can visit the school."

That evening, Anna discussed her plans with Ramón. At first she feared that he would oppose the idea. After all, she had her income from the Pompeii and he had more than enough money. It was not unusual for Cuban men to demand that their wives stay home and just devote themselves to running the household. To her surprise, Ramón thought that it was a great idea, that she should have other interests and responsibilities besides the house and himself. Maybe his association with Herminio Aguado, thought Anna, was a positive influence, making his outlook a lot more progressive than the one shared by the rest of Cuban society, especially the men. She threw her arms around his neck and kissed him, grateful for his support. That night they made love, but afterwards Anna could not fall asleep, anticipating the events of the next day, when another door would possibly open in this land that seemed to be filled with unexpected surprises.

The following morning she was up early with Ramón. When they came into the kitchen Flora had already prepared breakfast. They talked about the day while they ate and then Ramón left for the fields, but not before kissing Anna and wishing her good luck. Rather than returning to the bedroom upstairs, Anna stayed in the kitchen and helped Flora with the dishes; it was a way of passing the time.

A short while later, the sound of a car announced that Adriana had arrived. Not being able to control her impatience, Anna came out to the front of the house before Adriana had a chance to park the car. They greeted each other warmly, with a hug and kisses on both cheeks, and then came into the house. Anna, anticipating the visit, had prepared some coffee, so they sat down in the kitchen and went over their plans for the day while enjoying a cup of the strong brew. Flora was nowhere to be seen.

In less than half an hour they left the house and were on the road. Although the distance between the house and the center of town was not long and Adriana was not driving slowly, Anna thought that the trip that morning was taking longer than it usually did.

"I am nervous," she finally said.

"There is no reason to be," Adriana reassured her, "I am certain that you and señora Albet, the head of the school, will like each other; she is always looking for qualified people to add to her staff."

Adriana was right on both counts. As they walked into the school they were greeted by a combination of voices and sounds coming from different classrooms. At the end of the hall they found the main office. Sitting behind a desk there was a woman going over some papers. Anna guessed that she was in her late thirties. Resting on the desk, a metal plaque announced her name and title: *Dra. Blanca Albet, Directora.* She stood up and came out from behind the desk, greeted Adriana and then, turning to Anna she said, "I am Blanca Albet, the principal of the school." From that first moment, because of her affable manner, Anna realized that Adriana had been quite accurate in her assessment. Being in that position not only required academic preparation, but also those intangible skills that allowed her to deal with people on a regular basis and on different levels.

"You must be Anna; I have heard a lot about you," she said. "Please sit down," she suggested while pointing to several empty chairs in the office.

"I am grateful that you have agreed to see me," said Anna as they all sat down, "I have only lived in Pinar del Río for a few months."

"There is no need to explain," she said with a smile, "We all saw the pictures of your wedding to Ramón in the newspaper. Congratulations."

"Thank you," said Anna, "I really like living here, but I want to do something more than just sit home and take care of a house and a husband."

"I understand you perfectly," agreed señora Albet, "I also have a husband; I could stay home if I wanted to, but I believe that in life one must have a purpose. This school is my personal project; it takes a lot of time and energy. Fortunately for me, I have a superb staff and my husband is very supportive."

"So is mine," interjected Adriana. "They understand that having interests and responsibilities away from the house makes us more interesting persons and better wives. It is a winning situation all around."

"My area of expertise is cooking," said Anna, "I am sure that I can make a positive contribution."

"Adriana mentioned over the phone that you own a restaurant in Havana," said señora Albet.

"I do not fully own it anymore," explained Anna, "I now have a partner."

"In our curriculum, of course, we include cooking. If you like, to start, you could come three times a week. Let's see how that works out. Is that acceptable?"

"Yes, of course," answered Anna, relieved that she had been offered the job.

"You realize, of course, that your salary will not be very high. As a rule teachers do not make much."

"That is fine," said Anna, "The important thing is that I will have something to do."

"Very well then," concluded señora Albet, "We will expect you tomorrow morning. Now, if you will excuse me, I must get back to work."

It had been that simple. Of course, Adriana's recommendation had played an important part in señora Albet's decision to offer Anna a job, even if it was only a few days a week. She would still have enough time for herself, Ramón and the house. It was indeed, an ideal situation.

Rather than celebrating in a restaurant, Adriana invited Anna for lunch at her house. As usual, Dolores had everything ready, but instead of taking lunch in the huge dining room, they opted for the smaller, more intimate setting of the table behind the house and overlooking Adriana's garden.

"My husband has a meeting with a client today," said Adriana, "He will not be here for lunch."

"You are fortunate to be able to lead the life you do," commented Anna as she took the first bite.

"I think you should say that we are fortunate," answered Adriana. "We should never forget that we enjoy many privileges that other women only dream about, starting with the type of husbands who realize that we are more than mere extensions of themselves and allow us to pursue our own interests."

"You are right," agreed Anna, "But I have one concern about working at the Escuela del Hogar, something I had not considered before."

"Yes, what is it?" asked Adriana.

"I have no means of transportation, and I do not want to disappoint señora Albet."

"Do not worry about that," said Adriana with a smile, "I can pick you up in the mornings; I have to work too, you know."

"But I hate to impose on you," said Anna.

"It won't be for long, just until you get your driver's license," added Adriana in a matter of fact tone.

"I never thought about that," confessed Anna.

"Well, I think it is about time you did," answered Adriana. "I am sure that Ramón will not mind. In fact, once you start driving you will be able to help him even more with his business. Men can't do everything, you know, even if that's what they want you to think."

"As usual, you are right," agreed Anna, once again thinking how fortunate she was to have such a wise friend.

The following months proved to be pivotal in Anna's life. She found her job at the Escuela del Hogar most fulfilling; the students were enthusiastic about learning the recipes that she presented in class; the staff was most helpful and señora Albet herself made sure that her initiation into the teaching field was a pleasant one.

Ramón, after receiving the news that Anna had been offered a job, was most happy for her. He realized that his wife needed something to do while he put in all those long hours supervising the fields and dealing with the buyers that came from different parts of the republic. Upon learning that Adriana would come for Anna in the mornings, he suggested that she should learn how to drive. After all, he reasoned, he used the Jeep to get around in the fields and the Packard just sat idle in front of the house, sometimes for days. Anna was both happy and relieved, since the suggestion had come from Ramón and had not been a request on her part. "It will be fun," he said, "Besides, it never hurts to learn something new."

At first, Anna had certain reservations, since she did not want to damage either the internal components or the beautiful body of the Packard. Once again Ramón put her at ease by offering a most logical solution. "I will teach you in the Jeep," he said, "We will be off the highway and streets. Once you master the clutch, the transition to the coupé will be an easy one. I promise you," he said convincingly.

So every day in the evenings for several months, Ramón would take Anna into the fields with the Jeep and impart driving instructions. First he showed her the controls and explained that different speeds of the vehicle required different gears. Sitting behind the wheel he demonstrated every aspect of his lesson several times and then would ask her questions, just to make sure she was grasping the theory of what he said. Once he was satisfied that she understood the principles of a clutch, he had her sit behind the wheel and supervised her while she changed gears with the engine off.

"Just remember, it is coordination between your left foot and your right hand," he reminded her one last time, "If your are shifting gears, the clutch pedal has to be fully depressed."

It all seemed simple enough. Anna had watched how easily Ramón drove the Packard on the paved roads and the Jeep in the fields. Of course, there was a world of difference between watching an experienced driver and actually implementing the theory into practice. The first time she started the engine, making sure the transmission was in neutral. Then, as she had practiced so many times before, she depressed the clutch and placed the transmission in first gear. When she let out the clutch, however, the Jeep just jerked forward and the engine died immediately. It was not as simple as it seemed.

"Remember that as you release the clutch you must also depress the accelerator," reminded her Ramón.

Without saying anything, Anna put the transmission in neutral and started the engine again. She repeated what she had done a few moments before, except that this time she depressed the gas pedal as she released the clutch. The Jeep lurched forward, but it did not stall. Anna gripped the wheel firmly as they traveled the unpaved road that led to the tobacco fields.

"Change gears," shouted Ramón over the sound of the engine. Going from first into second gear was a lot easier than staring off. Anna depressed the clutch, released the accelerator, moved into second and then gave the engine some gas again. The Jeep now traveled at an even pace on the dirt road. As they gained speed, Anna shifted into third, repeating what she had done before. The Jeep gained speed, but Anna managed to keep it within the narrow confines of the road. Eventually she shifted into fourth as the sound of the engine became strained. They traveled the road for half an hour; during this time Ramón instructed her to slow down, thus forcing Anna to shift into a lower gear, and then speed up again. By the time they returned to the house, Anna had shifted up and down many times. She stopped the Jeep, making sure the transmission was in neutral, and then shut off the engine.

"I think you've got it," said Ramón with a triumphant tone. "Tomorrow we can practice some more."

"I am looking forward to it," said Anna with the excitement of a child, "It was fun."

Good to his word, Ramón kept up the driving lessons, for he knew that the key to good coordination was constant practice. In a short time, Anna mastered the controls of the Jeep. She became so proficient behind the wheel that when she was not teaching at the Escuela del Hogar, she drove Ramón around the different sections of the tobacco fields. On those days they would leave the house after an early breakfast, return for lunch and then go out again.

During one of these outings, Ramón asked her to stop at a small house located in a clearing and bordering a cluster of fruit trees. Anna noticed that it had been constructed of wood that had been painted white; the roof, rather than being made from the thatch of the royal palms that abounded throughout Cuba, was made of galvanized zinc plates. The ample porch, with welcoming rocking chairs, extended the entire length of the house and had a cement floor. Neatly structured flowerbeds offered a welcoming explosion of color to the visitors. Behind the house there was a small tower crowned with a spinning turbine that captured the energy of the wind and provided electricity to the dwelling. At once Anna realized that this house was quite different from the ones occupied by most agricultural workers. Although not luxurious, it had all the amenities that make daily living a little easier. There was a battered pickup truck parked in front of the house, an obvious clue that the occupant was home. A spotted dog, taking advantage of the cool cement floor, rested by the front door. As soon as they exited the Jeep, the dog raised his head and then came running towards them. By the wagging of his tail and absence of barking or other aggressive gestures, Anna also realized that the animal knew Ramón.

"This is my friend Moteado," said Ramón with a tone of joy in his voice as he stopped and knelt to pet the dog. The name suited him perfectly, for it meant spotted in Spanish.

"Who lives here?" asked, Anna, but before Ramón could give her an answer, a thin, elderly man wearing a hat came out to meet them.

"*Buenas tardes*, don Anselmo," said Ramón as the man approached them.

"*Buenas tardes*, señor Contreras," he answered while removing his hat, an unequivocal sign of deference to Ramón.

"I just stopped by to remind you about the buyers who are coming in tomorrow," said Ramón as they shook hands, "We want to make sure that everything is ready. I also wanted to introduce you to my wife, Anna."

"*Mucho gusto*, señora. I am Anselmo Castillo," he said as he extended his hand. Anna noticed that as he offered his hand he did not make eye contact, an unmistakable sign that he acknowledged being in the presence of someone who belonged to a higher social status. His handshake, she also noticed, was firm, denoting a straightforward manner of a man who valued his word above all else. The wrinkles on his face, acquired over years of living in the fields, displayed a topography of hard work and honest living. Anna liked him immediately.

"The pleasure is mine, don Anselmo," said Anna as she shook the man's hand. "Don Anselmo is my right hand man," explained Ramón, "No one knows this land and the tobacco business as he does; he taught me everything I know. In fact, he is the man in charge whenever I am away; there is no one else I trust," added Ramón.

Upon hearing these words, meant obviously for don Anselmo's benefit, he smiled widely. "Tobacco is all I know," he said, "It is in my blood. I just do my job, that's all," he said modestly. At that precise moment a tall man emerged from the house. He was much younger than don Anselmo—maybe twenty five—and his face did not show yet the wear and tear of the constant work in the fields. "My son Felipe is also in the business," added don Anselmo.

"*Buenas tardes*," said the young man as he approached the visitors slowly. He did not offer his hand or lower his gaze, but rather looked at the group with obvious concentration. Unlike don Anselmo, he wore no hat and Anna noticed that, for a fleeting moment, he had surreptitiously fixed his eyes on her from head to toe. Or maybe it had just been her imagination; everything had happened so quickly that she could not be quite sure.

"The tobacco is ready to be delivered," said don Anselmo, breaking the sudden silence. "I inspected and counted the bales myself early today."

"Very well then," said Ramón, "I will see you early tomorrow at the storehouse."

"I will be there;" he answered.

"It was a pleasure to meet you señora," he added, this time addressing Anna.

"The pleasure was mine," she said as she and Ramón got back into the Jeep.

On the way back to the house, while Anna drove expertly, Ramón told Anna how don Anselmo had taught him the practical side of the tobacco growing business after he had received his agronomy degree from the University of Havana. Despite the fact that he had been around tobacco all his life, there were subtle nuances that could never be learned from textbooks, but passed down from older growers who had spent their lives in the fields.

"In many ways," said Ramón, "Don Anselmo is the one responsible for the success we enjoy today; from the beginning he was willing to teach me all he had learned about this crop. I listened and I asked a lot of questions; I also worked side by side with him in every aspect of the business, something unheard of for the owner of the land."

"He must have liked that," commented Anna.

"You are right," answered Ramón, "I think at times he forgot who I was and almost treated me as if I were his own son. Not only did he teach me the practical side of the tobacco business, but also what it means to work for a living from sun up to sun down. Until this day we have maintained that relationship; even though the ultimate decisions concerning the business are mine, I always consult and discuss everything with him. His advice is invaluable."

"I am glad that he works for you, and not someone else," said Anna.

"From the beginning I realized that he was a tremendous asset, so I took him out of the fields and made him supervisor. I also had that house built for him, so he can be close to everything, and at the same time enjoy some of the comforts that he has earned. I make sure that he wants for nothing. He is almost like a father to me," reiterated Ramón.

"What about his son?" asked Anna.

"Felipe? Well, that is different story. I do not pry, but I do not believe that don Anselmo is completely satisfied with him. He works in the fields, but he lacks the passion that his father has. For him it is just a job, that's all. It is as if he were waiting for something better to come along."

"Well, that's too bad," commented Anna as she parked the jeep behind the house, "I really like don Anselmo."

"So do I," echoed Ramón, "So do I."

IX

Anna's life soon acquired a rhythm of its own, especially after receiving her driver's license. Several times a week she drove the Packard to her teaching job at the Escuela del Hogar. The most pleasurable aspect of her work was the interaction she had with all the young women who were eager to learn all about preparing satisfying, yet economical and nutritious meals. Anna soon realized that she, like señora Albet herself, was more than a teacher, but a role model and a living blueprint for what these young women wanted to achieve in the future.They knew, of course, that she was the wife of Ramón Contreras, one of the wealthiest and most successful men in the region, and that she had no need to work outside her home. Yet Anna never failed to appear, always prepared with her lessons and readily available whenever her students needed a sympathetic ear if they required advice on a personal matter.

Once a week she met with Adriana Aguado for lunch; they talked about their daily lives, their husbands, their jobs, the ongoing war in Europe. In short, they shared those daily concerns — both trivial and significant — that allowed their friendship to flourish because they kept abreast of each other's lives. These weekly meetings also gave them the welcome opportunity to speak Italian, yet one more component to their relationship.

Towards the end of each month, or whenever time permitted it, Anna and Ramón would drive to Havana in the Packard and spend a few days in the city. Don Anselmo, of course, stayed in charge and he had the telephone number of the restaurant, just in case anything urgent were to come up. Rather than staying at a hotel, they used the apartment above the Pompeii. They had decided to keep it because they needed a place to stay during their visits; it was close to everything and also part of the same building.

Anna would meet with Sergio and discuss the business, go over the ledgers and take care of other matters that had to be decided.The few doubts that she had harbored at first concerning the partnership had quickly vanished; not only was Sergio a superb chef, but he proved to be an excellent administrator as well. The Pompeii was turning a nice profit every month.

While Anna spent her time at the restaurant, Ramón met with prospective buyers and distributors from the different cigar manufactoring houses. Even though he was very much aware that his product was unsurpassed, he also had to make sure that the competition would not undercut his prices and that he could meet the exacting delivery dates. It all came out to a balancing act, but he had a keen sense for the business and everyone wanted the tobacco that he was growing. At the end of the day, when all their business dealings had been concluded, they would get a copy of the *Diario de la Marina* and search for the latest American movie, a concert or a play. Sometimes, if they had the energy, they would go out to one of the many clubs available in the city, order a bottle of champagne and dance until dawn. Anna could not remember a time in her life when she was happier; the war in Europe had finally ended and everything was exactly as she wanted it to be. She was also oblivious that the designs of fate would soon begin to deliver lethal blows — relentlessly and systematically — that eventually would dismantle a world whose foundation she believed to be rock solid.

The first of those unexpected blows came a year later. She and Ramón had come to Havana so he could meet with some of his potential buyers. That evening she had stayed behind because sometimes those meetings went well into the night and she wanted to use the time to go over her own business with Sergio.

They were sitting in her former office when the telephone rang. Sergio casually picked up the receiver and mechanically said 'Pompeii Restaurant' into the mouthpiece. There was a long pause; then, without any words, Sergio handed her the phone. Anna thought it strange, for she never received calls at the restaurant any more.

At the other end of the line she heard Ynaca Eco's familiar voice. She had called Pinar del Río first, and not finding anyone at home, had tried the Pompeii as a last resort.The news were not good; Oppiano Licario had died suddenly and the viewing would be that night. After giving Anna the particulars, the line went dead.

"Are you alright?" Sergio asked, noticing that Anna had suddenly turned very pale and that she was crying.

Anna relayed the news and asked him to tell Ramón that she had gone to the funeral home; he should not wait, since she did not know at what time she would be back. Then she stormed out of the restaurant.

Almost in a state of shock, Anna walked hurriedly towards the address that Ynaca Eco had given her. After a while she found herself in a section of Havana with which she was not familiar; in the distance she saw a house flooded with light. Involuntarily she quickened her pace, as if being pulled by a powerful and invisible magnet.

"The house itself seemed to be a supernatural forest. One could see the ornate grillwork that also served as a gate. At the center a very shiny metal square stood for the lock. Its size revealed that it required a huge key, as if to open castle gates. Beside the house, a breezeway was made visible by the lunar whiteness. One end joined a broad terrace surrounded by a garden in which the habits of pruning shears and voluptuous exercise had been neglected.

The breezeway was made of red bricks, as was its vaulted ceiling. Along its length could be seen mosaics with a white background, showing lances, keys, swords, and Holy Grails. The lance penetrated the ribs of the one climbing a pole, the key opened the entrance to an enchanted castle, the sword was for decapitations on a public square, and the knights of King Arthur were sitting around the grail of blood. The emblemata of the mosaics were executed in red cinnabar, the lance was transparent like a diamond, a steel gray shaped the sword stuck in the ground like a phallus, and every trefoil showed a key, as if nature and supernature had been united in something meant to penetrate, to jump from one region to another, in order to reach the castle and interrupt the feast of the hermetic troubadours.

The enchantment of the house was in the steps that its terrace offered. It had been built on a knoll and the steps leading up to it had to rise about six feet. At the top of the columns, squids poured down, twisting with every marine interpretation to receive the lunar advice. The advance of each column was interrupted by pedestals with stalactite pineapples, and on every leaf of their crowns, searching out and yawning, were lizards whose eyes restlessly traced infernal circles while their bodies languished in ecstasy all season long. Needles went in and out of the stone; the bees, the lynx, and the sloth played without shattering the nocturnal silence in a treetop formed by the crystallized light. A combination of octopus and stalactite climbed up those columns inundated with silvery reflections. The house seemed to be uninhabited, or its dwellers were asleep, like a lizard in autumn. As long as their dreams lasted, the drop of water that forms the stalactite and the drop of the squid's ink would join together, softening a stone that crawls and climbs in the middle of the night.

Anna climbed the stairs. She could see some rooms, while others were filled with the tiny murmurers who spoke their words close to the ear, as if silence should not be interrupted. On the third floor, she noticed that from one of those chapels an exacerbated lucifugous proliferation was bursting forth. A tightrope walker's spotlight reigned, as in the circus it follows the body that leaps like a bird; but here the light was beaded on the most extreme immobility. Coming off the stairs she was momentarily paralyzed, she noticed that a person was suddenly rising up from the circle of talkers. She squinted as if to recognize her and then signaled with a hand for her to come closer. It was Oppiano Licario's sister who had summoned her. "I knew you would come this last night," she said to Anna with desperate but serene pain.

"Come with me, let's go see him," Oppiano Licario's sister said. Dark, pale, with blue eyes that had the look of a scale holding up an unknown weight, perhaps a fish glimpsed in the shadows of its silver and the night perched on the coral tree. Her skin, extremely polished, showed the counterpoint of its pores, made visible the entry and exit of the needle that had woven that net. Her skin was the defense of her consciousness, and her organs of sight, penetration and rejection. Her name was Ynaca Eco Licario, her family called her Ecohé, and like her brother she showed a completely religious selfconfidence; her self was formed by two intersecting lines. The point of intersection was the coincidence of her chance and her destiny. Her mystery lay in the fact that at times her skin trembled without knowing what dictated that tremor.

She went over to the glass pane. Oppiano's face already showed an impassivity that was not that of his usual discretion, nor that of his infinite reply. Like a magic mirror it caught the radiation of *ideas, the column of selfdestruction of knowledge rose up with the flame's slenderness, was reflected in the mirror, and left its mark. It was the tail of Juno, the starry sky that was reflected in the parenthesis of the constellations. His body no longer strolled on the rooftop to fix the errant reading of the stars. His eyelids closed in a silence that stretched out like the tide, he surrendered the key and the mirror."[2]*

The two women stood by the coffin in silence, each trying to fathom how Licario's life had impacted their own. They realized that it went beyond words, that Oppiano's influence was as solid as a mountain range, but also as elusive as a silvery fish in the dead of night. Had it not been for him, Anna would not have found her way in this new country. It was impossible to ascertain how many other people he had helped, and in what circumstances.

After a while, Ynaca Eco returned to the growing group of mourners and left Anna by herself. She closed her eyes and said a silent prayer, entrusting the eternal rest of Oppiano's soul to The Maker of All Things. She had paid her respects; there was nothing else to do there, so she walked out of the lucifugous chapel. As she was about to leave the building, a familiar figure, completely dressed in white, caught her attention. It was none other than Mr. Ioso, the mysterious Greek whom she had met on top of Mount Epomeo.

"Do not be surprised," he said upon seeing Anna's expression, "All coordinates converge tonight in this city, in this house; Licario's hand has brought us all here, so we can acknowledge his life and say a last good-bye on his final night above ground."

"I thought of you from time to time and wondered about your fate," she said, "But we were separated at the immigration center and I had no way of finding you. How did you know about tonight; how did you know Licario?" asked Anna, truly curious about the odd circumstances.

"During the crossing I mentioned to him my familiarity with metals and the methods used by the ancient Greeks to mint their coins. Licario suggested that I should open an antiquarian shop, for

---

[2] José Lezama Lima, Paradiso. Farrar, Straus and Giroux pp.462-465.

that would be suitable to the talents I had. With his help I found the locale and before long my venture was up and running. As usual, he was correct; I have a steady clientele and my business is thriving."

"His death was very sudden," commented Anna, "Had you seen him recently?"

"He came to see me about six months ago," answered Mr. Ioso, "I saw him getting off a bus in front of the shop. He wanted me to authenticate a collection of Greek drachmas that he was carrying in a suede pouch. Once I verified that the coins were authentic, he did not stay long; he left and I saw him disappear through the plate-glass window. It was as if he were on his way to a meeting of the outmost importance. The impact of his death has brought us together again; it is impossible to ascertain how many other people he influenced during the course of his life," he concluded.

"You are correct," agreed Anna, thinking of those invisible forces that Mr. Ioso had mentioned for the first time at the Church of Saint Nicola. Then she proceeded to tell Mr. Ioso of the events that had taken place since her arrival in Cuba, from her first day at Tricornia to her marriage to Ramón and her new life in Pinar del Río. As she recounted these events, it became even more clear how influential Oppiano Licario had been in her life.

By the time Anna returned to the Pompeii it was almost dawn. Ramón had not gone to bed, but stayed up all night sitting by the window, immersed in darkness, watching the street below. When she came into the apartment, he did not say anything, but slowly walked up to her and held her in his arms for a long time. They went to bed still without speaking; then Anna cried until she finally fell asleep.

The journey back to Pinar del Río the following day was a quiet one, devoid of the conversation and comments in which the couple usually engaged during those trips. Although Ramón's association with Licario had been a casual one, he was aware of how he had helped Anna since the day of her arrival in Cuba, so he refrained from intruding into his wife's somber mood.

Several hours later, they were home. Flora, anticipating their appearance, had prepared dinner, but neither one of them was very hungry. After changing clothes Ramón got in the Jeep and drove to don Anselmo's house, just to make sure everything was alright and to let him know the results of his dealings with the buyers.

Anna, on the other hand, placed Immortal Arias in the small record player that she kept in their bedroom and then went out onto the terrace that looked over the tobacco fields. The wide, almost endless expanses of green—now beginning to fade with dusk—seemed a most improbable backdrop for the incomparable voice of Louis d'Amio. As the light of day gave way to impending darkness, Anna pondered about the life of Oppiano Licario. At that instant, she realized that one of the pillars on which her universe had rested—a pillar she had thought unshakable—had suddenly collapsed without warning, leaving behind a void that could not be filled.

Giacomo had told her once that people do not die all at once, but in installments, that the final breath was just the end of a chain. At that time Anna had not understood what he meant, but simply had accepted his words at face value. Now their meaning was crystal clear; it required no explanation. Fate had a way of dealing blows to people along the way; those blows gradually wore them down, until that final one eradicated all vestiges of life. Anna's life had surely been made less complete because of Licario's death. While looking at him in the chapel the night before, eyes closed behind the glass plate, she had also died a little. There was no question about that.

The record had concluded; Louis d'Amio's voice had been replaced by the repetitive sound of the needle on the last grooves of the record. Anna was enveloped by silence and darkness. But tomorrow, she knew, would be a new day and life would invariably go on. No one had any choice in the matter.

Despite a pervasive feeling of despondency, the following day Anna forced herself to get up and drive to the Escuela del Hogar. She taught her classes, consciously focusing on the lessons and managed to get through the morning without any major mishaps or outward signs of unrestrained emotions.

It was not until later that day, after driving to Adriana Aguado's house and relaying the news of what had happened during the past three days, that Anna finally lost the firm grip she had on her feelings and began to weep openly and question aloud the fairness of life. Adriana, older and more experienced, realized that Anna

297

was not looking for answers—those questions could only have been answered by The Creator—but for a sympathetic ear who would listen to her lamentations and a welcoming shoulder to shed her tears. Adriana let her cry, all the while patting her on the back, until her emotions were completely spent, her tears exhausted. Once Anna became more composed, Adriana asked the ever present Dolores to make some tea. They sat in the more intimate living room, drank the hot brew and spoke softly about Licario's sudden death, about his incomparable and inexhaustible knowledge of the most obscure subjects, about the helping hand he had offered Anna during her first day in Cuba. They also spoke in general terms about life and how fate had a way of derailing the most carefully conceived plans with unforeseen events that were beyond the control of mere humans. Just being able to share these concerns with Adriana made a world of difference to Anna; her older friend had now become, after Licario's death, the strongest pillar among her circle of friends.

Following Adriana's advice, Anna made an effort to return to her former life and put Licario's death into perspective, as something that would eventually befall everyone and over which she had no control. She continued teaching her classes at the Escuela del Hogar with renewed energy, had lunch with Adriana once a week and took up again her study of English with the set of records and books that she had bought in Havana and that, as of late, had been collecting dust in one of her cabinets.

Ramón, as observant as he was, realized immediately that his wife was trying just a little too hard to go on after Licario's death. Once, he had come home unexpectedly and had found Anna going over their wedding pictures that she had spread on the dining room table. Immediately he understood that not every picture was present, but only those in which Licario appeared. He did not make any comments, but at that instant made the resolution to spend more time with his wife and to take her places, even if his business had to suffer.

A few days later, putting everything aside, he took Anna to the Valley of Viñaes, one of the most beautiful spots in Cuba, for the weekend. Its unusual gelology, unique in the world, as well as its pristine and timeless charm, brought smiles to her face and comments of excitement upon watching the entire view from the strategically positioned overview. So pleased was Ramón with

Anna's mood that he asked an anonymous visitor to take their picture with the valley as a backdrop.

Coincidentally, on December 24, 1947 the Riesgo Theater — named after its owner, Joaquín Riesgo — opened its doors for the first time. It was touted as one of the largest in Cuba, and it boasted the latest technological innovations developed in the United States. Ramón saw yet another opportunity to distract Anna, so he bought four tickets for the opening night and invited the Aguados. Afterwards they went out to the Club Rumayor for a Christmas Eve dinner, the most sumptuous of the year, since it usually included an array of choices prepared to perfection, candies and hard cider imported from Spain.

Taking advantage that all schools would not reopen until January 7th, and that business was usually slow at that special time of the year, Ramón organized an impromptu trip to Havana. Leaving don Anselmo in charge, he and Anna left early one morning. There was no specific purpose to this trip, a fact that made it even more special. As usual, they stayed in the apartment above the Pompeii and spent their days wandering around the city or just sitting on the low wall of the Malecón, facing the sea and recapturing the magic of the time when they were just getting to know each other. At night, they took in a movie or went dancing in one of the many available clubs. Music was never in short supply in Havana.

To celebrate the coming of the new year, Ramón made reservations at the Tropicana, a club on the outskirts of the city, that usually booked the best national and international talent for its shows. The lavish productions included lines of chorus girls whose scanty costumes of colored feathers and sequins glittered under the spot lights and were impossible to ignore. For that special occasion, they had a full orchestra that played the most popular Cuban songs in vogue at the time.

On their last day in the city, even though Anna did not need anything, Ramón took her on a shopping spree to *El Encanto*. Although admittedly he did not enjoy shopping for women's clothes, he sat patiently for hours while Anna tried on and modeled for him what seemed to be an endless collection of dresses, blouses and skirts. It was yet another gesture that showed how much she meant to him. Suddenly realizing how many new items she had picked out, and how high the bill would be, she suggested putting some of them back, but Ramón would not hear of it.

"Merry Christmas," he whispered into her ear and then kissed her on the cheek.

A few days later, back in Pinar del Río and while having lunch with Adriana, Anna recounted the trip to Havana, all they had done and seen, and showed off one of her new dresses. Adriana was pleased to see that her friend had finally snapped out of the enervating despondency in which she had fallen after Licario's death. Anna also spoke enthusiastically about her classes at the Escuela del Hogar, about the progress she was making with her study of English, and about her restaurant in Havana. It was also unavoidable that the topic of politics should come up in their conversation. Even though elections would not be held until later on that year, the political parties had already begun to extol the virtues of their candidates. This activity would reach a feverish frenzy in the month preceding the elections, when flyers would be distributed, posters would suddenly appear on every available surface, and radio spots would become more frequent. On the last day, as a final assault, cars with loudspeakers mounted on their roof would traverse the streets and deliver a final message to those going to the polls.

From 1944 to 1948, under the presidency of Raúl Grau San Martín, Cuba had enjoyed—because of the war and postwar economic growth—one of the most prosperous times in its history. It was no surprise when Carlos Prío Socarrás, member of the same party and Grau's protegé, was handily elected to the presidency in 1948. Under his rule private industries, as they had under his predecessor, enjoyed record profits. This overall economic prosperity was also extended to thefreedom of expression — even dissen-ting voices were not silenced — that Cubans enjoyed. Much of the revenue that came into the national coffers was channeled into public works, so the money collected returned to the taxpayers, further stimulating the economy and bettering everyone's standard of living.

Because of her association with señora Albet at the Escuela del Hogar, Anna soon came to believe that the key to a better future rested on education. She saw an ample opportunity to make a small contribution, so she used her influence with Ramón to broaden the educational opportunities for the children of the men

300

who worked in the tobacco fields. It was not unusual for these children to work right along with their parents in order to supplement the family's income, but by doing so they forfeited any future opportunities for a different line of work. Anna convinced Ramón to pay the parents for every child they sent to school rather than to work in the fields. At first he was not so sure that the idea was a sound one, but in the end he gave in because he also realized that the prosperity and good fortune that he enjoyed should not be hoarded, but shared. He also realized how much the project meant to Anna, and for him that was good enough.

The task to make sure this innovative idea was implemented fell on don Anselmo's shoulders. He dealt directly with all the men on a daily basis, knew their families and his honesty and good intentions were undisputed. The men also knew that he had been working the land even before they were born and that he was a mentor of sorts to Ramón Contreras.

One evening Anna and Ramón had him over for dinner, just to make sure he understood what the project entailed. At the end of the evening, after hearing all the particulars, don Anselmo was convinced that it would be one of the best things that had ever happened to the workers. Soon thereafter, he gathered everyone in one of storage houses and explained to them that their children no longer needed to work in the fields, that they would earn the same amount just for attending school. Of course, he emphasized, no one was trying to tell them what to do, so the plan was completely voluntary. Some of the more incredulous ones asked about expenses for school supplies and uniforms, but were quickly convinced when don Anselmo told them that those expenses would be fully covered as well by señor Contreras.

So successful was the program that at the end of the school year the workers themselves organized a *guateque*, or country party, and asked don Anselmo to ask Ramón and Anna to come as special guests. Of course, nothing could have pleased them more; throughout the year, they had been following closely the progress of their educational project. It was one of don Anselmo's new duties to provide them with a monthly progress report.

On the appointed day, Ramón and Anna drove in the Jeep to a central clearing surrounded by the modest houses where many of the workers lived. There was a tacit agreement, in force even before Ramón was born, that the workers could live there free of charge. As they approached the clearing, the first thing they saw was a group of children wearing their school uniforms. Their teacher—a tall man wearing a white guayabera shirt—stood in front of the group. As Anna and Ramón exited the jeep, the group started singing. Apparently they had been practicing because their performance, although far from being professional, exhibited a great deal of unity and enthusiasm. After the song was over, the teacher walked over to where Ramón and Anna were standing and presented them with what seemed to be a scroll held together by a thin blue ribbon. In reality, it was nothing but a common sheet of paper that the clever instructor had rolled to make it appear more official. It contained a brief message, thanking Ramón and Anna for making it possible for the children to attend school. Below the message, each child had signed his name. This was, indeed, progress, thought Anna with satisfaction.

The parents of the children gathered around the couple, shyly at first, but then more at ease as Ramón inquired about their families and their jobs. They also voiced their gratitude that Ramón would pay for the children to attend school. It was at this point that he explained that it had not been his idea, but Anna's; she had convinced him of how important it was for the children to be in school instead of working in the fields.

A group of the men, guitars in hand, provided the music for the party. They sang traditional Cuban songs whose words everyone knew because they were so old and were never out of vogue. Most were *danzones*, a musical style that originated in the nineteenth century and that incorporated a nostalgic element in the cadences of the music and words that often spoke of lost loves. Ramón did not waste any time and asked Anna to dance. Upon seeing them, the workers clapped enthusiastically and they themselves followed suit with their wives or girlfriends. The party was a most welcome — if momentary — respite from the monotony of their daily lives.

Several tables, covered with colorful plastic tablecloths, had also been set up for the party. They held an assortment of trays containing the most popular Cuban dishes: rice, black beans, fried plantains, cassava, and roasted pork. There was also an abundant assortment of local desserts: guava shells in syrup, grated coconut, chocolate pudding and buñuelos, a Cuban version of donuts with anisette seeds. Of course, a variety of drinks was also present. For the adults there was wine, rum, and Guayabita del Pinar, the typical drink of Pinar del Río. For the children soft drinks and fruit juices had been provided. An array of torches had been lit after dusk, both to provide light as well as to keep the mosquitoes away.

The party went on until after midnight. By the appearance of the tables—the trays and bottles were empty—everyone had had more than enough to eat and drink. Eventually the parents took their sleepy children home, the musicians put away their instruments, and the only sound was that of the night insects. Ramón and Anna said good night to the few remaining guests and drove away in the Jeep.

Early the following morning, while they were having breakfast on the terrace, the sound of an old pickup truck caught their attention. They recognized the truck as don Anselmo's, but could not understand why he would be coming to the house, since at that time he was usually already in the fields. A few moments later the sound of the engine died and there was a knock on the front door. By then Ramón himself had come downstairs, curious as to the purpose of the unexpected visit.

"*Buenos días*, don Anselmo," said Ramón as he opened the front door and asked him to come in.

"*Buenos días*, señor Ramón," answered don Anselmo as he removed his hat. "Excuse me for showing up so unexpectedly, but I have been asked to deliver a message; I could have done it last night, but it was not the time or place to discuss business."

"Let's go in the kitchen," suggested Ramón while leading the way. As soon as they sat at the table, although she had not been asked, Flora silently placed two cups of coffee in front of the men. It was part of Cuban hospitality. Then, cognizant that they needed privacy, she left the room.

"So what's on your mind, don Anselmo?" asked Ramón, intrigued as to the purpose of the unexpected visit.

"You remember how happy the children were last night," he said.

"Yes, of course," answered Ramón, still without a clue.

"Well," continued don Anselmo, "Now that more children are attending school, the building is bursting at the seams."

"So what did you have in mind?" asked Ramón.

"This is not for me, you understand, señor Ramón," explained don Anselmo, "But the teacher and the children have been talking about adding a classroom to the school; it would certainly improve the quality of their education."

"I see," answered Ramón, "I still do not understand what it all has to do with me."

"They asked me to ask you if you would be willing to finance such a project," don Anselmo finally explained, "They reasoned that since you had taken such an unusual interest in the children, you might want to help them again."

"That is quite a request," said Ramón while sipping his coffee.

"They will understand if you say no," added don Anselmo, but they insisted that I ask you anyway.

"I don't think I can give an answer at the moment," said Ramón, "Let me talk it over with Anna first; she is the one who has taken an interest in the children. I can let you know in a few days."

"That's fair enough, señor Ramón. I won't say anything until I have a definite answer from you," said don Anselmo.

"I will talk to Anna today," Ramón reassured don Anselmo as he stood up to say good-bye.

A few moments later the sound of the pickup truck was heard and within minutes it faded into the distance. At that precise moment, Anna came downstairs. She was dressed and ready for her classes at the Escuela del Hogar.

"Was that don Anselmo?" she asked.

"Yes," answered Ramón, "He came to make a request on behalf of the children."

"What sort of request?" asked Anna.

At this point Ramón led Anna into the kitchen, poured her some coffee from the pot that Flora had made earlier, and proceeded to recount the details of the visit. Anna drank her coffee slowly, listening to Ramón without interrupting him.

"Are you going to do it?" she finally asked him.

"I told don Anselmo that I would speak with you; after all, this is your project," he answered noncommittally.

"Would the addition be very expensive?" inquired Anna.

"No," said Ramón, "I do not believe it would be that expensive. All they need is an extra classroom added to the existing building. I did not want to give don Anselmo an answer before discussing it with you. What do you think?"

"You saw how happy the children were last night," said Anna with a glow in her eyes, "The parents are also very grateful that you have provided this opportunity. This project would only corroborate before their eyes your commitment to the men who work for you," added Anna vehemently. "Besides, I would like to pitch in with my profits from the Pompeii. After all, as you pointed out, this entire project was my idea."

"Well, then it is settled," said Ramón, "If it makes you happy, then it makes me happy too."

"I love you Ramón," said Anna and then threw her arms around his neck and kissed him.

"I will tell don Anselmo today," said Ramón, still holding Anna in a tight embrace, "we can take advantage of the summer recess to start the project. It should be done by the beginning of the school year."

"Now I have to go to my classes," said Anna, kissing Ramón again. "I will see you later on today."

"Have a great day," answered Ramón.

As Anna drove to the Escuela del Hogar, she realized that her interest in the welfare of the local children went beyond selfless and altruistic motives, even beyond the influence that señora Albet had in her way of looking at education. No, it went much deeper than that; it was personal. During the time that she had been married to Ramón, even though he had never expressed the slightest reproach, Anna knew that one of his expectations was to have children eventually. They had talked about it during their courtship; it was something that they both wanted. During her marriage to Giacomo the thought had never crossed her mind. The age disparity was the first impediment, and the political unrest precluded bringing children into the world. The thought was inconceivable.

With Ramón it was different. After the first two years of marriage, she began to suspect that this could be the one aspect of their relationship that might go unfulfilled. Despite their frequent and intense lovemaking, every month the predictable conclusion of the menstrual cycle offered her tangible proof that she had failed to conceive.

She confided her fears in Adriana during one their lunch dates. After a brief silence her friend offered words of encouragement, telling her to stop trying so hard and just allow nature to take its course. She pointed out that Anna was only twenty-eight years old and that sooner or later, probably when she least expected it, she would be carrying Ramón's child. As usual, Adriana's words at the time made her feel better, but the years had gone by and nothing had happened. She compensated by being the best wife possible, but deep down she knew that their friends, especially the women, were wondering why they had not had any children yet.

Life continued its inexorable course; Ramón rose early every day and had breakfast with Anna, then went into the fields; she drove to the Escuela del Hogar to teach her classes. On weekends, they went to the movies or sometimes spent the night at nearby towns that Anna had not visited yet. Once a month, Ramón made it a point to drive to Havana. He insisted that Anna had to keep an eye on the Pompeii, but she knew this was just an excuse to get her out of Pinar del Río—Sergio's management of the restaurant continued to produce growing profits—so she could enjoy the offerings of the capital, especially the theater, and concerts. He also took her to the shows at the Tropicana Night Club, the most famous in Cuba. On those nights he would invariably order a bottle of champagne, and after the show, they would dance until dawn.

By that time, Ramón had traded in the Packard coupé for a jet-black Mercury that turned heads everywhere they went. No matter what he drove, his vehicle was instantly recognizable to the inhabitants of the city. For his work, of course, he continued to use the venerable Jeep that had served him well for so long.

Although their friendship with the Aguados had continued and strengthened throughout the years, they had not seen much of them for a few months. When Anna commented on their absence from the city, Ramón simply shrugged and conjectured that they were probably traveling abroad. Ironically, he was not too far from the mark, but the reason for their departure had not been motivated by a long anticipated vacation, but by a more serious and insidious motive.

The first sign was Adriana's gradual loss of weight and diminished energy. After consulting with Dr. Sotolongo, a friend of the family, he suggested that they should consult a specialist in Havana. Upon hearing his friend's suggestion, Herminio turned pale. He was well aware of Dr. Sotolongo's keen eye and his diagnoses were seldom wrong. In this instance, he had abstained from giving an opinion, but had deferred that burden to another physician. Herminio suspected that his friend had found something that could not be confirmed, but was probably not good if he wanted a specialist involved.

The following day, after informing his partners at the firm, Herminio and Adriana got under way. During the trip Herminio talked about his latest project, and promised Adriana than once it was concluded they would go on vacation abroad. Paris perhaps, or Venice, if she so preferred. Adriana, in turn, knowing that her husband was trying not to worry her, just went along with his suggestions of a memorable trip that would bring them even closer.

That week was spent in a secluded clinic in the company of the most brilliant doctors in the city. They ran endless tests, analyzed bodily fluids, and monitored Adriana's vital signs day and night. In the end, after the results were in and arriving independently at the same conclusion, they summoned Herminio into a small conference room. He did not sit down, but faced squarely the group of doctors. The look on their faces left no doubt as to the news they were about to relay.

"I wish there were something we could do," said the senior member of the team, "We ran the tests several times, but the results did no vary. The disease is far too advanced to respond to treatment; all we can do is make her comfortable." The physician had carefully avoided the dreaded word 'Cancer' in his explanation.

At that instant Herminio felt that he had been suddenly thrust into a whirlwind and would faint at any moment. He must have turned very pale, for one of the doctors moved closer, just in case he had to catch him. Herminio simply collapsed on the nearest chair; his entire world had been destroyed in a matter of seconds.

"What now?" he asked in a soft voice after a few moments, somewhat more composed after assimilating the initial blow.

"Now, as we said, all we can do is make her as comfortable as possible," reiterated the oldest doctor.

"How long?" asked Herminio with a tremble in his voice.

"It is impossible to tell for sure; I am also speaking for my colleagues. With every passing day she will become weaker; eventually she will be bedridden. If you like," added the doctor after pause, but fully cognizant that there was no one more qualified, "You can seek a second opinion."

"How long?" repeated Herminio, but now with a forceful tone.

"Two months, at the most," answered the doctor with the finality of doom.

"I would like to take her home," said Herminio softly.

"Of course," answered the doctor, "I will write down a set of instructions before you leave."

On the way back to Pinar del Río Herminio brought up again the subject of an extended vacation, but Adriana simply smiled and said that she would be happier spending the time at home. It was at that moment that Herminio realized that she already knew, that the expression on the doctors' faces, and probably on his own, had openly conveyed the terrible truth.

As soon as they were back in Pinar del Río, Herminio informed his partners that he would not be coming back to work for an indefinite period. He instructed Dolores that from that day on they would not receive any unannounced visitors. In short, Adriana was not to be disturbed for any reason at all. Herminio had decided that he would devote every minute of every day they had left next to her.

At first they went for walks, sat in the garden and looked at pictures of places they had visited together, trying to recapture happier times. Perhaps it was during those last weeks—despite their anguish—that they loved each other more than ever. Dolores saw to their needs silently, efficiently and unobtrusively. Towards the end, when Adriana was too weak to leave her bed, Herminio brought her fresh flowers from the garden and read to her from her favorite books.

It was around this time that she placed in its case the solid gold brooch depicting a gondola and gondolier, and instructed her husband that it should be delivered to Anna once she was gone. Herminio, eyes full of tears, promised her that her wish would be carried out.

On that dreadful day, upon opening the small velvet-lined box, Anna started to cry. She knew immediately that something tragic had happened, that the Aguado's absence for the past three months had culminated in tragedy. Her conjectures did not last long; that day Ramón came early from a business meeting, and the expression on his face left no doubt that he was the bearer of bad news. He told Anna what everybody already knew: Adriana had died peacefully in her bed; her husband had been with her until the final moments. At her request, there would not be a wake, but a simple ceremony at the San Rosendo Cathedral followed by the burial.

As she heard the details that corroborated what she already suspected, Anna began sobbing softly; she knew that for the rest of her days she would never have a friend as close as Adriana. Ramón, cognizant that there were no words that could console his wife, simply held her in his arms and allowed her to express her grief. Besides being a friend of Herminio, he had met Anna at the Aguado's home, so he also felt indebted to them for his good fortune. Everyone had lost; there was no question about that.

The following morning Ramón and Anna drove to the cathedral. She wore a black dress and no jewelry. The only piece she put on was Adriana's gold brooch; it was a silent pledge of friendship that went beyond the finality of death. Despite the early hour, a crowd had already gathered in front of the building. For an instant Anna thought of her wedding day, eight years earlier; it was strange how the same building, depending upon its use, could conjure up different memories and feelings. From this point on, whenever she thought of the San Rosendo Cathedral it would evoke a mixture of happiness and sadness.

Inside the church the smoke of burning incense collected in uniform and ascending strata and adopted indiscriminately the different colors corresponding to the light that came in through the stained glass windows. Then, suddenly disturbed by the people who were filling the pews, it dissolved in its upward journey, joined the elaborate flourishes of the capitals, and eventually exited through the concealed vents that led to the twin belfries.

Once everyone was seated, the priest—as clerics always did on those occasions—spoke of the mystery of life, the inevitability of death, and how Adriana had left this world a better place than she had found it. This last part, thought Anna, was entirely true. Adriana had helped many people throughout her life, including her. From her perspective, the void that her death had created would not be able to be filled. Of that much she was certain.

As Anna and Ramón exited the cathedral, she caught a glimpse of Herminio getting behind the wheel of his car. She had not seen him for several months, so the sight of him in his present state was nothing short of appalling. He had lost weight, his hair had noticeably thinned, and his face clearly displayed the constant anguish he had endured during the past year, giving the impression that she was looking at a much older man. What captured Anna's attention, however, were his eyes. Where before they were full of life, laughter and love, they were now but inanimate and dull globes, set deep in their sockets, evoking the lifeless gaze of a recent corpse. This impression, though a fleeting one, was one that Anna would always carry with her. Although Herminio had not died with Adriana, he had certainly stopped living after her disappearance.

The caravan made its sinuous and gradual way through town towards the cemetery. Once there the cars were parked outside the gate and the mourners started to walk to the site of the grave. Under the bright Cuban sun, the almost infinite sea of white marble glistened with the intensity of a colorless and lifeless ocean that eventually forced the mourners to turn their gaze away. A short distance away Anna spotted a momentary oasis of color created by the profuse number of floral wreaths that had been delivered to the grave earlier that morning. The cemetery workers had efficiently removed the heavy lid that covered the carved marble tomb. Right above the opening the casket rested on the clever mechanism that would eventually lower it into the ground with the aid of protesting cranks and creaky pulleys.

Shortly thereafter, the priest emerged from the crowd and stood beside the coffin. Once again, he reminded the mourners that Adriana had been called to the bosom of the Lord, and that it would be unwise to question His will. Anna, however, did not hear these words that were supposed to offer solace in a time of grief; her attention was focused on Herminio, who was standing next to the priest. Under the bright sunlight she was able to assess more fully the impact that Adriana's illness and eventual death had had on him. Gone was the vibrant man that she remembered, replaced by another whose emaciated, almost frail appearance resembled that of someone who had emerged from a long stay in a home for convalescents.

The graveside ceremony was brief. Everything had already been done; every word had been spoken. Taking a slight cue from the priest—Anna noticed that his brow was heavily beaded with sweat—the workmen slowly began to lower the coffin into the ground. Once everyone was gone they would replace the heavy marble lid and cover it with the flower wreaths. That temporary oasis of color in the white marble sea would signal that a household, somewhere in the city, had been touched by the hand of death.

The crowd began to disperse as they walked back to the parked cars. Anna, not able to contain herself, glanced back to the spot where Herminio was standing. She saw him crying inconsolably on the shoulder of Vicente Rodríguez, his best friend. Although she did not know it at the time, this would be the last occasion she would ever see him. From that day on he would become a recluse, locked in a house full of ghosts and memories, rejecting all contact with the outside world.

Fully aware of his wife's deep friendship with Adriana, Ramón was in a hurry to take her home and away from such depressing spectacle. Just as he had done earlier that morning, he drove in silence, not wanting to intrude in Anna's memories of her friend. From time to time he would look at her, just to confirm what he already knew: she had not stopped crying, although now it was just a steady stream of tears that silently rolled down her cheeks. As soon as he noticed, without a word, he took his immaculate handkerchief from his lapel pocket and offered it to her.

Although also deeply shaken by Adriana's death, Ramón tried to maintain an air of equanimity. He realized that he had to be strong for Anna, that at this moment more than ever she needed an assurance that there was something firm and immovable in her life. Just as he had done after the death of Oppianio Licario, Ramón cut down on his working hours so he could spend more time with her. In the evenings, they went for long drives in the Mercury, or they would just sit on the terrace and watch the sun as it set over the tobacco fields. Ramón would purposely allow the night to envelop them—he used the feeble excuse that insects were attracted to the light—because after eight years of marriage he knew that the darkness helped Anna, since it was conducive to a freer form of expression on her part. He would just listen to her and hold her hand, until it was time to retire for the evening.

It was during that time — on March 10th, 1952, to be exact — that a coup d'etat deposed the constitutionally elected government of Carlos Prío. General Fulgencio Batista, a former sergeant backed by the Cuban army, took control of the government. Most people, because of the freedom of expression they had enjoyed for the past ten years, quickly denounced the coup. Batista responded with a wave of censorship; he was not about to relinquish power so easily. The following year elections were held and Batista was elected by an overwhelming majority. The opposition cried foul. But this period of unrest, unbeknownst to Cubans, was but a mild preamble of the fate that would soon befall the entire nation.

Daily life went on as before, except for the curtailed freedom of expression and personal liberties. Foreign enterprises—especially American—were encouraged to come to the island and granted generous concessions. Under Batista's strong rule, the economic progress that the republic had enjoyed throughout the forties continued uninterruptedly. This apparent calm on the surface was nothing but a thin veil for the deep discontent and strong under-currents that now permeated Cuban politics; the clandestine opposition groups were growing in number and strength. The tipping point came in 1957, when an all-out assault on the presidential palace was staged. The goal of this operation was a simple one: kill Batista. At the precise moment when the armed men irrupted into his office, the president had stepped out, so all the planning and subsequent carnage on both sides did not produce any results. Batista had survived the attack.

From that day on the repressive measures against all potential conspirators became even stronger. The secret police swiftly tracked down the survivors of the attack against the presidential palace and either jailed them or executed them. Cubans were now living under an open dictatorship. Despite everything, business was good. The press was strictly controlled and foreign capital was flowing into the island. Graft and corruption among government official became rampant.Pinar del Río, being rather rural and remote, was perhaps the least affected by the ongoing events. There were rumors that a small group of men had landed in the province of Oriente, at the other end of the island, and that they had gone into the mountains to fight against the dictatorship. Another piece of news, more disturbing because it hit closer to home, was that Felipe Castillo, don Anselmo's son, had left the fields to join the rebels in the mountains. Anna was never able to corroborate anything, but don Anselmo now came to the house more frequently than before to confer with Ramón behind closed doors.

Both men continued to look after the tobacco plantation and by then Anna had become one of the veteran teachers at the Escuela del Hogar. Through señora Albet's connections, she also met with a tutor once a week to help her with her English pronunciation. Although she had accepted Adriana's death, it had certainly taken a toll on her. She still traveled to Havana once a month with Ramón to meet with Sergio and keep abreast of the Pompeii. A year earlier, Ramón had traded in his black 1950 Mercury for a silver Lincoln Continental Mark II. This car was, unquestionably, the most unique in the entire province. Anna understood, after fifteen years of marriage, that Ramón put in long and hard hours every day, and what many might have considered an unnecessary and extravagant expense was just a small way of rewarding himself for all the hard work. He had always enjoyed automobiles, and this was one of the few pleasures that he allowed himself.

But the deteriorating political situation in the country could not be ignored. Although Ramón always made a conscious effort not to approach that topic beyond the confines of his own house, once he was alone with Anna — either on their terrace or in the bedroom — he would discuss and analyze what little news filtered down to the general public. During one of their latest trips to Havana, while going over the books with Sergio Osorio, an obvious downturn in business had caught Anna's attention.

"People are not coming out as much," explained Sergio, then, lowering his voice, "They are afraid."

The resistance in Havana was much stronger than in the provinces. Hardly a night went by without a bomb going off or some other acts of sabotage. Batista's regime counteracted with even more brutal measures. The violence kept escalating on both sides.

"This situation cannot go on indefinitely," confided Ramón one evening while sitting on the dark terrace. "Batista knows that he can't hold on to power; his government is too corrupt."

"So what can he do?" asked Anna.

"I believe that he will try to stage some sort of elections where the candidate of his choice will assume the presidency. Once he transfers power to a successor, he will leave the country quietly."

"How do you know this?" asked Anna.

"It is not a matter of knowing," answered Ramón as he squeezed her hand lightly, "It is a pattern that has repeated itself throughout our history since the very beginning."

Ramón's words proved to be on target, but only partially. In 1958, under the auspices of the Batista regime an election was held and a new president, Rivero Aguero, was elected. On December 31st of the same year, under the cover of darkness and before the new president could be sworn in, Batista fled Cuba.

New years' day, 1959, Cubans woke up to a mood of chaotic jubilation. It was at that time that Fidel Castro, from the mountains of Oriente province, boisterously announced a victory march that would culminate in his revolutionary group taking charge when they arrived in Havana. Although they were not the only group that had opposed the Batista dictatorship, from the start they claimed to be victors in the struggle, thus relegating every other opposition group to the background.

This historic march, to further support their claim of victory, was broadcast on national television. In every town, there were stops for celebratory gatherings. A week later, the march ended at the José Martí Plaza in Havana. A long-winded speech—full of rhetoric, utopian promises and white doves—culminated the event. Free elections were supposed to take place within eighteen months. Cubans thought, now that Batista had fled, that their problems were over.

The year 1959 could accurately be described as a national blood bath. Anyone in any way associated with the Batista regime was rounded up and jailed indefinitely—a clear violation of the 1940 constitution. Many were tried by military tribunals and executed by firing squads. Free elections were no longer mentioned.

The new regime, drunk with power and without opposition — those who dared to protest at the abuses of power and violations of human rights, were quickly labeled 'antirevolutionary' and swiftly silenced or jailed — began its rampant roster of reforms aimed at overhauling the very foundation of Cuban society.

The first step was to seize control of the media. Newspapers, magazines, radio and television stations were seized in the name of the Glorious Revolution. Once in possession of all news outlets, the new government was in a position to control, suppress or modify the news that would be disseminated to the population. Even during the harshest dictatorships in Cuban history, when censorship had been imposed, the news media had remained in private hands.

Education was next. All schools in the nation now fell under the direct control of the government. Teachers had to sign statements of allegiance and adhere to a modified curriculum that oftentimes was nothing more than thinly veiled propaganda. Both teachers and students were exhorted to join the government sponsored 'voluntary' work brigades.

The Escuela del Hogar, where Anna had taught for the past fifteen years, was suddenly closed. Sra. Albet's husband had been arrested in the middle of the night and taken to jail, but the charges were never made clear.

"Things don't look good," confided Anna to Ramón one evening, while sitting on the terrace. If there was one lesson that she had learned well from Giacomo was that whenever the government seized all modes of communication, with the sole end of controlling the news, there was cause for alarm. Just as in Italy during Mussolini's rule, the government was also organizing the country's youth into brigades that they could command and control through indoctrination.

"I know," acknowledged Ramón, "but Cuba has gone through difficult periods before. Things are bound to get better." Perhaps Ramón did not believe his own words; Anna suspected that he was saying them not to alarm her. She had seen all the signs before; she did know that even more difficult times lay ahead.

Within months the self-appointed Cuban government took its next step to exert absolute control over the island. In an unexpected and sweeping maneuver, all lands in private hands, as well as businesses owned by corporations or individuals, were nationalized. Cuba had turned from a republic into a communist state. Popular protests were met with increasing military trials and firing squads that worked around the clock.

The dreaded knock on the door at the Contreras home did not take long. Anna, who was downstairs with Flora, opened the door herself. Standing in the threshold was a bearded man clad in an olive-green uniform; behind him, rifles in hand, were two much younger men. Anna guessed that they were barely out of their teens.

"We are looking for Ramón Contreras," said the older man, dispensing with any introductions or preambles of courtesy.

"May I ask what this is about?" inquired Anna.

"Official business," answered the man curtly.

"One moment. I will get him for you," answered Anna, but without asking the men to come inside. She returned a few minutes later with Ramón and then retreated back into the house. She knew that the men wanted to talk alone.

After a few minutes, Ramón joined her in their study. By the expression on his face, Anna knew that the news could not be any worse. He handed her an official looking piece of paper, replete with seals and illegible signatures.

"Our land has been taken over by the government," he said as he collapsed on a nearby chair. At that moment, Anna had the fleeting impression that the words had come out of the mouth of an old man. Ramón was completely deflated, close to the point of being broken. The land had been in the hands of his family for generations; many of the men who worked for him were descendents of former workers. Everyone had been treated fairly; the business had prospered. Until now. It was anybody's guess as to what would happen next. Most likely someone would be appointed to run the place, whether he knew anything about growing tobacco or not. The only prerequisite would be blind obedience to the dictates of the revolution.

"Did you recognize him?" asked Ramón after the men left.

"Who?" asked Anna.

"Felipe," answered Ramón, "don Anselmo's son. He spent time in the mountains with the rebels, so they have given him a lot of authority. More than he can handle, if you ask me. It is one thing to play hide and seek with the army; solving everyday problems is a different matter. Everyone recognizes that he will never be the man his father is."

"No, I didn't recognize him," answered Anna. "It was probably the beard and the long hair."

"A uniform does not make the man," answered Ramón, "He is still the same person. But now he is dangerous because of the control he has over others."

"What are we going to do?" asked Anna with an anxious tone in her voice as she held his hand.

"Do?" answered Ramón, "Nothing. At least for the moment. At this point we just wait; let's see what happens in the next few months. Things are bound to get better; maybe this government will not be in power much longer."

But once again Anna realized that Ramón was saying that so she would not worry; he wanted to take the burden off her shoulders. Elections had been put off and eventually forgotten, while the government tightened its grip on every aspect of everyday life. Just as Ramón had predicted, Felipe was made manager of the tobacco plantation. Don Anselmo, who had devoted his entire life to the betterment of the crops, was now relegated to the status of a second-rate employee who no longer had any say as to how things were done, no matter how much experience and knowledge he had. Still, the men looked toward him for guidance. Eventually, this situation led to a confrontation in front of the workers; there simply could not be two men in charge. This was one of the few times the workers had seen don Anselmo lose his temper. He simply told Felipe that no matter how much authority the government gave him, he would always be a *come mierda*—a shit eater—who would never know anything about growing tobacco. This was one of the worst insults in the Cuban vernacular. Some of the men thought that Felipe would hit his father, but the latter stood his ground and the young man walked away. There was a unanimous round of applause from the men.

This explosive exchange, of course, changed nothing. Felipe was the man in charge; he held all the trump cards and he knew it. His word was law. To further exert his authority, claiming that it was part of the farm equipment, he confiscated the Jeep that Ramón used to survey the fields. The change towards normalcy and order, where individual rights as well as private property were respected, seemed to be getting farther away with every passing day. Ramón's land had now become a state cooperative; no one had a vested personal interest in its success. At this point Anna thought that things could not get any worse, but the hand of fate was about to deliver the most brutal blow she would receive in her entire life.

Late one afternoon, Anna started to walk in the direction of don Anselmo's house, where Ramón usually was at that time of day. Normally she would have waited for him at home, but just minutes before some documents addressed to him had been hand delivered. Thinking the matter urgent, she wanted to place the papers in his hands as soon as possible.

She had traveled the road, both on foot and on the Jeep, a thousand times before, so she was familiar with every twist and turn. Along the way there were several storage houses where the tobacco leaves, after being harvested, were hung to dry.

As she walked by the one of these houses, she saw the familiar Jeep parked in front of it. For an instant she thought of Ramón, but immediately realized that he no longer had the use of that vehicle. Suddenly, a by now all too familiar figure, donning the olive-green uniform and the unkempt beard, appeared in the doorway. Anna did not intend to speak or acknowledge his presence in any way. As far as she was concerned, he did not exist, so she kept looking straight ahead. But Felipe Castillo would not be so easily deterred. Whether he had been waiting for Anna, or their encounter was a random one did not really matter. The expression on his face clearly showed his intentions.

"You've always thought you were better than the rest of us," he said with a voice that was really a hoarse whisper. Then he quickly blocked Anna' path and forcefully pulled her into the darkness of the storage house. As she unsuccessfully tried to fight him off, she felt on her neck the sickening warmth of his breath and his rough, hungry hands pawing at her dress and popping off its buttons. She tried to scream, but Felipe had anticipated this reaction and placed a hand on her mouth.

Almost without transition Anna found herself on her back, looking at the tobacco leaves hanging from the rafters. Time ceased to exist. What followed was a blur of images, sounds and smells underlined by the pain of a forced penetration and the unwelcome ejaculation.

Eventually, Felipe stood up—his animal appetite momentarily satiated—and began to arrange his clothes. He looked down at Anna with a patronizing look, as if he had just performed a kind deed for someone in need. Without a word, he exited the storage house. A few moments later, the sound of the Jeep engine coming to life reached Anna's ears. She did not get up right away, but stayed very still on the jute sacks that were scattered on the floor. She did not know how much time had passed, but it seemed an eternity. The shock of the entire experience prevented her from crying. It was as if she kept waiting to wake up from a nightmare, but could not cross into the world of wakefulness.

Finally she stood up and walked out. At that moment, she felt that she was standing beside herself, completely detached, watching that other Anna struggle to get to the house. Night was approaching fast, and by the time she reached the front door she heard the distinct calling of the owls from the top of the ceiba tree.

318

She stumbled into the house—the door was never locked during the day—and the heavy and irregular sound of her steps must have alerted Flora, for she came out of the kitchen, still drying her hands on her apron.

"Señor Ramón! señor Ramón!" she cried out at the top of her lungs at the ghastly sight as she rushed to help Anna to her upstairs bedroom. As they reached the foot of the stairs, Ramón came running downstairs. He literally jumped the last few steps and landed next to Anna.

"What happened?" he asked, despite the fact that he already had guessed the terrible truth due to Anna's torn dress and facial bruises, but received no answer. Anna kept shaking her head from side to side, as if by doing so she could erase the dreadful event that had taken place.

Once in the bedroom, Flora began to remove the torn and filthy garments that she had on. She had also guessed what had happened. In the meantime, Ramón began to clean the facial cuts and bruises with some disinfectant. After this task was accomplished, he went into his office and called Dr. Sotolongo.

The doctor arrived within the hour. After examining Anna, he produced a syringe and an ampoule of clear liquid from his black bag and gave her an injection.

"It is just a mild sedative," he explained to Ramón. "Just let her sleep through the night; I will be back early in the morning," he said as he walked out of the bedroom.

Ramón sat at the edge of the bed, holding Anna's hand and caressing her forehead. Flora had collapsed in a corner chair, not wanting to leave in case Ramón needed something. Just as the sedative was taking effect, Ramón whispered the question that had been burning on his lips all along.

"Who, Anna, who?" Ramón cried out.

"Felipe. Felipe Castillo," she whispered before slipping into the deep sleep induced by the injection. Ramón's face did not show any outward signs of emotion, but the fire in his eyes left no question as to his intentions.

"Stay with her," he told Flora and then left the bedroom in the direction of his office. From the bottom drawer of his desk, he produced a wooden case with a lacquered top. Inside there was .38 caliber revolver that had belonged to his father. Ramón used it occasionally for target practice, so he was more than familiar with the weapon. After checking to make sure it was loaded, he placed the revolver under his belt. At that time of day he was almost sure where to find Felipe Castillo, so he got behind the wheel of the Lincoln and drove into the fields.

No one knows exactly what happened then, for there were no witnesses. Several shots were heard coming from one of the storage houses. When some of the workers arrived at the scene, they found don Anselmo, still holding a gun, and Ramón and Felipe at his feet, both dead. He surrendered without any incidents and was taken to the police station in Pinar del Río. All the while he kept shaking his head, as if acknowledging that such a terrible event had truncated any possibility of a future.

After the preliminary booking was over, don Anselmo was asked to give a statement. To everyone who knew him what had happened seemed unthinkable; he was the most likable and peace-loving person around. Yet, two men — one of them his own son — were dead.

He explained that he had been taking inventory in the storage house with Felipe when he heard the sound of a car approaching. By then Felipe, who was wearing his uniform, had already drawn his weapon, as if he had known that trouble was coming. A few moments later Ramón, revolver in hand, came into the storage house. Don Anselmo did not know what was going on, so the first shot took him by surprise. He saw Ramón falling at his feet. Instinctively, guided by an inner desire to protect someone who had loved him like a father, he picked up Ramón's revolver and fired at Felipe. That was all he could remember.

The physical evidence fully corroborated don Anselmo's words. Ramón had been shot with Felipe's gun, and the bullet that had killed Felipe had been fired from Ramón's revolver. Now it was up to the courts to decide his fate. One thing was certain: he would never return to his beloved tobacco fields again.

The burden of breaking the news to Anna fell upon Dr. Sotolongo. He came to the Contreras' home early the following morning, holding his black bag and with a somber expression on his face. He had spent his career healing people and making them feel better, both with medical treatment and kind words. So he certainly did not look forward to the task at hand; less than twenty-four hours before, Anna had been raped, and now he had to tell her that her husband was dead. He was fully cognizant that his words would shatter a life that was already in pieces.

Flora opened the door before he had a chance to knock; it was apparent that she had gotten up early, or maybe she had not gone to bed at all. After the perfunctory 'Buenos días,' she offered Dr. Sotolongo a cup of coffee. He was more than happy to accept; it had been a long night and it would allow him a pause before facing Anna. He sat at the kitchen table, drinking the black coffee, while Flora went about her business, trying to hold back the tears. The tragic news had spread quickly, and Flora had practically raised Ramón after his parents' death. Dr. Sotolongo, being the family's physician as well as a personal friend, was well aware of the crucial role that Flora had played in Ramón's upbringing. There was no need for words; the grief floating in the air was almost tangible. After finishing his coffee, Dr. Sotolongo stood up and picked up his black bag from the table.

"Let's see Anna," he said. At that moment his voice was almost a sigh, crushed under the weight of the recent events and the news he was about to deliver. Under the influence of the sedative he had administered the day before, she had slept through the night. But now, as its effects wore off, Dr. Sotolongo could detect that Anna was regaining control of her senses. Although her eyes were still closed, she was tossing nervously from time to time, as if trying to avoid an invisible foe that kept stalking her relentlessly.

"Good morning, Anna," said the doctor, although he knew that it would be a terrible one.

After a few moments, Anna opened her eyes. Her gaze was distant and empty, as if she could not focus on the present moment or recognize anyone in the room. "Where is Ramón?" she whispered.

This was the very moment that Dr. Sotolongo had been dreading. He knew how close Anna and Ramón had been from the very beginning; some people even suggested that they had the closest thing to a perfect marriage. And now he had to deliver a blow from which she would never recover. Anticipating an episode of hysteria, he had come prepared to administer even stronger sedatives, if necessary.

"Ramón is not here," he said, trying to ease into the terrible news.

"When is he coming back?" asked Anna in a feeble voice.

321

"I am sorry, Anna," he said while holding her hand, "but he is not coming back. There has been a terrible accident..."

Dr. Sotolongo had purposely avoided using the word 'dead,' or giving her any particulars about the incident. She would find out soon enough. At this moment she had to deal with the harsh reality that Ramón was gone from everyone's life, especially hers. He felt the grip of her hand tightening, as if all her emotions were concentrated on that particular extremity. There were no tears or sudden outward bursts of uncontrollable weeping, but just a cool, emotionless shell devoid of all feelings that stared into space. Dr. Sotolongo let out a sigh of relief that the sudden hysteria he anticipated had not materialized. But he also realized that this seemingly calm reaction had the potential of being a lot more dangerous. Practical experience, as well his medical training, had taught him that tears were like a relief valve that maintained a manageable pressure of a person's psyche. If this natural avenue was suppressed, the pressure would eventually build to an intolerable level and do irreparable damage. The consequences were impossible to predict, and even more so in this case.

"I want to see him," she said while letting go of Dr. Sotolongo's hand, "He needs me now more than ever."

"Of course," he answered, "I will take care of everything and wait for you downstairs."

Flora, who had come up with Dr. Sotolongo and was standing in a corner, helped Anna out of bed and with her clothes.

"I will prepare breakfast," she said, "You need your strength."

Anna did not answer, but followed Flora downstairs into the kitchen. Dr. Sotolongo had made himself at home and was drinking a second cup of black coffee, surely one of many before that day came to a conclusion. Anna sat across from him at the kitchen table, also drinking a cup of coffee, waiting for the food that Flora was preparing. The fact that she had acceded to eat was an excellent sign. Despite the circumstances, he realized, the body had to be nourished.

"Where is he?" she asked in an even, emotionless tone.

"I will take you to him, if that's what you want," said Dr. Sotolongo.

"Yes, that is what I want," answered Anna without hesitation, but still without any traces of emotion in her voice. Once again, the doctor realized that she had not come to grips yet with the enormity of the situation, that somehow she had been able to repress her feelings in order to cope with Ramón's sudden death. At that point there was nothing more to be said; he would take her to the funeral home so she could have some private time with her husband before the public began to arrive. As a friend of the family, and also as their physician, Dr. Sotolongo felt that it was his responsibility to look after Anna until the more pressing matters at hand were settled.

Although still early in the day, the funeral home where Ramón's body had been taken was open. Dr. Sotolongo parked his black sedan in front of the building — its white, welcoming façade was almost a contradiction, given the somber purpose of the enterprise — and opened the car door for Anna.

The main door opened onto a vestibule, which in turn led to the different chapels into which the building had been divided. The inside walls, reflecting the theme that was stated outside, were white and plain. For a moment, Anna remembered the strange house in Havana where Oppiano Licario had spent his last night above ground.

As if they had been expected, a thin, tall man wearing a dark suit materialized in the room. Apparently he knew Dr. Sotolongo, for they shook hands and had a brief and subdued exchange of words. The man introduced himself to Anna and led them into a room where the wakes took place. The first thing that Anna noticed was that all the lights were out, and that the room was softly illuminated by the natural light that came in through a small side window. All sounds from the outside world had ceased to exist. In the back of the room, surrounded by floral arrangements, there was an open coffin. In the soft, almost nonexistent light and the deep silence, the resting figure seemed to enjoy a placid sleep. Instinctively Anna held on to Dr. Sotolongo's arm, as they slowly approached the casket. Ramón Contreras looked just as handsome in death as he had in life. His light complexion contrasted sharply with his dark hair; for an instant, Anna thought that she detected the regular rhythm of breathing under the immaculate suit and tie. It seemed that Ramón was about to open his bright blue eyes and greet her with a smile, but immediately she realized that it was her imagination. Ramón's heart had been pierced by a bullet.

As Anna stood by the coffin, looking at her husband, Dr. Sotolongo, out of respect, retreated into the shadows. He knew that

Anna needed this very private time with Ramón; it was the only time she would be alone with him. Later on that day she would be forced to face the onrush of friends who would come to pay their respects and offer their condolences. For a while she stood by the open casket, perhaps offering a silent prayer for her husband's soul, but fully conscious that she would never see him again. Once she was finished saying her silent good-bye, she turned around and looked for the doctor.

"I am ready to go home," she said softly, as if she feared disturbing Ramón's rest

.Dr. Sotolongo, as solicitous as ever, silently led Anna out of the funeral home to where his car was parked. The journey back to the house was just as quiet as when they had come into town. From time to time the doctor would momentarily take his eyes off the road to see if he could detect any sign of emotion in Anna's face, but he was not successful.

They found Flora in the kitchen, going about her duties but still visibly shaken by the events that had taken place during the past twenty-four hours. From time to time, she would raise a hand to her face to wipe the tears that she could not hold back.

"Lunch will be ready soon," she said. Then, addressing Dr. Sotolongo, "Will you be staying?"

"I had not thought about it," he answered, "but I think I will." In reality, he wanted to stay close to monitor Anna's progress and make sure that she ate before returning to the funeral home. At this point, however, the doctor's main concern was the fact that she had not shown any outward signs of emotion about the tragic events that had taken place.

While he waited downstairs, Anna went up to her room to freshen up. Flora continued with her work in the kitchen; from time to time, as she had done in the morning, she would wipe a tear, making an effort to hold back her emotions. The burial was scheduled for five in the afternoon; in her mind she could not conceive of life without señor Ramón. She had always worked for the Contreras family; she was present on the day of his birth and on the day his parents were killed. Back then she called him Ramoncito—little Ramón—a term of endearment in Spanish. It was not until he returned from Havana with his degree in agronomy and officially assumed control of the business that she started calling him señor Ramón. As the years passed, her love and loyalty had increased. She remembered fondly how every year, at the end of the school term, he would bring her a present from Havana when he returned to Pinar del Río for the summer. And now he was gone.

Even though there was only one guest for lunch, Flora set the table in the dining room. As she went about this task, she almost prepared a place at the head of the table, where Ramón would have sat had he been there. Anna's place was to the right, and she set the other plate across from it.

Anna had changed into a sober, darker dress with long sleeves that perhaps was a little excessive for the warm Cuban climate; without a word, she occupied her usual place, across from Dr. Sotolongo. Lunch proceeded at a slow, leisurely pace that denoted the fact that Anna was consciously trying to put off going back to the funeral home and facing all the people who would come to give her their condolences. It was Dr. Sotolongo who, after looking at his watch, announced that it was time to go. Flora had also changed into a more suitable dress, for she would be riding with them into town.

As they stepped out of the house, despite the shade provided by the cluster of surrounding trees, they felt full force the heat of the early afternoon sun. Even the birds, so active in the morning, had taken refuge on the highest fronds of the ceiba tree in order to find a respite from the rising temperature.

Dr. Sotolongo opened the door for Anna, and then the one right behind her for Flora. Just as before, there were no words exchanged during the trip into town. And just as before, he occasionally glimpsed at Anna, unsuccessfully trying to detect a visible sign of grief. Flora, on the other hand—Dr. Sotolongo observed this through the rearview mirror—was now weeping openly and wiping her eyes with an embroidered handkerchief she had taken out of her purse.

Outside the funeral home a crowd had already gathered. Anna recognized some of his friends and business associates. She also recognized the teacher in charge of the school near the tobacco fields. For an instant she remembered the party, years ago, to celebrate Ramón's decision to make sure every child whose parents worked in his land attended school.

In front of the building a space had been reserved for Dr. Sotolongo's car, so Anna would not have to walk. After parking, once again he opened the door for Anna and Flora and led them into the familiar vestibule. The funeral director, in turn, led the party into the central room—the most spacious of the three available—where Ramón rested in his casket. Nothing had changed, except that more flower arrangements had been delivered since their more private visit that morning.

Almost immediately the many mourners began to enter the chamber. The funeral director expertly controlled the traffic, fully aware of the capacity of the room. They came, delivered their condolences to Anna, and then moved on to view the deceased. Afterwards they were ushered through a side door that led to another room. The human flow came uninterruptedly for two hours. At precisely four o'clock, Dr. Sotolongo was alerted that the coffin would be taken to the San Rosendo Cathedral, where a requiem mass had been scheduled. He moved slowly among the mourners to where Anna was still receiving the people who had been coming to pay their condolences since their arrival. He whispered something in her ear and then led her out of the funeral home. On the way out they retrieved Flora and walked to where the car was parked.

"Are you ok?" Dr. Sotolongo asked Anna as they drove in the direction of the cathedral.

"I am fine," she answered softly, "A little tired; that is all."

The San Rosendo Cathedral had not changed in all the years that Anna had lived in Pinar del Río. Its twin towers impassively loomed over the city; its massive carved wooden doors always ready to welcome anyone in need of solace or to celebrate a joyous occasion.

To symbolize the significance of the event taking place that afternoon, the twin wrought iron gate had been decorated with white flowers. As Dr. Sotolongo parked the car in front of the building, Anna could not help remembering the day of her wedding to Ramón, and the floral arrangements that he had ordered placed around the entire perimeter of the fence that surrounded the cathedral. It all seemed so long ago, as if she were recollecting a fairy tale she had heard as a child and not a chapter of her own life.

Inside the cathedral, thick and lazy strata of smoke from the burning incense filled the atmosphere. At the foot of the altar Ramón's casket had miraculously appeared, except that now it was

326

closed. Without any warning the attending priest materialized from the side door that led to the sacristy. After genuflecting reverently, he started the mass. When the time for the homily came, he approached the pulpit slowly and then began to deliver words that had to do with the fragility and briefness of life, with the unfathomable will of God, and with the exemplary life led by Ramón Contreras. He went on to expound on the numerous charitable contributions that the deceased had made to the different organizations, including the church itself. He concluded by urging everyone to put aside their natural feelings of rage, and to honor Ramón's memory by performing as many acts of kindness as they could. Throughout the entire service, Anna sat impassively, looking straight at the priest, but without betraying any signs of emotion. Flora, on the other hand, had not stopped crying. After the mass was concluded, once again Dr. Sotolongo led Anna and Flora to where his car was parked, but had to stop several times to accommodate the people who wanted to deliver their condolences.

A hearse had materialized out of nowhere—the efficient workers had already loaded the casket—and it soon began to move slowly on its way to the cemetery. Dr. Sotolongo turned on his headlights and followed the hearse. The funeral cortege made its way from the cathedral to Independence Park and then on to the other side of town, where the cemetery was located. As the procession made its sinuous way through town, people stopped on the sidewalks or peered out of shutters that had been closed after lunch to protect them from the midday sun. By the time they reached the cemetery, the oppressive afternoon heat was beginning to wane. The ever efficient employees from the funeral home, aided by the cemetery workers, did not lose any time in trans- porting the coffin to the Contreras pantheon, where Ramón's parents were buried.

After parking his car close to the gate, Dr. Sotolongo, along with Anna and Flora and followed by other mourners, started to walk towards the burial site. At that hour of the day, when the atmosphere was beginning to cool off, she could feel the heat being released by what seemed to be infinite expanses of white marble as they made their way through the narrow paths of the cemetery. Anna was familiar with the place, for she had often come with Ramón to bring flowers to his parents' grave. During those occasions she could not have imagined that eventually

327

she would be present the day Ramón joined them in the recesses of their mausoleum.

On that bright afternoon, anyone in the cemetery could have identified the Contreras burial place; its solid carved marble lid had been removed, and the floral arrangements, brought from the cathedral, had been placed strategically nearby. Once the coffin was in the ground and the lid back in place, they would add a dash of color to the marble landscape—a cruel mockery to remind everyone that a new resident had been added—until they quickly wilted under the relentless Cuban sun. Dr. Sotolongo stopped walking, produced a handkerchief from the lapel pocket of his suit and wiped the sweat off his forehead. After a few minutes of silence, all the mourners arrived.

The local priest, also with a handkerchief in his hand, emerged from the crowd. He was understandably anxious to conclude his duties, return to the rectory and exchange his asphyxiating cassock for some cooler garments. At this point things moved rather quickly; everything had been said during the requiem mass; the cemetery workers were ready to lower the casket into the open grave. All that remained was for the priest to deliver a brief invocation and the final blessing. It was a mere formality, but a necessary one. He understood this better than anyone else present that afternoon.

Making a supreme effort, he repeated some of the words of praise for Ramón's life as he made the sign of the cross over the casket, entrusting the deceased man's soul to the infinite love and mercy of God.

It was over.

From this point on, the workers would complete the task at hand, replace the marble lid and place the flower arrangements on its surface. The crowd began to walk back to the entrance of the cemetery, where the cars were parked. There was a subdued and general whispering as the people remembered their own stories about Ramón and shared them with those within reach.

Once again Anna and Flora rode in silence with Dr. Sotolongo. It was not until they arrived at the house, that he spoke. "Is there anything else I can do for you?"

"No," answered Anna in a tired voice, "You have been most kind. Now I would like to rest."

"Of course," agreed the physician, "I will return tomorrow. Now I have other patients to see."

"Until tomorrow, then," said Anna, "And thank you again."

They watched Dr. Sotolongo's car disappear, and then the two women went into the house. The silence that welcomed them was almost palpable. Each, in her own way, carried very personal and intimate memories of Ramón; they were now united by his absence.

"Would you like something to eat, señora?" asked Flora, looking at Anna with watery eyes.

"I am not hungry, Flora; maybe later," she answered while placing a hand on her shoulder. With this seemingly trivial gesture she acknowledged that the loss was not only hers, but Flora's as well. "I think I will go up to my room now," Anna said softly.

"Just let me know if you need anything, señora," answered Flora and retreated into the kitchen.

When she walked into her room, Anna was greeted by silence and the certainty that Ramón was never coming back. But still, there was something indefinable, something else that she could not pinpoint... In order to dispel the oppressive stillness, she walked over to the stand where the record player was located, placed Immortal Arias on the turntable and then collapsed on the bed.

As the incomparable voice of Louis d'Amio filled the room, the emotional barriers that Anna had erected during the past twenty four hours began to collapse, allowing the harsh reality to rush in while simultaneously releasing her repressed feelings of sorrow. At first a soft stream of tears rolled down her cheeks, but as the music progressed, as if reflecting its unbound intensity, she wept openly, until her crying became a loud wailing at the realization of the finality of all that had happened, of the uncertain road ahead. Finally, completely spent emotionally, she fell asleep.

It was not until the following morning, still surrounded by the deep silence of her room, that she figured out what was missing. The unmistakable and intoxicating fragrance that had surrounded her since her first encounter with Ramón and that had permeated her life for the past sixteen years, was now completely absent. Anna realized then, for the first time, that Ramón indeed did not wear any type of cologne, and that the fragrance was not his, but an emanation that her own body released as a reaction to his unique presence.

Just as he had promised, Dr. Sotolongo returned at midmorning the following day. Flora opened the door and led him to the kitchen, where she had brewed a fresh pot of coffee. Anna was still upstairs, so after pouring him a generous cup — black, no sugar — she went up to let her know of his arrival. As it turned out, Anna was ready to come downstairs, so he did not have to wait.

She joined the doctor and offered him a faint smile as they exchanged greetings. From the first moment his keen professional eye looked for signs of stress, but the look on her face made him realize that Anna must have slept the night before. This did not mean, of course, that he was not still worried about her well being; the repercussions — emotional, physical and financial — of Ramón's sudden death would be felt for years to come, probably for the rest of her life.

At first the conversation was subdued and centered around trivial concerns; Dr. Sotolongo was slowly but skillfully leading up to what Anna's plans were for her immediate future now that Ramón was gone. Before he could approach this area, a loud knocking at the front door was heard. This was unusual; Anna was not expecting anyone, especially at this time of the day. She started to get up from her seat to open the door herself, but Flora was closer and already on her feet, so she was the one who answered the call.

Standing in the threshold, a uniformed man was asking to see Anna. By then Dr. Sotolongo had walked to the door and asked the man the purpose of his visit. There was no immediate answer; the man simply handed over a sealed envelope with Ramón's name prominently displayed on its surface. "These documents were delivered several days ago," he explained, "Since we have received no answer, we are delivering them again. Just make sure they get to the right person." Then he simply turned around and got into the car where another soldier, with the engine running, was waiting for him. Dr. Sotolongo watched them disappear and then went back into the house.

"An envelope was just delivered," he said while handing it to Anna, but omitting Ramón's name. "The man said that these documents had been delivered previously."

"Yes, I remember," Anna said. These were the same documents that she had attempted to take to Ramón two days earlier; apparently their urgency had not diminished, given the fact that they had been hand delivered a second time.

Using a kitchen knife, Anna carefully opened the envelope. Inside she found an official looking document, complete with illegible signatures and official seals. As she read the tight lines, she became pale and involuntarily her hands began to shake. Without any explanation she offered the documents to Dr. Sotolongo. The information contained within was clear and to the point: the house now belonged to the government and the current tenants had two weeks to vacate the premises. This was part of the so called 'Urban Reform' program that the current regime had undertaken. It was but an extension of their 'Agrarian Reform' program. First they had appropriated all privately owned land, and now all the houses in the country were being taken over as well. Dr. Sotolongo knew that there were no appeals, so he found it difficult to offer Anna a solution to her dilemma. Cuba had never experienced anything like this before. The news, of course, could not have come at a worse time. Her entire world was quickly collapsing around her.

But it was Anna who spoke after a few moments; somehow she had regained her composure. "Things will be alright," she said to Dr. Sotolongo. "There are too many memories in this house; the place is much too big for just one person, especially without Ramón."

"How can I help?" asked the doctor.

"You have done more than anyone else," she answered. "There is nothing for me anymore in Pinar del Río. I think it is best if I were to return to Havana."

"Are you sure?" asked Dr. Sotolongo, "What would you do there?"

"The same thing I did when I came to Cuba almost twenty years ago; I will work at the Pompeii and live upstairs, in my old apartment. I think a change of scenery will be good for me anyway," she added after a brief pause.

"It sounds as if the decision is made," said the doctor.

"There is no other way; I think you know that," answered Anna.

"I don't need to tell you that you can always count on me for whatever you need," added Dr. Sotolongo.

"And for that I will always be grateful; you are indeed a rare friend."

The next few days were spent deciding what Anna would take with her. Somehow she realized that her return to Pinar del Río was very unlikely. On the day of the trip, she rose early and came down to the kitchen; Flora had been up for a while and had breakfast ready for her. There was not much to be said, so Anna simply walked up to the old woman and embraced her.

"Thank you so much for everything, Flora," she said.

"No, thank you señora. You made Ramoncito very happy; that was enough for me."

At that moment Anna was reminded of how much Flora loved Ramón; she also felt her anguish at the thought that he was never coming back.

After a brief breakfast—black coffee, hot buttered toast and orange juice—Anna walked out of the house to where the Lincoln was parked. The suitcases were already in the trunk; although there was nothing else for her to do there, she hesitated for a few moments, paralyzed by the weight of her memories. Eventually, with a lethargic motion, she engaged the ignition; the powerful engine came to life at once and she guided the car expertly through the lane that led to the main highway. Reflected on the rear view mirror, standing by the door, was Flora.

Anna drove purposely, just as Ramón had taught her, watching everything around her and anticipating the maneuvers of the other motorists. Within minutes she reached the outskirts of town and the central highway that led to Havana. She realized that as many times as she had made this trip, she had never done it without Ramón. She also realized that her life from this point, in every respect, would be diminished because of his absence. As she drove through the town of Artemisa, she unavoidably recalled the first time she and Ramón stopped there for lunch, and she secretly wished that she could turn the clock back to that particular instant and relive the last eighteen years. She did not stop, but gripped the steering wheel firmly and sped on, allowing the Lincoln to devour the miles that separated her from Havana.

Around one o'clock that afternoon, she arrived in the city. The first thing she noticed was the number of soldiers in the streets and the military vehicles that had joined the busy traffic. Eventually she pulled up in front of the Pompeii and parked the car. The building itself had not changed much, but as she walked in she realized immediately that the place was not as busy as it should have been for a restaurant in the Prado during the lunch hour. It had been almost six months since her last visit.

Sergio Osorio was, as always, in the kitchen preparing one of the Italian dishes for which the house was famous. When he saw Anna, a look of surprise came over him; then he smiled and put down the kitchen utensils. He did not say anything, but simply approached her and embraced her, letting her know how sorry he was and that she could count on him unconditionally. Dr. Sotolongo had called that morning, after Anna's departure, to make him aware of all that had happened. Leaving one of his assistants in charge, Sergio led Anna into her former office.

"Sit down," he said, "I am happy to see you; it has been a while since you came to Havana."

"Yes Sergio, I know," answered Anna, then proceeded to describe the events that had taken place during the past several months, only omitting the dreadful encounter with Felipe Castillo in the storage house. Even though Sergio already knew of these events, he listened attentively, cognizant that Anna needed a sympathetic ear to listen to her tribulations.

"Your apartment upstairs is exactly the way you left it," he said, "and there is always work to be done in the restaurant. I think it will do you good to stay busy," he added.

"I agree," said Anna with a faint smile. "Speaking of the restaurant, today it looks a little slow. It is lunch time, after all." Upon hearing this, Sergio shook his head slowly from side to side, as if he didn't know where to begin.

"Things are going from bad to worse," he said lowering his voice and getting closer to Anna, as if he feared that his comments could be heard. "And I am not talking just about the restaurant. Many of our suppliers have gone out of business, and those that are still operating keep raising their prices; they claim that they just can't get what they need, since their sources have dried up. There is a general feeling of uncertainty," he continued, "All the executions and jailings have made people nervous; no one knows what is going to happen next. People stay at home more, consequently businesses that depend on the public suffer."

"Can we still keep the doors open?" asked Anna.

"For the moment," said Sergio, "We are still turning a profit, but who knows what the situation will be a month from now," he concluded with a tone of pessimism in his voice.

"We will talk again tonight," said Anna. "Now I would like to go upstairs and unpack; could you get one of the waiters to bring my suitcases upstairs? Oh, yes, one more thing," she added before exiting the office.

"What is that?" asked Sergio.

"Thank you for listening; you have always been a lot more than a business partner; you have also been a good friend."

"Don't mention it," said Sergio, "I feel the same way."

The upstairs apartment, just as Sergio had said, was exactly the way Anna and Ramón had left it during their last visit to the capital. She walked slowly to the windows that faced the Avenida del Prado below and tried to take it all in. Yes, Sergio was right, things were changing, and not necessarily for the better. She remembered her arrival in Cuba at the beginning of 1941. At that time there was an enthusiasm in the air, a feeling of collective optimism that was lacking now. The promises of the revolution had metamorphosed into massive executions, confiscation of private property and censorship of the press. The changes, without exception, had impacted the lives of everyone on the island. She was no exception. The important thing, however, despite all the reverses of fortune, was to piece her life together and go on. This was one of the more important lessons that she had learned from Giacomo in the face of adversity.

But if Anna thought that she had endured all misfortunes that fate could possibly send her way, time would prove her wrong. Almost a month passed after her return to Havana; she had settled into a comfortable and predictable routine, putting in long hours at the Pompeii and trying to devise ways to keep the business afloat.

One morning she suddenly realized that her menstrual cycle, always so regular, was conspicuously absent. At first she attributed this anomaly to the stress that she had endured recently, but when the second month came around and there was no change, she had to face the reality of the situation. Even though she had always had dreams of becoming a mother sometime in her life, this was a most inopportune time. But what bothered her the most was the ambivalence of her condition: there was no way to ascertain the identity of the father; she could be carrying Ramón's child, but there was also the possibility that she could also be carrying the child of Felipe Castillo. Just the thought of this prospect made her shudder, so she tried to put it out of her mind and think about Ramón.

At first she did not confide in Sergio, but after suffering a few bouts of morning sickness and sudden fainting spells during the day, she finally told him about her condition one evening after closing time. He assumed, of course, that the child was Ramón's, and Anna did not confess her gnawing uncertainty about the identity of the father.

"Have you seen a doctor yet?" he asked.

"No, not yet," she answered, "I don't know any doctors here in Havana."

"Let me recommend someone," said Sergio as he wrote down a name and an address on a piece of paper. "Go and see him tomorrow; promise me that you will," he concluded with a tone of concern in his voice.

"I promise; I promise," said Anna as she took the piece of paper and left the office.

The following morning, Anna drove to the address that Sergio had written on the piece of paper. The white stucco building, with its ample windows and welcoming façade, turned out to be a private clinic where a group of doctors of several specialties worked. After parking the Lincoln, Anna walked in and asked the receptionist where the office of Dr. Iturriaga was located.

A few doors down, she was received by Dr. Iturriaga's nurse. Anna explained the purpose of her visit and then filled out some forms that detailed her medical history. There was not much to put down; she had never been sick or been involved in any accidents. After handing the papers back to the nurse, Anna noticed that there were other women in the waiting room, and that they were all in different stages of pregnancy. Approximately half an hour later, the nurse — part of her job was to direct the patients who came to see the doctor — led her into an adjacent room, where the examinations were conducted.

Dr. Iturriaga was tall, thin and had blue eyes and blondish hair. Anna thought that he did not look like the average Cuban, but immediately deduced by his name that his family was of Basque ancestry. He introduced himself, asked Anna to sit down and then gathered some information about her medical history. Somehow he had gone over the papers before she came into the room and wanted to clarify some points. After the brief exchange was over, he took her pulse, blood pressure and listened to her heart with a stethoscope.

"Everything seems normal," he said, "There is no reason why there should be any complications; you are a healthy woman, after all. Of course, it is always best to monitor the pregnancy every step of the way." Anna understood that Dr. Iturriaga was being polite. He was letting her know that she was past those years in which most women become mothers, and that at thirty-nine years of age one had to be careful and vigilant to possible complications.

She left the clinic with a feeling of relief that made her realize how concerned she had been before seeing a doctor. As per Dr. Iturriaga's instructions, she was to return once a month in order to monitor her progress. In the meantime, there was no reason that she could not carry out her duties at the restaurant, just so long as she did not overdo it.

Life continued as before, but fate had yet another surprise for Anna, one that she neither expected nor imagined. A few months later, during one of her routine visits to Dr. Iturriaga's office, she received the news. As usual, he was listening for the fetus's heart beat as part of the regular check up. For an instant a puzzled look came over his face as his blue eyes seemed a little larger, since he had raised his eyebrows. He repositioned the stethoscope on Anna's exposed abdomen and listened with a look of absolute concentration.

"There is no doubt," he said with a definitive tone, "There are two heartbeats, not one. You are expecting twins." Upon hearing these words, Anna was so surprised that she did not know what to say. Twins! She could never have imagined it. "This does not change anything," continued Dr. Iturriaga, "but the delivery date may be sooner than we had anticipated. The only problem for you," he added with a smile on his face, "is that you will have to come up with two names instead of one."

Anna left the clinic almost in a state of shock. She could still not get over the fact that she was carrying twins. For an instant she was filled with an irrational fear; she had no husband, her resources were meager at best and the situation in Cuba was deteriorating by the day. But this feeling was a fleeting one, quickly swept away by the certainty and joy that the hearts that beat within her were nothing short of a miracle.

When she returned to the restaurant, rather than going upstairs to her apartment, she walked directly to the kitchen to give Sergio the news. He had two children himself, so he could fully appreciate the thrilling news. Just as Anna had expected, he was very happy about the revelation.

"This calls for a celebration," he said, "Maybe some champagne; after all events like this don't happen very often." On his way to one of the shelves where the bottles were kept, he stopped. "I forgot that you should not drink alcohol," he said and tapped his foreheaixd with his open hand, "but we can still celebrate with a glass of grape juice," he added and produced two glasses. From another shelf, he took the bottle of juice, poured until the glasses were filled half way, and gave one to Anna.

"To the twins," he said, "May they have a happy life," he added.

"To the twins," echoed Anna as she raised her glass.

During the subsequent months, as Anna's pregnancy grew more advanced, her workload in the restaurant decreased proportionally. She continued with her visits to Dr. Iturriaga, who monitored her condition even more closely as the time of delivery came closer. Toward the end of the final month, she joked with Sergio that it was almost impossible for her to climb the stairs that led to her apartment. The restless kicking inside her belly seemed to reflect the turmoil that had gripped the entire nation. Not a day went by without some sort of news about threats of an embargo or the impending invasion originating in the United States.

A few days later, during the lunch hour, Anna felt the pain of contractions telling her that the time had arrived. Sergio, who kept an eye on her constantly, left one of the head waiters in charge and rushed her to the clinic in the Lincoln. From the Pompeii someone called to alert the staff that she was on her way, so by the time she arrived they were ready. She was placed in a room and within minutes Dr. Iturriaga came in to examine her and ascertain the degree of dilation. It was always difficult to determine how long it would be until she went into the delivery room, and being a first-time mother made it even more difficult to predict. The fact that she was carrying twins also had to be taken into consideration. Anna was definitely glad that she had been seen by a doctor on a regular basis; up to the last visit he had assured her that everything was normal.

After the initial examination, the doctor left; Anna was not ready yet. Then it was a constant parade of nurses who came in at short intervals and offered words of comfort. They had seen it all before and realized that women about to give birth, especially a first timer like Anna, needed constant reassurance and support. They also told her, as they applied cold compresses on her fore-head, that afterwards she would not remember the pain, but due to its increasing intensity Anna did not believe them.

Sometime later—by then Anna had lost all track of time—after a second examination by Dr. Iturriaga, she was taken into the delivery room. The pain had not decreased, but become more concentrated and frequent. For an instant Anna asked herself what she had done to deserve such punishment, but the thought was quickly replaced by the eager voice of the doctor and nurses urging her to push, to aid the new lives that were eager to come forth and join the world. Anna complied, not so much because of their exhortations, but because she wanted the pain to end. Before long the enclosure was filled with the loud and constant crying of the newly born twins.

"They are beautiful," she heard one of the nurses saying as she cleaned them up and wrapped them in small sheets.

"Congratulations," this time it was Dr. Iturriaga, "You have two beautiful daughters."

"Thank you," Anna said, not because of the compliment, but because the pain had ended. Through her tears she saw the faces of her daughters, just minutes old, and she was instantly filled with a joy that was beyond words. Their crying, however, made her aware that from that day on she had acquired the awesome respon-sibility of caring for them, guiding them in the world and making sure that their needs were met, even if it meant denying herself. In short, her life had ceased to be hers; it now belonged to the twin girls that the nurses were holding close to her face.

The next few days were spent at the clinic, recuperating from the delivery and receiving a few visitors. Of course, Sergio came to see her and brought a huge bouquet of flowers that one of the nurses placed in a vase by Anna's bed. He was thrilled when one of the nurses brought the twins into the room and he insisted in holding them, but one at the time.

"Have you decided on their names yet?" he asked.

"No, not yet," answered Anna, although she had secretly made up her mind. The older one—if she could be called that—would be called Francesca; the other would be named Adriana. In Anna's mind, there could be no better names.

"Well, let me know when you do," said Sergio, "I have to know what to call them."

"You will be the first to know; I promise," she said.

A few days later, Anna was discharged. Dr. Iturriaga came in for a final consultation, and after ascertaining that everything was in order, told her that she could take her daughters home that afternoon. Anna was anxious to get out of the clinic, so she welcomed the news. She called Sergio at the Pompeii and asked him to come after lunch. For the past several months he had been driving the Lincoln; Anna found it too uncomfortable — the steering wheel pressed against her protruding abdomen — as the pregnancy advanced. Around two o'clock, the Lincoln appeared in front of the clinic. Sergio was wearing his black pants and white shirt; this was the busy hour at the Pompeii, so he had taken off directly from there. As he was getting out of the car, he saw Anna coming out of the clinic, holding one of the babies. A nurse was behind her, holding the other.

Sergio went around the car, opened the passenger door and helped Anna onto the seat. Then the nurse placed the second baby into the crook of her free arm. After wishing her good luck with her daughters, she went back into the clinic.

The drive to the Pompeii was not a long one, and Sergio purposely took extreme care not to make any abrupt turns, lest he awaken the twins. His curiosity, however, would not permit him to arrive at Anna's apartment before asking their names.

"Aren't you going to introduce me?" he asked, but still with his eyes on the road ahead.

"This is Francesca," said Anna raising slightly her left arm, "I named her after my mother." At this point Sergio made a sign of approval. "And this is Adriana," continued Anna, now raising her right arm, "She was named after my best friend."

"They are both beautiful," commented Sergio taking his eyes off the road for a second, "And I think the names are most appropriate; you are very lucky to have them," he concluded. What Sergio had said was true, but what he did not voice was just as valid. Anna no longer had the support—emotional or financial—of a husband; her apartment above the Pompeii was really too small for three; the earnings from the restaurant were declining every month. In short, he foresaw difficult times ahead.

Sergio's concerns were not unfounded. The twins required constant attention, so Anna had to reduce her working hours. The days when she worked one of Sergio's cousins came to the apartment to watch the girls, so much of what she earned at the restaurant was spent in their care. At the end of each day, when the girls finally went to sleep and she sat by the window overlooking the Prado, what she missed the most was Ramón's company. Somehow he had always known what to do; his unbridled enthusiasm for life made every goal, no matter how difficult, seem attainable. Now all she had left was silence and memories. Of course, Ramón had left her a sizeable amount of money, but by then foreign banks had fled the island and people had lost confidence in the financial institutions controlled by the new regime, so she kept the money hidden in the bottom of a suitcase and covered it with some old blouses and skirts. All this money, however, could not even begin to compensate for his absence. In the meantime, all she wanted was to look after her daughters. Little did she know that what life had in store for them was so farfetched that she could never have imagined it in a hundred years.

Two events in particular shook Anna's belief that her daughters had a future in Cuba. The first took place during the month of April of 1961. An ill planned and executed invasion by Cuban exiles, sponsored by the U.S. government, made everyone realize that the current Cuban regime had no friends in Washington. Before the Cuban people had a chance to react, a massive wave or repression descended over the island. Anyone who was even

340

slightly suspected of not being a follower was incarcerated. People were hastily herded into stadiums or any other large enclosures where they could be kept confined. When the landing forces, after air cover provided by American pilots was suddenly withdrawn, were easily captured by the Cuban army and subsequently publicly humiliated on national television, Anna knew that all semblance of law and due process had completely broken down and that reason no longer applied.

The second event took place in August of the same year. This one was not as violent as the first, but one that reached further into the life of everyday citizens. The government, without any type of warning and in a sweeping move, decided to change the country's currency. This meant, of course, that the money that people had placed in bank accounts or hoarded in secret places became, practically overnight, completely worthless. The old currency could be exchanged for the new one, but each person had a limit as to how much could be exchanged. What was left of fortunes that had been built over a lifetime was gone in less than twenty-four hours. She was destitute.

After that day, only one thought occupied her mind: get the twins out of Cuba. One night, after closing time and going over the books with Sergio in the small office, Anna brought up the subject of traveling abroad with the children. Fearful to be heard, even though all the employees had already left, Sergio closed the door and lowered his voice. "Many parents are sending their children out of the country," he said almost in a whisper, "They fear that the government is going to take away their parental rights. It seems unimaginable, but so many things that we thought impossible have already taken place that it would not surprise me," he added with a serious tone.

"And how are they getting the children out?" asked Anna, hoping that her prayers had been answered.

"The Catholic Church and the United States Government have organized a program to bring minors out of Cuba. When they arrive in Miami they are placed in homes in different parts of the country. Once their parents come, they are reunited and given help to start a new life in that country."

"And how do you know all this, Sergio?" asked Anna.

"Unfortunately, or maybe fortunately, one of my cousins just sent her nine-year old son to the United States."

"Why didn't she go with him? It was only logical," said Anna.

"That may very well be," answered Sergio, "But the Cuban government will not issue visas to the parents. It is a cruel ploy to prevent them from sending the children abroad."

"I should not have any problems in that respect," answered Anna, "Even though I was married to Ramón, I never gave up my Italian citizenship; my passport is still valid."

"Well, in that case," concluded Sergio, "All you need to do is get the proper documents from the Cuban authorities. There should not be too many problems."

Sergio, as usual, was correct. Anna did not encounter any real impediments to the twins' departure. After all, they were toddlers who were traveling with their mother, a foreign national. Within a month,

she had all the required documents in her possession. Of course, that did not mean that they could leave right away. The Cuban government only allowed two flights a day to Miami; the demand for a seat was so great that a waiting list had to be created. All she could do now was sit home and wait for a telegram that would tell her the date of their flight.

The business at the restaurant had taken a turn for the worse. The government kept alive rumors of another invasion from the United States in order to justify their ever-increasing repressive measures and flagrant violations of human rights; people were fearful and kept to themselves. Best not to be out too much, lest they call attention to themselves and be thrown in a Cuban jail and kept there indefinitely, without formal charges or due process.

Six weeks after requesting permission to leave Cuba, a telegram was delivered to Anna's apartment. At that moment she felt a sense of relief; once they were in a more stable environment, Anna could begin to forge a future for her daughters. That feeling of elation, however, was short lived.

The telegram succinctly informed her that Francesca and Adriana Contreras had been granted permission to leave on a flight to Miami, but there was no mention of her own name. Thinking it had to be a mistake, she walked downstairs, holding the twins in her arms.

"No mistake," said Sergio after looking at the contents of the telegram, "This is one way of dissuading you to send the children to the United States; they can't stop you from leaving, but they can make it difficult for you. The proof is in your hand," said Sergio. Then, after a pause, "Just think about everything and do what you think is best for your children. In the end, that is all that matters."

Back in the apartment, while the twins took a nap, Anna placed Immortal Arias on the turntable while considering the situation. If she did not seize this opportunity, there was no guarantee that in the future she would be assigned the same flight as the twins. For them that telegram, stating the date and time of the flight, was a solid foundation on which they could build a future life. Sooner or later, she told herself, she would join them, no matter where they were, even if they had to be separated for a while. Thinking about this impending separation and the absurdity of the situation made her cry uncontrollably; many other parents in Cuba, she also thought, were going through the same anguish. Sergio was right; the most important thing was the welfare of the girls. There was no alternative.

The following days were spent in preparation for the trip. Francesca and Adriana, only a little more than a year old, were completely oblivious to their mother's distress. They ate, slept and played, just as children their age were supposed to do. Anna, on the other hand, spent all her time with them, strolling down the Prado with a twin baby carriage and at times even venturing as far as the Malecón. In the evenings, before putting them to bed, she would sit in an easy chair while holding them in her arms. She would softly sing to them Italian lullabies that she thought completely forgotten, until they fell asleep. After placing them in their cribs she would crawl into bed herself and cry softly and call out for Ramón in the darkness and the silence of the apartment.

The date stated in the telegram inexorably arrived. On that November morning, a cooler than normal breeze was blowing in from the ocean, perhaps auguring the winters to come away from this tropical island. Anna made sure that the twins were dressed appropriately and at eight o'clock walked downstairs to meet Sergio, who had agreed to drive them to the José Martí Airport. Although the flight was not scheduled to leave until ten in the morning, Anna had gotten up at six after a sleepless night.

The Lincoln was parked in front of the Pompeii, and Sergio was standing by the door. At that moment there was no need for words; they were both painfully aware of the seriousness of the situation, of the fact that they were about to send two infants to a foreign country where they would be received by perfect strangers. Even though those unknown people had the best intentions, they were strangers nonetheless.

The drive from the center of Havana to the airport took only twenty-five minutes. Anna sat in the front, holding the twins, while Sergio drove at a leisurely pace on the almost deserted highway. It was a bright, sunny day, but the temperature had not risen yet. In the distance Anna saw the main control tower of the airport and then the building itself. Sergio slowed down and then maneuvered the Lincoln into the parking area. The walk from the parking lot to the main entrance of the airport was a short one, but Anna's eyes once again filled with tears as she held the twins close to her, for she knew that shortly they would be gone.

Inside the main terminal, in a stark contrast to the calm outside, there was frantic activity. People walked to and fro, carrying suitcases or long duffel bags. Anna noticed that there were children of all ages accompanied by their parents. They all had in common that universal look of concern that parents show whenever there is anything of consequence that affects their offspring. This situation was, for all practical purposes, a big gamble. On the one hand, the children would have stable environments and better lives. The downside, of course, was the very real possibility that they might never be reunited. Or worse, if that day was too distant, by then parents and children would have become perfect strangers. But Anna did not want to think about the possible risks; she was only considering the immediate and tangible reality of the deplorable Cuban situation that clearly dictated that the children should leave the country.

Locating the gate from which the passengers bound for the United States departed was not difficult. All they had to do was follow the other parents with children in tow down the long corridor. Eventually they found themselves in front of a waiting room whose walls were made up entirely of glass. Once the passengers entered this room there could be no further communication with their families, unless they wanted to avail themselves of hand gestures. Anna had heard of such a room; Cubans called it 'The fish bowl.'

Standing by the door, a uniformed man with a clipboard in his hand was calling out names of the people scheduled to travel that day. Once they went into the waiting room, their names were checked off a list. But this was just a preliminary requirement. Once inside, their documents were checked while, in a separate room, someone else went through their luggage. The Cuban government would allow people to leave, but not before stripping them of anything of value they carried on their person.

Eventually, the names of Francesca and Adriana Contreras were called. Anna walked up to the man holding the clipboard and informed him that he had called two infants. He did not seem surprised, further evidence that it was a common occurrence for toddlers to leave the country.

"You can go in with them and present their documents, but then you will have to leave the waiting room," he said in an emotionless tone of voice, as if he were merely referring to merchandise and not children.

The waiting room was abuzz with the whispers of those waiting to depart. Anna walked over to the clerk responsible for checking the exit documents and placed the telegram and the visa waivers on the narrow counter. The agent quickly checked the names on the master list he had on the counter.

"Everything seems to be in order," he said in the same emotionless tone as the man at the door, "The children will have to stay in a special area, until the flight leaves," he said and pointed out a side door. Anna started to walk across the waiting room, but before she could reach the door that the man hand pointed out, she heard a voice coming from behind.

"Excuse me," said a middle-aged lady wearing a gray dress and dark shoes, "I could not help but overhear your conversation; if you like I can hold your children until it is time to board the plane; that way you will be able to watch them through the glass until the last moment."

"That is very kind of you," said Anna, trying to hold back the tears, "but I do not want to impose."

"It is no imposition," answered the stranger, "I know how difficult this moment must be for you; my own son left two months ago and I hope to be reunited with him soon."

Even in this room, full of desperate and anxious people, thought Anna, acts of kindness were still possible. The woman extended her arms, and Anna carefully handed over the twins and then kissed them with an infinite love of which only a mother is capable.

"I will stand with them next to the glass," said the woman as she walked next to Anna towards the door that led to the inside of the airport. For the next twenty minutes Anna watched her daughters, now asleep in the stranger's arms, through the sheet of glass. They were only inches away, but at this moment an entire universe stood between them. Then there was a call for the passengers to board the plane; everyone in the waiting room exited through a door that led to the tarmac, where the plane was already waiting. Suddenly, weighed down by the realization that they were leaving, but mostly by the fact that she might never see them again, Anna began to weep, joining the chorus of mothers whose children now faced an uncertain future in a distant land.

By the time the lunch crowd started to arrive at the Pompeii, Anna and Sergio were back. The return journey from the airport had been a somber, quiet one. Sergio kept assuring Anna that as soon as she landed in Miami, she would be reunited with her daughters. She shook her head affirmatively, but deep down she knew it would not be that simple. Once the twins arrived in the United States, they would be turned over to Social Services. They, in turn, would place them in suitable homes. Anna knew that before her daughters were returned to her, she would have to prove that she was financially solvent and that she could provide a stable environment. But it didn't matter; the girls were out of Cuba and somehow she would find a way to get them back. Around three thirty, after the lunch crowd had dispersed into the city, Anna went up to her apartment. As she opened the door and stepped into the small living room, she noticed the envelope on the floor. Even before picking it up, she knew it was the telegram telling her when her departure date had been scheduled. With nervous hands she tore open the envelope; all she could think about was that at least this was a starting point on the road to that day when she would reunite with Francesca and Adriana.

The telegram was as succinct as the one that had been sent to the twins. It contained her name and the brief message that she had been assigned a seat in three weeks. That was all. For an instant,

Anna thought that she was dreaming; she did not dare get too excited, lest she wake up at any moment. Making an effort to restrain her emotions, she walked downstairs to look for Sergio. At that time he was in the small office of the Pompeii going over some invoices, and by the expression on his face, he was surprised to see Anna.

"It came today," she said. There was no need to explain what 'it' meant.

"When?" he asked.

"While we were at the airport," she answered, "It almost seems that someone wants to play a cruel joke on me," she added, "The flight is in three weeks."

"Not much time," said Sergio.

"It will seem an eternity," answered Anna, "What I care about the most is no longer in Cuba."

"I understand," said Sergio, "Of course, if you want me to do or help with anything in the meantime, just say it."

These last words had not been necessary. Throughout the years, but especially after Ramón's death and Anna's return to Havana, her friendship with him had grown stronger, until Anna came to rely on him for almost everything.

"Thank you Sergio; you are a true friend," she said and briefly placed her hand on his.

"Don't mention it," he said while shrugging his shoulders and looking down, a little embarrassed. There was nothing more to be said, nothing more to do except wait.

During her remaining days in Cuba, even though she did not have to, Anna kept working at the Pompeii. She knew that soon it would be behind her and that she would miss Sergio and the other people who had worked there for so many years. In the evenings she took long walks along the Prado, trying to etch every feature, every building and every sound of that unique avenue that had been the location of her restaurant for so many years. Sometimes, just as she had done with Francesca and Adriana, she would stroll down to the Malecón and sit on the wall, facing the ocean. She remembered how much Ramón loved this place, the sea, even though he had been born and raised away from it. She pretended that he and the twins were waiting for her, counting the hours until her arrival. But invariably reality intruded in her reverie and she found herself sobbing softly in the darkness, listening to the waves break against the rocks below.

On the eve of her departure, along with her clothes and personal articles, she packed those items that meant the most to her in a suitcase. Before closing it, just as she had done the day of her arrival in Havana, she placed Immortal Arias on the turntable. Louis d'Amio's voice guided her from dusk to night, providing an oasis of solace in that lonely and barren landscape that her life had become. After closing the suitcase, she went to bed. Soon she would be reunited with her daughters. With that thought on her mind, she fell asleep.

The trip to the airport the following morning was just like the one three weeks before, except that this time Sergio drove at a brisk pace. They were not late; the road was not congested, but Anna was anxious to get there, as if her presence would make the flight leave sooner than scheduled. For the third time that morning, she checked her documents.

The atmosphere at the terminal was identical to the one they had seen a few weeks before; crowds of families saying good-bye to children who would be leaving for the United States. The expressions of sadness, the hugs and the tears were just as poignant. Only the people were different. As she and Sergio walked down the corridor that led to the waiting room, Anna suddenly felt a sense of relief, almost numb to all emotions. She only thought about the fact that at the end of the flight her daughters were waiting for her.

"Thank you for everything," she said as she hugged Sergio before handing her papers to the man at the door.

"It has been a privilege to be your friend," he said in a faint voice. For an instant Anna thought that he might break down, but he managed to compose himself.

"Keep the Pompeii running," she said, "I will be back soon."

"I look forward to that day," he said, "I just hope it is not too far into the future."

"It will be here before you know it," answered Anna as she went into the waiting room. Then she was surrounded by strangers just waiting for the call to board the plane that would take them out of Cuba. Behind each face there were sketchy plans, unrealistic dreams and unfounded aspirations that most likely would never come to pass in their new land. But at this point it really did not

348

matter, not for any of them. The undeniable reality was that in a few minutes they would be flying away from the island.

Suddenly, the impersonal voice coming through the loud-speakers summoned the passengers to start boarding. As she exited the waiting room on her way to the plane, Anna turned around briefly. Sergio was still there, his face pressed against the glass, waving slowly.

By then the plane had already taxied to the runway close to the departing gate. Its white fuselage bore the familiar Pan American sign in blue letters. The line of travelers slowly disappeared into the cabin and took their seats. At that moment, just before takeoff, an eerie silence came over the passengers. Eventually, once everyone was on board and seated, the door closed and the humming of the already running engines intensified as the plane gained speed. At the moment of takeoff, there was a spontaneous burst of applause.

But Anna was busy looking out the small window, watching the city, the island itself, become more distant and faint. At that instant, one thought came into her head: For the past twenty years, she had been truly happy.

Book Three: United States

X

Miami International Airport extended almost to the horizon—or so it appeared from the distance and seen through the small windows of the Pan American plane about to land. The flight from Havana had taken less than an hour, but because of the general excitement, it felt that just a few minutes had passed since the plane had taken off. The passengers peered down curiously, eager to catch their first glimpse of the new country that had occupied their imagination and given substance to their dreams for so long.

As the plane landed and taxied down the runway, once again there was a spontaneous burst of applause from the passengers. Anna could clearly see that some of them were visibly shaken and overcome with emotion, now that they were faced with a moment they had anticipated so often and for so long. Behind every face was a story—probably one filled with sadness and heartbreak. She also realized at that moment she was not the exception, but the rule of that tragic and poignant reality.

The stewardesses, experienced with this type of emotional outbursts, urged the passengers to remain in their seats with their seat belts buckled until they were instructed by the pilot to disembark. Because of the apparent organization every step of the way, Anna realized that the American officials had previous experience in handling the influx of immigrants. After leaving the plane, it was only minutes before she was standing in front of one of the immigration clerks with her passport and other papers in hand. By the sudden look of surprise that came over his face she realized that he was used to receiving and inspecting the light blue Cuban passports, and not the bright burgundy Italian ones.

"What is the purpose of your visit?" the officer asked.

"I have come to be reunited with my daughters," Anna explained, "They came three weeks ago."

Everything was in order; as to why this Italian citizen was entering the U.S. with a group of soon to be Cuban exiles—even if she was looking for her daughters—was a mystery to him, but one that would not cause him to lose any sleep.

As Anna moved away from the desk of the immigration officer and down the corridor that led into the airport itself, she spotted two nuns in a booth with a prominent sign that proclaimed 'Catholic Relief Services.' This was precisely the station that she needed to find; the nuns had probably received Francesca and Adriana after their arrival three weeks earlier. Now it was just a matter of tracking down her daughters.

"Good afternoon," said Anna in English, but the nuns returned the greeting in Spanish. They had been expelled from Cuba — along with other nuns and priests — a few months earlier; the Church had stationed them at the airport to welcome and give some guidance to the waves of refugees that arrived on a daily basis.

"How may we help you?" asked one of them.

"I sent my daughters three weeks ago," she explained, "I would like to see them as soon as possible."

"That is perfectly understandable," agreed one of the nuns, "But first we must ask you if you have a place to stay. Do you know anybody in this city?"

"No, no one," answered Anna. "My most pressing concern was to get my daughters out of Cuba, so I sent them in the care of the Catholic Church."

"Your case is not unusual," added the younger one. "In fact, it is quite common."

"Can you help me find them?" insisted Anna.

"That is what we are here for," interjected the older one, "Our organization has contracted with a downtown hotel where we send those Cubans who have no family or a place to go. We can send you there and tomorrow we will have the information about your daughters. How does that sound?" she concluded with a smile. Anna did not consider telling the nuns that technically she was not Cuban; all she wanted was to find Francesca and Adriana, so she agreed readily to what the nuns proposed. As soon as she became settled, she could start the process of reclaiming her children.

"You are most kind," said Anna, realizing that she had no other course of action.

"We have a van that takes our guests to the hotel; it will be leaving shortly, as soon as we take care of the passengers that came in today."

While the nuns turned their attention to the other people needing their help, Anna concentrated on her surroundings. The Miami airport, or at least what little she had seen of it, gave the impression that it had expanded since she had first visited almost twenty years before. This time, however, the travelers were not well to do Cubans with pockets full of money seeking a holiday away from Havana, but a veritable wave of humanity that had been forced from their homeland by circumstances beyond their control. They scurried about, clutching their meager belongings and trying to get a sense of direction in this new land. The stories could clearly be read on their faces, and showed signs of relief and happiness whenever relatives or friends appeared. They hugged, kissed and shed tears of joy and then the newcomers were whisked away to distant houses in the city, where they would celebrate with an elaborate dinner that would go on into the late hours of the night as stories of other family members, close friends and the overall political situation in Cuba were told.

At last the last passengers from that day's flight were gone. A small group remained around the Catholic Relief Services booth, patiently waiting for the nuns. The older one signaled the group to follow her down the corridor that led to the outside. Parked by the curb was a white van with the sign 'Catholic Relief Services' painted on its side in bright blue letters. As he saw the group approaching, the driver stepped out and opened the sliding side door.

"The suitcases can go in the back," he said while opening the rear doors of the van. After all the luggage had been carefully stacked, he closed the doors and got behind the wheel. Anna noticed that he did not receive any instructions from the nuns, but placed the van in gear and started to drive. It was apparent that he made the trip often, so instructions were unnecessary.

The traffic at that hour was getting heavier, but the driver skillfully guided the van as they made their way away from the airport and toward the center of Miami. As they approached their destination, the buildings became taller and the distance between them diminished, as if every square foot of space needed to be utilized. Even though it was November, through the open windows

355

of the van Anna could feel the waves of hot air rising from the pavement and reflecting off the concrete sides of the buildings. No one spoke, but simply looked at the surroundings, trying to fathom this new and foreign reality that from this day on they had made their own. At last they pulled up in front a two-story building. The Rice Hotel was located in the very center of Miami, almost at the intersection of Miami Avenue and Flagler Street. The hotel proper was on the second story of the building, and a narrow stairway led from the street level below to its lobby. Anna and the other random passengers, led by the two nuns, slowly made their way upstairs, suitcases in hand and a feeling of unknown expectations that manifested itself in a knot at the pit of their stomachs.

As they emerged from the top of the stairs, they found themselves in an ample lobby. The first thing that Anna noticed was the carpet; it had certainly seen better days and it could have used a cleaning. The eclectic furniture—a couch upholstered in green vinyl, several easy chairs of different colors—had probably come from a second hand store. The chairs and couch were arranged around a wooden stand with a black and white television set with rabbit ears on top. At the back of the lobby, almost taking the entire length of the wall, was the desk. The man behind it did not show any surprise as the nuns, followed by the group of travelers, emerged from the street below. He had probably been alerted from the airport that they were on their way, for he already had some keys ready on the Formica counter. Since most of the passengers had come by themselves, they would be given single rooms. After registering the guests, the man handed out the numbered keys and explained that there were two communal bathrooms in the hallway. The rooms were just that, rooms. Before walking down the narrow hallway to the one that had been assigned to her, Anna turned to one of the nuns and confirmed the appointment the next morning.

"The refugee center is within walking distance of the hotel," one of the nuns explained. "In the meantime, here is our telephone number, just in case," she said while handing Anna a small card.

"Thank you," she answered, "I will be there early tomorrow morning."

There was nothing more to be said, nothing more to do except wait until the next day. With the key in one hand and her suitcase in the other, Anna made her way to her room and opened the door.

To say that the place was minuscule would have been a gross understatement, for she found herself in what would more accurately be described as a large closet. The single bed occupied most of the floor space; next to it there was a nightstand with a small oscillating fan that propelled the stagnant air in every direction. At once Anna understood its purpose, for there were no windows. For an instant she could not help but to compare this room with the ample corner suite, overlooking the ocean, that she had shared with Ramón at the Cardozo Hotel during their honeymoon. But it didn't matter, she told herself; this was just a temporary situation and soon, somehow, she would be reunited with her daughters and get on with her new life in the United States.

After closing the door behind her, she placed her suitcase on the bed and opened it. On the opposite side of the nightstand there was a makeshift rack, full of empty hangers. Anna took her time, arranging the few garments on the rack and the rest of the items in the drawers of the nightstand. Finally the only thing left in the suitcase was a box where she had neatly arranged those items that carried a special significance to her. She wished for a record player, so she could play Immortal Arias, but she had to settle for the memory of Louis d'Amio to comfort her in this stuffy room of a rundown Miami hotel. After running a mental inventory of the contents of the box, she closed it, slid it under the bed and left the room.

The activity in the lobby had not waned since Anna's arrival earlier that day. Some of the guests were talking to the man at the desk, while others were watching the black and white TV set. Most of the guests, Anna soon realized, were sitting on a covered terrace that spanned the entire length of the building and gave an ample view of Miami Avenue below. They enjoyed the cooler air while conversing loudly—as Cubans tend to do—mostly about the political situation in the island and the impending collapse of the current regime. Anna also noticed that the group was an eclectic one; they were young and old, male and female, but were now united by the common fate of having been displaced from their homeland and the prospects of an uncertain future. Most wanted to believe—as Anna did herself—that their stay in the United States would be a brief one, and that before long their lives would resume their usual course in Cuba. There were several empty chairs, so Anna did not hesitate and sat down. For a while, with the incessant chatter as a background, she looked at the traffic below. Many of the cars were shiny convertibles with young drivers who kept the radio tuned to music stations at high volume. Even though they were only ninety miles away from Cuba, Anna thought, they were in a different world.

Sitting by himself at the far end of the terrace, reading a book, was a thin teenager. He had black hair and wore a short-sleeved shirt with light patterns. Somehow he seemed familiar, but Anna could not quite place him. For a few minutes she studied the young man; yes, she was sure that she had seen him before. It was not until he raised his head, in order to look momentarily at the avenue below, that Anna was able to place him. Although she had never actually met him, she had seen him occasionally at the Escuela del Hogar with señora Albet. He was one of her children. For an instant she hesitated, but then stood up and walked to where the young man was sitting.

"Hello," she said.

The young man raised his head from the book and then there was no doubt in Anna's mind. Señora Albet's features were neatly repeated in the boy.

"Hello," he said timidly, perhaps taken aback by Anna's unexpected appearance. He also showed a look of puzzlement, since he did not know the person standing next to him.

"I am certain that I have seen you before," explained Anna, "What region of Cuba do you come from?"

"I am from the city of Pinar del Río," he answered.

"So am I," exclaimed Anna. "I believe I saw you occasionally at the Escuela del Hogar;" then, after a pause, "Not as a student, of course, but just visiting."

"My mother used to be the head of it," the young man answered, "before they shut it down."

"What became of your mother?" asked Anna with genuine curiosity.

"Nothing happened," answered the young man with a pensive look on his face. "My father was taken to jail without any charges. A few months later they released him without any explanations. They are both in Pinar del Río, trying to get by and waiting for this nightmare to end."

"I know exactly what you mean," answered Anna, but without offering any concrete details. "By the way, my name is Anna. I used to work with your mother; she is a fine lady."

"Thank you for saying that," said the young man, "We all need to hear those things from time to time."

"It is true," continued Anna, "She gave me a job at her school and always treated me kindly and with respect."

"That's the way she is," he said with obvious pride in his voice.

"By the way," said Anna changing the subject, "Is there a place to eat around here? I arrived today and I am not familiar with the surroundings."

"There is a Royal Castle on the next block," answered señora Albet's son. "A lot of people go there."

"What is a Royal Castle?" asked Anna.

"It is just a small place where they sell hamburgers and other fast foods," he explained, "There is nothing like that in Cuba."

"I think I will go there," said Anna. "Thank you for the information."

"It was nothing," answered the young man and then returned to his book.

Anna was not really that hungry, but she wanted to take a walk, and this was just as good an excuse as any. On the way to the hotel, the nuns had given each of the occupants of the van a five-dollar bill so they could get something to eat that evening. Tomorrow, once they arrived at the refugee center and registered, they would be given other means of aid.

As Anna walked through the lobby, she noticed that the group around the television set had increased, and they had huddled tightly around its stand. They were hungry for any type of news that had to do with Cuba, for a clue that would suggest that soon they would be going home. She did not stop, but walked directly downstairs. At the foot of the stairs, next to the entrance of the hotel, there was a record shop. In the window, prominently displayed, Anna saw long-playings by Nat King Cole, Elvis Presley, Ray Charles and other performers who were in vogue at that time. She walked slowly, trying to assimilate everything—it was all new and so different from the Paseo del Prado—until she reached the corner of Flagler and Miami Avenue, where the pedestrian crossings were located. The signs either invited one to 'Walk' in white luminous letters or displayed the admonition 'Don't

Walk' in red ones. Anna crossed the street in the direction of Biscayne Boulevard, and suddenly found herself in front of the ample display windows of Burdine's, one of the most exclusive department stores in Miami. As she surveyed the merchandise and the latest fall fashions she had to recall one month of December, long ago, when Ramón had taken her shopping to *El Encanto* in Havana. He had endured, patiently and without protest, hours in the women's department while she tried on an array of dresses and blouses. At the end, when she attempted to return some of the items to their shelves, he would not hear of it. That was true love, she concluded.

As she continued her leisurely exploration of that city block, Anna passed another record shop, a shoe store, a travel agency, and a small restaurant called Marakas. The one thing they had in common was that they were all busy. People were coming in and out constantly with packages in hand. Once again, she thought of Havana and how as of late all the goods had disappeared from the store shelves. Eventually, just as señora Albet's son had told her, she found herself in front of the Royal Castle. The establishment was neither royal nor was it a castle. It could better be described, simply, as a hole in the wall. Along the single Formica top counter there were ten stools affixed to the floor, and the walls were covered with white tile. Facing the customers was a simple menu displayed in black letters. A man dressed in white skillfully operated a grill and also took the orders from the customers. What stood out immediately was the more than reasonable prices of the available items.

Anna sat down on one of the vacant stools and read the menu one more time. Although she was not really hungry, it was important to eat something. When the man at the grill came over, Anna ordered a cheeseburger and a birch beer. She had never tasted this type of soft drink, so she decided that this day would be a good one to start. While her food was being prepared, she looked at the other customers sitting at the counter. Although they were of different ages, they were clearly not well to do individuals; their clothing and shoes clearly told her that. Further, the expression on their faces gave away the fact that they were struggling. In all probability they would have to count their pennies in order to make sure they had enough money for the simple meal. As they ate they looked straight ahead or their attention was focused on newspapers folded in half to accommodate the narrowness of the counter and not intrude into the space of other customers.

Anna's food arrived within minutes of her placing the order. First, the birch beer came in a large glass mug that had obviously been placed in a freezer, for its surface showed frozen condensation, then the cheeseburger on a white plastic plate.

"Thank you," she said, uttering her first words in English as she paid for the meal. The total amount was twenty cents.

"No problem," said the man at the counter as he returned to the grill.

Anna ate slowly at first, and then with more enthusiasm as she realized that she was hungry after all. The cheeseburger had just been made and the pickles and onions gave it extra flavor. When she took the first sip of the birch beer, however, she had to stop. This was nothing like she had ever tasted before. Even though it looked like Coca-Cola, it did not taste like it. She tried to recall the different soft drinks available in Cuba to establish a credible comparison, but gave up after a few seconds. All she could conclude was that it did not taste like any other beverage, especially *Materva*, arguably the most popular of all Cuban soft drinks.

After finishing the meal, Anna stood up and continued her walk around the city block, stopping occasionally to look at the merchandise in the store windows. They had magically come to life with cleverly concealed lights that both illuminated and highlighted the sundry items on display. It was apparent that this was not a residential area, but one devoted to business. She kept thinking about the meeting at Catholic Relief Services the following morning, about the myriad of questions she had for the nuns, not just about the whereabouts of the twins, but also about all those things that we take for granted until they are taken away, those things that make up a daily routine: where to eat, where to do laundry, basic transportation, etc. It was almost too much to contemplate, but she knew that she would have to overcome those obstacles if she hoped to be reunited with her daughters.

Despite the deliberate slow pace of her walk, she found herself once again in front of the stairs that led to the lobby of the Rice Hotel. Even at street level she could hear the voices of some of the guests as they energetically debated a political point of view. As she ascended the stairs, the sound of the ever-present television set also reached her. The familiar scene at the lobby had not changed;

guests huddled around the TV set. Some sat on the green couch or the adjacent chairs, while the latecomers sat on the floor. On the open terrace another group occupied the chairs that overlooked Miami Avenue. Those were the ones who preferred conversation over television. Anna instinctively looked for señora Albet's son, but the young man was not there. At that particular moment, surrounded by the lively group on the terrace and the eclectic crowd around the television set in the lobby, she realized how alone she was.

The Cuban Refugee Center, despite the early hour, was already crowded. Even though Anna had left a six o'clock wakeup call at the front desk, it had been unnecessary; she had spent most of the night anticipating this day. When the knock on the door finally came—there were no room telephones at the Rice Hotel—she was already up. After dressing and using the bathroom in the hallway, she walked into the lobby to ask directions to the Refugee Center. That, too, proved unnecessary. A small group of people had already gathered there, so they could walk together. Some would go directly to their destination; others would stop to have breakfast on the way.

"Good morning," said someone from Anna's left. At first, she did not know if the person was addressing her, but there was no one else on the spot where she was standing. The voice belonged to a slender woman with graying hair and an affable smile; she looked vaguely familiar, but Anna could not readily place her. That casual encounter, although neither woman realized it at the time, would be the beginning of a friendship that would only be severed by death, many years later and in a distant city whose name they had yet to hear.

"Good morning," answered Anna, not wanting to appear rude to the woman.

"By the expression on your face I see that you do not recognize me," she said.

"You seem vaguely familiar, but you are right, I can't remember where I have seen you before," admitted Anna.

362

"That's alright," said the woman as she smiled. "We were in the same flight yesterday and the van from the airport brought us here together. By the way, my name is Silvia Delgado."

"It is a pleasure, Silvia; I am Anna d'Amio. Forgive me for not recognizing you, but I have a lot of things on my mind," she explained.

"No need to apologize; I realize that we all have problems and matters that must be resolved," she added.

"Are you going to the Cuban Refugee Center?" asked Anna.

"Where else? It is the first stop we must make in order to get a sense of direction in this country, but before going I would like to have some breakfast."

"I know just the place," said Anna thinking of the Royal Castle, "It is on the way and the prices are very reasonable."

"Then, lead the way," said Silvia as she walked to the stairway that led to the street.

The two women made their way down, but when they reached the sidewalk, rather than walking towards Flagler St., Anna walked in the direction of 1st St. N.E., where the Royal Castle was located.

"Are you sure you know where we are going?" asked Silvia after a few minutes.

"Of course," answered Anna confidently, "I took a walk yesterday and had dinner at that very restaurant." By that time the familiar white tile façade of the Royal Castle was in view, so Anna smiled and pointed it out to Silvia.

Although it was early in the morning, the Royal Castle had been open for hours. Its breakfast menu catered to those people who left home before dawn and did not want to prepare breakfast for themselves; it was a quick and economical alternative that freed them from that early chore. In this case, it also fit the bill because neither Anna nor Silvia had any means of cooking at the Rice Hotel.

They sat down on the silver stools and started to study the menu. "You have to help me," said Silvia suddenly.

"What is it?" asked Anna, not knowing what the problem could be.

"I can't read the menu," confessed Silvia.

"The breakfast menu is a simple one," explained Anna, "You have your choice of eggs cooked different ways, toast, grits, hash brown potatoes and then your drink: coffee, milk, or juice." By then the man behind the counter was already standing in front of them to take their order.

"I will have whatever you are having," said Silvia, so Anna ordered the scrambled eggs, light buttered toast, hash brown potatoes and black coffee.

"Where did you learn to speak English?" asked Silvia in a tone of awe.

"I don't speak English that well," explained Anna. "I have been taking classes for the past few years, but I can read it better than I can speak it."

"Well, that is a lot more than I can do," said Silvia, "It always amazes me how people can actually communicate in that language."

"I am sure Americans must say the same thing about Cubans," offered Anna, "I suppose it depends on what a person is used to. When I arrived in Cuba, twenty years ago, I thought that I would never get the hang of Spanish, but constant practice made all the difference."

"I can't believe you were not born in Cuba," said Silvia, "I cannot detect any accent at all. Where is your home?"

"I consider Cuba my home," Anna was quick to clarify, "But I was born in Italy."

"And now you are living in a hotel filled with Cuban refugees," commented Silvia, "It is amazing."

"It is not as farfetched as it sounds," explained Anna, "My husband was Cuban, and my daughters were born in Havana; for many years I have been a Cuban resident. But as I said before, I consider Cuba my home."

"What about your family?" asked Silvia, obviously interested in Anna's life.

"My husband is no longer living," Anna explained, but without going into details. "My daughters came to the United States three weeks ago. That is why I am here, to be reunited with them and put our lives together, until we can return to Havana."

"That's what we all want," echoed Silvia. The two women would have continued their conversation, but breakfast was over and it was time to go. "Do you know how to get to the Refugee Center?" she asked.

364

"I have never been there, but I was told it is about seven blocks away on Biscayne Boulevard; I am sure we will find it," added Anna.

The Cuban Refugee Center, just as Anna had said, was located on Biscayne Boulevard. Its location was a building called Freedom Tower; this structure had been used throughout its life for different purposes. At this particular time, it was a hub where the influx of Cuban refugees were welcomed, registered for different services, and given counseling as to what shape their lives could take in the United States.

As they made a left from 1st Street onto Biscayne Boulevard, they realized that there were other people—some by themselves, others in small groups—walking in the same direction.

"This reminds me a little bit of Havana," commented Anna.

Although the resemblance was not that pronounced, she was referring to the fact that Biscayne Boulevard—just like Avenida del Prado—was open and wide, and the traffic was separated by a median where coconut trees and royal palms had been planted. Then, of course, was the bay, always there, like the harbor in Havana. "Too bad they don't have a Malecón," she said to Silvia, "but I guess that would be too much to expect."

"I have never been to the Malecón," confessed Silvia, "but I have seen pictures of it. In fact, the only time I visited Havana was this week, when I left Cuba. My entire family is from the province of Camagüey."

"That is a shame," said Anna, "I mean the fact that you never visited Havana; it is a wonderful city."

"Well, maybe someday; everyone says that within a year we will be back in Cuba."

"I hope they are right," said Anna, "For everyone's sake."

In the distance, the unmistakable silhouette of Freedom Tower was now visible. As Anna and Silvia approached the building, the sound of people speaking Spanish became more prevalent. Covering the walls in the lobby were signs directing the visitors to the different offices where the services provided by the center were dispensed. Having just arrived in the United States, both Anna and Silvia would go first to the office where emergency financial aid was provided. This procedure was routine; the U.S. Government wanted to make sure that the refugees got settled as soon as possible, found work and stopped receiving the emergency aid.

After all, the entire program was funded with taxpayers' money. Contained in the same building was a branch of the employment office; their job was to assess the type of skills the refugees possessed and try to match them with the available jobs. Those who were willing to accept work in other states would be relocated. To that end, and reiterating the American reputation for efficiency, there was even a Social Security branch on the premises, where prospective workers could register and receive their cards. Every contingency had been foreseen; every need had been anticipated. Anna's ultimate goal, of course, was to reunite with her daughters, so she knew that the sooner she dealt with the red tape, the sooner she would be with Francesca and Adriana again.

Despite the early hour, a line had already formed in front of the door labeled 'Emergency Aid.' These first few days would be spent mostly waiting in line, but it was an unavoidable situation. In fact, most refugees were grateful that the United States Government had opened its doors and provided so many services during this time of need, so they did not mind waiting. These occasions provided fresh opportunities to strike up new friendships or resume interrupted conversations with old acquaintances. That meant that the waiting room was filled with multiple exchanges that combined into a loud cacophony often underscored with gesticulating hands, exaggerated facial expressions, or pierced by the staccato sound of sudden laughter. In short, it was a room full of Cubans.

Eventually Anna and Silvia found themselves inside the office proper. There were several desks where the clerks gathered and processed the information they collected from the seemingly endless parade of prospective recipients.

"Let's meet outside at noon," said Anna.

"Agreed," answered Silvia, "It is hard to tell what we will have to face this morning."

At that very instant, one of the clerks signaled Anna to approach his desk. "Sit down," he said, and then asked her for her papers. She noticed that even though the clerk was obviously an American, he spoke fluent Spanish, but with a tinge of an accent. After taking down all the particulars, including the address of the Rice Hotel, he explained to her that the purpose of the aid was to get people on their feet until they could get a job and support themselves. She would have to come to the refugee center on a

366

weekly basis in order to pick up her check. The first one would be issued that very day, so she could cover her expenses for the week. To Anna this made absolute sense; she did not want to depend on welfare aid indefinitely, but was anxious to start earning a living and regain custody of her daughters.

After leaving that particular office, Anna looked for the small office that the Catholic Relief Services had in the refugee center. There were not as many people waiting in line, so it took her less than half hour to meet with one of the representatives. Once again she showed her documents, along with the birth certificates of Francesca and Adriana, and gave all the details as to when the twins had flown into the United States. "All I want is to be with my daughters," she added.

"That is what we all want," said the woman sitting behind the desk, "To reunite parents and children as soon as it is feasible."

"Can you tell me where they are?" pleaded Anna.

"Let's see," said the woman as she opened the top drawer of an immense file cabinet. From where she was sitting Anna could see the letters A-D. "Yes, here they are," exclaimed the clerk, "Francesca and Adriana Contreras arrived three weeks ago; they were received by Catholic Relief Services and sent to a temporary home until more permanent accommodations could be found."

"Are they close by?" pleaded Anna again, "I must see them."

"According to the files," said the woman after a pause, they remained in Miami for two weeks, then they were sent to two separate homes, one in Virginia and the other one in New Mexico."

Although Anna was not quite sure exactly where those states were, she did know that they were located a great distance from Miami. The woman behind the desk must have read Anna's look of desperation, for she wrote something on a sheet of paper and then handed it to her.

"These are the addresses and the telephone numbers. You can call any time you like." Then, after a short pause, as if wanting to reassure Anna that her children were all right, "We screen all our prospective foster parents very carefully, and we also have unannounced visitations, just to make sure that the children are in a proper environment."

"Why were they not kept together?" asked Anna. It was a fair question.

"Our organization has to place the children as the spaces become available. Of course we try our best to keep the siblings together, but sometimes that is not possible, especially now with the daily influx of children that we have experienced lately."

"I understand," said Anna, "How do I get them back?"

"As soon as you have a steady income and the proper means to care for them, come back to see me. I will personally file the necessary requests; in the meantime, just think that your children are in good hands," she assured Anna.

"Thank you," said Anna as she stood up and left the office. The meeting had left her with mixed feelings. On the one hand, she knew exactly where her daughters were, and also that they were being cared for. On the other hand, they were many miles away and the only way to get them back would be to find work, so she could get back on her feet financially.

Anna's next stop was the branch of the employment office. The line that had formed in front of that particular door was much longer than the previous one. No one liked to wait, but there was no choice. While she waited in line, she considered the progress that had been made: she had a check in her purse and a piece of paper with the addresses and phone numbers of the families that were caring for the twins. The rest was up to her; she would take advantage of all the opportunities that were being offered to the incoming Cubans, until the twins were back with her.

Although the line for the employment office was longer, Anna noticed that it was moving faster than the previous one. When she finally walked through the door, she realized that there were more clerks in this department; this also made sense, since the government wanted to make the period of financial aid as brief as possible.

Once again, Anna found herself sitting across the table from another clerk. This one was a man wearing a short- sleeved shirt and a bow tie. He looked at her from above his horn-rimmed glasses and asked her for her papers. Just as the other clerks, he spoke Spanish fluently, but with a trace of an accent. He frowned slightly as his clear blue eyes, magnified by the lenses, expertly scrutinized the documents that Anna had handed to him.

"What type of employment are you looking for?" he finally asked.

"I had not given it much thought," answered Anna, "In Cuba I used to be a teacher."

"I am afraid," said the clerk in a matter of fact tone of voice, "That teaching here is not a very feasible prospect. First of all, you would have to become certified again. That is a long process, especially for someone who has no credentials. The other barrier, of course, is the language."

"I do speak English," answered Anna softly in that language.

The clerk looked up, visibly surprised, and smiled faintly. "And how did you learn, if you don't mind my asking?" Anna could tell that he was curious; apparently she was an exception to the droves of immigrants that he saw on a daily basis. He had also switched languages, maybe to further ascertain Anna's fluency.

"I have always been interested in languages," she said, "In Cuba I met with a tutor once a week; I also speak Italian."

At this point the clerk wrote something in Anna's file, perhaps a reminder to himself. "Come back to see me tomorrow morning," he said, "Maybe by then I will have found something for you. Of course, you understand that jobs are hard to come by; I do not want to offer you any false hopes."

"I understand," said Anna, still using English. "My primary concern is to start working as soon as possible; I will be back in the morning."

"I look forward to seeing you again," said the clerk as Anna stood up and prepared to leave the office.

The morning had passed quickly, and Anna was glad that it had not been a total waste of time. She had registered with the refugee center, had a check in her pocketbook, had found out where the twins were and prospects of employment seemed bright. Not bad for one morning.

The commanding clock in the main lobby of the center told her it was almost time for lunch, so Anna walked over to the main door, where she and Silvia had agreed to meet earlier that day. A few minutes past twelve, Silvia appeared, and by the smile on her face Anna deduced that things had gone well for her that morning.

"Were they able to help you?" asked Silvia, aware of Anna's urgency concerning the twins.

"You go first," answered Anna, "Tell me what happened."

"Well, they gave me some emergency money, and as long as I keep looking for work they will continue to help me. It is not much, but at least it is an assurance that I will have some money coming in," she said.

"I know," Anna agreed, "They also gave me some money for this week.

"I am not so sure about employment though," continued Silvia. The sudden change of expression on her face left no doubts that she was not encouraged.

"What do you mean?" asked Anna.

"The gentleman explained to me that the two main obstacles that Cubans face, and all refugees for that matter, is the lack of credentials and not knowing the language. No matter how well qualified we are, those two hurdles must be overcome first, if we are to find suitable employment. In the meantime we have to settle for whatever is available," she concluded with a sigh.

"I know," said Anna, "But we must be patient; I am sure that better times are ahead." This last statement, although she was not so certain of its validity, she had made for Silvia's sake. She did not want to sound pessimistic in front of her friend.

"How about you?" asked Silvia.

"Things went well," answered Anna with a smile. "I know where my daughters are, and I have to come back tomorrow to the employment agency. I am hoping that this situation is just temporary," she added after a pause.

"Well, it appears that your morning was most profitable," she said.

"It is a start," conceded Anna, "But at least we are on our way to getting settled. In my mind, there is nothing worse than uncertainty. I think that is the reason we all left Cuba; one never knows what is going to happen there from one day to the next."

"Yes, I agree with you," said Silvia in a more pensive tone, as if Anna's comment had awakened some recent and painful memories.

"It is time for lunch," said Anna, purposely trying to steer the conversation to lighter and more immediate matters, "We can stop at the Royal Castle on the way back to the hotel, if you like."

"That will be fine," Silvia agreed.

As they walked to the restaurant, Anna noticed that the amount of traffic on Biscayne Boulevard, both vehicular and pedestrian, had increased since earlier that morning. They also heard some other people—obviously Cubans—speaking Spanish.

The Royal Castle, now that it was lunchtime, was experiencing its busiest hour of the day. Since all the stools were occupied, Anna and Silvia had to wait for some of the patrons to finish their lunch before they could sit down, but it did not take long. Everyone there knew that there were other customers waiting, so they did not linger reading the paper or engage in unnecessary conversation.

Once Anna and Silvia sat down, the man behind the counter came over right away. The lunch menu, just like the breakfast one, was limited, so Anna ordered cheeseburgers and birch beer for both of them. By the look on Silvia's face when she tasted the birch beer Anna could tell that the new soft drink was not completely to her liking, but she held the frosty mug firmly and eventually finished all of it.

"I really miss Cuban food," she said, "I hope we don't have to come here every day to eat."

"We won't," said Anna as they got up from the stools and resumed their walk back to the hotel.

"What do you mean?" asked Silvia.

"I heard some people talking last night, while I was sitting on the terrace, about having a *cantina* delivered every day. Apparently it is not uncommon at the hotel."

"That's more like it!" said Silvia enthusiastically, "I don't know if I could ever get used to eating American food all the time."

Besides the language, food was another one of many hurdles that Cubans had to overcome during the process of assimilation into American culture. With the sudden influx of refugees into the United States, but especially into the city of Miami, and their longing for their native foods, the proliferation of cantinas was inevitable. A cantina, simply put, was a food service to which one subscribed for a modest fee and that was delivered to a specified destination on a daily basis. Once a week the possible menus were distributed to the subscribers, who simply checked the items that they wanted to eat for each day of the following week. The food was delivered in round, stackable containers made of aluminum that were returned the following day, when the new delivery was made. This, of course, was not a new idea. It was commonplace in Cuba for people who were too busy to cook to avail themselves of this service, so it was no surprise to anyone when the same service sprang up in Miami.

"I only see one obstacle," said Silvia. "What is it?" asked Anna.

"Well, you saw how small the rooms are at the hotel. One can barely sleep in there, let alone eat."

"I have already thought of that too," answered Anna, "The Rice Hotel also has bigger rooms, which they call efficiency apartments. They have two beds and room for a small table and a hot plate."

"That would be a lot better," agreed Silvia, "but I am sure they cost more than a single room. There is no way to afford it with the little money from the refugee center."

"We can, if we combine our resources. Think about it; we will be more comfortable and will have the convenience of the cantina. We will save money on the room and also on food. Besides, it is hard to tell when we will find work."

"Everything you are saying makes sense," agreed Silvia, "We have to look out for ourselves."

"Then it is settled," said Anna, "As soon as we get back to the hotel I will speak with the man at the front desk. I am sure there are people moving out all the time."

"You are probably right," concurred Silvia, "The Rice Hotel is not a place where people would stay voluntarily, but a stepping stone on their way to better accommodations."

"It serves its purpose," said Anna. "It is place that shelters recent immigrants, but it also serves as a stimulus so they try to find work as soon as possible. As you said, it is a stepping stone to a better life."

But the Rice Hotel was a lot more than a rundown place where Cubans with nowhere else to go ended up. As the lights dimmed, the loud conversations subsided and the guests went to sleep, their memories, hopes and aspirations came to life in their dreams.

Absent or deceased relatives roamed the halls, imparting with their voices and occasional laughter a new character to the building. Ghosts of their own selves in a previous life, when they enjoyed the plentiful bounty of youth, readily joined them to create a unanimous and joyful whispering that extended into the dawn.

With the rising of the sun and the abrupt sound of alarm clocks that ushered the beginning of the waking hours, the fleeting phantoms of previous lives fled the hotel. Once again they became nothing but latent memories in the minds of its tenants as they yielded to the reality of the new day.

As Anna and Silvia approached the street level entrance to the stairway that led to the lobby, the perennial sound of the television was heard from above. No matter what the time — day or night — there was someone sitting on the green vinyl couch watching something. If they got tired, they just went over to the terrace, sat in one of the chairs and watched the traffic on Miami Avenue or tried to engage another guest in conversation, usually about how all the evidence pointed to the fact that the current regime in Cuba would collapse at any moment. Other guests, in search of air conditioned relief during the hot Miami afternoons, would cross the street and take refuge in the cool atmosphere of the Walgreens drugstore. There they would sit at the soda counter and enjoy a Coke, or just wander between the aisles, pretending to be looking for an elusive item. All these rituals, of course, were nothing more than a way of passing the time, of getting through one more day, hoping that the next one would bring the news that they believed imminent.

As soon as they found themselves in the lobby, Anna approached the man behind the desk. She asked about the larger efficiency rooms and then explained that she and her friend Silvia would like to share one.

"Sure," he said, "It makes sense; I get that request all the time. It just so happens that a unit just became available. When would you like to move in?"

"We could do it today," said Anna after getting a nod of approval from Silvia.

"So today it is," said the man at the desk, "Just bring your stuff out of your rooms and when you are done turn in the keys," he said while handing Anna the key to the new unit. It had been that simple.

The rest of the afternoon was spent moving the belongings from the old rooms into the new apartment and then arranging their scant belongings in the available shelves and closets. The accommodations were a far cry from what Anna had left behind in Havana, but they were an improvement over the windowless room where she had spent the first night at the hotel. Silvia, too, seemed to be pleased with the change. Perhaps the fact that at this moment they owned nothing and had no one forced them to find strength in the other. It was only natural.

Although at this point Silvia had mentioned little about her life in Cuba, she would soon confide in Anna the dreadful circumstances that had brought her to the United States, and finally to this third-rate downtown hotel. Her family, although not wealthy, could be placed in the category of comfortable middle class; all the Delgados were law-abiding citizens and well respected in their community. They did not aspire to riches or to fame and fortune, but simply wanted to lead private, almost anonymous lives surrounded by family and friends. They worked hard, and from time to time they took vacations in other parts of the island. Silvia and her younger brother Evaldo grew up in what could be described as a typical Cuban family. They attended public schools and developed a wide circle of friends. There was nothing in their upbringing that could be considered out of the ordinary. At twenty-three, after finishing a degree in accounting, Silvia married Emilio, her high school sweetheart and local journalist. Just like the rest of their families, Silvia and Emilio just wanted to live their
lives, one day at a time, and travel the same stable path that their parents had before them.

What derailed their plans was the collapse of the Batista regime and the subsequent takeover by the thinly disguised communist government of Fidel Castro. The Delgado family was not singled out in any way by the new regime — they were after all, people who mostly stayed to themselves and minded their own business — but the pervasive barrage of propaganda had a most insidious effect in their daily lives. As it happened with many Cuban families, they were soon irrevocably split along ideological lines.

Silvia, who was newlywed but still living in the same house as her parents, did not take long to recognize the new regime for what it was. Despite the heavy rhetoric and the grandiose utopian promises, the daily reality told her a different story. Things were not getting any better. In the privacy of their bedroom, she and Emilio often discussed the changes taking place in the country and all its different possible ramifications. They both agreed that those changes were eroding the constitutional rights of every Cuban citizen.

Unbeknownst to her, even though they shared the same bed, Emilio had joined a clandestine cell whose purpose was to undermine the authority of the current government and restore freedom of the press. This secrecy on his part did not imply a lack of trust, but rather a deep love. Should anything happen he did not want his wife to be compromised in any way.

The means that Emilio's clandestine group utilized to achieve its goal were not violent at all. No, they did not have to resort to planting bombs or sabotaging public works. These methods, after all, although successful in drawing momentary attention, would soon be forgotten by the public and could backfire; there was always the possibility that innocent bystanders could be hurt or killed. This was precisely what they did not want.

So, what better way to combat censorship than with a publication that clearly and systematically dissected the policies that were being implemented, refuting their logic and pointing out their folly? But this enterprise, everyone knew, was more dangerous than planting bombs, for its effects went well beyond the immediate moment and extended beyond time and place.

With the aid of his journalist friends, Emilio set up a makeshift press in the back room of the house. This room was used as a repository for the eclectic collection of objects that the family discarded, so no one ever went in it unless it was to add one more item to the dusty collection. On a table, behind a massive armoire, and covered by a ragged tarp, Emilio hid the small mimeograph machine. Its rudimentary mechanism was powered by a hand crank, so no electricity was necessary for its operation. All that was needed was ink and paper. So much the better, for it made the small machine completely portable.

The clandestine operation got underway with an initial one page pamphlet, printed on both sides, where the anonymous author simply asked one hundred questions — from constitutional violations to private ownership of property — for the citizens to consider. This first issue was clearly meant to raise awareness among the citizens, not to provide any answers in particular. There would be time for that in future issues. The underground leaflet — efficiently distributed under the cover of darkness by the members of the group — readily made its way into parked cars, restroom stalls and any other public place where it was easily picked up, read, and left behind for someone else. It could also be folded many times and tucked away into the recesses of one's underwear to be studied more carefully at a later time. Everyone knew of the consequences if such a paper were to be found in one's possession, so it was never held for any length of time.

Although Silvia sensed that there was something going on, she did not dare ask, and Emilio did not volunteer any information. The unauthorized publications continued to appear at random dates at the most unexpected places. Each new issue was a fresh indictment of the policies that the new regime was putting in place. But above all, it was a loud cry of protest at the lack of freedom of expression.

In April of 1961, the failed Bay of Pigs invasion and the subsequent capture of the invading troops triggered a new wave of repression; many citizens were arrested just on suspicions of not being sympathizers of the regime. Those in power saw behind every face a potential conspirator, behind every closed door a plot to undermine their authority. During this heightened state of paranoia, the so-called 'Committees for the Defense of the Revolution' were formally organized and put in place in every neighborhood across the nation. Their mission was a simple one: keep an eye on any suspicious activity and report it to the authorities, even if those involved were relatives or friends.

Silvia's younger brother, Evaldo, seduced by the empty rhetoric of the revolution, readily joined the committee in his neighborhood. His radical views, adopted during the indoctrination meetings, were often manifested at the supper table, where all the Delgados made it a point to gather every evening. He had placed himself, by blindly adopting the party line, squarely against the tradition of common sense that hadcharacterized the Delgado family for generations. As time went by and he ascended in the ranks, the tension during those times when the family came together became almost intolerable. No one dared approach the subject of politics, lest an inevitable and heated argument ensue.

Silvia and Emilio went about their business, hoping that the political climate would soon change, as it often did in Cuba. This did not mean, of course, that Emilio and his friends backed off and stopped printing their subversive pamphlets. On the contrary, they believed that at this crucial moment, more than ever, the Cuban people needed to hear the truth, even if they had to take greater risks in order to disseminate it.

It was inevitable, given the ever-tightening grip of the regime on personal freedoms and their growing efforts to curtail the unrestricted movements of the population, that the clandestine press should be discovered. What made it worse was the fact that Evaldo was the one who set everything in motion.

Late one night, after the rest of the family had gone to bed and the doors were locked, Emilio abandoned his bed and walked in the dark to the back room, where the now forgotten items that the family had discarded were kept. He had written what he thought to be a particularly lucid editorial, which he intended to print and distribute the following day.

In the darkness, he found the doorknob and went into the room, closing the door behind him. He never turned the lights on until he was completely sure that the door was closed. One could never be too careful these days, even in one's own home. But when he turned on the lights, the figure sitting in a broken chair startled him. It was Evaldo, still wearing his uniform and holding a piece of paper in his hand. His face showed a mixed look of hate and reproach. For a moment neither one spoke, perhaps trying to guess what was going on in the other's mind.

"You are a traitor to the revolution," Evaldo finally said, still holding in his hand the document that Emilio wanted to release the following day.

"My allegiance is to Cuba," answered Emilio calmly.

"Cuba and the revolution are one and the same," answered Evaldo.

"That is what they want you to believe, so you don't question the policies of the regime. I refuse to stop thinking for myself," added Emilio softly after a brief pause.

"We have to trust in the revolution," answered Evaldo.

Emilio knew that there was no point in trying to argue with Evaldo, or explain the obvious. He would merely regurgitate the slogans that had been drilled into his head during the weekly meetings organized by the members of the party. At that moment, Emilio knew that they were at an impasse. There was nothing he could do or say; the evidence against him was undeniable. After giving Emilio a long look, he carelessly tossed the paper he was holding at his feet, and walked out of the room. His fate was in Evaldo's hands. His only hope was that he would overlook for Silvia's sake what he had discovered. He also knew that there was no point in running; there was no place to hide. There was also no point in alarming his wife; whatever was going to happen would happen, no matter what.

Evaldo's decision soon manifested itself. Just as the family was about to sit down for their midday meal — Evaldo was conspicuously absent — a loud knock on the front door caught their attention. It was Silvia who answered the unexpected call. At first she was surprised to see her younger brother, in full uniform, with two other men. He walked into the house, followed by his companions, until they were standing next to Emilio.

"You better come with us," he said, trying to make his voice as deep and as official as possible.

Emilio wiped his lips with his napkin and then stood up very slowly.

"Don't expect me for dinner," he told Silvia, who by now was standing next to him. Then he walked out, flanked by the uniformed men. It was the last time the family would ever see him. In fact, it was the last time they would see Evaldo as well. Fully cognizant of the decision he had made, he did not return home that night. From that point on, all ties with his family had been broken; he now truly belonged to the revolution.

When she realized that neither her husband nor her brother would be back that day, Silvia went directly to the police station in search of news. The least they could do, she reasoned, was to let her know where he was being detained and what the charges were, since he had not been accused of anything in particular at the time of his arrest.

The man at the front desk in the police station listened to her politely, checked in a logbook and then shook his head negatively. No one by the name of Emilio Delgado had been booked that day. This was, indeed, bad news. Silvia had heard stories of people being detained, but not taken to a station and formally charged. They were whisked away to clandestine houses where secret and painful sessions were held in order to extract information from the suspects in the shortest amount of time. Sometimes the men were never heard from again. She only prayed that this would not be the case with Emilio.

From that day on Silvia returned to the police station every morning, but always received the same answer. There was no news of her husband. A month later, when she thought she would go mad with uncertainty, the phone rang. It was Evaldo. He just wanted to tell her that Emilio had been tried and convicted of conspiring against the government. He gave her no details of the

378

past month, but simply told her that he was in a prison in the province of Oriente. She could write to him there. Then he hung up.

The first thing Silvia needed to do was to confirm the veracity of the information her brother had given her. Once more she returned to the local police station; the man at the desk by now had become used to seeing her, and as he did every day, he was prepared to tell Silvia that he had no news of her husband. When confronted with the new information, however, at first he seemed a little puzzled, and then annoyed.

"If what you say is true," he said in a tone of disbelief, "I should have been notified; I don't like anyone going over my head." The abrupt, almost arrogant demeanor of the commander gave away the fact that he was used to being in control.

"Perhaps you can check it out," suggested Silvia in a soft tone of voice, not wanting to antagonize the officer.

"Of that you can be certain;" he said forcefully, "I will get to the bottom of it. Come back tomorrow and I will have a definite answer for you."

Silvia returned home with mixed feelings. On the one hand, she wanted to know of Emilio's fate, but on the other she feared that the news would not be good. In the end, she concluded that whatever it was, she wanted to know. It was the only way to help him in whatever way she could.

Early the next morning she returned to the police station. When the sergeant saw her, rather than talking with her in the open, as he had done every time she had visited, he asked her to come into his office. The arrogant demeanor of the previous day had disappeared.

"The information you gave me was accurate," he said, "Your husband is currently serving time here," he added while handing Silvia a piece of paper. "You can write to him or visit him once a month. That is all I can tell you." He would say no more.

Silvia left the station with the piece of paper in her hand and with the certainty that at least Emilio was alive. She also deduced that it had been the G2, as the Cuban secret police was called, who had picked him up and interrogated him, bypassing completely the local authorities. Apparently the local official, after filing a protest, had been called aside and chastised in private. No one dared interfere with the G2. Cubans commented jokingly that the security force had been aptly named, for it was as ruthless as a second Gestapo.

That afternoon Silvia wrote a long letter and delivered it to the post office herself. She did not mention any of the events that had taken place, but concentrated in ways in which she could help her husband. Until she had a reply, all she could do was wait. In spite of the deteriorating mail service, a letter from Emilio arrived a week later. Although his letter was not as extensive as hers, it contained some very explicit instructions as to how she was to proceed. First of all he spoke of the conditions in the prison, referring to them as 'A lot less comfortable and amenable than what I am used to.' Emilio also mentioned that they would have to postpone celebrating their wedding anniversary indefinitely. Silvia did not have any trouble reading between the lines. Things were not good and he had no hope of being released. At the end of the letter he suggested that Silvia should stay with uncle Samuel for the time being. Of course, there was no such person; this was simply a thinly disguised code they had devised for people who had left for the United States. Any time one of their acquaintances suddenly left town, to later reappear abroad, they would simply say that he or she was visiting uncle Samuel.

At first Silvia was reluctant to follow her husband's wishes. She kept writing to him, asking him what she could do to help him and always mentioning the fact that her uncle had a full house at the moment, so she had to delay her visit.

With every passing letter — they were becoming more sporadic — Emilio reiterated what he had said in the first one, and insisted that there was room for Silvia at her uncle's house. He also promised Silvia that he would join her as soon as possible. In view of his insistence, she got her passport and very discreetly filed all the necessary documents so she could travel abroad. As with the rest of the Cubans who intended to leave, there was a long wait. No one could tell her when the telegram with the date of departure would arrive. Silvia kept hoping that something, anything, would happen before the telegram came, and she would be reunited with Emilio, thus making her uncertain journey unnecessary.

There were always rumors of another invasion, this one staged by U.S. Marines and not Cuban refugees, as the one that had taken place at the Bay of Pigs. Of course, Silvia realized that these were just rumors, wishful thinking on the part of a population that with each passing day, with each execution, grew more disenchanted with the current regime.

The days passed; she wrote to Emilio and tried to face life without him the best she could. Two months after she had requested permission to leave the country, the telegram finally arrived. She had a week to say good-bye to relatives and friends and make the trek to Havana. Although the capital city was not too far from her native Camagüey, she had never been there before. This was not any sort of impediment, for there were people whose business was to drive passengers to that city every day. When the day came, she already had a single bag — it was all the government allowed travelers to take — packed with her most essential possessions. The following morning — it all seemed a dream — she found herself at the José Martí Airport, in a room with glass walls, anxiously awaiting the departure of the plane with other Cubans who had come from every corner of the nation. From that point on everything seemed like a dream: the flight, the landing in Miami, the meeting with immigration officials and the surreal ride in a van that took her, along with other Cubans, to a third-rate hotel in the downtown area of Miami. And now here she was, sharing an efficiency apartment with a woman she hardly knew, but on whose strength and sense of optimism she was relying more with every passing hour.

By midafternoon, Anna and Silvia had finished moving and arranging their belongings in their new apartment. This particular hour coincided with the deliveries of the cantinas to the Rice Hotel, so they made arrangements to have one delivered, starting the next day. That evening they had no choice but to return to the Royal Castle and repeat the meal they had had the day before. After leaving the restaurant, they walked around the downtown area and eventually went into Walgreens, where they bought a hot plate and plastic bowls, cups and silverware.

By the time they returned to the hotel the multicolored neon lights of the different stores were lit, casting on the sidewalks an almost festive air. At that hour many of the guests sat in the balcony of the hotel, so Anna and Silvia did the same. For a while they talked about Cuba, but most of their conversation centered about their immediate plans to get their lives in order again. Although it was not late, it was time to sleep; the following morning they would get up before dawn and join the group of refugees who made the trek to a nearby church that distributed milk and bread—free of charge—to those who showed up at their door. They could make breakfast in their efficiency and then go back to the Refugee Center.

But at least for Anna, the day had not concluded yet. There was one more task to be completed before she could get some rest. At the desk of the hotel she changed several dollar bills into coins, and then walked over to the cubbyhole that enclosed the public telephone. From her purse she retrieved the paper that the social worker had given her that morning, and then dialed the number in the state of Virginia. The impersonal voice of the operator instructed her to place more coins in the slot in order to complete the call. After she had complied with the request, she heard the insistent ringing and then a distant voice answering the phone. At first, she did not know what to say, but it was a fleeting moment. She then identified herself, making sure to pronounce the words carefully, and asked about Francesca. Of course, she wanted to know everything.

The lady at the other end of the line, aware of Anna's predicament, assured her that the baby was fine, and told Anna to feel free to call anytime. Then she went on to tell her about Francesca's progress. The conversation was abruptly interrupted by the operator, informing Anna that her time would be up in one minute. Anna said good-bye and promised to call again. After hanging up, she realized that her hands were trembling, and that tears were rolling down her cheeks.

The call to New Mexico went as well as the one to Virginia. The woman on the other end of the line told her that Adriana was a perfect baby, and that she had adapted to her new surroundings quite well. She also told Anna to call any time, but to keep in mind that they were in a different time zone.

After speaking to the ladies who were looking after her children, Anna felt a lot more at ease. She made the resolution to call at least once a week. Now the rest was up to her; she had to find a way to recover financially in order to get them back. With this certainty on her mind, she did not have any problems falling asleep that night.

After a meager breakfast prepared at their efficiency apartment with the items that she and Silvia had procured at the church earlier that morning—bread, milk, instant coffee—Anna left the Rice Hotel again in the direction of the Cuban Refugee Center. She was hopeful about the possibility of employment that the clerk had mentioned the day before. It made no difference to her what it could be, just so long as she started generating revenue that would place her on her way to financial independence and a permanent reunion with Francesca and Adriana.

As she walked towards Freedom Tower, just as the day before, Anna realized that there was a constant flow of refugees going in that direction, no doubt seeking the different services and aid that the organization had to offer. The main lobby, also like the day before, was full of people talking loudly and trying to get to the right office. Anna went directly to the door of the employment office and got in line. Before long, she found herself sitting across from the same man who had asked her to return the day before.

"I am glad you decided to come back," he said after the perfunctory courtesies, "There is a job available."

"Well, that is good news," said Anna, "The sooner I start to work, the sooner I will get back on my feet."

"This job is not exactly a top paying job," he said after a short pause, almost in an apologetic tone of voice.

"At this point, I will take anything," said Anna decisively, "What kind of job is it?"

"They need somebody to clean the rooms in a Miami Beach hotel," he explained, "Would you be willing to do that?"

"Of course," said Anna without hesitation. At that moment, she was thinking of Francesca and Adriana, and how any job would bring her closer to reuniting with them.

"In that case," said the clerk with a faint smile, "You can report here tomorrow morning at seven," he said while handing Anna a piece of paper with the address on it, "I will call them ahead and let them know that you are coming. By the way, there are busses that go to Miami Beach every half hour; you should not have any problems getting there."

"Thank you so much," said Anna, grateful that she had found employment so quickly. She tried to imagine the day when her daughters would be returned to her; it was the one thought that sustained her.

She arrived at the Rice Hotel in a buoyant mood. Somehow the faces of the people she saw on Biscayne Boulevard seemed brighter, and the salt air that came in from the bay fresher. As she walked into the apartment, she found Silvia in the process of taking apart the different containers of their cantina, which had been delivered a few minutes before, just in time for lunch.

"How did it go?" she asked, but the question was not necessary. The expression on Anna's face clearly proclaimed that the interview had been a success.

"It is not much," she answered, "but at least it is a job. Tomorrow morning I have to be in Miami Beach; I will be cleaning rooms in a hotel."

"That does not sound too difficult," said Silvia, "Everybody knows how to clean; maybe they will have something for me too," she added.

"I will certainly ask," said Anna, "But now, I am starved. Let's eat lunch."

"Good idea," agree Silvia as she started to set the plastic plates on the small table.

The following morning Anna was up before dawn. After waking to the church with Silvia to receive their daily quota of milk and bread, she stood on the corner of Flagler St. and Miami Avenue, waiting for the bus that would take her to Miami Beach.

Obeying its predetermined schedule, the bus soon appeared. It stopped with a pneumatic hiss and the door opened. At that early hour, Anna noticed, there were not that many passengers on board. She paid the fare and sat down, thinking about the day ahead.

The ride to Miami Beach was not an unpleasant one. The bus traveled quickly on Biscayne Boulevard, next to the bay, and eventually turned onto one of the causeways that connected the two cities. As they approached Miami Beach, Anna had to think of Ramón, and the picture-perfect honeymoon they had enjoyed in that city almost twenty years earlier. Those memories would never change or fade; it had been one of the happiest weeks in her life.

Twenty-five minutes later, Anna got off at her stop on Collins Avenue. The hotel was located one street up, on Ocean Drive, so she crossed the street and walked a block in the direction of the ocean. The paper that she had been given by the clerk at the employment office said 1300 Ocean Drive. Since all the hotels were relatively close to each other, it was not difficult to find the one she was looking for, but the surprise brought tears to her eyes. She was standing in front of the Cardozo Hotel, where she and Ramón had spent their honeymoon. She thought it was a cruel joke of fate to bring her back here, but now as the lowest employee of the Cardozo and not as a guest.

As soon as Anna walked into the lobby, she became aware that twenty years had taken its toll. Although she readily recognized the place, for a moment it was hard to reconcile her memories with the present reality. Gone were the tasteful paintings, the graceful wooden furniture and the hand carved counter where the guests checked in. The paintings had been substituted by mass-produced reproductions set in cheap frames; the furniture was clearly second hand and covered in vinyl; the sides of the plastic top counter showed a tropical motif. All this, however, paled in comparison to the guests that were sitting in the lobby. Those young, affluent and vibrant people that Anna remembered seeing during her stay in 1943 were gone. They had been substituted by elderly visitors whose clothes clearly denoted their lower station in life. The Cardozo Hotel languished under the semitropical sun and the salty air, in a downward spiral of decay that no one seemed to notice, catering with every passing day to guests of scant economic means. It was an absolute shame, she thought.

The man behind the front desk, at that moment busy with a stack of what appeared to be receipts, did not look up right away as Anna approached him.

"Sorry about that," he said, "I just didn't want to lose count. I am Gene, the manager."

"I understand," Anna said, "The employment agency sent me; they said that you were expecting me."

At this point the man reached under the desk and handed Anna some papers. "You need to fill these out," he said, "After you are done I will give you a uniform and then you can start work."

Anna did not bother to sit down, but took the documents to the end of the counter and began to place her personal information in the empty boxes. Once she was done, she returned to where the manager was still going over receipts and handed him the papers.

"Come with me," he said after putting the papers away.

Anna followed him down a corridor to a small room located at the back of the hotel, which he opened and then turned on the lights. Besides an array of brooms, mops, several vacuum cleaners and other cleaning supplies, there was a shelf with uniforms of different sizes.

"Pick one," he said, "You can change right here, then come to see me at the desk," he added before leaving the room.

The starched uniforms were neatly arranged on the shelves, according to size. After finding one that would fit her, Anna changed quickly and then returned to the lobby.

"You can start on the second floor," the man said when he realized that Anna had returned, "Change the sheets on the beds, clean the bathrooms and vacuum the carpet. Everything you need is in the room with the uniforms. Oh, yes, one more thing," he said after a pause, "You can leave your things there today, until I get you a locker. If you need anything, just come to see me."

There was nothing more to be said. Anna returned to the room with the cleaning supplies and loaded one of the small carts that were used to carry whatever was needed to do the job. She pushed it onto the hallway, towards the elevator, and made her way to the second floor. Since the manager had not told her to follow any certain pattern, she decided to start at the back and work her way towards the front of the hotel, to the rooms that had a view of the ocean.

Some of the rooms had a 'Do not disturb' sign hanging from the doorknob. These were the guests who had stayed out late the night before and wanted to sleep into the morning. Most, however, rose early and went to the beach or enjoyed an early breakfast in one of the many establishments that were so common in that area of Miami Beach. Just in case, Anna knocked cautiously and announced herself as 'Housekeeping' before opening the door with the master key that had been supplied by the manager.

The task at hand was not difficult, but Anna took her time, making sure that every room was spotless and orderly. She even took the time, before leaving, to spray from a can of orange scented mist, so the fragrance would linger in the room and at the same time counteract the musty smell that seemed to pervade the entire hotel.

If Anna had thought the Cardozo had changed when she first walked in, what she was about to see would be almost shocking. The front rooms were usually more spacious than the rest, and consequently more expensive. She remembered well the corner apartment where she and Ramón had spent their honeymoon. As she approached what had once been the honeymoon suite, where once was a door, now there were two. The wonderful corner apartment had been divided into two separate rooms. It was a cost-cutting measure implemented by the management so they could fit more tenants into the hotel. The caliber of guests that now visited the Cardozo had declined; everything that Anna had seen so far corroborated that fact. This, of course, did not deter her from doing her job; she went about efficiently cleaning the rooms, replacing the linen and making sure the bathrooms were clean. It was her job. At noon she took a lunch break and at the end of her shift reported back to the manager.

"You've done a good job today," he said, "I will see you tomorrow morning."

"Thank you for everything," said Anna.

"You're welcome," answered the manager, not knowing exactly why he was being thanked.

The ride back to the hotel was not much different from the earlier one. Now that she was sitting on the cushioned seat of the bus, Anna realized that she was tired, but also glad to have found a job. At that moment all she wanted to do was take a hot shower, put on some clean clothes and have something to eat. Her thoughts went no further.

When she walked into the efficiency at the Rice Hotel, Silvia was in the process of taking apart the cantina for the day.

"How was it?" asked Silvia, momentarily looking up from the cantina.

"Tiring," answered Anna, but at least it is a job, "How about you?"

"No luck," answered Silvia. "After you left this morning I went back to the refugee center, to talk to the man at the employment office. It seems that no matter how well qualified one is for the available jobs, the knowledge of English is essential. I suppose that leaves me out; many other people are facing the same situation."

"I know," said Anna, thinking of the many hours she had spent listening to records and practicing conversation with a tutor in Pinar del Río. "What do we have for dinner tonight?" she asked, purposely changing the subject.

"Rice, lentils, fried plantains and chicken," answered Silvia, "Just like in Cuba," she added.

"It smells delicious," commented Anna, who had learned to like all the simple Cuban dishes during her stay on the island, "Or maybe it is because I am so hungry."

"Maybe both," she suggested.

"Yes, but I would like to take a shower and get into some clean clothes before I eat," Anna explained.

"Go ahead," said Silvia, "While you do that I can heat up dinner; I know that you are tired."

Anna's least favorite thing at the Rice Hotel was the lack of individual bathrooms. One had to carry a bathrobe, towel, and other items from the room. Fortunately for her, at this time of the day the women's bathroom was not extremely busy, so she had no problems getting into the shower right away. She returned to the apartment, wearing the robe and her head wrapped in a towel a short time later. Silvia had already set the small table and served the food. Even though it was still early in the evening, the two women had gotten up before dawn and had had an early breakfast and lunch, so in reality it was not too early to have dinner. On a side table Anna noticed a small radio, now broadcasting news in Spanish, that had not been there when she had left for work that morning.

"Where did that come from?" she asked Silvia after sitting down and taking the first bite.

"Someone who was moving out this morning no longer had a use for it, so she gave it to me," she answered.

"Lucky for her," retorted Anna.
"She is moving in with her son and his wife, who just bought a house near the airport," clarified Silvia. "You are right, she is lucky to be with her family and out of this hotel."
"That's what we all want, to be with our families," said Anna thinking about the twins.
"And we have only been here three days," lamented Silvia.

"Be patient," said Anna in a low tone of voice, "Sooner or later we will also leave the Rice Hotel."

One cool and sunny morning in February, after several months of working as a maid at the Cardozo Hotel, Anna came to the realization that she was no closer to getting her daughters back than when she first arrived. She had settled into an almost comfortable routine, going to work, coming back to the hotel and calling Virginia and New Mexico once a week to keep abreast of the progress her daughters were making. Since she had a steady job, the financial aid she received at first from the refugee center had stopped. From her meager earnings, she had to pay her share of the rent at the Rice Hotel, half of the cantina, her fare back and forth to Miami Beach every day, along with other sundry expenses. The few dollars she had been able to save would not be enough to rent an apartment where she and the twins could live comfortably, if not luxuriously.

From time to time she and Silvia would go to a movie in one of the downtown theaters and stop at a restaurant afterwards for a snack. Thank God for Silvia; during the past months Anna had come to realize the type of person she was, so she considered herself lucky to have her as a friend. Even after finding out the terrible fate that had befallen her family, Anna never heard her complain. Maybe she could be classified as a modern-day stoic; no matter what fate handed her, she just shrugged and accepted it as something inevitable over which she had no control.

Contributing to Anna's growing sense of dissatisfaction were the letters from Sergio Osorio that occasionally made it to Miami. Although he could not be very explicit in his criticism of the government, Anna could easily read between the lines. Things had changed for the worse—if that was possible—since her departure. He kept telling her that he missed her, but that she had made the right decision to go.

It was during that bus ride, while pondering over these things on her way to work, that Anna had an idea that she hoped would allow her to break the vicious cycle into which she had fallen. Throughout the time she had been working at the Cardozo, she had observed that the hotels hired their cleaning crews—mostly women with no other marketable skills — through the state employment agency. Because many of them soon found transportation a problem, the turnover was quite high. Most just wanted a job until something better came along. The hotel managers put up with this situation because they had no alternative; rather than dealing with one entity, they had to deal with many independent individuals. What if, Anna reasoned, she could provide something better? Her organizational skills, she was sure, would come in handy in assembling a hand-picked cleaning crew that would be assigned to the different hotels. The managers would be dealing with a more stable work force and all the business would be conducted through her. Although the idea was appealing, she also realized that to launch any business endeavor a certain amount of startup capital was needed. This was different from her situation twenty years earlier, when she had arrived in Havana with a sizeable amount of money that Giacomo had had the foresight to put at her disposal. She had heard stories, while sitting on the terrace at the Rice Hotel, of Cubans who had started businesses with loans granted by the United States Government. What qualifications had to be met was a mystery.

That very afternoon, after leaving work, she did not return to the hotel, but got off the bus in front of the refugee center. There was no line at the employment office—most people conducted business in the morning—so she was able to see the clerk who had found her the job at the hotel.

"Is there anything wrong?" he said when he saw Anna standing in front of his desk, thinking that she, like many other of his clients, had quit her job and was back in his office looking for something else.

"No, there is nothing wrong," she said smiling, "I just need some information." Then she proceeded to explain what she had in mind, trying to be as convincing as possible as she went through all the little details of the operation.

"I think it is an excellent idea," said the clerk after a short pause, "In fact, what you heard about business loans is true; the government is going all out to help the Cuban community. I have all the information here, but you will have to go to another office, file the appropriate papers and submit a detailed proposal."

"That is not a problem," she answered as she received the papers and started to leave, "Once my business gets going I am sure some of your clients will no longer need assistance."

"That's the whole idea," he answered enthusiastically as Anna was exiting his office, "to get everybody working as soon as possible."

XI

While waiting for the approval of the loan, and the processing of the inevitable red tape involved before the issuing of the sundry licenses necessary to operate a business, Anna devoted the time to planning the different aspects of its implementation. First of all, she had to come up with a name. She realized that it had to be a name that would clearly convey the nature of her business, but at the same time one that the public would readily remember. After much thought and consideration, she decided on one that cleverly combined both letters and numbers and left no doubt as to what the business was about: WE KLEAN 4U.

The next thing that Anna had considered was the issue of transportation. If she was going to employ and manage a cleaning crew, she could not possibly rely on the busses. The proceeds of the loan would go towards the purchase of a van as well as uniforms for her workers. It was important not only to be professional, but to present that image to the public as well. As far the driving of the van was concerned, Anna was not too concerned. She had had ample driving experience in Cuba, and by now she had become very familiar with the route from downtown Miami to the south end of Miami Beach, so getting her driver's license would be but a formality.Anna had purposely refrained from telling Silvia about her idea; there was no point, lest she be disappointed in case the loan was denied. After all, she had no collateral to offer, so she felt it was a long shot. She only hoped that what the clerk had said about the federal government wanting to help Cubans was true.

One afternoon, after returning from her job at the Cardozo Hotel, the man at the front desk signaled her to approach him as soon as she emerged from the stairs into the lobby. One of his duties was to deliver the incoming mail, since all the guests had the address of the Rice Hotel. Anna did not find it strange; she occasionally received letters from Sergio. Today, however, the postman had delivered a hefty manila envelope. Without opening it, Anna knew that it came from one of the offices where she had filed for the loan and the business permits. She thanked the man at the desk, fearing that he could hear her heart racing from excitement at the prospect that everything had been approved.

Rather than going into her efficiency apartment, she sat on the green vinyl sofa and tore open the envelope with nervous hands. Inside, besides the official documents, she found a cover letter congratulating her on the approval of her loan and wishing her the best of luck in this new endeavor. Of course, along with this letter a repayment schedule had been enclosed, just a reminder that this was a loan, and not a gift from the American taxpayers. All in all, Anna thought, it had been easier that she had expected. All the possible impediments that she had imagined had not materialized. The check had been deposited into her personal account; all that was left to do was to get the business up and running.

When she walked into the apartment, the expression on her face reflected the good news she had just received. "You must have won the lottery," said Silvia, who by now was getting to know her friend rather well.

"Not quite," answered Anna, "But I might as well have."

"I don't understand," said Silvia with a puzzled look on her face.

"Sit down," said Anna, "I have some great news to give you." Then she proceeded to tell her friend about the idea for a business, how she had applied for a loan and the necessary permits to operate it. "Everything is right here," she said holding the envelope tightly, "Now the rest is up to me."

"That is great news," said Silvia in a tone of voice that denoted she was in awe of her friend. "What is the next step?" she asked with genuine curiosity.

"Now that all the paper work is done," explained Anna, "I need to get a reliable crew together; this week I plan to start looking for a van and I want to get my driver's license as soon as possible. I already have a few leads for clients at the beach, starting with the Cardozo. Gene, the manager, is tired of having to call the employment office for replacements that do not last; he wants to have a reliable and stable work force, even if he has to pay a little more."

394

"I can help you find the workers you need," interjected Silvia, "There are many women here at the hotel who would like to work, but they have no real skills, don't have transportation and their English proficiency is nil."

"A willingness to work is all I am looking for," said Anna, remembering the lessons she had learned from Ramón while dealing with the hired hands at the tobacco plantation.

"Then leave it up to me," agreed Silvia, "I will find you as many workers as you want."

"It's in your hands then," said Anna. "By the way, I think this calls for a celebration; let's go out to dinner tonight. We can save the cantina for tomorrow. Besides, I just got paid," she added, knowing that Silvia was thrifty by nature.

"That's a great idea; we can talk about the business some more," said Silvia enthusiastically.

"First I need to take a shower and get ready," said Anna, "Somehow my clothes and hair always pick up that musty smell of the hotel, but I won't be long."

"Take your time," said Silvia, "I'll put away the cantina while you get ready. I think that this is truly a significant day for you; in fact, I think it may change your entire life from this point on."

"I hope so Silvia," said Anna, "I truly hope so."

It was impossible to fathom how true Silvia's words would be, and how this venture would eventually take Anna from the blue skies and warm shores of Miami to the gray days and icy winds of the city of Pittsburgh. But for the moment, all her energies were focused on the launching of the new enterprise, oblivious to the fact that with every phone call she made, with every new problem she solved, she was getting one step closer to her ultimate destiny in a city whose existence she had yet to discover.

With Silvia's help, she put together a crew of women who were anxious to start earning some money and, at the same time, get out of the rut that made them feel utterly useless. They were all staying at the Rice Hotel, so that would make the logistics of transportation a lot easier to solve. To that effect, Anna had bought a second-hand van and the manager of the Rice Hotel had driven her to the Department of Motor Vehicles. The test had been a lot simpler than she had expected: the examiner asked her to drive around Miami for about fifteen minutes, making sure she observed all the traffic laws and gave the appropriate signals to other motorists. After driving in the often chaotic traffic of Havana, a city like Miami, where all the traffic laws were strictly observed, was not much of a challenge. After the exam, she took the wheel and drove back to the hotel herself. When she walked into the apartment she shared with Silvia, the latter once again read the expression on Anna's face, for she did not even ask if she had passed the test. Everything seemed to be falling into place for Anna. From that day onward, there did not seem to be enough hours in the day to attend to all the details of her new venture. She also took the van to a paint shop, where the logo of her new business was brightly painted on both sides. Silvia had also been busy; after recruiting the women who would be performing the work, she contracted with an old Cuban seamstress to manufacture the uniforms that the cleaning crew would be wearing. On the upper left of the chest, an embroidered patch in red proclaimed the name of the business: WK4U. It was a simple touch, but one that readily identified the workers and gave the business an air of professionalism.

That first day on the job, Anna and Silvia were up before dawn. After a quick breakfast of café con leche and toasted Cuban bread with a thin layer of butter, they gathered the other women at the hotel. By six fifteen they were in the van on their way to Miami Beach, and a few minutes before seven they descended on the Cardozo Hotel, like a systematic and unstoppable colony of ants with a single goal in mind. By the end of the day, the task at hand had been accomplished. Just to make sure that everything was up to par, Anna and Gene walked walked through the different rooms, exploring the most remote corners of the hotel.

"Nice, very nice," pronounced Gene once they were back in the lobby. "I knew you were different since the first day you walked in."

"I am glad you approve," said Anna, "From now on you only have to deal with me, so I can assure you that whatever needs to be done, will be done right away."

"That will make my life a lot easier," he said, "I already have enough work as it is."

"Today is only the first day," said Anna, "Before long my crew will be more familiar with the hotel, so they can be even more efficient."

"Good," said the manager, "As I said, I am for anything that will reduce my work load."

"Until tomorrow then," said Anna, "We will be back before seven."

On their way back to the Rice Hotel, the women in the van could not stop talking, bubbling with excitement over the fact that they were actually employed. For many of them, it was the first time they had visited Miami Beach or left the Rice Hotel for any length of time. The experience went beyond money, but it provided them with a sense of purpose and self-worth since their arrival from Cuba.

Once in their apartment, while preparing the cantina that had arrived earlier, Anna and Silvia began to discuss the day and other more technical aspects of the business. They realized that now that they were responsible for a payroll, they were also responsible for making all the different deductions—federal taxes, social security, etc.—that the law required—before issuing the checks.

"Remember that I used to be a bookkeeper in Cuba," said Silvia, "I can take care of all that; figures are figures, no matter where you are."

"I guess you are right," agreed Anna, "I will leave that side of the business in your hands then."

"Don't worry;" said Silvia in a reassuring tone, "I will not let you down."

"The thought never crossed my mind," answered Anna, "I am just trying to make sure that we do everything by the book; somehow I feel that there is something that I am overlooking."

"There is something we have not talked about," said Silvia.

"Yes? What is it?" asked Anna, not wanting to miss anything that might affect the outcome of her venture.

"Advertising," said Silvia, "It is at the core of every successful enterprise."

"That is true," answered Anna, "But I don't want to get in over my head. I rather start slowly and build the business over time. Besides, I already have other leads through the manager of the Cardozo. Don't forget that this is only the first day."

"You are right," agreed Silvia, "Let's see how things develop and then we can decide about advertising or not."

The rest of the evening, after eating the meal that had been delivered that day, was spent going over the different information that Silvia had collected from the women and making sure of its accuracy. After receiving her loan, Anna had opened a business account at a local bank. Along with the checks, the bank had provided her with a ledger where she could keep track of all the different transactions for the account. This empty ledger, she thought, was representative of the days and months to come; only time would tell whether income would be superior to the expenditures. And just as in life, there were bound to be unexpected circumstances—both good and bad—that no one could possibly foresee.

After finishing the paper work, Anna and Silvia decided to sit on the terrace of the hotel for a while. It had been a long day—the first of many more to come—and they needed some fresh air before going to bed. As usual, people came and went, talked about the latest news from Cuba and speculated about how long before the government collapsed. By nine thirty, they felt that it was time for bed. Tomorrow, they were certain, would be just as busy as today.

As the weeks progressed, the women who made up WE KLEAN 4U, as they became more familiar with the inner workings of the Cardozo Hotel, settled into the routine of the job. Both Anna and Silvia worked side by side with them, setting an example of what they expected from everyone. Gene was delighted that he only had to deal with Anna, and not with the entire crew. If there was a special event or a block of rooms that had to be ready ahead of time because of arriving tourists, he had the certainty that after mentioning it to Anna, the job would be done. In the evenings, after driving back to Miami and dining from the cantina, Anna and Silvia would go over the events of the day and discuss the direction in which the business was going. By all indications, everything was going well, for several women at the hotel had approached Silvia to ask her if she needed more workers in the crew. This, of course, pleased Anna. Although she had no plans to expand for the moment, it was always nice to find out that her business was starting to get noticed.

The tipping point came two months later, during her lunch break at the Cardozo. "I need to talk to you," said Gene, calling her aside. Anna thought nothing of it, for he often talked to her throughout the day to make sure that certain cleaning duties in the hotel were carried out, especially whenever a large group of guests was expected.

"What's on your mind?" she asked.

"I got a call from a friend of mine this morning; he also manages a hotel here on Ocean Drive. I ran into him a few weeks ago, and told him about your crew. He would like to know if you would take care of his place. Of course, I told him that I would speak with you. Either way, I think you should give him a call," he said while handing Anna a business card.

"Thank you, thank you very much. I will certainly call him. But as you know, all the women in my crew are busy with the Cardozo," she explained unnecessarily.

"Maybe you should think about expanding the business," the manager said, "You do good work and the demand is out there. You might as well take advantage of it."

"Thank you again, Gene," said Anna, "I will give it some thought and then call your friend."

That night Anna shared with Silvia the brief conversation she had had with Gene. By that time they had moved out of the Rice Hotel into a small three bedroom house on Brickell Avenue, right on Biscayne Bay, and finally had their own telephone installed. This had always been a priority for Anna, since she called Virginia and New Mexico a few times a week without fail. Now she did not have to have a pocketful of change every time she wanted to check on Francesca and Adriana. Since they were both busy working during the day, they continued to receive the cantina, as they had done since the beginning when they first started rooming together at the Rice Hotel.

Upon hearing the news, Silvia's usually serious face lit up with a smile, Anna knew that she was pleased. On more than one occasion, Silvia had suggested that Anna should hire more workers, but she had always been reluctant.

"So what are you going to do?" Silvia asked her friend.

"I am not sure," she answered, "I realize that this is a great opportunity, but there are other considerations."

"Such as?" asked Silvia.

"Well, for one, we would need more workers; I don't know where we would find more women willing to work for us."

"Just leave that to me," said Silvia, "I have some friends who live in another hotel; I am sure they will be interested. Besides, all those objections are rather feeble excuses, if you ask me."

"Maybe you are right," conceded Anna, "I am cautious by nature."

"I know that you have lost a lot throughout the course of your life, but you can't be afraid to take advantage of the opportunities that land on your lap," Silvia said.

She was referring to Anna's early life in Italy and how the war had wiped out everything, including her family, and the more recent events in Cuba. After several months of living and working together, they had confided in each other the details of their past. At this point, they saw in the other the closest thing to family they had. But more important, they were also united by the fact that they had both lost their husbands in the prime of their lives.

"Let's do it then," said Anna, "I will call the manager of the other hotel tomorrow and make the necessary arrangements. Besides, we have been driving a half empty van all these months; maybe it was meant to be anyway."

"And I will find the people we need," said Silvia for the second time in order to reassure her friend.

Once the decision was made, it was just a matter of working out the small details to carry out the expansion of WE KLEAN 4U. The following day Anna went personally to see the manager of the hotel and took with her all the necessary papers that would make the agreement official. Silvia, on the other hand, was busy with her friends at the Tamiami Hotel, where she had no problem recruiting the women she needed to take care of the increased business.

The transition from one hotel to two did not run into any major glitches. Just to make sure, Silvia stayed with the original crew at the Cardozo while Anna took care to supervise personally the new employees that had just been hired. As always, she wanted to make sure that everything went as planned, since first impressions usually were the ones that people remembered. Just as she had done months before with the original crew, she worked side by side with the women, thus ensuring that their duties were carried out to the letter. At the end of the day, she drove the van back to Miami and made the usual stops at the Rice and Tamiami hotels to

400

let the workers off. Then it was back to the house on Brickell Avenue, where she and Silvia went over the business after eating the meal from the cantina. Twice a week Anna called the families in Virginia and New Mexico who were taking care of the twins. Before going to bed, they usually watched the Spanish language news, eager to hear anything that might indicate that what they both considered a temporary stay in the United States would soon end. From an economic standpoint, life had taken a turn for the better; the business was expanding and they were showing a profit, but secretly they both kept hoping that things would change. As to how, they didn't know.

With the increased amount of work and responsibility, also came more money. After going over the business ledger with Silvia, Anna decided that she was finally in a position to petition the agency that had taken care of her daughters to return them to her. To that effect, she went back to the Cuban Refugee Center to speak to the clerk who had provided her with the information about the location of the twins. In order to substantiate the claim, she carried with her bank statements, showing that a certain amount of money was coming in on aregular basis. Along with these documents, she also had a copy of the lease of the house that she and Silvia were renting on Brickell Avenue. It was all tangible proof that now she had the means to provide for her daughters. Almost a year had passed since her first visit to the office.

"Everything seems to be in order," said the clerk after looking over the documents, "I am glad that you are doing so well. I will file the petition to reinstate custody right away."

"I am grateful," said Anna, "This is all I have thought about all these months. Children should be with their mother."

"And we want to facilitate that process," added the clerk, "As soon as I have some news, I will call you."

"Thank you again, for everything," said Anna, "All I want is to resume a normal life with my family," she added unnecessarily before leaving the office.

One random event, however, would soon precipitate a chain reaction whose ultimate outcome was impossible to predict, but that it would irrevocably change the course of Anna's life. One Saturday afternoon she had returned to the Cardozo Hotel by herself; she was not in the habit of spending her time off in Miami Beach, but the previous day the check that was usually delivered every Friday was late. Rather than staying, and making everyone else wait, she had decided to return the next day and pick it up herself. That way she would be able to deposit it in her account and Silvia could do the payroll for the week.

While waiting in the lobby, an unusual commotion was heard coming from within the hotel. A few moments later, and to everyone's surprise, a boy of about twelve or thirteen, stark naked and forcefully blowing into a kazoo, irrupted into the lobby. He stopped in front of Anna and started to play his own personal interpretation of *O Come To Me My Love*. The guests sitting in the lobby did not know how to react; the whole scene was so ludicrous that it inspired laughter, but it also violated all the established rules of decorum. Before anyone could react, two burly men literally picked up the young man and carried him away back into the hotel. The entire incident had taken less than a minute, not enough time for anyone to recover from the initial surprise. Anna just shrugged, thinking that the boy was pulling a prank, and waited until the payroll check was delivered.

Later that day, as she and Silvia were about to sit down to dinner, the sound of the doorbell interrupted them. They looked at each other with a puzzled look; they were not expecting anyone. Silvia stood up and answered the door; standing in the threshold, she found a man wearing a dark suit and holding some red roses in his hand. She guessed that he was in his late fifties or early sixties. "I am looking for Anna d'Amio," he said politely.

"One moment," said Silvia, "I will get her for you," then went back into the house. A few moments later, Anna came to the door.

"How may I help you?" she said, not being able to hide the puzzled look on her face.

"My name is Harold Wilson, and I have come to apologize for that unfortunate incident this morning," he explained while handing Anna the flowers.

"I do not understand," said Anna, still with a puzzled look on her face.

402

"It was my son Thomas who burst into the lobby of the Cardozo this morning," he explained. "I am sorry."

"Oh, that," said Anna, "It was nothing; I figured that he was just confused. No harm was done."

"My son is not well," continued the stranger, "But he is the only son I have, and since I value family above all things I am afraid that sometimes I am not as firm as I should be with him."

"Well, apology accepted," said Anna, "But it was not really necessary for you to come here in person. Thank you for the flowers; they are lovely."

"I hope the next time we see each other, it will be under better circumstances," said the man as he started to turn around, "Good bye."

"Good-bye, and thank you again," said Anna.

It was not until that moment that Anna noticed the black, shiny car parked by the curb. The man did not get behind the wheel, but in the back seat. As the car pulled away Anna realized that Harold Wilson had a chauffeur.

Anna did not give any more thought about the strange and brief visit. After Harold Wilson's departure, she put the flowers in a vase with water and returned to her interrupted dinner with Silvia. As far as she was concerned, she would never see him again.

The following day, as Anna was about to prepare lunch—she enjoyed Sundays because she had ample time to cook—the phone rang. When she picked up the receiver, although the voice at the other end sounded vaguely familiar, she did not know who it was until the man identified himself as Harold Wilson.

"How may I help you?" said Anna, not wanting to seem rude, but fully aware that there was no reason why he should be calling.

"I have a business proposition for you," he said, but without disclosing any details.

"Well, I am all ears," said Anna, somewhat annoyed that her cooking time had been interrupted.

"I would rather not discuss it over the phone," said Harold, "If you are not too busy, we can talk about it over lunch."

"You mean today?" asked Anna, a little surprised.

"Yes, I can be at your place in about half hour," he explained. "It will be worth your while," he added after a brief pause, to further arouse Anna's curiosity.

"Very well," she agreed, "I will see you in half an hour."

"Thank you," was Harold's answer before hanging up.
Suddenly Anna realized that she was not even dressed properly; Sunday was her day to relax at home and call the families that were caring for the twins. Silvia usually went out to see some friends she had made since her arrival in Miami, so she spent the afternoons by herself.

As Anna hurriedly began to dress, do her hair and put on her makeup, she realized that she could have declined this invitation altogether, or told Harold Wilson that she was busy on that particular afternoon. Yet, it had not taken much insistence on his part for her to accept. Just the fact that Gene had been the one to provide Harold with her address and phone number was reassuring. It was obvious that he knew the man. Anna's curiosity had also played a part on her decision to accept the lunch invitation.

Exactly half an hour later, the same black sedan that she had seen the day before pulled up in front of the house, and one of its back doors opened. Harold Wilson wore a dark suit of an impeccable cut, silk tie with a matching lapel handkerchief and perfectly pressed shirt. The ensemble bestowed upon him and air of understated elegance and wealth, but also readily identified him as a non-Floridian. As he walked towards the front door, the rays of the late morning sun highlighted his salt and pepper hair. Although not particularly good looking, Harold Wilson was always noticed because of his self-assured demeanor and the fine clothes that he wore. As he was about to ring the bell, Anna opened the door.

"Good afternoon," he said while offering a wide smile, "Thank you for agreeing to my invitation."

"I normally would not have accepted, but you were rather convincing over the phone," said Anna.

"I feel honored," said Harold, still smiling. "And I am curious," answered Anna.

"All things in due time," retorted Harold, "Let's have lunch and then we can talk business," he said while leading Anna towards the car. He opened the back door for Anna, and then sat next to her.

"To the Fontainebleau," he told the chauffeur, who acknowledged the request with a subdued 'Yes, sir.' This was yet another sign that this man was serious, thought Anna, for the hotel where they were going was perhaps the most exclusive in Miami Beach. Although Anna had been by it several times, she had never had the desire to go in, since she knew without asking that she could not afford such a place.

"Why the Fontainebleau?" she suddenly asked.

"And why not?" answered Harold, "That's where I am staying; they have a superb chef. I am sure you will be impressed."

On that bright Sunday afternoon, the traffic on Biscayne Boulevard was light, so they soon reached one of the causeways that led to Miami Beach. In the distance, rows of beautiful houses lined the shoreline. Most of them had private piers where small boats were available for the occupants. The bay proper was busy with yachts and other vessels.Even though the windows of the car were closed — apparently Harold Wilson preferred air conditioning — the smell of salt air managed the reach Anna in the back seat of the car.

"What a beautiful view," she commented, "The people who live in those houses are lucky, but I am sure that real estate on the bay must be expensive."

"It is a paradox," answered Harold.

"What is?" asked Anna, puzzled by his odd answer.

"The people who can afford to buy those houses usually don't have the time to live in them and enjoy the view. As a rule they are too busy with other affairs," he explained.

"And how do you know that?" asked Anna.

"Because I used to own one of them," stated Harold in a matter of fact tone, "I thought it would be nice to come down here with my son, especially in the winter, but my business commitments prevented me from it; I think I used the house once or twice. After a year I decided to sell it."

"I suppose that makes sense," Anna agreed.

"It makes sense from a business point of view, since the house was a financial drain; from a personal point of view, it didn't. I could have made the time to come down here, if I had really tried."

"I suppose it comes down to priorities," offered Anna. "That is correct," concurred Harold.

This brief exchange made Anna realize several things about Harold Wilson. First of all, he was wealthier than she had thought. Second, making money was no longer the prime force in his life, but something he did because he enjoyed the financial world. He was, above all things, a businessman.

"Whenver I come to Miami Beach I just stay at the Fontainebleau," continued Harold, "I enjoy all the amenities without the constant burden of an empty house. I find it to be more cost effective."

"So what brings you to Miami this time?" asked Anna.

"We are already here, so let's save that for lunch," answered Harold. As the car pulled up in front of the Fontainebleau Hotel, Anna understood why it was the highest rated hotel in Miami Beach. The semicircular driveway led to a set of double glass doors that opened onto the ample air-conditioned lobby. Through those doors Anna could see the constant activity within. The cars that were parked in front of the hotel, or the ones that pulled up to let people out, were far from the ordinary vehicles found on the streets. They were mostly Cadillacs, Lincoln Continentals, Buicks, and even an occasional Rolls Royce. Many were convertibles painted in pastel colors with their tops down.

The chauffeur stopped the car in front of the hotel, got out and came around to open the back door for Harold and Anna. Once they had exited, he quickly returned to his seat behind the wheel and left.

"We can either have lunch on the terrace, overlooking the pool, or inside, where it is air-conditioned," said Harold as he opened the glass door for Anna.

"Let's eat inside," answered Anna, "It will be quieter, and I don't want to miss a single word of what you have to say."

"I am glad you are interested," answered Harold as he led Anna in the direction of the dining hall.

"Intrigued would be a better word," she replied.

"I just hope you are not disappointed when you hear my proposal," answered Harold as they stepped into the ample and well-lit dining area. The tables, Anna noticed at once, were not covered with synthetic materials, but with white tablecloths made of fine linen that looked freshly pressed. Next to the matching napkins—neatly rolled and held in place by a metal ring—the silverware had been carefully laid out. Before they had a chance to sit down, a uniformed waiter appeared, greeted them and pulled out the chair for Anna. Once they were seated, he handed them the menus. As she began to look over the dishes that were available,

406

Anna also realized that there were no prices listed with the different items. These were the menus given to the ladies, so they would not be concerned about the price of the meals; those handed out to the male companions, on the other hand, had the prices clearly marked. This was further proof, thought Anna, that Harold Wilson moved in the highest economic circles. After she finished looking over the offerings in the menu, Anna opted for the salmon and a salad.

"I will have the same," said Harold as he took Anna's menu and returned both of them to the waiter, "And bring us a bottle of white wine."

"This is a very nice hotel," said Anna, stating the obvious. At that moment she felt a little awkward, and just for a fraction of a second she asked herself if accepting Harold's invitation had been the right thing to do.

"The best in Miami Beach," answered Harold. "But let me tell you why I've asked you here," he said suddenly and without transition, "As I already mentioned, I come down to Miami from time to time. These trips are usually business, and a few days ago I bought a hotel on Ocean Drive. At the moment, it is closed, but I plan to have the entire building refurbished. If everything goes well we should be able to open next year."

"That is fine," said Anna, "But I still do not understand what it all has to do with me."

When the waiter returned with the wine, he uncorked the bottle and poured some into Harold's glass, for him to approve it before serving Anna. Once Harold nodded, her filled both glasses and retreated from the table.

"Let me explain," said Harold while taking another sip of wine, "I know that you have a small cleaning business, and that your reputation for efficiency and reliability has been growing."

"And how do you know these things?" asked Anna.

"I just happen to be friends with Gene, the manager of the Cardozo. When my son came into the lobby we were visiting; he is the one who told me about you."

"I see," said Anna, but she refrained from making any comments about Harold's son. Even if she had wanted to, the incident had been too odd. What could she possibly have said?

It was Harold, perhaps guessing her thoughts, who brought it up. "Thomas is not like other children; in fact, he never has been and never will be. I keep people on the staff to look after him twenty four hours a day".

"What do the doctors say?" asked Anna.

"It happened during birth," answered Harold, "His behavior is erratic at times, but I assure you that he is completely harmless. Once I thought of having him institutionalized, but I concluded that he would be better off with me, even if there is no progress."

"I agree with you," said Anna, "Family is very important. What about his mother?"

"She died during childbirth," explained Harold.

"I am so sorry," said Anna in a soft tone of voice, intimately familiar with the pain of losing a spouse.

"No need to be," said Harold, "That was a long time ago, and maybe she would have suffered more seeing her son like that, without any hope of reaching full maturity.

"I wish there were something I could say," Anna almost whispered.

"Forgive me," said Harold, "I did not mean to burden you with my personal problems. I started to tell you about the hotel; I want you to manage it for me."

"I don't know what to say," confessed Anna, "I have never managed a hotel before."

"But you must have a business background," insisted Harold, "How else would you have put together the cleaning business you are currently running?"

"I used to own and manage a restaurant in Havana," confessed Anna.

"And I bet it did very well," exclaimed Harold.

"Well enough," admitted Anna, remembering fondly all the work she had put into the Pompeii.

"Then there should be no doubts in your mind," concluded Harold. "I do not expect an answer right now; there is plenty of time. I just wanted you to think about it; once you decide, we can talk about money."

"I promise I will consider it," said Anna, acquiescing to Harold's wishes.

"Good," said Harold after sipping leisurely on his wine. Now that the matter had been settled, he could concentrate on his meal and make small talk. Once lunch was over, Harold showed Anna around the hotel. By the way he was greeted by the different members of the staff, and by the familiarity he showed with the premises, Anna realized that he was a regular.

"This is quite different from the Cardozo," commented Anna.

"Yes, quite different," agreed Harold. "As you probably know, the Cardozo was built in 1939, at the height of the art deco era. At that time it was cutting edge and considered one of the best in Miami Beach. The Fontainebleau," he continued, "came much later. It is the product of a different era; it was meant to meet the needs of the corporate world and accommodate an international clientele."

"Yes, I see what you mean," said Anna.

"Now, before I take you home, I would like to show you something," suggested Harold as they made their way through the lobby.

"What is it?" asked Anna with genuine curiosity.

"You will see," answered Harold as he looked at his watch. Precisely at that moment, his black sedan appeared in front of the hotel and stopped in front of the double glass doors. Harold opened the back door for Anna, and the got into the car after her.

"To the new hotel," Harold instructed the driver, who acknowledged him with a slight nod. As they made their was through Miami Beach, Harold expertly pointed out to Anna the different landmarks that he considered worthy of notice. Eventually they arrived at the southernmost section of Miami Beach and stopped in front of a building in obvious need of attention.

"We can't go in today," explained Harold, "but I wanted you to see it before all the renovations begin. Just think about it; before long you may be running the place," he said enthusiastically.

"I will think about your proposal," said Anna, "I must admit that it is very tempting."

"I hope so," said Harold, "I don't want to start looking for another manager; just consider the possibilities."

By then it was almost five o'clock, so Harold instructed the driver to take them back to Anna's house in Miami. During the trip back, Harold spoke about his plans for the new hotel, and the vision he had in mind when it opened after all the renovations were completed. It would certainly be no competition for the Fontainebleau, but it would cater to middle class families looking for modern and comfortable—yet moderately priced—lodgings in Miami Beach. Anna listened attentively and had to agree that

Harold's purchase would probably be returning a profit before long.

"Thank you for a lovely afternoon," said Anna as they pulled up in front of her house on Brickell Avenue.

"No, thank you for accepting my invitation and listening to my offer," answered Harold and then he exited the car to open Anna's door on the other side. "I will be in touch," he finally said before getting back into the car and instructing the driver to go.

So absorbed had Anna been, that she had not noticed that Silvia was standing in the doorway; apparently she had been watching the brief exchange between Anna and Harold.

"So tell me all about it," she said with her typical smile.

"There is not much to tell," answered Anna, "We had lunch and then he asked me if I would consider managing a hotel he just bought, but it won't be ready for at least a year; it needs a lot of work."

"Is that all?" asked Silvia, with an incredulous tone of voice.

"I don't know what you mean," answered Anna.

"Then you must be blind," retorted Silvia, "First the flowers, then the lunch invitation, and now the job offer. I noticed the way he was looking at you; it reminded me of a teenager in love."

"You are imagining things, Silvia," answered Anna. "Besides, you know I have no time for such things; getting my daughters back is all I think about."

"Some things in life just have a way of happening, even if we do not plan them. Trust me; I know," Silvia said confidently.

"Time will tell," answered Anna, also confident that her friend was seeing things that were not there, "Only time will tell."

Harold Wilson was born with a silver spoon in his mouth. This does not mean necessarily that his life was without hardships, since material wealth does not guarantee an existence exempt from the reverses of life that, at one time or another, befall every man.

Born at the turn of the twentieth century into one of the richest and most respected families in Pittsburgh, his early childhood was filled with family outings and other social events, where he mingled with other children whose parents came from the highest strata of society.

410

His father, Dexter Wilson, as did many other Post Civil War industrialists, had accumulated unprecedented wealth in a relatively short time. But unlike some of his contemporaries — Washington Duke, Leland Stanford, Cornelious Vanderbilt and Andrew Carnegie — he had dismissed the idea of creating an institution of higher learning that would bear his name; the very idea went against his upbringing, where modesty had always been one of the cardinal rules. This did not preclude him, of course, from engaging in other philanthropic activities, which he preferred to carry out anonymously. Aided by his wife, Cora, they donated and raised considerable amounts of money for their favorite charities. The fact that they had direct connections to the most prominent families in the country just made matters a little easier.

During the summer of 1910, as was his custom, Dexter Wilson took his family for a summer vacation at a lodge he owned in the Allegheny Mountains. The cool air, the nearby lake and the peacefulness of the remote area made it an ideal retreat from the sweltering Pittsburgh heat. The lodge was also large enough to accommodate guests should he wish to invite some of his friends or business acquaintances.

Young Harold always looked forward to these times up in the mountains, for he especially enjoyed hiking and canoeing. Behind the lodge were the stables where a full time caretaker looked after the horses. In the evenings, away from the noise of the city, he would listen in bed to the nocturnal sounds that came in through his open window, and wondered if there could be a more peaceful and serene place in a remote part of the world. Up to the end of his life, he would always remember these times fondly. But that fateful summer would irrevocably change the course of his life.

Early one Saturday morning, the entire family rose, had breakfast and headed for the stables. Both Dexter and Cora were avid riders, so they were completely at home around horses. Harold had learned to ride the previous summer, and this was one of those activities that he also loved because he only practiced it at the lodge; it was obviously impossible to have a horse in the city.

After saddling the horses, the family started out on a familiar trail that led to the lake and then upwards towards one of the ridges that had a commanding view of the valley below. Dexter led the way, followed by Harold, and Cora was at the rear. The family enjoyed these times together, for it afforded them an opportunity to spend time with one another, away from the constant interruptions so prevalent in city life. Harold in particular loved these rides because he felt that then and only then he had his parents to himself. He talked freely about his school activities, his friends, and anything else that was on his mind. From time to time, his parents would point out to him some of the more interesting features of the landscape, or tell him about the next social gathering they were planning.

Neither Dexter nor Harold saw what happened. They heard Cora's horse neighing; by the time they turned around, suddenly startled by the sound, they saw the horse standing on its hind legs and Cora, unable to hold on, falling to the ground. By the time they dismounted and rushed to her side, she was unconscious and her head was bleeding. Faced with a crisis, Dexter did not hesitate. With the aid of his son, they got Cora up on his horse; sitting behind her and holding her inert body they made it back to the lodge as fast as they could. One of the stable hands was sent to fetch a doctor, so Dexter and Harold could look after the still unconscious Cora. While they waited, Dexter cleaned the wound and applied cold compresses to his wife's head.

The doctor arrived almost two hours later. From the bedroom Dexter and Harold heard the horses outside, so they rushed out to meet the him. Although he had been briefed by Dexter's employee, the doctor wanted to hear a first hand account of the events.

"What happened?" he asked as he came into the lodge, dispensing with all courtesies.

"We did not see it happen," answered Dexter, "Something spooked her horse; maybe a rattlesnake. She was thrown and hit her head on a rock; she has been unconscious ever since," he explained while leading the doctor into the bedroom.

Cora had not moved since earlier that day; although her respiration was regular, it lacked the depth of a person who was just sleeping. Its diminished capacity was barely enough to keep the body alive, a fact that did not escape the keen eye of the physician. From his black bag he produced a small flashlight, raised the eyelids of the patient with his thumb and shone the light on the pupils, looking for a reflex. Afterwards he took Cora's pulse and finally felt her head with a gentle motion of his hands.

"She has suffered a severe concussion," he finally declared. "The danger in these cases," he continued, "is the pressure that can

412

be exerted on the brain by the potential internal bleeding. She should be taken to the city right away, where she will have access to the most modern care," he concluded.

"Thank you doctor," said Dexter, "We will make the preparations immediately."

The journey back to Pittsburgh was not an easy one. First, the patient had to be placed in a horse drawn carriage that would take them from the lodge to the main highway. From there, they transferred her to one of the new gasoline powered cars that were now becoming so popular throughout the country. Harold stayed with his mother in the back seat, holding her hand, while Dexter concentrated on the road. They arrived at the hospital just before midnight, still wearing the clothes they had put on that morning for the ride to the mountain ridge. Cora was admitted into a private room, and Dexter, after speaking with the team of doctors, gave instructions that no expense should be spared to bring his wife back to health. This, of course, was completely unnecessary, for everyone knew that he was one of the wealthiest men in the state. The rest of the night was spent in one of the waiting rooms, while the doctors tried to ascertain the next course of action that would place the patient on her way to recovery. While Dexter waited, young Harold fell asleep on one of the sofas.

Just before dawn, one of the doctors came into the waiting room. At once Dexter stood up and walked over to meet him. "How is she?" he asked.

"She is resting at the moment," the doctor answered, "We tried to relieve the pressure on the brain. All we can do now is wait. I suggest that you and your son go home and get some rest; there is nothing you can do here. If there is any change, we will let you know."

"Please do," said Dexter, "We will be back after we rest and clean up."

"Our door is always open," said the physician. "Now, if you will excuse me, I have other patients to see."

"Thank you doctor," said Dexter, "We will talk again later."

For the next five days Dexter stayed by Cora's bed. He would only go home briefly to bathe, change clothes and get something to eat. All his business appointments had been canceled. Being summertime, Harold was not attending school, so he usually accompanied his father to the hospital. While they sat by Cora's bed, Harold usually read a book. He especially liked the novels of Jules Verne, because of his fertile imagination and his fantastic projections about the future. This love of literature, acquired so early in life, would always stay with him.

On the morning of the fifth day, Cora opened her eyes. Although Dexter and Harold were sitting by the bed, she did not seem to see them. "Harold, where is Harold?" she asked, as if looking for a lost child. Harold put down his book immediately, but before he could reach his mother she closed her eyes again. The moment had been so unexpected and fleeting that for an instant they doubted that Cora had actually awakened and had called out her son's name. That was the last time they heard her voice. From that day on her vital signs became weaker, and despite all the efforts of the doctors on the staff, she died three days later.

Dexter was devastated; he could not conceive life without Cora. After the funeral, alone with his son in his house on the North Side of Pittsburgh, he began to think about the future. The stone house, adorned with decorative woodwork, ceramic tile, slate roof and stained glass, had been constructed to Cora's specifications. Everywhere he looked he was reminded of her, of happier times. Although Dexter returned to work and friends of the family visited often, every night he came home to a house that was a constant reminder of Cora's absence. How heavy is the burden of solitude, he thought as he moved from room to room at the end of the day, desperately trying to postpone the time when he would retire to the bedroom that they had shared.

Then, of course, there was Harold. A boy needed his mother, especially with a father whose business in the steel industry took most of his time. At first Dexter hired a governess to look after Harold, but he knew that sooner or later some hard decisions would have to be made. By the end of summer, he had decided on a course of action. He sold the house on the North Side and enrolled Harold in a boarding school in Philadelphia. There he would not only get a proper education, but the guidance and attention that he could no longer find at home. Without Cora's cohesive influence, the family had quickly fallen apart.

Being as young as he was, Harold could not oppose the will of his father. Although he did not dislike the school—his classmates were mostly boys whose families were too busy to take care of them—there was a deep sadness reflected in his eyes. Harold had

414

never been away from home, and having just lost his mother did not make matters any easier.

He found a refuge in books; the school library was replete with the best literature from around the world. He read incessantly and voraciously, and before long became the top student in his literature classes. His teachers were both delighted and amazed to have such a pupil. What they never stopped to consider was the reason Harold loved books so much; they just accepted the fact at face value. With every story, with every novel he read, not only did Harold escape his own present condition, but came to understand that the fabric of life was composed of an infinite number of intertwined threads, which in turn reached out and joined the threads of other lives.

During Christmas and summer recesses he returned to Pittsburgh — those were times that he looked forward to and cherished — but with the passing of time came to miss the visits less and less. After Cora's death, Dexter had thrown himself more than ever — if that was possible — into his work, so Harold hardly ever saw him. On those occasions that he did, which was mostly at the supper table, there was not much to discuss, since they were living in different worlds. This is not to say that Dexter did not love his son, or vice versa, but although their relationship was affable enough, their interests had taken them in different directions.

Tangible proof of this fact came during Harold's last year at preparatory school. By then, he had decided to enter Yale and follow a career in writing, a decision applauded by his teachers and classmates. His academic performance, along with letters of recommendation, almost assured him admission into any school of his choice. The one thing he had not considered was his father's reaction to his choice of study and the institution in which it would take place.

Because of Dexter Wilson's involvement with the steel Industry, and because of his friendship with Andrew Carnegie, he had decided that his son would attend the Carnegie Institute of Technology. Many years later this institution would become the now world famous Carnegie Mellon University. Dexter, who by then realized that he was aging, saw a last opportunity to become closer to his son and teach him all he knew about the business.

Upon hearing his father's plans, Harold was deflated. On the one hand, aware of how much he had suffered after Cora's death, he did not want to disappoint him. Although many believed that eventually Dexter would marry again, he chose a life of work and celibacy. The other alternative was to openly oppose the will of his father and follow the path that he loved, even if it broke Dexter's heart. Ultimately, and after a long period of inner struggle, he acquiesced to his father's wishes and enrolled at the Carnegie Institute of Technology.

Although Harold did not find the coursework completely to his dislike, and his grades were at the top of his class, he knew from the beginning that he could never love this career as much as he loved literature. He still tried to read as much as he could, but his technical courses at the Institute left him little time for personal pastimes. His dream of becoming a writer had ended before it had a chance to begin.

By the time Harold received his degree in 1922, Dexter had begun to entrust him with some of the more important decisions in their company. The demands of World War I had brought an unprecedented prosperity to the steel industry, and that prosperity, now that the war had ended, seemed to have spread to the entire nation. Because of his prominent position in Pittsburgh's society — not to speak of his family's wealth — Harold was considered one of the city's most eligible bachelors.

But this exuberant prosperity of the roaring twenties did not fool Harold. He knew that sooner or later this artificial bubble of affluence could not be sustained, that it would burst eventually. Every day, as he watched the ticker from the stock market climb ever higher, he shook his head in disbelief. Of course, he knew that there was no point in warning his friends and business acquaintances; they would not want to hear what he had to say. They preferred to remain in that state of euphoria fueled by easy money, bathtub gin, and late-night parties where they danced the Charleston until dawn with easily accessible flappers.

Harold's introspective, almost taciturn character — undoubtedly tempered by Cora's unexpected death while he was still a child — had made him aware of the sudden reverses that life often has a way of handing out. This tendency had been further honed by the many stories and novels he had read; all plots — whether real or fictional — had to come to a logical conclusion.

416

He found a sympathetic ear, of all people, in his father. One evening, while sipping brandy in the older Wilson's office, Harold laid out all the concerns that he had regarding the economy. He offered, in a logical and systematic fashion, what he believed was irrefutable proof of what was to come. When he finished, there was silence. For a moment, he thought his father would dismiss his concerns as pure folly. Dexter had not gotten where he was in life by not paying attention to the circumstances that surrounded him. During the past few years, as he had given his son more responsibilities, he had come to realize that Harold had a keen sense of business, even if his true love lay elsewhere.

"I agree completely," he finally said. "The question is, what are we going to do about it, in order to shelter our assets and make sure our company survives?"

Harold was ready for this question. He had pondered long and hard what the new situation would bring, and he had come to one conclusion.

"Gold," he said simply. "The market is overpriced; once the collapse comes, the investors will be left with nothing but worthless pieces of paper. It is my opinion that we must begin to liquidate our holdings, now that the prices are at their highest levels, and invest in a vehicle whose value will always be beyond the fluctuations of the market. As I said, gold is the most viable alternative."

"What you suggest is a very radical measure," said Dexter, perhaps still not quite convinced.

"It is either that or be left with nothing," answered Harold calmly, "But since we have to liquidate gradually, we should start right away; it is impossible to tell how long before this unstable bubble bursts."

"Very well then," agreed Dexter, "Let's meet again tomorrow morning and we can go over the details."

"Good night," said Harold as he left his father's study. "Good night, Son," answered the older Wilson.

This last word took Harold by surprise. His father had not called him son since the times when they used to vacation in the Allegheny Mountains. After Cora died, Dexter always addressed him by his given name. Perhaps this was a subtle indication that the old man trusted him more with every passing day.

After that initial meeting, with Dexter's approval and under Harold's direction, they gradually liquidated all their stock market holdings. The proceeds were immediately invested in gold. For an entire year the market continued its dizzying upward trend; people thought that the party would never end. Even Dexter himself secretly began to doubt Harold's predictions; everyone's stocks kept climbing higher, while he had opted to step out of the market and watch the frantic action from the sidelines. When October 29, 1929—a day better known as Black Tuesday—arrived, with stocks plummeting and entire fortunes evaporating overnight, he knew that his capital was safe. Harold had been right all along. This dreadful day would usher the country into one of the worst economic decades in its history. The great depression had begun.

Because of Harold's foresight, they were in a better position than ever before. It was not so much that their assets had increased, but that everyone else's had decreased drastically or completely disappeared. This unprecedented position of strength gave them a superb advantage over their competitors, many of whom had filed for bankruptcy or were fighting for survival. After this day, Dexter never doubted Harold again. He now had the certainty that whenever he died, his company would remain and the Wilson fortune would continue to thrive. It was not until ten years later, with the United States being drawn into World War II, thanks to the war effort, that the economy would begin to recover. But Dexter, now getting on in years and in failing health, would not live to see the direction in which his son would take the company that he had founded. He passed away peacefully in his own bed in 1935. When Harold came to wake him, as he did every morning, he knew at once that death had come. It was not until that moment that he came to realize how much he loved his father, and how similar they were in so many ways. Even though they had lived in the same house since Harold finished his degree, and spent time together every day, they had never openly expressed their feelings for each other.

The funeral was attended by the most prominent businessmen in the country, as well as many other important citizens. Everyone knew that Dexter Wilson's philanthropy extended far beyond the Pittsburgh city limits, as they also knew that because of his modesty most of his works were done anonymously. They all paid their respects to Harold, acknowledging that he was now in full control of the Wilson fortune, but privately wondered in which direction he would lead the company now that his father was gone. At thirty-five years of age, Harold Wilson was not only one of the wealthiest men in the United States, but also one of the most influential as well.

Ironically, this was not how Harold felt about himself after returning home from the cemetery. As he stepped into the empty house, the full-length Venetian mirror in the parlor reflected a tall man with circles under his eyes. He realized that he looked somewhat older than his years, and that he resembled Dexter more than he cared to admit. He also realized that he was completely alone, that despite all his wealth, power and influence, he had no one to come home to at the end of the day.

Work was a relief; just watching over the company, presiding over meetings and making a myriad of decisions made the day seem like a blur. In the evenings, after a late supper, he retreated to his library and tried to put aside everything remotely related to business. Once again he found solace in literature; he reread many of the classics with which he had become familiar during his youth, and found many passages that now spoke to him, but that he had missed during the first reading because he lacked maturity. It was also during this time that he became fond of jazz, a passion he would cultivate until the end of his life.

Everyone thought that after a reasonable period of mourning, Harold would find a suitable mate, marry and start a family. There was no shortage of candidates who would have gladly accepted his advances. As it was customary, he attended all the social balls, enjoyed the music and the company of young eligible young women, but never called on any of them with any regularity. With the passing of time, most people came to believe that Harold was a confirmed bachelor. This, or course, was not the case.

In 1941 the United States was drawn into World War II, and everyone's attention turned from social functions toward the war effort. Four years later, after the conflict was over, the city of Pittsburgh launched a clean air and civic revitalization project know as The Renaissance. The success of this project hinged on engaging every citizen at one level or another. Harold was one of the leaders of such a project. In a way, he thought, it was ironical that the fortune that Dexter had amassed through steel and its polluting byproducts should now be used to reverse the damage and restore the city and the environment to a more pristine condition. To kick off this endeavor, a ball was organized. The proceeds of this event would go directly toward this process of revitalization. As a member of the board, Harold Wilson was one of the most distinguished guests scheduled to attend. Although he had never been that fond of such gatherings, he realized that his presence would enhance the validity of the event.

As fate would have it, Caroline Ashburn had also been invited to the ball. Only daughter of Dr. Peter Ashburn and a graduate of Wellesley College, she had recently returned to Pittsburgh to start a new career as an artist after spending a year in Paris. Although it could not be said that Harold Wilson and Dr. Ashburn were friends, they were not complete strangers; their paths had often crossed because of Harold's continued endowments to local hospitals.

On the appointed night, Harold put on a dark suit, white shirt, and a gray silk tie. He arrived at the ball around ten o'clock, and gave the chauffeur instructions to wait. Although his presence was important, he did not intend to stay the entire night. As soon as he walked in, he was instantly greeted by some of the most prominent citizens of Pittsburgh. Among them were Dr. Peter Ashburn and his daughter.

"Allow me to introduce my daughter Caroline," he said, "She returned to Pittsburgh last week," then after a pause, "I hope this time is for good."

The first thing Harold noticed about Caroline was that she was young and very beautiful. After that first impression subsided, he also realized, by her expression and the incipient smile on her face, that she seemed mildly amused by the gathering of well-to-do individuals in the huge hall. It was as if she were subconsciously flaunting a certain degree of disdain for old money and high social standing.

"It is a pleasure," said Harold while shaking lightly the young woman's hand. "Were you away very long?" he asked, making a reference to Dr. Ashburn's comment.

"No, not really," she answered, "Just a year. My father wanted me to come back to Pittsburgh right after graduation, but there were some things that I had to see for myself before returning."

"I don't quite understand," confessed Harold.

"Above all things, I am an artist," said Caroline in a vehement tone, "I spent some time in Paris, immersed in the great works of European art; I felt it was essential before launching my career."

"I can accept that," said Harold, "The creative process must be nourished constantly." At this point in the conversation, Caroline made a pause, as if she were organizing her thoughts.

"You do not sound like a businessman," she finally said, "I was under the impression that in your world making money was the most important thing."

"I am not a typical businessman," answered Harold, "But that is a long story," he said enigmatically after making a pause himself.

"I have all evening," answered Caroline.

"I am afraid you might be bored," said Harold, somewhat intimidated by her forward demeanor.

"Let's dance and you can tell me all about it," she insisted as she took Harold's arm and led him onto the dance floor.

As soon as they started to dance, Harold inexplicably realized that Caroline Ashburn, whom he had just met, would play a pivotal role in his life. Her perfume, the touch of her hand, the gleam in her eyes and her easy smile made him feel as he never had before in the presence of a woman. Perhaps she subconsciously took him back to when he was a boy and Cora would come into his room to tuck him in and kiss him good night before turning off the lights. That closeness, that tender touch underscored by the subtle fragrance had almost been forgotten. Until tonight.

By the time Harold looked at his watch, he realized that it was almost three o'clock; the ball was about to conclude. He had spent the entire night with Caroline Ashburn; they had danced and they had talked. Throughout the course of the evening, Harold had confided in her that during his youth he intended to pursue a career in writing, but that circumstances had turned him into the businessman he had become. Caroline, in turn, told him about her stay in Europe after graduation, the days spent looking at art in museums, her plans to become an established artist in her own right, and her return to Pittsburgh at her father's insistence. "I have an idea," said Harold as they were walking out of the building, "I would like to be your first client; I want you to do my portrait." This suggestion was nothing more than a feeble excuse on his part to see her again. Somehow he found her presence exhilarating.

"But you have not seen any of my work," she said, "How do you know I can do the job?" Her question, of course, was a valid one, but Harold would not desist.

"Call it my businessman's instinct," he answered readily. "Besides, as passionate as you are about art and your career, I have to trust you," he added, "Have lunch with me tomorrow and we can discuss all the particulars."

"Very well then," agreed Caroline, "Come by around one o'clock; I will be waiting. Good night."

"I am looking forward to it," said Harold, "I will see you then."

As Caroline disappeared into her father's car, once again Harold felt that she would somehow play a very important part in his life. He had certainly never met anyone like her. In the parking lot his chauffeur had fallen asleep behind the wheel, so Harold shook him gently on the shoulder to wake him. He remembered that he had not intended to stay beyond midnight.

The following morning, after a late breakfast, Harold went into his library. He usually read the Sunday paper while listening to jazz and enjoying a second and even a third cup of coffee. It was a time that he liked to reserve for himself, before having to meet with friends or business associates in the afternoons.

But this Sunday morning was different. His mind drifted from the financial section of the newspaper as he recalled all the things that Caroline Ashburn had revealed about herself and her dreams. He closed his eyes and saw her face while he tried to evoke the gentle touch of her hand and the subtle perfume that she wore. She had reached a part of him that he had shielded for many years.

Around eleven thirty he put aside the unread newspaper, went up to his room to dress, and then left the house. This time, rather than using the chauffeur, he drove the car himself. Although he had never visited Dr. Ashburn's house, he knew precisely where he ived. During his leisurely drive, he saw people coming out of churches wearing their Sunday's best, and children on their bicycles as well as pedestrians dressed more casually on their way to the early matinees where double features were offered.

Dr. Ashburn's house sat on a promontory overlooking the Allegheny River. It was built in the English Tudor style, and the grounds surrounding it were perfectly manicured. As he approached the long driveway that led to the house, Harold slowed down and then parked in front. At that moment, he felt a little apprehensive; although his intentions were nothing but honorable. Despite the obvious affinity that existed between him and Caroline Ashburn, he realized that there was a large gap between their ages. He walked up to the main door, but before he could knock, it opened.Caroline was in the threshold, smiling widely. Apparently she had been watching through the window, to make sure she would be the one to open the door for Harold.

"Come in," she said, taking Harold's hand and leading him into the living room, "I want you to say hello to my father before we go." As if waiting for a signal, Dr. Ashburn appeared from another section of the house.

"Good afternoon," he said while shaking Harold's hand, "It seems that you have made quite an impression on Caroline. Not an easy feat, if I may say so myself."

"I just suggested that she could do my portrait," answered Harold, not knowing exactly how to answer the comment.

"Whatever the reason," retorted Dr. Ashburn, "I am glad the two of you have hit it off so well." With this comment, Harold understood at once, Dr. Ashburn was giving his approval to a friendship that might turn into something more, and if it did, Caroline would settle in Pittsburgh and stay close by. Nothing could make her father happier. "Now, if you will excuse me, I must make my rounds at the hospital," he said, "Enjoy your lunch."

"We will," answered Harold, "It was good to see you again."

"Are we ready?" asked Caroline while holding on to Harold's arm.

"Yes, anytime," he said while looking at his watch. "I made reservations for one o'clock. The restaurant is not far from here," he added as they walked out to the car.

That first luncheon went on until the late afternoon. After the meal, Harold ordered a fresh pot of coffee and they picked up their conversation where they had left off the night before. With every passing minute they both realized that, despite the difference in age, they had quite a few things in common. Besides art and literature, they also loved jazz.

"I must confess," said Caroline, "that you are as far as one can get from a businessman."

"You already know the story," said Harold, "It was because of my father that I took on this responsibility; I suppose someone had to do it."

"And from what I can see, you do it very well," added Caroline.

"That does not mean that I stopped being the same person I always was; it is just a little more difficult."

"But now you have me to help you," said Caroline with a smile as she placed her hand on his, an unmistakable sign that the incipient friendship was quickly changing into something more intimate.

From that day on they became inseparable. The following week Caroline came to Harold's house to start working on his portrait, and after the posing sessions she usually stayed for dinner or they went out. Shortly thereafter, with Harold's help, she opened an art studio where she painted, exhibited her work and also gave art lessons to the children of Pittsburgh's most prominent citizens. On weekends she and Harold would attend cultural events, especially poetry readings and jazz concerts. They had become an item.

Dr. Ashburn could not be happier. His daughter had opted to stay in Pittsburgh and apparently Harold Wilson was quite taken with her. So the doctor was not at all surprised when one evening, six months later, Harold came calling to ask for Caroline's hand in marriage. This was just a formality, for Caroline was of age, but being old school Harold had insisted that things should be done properly. Somehow he felt that omitting this step would have been disrespectful to his soon to be father in law.

After giving his approval, Dr. Ashburn kissed his daughter, opened a bottle of champagne and offered a toast for the happiness of Caroline and Harold. This marriage, he knew, not only would keep his daughter close by, but it would also consolidate his standing in Pittsburgh's high society. It was a win win situation all around. So much the better that Harold and Caroline seemed to be so much in love.

The wedding took place three months later; it had been, by all standards, a whirlwind courtship, but one that augured continued happiness for the couple. After a honeymoon trip to Paris — Caroline had insisted that she wanted to show Harold all that city had to offer — the couple returned to Pittsburgh. Harold attended to his business endeavors; Caroline's career as an artist and teacher was beginning to take off. She also undertook a renovation of the house where Harold had lived alone for so many years and that reflected the whimsical taste of someone who had been a confirmed bachelor.

Every Sunday the couple had dinner at Dr. Ashburn's home. For the doctor, this was an opportunity to see his daughter, but also to discuss with his son in law the different needs of hospitals and clinics in the city. Now that Harold was part of the family, he felt freer to enlist his help in raising the money needed for the philanthropic work that occupied much of his time.

It was during one of these Sunday dinners, less than a year later, that the couple announced that Caroline was expecting. She had a special glow—a combination of fulfillment and hormonal changes—that made her look absolutely radiant. Upon hearing the news Dr. Ashburn stood up, kissed his daughter and shook Harold's hand. This was the best news that both families had received in a long time. To celebrate, Dr. Ashburn brought out a bottle of champagne, but would not allow Caroline to drink.

"From this moment on," he announced, "You must remember that anything you do will affect the health of the baby."

"Yes, doctor," she said and smiled.

The next few months were spent preparing for the arrival of the new heir. One of the bedrooms in the house was turned into a nursery, and every item was chosen personally by the proud parents to be. Even though Caroline was under the care of one of the most prominent obstetricians in the city—also a personal friend of her father—every Sunday, during the dinners at Dr. Ashburn's house he insisted on having a detailed report of that week's progress. She indulged her father, for she knew how much it all meant to him, and recounted all the trivial details of the previous week.

The impending birth of Thomas Wilson, rather than bringing joy to both families, would leave them filled with pain and consternation. One evening, as they were about to sit down for dinner, Caroline felt a sudden stream coming down her legs and contractions in her lower abdomen. The couple had been forewarned by the doctor that this would happen, so Harold quickly rushed his wife to the hospital, where she was immediately placed in the delivery room. While he waited, Harold called his father in law, who appeared shortly and joined Harold in the waiting room. Harold's nervousness was outwardly manifested in the short walks around the room and the frequency with which he looked at his watch. Dr. Ashburn, more experienced in these matters, explained that every baby had his own schedule, and that first born babies usually took a little longer. It was ten o'clock in the evening.

The rest of the night was spent in anxious waiting, but by four in the morning Dr. Ashburn knew that there was something wrong. Not wanting to alarm Harold, he left the waiting room alleging he had to visit the rest room. In reality he wanted to speak to the head nurse in order to find out exactly what was going on in the delivery room. The nurse, of course, knew who he was, so there was no point in trying to hide the details of the situation. There had been some complications; the position of the baby was endangering the mother's life. The doctors had spent hours trying to reposition the unborn infant, cognizant that the umbilical cord could easily strangle him. In the meantime, the mother was becoming weaker.

Upon hearing the news, Dr. Ashburn did not say anything, but simply thanked the nurse and returned to the waiting room. He knew the doctors personally and was certain that they were doing all that was possible to ensure the safety of Caroline and the baby. In the meantime, there was no point in alarming Harold unnecessarily. But when the first rays of the morning sun came in through the window and still there were no news, Dr. Ashburn did not have to be told that something was very wrong. His speculations did not last long, for a short time later one of the doctors came into the waiting room. His somber face augured the worst possible outcome. Upon seeing him both men approached him, eager for news about Caroline.

"The baby is fine," said the doctor, attempting to ease the blow he was about to deliver.

"How is my wife?" asked Harold, justly alarmed by the doctor's dim expression.

"We did everything we could; there were complications," he explained in a feeble tone, not wanting to utter the word that was in everyone's mind.

Dr. Ashburn had retreated to a corner of the waiting room. His back turned, as he seemed to be looking out the open window that faced the front of the hospital, with its manicured lawns and immaculate landscaping. Harold, now aware of what had taken place, approached him and placed a hand on his shoulder. As Dr.

426

Ashburn turned around to face him, Harold realized that he had been crying quietly, then he felt his own tears streaming down his cheeks. There were no words that could convey the grief that both men were experiencing at that moment; Caroline's irrepressible life force had been snuffed out in a matter of hours. Yet, another life had taken her place, a life not yet bruised by the reverses of living and whose course was yet to be determined by the hand of fate.

Caroline's funeral, given Harold's and Dr. Ashburn's station in Pittsburgh's society, was attended by the most prominent families. Her contemporaries, still reluctant to believe the news, quietly came to pay their respects and offer condolences to her father and husband. It seemed that just yesterday they were attending birthday parties and school functions. It did not seem fair that such a young life had been cut short, leaving behind so many unfulfilled dreams, incomplete plans and a loving family.

The most difficult part for Harold was returning home. Caroline's hand was visible everywhere; in her studio there were several paintings still unfinished. He felt that sh e would walk in anytime. The most persistent reminder, however, was not an object, but the loud crying of the newly born baby that was now heard throughout the house.

Aware that he was not capable of taking care of his son, Harold hired a live-in nanny that would look after the boy's needs. Every Sunday evening, as he had done when Caroline was alive, he drove to his father in law's house for dinner, with the baby usually asleep in a bassinet safely placed in the back seat of the car. Both men were now joined not only by the common loss they had incurred, but also by the joy of having Thomas Wilson be a part of their lives. The baby's presence mitigated their sorrow and reminded them how much Caroline had loved life.

But as time passed, as if the cruel hand of fate were not satisfied with the pain inflicted upon the men, a new round of sorrow was about to begin. This one would not be as quick and definitive as Caroline's death, but slower and increasingly painful.

It was Dr. Ashburn's keen eye that first spotted the first signs that there was something not quite right with Thomas. Well aware of the stages of development in infants, he realized that his grandson was behind in both motor coordination and language acquisition. Not wanting to alarm Harold, he kept his suspicions to himself, but quietly alerted Thomas' pediatrician, a colleague

427

whom he had known for years. The toddler' routine checkup was coming up, so when Dr. Ashburn received a call from his friend, confirming what he had suspected all along, he was not at all surprised. He asked his friend not to say anything to Harold, since he felt that he should be the one to break the news to his son in law.

That Sunday, as the two men sat at the table for their traditional dinner, the doctor explained to Harold in detail about Thomas' condition. The boy would develop physically, albeit at a slower rate than other boys, but his intellectual and emotional development would most likely peak at age twelve or thirteen. He conjectured that during his difficult birth, the oxygen supply to his brain must have been cut off, causing irreversible damage. Dr. Ashburn went on to explain that there was nothing anyone could do, no treatment available that would turn Thomas into a normal boy. He would need constant care and supervision the rest of his life.

Upon hearing the news, Harold was deflated. After Caroline's death he had placed all his hopes on Thomas, dreamed of all the things that he would be able to teach him and share with him. How his condition would affect their lives, with all its ramifications, was too early to tell.

For a moment, Harold was transported to that time in his life when his mother had died and how his father had found refuge in his work. He also remembered how he had been sent to a boarding school in Philadelphia, the loneliness of separation and the constant yearning to be with his family. At that instant, he told himself that no matter what, Thomas would always be with him, that he would not send him away to an institution to live out the rest of his life among strangers. No matter what, Thomas was his son; further, he was Caroline's son, and he would not insult her memory by rejecting him. Life would go on. It would no doubt be difficult at times, but he would always be with his son.

Money was no object, so Harold hired full-time help with the best credentials to help him with Thomas. Since he wanted his son to have as close as possible to a normal childhood, a private tutor worked with him on a daily basis. Although progress was slow, Thomas eventually learned to read and to do simple arithmetic problems, but like his father, he had a preference for literature that he expressed by writing simple poems, mostly about the animals he saw in his backyard or between the pages of a natural history book. Every night, before putting Thomas to bed, Harold would read to him some of the best English language poetry — Wordsworth; Shakespeare; Byron; Blake; Frost — or fantastic tales such as The Thousand and One Nights, and Ali Baba and the Forty Thieves.

Thomas also showed an interest in music, so Harold would take him to classical concerts as well as jam sessions in some of Pittsburgh's jazz clubs. During these outings Thomas would clap enthusiastically—often at the wrong time—showing a complete lack of inhibitions. This tendency manifested itself in all areas of his life; he found it difficult to wait for dinner when he was hungry, or to get up in the morning when he had to meet his tutor. During winter, he would wear more than one coat, while in summer it was not unusual to see him walking around the house completely naked.

But in spite of his shortcomings, Thomas was very much loved by his father and grandfather; they saw in him an innocence and exuberance that was slowly worn away in other boys as they grew older. Sunday dinners at Dr. Ashburn's home had never ceased, and Thomas always looked forward to visiting his grandfather. He especially liked the fact that the house was located on a small hill and he could see the river below from the comfort of the living room, no matter what the weather was outside.

Harold Wilson's life had acquired a comfortable and steady rhythm that was as predictable as the seasons themselves. He went to work; spent time with Thomas; continued with this philanthropic work and had dinner every Sunday with his father in law.

In 1962—Thomas had just turned thirteen—Harold decided to invest in a hotel in the art deco section of Miami Beach. Years before he had owned a house on Biscayne Bay, but had sold it a year later—at a profit—because it sat empty most of the time. The time he had spent in Miami Beach made him realize that the properties were undervalued, so this would be an ideal time to acquire some real estate there. Thomas had always enjoyed the weather in Florida, so this would be another opportunity to spend time with his son, perhaps go to the beach or spend a day fishing. Just the thought of it brought a smile to his face. Yes, he concluded, a trip to Miami would be good in every respect.

Now that he had a valid reason, Harold Wilson called Anna on the phone several times a week, and came to visit whenever he was in Florida. It was during one of these meetings, after their business dealings were finished, that the topic of children came up. Harold talked more openly about Thomas and recounted the story of how his mother had died during childbirth, leaving him to care for their son. He also told Anna how his own mother had died tragically when he was very young, and how he had spent many years away from home in a boarding school in Philadelphia.

As she listened to Harold's story, Anna felt tears coming to her eyes. She could sympathize with him at a very personal level, since Ramón had also died unexpectedly, leaving her with the responsibility of two daughters. At that moment she realized that despite all his money and influence, there were things in life that not even Harold Wilson could control; he was at the mercy of fate as much as anyone else. In fact, Anna concluded, his life had not been a happy one at all.

Although in the past she had never revealed any details about her personal life, the fact that Harold had shown her a side of him that he usually kept to himself, prompted Anna to talk about her daughters. She told him how they had left Cuba, and that the girls were in separate foster homes in Virginia and New Mexico.

"Children should be with their parents," was his only comment.

"I have already filed the papers to regain custody," she explained, "but the bureaucracy moves at a slow pace."

"Perhaps I can be of some assistance," he said.

"I do not understand," said Anna, "What can you do?

"Just leave it in my hands," said Harold as he took his pen and a small pad out his coat pocket.

Barely a week had passed when Anna received a call from Social Services during the late afternoon. The clerk informed her that her petition to regain custody of her daughters had been approved, and that the girls would be arriving in Miami that weekend. Anna was both astonished and overjoyed. After hanging up, she ran into the kitchen, where Silvia was busy preparing dinner.

"They are coming!" she shouted, "They are coming!"

"Who is coming?" asked Silvia, putting down a kitchen knife.

"Francesca and Adriana," answered Anna excitedly, "They will be here this weekend."

"I thought you told me the process took a lot longer," said Silvia, "How did you manage that?"

"I don't know," answered Anna, "All I know is that the twins will be flying in this weekend." Then she remembered that Harold Wilson had promised to look into the situation and try to expedite matters. As she was about to relay this information to Silvia, the phone rang again. Thinking that it would be Social Services with more details, Anna picked up the receiver before it rang a second time.

"Hello," she said with an anxious tone of voice.

"Congratulations," said the familiar voice at the other end of the line. It was Harold Wilson.

"How did you know?" asked Anna.

"That does not really matter," he answered, "I am just glad that I could move things along."

"Are you in Miami?" asked Anna, "I would like to thank you personally."

"Not at the moment," Harold answered, "But I will be there this weekend; I would like to take you to the airport, if you don't mind."

"You already have done so much," said Anna.

"It was nothing," answered Harold, "I will call you as soon as I am in Miami. I have to go now; business, you know."

"Thank you again," said Anna. Then the line went dead.

"That was Harold Wilson," she said to Silvia, "He will be coming in this weekend."

"I am not surprised," she answered, "I told you he was interested in you since the first day."

"He is just a business partner who has become a friend," retorted Anna, dismissing the comment "but I am glad that he has taken an interest in us."

"I suppose that in a way that is good," agreed Silvia, "We can use any help until we return to Cuba."

"I've just realized that I don't have any clothes for the twins," Anna said suddenly in a tone of alarm.

"I would not worry about that," said Silvia, "I am sure they will have some clothes with them. Besides, you don't know how much they have grown since the last time you saw them."

Silvia was correct. Anna had not seen the girls since the day she put them on a plane to the United States at José Martí airport in Havana. Children, especially at that young age had a way of outgrowing their clothes very quickly. There would be plenty of time to go shopping and find whatever they needed. The main thing was that they would soon be together.

Since the day Anna had moved into the house on Brickell Avenue, she had begun preparing a bedroom in anticipation of the day when Francesca and Adriana would be returned to her. Although not very large, it contained everything that the girls would need. She wanted them to feel at home from the first day. Despite the fact that she knew they were in good hands, she also realized that the longer the separation lasted, the more difficult it would be for the twins to feel that they were a part of a family, even though they would be with their mother.

Before going to bed, she placed her copy of Immortal Arias on the turntable of the secondhand record player she had bought right after moving out of the Rice Hotel. As she listened to Louis d'Amio's incomparable voice, she closed her eyes and imagined him smiling at the prospect of his granddaughters finally coming home. She also tried to imagine how the girls would react when they saw her. Would they recognize her right away? Would they recognize her at all?

That night Anna did not sleep well. She kept having a reoccurring dream that she was at the airport, but the plane would not land. Then she would wake up and imagine the meeting and the possible outcomes that it could have. She feared that the girls would cry for the women who had become their mothers during the past year.

Even though it was Sunday and she did not have to work, Anna got up early. As she walked into the kitchen to start breakfast, she realized that Silvia was already up and had made some coffee.

"Today is the big day," said Silvia as she handed Anna a cup.

"I know," answered Anna, "I did not sleep well last night in anticipation."

432

"I figured as much," said Silvia, "Everything will be fine; sometimes you worry too much about things."

What Silvia said was true; she had discovered from the beginning that Anna had a tendency to allow small details to grow out of proportion in her mind. It had been like that before she decided to open her cleaning business, yet everything had fallen neatly into place and WE KLEAN 4U was making a nice profit. his she knew because she kept the books and handled the payroll. Anna had also had some reservations about moving into the house where they currently lived, citing that the rent was a lot higher that what they were paying at the Rice Hotel. Maybe having lost everything in Cuba had made her overly cautious about her expenditures. Once again, Silvia reassured her that they were on firm financial ground and they made the move into the new house.

Around nine o'clock the phone rang. When Anna answered it she heard Harold's familiar voice. He was calling to tell her that he was in Miami and that he would come to pick her up after lunch. At that moment, Anna felt a sense of relief, knowing that he would be at the airport with her when her daughters arrived. She also realized that not only did she enjoy his company, but that she was also learning to depend on him.

The rest of the morning was spent in making sure the twin's bedroom was ready. This was completely unnecessary, since Anna had done the same inventory several times since receiving the call from Social Services about the arrival of her daughters. It was a way of traveling those nervous hours before going to the airport. While Anna inspected the girls' bedroom one more time, Silvia stayed in the kitchen drinking a second cup of coffee and going over the payroll for the following week. Around eleven thirty she prepared some sandwiches and called Anna. She had purposely refrained from cooking a large meal; she knew that Anna would be too nervous and anxious to eat.

During lunch Anna talked excitedly about all the things she wanted to do with the twins, all the places she wanted to visit with them. Silvia listened attentively, knowing how much this day meant to her friend. Silvia was well aware of Ramón's tragic death, and all the subsequent hardships that Anna had endured before leaving Havana. All she had left were her daughters and the hope of providing for them a better future than they would have had if they had stayed in Cuba. After they finished eating, Anna made some coffee and they talked some more about the changes that would have to be made once the children were actually in Miami. In the middle of the conversation the doorbell rang, and Anna almost jumped out of her seat.

"He's here," she said, referring to Harold.

The familiar black sedan was parked in front of the house. Anna grabbed her purse and dashed towards the front door; the day she had dreamed about for so long had finally arrived.

"I will be here when you get back," said Silvia as Anna left the house.

As usual, Harold Wilson had come out of the car to open the door for Anna. Despite the warm weather, he wore a dark suit and tie; the familiar outfit made him stand out as someone who had just flown in from elsewhere. He greeted her with a wide smile, waited for her to get in the car and then sat next to her in the back seat. Apparently he had discussed the itinerary with the chauffeur, for the latter started the car and drove off without any instructions from Harold.

"How is your business in Pittsburgh?" asked Anna, not knowing what else to say.

"Everything is good; I am just very busy," answered Harold, "There are always meetings and other details that have to be attended to."

"It must have taken a great effort to get away," commented Anna,

"I want to thank you for what you are doing, and for what you have already done."

"There is no need to thank me," he answered modestly, "I am just glad that I can be of service. Besides, there is nothing more important than children."

"I am glad you feel that way Harold," answered Anna. This was the first time; she realized immediately, that she had used his first name. Even though they had been spending time together every time he was in Miami, she always addressed him without using his given name. This was not a conscious effort on her part, but something that just happened.

"I do," he said, "You know that." He was referring to Thomas and how he tried to spend as much time as possible with the boy. Anna wondered if Harold brought him to Florida every time, and what he did when his father was not with him. She had not seen him again since that day in the lobby of the Cardozo Hotel. Maybe Harold was purposely keeping him away from her, since that first encounter had been less than auspicious.

On Sundays the traffic was lighter than usual, but as they approached the airport it became a little heavier; the city of Miami was a hub that travelers used on their destination to and from other places, so it was busy twenty four hours a day.

"Do you have the information about the flights?" asked Harold as they stopped in front of one of the entrances to the airport.

"Yes, of course," answered Anna, "The first one arrives at two, and the second at two thirty."

"Well, we have plenty of time," commented Harold while looking at his watch and exiting the car, "It is only one thirty," he said while extending his hand to help Anna out of the car. As they walked into the airport, Anna's nervousness became more apparent, for she kept looking at her watch every few minutes; no matter how many times she imagined the moment, there was no way to be absolutely sure of how that reunion would turn out.

"Everything will be fine," said Harold, leaning closer to Anna and leading her to the gate where the first plane was scheduled to arrive from New Mexico.

Gathered by the gate, and seated in vinyl-covered chairs, a group of people waited for the plane to arrive. Some read the paper; some just looked out the huge glass sheet that faced the runway. Anna looked at her watch again, as if by doing this she could speed up the passage of time.

"Let's sit down," said Harold pointing to a couple of empty seats, "The plane will be here shortly."

"I want to thank you one more time for accompanying me," said Anna, "I realize that you are a very busy man."

"You are a very special woman Anna," he answered softly, "I have come to realize that during the past few months; I am glad that I can be here with you."

At once Anna thought of Silvia's words; she had repeatedly expressed the opinion that Harold 's interest in Anna went beyond business matters. Everything, Anna had to admit, pointed in that direction. And perhaps it was not such a farfetched conclusion; after all, Anna was, at forty two, still a very beautiful woman despite all the hardships that she had had to endure during the past three years. But whether Silvia was right or not, at this moment it was irrelevant. All that Anna could think about was that in a very short time she would have her daughters back. This was the goal for which she had labored and sacrificed since her arrival in the United States.

"The plane should be arriving about now," said Harold while standing up, "Let's walk over to the window; maybe we will be able to see it land."

Anna did not answer, but also stood up and walked with Harold toward the ample glass plate window. She soon realized, however, that it would be impossible to ascertain in which plane Adriana was traveling, since the sheer number of planes landing and taking off every few minutes was really dazzling. They would have to wait for it to land and for the passengers to disembark through the assigned gate and into the airport.

The wait was not a long one; apparently the plane had already landed, for it taxied slowly to the gate and soon the stream of passenger began to appear. Some disappeared immediately into the airport; others were greeted by friends or family and after a series of effusive hugs and kisses, were escorted away to awaiting cars. As the stream of passengers progressed, Anna felt the tension rising, and instinctively held on to Harold's hand. He, in turn, squeezed her hand lightly, as if silently reassuring her that her daughter would appear at any moment. It was not until the last passenger had left the plane that one of the stewardesses appeared, holding a little girl. At this moment, losing all self-control, Anna ran towards her daughter, anxious to hold her in her arms after such a prolonged absence. It was not necessary to identify herself as the girl's mother; the expression of joy and relief on her face, mixed, with her tears, were enough. As she held her daughter, after such a long time, Anna felt that the tears streaming down her cheeks would not stop. She held her close as she caressed her hair, without saying a word. This was not an uncommon scene at the Miami airport; parents were often reunited with their children after a long separation. After a few minutes, it was Harold who spoke. "We have to go and meet the other plane," he said softly as he led Anna in the direction of the gate, "It will be here momentarily."

Anna did not say anything, but kept clutching Adriana very close, as if fearing that she would have to let her go one more time. Harold understood this and did not intrude in that most intimate moment that Anna had imagined so many times and for so long.

The waiting area for the second gate, where the plane would be arriving from Virginia, was no different from the first one. The same chairs were used throughout the airport, and just as before there was a group of people, reading or talking, waiting for the plane to land. Rather than sitting down, Anna kept pacing back and forth in front of the window, holding her daughter. After a short wait, the passengers coming in from Virginia began to appear. Anna and Harold knew that a stewardess would be last to exit, holding the girl in her arms. Despite this certainty, Anna still feared that her second daughter would not show. At last, once all the other passengers had left the plane, Francesca came into view. Rather than putting down Adriana, or handing her over to Harold, Anna received her with her free arm. For the first time, one of the girls—she did not know which—uttered the word 'Mama.' The other echoed the word, and soon Anna was crying uncontrollably once again as she kissed her daughters. At that moment, while holding both girls she felt Harold's arms embracing the three of them, silently sharing that moment of infinite joy.

XII

On the day when Francesca and Adriana were returned to her, for the first time since her arrival from Cuba, Anna felt at peace. Even though her daughters had been well cared for, she had always felt that as a mother one of her primary responsibility was to be by their side.

From the beginning Silvia proved to be an invaluable help; when they returned from the airport, Anna found the living room decorated with colorful balloons and a cake next to a punch bowl on the kitchen table, as well as some carefully wrapped presents. Silvia had organized a small welcome home party. Anna, of course, had no idea, but she thought it was a wonderful gesture. At first the twins were a little intimidated, but it did not take them long to make themselves at home and enjoy the cake and punch that Silvia had prepared for them. Even Harold, usually so serious and proper, had a piece of cake and smiled broadly as he watched how the twins hugged their mother and started to become acclimated to their new surroundings.

That evening, as she had done every Sunday, Anna called the families that had cared for Francesca and Adriana to let them know that the girls had arrived in Miami, and also to thank them for all they had done. She realized how fortunate she was, but was also aware that many other people—people she had never met—had had an active part in making this happy ending a reality.

From that day on, Harold called from Pittsburgh every night to ask about the girls. At this point, Anna soon became aware that their daily conversations centered less and less on business and more on personal matters. Using the feeble pretext of overseeing the renovation of the hotel, he also came to Florida more often. On those occasions, he always brought presents for the twins and came to pick up Anna so she could help him assess the progress being made. After those inspections, he would have the chauffeur drive to have lunch or take the girls to the beach. One of their favorite spots was Crandon Park because of its proximity to the house, its inherent beauty and pristine conditions. Francesca and Adriana were always amused watching the hermit crabs crawl back into the s hells whenever they got too close, and they also liked collecting the small coconuts or seashells they found on the beach.

While swimming in the warm, clear water, or sitting on a beach towel, Anna realized that these were the only occasions that she ever saw Harold without his dark suit and tie. His tall, muscular body and the absence of the formal attire made him look ten years younger; he certainly did not look like a man in his early sixties. It was during one of these outings, while the twins were playing on the beach, that Harold asked Anna what she thought was a rather strange question.

"Do you like jazz?" he said.

"Well...I really don't know," she answered, taken a little aback by the unexpected question. "You know I grew up listening to opera and classical music, but I know very little about jazz."

"Then I would like to take you to see a live performance," said Harold, "I am sure you will find it interesting."

"When?" asked Anna, "You know that I have responsibilities, and now that the girls are back with me it is not as easy to get away."

"Next Saturday night," he answered, "I promise to make it worth your while."

"Well," said Anna in a hesitant tone, "I suppose that I could ask Silvia to watch the girls for one evening."

"The performance is not in Miami," added Harold casually.

"I do not understand," said Anna with a puzzled look on her face.

"It is in Pittsburgh," he explained, as if he were taking about a short ride to the next county.

"I can't go to Pittsburgh," protested Anna.

"And why not?" asked Harold, "I do it all the time; it is not as difficult or complicated as you may think."

"But what about the girls?" asked Anna, looking at the twins who were at the moment playing in the sand.

"You just said that Silvia could look after them," said Harold convincingly, "I can have my chauffeur pick you up and drive you

440

to the airport Saturday morning. I will wait for you in Pittsburgh and you can fly back on Sunday."

"Won't that be expensive?" said Anna.

"What good is money if it does not provide certain freedoms and options?" he retorted, "Just say yes and I will take care of the rest."

"I will consider it," answered Anna in a noncommittal tone, "Besides, I have to ask Silvia before I give you an answer."

"It will not be that long of a stay," insisted Harold, "You can fly out of Miami early Saturday morning and you will be back Sunday evening," he repeated after a pause.

"I will call you tonight, before I fly back to Pittsburgh; you can let me know then."

"That's fine," agreed Anna and then turned her attention to the twins.

That evening, while having dinner with Silvia, Anna told her about Harold's invitation to visit Pittsburgh so they could attend a jazz concert. Silvia listened intently to her friend, shaking her head affirmatively from time to time as Anna gave her all the details.

"I am not surprised," she finally said, "I have told you before that since the very beginning he was interested in you."

"Harold is a nice man; he also loves the girls," said Anna, "But I think he is just lonely; he has endured some reverses in his life."

"I am not saying that he isn't," retorted Silvia, "But being nice to Francesca and Adriana is another way of getting close to you; I hope you realize that."

"Yes, I do realize it," said Anna, "But I don't think his intentions are less than honorable."

"Just be aware that if you accept this invitation," admonished Silvia, "You will be opening the door to an entire new dimension in this relationship. As far as taking care of the girls, you know there is no problem; I am more than happy to do it."

"Thank you Silvia," said Anna, "I know that I can always count on you." What Anna meant was that not only Silvia was willing to help her, but also to give her opinion about the possible outcome of any decision that she made. This was the main pillar of their friendship, the fact that they were honest with each other.

Good to his word, before flying back to Pittsburgh that evening, Harold called. Anna had done nothing but think about the invitation, and the possible ramifications if she accepted. Ultimately, however, she concluded that attending a concert, even in a distant city, did not commit her to anything. Besides, she enjoyed Harold's company as much as he seemed to enjoy hers.

"Have you thought about my invitation?" asked Harold, getting right to the point.

"Yes, I have," answered Anna, "I accept; I think it will be fun. Silvia will take care of the twins until I return."

"Excellent," said Harold with an obvious tone of satisfaction, "I will call you tomorrow with all the details. Now I have to catch a plane; I will see you soon."

"Until then," said Anna. Although Harold had hung up, she did not put the receiver down immediately, perhaps considering further the possible implications that accepting this invitation entailed. Silvia was right; there was no telling where it would all lead.

Between work and caring for the girls, the week went quickly. Harold had called on Monday night to give her the particulars about the flight, and to let her know that his chauffeur would pick her up at seven on Saturday morning to take her to the airport. But even though Anna already had all the information necessary, he also called every evening, not to talk about anything in particular, but just because he wanted to hear the sound of her voice. During those conversations, he would tell her about his latest business deals or ask about the girls and her cleaning business. Anna came to understand that for Harold it was not so much what she said, but the fact that she was saying something, anything. In the past he had told her how much he liked the timbre of her voice and her accent whenever she spoke English. He also never seemed to get tired of looking at her. Even on those occasions when she wore no make-up or her hair was not perfectly brushed, she was conscious that his gaze never wandered too far. Anna had never made a big deal of it, but deep down she felt flattered that Harold would find her so attractive. After all, she was not twenty any more, and the inevitable traces that the years were taking their toll were clearly visible, no matter how skillful she was at applying her makeup. She also realized, because of Harold's wealth and social standing, that he could probably have any woman he wanted. Yet, he chose to spend his free time with her whenever he was in town and call her on the phone as much as his time permitted. As to why, she had not clue. Perhaps not even Harold himself knew; the only certainty that Anna now had was that she had unwittingly awakened in him feelings that seemed to be gaining strength with every passing day.

As Saturday approached, despite Harold's phone calls, Anna felt a little apprehensive. She would be flying hundreds of miles, going to a city whose existence had been unknown to her until very recently. Just to make herself feel more at ease, she wrote down Harold's address, telephone number, and the time of her departure and return. Knowing that Silvia had this information made her feel better.

"You are not going to the end of the world," said Silvia as Anna handed her the paper with all the information. She knew her friend and had learned that sometimes Anna exaggerated things in her own mind, "You will be back before you know it. Besides, you could have said no."

"You are right," agreed Anna, but she still felt a little uneasy.

But by the time Saturday arrived, Anna felt completely calm. Aware that Harold's driver would be arriving promptly at seven o'clock, she got up early, took a shower, placed her small suitcase by the door, and made breakfast for Francesca and Adriana. A few minutes before seven, she saw the familiar black sedan pull up in front of the house. She hugged and kissed the girls and told them she would be back soon.

"Just go," Silvia urged her, knowing that it was the most sensible thing to do.

"I will call you tonight," shouted Anna as she was getting into thecar.

As the plane made its descent over the city of Pittsburgh, the first thing that Anna noticed was the color of the sky. Or rather, its lack of color. Throughout her entire life she had lived under the deep blue skies found in tropical or semitropical areas, where white, fluffy clouds usually drifted lazily close to the ground. This was different; as she looked out the window, she had the fleeting impression that somehow the sky had been bleached of all color and had been left with a drab gray that became almost white towards the line of the horizon. The clouds were also different;

they appeared more distant, higher, as if they feared getting close to the ground. She also noticed, as they approached the airport, that the city was located next to a robust river.

Harold was already waiting at the terminal when she exited the plane; she saw him standing among a group of casually dressed people, wearing the usual dark suit and tie. As soon as he located Anna in the line of arriving passengers, his face seemed to light up. This was the reaction she always evoked in him; in her presence, Harold stopped being a disciplined and successful businessman and became simply a man in the company of the woman that seemed to occupy a special place in his heart. Even if he had tried, he would not have been able to hide how he felt; the gleam in his eyes would have surely given him away. Making his way through the crowd awaiting the arriving passengers, Harold reached Anna and then hugged her affectionately, perhaps a little longer than necessary, to show his joy.

"I am so glad you came," he said, "How was the flight?"

"It did not take as long as I thought it would," she answered, "Everything was very smooth; I even saw a river as the plane approached the city," she explained, but left out her first impression that everything was gray and drab in comparison to Miami.

"The city of Pittsburgh is built on the confluences of the Allegheny and the Monongahela Rivers," explained Harold, glad that he could give her details about the city, "They join to form the Ohio River."

"That is interesting," said Anna, not knowing how to answer the comment.

"It is an ideal location for commerce and industry," continued Harold, "Fortunes have been made in this city," he further explained, but did not mention his own family. It was just idle conversation.

"Is your house far from the airport?" asked Anna.

"Not very far," answered Harold, "Let's get your luggage and then we can be underway."

As they walked out of the main building, Anna kept looking for a black sedan with a chauffeur, but it was nowhere to be found. "I drove myself today," explained Harold, "I am a lot more familiar with Pittsburgh than I am with Miami."

Harold's car—another black sedan—was parked near the exit. After placing Anna's small suitcase in the trunk, he opened the door for her and then got behind the wheel. As they exited the parking lot, Anna realized that this was the first time she had seen Harold driving a car. She also realized that there were many other things she did not know about him, things that only time would allow her to discover. The only thing that bothered her a little was the fact that Harold had never introduced her to Thomas. Even though his son traveled with him to Florida, he had never made any attempts to bring the two of them together.

"Besides the jazz concert, there is another reason I wanted you to come," said Harold, as if he could read Anna's thoughts.

"And what that might be?" asked Anna.

"I want you to meet Thomas, my son," he said while keeping his eyes on the road ahead. "I think the two of you got off to a wrong start at the Cardozo; I am hoping this time it will be different."

"And why did you wait so long for this meeting?" asked Anna.

"I just felt that if the two of you become acquainted at our house, where the surroundings are more familiar to him, things will be easier. Whenever he travels with me away from home he tends to become overexcited. By the way, I told him last night that we had a very special visitor and he is looking forward to seeing you."

"I am glad," said Anna, "I think it is important that we become friends. What else can you tell me about him?"

"Thomas loves meeting new people," said Harold, "But I warn you that sometimes he goes overboard; just be prepared."

"You don't have to remind me," said Anna with a smile, thinking about their first encounter in the lobby of the Cardozo.

"He likes learning about many things, although sometimes he becomes frustrated. For the past year he has become interested in painting, so I let him use his mother's old studio. I would like to think that he has inherited some of her talent. Besides meeting his regular tutors," continued Harold, "I have been sending him to art school. I believe that he is making progress, and socializing with people who share the same interest is good for him."

"I would love to see his work," said Anna, "Although I am not an expert, I have always enjoyed art."

"You will," said Harold, "But don't expect to see masterpieces; he has a long way to go yet."

"You are a good father, Harold," said Anna as she briefly placed her left hand on his right.

"I do what I can," he answered, still looking straight ahead, "I just wish there were more that I could do for him."

"We all want to give everything to our children," answered Anna, "so we do the best we can and hope for the best."

"You are right," said Harold after a moment, "Thomas is not unhappy with his life."

"And you make that possible every day," Anna reminded him.

By this time, after leaving the airport, they had traveled through busy roads and crossed several bridges, to arrive eventually at a large house that reminded Anna of the mansions she had seen in movies and magazines. The colonial style structure sat amidst beautiful landscaping, where hollies, English boxwoods and junipers predominated. Farther back, there were oak, maple and walnut trees. To Anna's untrained eye they were just trees that she had never seen before, but she found the view most appealing.

"I used to live inside the city of Pittsburgh, but that was years ago," explained Harold

"The place is lovely," commented Anna as they drove up the driveway that led to the house.

"It is a quiet and private place," said Harold, "But still close enough to the city so I conduct business or meet with my associates right here. It is also good for Thomas," he added after a moment, "He likes the open spaces; I hope you like it too."

After parking the car in front of the house, Harold went around and opened the door for Anna; at the same time he chose a key from the ring he was holding and placed it in the lock. With an almost inaudible 'click' the massive double door yielded readily, giving way into an ample foyer with tiled floor, a coat rack and a huge Venetian mirror. Towards the back there was a stairway that led to the upper floor. Before Anna could take it all in, she heard someone coming from the back of the house and an elderly woman, dressed in an austere gray dress, appeared in the foyer.

"Welcome back, Mr. Wilson," she said in a familiar, yet respectful tone, "How was the traffic?"

"Not too bad," answered Harold, then proceeded to make the introductions. "This is Anna d'Amio, our guest for the weekend," then, looking at Anna, "This is Mrs. Gregory; she oversees this entire house and also looks after Thomas."

446

"Very nice to meet you," said Anna, looking at the woman.

"Likewise," she answered, "I hope you have a pleasant stay. By the way," she added, now looking at Harold, "Will you be having lunch here?"

"Yes," he answered, "I want Anna to meet Thomas; where is he?"

"In the studio, painting. Should I get him for you?"

"That will not be necessary," said Harold, "I will get him myself whenever it's time for lunch."

"It will be ready in half an hour," answered Mrs. Gregory, "If you excuse me, I must go to the kitchen."

"Mrs. Gregory has been with us for a long time," explained Harold after she had disappeared to the back of the house, "In fact, it was my father who hired her. She pretty much takes care of everything in this house and, as I said, also helps me with Thomas."

"I am sure she is invaluable," commented Anna.

"Indeed," concurred Harold, "She is the one person I can trust to carry out my instructions to the letter. Although she has been in our family's employ for many years, she is a lot more than a servant."

"Yes, I understand," said Anna, thinking of Flora and the role she had played in the Contreras family.

"But let me show you the rest of the house," said Harold as he led Anna into the adjacent living room. Presiding over the solid wood furniture, Sevres porcelain vases and a central Persian rug of intricate designs, was a portrait of a man in a dark suit and tie. "This was my father, Dexter Wilson," he explained, but Anna had already deduced the identity of the man in the portrait. "Through hard work and perseverance, along with a measure of good luck, he built the Wilson Empire," Harold explained. "We hardly ever use this room; most of the time we are in the library. Let me show you," he said while leading Anna down a short hallway. Everything in the library was pretty much the way Anna had imagined it from Harold's description during previous conversations. The walls were lined with wooden bookcases that reached the ceiling; most of the back wall was a huge window from which pines and other deciduous trees could be seen. No doubt a variety of wildlife populated that forest and the inhabitants of the house could watch them at their leisure. Facing a massive fireplace with a stone hearth, a couch and easy chairs extended an invitation to spend time with a book. What Anna noticed immediately, hanging above the mantelpiece, was the large portrait of Harold, done in oil. He was much younger then, and the expression on his face, especially the faint smile, conveyed one of complete happiness and underlying confidence.

"That is a very nice portrait of you," commented Anna.

"It was done a long time ago," said Harold, "I have come to think of it as someone else's portrait. I was a different man then."

"How so?" asked Anna.

"As I said, I was very young. Back in those days I was arrogant enough to believe that I could control everything, even life itself. Of course, I was wrong. No one can foresee and shape the events of life; you know that yourself."

"Yes, I know," agreed Anna, thinking back to the events that had brought her to this point in her life.

"Thomas and I spend a lot of time in this room," offered Harold, "We read every day, look at the animals in the forest or sometimes, during winter, build and fire and watch the snow fall."

"That sounds lovely," commented Anna.

"It has brought us closer together; sometimes I just sit and listen to him talk. He usually does not hold back, so it gives me a very good idea what is on his mind, or if he is concerned about anything. Lately he is mostly involved with his paintings. But let's go find him," he after a pause, "It is time for lunch."

The room where Thomas did his painting was at the end of a corridor, towards the back of the house. In order to reach it they had to go through the dining room first and then in front of other rooms whose doors were closed. Once they were in front of the right door, rather than opening it and just walking in, Harold knocked softly on the wood.

"Come in," said a youthful voice from within, "I am almost finished."

"I have taught Thomas the value of privacy," said Harold, "If I am working in my office he also knocks before coming in," he explained further before opening the door.

The studio was almost devoid of furniture, except for a few random chairs and a small table whose bare surface showed an assortment of paint tubes, brushes, and other materials. High above the center of the room there was a massive skylight that captured an abundant amount of natural light.

Thomas Wilson was thin and almost as tall as Anna. He wore jeans and a shirt stained by the different colors of the paints he handled regularly. At that moment Anna tried to reconcile the image of the young man standing in front of her with the memory she had of their brief encounter in Miami Beach, but they did not seem to have any points of contact.

"You must be Anna," he said as they walked in, "My dad told me all about you," then, unexpectedly, he walked over and gave her a hug. Anna did not exactly know how to react; still in Thomas' embrace, she looked at Harold, trying to find an answer. He simply shrugged, as if letting her know that this was not at all unusual. After a few moments Thomas released her. "Come look at my paintings," he said enthusiastically, taking one of Anna's hands and leading her to a corner of the room, where a series of canvases were neatly arranged against the wall.

Thomas' work was not what she had expected at all. When Harold told her that he had become interested in painting she had imagined a series of random splatters, without any control or discipline, not unlike those of a very young child who is simply experimenting with colors and shapes. What she saw was indeed surprising. They were landscapes depicting the different seasons, as well as several still lifes. But what surprised Anna was not the subject matter of the paintings, but the obvious mastery that Thomas had over the compositions. He had captured perfectly the bright colors of autumn, the soft hues of spring and the elusive play of light and shadow that was often present during clear, winter days. Yet, there was something more to his paintings beyond the mastery of technique. After looking at the canvases again, Anna realized that there was unique perspective to them, as if the artist were seeing everything for the first time. That fresh-ness — innocence — had been translated onto the work. Thomas' work was not cluttered by the subconscious baggage that other artists often brought to their creations. Yes, innocence was the word that Anna finally settled on; they were beautiful works as seen by the unfettered eye of a child.

"These are truly wonderful, Thomas," she heard herself saying.

"Thank you, thank you very much," he answered, as if he were receiving the praise of the most learned art critic in the country, "I take lessons, you know; my teacher says that maybe I can have a showing of my work in the future, and I want you to come. Will you promise me?"

At this point, a little overwhelmed by Thomas' exuberance, Anna looked at Harold. It was also very obvious that he had no recollection of their brief encounter in the lobby of the Cardozo Hotel.

"Of course Thomas, I would be delighted," she agreed.

"It is time for lunch, Thomas," interrupted Harold, coming to Anna's rescue, "Go wash your hands and we can talk more about your paintings in the dining room."

"He really has talent," commented Anna after Thomas had left the studio, "His paintings are truly amazing."

"That is what his teacher tells me," said Harold, "But I am never sure if it is true or if he simply wants me to keep sending Thomas for more classes. What matters to me, however, is that he is very enthusiastic about his work. That alone is worth the money."

"Of course," agreed Anna, "But I can tell you that his paintings are unique."

"Well, that is reassuring," said Harold, "I know that you would not say anything you did not think was true. By the way, I am certain that Thomas did not remember you, so I would like to think that the two of you have just met for the first time."

"Yes, I think that is best," agreed Anna.

"But now let's have lunch," said Harold as they walked out of Thomas' studio. The smell of the food reached them before they came into the dining room. Mrs. Gregory had set the table with an immaculate linen tablecloth and silverware whose handles showed intricate carvings. The plates were also of the highest quality, and their delicate designs reminded Anna of European designs she had seen in Italy during her youth. The dining area, like the library, also had a huge window that faced the woods behind the house, thus benefiting from natural light but also enjoying the privacy conducive to the enjoyment of a good meal, and the walls were tastefully covered with paper that depicted bucolic scenes. In the evenings, after the sunset and sunlight faded, they would turn on the massive chandelier imported from Austria that hung above the table. Once again Anna realized that every-thing in Harold's house exuded that ineffable essence that quietly proclaimed that this was the product of old money, and not the tawdry result of someone who had suddenly come into a sizable fortune and lacked the finesse or refined taste to disburse it in a sober and judicious manner.

After pulling a chair out for Anna, Harold sat at the head of the table, and a few moments later Thomas came into the room. He had combed his hair and changed his paint stained shirt for a clean plaid one. He sat on Harold's left, right across from Anna and smiled at her. Once again she was certain that he had no recolecttion of their first encounter in Miami Beach.

Mrs. Gregory, with an unobtrusive efficiency acquired over many years, served the food and then left the dining room. She would reappear, no doubt, if they needed anything, but for the moment it was just Harold, Thomas and Anna in the room.

"Mrs. Gregory is an excellent cook," commented Harold, just trying to make conversation.

"I like her desserts best," interjected Thomas before Anna could answer.

"Maybe she will have a surprise for us later," said Harold, addressing his son directly, "But now I want to know Anna's impressions of what she has seen so far."

This last comment took Anna off guard. She had only seen the airport and part of the city as they drove to Harold's house. Besides, her opinion could not be that important.

"It is different from Miami," she said, stating the obvious. As they made their way through the city earlier she had noticed how different the architecture was, and came to the logical conclusion that no matter where one lived, the weather was the most important factor in determining how buildings were constructed. Although the temperature was rather mild at the moment, the massive fireplaces she had seen in this house gave a clear indication that winters could be long and severe. As to how people dealt with these abrupt changes in the weather, she did not know.

"Indeed," said Harold, "This country is so vast that every type of climate can be found. Personally I prefer the change of seasons."

"Yes, me too," said Thomas, "I like autumn because the trees have many colors, just like a painting."

"How about you, Harold?" asked Anna, "Do you have a favorite season?"

"I love spring," answered Harold without hesitation, "During winter the sky is gray and the trees are devoid of leaves; everything seems to be dead. Then the days begin to get longer and everything is reborn; suddenly the trees are green again and the birds are singing and making their nests. I think it is nothing short of a miracle."

"I still like autumn best," reiterated Thomas abruptly, "Spring and summer are too green."

The rest of lunch was spent in small conversation. Thomas spoke about his paintings and Harold gave Anna a brief lesson about the history of Pittsburgh and, more specifically, how the roots of the Wilson family went back several generations and the impact its members had had in the development of the city. Just at the right moment, Mrs. Gregory returned to the dining room carrying a tray with dessert. After placing the individual dishes on the table, she left the room again.

"This is my favorite part of the meal," exclaimed Thomas excitedly and began to eat his baked Alaska with unrestrained gusto.

"Tell me about the concert tonight," asked Anna while tasting the dessert.

"Have you ever heard the name Billy Strayhorn?"asked Harold.

"No, I can't say that I have," admitted Anna.

"Well, don't feel bad," said Harold with a sigh, "Even many Americans have no idea of who he is. Let me just say that he is, in my opinion, the most underrated jazz arranger and composer in this country. He collaborates with Duke Ellington, another giant in the field, but seldom gets any of the credit. At any rate, although Billy Strayhorn was born in Ohio, he came to Pittsburgh when he was very young, so the city claims him as one of its sons. The club where we are going tonight, appropriately enough, is called *Billy's*. Although different groups will be there, they will all play nothing but Billy Strayhorn's compositions. It should be a memorable evening, especially meaningful for jazz lovers."

"I love jazz," said Thomas suddenly, looking up from his empty dessert dish.

"It is true," said Harold, "Thomas and I spend time together listening to jazz."

"Coltrane is the greatest," added Thomas, as if he were talking about a personal acquaintance who visited the house on a regular basis.

"John Coltrane is one of the most innovative and dynamic saxophone players in the scene today," explained Harold, "Thomas is correct in his assessment concerning his talent."

"I see that I have a lot to learn," said Anna, "I must confess that my knowledge of this music is nil."

"In your case, it is perfectly understandable," said Harold, "But I would say that most Americans are completely unaware of what I consider to be a national treasure."

"You sound very passionate about it," said Anna, given the vehemence in Harold's voice.

"I am passionate about jazz," admitted Harold, "And there are several reasons. I recognize its inherent aesthetic value, but it goes beyond that. That music helped me to overcome some very difficult periods in my life; I will tell you about it another time". Anna understood that Harold did not wish to discuss such personal matters in front of his son.

"May I be excused now?" said Thomas after finishing his desert, "I want to get back to my painting."

"Of course Thomas," said Harold, "We will see you later."

"And I want to see Anna again," he said before leaving the room.

"He still has to work on his social graces," explained Harold unnecessarily, "But I believe we make a little progress every day, and I think he likes you a lot, otherwise he would not have said that he wanted to see you again. As you know, he does not hold back much."

"In a way," said Anna, "It is a wonderful quality; he has a spontaneity about him that most people lose as they enter the adult world. Perhaps it is a part of that inevitable price we have to pay to function successfully in society."

"You are correct," agreed Harold, "But that very quality of which you speak will prevent him from opening many doors; I am completely aware of that."

"But it will open others," said Anna, "Just look at his paintings; that ineffable quality that permeates his personality shows in every brush stroke that he makes. If he pursues this interest and keeps sharpening his talent, I predict a very successful career."

"I hope you are right," said Harold, "Needless to say, I will give him my personal support and provide every opportunity so he can achieve those goals."

"You don't have to tell me that," said Anna, "I know how much you love your son. But tell me more about the concert tonight; you said that the music of Billy Strayhorn would be featured. Who is playing?"

"There will be several groups there tonight," explained Harold, "But I am very excited about a tenor sax player that has come on the scene lately; his name is Jack Stewart and he is traveling from New York just for this engagement."

"Do you have any of his records?" asked Anna.

"Unfortunately, he has not recorded anything yet, but I believe that soon there will be a break in his career."

"How do you know about him, if he has not recorded anything?" asked Anna.

"Whenever I travel to New York for business, I always make it a point to visit jazz clubs in the evening. A friend of mine runs a club called *The Empty Hand*; he keeps me abreast of the new names coming up. That's how I heard of Jack Stewart. I have seen him perform several times, and I can assure you that sooner or later his name will be known in the world of jazz."

"I believe you," said Anna with a smile.

"I am not the only one who holds that opinion," answered Harold, "Just wait until you hear him play tonight."

"You realize, of course, that my opinion does not really matter. I know nothing at all about this music."

"You will see," insisted Harold, "You will see."

At that moment, Mrs. Gregory reappeared, this time with a tray of steaming coffee. After placing the tray on the table, she retreated to the back of the house.

"I take mine black, but I know that you like yours on the sweet side," said Harold while adding two spoonfuls of sugar to Anna's cup. This little detail was but one of the many indications that Harold had made a conscious effort during the past year to learn as much as he could about Anna's likes and dislikes, an unequivocal sign that his interest in her went beyond a mere friendship.

After finishing their coffee, Harold led Anna to the flower garden next to the house, where they sat on a rustic bench under a pergola whose thick vegetable cover became a shield from the sun and created an intimate cocoon that isolated them from the rest of the household. For an instant, she remembered Giacomo's garden in Naples, and later on the island of Ischia.

"Have you lived here long?" asked Anna.

"Most of my life," answered Harold, "I mentioned that we used to live in the city of Pittsburgh proper, but after my mother died my father sold that house and bought this place. I suspect that he could not bear to live with the memories, so it was a way of having a fresh start. He remained single until the end of his life; his work became his entire universe."

"What about you, how did you fit in?" she asked.

"I believe that my father loved me a great deal," answered Harold softly and without looking at Anna, "But after my mother died, I don't think he really knew how to deal with a child; that is the reason he sent me to the boarding school in Philadelphia. Or maybe I reminded him of my mother too much; most likely a little of both."

"That is very sad," commented Anna, aware that life had a way of dealing people hard blows when they least expected it.

"Everyone is entitled to a second chance at happiness," commented Harold in a pensive tone of voice, "But sometimes that second chance never arrives."

"Or worse," added Anna, "It arrives but it is not recognized as such."

"You are absolutely correct," agreed Harold, "Especially as the years pile on, there is more urgency. Life does not go on forever, unfortunately."

Although Harold was speaking in abstractions, Anna sensed that he was referring to them and about that particular point in their lives. There was still time, but as Harold had stated, they no longer had the luxury of youth, when life appears to go on indefinitely, and time lost or squandered in senseless pursuits seems of no consequence. Anna had always known how important family life was for Harold, but with this first visit to his city and into his house that point was driven home even more. He was, in every respect, a very traditional man yearning for the emotional stability that can only be found if one is part of a family unit.

"When things are meant to be," said Anna philosophically, "No matter what we do to attain them or to avoid them makes no difference. They will happen, regardless of our preferences."

"You almost sound as if you do not believe in free will," said Harold, suddenly tuning his gaze from that invisible point in space to Anna's face.

"I have often wondered about that myself," she answered, "Maybe those decisions that we make are nothing but steps that lead us in the direction of our destiny. I realize that it is a paradox, but I still believe that some things are meant to happen."

"Men have been struggling with that question since the beginning of time," added Harold, remembering a course in introductory philosophy he had taken during his youth, "I do not believe we will find an answer this afternoon."

"You are right, of course," said Anna as she patted Harold's hand softly.

"Now I think you should get ready for the concert; I will show you to your room so you can change," he said as he stood up and reached out to take Anna's hand.

"Thank you for a lovely afternoon," said Anna, "Before I get ready I must call Silvia; I promised her that I would check in when I arrived."

"The day isn't over yet," said Harold as they walked back to the house and led Anna into his office, where the telephone rested on his desk.

After a simple dinner served by Mrs. Gregory, Harold and Anna got ready to leave for the concert. Throughout the meal, Thomas talked excitedly about his new painting, and made Anna promise that she would see it before her return to Florida. She did so gladly, for she was happy that Thomas liked her to the point of wanting to share his art with her. She also made a mental note to send Thomas a note telling him how much she liked his paintings and to urge him to continue with his studies.

As they were about to walk out, Harold embraced his son and kissed him on the forehead, further proof of how much he cared for the boy. In the background, Mrs. Gregory allowed herself a brief smile, for she witnessed on a daily basis the type of relationship that Harold and Thomas had. She would look after him until it was bedtime, making sure that he did not stay up too late in the studio. That particular evening Harold had dispensed with his usual suit and tie and had substituted them with more casual slacks and a light sweater with brief and tasteful designs. Although Anna could not help but notice the change, she did not make any comments, but thought that the change of garb made him look younger.

"Thomas worships you," said Anna as they got under way.

"I know," answered Harold, "That is why I told you that I always want to be present in his life," then fell silent.

Anna did not know if this silence contained an unspoken indictment of Dexter Wilson's decision of sending young Harold to a boarding school, away from the only family he had left, at such tender age and so soon after his mother's death. This was not the first time that Harold had expressed such feelings about his son. Perhaps he wanted to prevent a certain spiritual void in Thomas that was such an integral part of himself. Since the time Anna had met Harold, she had noticed that from time to time he would become silent and distant, as if he were suddenly transported to another time, another place and for a few minutes were reliving those early years after becoming an orphan. She never intruded in those reveries, nor asked him where his mind had been at such times, for she understood that there were certain recesses in a person's mind and heart that are to remain completely private. Eventually he came out of it, smiled at her with the kind of smile a father offers a child, and resumed the conversation that had been momentarily halted by his memories.

"Is the club far?" asked Anna.

"Not very far," answered Harold, "It is located in downtown Pittsburgh; we go back the same way we came in today."

As they approached the city, Anna had the impression that she was looking at a different place. Somehow the streets and avenues, illuminated by the street lamps, seemed narrower. What struck her as being odd was that there were more people about than during the morning hours. Harold must have guessed her thoughts, for he explained that after undergoing a recent renovation, the downtown area of the city had experienced a resurgence in popularity. Especially on weekends, people came out to enjoy the different offerings or simply to sip a cup of coffee or a glass of wine in one of the sidewalk cafes so prevalent in the area. What Harold failed to mention was that he had been one of the persons instrumental in bringing about that resurgence.

After parking the car in a side lot, they started to walk toward the club as Harold, picking up where he had left off that afternoon, kept telling Anna about the jazz world, the work of Billy Strayhorn in particular, and how they were fortunate in Pittsburgh to have clubs that brought musicians directly from New York. The enthusiasm in his voice, thought Anna, was reminiscent of a man in his twenties or thirties, and not of someone who would turn sixty-five in less than three years. This no longer surprised her; whenever Harold conducted business he adopted a serious and confident demeanor, which combined with his dark suits bestowed upon him an imposing presence. Tonight, without his suit and on his way to a concert of the music he loved most, miraculously he had turned into a much younger version of himself. Because of the excitement in his voice and the gleam in his eyes, Anna had to think of Thomas and how he approached his art without reservetions or inhibitions. Maybe this quality was inherent in Harold all along, but it had been squelched by his mother's death and the subsequent events in his life. Yet, here it was, still alive after all these years and plainly visible whenever he did something he truly loved.

For the first time since they had first met, Anna conjectured about the type of relationship he and his late wife had had. That was a long time ago, so Harold was much less experienced and most likely full of dreams that accompany one's youth. One thing was certain: if he had put as much energy into that relationship as he had into his business, not doubt it had been a very passionate one. Conversely, concluded Anna, the pain of losing someone so close must have been almost unbearable. This she knew from personal experience.

"The club is just ahead," said Harold pointing at a blue neon sign that proudly proclaimed *Billy's*. There were other people already going in, aware that this was to be a special night in the annals of Pittsburgh jazz.

Anna was a little surprised at the appearance of the place. From the outside it did not seem to be anything special, just a wide wooden door set in the plain concrete façade painted a bright crimson color. But once Harold held the door open for her that first impression vanished immediately, for she found herself in room whose large dimensions were impossible to tell from the outside. There were small tables with their corresponding chairs and at the back of the room stood a platform where some musicians were already setting up their instruments. To the right side of the door there was a bar, and to the left were the rest rooms as well as an emergency exit. It was a typical layout for a club in order to maximize space and facilitate the traffic of the patrons. What Anna found most unusual was the lighting. Recessed in the walls and the ceiling, concealed from view, were blue lights that matched the blue hue of the neon sign outside. Bathed in this diffused illumination, the entire club—including the patrons—acquired a surreal, dreamlike quality, as if they had suddenly been transported into a prehistoric cave. When Harold had mentioned a jazz concert, the image that had come into Anna's mind was that of a regular concert hall, where classical music was performed, so this particular setting was a surprise.

One of the employees, after exchanging a few words with Harold, led them to one of the small tables in front of the stage. It was obvious that he was known in the club and that the table, with its advantageous location, had been reserved beforehand. Looking at Harold in the unusual light, wearing a casual attire and showing a smile of satisfaction, made Anna think again that he looked twenty years younger.

"The first set should start momentarily," said Harold with anticipation and looking in the direction of the musicians. At that moment, the employee of the club returned with some drinks, which he expertly placed on the small table. This coincided with the appearance of a man on the stage wearing casual clothes and a relaxed demeanor. He proceeded to welcome everyone present, and then introduced the first group that would be performing that evening, a quartet made up of local musicians. Individual spotlights shone on each of the performers, and as soon they started to play there was a loud round of applause coming from the crowd.

"That's *Chelsey Bridge*, one of Billy Strayhorn's better known compositions," explained Harold. From that point on, there was a succession of groups coming on stage—trios, quartets and even a sextet—each with its own vision of the work of Billy Strayhorn. They were all received with varying degrees of applause by the audience, and their performances could be classified from lukewarm to red hot. Between sets Harold, as expected, provided expert and accurate comments about the compositions being performed. Anna found the overall experience not at all unpleasant, although to her ears, brought up listening to opera and classical music, the sound of jazz seemed erratic, disorganized, and even chaotic at times. As the evening progressed, despite Harold's comments, it all became a blur of sound that became very much the same.

The last group to perform that night would be The Jack Stewart Quartet; this was the main the reason why Harold had wanted to attend this tribute to the work of Billy Strayhorn. Anna, after listening to the other performers, did not expect this group to be any different, regardless of Harold's previous words of praise.

As the quartet came onto the small stage and the MC made a hasty introduction, Anna thought that its leader, Jack Stewart, seemed rather young to be the head of the group. Suddenly, there was a spontaneous wave of applause, and the people sitting — including Harold — stood up. Even though they had not played a single note yet, their growing reputation had preceded them.

Silence.

Then, the music. They started the set with *Take the A Train*, a composition that everyone knew. Once again there was a spontaneous wave of applause. Even her lack of knowledge about jazz did not prevent Anna from recognizing from the start that this particular group was far superior to the others that had performed there that night. Somehow they seemed more together, more in tune with what the other members of the quartet wanted to convey. They gave each other room to expand on a theme, and they delivered unexpected variations during the solo parts.

But it was not until Jack Stewart himself stepped forward with his tenor saxophone and began to play that Anna understood why Harold was so impressed with this young man. From the first moment she could tell that he had an absolute mastery of his instrument. But it went beyond technical execution; he possessed a passion, a fire, that translated into the sheer inventiveness of the passages that he was playing, whether they were up tempo compositions or more mellow ballads. The quartet kept up the pace for almost forty-five minutes—as long as the house would allow because of time constraints—and ended the set with *Star Dust*, a soulful, melancholic ballad. When the last note faded into silence, the crowd once again was on its feet, clapping wildly. Without realizing it, Anna was on her feet herself, standing next to Harold and showing her approval of the performance they had just seen and heard.

"I told you he was great," said Harold with a childlike excitement he did not bother to conceal as the lights came on, "That interpretation of *Star Dust* was pure genius," he added.

"It is too bad they have not recorded anything yet," said Anna, "I would like to hear them again."

"We can always go up to New York," retorted Harold, "They are always performing in Greenwich Village."

Anna realized that with every passing day, Harold became more and more comfortable with her, sharing some of his past and making her a part of his present. As for the future, she did not want to think too hard about it.

After exiting the club, they walked randomly in the downtown area and ended up at an all-night cafe. They ordered some coffee and light pastries, and Harold told her some more about Jack Stewart and how he had listened to him several times before in New York. He also augured a bright future for him in the world of jazz. All this, of course, he had expressed before, but Anna just let him talk about the music that he loved so much, until Harold himself, realizing that it was almost two in the morning, decided that it was time to go home.

During the drive back Harold once again expressed his belief that a record contract for Jack Stewart and his group was imminent. "He has too much talent to remain in the shadows for long," he said. He also assured Anna that whenever that recording became available he would buy her a copy. Anna answered that she would like that very much, and she meant it.

Despite the late hour, all the outside lights of the house were still on; Mrs. Gregory would not turn them off until everyone was home for the evening. Harold opened the door and they walked into the foyer, where a small lamp had also been left on.

"Thank you for a wonderful evening," said Anna, "It has been a long day."

"No," answered Harold, "Thank you for agreeing to come all the way from Miami to accompany me to the concert. I know you must be tired; we will talk some more tomorrow. Good night."

"Good night, Harold," she answered as she left the foyer in the direction of the bedroom Mrs. Gregory had shown her earlier in the day.

For a few minutes, Harold stood silently in the foyer, smiling and thinking of what the days to come would bring.

Despite having gone to bed rather late the previous night, Anna woke up early. After taking a quick shower, putting on a dress, and doing her hair and makeup, she left her room. Harold was already up, going over some papers at his desk. The casual clothes he had worn the night before had been substituted by his traditional dark suit, white shirt and sober tie.

"Good morning," said Anna from the threshold of the office.

"Good morning," he answered, looking up from the documents and smiling widely, "You are up early; did you sleep well?"

"Yes, thank you," she answered as she came into the room.

"Breakfast will be ready soon," said Harold, "Thomas is still in bed, but I will get him up shortly, so we are not late for church. Sunday is always a special day for us."

"In what way?" asked Anna.

"Since Thomas was a baby," explained Harold, "we have a Sunday meal with his grandfather. We would like you to come with us today." Although not completely unexpected, this comment surprised Anna a little. She was prepared to meet Thomas, but had no idea about his grandfather. Apparently Harold wanted her to meet everyone in the family. She was also somewhat surprised that Harold was a regular churchgoer, since he had never mentioned it before.

"I would be delighted to meet Thomas' grandfather," answered Anna, for she welcomed the opportunity to meet another member of the family.

"It's all settled then," said Harold, "Just give me a moment to get Thomas," then left to get his son. He reappeared a few minutes later with the boy; apparently he had been up for a while, since he was wearing dress slacks, a white shirt and tie and a jacket.

"Good morning Anna," he said in his usual exuberant tone, then without a transition, "I love Sundays; my dad and I go to church and see lots of friends. In the afternoons we drive to my grandfather's house."

"That is very nice, Thomas," said Anna, "It is important to have friends."

"Let's have breakfast," interrupted Harold, "We do not want to be late for the service."

"I love breakfast," said Thomas, leading the way to the dining room. Harold smiled and followed him, and once again Anna realized how much Harold loved the boy.

During breakfast, Thomas monopolized the conversation, telling Anna again about his paintings and showering her with details about his weekly visits to his grandfather's house. Harold indulged him since he knew, because of his extrovert personality and lack of inhibitions, how easy it was for Thomas to share all aspects of his life. Anna concluded that despite all the odds against him, Harold had tried—and succeeded—in giving his son a sense of belonging, to make him feel that he was a part of a real family and not just a boy who was looked after by a stranger his father had hired.

As they left for church —Harold behind the wheel, Anna sitting next to him and Thomas in the back seat—they could have easily passed for a regular family on its way to Sunday services.

"We attend the Church of the Epiphany, in the center of Pittsburgh, explained Harold as he expertly made his way into the city. It is a very old church with a very stable congregation." From these comments Anna surmised that all significant events in the Wilson family had taken place in that church: Harold's baptism; a requiem mass for his mother; his marriage to Caroline; another requiem mass after her death and then Thomas' baptism. It was one more component that contributed to the stability and sense of continuity that every family needs, if it is to remain together.

"There is it!" suddenly shouted Thomas from the back seat as he pointed excitedly to a building on his right.

The Epiphany Catholic Church was a massive brick building with two imposing belfries. The beautiful façade showed obvious Byzantine details—the most prominent being a huge circular stained-glass window that crowned the three romanesque arches of the separate entrances below. Without wanting to, Anna had to think of the smaller and more humble San Rosendo Cathedral, in

Pinar del Río, the baroque cathedral in Havana, with its elaborate stone work, and the simpler Church of Santa Chiara in Naples. Different styles, different languages, but with one common purpose: offering guidance and solace from the often confusing business of living and strength against the inherent myriad human frailties buttressed by the hope of eternal life.

Although the adjacent parking lot was already crowded, Harold did not have any difficulties in finding a space. As they walked towards the church, he was immediately recognized and several people approached them to say good morning. The vestibule of the church sported a holy water fountain, hand carved from a single block of marble, and another set of wooden doors with panels depicting biblical scenes. Once inside, seated next to Harold, Anna took time to appreciate the splendid work that had gone into the building: the stained-glass windows; the magnificent altar, the elaborate pews. It was apparent, as Harold had said, that all this had taken many years and several generations of worshippers to achieve. The service started right on time as the priest gave the opening blessing, and during the homily he spoke about the power and difficulties of love, the very foundation on which Christian doctrine rested. He was right; sometimes in life, for many reasons, it was difficult to love. Harold seemed to be concentrating on the homily, while Thomas, although quiet, inspected with his errant gaze the architectural details of the building. Then came the consecration of the host and the subsequent communion.

After the final blessing, as they were walking out of the church, just for an instant and with the corner of her eye Anna thought that she caught a glimpse—absurd as it was—of a figure that took her back many years. When she tried to ascertain if she was right, the man was gone. The rational part of her brain immediately took over, telling her that what she thought she had seen was not possible, that too many years, too many miles and too many events made it impossible, so she quickly dismissed it and returned to the immediate reality of that day.

Outside the church, the worshippers lingered, greeting each other and perhaps exchanging anecdotes or catching up on one another's family news. It took them a while to reach the car, since many people wanted to talk to Harold, especially on this Sunday morning, when he had shown up with a woman nobody had seen before. He introduced her as Anna d'Amio, a friend of the family, but gave them no further details as to what she was doing in the city, how they had met, or what kind of relationship they had. Thomas, in the meantime, did not waste any time in telling anyone who would listen about his art work and the projects he wanted to do in the future, but eventually they found themselves back in the car. Even though Anna was not familiar with the city, she realized that they were not heading back to Harold's house, so she asked him where they were going.

"Nowhere in particular," he answered, "I just thought I would take you around the city; you did not see much of it last night. From here we can go directly to see Thomas' grandfather."

"I love my grandfather," said Thomas from the recesses of the back seat, "He always listens to me and tells me stories. I also like the food at his house," he added after a pause.

After riding around the city for almost an hour, Harold took a road that led away from the center of Pittsburgh to Dr. Ashburn's house. The tall buildings gave way to smaller, clearly residential structures set in the center of well-groomed lawns sheltered by trees and adorned with decorative shrubbery and colorful flower-beds.

"There it is," shouted Thomas from the back seat, just as he had done when they were approaching the church. "You are going to like this house, Anna," he added as Harold expertly guided the car into the long driveway. As soon as the engine was off, he opened the door and stepped out of the car; another obvious sign of how much he enjoyed the visits. Before they had a chance to ring the bell, the door opened and a tall, gray-haired man wearing a tweed jacket stood in the threshold, smiling widely and arms wide open as he saw Thomas approaching him. As they embraced, Anna felt that the love between Thomas and his grandfather was almost palpable. It was a simple action that expressed what words never could. Dr. Ashburn then turned his attention to Harold, and after the initial introductions, they went in the house. As they walked in, an inviting aroma emanating from the kitchen welcomed them; no wonder Thomas enjoyed these visits so much.

"We are having spaghetti today," he said, "It is one of my favorites."

"Everything is one of Thomas' favorites," explained Dr. Ashburn as he led Anna and Harold towards the dining room and proceeded to open a bottle of wine, pour it into glasses he took from a side cabinet and handed them to Harold and Anna.

"Where is my glass?" protested Thomas.

"We go through this every week," explained Dr. Ashburn, speaking directly to his grandson, "When you get a little older you can have a glass too."

"But I am older today than I was last week," he argued. At this comment they all had to laugh, because he was technically correct.

"So what brings you to Pittsburgh?" asked Dr. Ashburn as he sipped his wine, "You are a long way from home."

"You are right," answered Anna, "But Harold insisted that I come to this jazz concert; I have to admit that it was worth it. Besides, this trip has given me the opportunity to meet Thomas and to share some time with you as well."

"Jazz has always been one of his passions," said the doctor, "I can't claim to understand it; I think it is an acquired taste. At any rate, I am glad that you came."

"Me too," said Thomas, "I hope you come back soon."

"I would love to, Thomas," answered Anna, "But Miami is a long way from here."

"Thomas can come with me the next time I fly to Florida," said Harold.

"I think that is a great idea," said Dr. Ashburn, "There are no beaches in Pittsburgh, and sunshine is in short supply."

After that short exchange, they sat down for lunch. Dr. Ashburn occupied the seat at the head of the table, with Harold to his right and Anna to his left. Thomas sat next to his father. As they passed the dishes around, commented on the food or occasionally reminded Thomas not to eat so fast, Anna realized how well balanced were the dynamics of that special relationship Dr. Ashburn, Harold and Thomas shared. After so many years they knew each other as well as one human being can know another, shortcomings and all, and had become closer. Had Caroline Ashburn been present, Anna also thought, she would have been most pleased.

After desert was served—Thomas' favorite part of the meal, we repeat—Harold looked at his watch and reminded everyone that the visit had to be cut short, since Anna had to fly back to Miami.

"I hope to see you again," said Dr. Ashburn as they were leaving the house, "You are welcome here anytime."

466

"Thank you for everything," said Anna, "I hope to come back soon."

On they way back to their house, Thomas sat quietly in the back seat, refraining from making any comments about the different landmarks that were visible on the way. Harold, knowing his son as well as he did, realized that something was bothering him, so he asked if there was anything wrong.

"I don't want Anna to go," he said in a sullen tone.

"She can come back," said Harold, "Or we can go and visit her; you were there when I suggested it to your grandfather."

"How soon can we go?" he asked, now with excitement in his voice.

"Soon," answered Harold, "I promise you."

If there was one thing that Anna had learned about Harold, whether in business or personal matters, was that he always kept his word, so she expected to see Thomas the next time he came to Florida to check on the progress of the hotel he had bought in Miami Beach. This trip had also further demonstrated to Anna how important the concept of family was to Harold. It was perhaps the most important thing they had in common, for she felt the same way about Francesca and Adriana as he did about Thomas.

"We should get going soon," said Harold as he parked the car in front of the house.

"I will gather my things and be ready in a few minutes," answered Anna as they walked into the foyer, but before she had time to go into her room, Thomas took her by the hand and pulled her in the direction of his studio.

"You promised to look at my painting before you left," he said.

"So I did," she answered as he allowed herself to be led into the room where Thomas had set up his studio.

The work in question was still resting on an easel in the center of the room, just below the skylight. With a decisive motion, Thomas removed the cloth that covered it.

If Anna thought before that Thomas had talent, this particular painting dispelled any doubts that she might have still harbored. The canvas depicted a jungle scene, replete with wild animals and exuberant vegetation. What amazed Anna was the details that Thomas had been able to recreate on the canvas: the mane of the lions; the stripes of the zebras; the spots of the leopards. The flora was also as detailed as the fauna, for the pistils of the flowers and the blades of grass were also clearly visible. In a way it reminded her of the work of Henri Rousseau, but full of the innocence that filled Thomas' work.

"Amazing, truly amazing Thomas. I love it," Anna said in awe, and she meant every word.

"That makes me very happy," then he walked towards a side shelf. "I have something for you," he said to Anna while handing her a small painting. It depicted a winter scene, with a frozen river and snow covered spruces. In the distance, crossing a bridge, two boys could be seen carrying a sled. This painting perfectly conveyed what Thomas was about: besides an obvious command of his craft, it also showed an unencumbered simplicity mixed with the innocence of a child.

"Well, thank you Thomas," she said, "I will treasure this forever," then, without thinking, gave him a kiss on the cheek. He did not say anything, but simply looked at the floor and blushed a little. It was also evident that he was not used to receiving the affections of a woman.

"I will wait for you in the foyer while you get your suitcase," said Harold, who had been standing silently in the doorway, reminding her once again that it was time to go.

"I will not be long," she said and disappeared in the direction of her room.

By the time she reappeared in the foyer, just a few minutes later, she was puzzled by Thomas' absence. Harold explained, as he picked up Anna's suitcase, that he was still in his studio, so he would not be coming with them. On the way to the airport, they talked about Anna's visit, starting with the jazz concert, the mass at the Church of the Epiphany, and the visit to Dr. Ashburn's house. But these were just physical places; what Anna found most worthwhile—and Harold concurred—was the fact that Thomas had taken an instant liking to her.

"That tells me a lot," said Harold, "He has a way of seeing through people and determining if they are genuine or if they are just putting up a front. I was surprised that he should part with one of his favorite paintings and give it to you."

"I like him a lot too," answered Anna, "In a way he reminds me of what you could have been, had you taken a different path in your life." In the past Harold had confided in Anna about his early ambitions of becoming a writer and how he had given up those

468

dreams in order to please his father, so there was no need to be more specific; they both knew what she was referring to. Harold did not answer, at least not with words, but his brief smile was clear evidence that in the past he had considered that possibility himself.

"The traffic is lighter today," he said, opting to keep his thoughts to himself. By then Anna knew him well enough to know that there was no point in pursuing that line of conversation; he would tell her how he felt whenever he was ready.

"Sundays are the same everywhere," she answered, "Most people want to stay home with their families."

The number of cars in the airport parking lot was just as light as on the streets; Harold found a spot close to the main terminal, turned off the engine and went around to open the door for Anna. After retrieving her suitcase, they made their way to the check-in counter. The plane would not leave for another forty-five minutes, so there was no need to hurry. After checking in with the airline, they slowly walked over to the gate from which the plane would be leaving. Other passengers had already gathered there, speaking softly to family or friends, checking their watches for the tenth time or just smoking silently. Harold and Anna opted to watch the incoming and outgoing planes landing or taking off through the glass window facing the runway. Less than ten minutes had elapsed when the announcement to start boarding came over a loudspeaker. Anna picked up her bag and started to get in the line that had formed in front of the gate. Harold, in turn, walked with her, until he could go no farther.

"Call me tonight," he said.

"I will, of course," she answered.

Then, as if it were the most natural thing to do, he simply bent down and kissed her, ever so softly, on the lips.

Even before landing in Miami, Anna knew that everything between her and Harold had changed. No words had been exchanged, but just that simple act of touching lips had catapulted their relationship to a new, more intimate level. Where before there had been a solid friendship, based at first on a business agreement and later in the discovery that they enjoyed each other's company, now there was the uncertain reality of a romantic involvement with all its future and unpredictable ramifications, both good and bad.

That is not to say that Anna was opposed to having a relationship with a man, but she knew that more often than not men were interested in just one thing, and after they finally got it, they lost interest and moved on to their next conquest. She had had one of those unpleasant experiences a year and a half before, while trying to put everything together in order to get her cleaning business off the ground.

The man who sold her the van, a Cuban by the name of Rogelio Díaz, ran a successful auto parts delivery business. Although there was nothing wrong with the van, he was ready to upgrade to a larger and newer model, so he placed a classified ad in the paper and waited for the prospective buyers to call. Since he wanted to make a quick sale, he was happy when Anna, from the pay phone at the Rice Hotel, called to inquire about the vehicle. At this point, his concern was only financial. But when she took a bus to his house to inspect the vehicle, from the instant he saw her he developed a more personal interest.

He introduced himself not just as a seller, but as a fellow Cuban who was always glad to help other refugees, and he cited the fact that he had other Cubans in his employ. Anna found him affable enough, and because of his obvious good looks and apparent success, she assumed that he was a family man with a wife and children. She did not have to conjecture long, for as he showed her the van, he also began to tell her the story of how his late wife had died in a Cuban hospital before her permission to leave the island had been granted by the authorities. Anna, of course, felt sorry for the man and had no reason to doubt what he was telling her. It was a plausible story, but in this case Rogelio was using it to elicit sympathy from Anna. From that point on, as he gave the particular details about the van, in passing he asked about Anna's life, as Cubans usually do.

Since the vehicle was in excellent condition, had a new set of tires, and Rogelio had kept meticulous records of its maintenance, by the time she left, they had made an agreement of sorts about the price. This was exactly what Anna needed to transport the workers for her cleaning business, but because she still did not have a driver's license, she would have to return with a friend and the oney. "No problem," said Rogelio and they agreed on a time and day for the exchange.

The only person Anna knew with a driver's license was the manager of the Rice Hotel, a kindly gentlemen in his sixties who had taken that job to fill his idle hours after his retirement as a high school Spanish teacher. That job was a perfect fit for him, since it provided a steady source of income, was not too difficult and it allowed him to use his language skills on a daily basis, although once in a while he was thrown off by certain phrases in the Cuban vernacular that could not be found in any dictionary, or by the staccato tone in which Cubans communicated whenever they got excited.

When Anna approached him and asked him for that favor, he was more than happy to oblige. From the moment of her arrival at the hotel, he had identified her as one of those hardworking individuals who is always looking for ways to improve their situation. If he could help her in a small way, he would. On the appointed day, they took the bus that stopped at the corner of Flagler and Miami Avenue and within half an hour, they were at Rogelio's doorstep. The van was in the driveway, and Anna noticed that it had been washed and waxed since her initial visit. This was not necessary to carry out the transaction; they already had a deal, but she thought it was nice that Rogelio had taken the time to clean out the vehicle and make it as presentable as possible. As they approached the house, Anna noticed the look of approval on the manager's face as he stopped for a few minutes to walk around the van and give it visual inspection. Anna had told him all about it, why the owner wanted to sell it and that all the maintenance records would come with it. Before he had a chance to comment on the excellent shape of the van, the front door of the house opened and Rogelio stepped out with a grin on his face.

"I am so happy to see you," he said looking at Anna, his gaze lingering on her body longer than necessary. "And you must be the friend with the driver's license," he finally said while looking at the manager and extending his hand.

"*Mucho gusto*," the manager said as he shook Rogelio's hand, but he knew that it was just a formality before a business transaction. The exchange only took minutes; Rogelio had all the papers, including the title and registration, in a brown folder.

Anna, in turn, had the money in her purse, and as soon as it was counted, Rogelio signed the title and gave her two sets of keys.

"It was a pleasure doing business with you," he said to Anna and shook the manager's hand one more time. When they drove away, Rogelio was still standing in his driveway, watching them disappear into the busy traffic of the North West section of Miami. From there, rather than returning to the Rice Hotel, they drove directly to the Department of Motor Vehicles on North Miami Ave, so Anna could take her driver's test. In anticipation of this day she had already passed the written exam a month before.

A week later, after coming in from a day of work at the Cardozo Hotel, the manager signaled for her to approach the front desk, then handed her a piece of paper folded in half, where he had taken a message for Anna. The message was from none other than Rogelio, asking her to call him, but without any further explanations. Thinking that it probably had to with something related to the van, she went directly to the pay phone in the hallway and dialed the number written on the paper. Her call was answered on the second ring, as if the person on the other end of the line had been waiting by the phone. Anna identified herself and asked Rogelio about the meaning of her message.

"I am so glad you called," he said, "I found some other papers that go with the van, and I thought you should have them. I will be hosting a small party this evening, so I will be home, just in case you want to pick them up; you are less than fifteen minutes away."

For an instant, Anna thought to ask Rogelio to put the papers in the mail, but picking them up in person would be a lot faster. Besides, she wanted to have all the information together in the folder he had given her on the day of the purchase.

"That is fine; I can be there around eight o'clock," she said, then after a pause, "But I do not want to disrupt your party."

"That's not a problem," answered Rogelio, "I am looking forward to seeing you again."

Although it had been a long and hard day, after taking a shower, changing into some clean clothes and eating dinner from the cantina, Anna felt renewed. Around seven thirty she left the hotel, got into the van and made a right hand turn onto Flagler Street. The rush-hour traffic had waned somewhat, so within fifteen minutes she was pulling into Rogelio's driveway. Over the phone, he had said that he was having friends over that evening, so

Anna found it strange that there were no other vehicles parked there or in front of the house. Maybe they were coming later, she surmised. Before she had a chance to ring the bell, the door opened and Rogelio, with a drink in his hand, appeared in the threshold.

"Come in and sit down while I get your papers," he said, stepping aside and leading Anna into the living room. His entire body exuded the smell of an eau de cologne whose brand Anna failed to identify, but that he had — in the purest Cuban tradition — used in excessive amounts. In the background, the unmistakable sound of Olga Guillot's sultry voice, delivering one her incomeparable boleros, emerged from a stereo sound record player.

"It was nice of you to meet me this evening; you told me that you have company coming," said Anna as she sat on the couch.

"Let me fix you something to drink," said Rogelio and without waiting for an answer walked over to the Formica counter—replete with bottles—that served as a divider between the kitchen and the living room. Anna watched him as he expertly used a set of tongs to pick up the ice cubes from a metal bowl, place them in a tall glass and then pour the liquor from one of the bottles. "Rum and Coke ok?" he asked, but by then he was already walking back to the couch where Anna was sitting.

"Yes, thank you," she answered as she took the drink from Rogelio. Although Anna had never been a drinker, she did not want to appear rude, especially to someone who had gone out of his way to make sure she had all the information about the vehicle she had just bought.

"I will be right back with your papers," said Rogelio as he put his drink down on the counter and disappeared into the back of the house. This pause gave Anna the opportunity to pay more attention to the decoration in the living room. Although it could not be classified as tawdry, the furnishings, although of high quality, denoted a certain lack of sophistication, as if the entire room had been put together without much thought about the end results. Anna attributed this to the fact that Rogelio lived alone and that he probably spent most of his time thinking about his business and not about the decoration of his house.

He returned a few moments later, holding what appeared to be a booklet of some sort. "This is the owner's manual," he explained while picking up his drink and sitting down next to Anna, "I was checking out some things last week, before placing the ad in the paper, and forgot to put it back in the glove box; I found it after you had gone, so I called and left you a message." At this point he made a pause to take a sip of his drink before continuing with his explanation, "Here, on the inside of the back cover, I have written the name and phone number of the mechanic who has done all the work, just in case you need to have the van serviced in the future."

As he spoke, holding the open manual in his hand and using its information as a pretext, Rogelio had slid on the couch as close as possible to Anna. He had also extended his free arm, although not actually making contact with her, over the back of the couch. "So tell me more about your business," he said in a casual tone, not wanting to unduly alarm Anna or give away his intentions.

"It is just a small cleaning business," she explained, "Nothing as big as what you have."

"You don't have to be modest," he said as he offered her his best smile. "Everyone has to start small and give themselves time to expand; this is the land of opportunity."

"You seem to be doing very well for yourself," she said.

"If you mean financially, I guess I am not doing too badly," he said with a smile of satisfaction, "But not everything can be measured in terms of dollars and cents," he almost whispered while letting out a sigh and lowering his head. Suddenly the expression on his face had gone from one of contentment to one of unfulfilled longing.

"What do you mean?" asked Anna, "You seem to have a perfectly fine life."

This was the moment that Rogelio had been waiting for. Taking another sip from his glass and trying to get even closer to Anna, he raised his head and looked into her eyes. For an instant, the image of a lost puppy looking for a home came into Anna's mind. These were exactly the feelings that he wanted to evoke, of someone who was sincere and vulnerable, someone who was about to reveal the innermost secrets of his soul.

"I already mentioned about my wife; God rest her soul," he said in a mournful tone, "What good is all this if I have no one with whom to share it? When I come home at the end of the day all I find is an empty house, full of meaningless gadgets. There is more to life than work." As he said this Rogelio put down his glass on the coffee table and took Anna's free hand in his. "Since the moment I saw you I knew there was something very special about you," he said, leaning even closer, "We can build something beautiful, starting tonight," he whispered while he tried to put his arms around her and kiss her.

It was then that Anna saw Rogelio for what he really was: a pathetic man who had staged this charade with the ultimate purpose of getting her in bed. His party was nothing but a fabrication; the nonexistent guests were never meant to arrive, giving him ample time to carry out his designs. In all probability this sleazy ploy had worked in the past; after all, there were enough desperate and gullible women out there eager to latch on to such opportunity, even if it eventually turned out to be nothing but a mirage.

With a forceful gesture, Anna broke the incipient embrace, stood up and stormed out of the house, not even bothering to close the door behind her. On the way back to the hotel, she reminded herself that the most pressing thing in her life was to get back on her feet financially. That was the key to regaining custody of Francesca and Adriana. As for men in general, this was the furthest thing from her mind; she could not even begin to conceive of a romantic liaison after being married to Ramón for almost twenty years. It was an aspect of her life that she did not contemplate at this point; only time would tell.

Harold Wilson was different; he had proven that from the very beginning. With all his wealth, status and connections he could have married any time he wanted to. He also could have chosen to enjoy the company of one woman — or several, for that matter — without the legal constraints of a formal marriage. Yet, he had opted to devote his time to his son, his business and his charitable work. And now, all his actions proved that he was interested in more than a simple friendship. Anna also realized that she had never given him any indications that all his displays of attention — both toward her or the twins — were in any way unwelcome. On the contrary, she enjoyed Harold's company tremendously, and the fact that he seemed to love the girls made him even more special in her eyes. Unquestionably, she had eased herself into a situation that had inevitably led to the point where she now found herself. Yes, everything had suddenly changed, and she knew that from this day on Harold would want to take their relationship — and rightfully so — further.

When Anna arrived from the airport at her house on Biscayne Boulevard, the twins were already asleep. She tiptoed into their room, so as not to wake them, and watched them for a few minutes, oblivious to the world; thinking of the time they had been away, living with strangers, brought tears to her eyes. It was impossible to conceive a future, no matter where, without them. Back in the kitchen, Silvia was already waiting for her with a sandwich and some coffee. There were times when Anna thought that Silvia could almost read her mind, for she was able to anticipate her words or even her changes of mood.

"He already called twice," she said while pouring herself a cup of coffee. There was no need to clarify; they both knew she was referring to Harold.

"And what did he say?" asked Anna while taking a bite from her sandwich.

"Nothing much," answered Silvia, "He just wanted to know if you were home yet."

"He feels responsible for me," Anna offered, "I will call him in a few minutes; there is no reason for him to worry unnecessarily."

"I understand," said Silvia, "How was the trip?"

"The trip was fine; I met his son, and we went to the concert. This morning the three of us went to mass and then he drove me around the city. Afterwards we had a late lunch at his father in law's house."

"Father in law?" Silvia was puzzled.

"Well, his former father in law. After Harold's wife died he and Thomas kept going there for dinner every Sunday. I think it is a nice tradition."

"I am not surprised," said Silvia, "From the moment I saw him I got the impression that he was a rather conventional man, one who likes to have a set pattern for every aspect of his life," she continued after finishing her coffee.

"As usual, you are correct," agreed Anna, "Maybe that is one of the cornerstones of his success. But now I have to call Pittsburgh; after all, I don't want him to worry about me."

"No, of course not," said Silvia in a slightly sarcastic tone and then smiled widely.

After Anna's visit to Pittsburgh, Harold's calls became more frequent and longer. At this point, they seldom talked about business, but about personal matters. Harold kept telling Anna how impressed Thomas had been with her, and that he kept asking when she would return. It was an indirect way for Harold to find out about her plans and how she felt about Pittsburgh. There was no need for him to be oblique about it; Anna had always been straightforward with him and by then their relationship had progressed to the point where they could discuss just about anything. Right after her return to Miami, she had written a short note to Thomas, thanking him for the painting and encouraging him to keep up with his artistic endeavors.

One Saturday morning three weeks later, just out of the blue, Harold called to tell Anna that he and Thomas were at the Fountainbleu, where they had taken a suite for the weekend. He wanted her and the twins to join them; there was an adjacent bedroom where she could stay with the girls. Anna did not think about it twice; she had no plans for the weekend, and she had to admit to herself that she missed Harold. Their regular phone conversations every evening, even though they sometimes went on for hours, were no longer enough. He also sent presents for the girls on a regular basis, who by then referred to him as Papa.

The familiar black sedan arrived about an hour later, but without Harold; he thought it best to remain at the hotel with Thomas and wait for the three of them. Thomas was excited enough to be in Florida, so he did not want to add to it by introducing him to the twins at Anna's house; the hotel would be a more comfortable setting.

As they made their way from Biscayne Boulevard over the causeways that joined the cities of Miami and Miami Beach, the twins excitedly pointed to the boats below, or to the people who water skied on the bay, leaving behind them furrows of white foam that eventually dissolved in the waves.

Harold was in front of the hotel waiting for them; at first Anna did not recognize him because he had dispensed with the dark suit and wore cream-colored slacks and a light blue shirt. It was Thomas who spotted them first as they exited the dark sedan. He ran towards them and, with his usual effusiveness, gave Anna a hug and a kiss. By then Harold was standing next to them too; he also kissed and hugged Anna. The expression on his face left no doubt as to how happy he was to see her. Then, as if it were the most natural thing to do, he picked up both twins and kissed them on their cheeks. Anyone looking would have assumed that this was just a regular family enjoying a vacation in Florida.

"I have a surprise for everyone," he said, obviously pleased to be with Anna, Thomas and the girls.

"I love surprises," said Thomas before Harold had a chance to explain or Anna the opportunity to ask. Anna and Harold looked at each other and broke out laughing. Adriana and Francesca, echoing their mother, laughed too.

"What is so funny?" asked Thomas, completely clueless that his abrupt comment was a source of amusement.

"As I was saying," Harold went on, "I think everyone would enjoy a boat ride around Biscayne Bay, so I made the arrangements for this afternoon."

"What a nice surprise Harold," said Anna. Then, without much thought, kissed him on the cheek.

"I have never been on a boat," said Thomas, "And I can't swim either."

"Well, we will have to teach you," said Anna, "I am sure you will not have any problems learning."

"Before we go we should have lunch," said Harold, who was still holding the twins, and had started walking in the direction of the hotel terrace, where other guests enjoyed the view and their meals under multicolored umbrellas.

That weekend turned out to be the most memorable in the growing relationship between Harold and Anna. They both realized that it was the first time that all the children were together, and how they interacted would have a profound influence on the future of that connection. But if that day was an indication of what was to come, they had no cause for concerns. Thomas took to the twins immediately — perhaps that inner child in him identified with them — and especially once they were aboard the boat that took them on the leisurely cruise of the bay, his comments about the mansions, the other boats and everything else were no longer directed at Harold or Anna, but at them. The twins, in turn, giggled, laughed or just pointed at whatever Thomas was showing them, repeating some of his comments as best they could. In the meantime, taking advantage that the children were busy, Harold pointed out to Anna some of the highlights located on Biscayne

Bay. He particularly liked Vizcaya, a magnificent estate built by millionaire James Deering, of the International Harvester fortune, at the turn of the century. After his death in 1925 the property had been turned over to Dade County and it was currently a museum. Harold gave Anna other details about the owner, about its construction, and how it had finally become a public place. He also promised her to take her there in the future, so she could admire from within all the marvels that the place held. What he failed to mention was that the original owner and Dexter Wilson had been friends, and that during the summer of 1918—the estate had been completed just three years before—he had traveled to Florida by train with his father and during that visit he had met James Deering himself. These were details about Harold Wilson's life that Anna would find out during future conversations, as they learned more about each other's lives.

Several hours later, back in the hotel, they decided to go swimming in the gigantic pool. Thomas, as it turned out, did not have any difficulties in the water, and before long he was floating and moving about as if it were a most familiar medium. Harold and Anna, each holding one of the twins, opted to remain in the more shallow end of the pool, where the water only reached the waist. They talked and laughed when the girls splashed about or — as they watched Thomas — tried to let go and swim by themselves. At this point Harold held each of them by the hands, opened his arms and spun around in the water, making quick circles and reversing direction from time to time. The girls laughed even more and squealed with delight as he increased the speed of the turns and the frequency of their reversal. It was moments like this when Anna felt closest to Harold, watching him play with the children and momentarily forget all the business concerns that always preoccupied him. He stopped being a businessman to become just a man, enjoying the company of the people he loved. Just as before, she thought that they must have looked like the typical American family on vacation.

The boat ride around the bay, and lunch by the pool were not the only surprises that Harold had in store for Anna and the twins. That evening, rather than having dinner at the hotel or one of the many excellent restaurants located nearby, he had his chauffeur drive them to Lincoln Road. Since the road was closed to vehicular traffic, they all got out of the car after arranging a predetermined time for a pick up. Even though Anna had worked for some time now in Miami Beach, she had never visited this particular section. The charm of Lincoln Road resided in the fact that it was only open to pedestrians. Along its center there were beautiful flower pots, playful fountains and benches, in case the public got tired or just wanted to take a respite while eating an ice-cream cone or drinking one of the fresh juices that were dispensed at various establishments. It was, in short, a place where all sorts of people congregated, coming together to enjoy the outdoors and do a little shopping.

As they started their exploration, Anna felt Harold's hand reaching for hers, completing a gesture that by now had become second nature. During the past few months, she had also learned that Harold yearned not only for emotional closeness, but for frequent physical contact. At times, whenever he caressed her hands or face, Anna sensed a certain urgency, as if he were trying to make up for time lost during past years and fill that inner void that she suspected he had always carried with him.

It took them most of the evening to walk the length of Lincoln Road and back. Not that the distance was so great, but the shops were so enticing that they had to stop many times. Besides the aforementioned businesses, there were record shops, bookstores, clothing stores and, of course, art shops with their corresponding galleries. Thomas, as exuberant as ever, wanted to go in right away and inspect what they had to offer. Knowing that he would not be deterred, and wanting to make that weekend as memorable as possible, Harold acceded. They bought some art supplies — mostly oil tubes — whose colors Thomas claimed could not be found in Pittsburgh. He also engaged the owner — an artist himself — in a conversation about the influence of Picasso on twentieth century art. After a while, knowing that they did not have all night, Harold had to pry him away, lest he spend all night in conversation. But secretly he was proud of his son; he had expressed some of the insights that they had explored together in their library while looking at countless color reproductions, as a fire burned in the massive fireplace and the snow blanketed the woods outside their window.

About ten minutes after leaving the art shop, Harold stopped in front of a jewelry store. "Let's go in," he said as he led Anna and the children into the shop. She knew that he did not enjoy

480

shopping that much, especially for jewelry—in fact, he wore no rings or chains, only a watch—but apparently something had caught his eye. Once in the store, he did not wander around looking at the other merchandise, but simply called a clerk aside and spoke briefly to him. The young man opened the showcase that faced the outside of the shop, retrieved something from its contents, and then showed it to Harold. He nodded and asked the clerk to put it in a box and wrap it. The entire exchange had taken only minutes, and once the transaction was concluded, they were back walking with the rest of the visitors. The children had not even been aware of what had taken place. Although Anna suspectted that Harold's purchase was for her, she did not say or ask anything, lest she ruin the surprise.

Since it was getting late, they decided to have dinner in a little pizza shop that, if the crowd outside was any indication, provided the customers with top-rated food. The place was already filled to capacity, so they opted for one of the outside tables under a colorful umbrella. It was just as well, for they all liked to watch the constant activity of the people who visited Lincoln Road.

Once the waiter came to their table—they had already decided on a pepperoni pizza—Thomas could not help himself and asked him to put extra cheese on their order. While they waited, he took a pencil out of his shirt pocket and started to do a sketch of the twins on a paper napkin. Even in such an impromptu setting, thought Anna as the drawing progressed, his talent—although still rough and unpolished—was apparent. The girls, who were sitting on either side of Thomas, peered curiously at what he was doing, not knowing exactly what to make of the whole thing. What emerged after a few minutes was a sketch of Francesca and Adriana; at this point both Harold and Anna nodded approvingly, for it showed once again how much Thomas had taken to the girls.

Towards the end of the evening, they met the chauffeur and returned to the Fountainbleu. It had been a long day, so after giving them a quick bath, Anna put the twins to bed. Thomas was also tired, so a short time later he also decided to retire for the day. After kissing Harold and Anna good night he went to his bedroom.

"I have something for you," said Harold while holding Anna's hand and leading her out to the balcony, "But first I want to tell you how happy I am that you decided to come and join us this weekend; Thomas is very happy too." There was no need for

Harold to tell Anna what she already knew, but she knew that he was the type of man who needed to verbalize what he felt, even if it was obvious to everyone around him. This need probably arose from having to always present an emotionless, logical and even calculating facet of his personality during his business dealings.

"You know there is no need to thank me," Anna answered, still holding Harold's hand, "We enjoy your company and seeing Thomas again has made this visit extra special."

"Here," said Harold releasing Anna's hand, reaching into his pocket and handing her a small box, "I hope you like it."

"Harold, you didn't have to get me anything," protested Anna.

"It was really nothing," he retorted, "Just a little token so you will always remember this weekend," he added while shrugging his shoulders and smiling.

Inside the box, resting on a black velvety case, was a pair of red coral earrings. The delicate pieces had been painstakingly joined together with a thin strand of sterling silver wire, creating the impression of a descending cascade about two inches in length.

"Harold, they are beautiful!" exclaimed Anna, "I have never seen anything like this before. Thank you."

"I thought you would like them, not just because they are beautiful, but because they are unique and are made of something natural that could never be replicated by man," he said. "Let me put them on," he added as he took one of the earrings out of the case. Anna, not wanting to say no even though the sun had already set and it was dim on the balcony, removed the single pearl studs that she wore. Harold, not being able to find the piercing on her earlobe, hesitated for a moment, so Anna took his hand and guided it until both earrings were in place. Because of the close proximity, Anna's discreet perfume enveloped him; he lowered his hands from her ears to her face, caressing it softly. "You are so beauty-ful," he said softly, then kissed her repeatedly on the lips and then held her very close, without any words, as if he were trying to satiate an inner hunger for love that had been with him for many years.

This particular trip to Miami was the first of many. Somehow, especially now that Thomas had met Anna's daughters, Harold either found or made the time to fly down at least once a month. Those visits always centered on family oriented activities, so the children would enjoy themselves and become more used to each other's company. On one of those occasions, they visited Parrot Jungle, a hit with Thomas, who lost no time making comments about the colorful and playful birds, and then produced a sketchpad where he collected ideas for future paintings. They also had the opportunity to spend one afternoon touring Vizcaya, the estate they had seen from the boat during an earlier visit. Anna particularly enjoyed the tapestries and porcelains on display, but her favorite room was the atrium in the center of the mansion. The plants, wicker furniture and unique floor gave the room a certain old-world charm that she found irresistible. They were settling into a routine that everyone liked, and especially the children always looked forward to the next visit.

This pattern, however, would be shattered by an unexpected event, perpetrated by the hand of a stranger, that would forever change how the American public felt about their country. In November of that year, 1963, young president Kennedy had scheduled a visit to the state of Texas. This was supposed to be a routine stop, one of many that all presidents make during their term in office. When the news broke that the president had been fatally shot, a state of shock descended upon the entire nation, if not the world. Harold had met John F. Kennedy, because of his connections with the family, several times in the past, and although he had not seen him since he had moved into the White House, he felt as outraged as any American that the president had been assassinated so openly and with absolute impunity. Harold was also aware that many in the Cuban community blamed Kennedy personally for the failed Bay of Pigs invasion two years earlier, and that they held ambivalent feelings toward him. But all that was in the past; the bottom line was that an American president had been assassinated and that the event would have far reaching repercussions. Harold, knowing that he would have to attend the funeral, called Anna immediately to let her know that he had to cancel his trip to Florida that week. For the first time since she had known him she detected something in his voice that she had never heard before: grief. It made him sound distant and detached, as if he were struggling to keep his feelings from overwhelming him. "I will call you soon," he said and then hung up.

During the next few days Anna went to work as usual, and along with the entire country, watched the endless stream of broadcasts on television; they were a mixture of news and conjectures as to the assassin's motivations and the direction the nation would take from that point on. She was sure that Harold would have more solid news, but he had not called. Trying to reach him at his Pittsburgh number, she knew, would be a waste of time.

When he finally did, ten days later, the first thing she noticed was that the tone of his voice had changed; somehow he sounded more decisive, as if he had finally found something that he had been missing for a long time. "I want you to spend Christmas in Pittsburgh," he said. Although it was not a command, it was not a request either. Harold was expressing a desire he knew would be met. "Bring Silvia too," he added after a short pause. At first Anna thought this was strange, but then realized that Harold wanted her to have everyone who was important in her life. "I will make all the arrangements and will call you again soon, but now I have to go."

"I will wait for your call," said Anna and then the line went dead. He had not even told her how much he missed her, but she knew how much he disliked expressing his feelings over the phone. What she found most strange was that he had not asked about the girls or mentioned Thomas. President Kennedy's funeral, thought Anna, must have really made an impact on him.

The prospect of spending the Christmas holidays in Pittsburgh somehow appealed to Anna. Just the idea of seeing snow for the first time was motivation enough; although she had seen pictures and movies, she could still not imagine being in a climate as cold as an ice box. The image of the massive fireplace in Harold's library came to mind. She looked up at the painting that Thomas had given her, depicting a winter scene and two boys carrying a sled. Harold's world was indeed far removed from Italy and Cuba, even from Florida. Yet, with every passing day he wanted her to make it her world as well.

When she told Silvia about Harold's invitation, she was a little surprised at first, but then simply smiled and agreed that it would be an interesting trip. Since her arrival from Cuba, she had not left Miami, so she was understandably curious about other parts of the United States. Besides, Anna and the twins were the closest to family she had, so spending Christmas away from them was not an appealing prospect. With time she had come to realize that Harold's interest in Anna was genuine and did not conceal any ulterior motives, that for whatever reason he had chosen her over other women. Further, she had also noticed that he doted upon the twins as if they were his own daughters. What more could a woman want?

A week later Harold called again. He did not offer any explanations why it had taken him so long, nor did Anna ask for any. When the time came, he would tell her. This time he gave her all the particulars about the trip, and assured her that his chauffeur would come to their house to pick them up. All this, of course, was unnecessary. Being the good businessman that he was, one of Harold's qualities was reliability. After getting all the details out of the way, he moved on to more personal matters, and told Anna how much he was looking forward to their visit.

The month of December brought with it cooler temperatures, forcing Floridians to bring out sweaters that only saw the light of day a few times a year; the change also encouraged them to complain about the unbearable cold weather. Anna was mildly amused, realizing that everything was relative and that by then many parts of the United States already had snow on the ground.

When the day of the trip finally arrived, they were more than ready. A week earlier, during a shopping spree, Anna and Silvia had managed to find long and heavy coats at bargain prices, since no one had any use for them in southern Florida. The twins were a different story; no one seemed to stock winter coats for children, but once again Harold's foresight saved the day. A box was delivered to the house and not only did it contain identical coats in the right size, but also matching gloves and hats.

As expected, Harold's chauffeur arrived with a few minutes to spare, and shortly thereafter they were on their way to the airport. Anna could easily tell how excited Silvia was; this would only be the second time she had been on a plane, and her first on a jet. But it was more than that; she had never left her hometown in Cuba until coming to Havana and then Miami, so the prospects of visiting the city of Pittsburgh—a name that in itself she found exotic—during a time of the year when the climate was so different filled her with excitement.

The plane ride was completely uneventful, but as the pilot began the descent approach over the city, breaking through a thick bank of clouds, they realized that the ground below was completely covered with snow as far as the eye could see. Quite a different landscape from what they were used to. The fresh snow bestowed upon the land a clean, virginal quality that they found rather beautiful. But the shock came when they finally landed and exited the plane; even though they had put on their overcoats, they were not ready for the blast of cold air that welcomed them as they made their way into the terminal.

Harold and Thomas were already there, and as soon as they saw the group they rushed over to greet them. In an open and unusual display of emotion, Harold kissed and hugged Anna openly, then kissed the twins and hugged Silvia. Thomas, as effusive as ever, hugged and kissed everyone, including Silvia, and started to tell everyone how much he liked Christmas as they walked to the baggage pick up.

"How was the trip?" asked Harold, who had kept his arm around Anna.

"Nothing out of the ordinary," answered Anna, "But we did not think it would be this cold."

"But of course it is cold," said Thomas, "It is December!"

After retrieving their suitcases, they walked to where Harold had parked the car. Both Anna and Silvia were visibly shivering, but Francesca and Adriana—who had their hats and gloves on—did not seem to mind the cold temperature. "Don't worry," said Harold smiling, "I will turn on the heat in the car."

"Please do," pleaded Anna as she settled in the front seat, between Harold and Thomas; Silvia sat in the back with a girl on either side, still unable to stop shivering. As they got underway, they noticed that the streets were still partially covered with snow. Some people were shoveling sidewalks or driveways, trying to clear a path for pedestrians or making sure their cars would make it onto the streets. In a nearby park some boys had organized a snowball fight and seemed to be having a great time. For an instant Anna wondered if Harold had ever done this as a boy, if he had sled down a hill with complete abandon, laughing with joy as the sense of speed filled his entire being. Somehow, she found it difficult not to think of him being completely serious and in control of himself, but she could be wrong. As she got to know him better, she also realized that he was a man of contradictions, thus a man full of surprises.

Thomas, perhaps thinking that the atmosphere inside the car was too quiet, turned on the radio without warning. Right away the car was filled with the joyful sound of Jingle Bells. Anna, of course, was familiar with this carol, and knew the words in Spanish, but she had never heard the song in English. Immediately Thomas started to sing along, and his enthusiasm was so contagious that Harold joined him after a few bars. Anna also tried to sing with them, but not knowing the words made it an almost impossible task.

As they drove up the snow-covered hill, Anna recognized Harold's colonial style house, but it looked completely different from the first time she had seen it. The dark roof was now white; the trees surrounding it, except for the blue spruces, were completely bare, and a soft plume of smoke rose from the chimney. What immediately caught her attention was the snowman in the front yard. It wore a hat, a colorful muffler, and the eyes and mouth had been made from items found in the yard. The long nose, however, was a bright orange carrot provided by Mrs. Gregory.

"How do you like our snow man?" asked Thomas in a joyful tone, "My dad and I built it two days ago," he explained, without waiting for an answer.

"I love it, Thomas," said Anna, still in awe that Harold had helped his son with such a project. This further corroborated the fact that Harold would do anything for Thomas. Still, Anna found it difficult to imagine Harold putting everything aside to play in the snow with his son. With the corner of her eye Anna detected a brief smile of satisfaction on Harold's face.

Inside the house, the smell of home cooking reached out from the kitchen all the way to the foyer, no doubt a special recipe that Harold had asked Mrs. Gregory to prepare for that evening. Rather than waiting for her to come out, Harold himself picked up Silvia's suitcase and showed her to her room, which was located next to Anna's.

"We have made some changes to your room since you were here," he said to Anna, who was closely behind.

"What kind of changes?" she asked.

"See for yourself," answered Harold as he led them into Anna's room. The changes, although small, were significant. Next to Anna's bed, there were two identical cribs with pink sheets and blankets. Harold had thought of everything, she concluded.

That visit, as it turned out, would be one of the most memorable, not just because of the special season, but because of all the surprises that Harold had in store for them. First of all, he had cleared his busy calendar so he could devote uninterrupted time to his guests. After everyone had settled in, he and Thomas took them into the library, where a tall Christmas tree had been erected next to the fireplace. It was a family tradition, Harold explained, that he and Thomas spent one evening decorating the tree while listening to music. Countless presents, carefully wrapped and each with a colorful bow, patiently awaited under the tree for that special morning.

The days leading to that most special holiday were full of activities. Taking advantage of the fresh snow, Harold took everyone to a park so Thomas and the twins could go sleigh riding. At first Anna was a little apprehensive, but after watching Thomas, she let the girls get on the sled, one at the time, and ride down a small hill. As they came back up, laughing and dragging the sled, Anna could see the breath in front of their faces. For a moment, she felt as if they had always belonged there, enjoying Thomas' company and with Harold making sure that they were safe; it was a feeling of peace and contentment that she had not experienced for a long time. After the children finished playing in the snow, they drove to a small nearby restaurant and Harold ordered hot chocolate for everyone, a perfect drink after spending an afternoon outdoors.

These were days that Anna would never forget, not just because of their first experience with winter, but because Harold had scheduled a series of activities to keep them entertained. Another afternoon he took them to see an ice skating show; the ensemble had come down from New York, and according to Thomas' comments they had been coming to Pittsburgh for several years. Not having seen ice skating before, Anna and Silvia were both amazed and delighted at the graceful movements and pirouettes that the performers were able to execute, to the rhythm of lively music, while gliding on the ice.

But the biggest surprise of all came on Christmas Eve, after an elaborate meal prepared by Mrs. Gregory for that special occasion. The children had gone to bed and Silvia had also retired for the evening, so Anna found herself alone with Harold in the library. The room was dim, making the myriad of lights on the Christmas tree stand out even more; from the hearth the occasional popping of wood as it burned punctuated the silence.

"Anna," said Harold, stepping closer and placing his hands on her upper arms, "I have something to ask you; please hear me out before you give me an answer."

"Of course," she answered, thinking perhaps that he would want them to prolong their stay past the new-year so they could attend one of the charity balls to which he was always invited.

For a moment Harold was silent, as if he did not know exactly how express what he had in mind. Then, with an aplomb developed over decades of business dealings, he looked at Anna directly in her eyes and made his request. "I would like you to marry me."

Although not a totally unexpected turn of events, she was truly surprised. It must have shown on her face, so before she could react Harold went on, "I realize that the timing may not be perfect, that we live many miles apart and that you would have to make a drastic adjustment by moving to Pittsburgh, but I do promise you that I will be a good husband to you and a good father to Francesca and Adriana." Anna started to say something, but Harold raised his hand and stopped her before she could even utter the first word. "I know that I am asking you to make a life changing decision, one that will also affect the future of your daughters, so I do not expect an answer now. Sleep on it and let me know tomorrow; whatever you decide, I will not love you any less," he concluded and kissed her softly on the lips, consciously attempting to convey in a non-verbal way the feelings that he had just tried to put into words.

Back in her room, Anna knew that she would not get much sleep that night; one way or another she would have to give Harold an answer the following morning. As she tried to sort out the different ramifications of such a decision, she evoked mentally the voice of Louis d'Amio as he sang his Immortal Arias.

First and foremost, she had to think of her daughters. Were she to accept Harold's proposal, they would grow up in a stable environment and with the presence of a father figure that all children need. Another consideration was Thomas; the twins already considered him a big brother, so for all practical purposes he would become her son. Harold had also brought up a point that she also had to consider. They would live in Pittsburgh, away from Miami and the Cuban community, so Francesca and Adriana would grow up away from the customs, language and traditions that were rightfully theirs. In a way she would be trading off her daughters' heritage for a stable and sheltered life, since living in Pittsburgh they would want for nothing.

And what about herself? Although she had strong feelings for Harold—after all, he was crazy about her and showed it at every available opportunity—they were not the same passionate feelings that Ramón had awakened in her. There was also an age difference of twenty years; she envisioned a marriage to Harold as a comfortable and secure one, a steady relationship with few ups and downs and without any surprises. This, of course, was not necessarily bad; it would just be different from the marriage she had enjoyed with Ramón. Another consideration was Harold's circle of acquaintances; from the start Anna knew that, although this was not true at all, many would judge her harshly and assume she was marrying him for his money.

There was also Cuba. Just as every other refugee, she still clung to the distant hope of returning to Havana soon and resuming a normal life. This appealing prospect would have to be discarded completely if she agreed to marry Harold.

As she considered all the different aspects that her decision involved, and still listening in her mind to Louis d'Amio, she fell asleep.

No one was surprised when Anna d'Amio agreed to marry Harold Wilson, a man many years her senior and not particularly good looking. Sole heir to a fortune whose origins could be traced to the steel mills around Pittsburgh, his wealth and social connections still made him, in the eyes of many, a great catch.

The unexpected announcement was received with dismay and consternation among his friends and acquaintances. He was, after all, a wealthy and influential industrialist who moved in the highest circles of society; she was, in their opinion, a nobody whose fortune—or rather, her late husband's fortune—was nothing but a remote memory from a distant Caribbean island. Her only assets were her physical beauty, now clearly beginning to decline, and an innate charm that men found irresistible due in part to her indefinable accent whenever she spoke English. Anna d'Amio, they agreed, was a social climber.

As for Anna herself, how they felt was completely irrelevant. Deep down she knew that Harold's fortune had not played a role in her decision to marry him; in him she had found those qualities that from an early age she considered desirable in a man, especially if that man was to become her spouse and a father to her children. In many ways, she thought, Harold was no different from Giacomo or Ramón, her previous husbands. She had given each his due, socially, emotionally, and sexually, as she was prepared to do with him.

While sitting at the kitchen table in the house on Brickell Avenue, going over those particulars that had to be attended to before the wedding, and listening to Immortal Arias, Anna took a mental inventory of the past few months. After Harold's proposal and her acceptance on Christmas day, they both realized that there were quite a few details to take care of before the wedding day. On the one thing they agreed from the beginning, was that it should be a small, intimate ceremony at the Church of the Epiphany, since they were beyond the extravagance usually found during one's youth. (Anna had to think of Ramón's gesture of decorating the entire wrought iron fence of the San Rosendo Cathedral with fresh roses.) There was also the matter of Anna's move to Pitts-burgh and her business in Miami, but fortunately Silvia would be taking over the helm. Then, of course, there was the wedding itself: a gown, invitations, the reception, the guest list, etc. Right after Christmas they had visited the church to speak with the pastor and make all the necessary arrangements. Banns of marriage would have to be announced to the congregation for several weeks before the ceremony. Finally, everything was done; now all she had to do was wait for the appointed day.

Almost hidden from view in a stack of correspondence, a letter caught Anna's eye. It had no return address and her name and address were not typed, but hand written. For an instant, she thought of Sergio Osorio, but the stamp was not Cuban, but American. The only clue as to its origin was the cancellation mark: Pittsburgh. Harold's? No, by then she was familiar with his handwriting and it was certainly not his.Anna was not prepared for the letter she was about to read. In fact, nothing could have been further from her mind, especially now that she was so busy with moving and wedding preparations. The letter, just as the envelope, was not typed, but handwritten in the language of her childhood.

My beloved, my never forgotten Anna, I hope this letter finds you well. Please forgive my boldness for contacting you, but a force much stronger than I compelled me to do so. You must be wondering the why and how of this letter: I, too, have pondered and anguished for days before putting pen to paper. Where do I begin? Perhaps a thank you for saving me from my mother's insidious plans for my life would be a start. But more important than that, I must thank you for showing meso early in life the meaning of love. After that last night we shared (it seems so long ago, yet still so vivid) I ran away from home and ended up at Father Benito's door. I had no place else to go. Through him I was able to enter the seminary in Rome, where I took refuge from the world, but mostly from myself. In case you are wondering, I gave up singing; it was a way of offering a small sacrifice for my good fortune.

When the war broke out, I heard that Naples had been bombed without warning, and that many people had perished, among them your mother (may her soul rest in peace). I assumed that the same fate had befallen you, so my only solace was the religious life and those memories of the times we spent together. I must confess (and may God forgive me) that the church could never fill the void, that infinite emptiness the absence of your love left in me. Anna, I have carried you in the innermost recesses of my heart and soul all these years, as I surely will continue to do so until the day the Lord decides to call me to His bosom.

Although several attractive opportunities presented themselves throughout my ecclesiastical career (I was even offered a post to serve at the Vatican), I always turned them down, for I preferred to remain a lowly and humble priest, unknown to the world around me. A few years ago I put a request with my superiors to be sent to a remote place in the world—yet another effort on my part to get away from everything that reminded me of the loss of your love—hoping to be placed in the missions in Africa or South America. I was both disappointed and dismayed when I was informed that my next assignment would be in the United States, where I would serve at the Church of the Epiphany in the city of Pittsburgh.

It is written that the Lord works in mysterious ways. Imagine my surprise (shock would be a better word) when I first saw you last year during Sunday mass. At first, I believed that my eyes were deceiving me, that it could not possibly be you, alive and so far away from Naples. For a time I convinced myself that I was mistaken, that my eyes and my mind were playing tricks on me. It was not until I saw your name (and your address) in the list of upcoming nuptials that I knew that I was not dreaming.

Anna, I believe that He has brought us together again, after all these years, for a reason. Let us fulfill His will and spend the rest of our lives together. I implore you not to go through with this marriage; I am fully prepared to renounce all my vows and start anew with you. We can make it work; we can finally achieve the happiness that has eluded us for so many years. To you I pledge my eternal love and surrender my life.

Yours forever,
Paolo

By the time Anna finished reading the letter, her eyes were flooded with tears and her hands were trembling. At that moment she was seventeen again, mad with love and crazy with the anticipation of sharing another intimate session with Paolo. All those feelings, suppressed for so long, came to the surface and erupted into a mournful wail, announcing that what she had felt then was not dead, but dormant, still as strong and overpowering as ever. In a flash, she envisioned a life with Paolo, perhaps in Florida, where they would both work at her business and share what could be an idyllic life, looking after the twins and regaining those precious and intimate moments they had missed since their abrupt separation. They would turn back the clock and be young again, erasing the past thirty years. Yes, it could work, she told herself, just as Paolo had suggested in his letter. Nothing was impossible, especially with the power of love.

But the sudden chimera, produced by the unexpected letter and the onrush of memories from her youth, did not last long. Anna recognized it for what it was, a nice fantasy that could never be realized. At this point she had learned that life always moved forward and there was no way to turn back the clock—except through memories—that as the years accumulated, even if one did not want to or acknowledged it, so did the baggage one carried.

Every hour, every day, inflicted unavoidable injuries, left its indelible scars, slowly but inexorably turning people into beings often unrecognizable even to their former selves. That was the price of living; no one was exempt from it.

Somewhat more composed, she reread Paolo's letter. This time, rather than evoking tears, it made her smile faintly, secretly flattered by the knowledge that young, beautiful and innocent Anna d'Amio would always live in someone's heart and memories, beyond the cruel reach of aging and its inevitable conclusion.

Then, putting the letter aside, she turned her attention once again to the more pressing matters of living.

Book IV: Post Mortem Correspondence

Taos, New Mexico
May 12, 2005

Dear Francesca,

It was good to see you again, although I wish the circumstances had been different. How sad and ironic that families always come together at funerals, foregoing all other opportunities that are often available to see each other.

I must confess that along with the grief over Mother's death, I also have some feelings of guilt for not having been there with you, Thomas and Aunt Silvia during her final days. I realize that Robert's work is here, and that my duty as his wife is to be with him, but somehow that does not make me feel any better. I keep telling myself that we always visited at Christmas and during the summer, but now that she is gone, that seems far from adequate. Although she never said so, I know that she would have liked to have us closer. As you know, Mother believed that in life each person has a path to follow, and that it was futile to oppose the designs of destiny.

Even though my work will suffer, I have made the resolution to return to Pittsburgh more often. I mentioned it to Robert on the way back and he was in complete agreement. Once again, it was nice to see all of you again.

A hug and a kiss.
Your sister,
Adriana.

Pittsburgh, Pa.
May 20, 2005

Dear Adriana,

I, too, was also very happy to see you, and share your opinion that we should make the effort to spend more time together.

Please do not feel guilty about anything; of all people, Mother understood—and approved—of your decision to move away after graduating from Carnegie Mellon. Remember how she would always say that it was important to 'Follow your heart.' By then you had met Robert, the love of your life, so it would have been impossible for you to stay.

I also want you to know that no one suspected that Mother would pass so suddenly; that is the reason I did not call until we found her. As you know, during these last few years she spent more time in her room, not really wanting to see anyone except Aunt Silvia and Thomas. I believe that it all started in 1981, after Harold's death, but we were just too young at the time to realize what was going on. Take solace in the fact that she passed peacefully, while listening to Immortal Arias.

While going through her personal possessions, I found a box with an assortment of items that must have meant a lot to her. As I tried to sort them out, I came to the realization of how little I really knew her. Perhaps between the two of us, and with Aunt Silvia's help, we can decipher their meaning and see how they fit into her life. Give my regards to Robert.

Love,
Francesca.

Taos, New Mexico
May 29, 2005

Dear Francesca,

Thank you for your kind words; they made me feel a little better. You are right in saying that I heeded Mother's advice and followed my heart; I have no regrets and for the past twenty years I have been infinitely happy with Robert. Yet, I still wish we did not live so far away, but I suppose one can't have everything in life.

Concerning Mother's last years, I concur with you that she began to withdraw into herself after Harold's death. I remember one instance, just before my wedding in 1985, when I found her in her room looking at old pictures. The expression on her face was one of complete happiness, as if she were a young woman about to be married herself. As soon as she realized that I was standing in the doorway, she closed the album and asked me to come in. 'Adriana, never forget that the only thing that survives is love,' she said to me and smiled. At that time I just assumed that it was an idle comment meant for a soon to be bride, so I never gave it a second thought. Perhaps she was trying to tell me that as one ages, and our tomorrows turn into yesterdays, we are nurtured by memories of times past and that love is the most enduring; I assure you that with every passing day I agree with her more.

In your letter you mentioned a box with personal effects. What sort of items did you find? Without seeing them, I would suggest that there are three ways in which they could be organized: chronologically, by category, and by language. Let's hope that these items will provide us with some clues as to Mother's life before coming to Pittsburgh.

Your loving sister,
Adriana.

Pittsburgh, Pa.
June 8, 2005

Dear Adriana,

I am glad that you are feeling better; undoubtedly Mother's passing was a shock to everyone. We all make decisions and then must live with the consequences. Just as you chose to leave Pittsburgh, I chose to stay and work as an accountant after finishing my degree. Perhaps it was just an excuse on my part to stay close to the family and keep an eye on Thomas. I don't need to tell you how successful he has become with his paintings. By the way, he is doing better; you saw how distraught he was during the funeral. I have only seen him like that when his grandfather and Harold died. Besides Mother, they were the two people to whom he felt closest, because he knew how much they truly loved him.

I find most interesting the comment Mother made to you before your wedding. Although she never voiced it, I always suspected that a part of her secretly yearned for another time, another place, where she was more fulfilled. Money was never important to her, proof of that is the significant charitable work that she did until the very end of her life. I do know for a fact, because of my conversations with Aunt Silvia, that the years she spent in Cuba married to our father were the happiest of her life.

Some of the objects that I found in her box were already known to us: the recordings that our grandfather made almost a hundred years ago, his inscribed Breguet pocket watch, and the handwritten cook book that our grandmother passed on to her. You remember how much pride she took in her cooking, and how excited she was during holidays, when everyone was home.

Your suggestion for classification of these objects is a good one. There are three photographs (fortunately, they are dated), of which I am enclosing copies, and I thought we might start there. One is of her wedding day to our father in November of 1943. The wedding party, as you can see, is posing in front of a church. Mother, of course, looks radiant, but for some inexplicable reason, although she appears very happy, Dad's white suit is completely soiled. The tall, thin man with black hair standing next to them, according to the information on the back of the picture, is one Oppiano Licario. I asked Aunt Silvia, and she said that he was the

500

best man at their wedding, but that is all she knew about him. In the second photograph, this one dated December of 1947, Mom and Dad are standing together, and in the background one can see very unusual mountains that seem to erupt vertically from the ground. Although he has an arm around her shoulders, and she is smiling, notice that her smile is a little contrived, as if she were battling to overcome an inner sadness. The inscription on the back reads 'Valle de Viñales, diciembre de 1947.' I do know that this is one of the most beautiful spots in Cuba, and that it was not far from Pinar del Río, the city where they married and lived.

The third photograph, dated July of 1937, is the one that really shocked me, so I ask you to examine it closely. Mother is wearing a wedding gown, and is standing in front of a church with a much older man, a middle-aged woman and a very young man with an obvious sullen expression on his face. On the back of the photograph is the inscription 'Giacomo and I on our wedding day, with my mother Francesca and my brother Guido.' I said that I was shocked because I never knew that Mother had been married before or that she had a brother. Somehow, I always assumed she was an only child, since she never mentioned any siblings. Of course, Aunt Silvia knows nothing about this. When I showed her the photograph, she said it was the first time she had ever seen it.

Perhaps you will come up with a plausible explanation to this mystery. I also find it strange that Mother never expressed a desire to go back to Italy, even for a visit. All this strengthens my belief that deep down we knew very little about Mother's personal life.

A kiss and my best to Robert,
Francesca.

Taos, New Mexico
June 14, 2005

Dear Francesca,

Thank you for your letter with copies of the three photographs you found in Mother's box. To say that I was surprised would be an understatement. Obviously, I did not find it strange that she should have a photograph of the day she married our father. As to the matter of his soiled white suit, I suppose we will never know, but it must not have been very important, since they both seem so happy. It is not until now that I hear the name Oppiano Licario; Mother never mentioned him to me, but he must have been very close if she asked him to be the best man at her wedding. As far as I know, she did not know anyone in Cuba when she arrived there at the beginning of 1941, so he must have been someone she met on the island. The photo taken at the Valley of Viñales does not surprise me either. According to what I have read, it is a popular tourist attraction; you said that in your letter. Somehow that particular day must have held a special significance for Mother, since she chose to keep the picture all these years. I am afraid though, just like Dad's suit, we will never know what was going on with her at that particular time. Oftentimes photographs hide more than they show, and this seems to be one of those cases.

Just like you, I was shocked by the 1937 photograph. Mother almost looks like a child wearing a first communion dress, and especially more so standing next to Giacomo. I can only conjecture that because of the uncertain times in Italy just before World War II, her family must have agreed to a marriage of convenience, although I cannot imagine what circumstances could have precipitated such an event. Surely, she had to leave her family and stop her studies in order to assume her duties as a wife. She must have been desperate to take such a course of action. Whatever happened, I am certain, it was serious. As you know, Mother was always a very sensible woman.

While comparing the two wedding photographs, what I found most significant is the expression on Mother's face. In the earlier one she is not smiling (as one would expect on such a significant date), but her face is serious, almost sad, as if she could hardly wait to be done with the whole affair. In the second one her happiness is almost palpable, and everyone present reflects that happiness. Our uncle Guido is also another mystery. Although Mother often spoke of her parents, she never mentioned a brother. I also find puzzling the fact that she never returned to Italy, even though she had plenty of opportunities to do so. Perhaps she did not want to reopen a chapter of her life that she considered particularly painful. What a shame that she did not keep a diary! As we both know, she was not one to linger on the past.

Once again, I thank you for the photographs. Please send me copies of whatever else you find appropriate, and with some luck we will be able to piece together some of her earlier years.

All my love to you,
Thomas and Aunt Silvia,
Adriana.

Pittsburgh, Pa.
June 27, 2005

Dear Adriana,

No need to thank me for the photographs. Somehow it seems that Mother left us (I am sure not intentionally) pieces of a puzzle that represent significant moments of her past. I also wonder if she just left us the tangible pieces, those that were mere conduits to her memories of other times. Let us hope that through them we can at least create a sketch of her life.

In a previous letter I mentioned that the name Oppiano Licario meant nothing to me, but that he had been the best man at Mother's wedding in Cuba. Well, it appears that the connection goes back to the beginning of 1941. While going through her passport, (of which I am sending a copy) I found that a card (copy also enclosed) had been stapled to one of the pages where he vouched for her when she immigrated to Cuba. I also gather that he must have had some influential connections in Havana at that time.

I am also enclosing a copy of post card showing the ruins of Pompeii (the original is dated 1937 on the back, but contains no other writing), along with a newspaper advertisement for a restaurant with the same name. Since the newspaper *Diario de la Marina* was published in Havana, it leads me to believe that at one time during her stay in Cuba Mother owned this restaurant. What I find most interesting, though, is that the photograph shown in the advertisement is a faithful replica of the 1937 postcard. I asked Aunt Silvia, and she vaguely recalled something about a restaurant in Havana, but was not too sure. (Between you and me, I think that old age has taken a toll on her memory.)

Thomas sends his regards and is looking forward to seeing you again. My best to Robert,

All my love,
Francesca.

Taos, New Mexico
July 12, 2005

Dear Francesca,

   With every passing letter, I am more amazed as I conjecture about Mother's life. So far, we know that she lived in Italy until 1941, when she came to Cuba. We also know that she married at seventeen due to unknown circumstances, and that we have (had?) an uncle named Guido. We also know that she worshipped our grandfather. As to the postcard depicting the ruins of Pompeii, maybe she visited there at one time or another, since the site is not far from Naples. I can also surmise that if she owned an Italian restaurant in Havana, she would have chosen a name that would have immediately identified it as such.

   The name Oppiano Licario seems to pop up at the most unexpected places. I just have to wonder if she had met him (and how) before arriving in Cuba, but that possibility seems remote, since at that time Italy was in the midst of a war. While examining the copy of her passport, I noticed that there was no visa to enter Cuba. Why would Licario then offer to vouch for her? Further, what would he be doing at a place where foreigners came into the country? Maybe he worked there; I don't know. I also noticed that Mother traveled to Miami in the fall of 1943, right after her marriage to our father. As you know, he owned a tobacco plantation in western Cuba and was rather well-to-do, so that they should spend some days in Miami does not surprise me. Perhaps she mentioned something to you, since you saw her on a daily basis.

   Give my love to Thomas and Aunt Silvia. Robert sends his regards.

Love, Adriana.

Pittsburgh, Pa.
July 20, 2005

Dear Adriana,

How right you are in saying that Mother's life is shrouded in mystery. The more I think about it, the more convinced I am that she never spoke about her life to us so we would look forward and not back. Even though we were born in Havana, she wanted us to be Americans, especially after Harold legally adopted us. I also suspect that she wanted us to have the sense of stability that, for circumstances beyond her control, was lacking in her life.

With this letter, I am enclosing photographs of three pieces of jewelry I also found in Mother's box. The first is of a metal plaque (probably silver) depicting a saint. The small engraving reads 'San Nicola.' The second is of a medallion with the silhouettes of a male and female faces on opposite sides. The curious thing is, if you make it spin (it is mounted on an axis), the two figures appear to kiss. Engraved on the handle is the inscription 'Through love two become one.' Notice that it is written is Spanish. The third photograph is of a brooch in the shape of a gondolier. There is no inscription of any kind on the back. I know that it is not much to go on, but I value your opinion, even if it just a conjecture.

On a more personal note, Thomas is back on track, painting as much as ever. You know how close he was to Mother, and how deeply her death affected him. I think he believed that she would always be around. Aunt Silvia is also doing well; she and Mother were like sisters, and I know that she misses her terribly. As for myself, I stay busy with my accounting job. It helps me pass the time.

> All my love to you and Robert,
> Francesca.

Taos, New Mexico
August 15, 2005

Dear Francesca,

Forgive me for not answering your last letter immediately, but we just returned from California, where Robert met with some of his clients. We had the opportunity to visit the Napa Valley and taste some of the wine that is produced there. It is a very beautiful place with a much slower pace of life than Los Angeles, where people seem to be running all the time.

The photographs you sent me are most interesting. I did a little research and the Church of San Nicola is located on top of Mount Epomeo, on the island of Ischia. It is plausible that Mother visited that island some time before leaving Europe. At first, I thought that the metal plaque was some sort of souvenir, but I could find no reference to such item. I gather that it is a one of kind piece that she acquired from a local artisan. The question, then, still remains, why was it so important to her? A gift, perhaps?

When I looked at the photograph of the spinning medallion, although I knew it was not possible, somehow I felt that I had seen it before. It was not until yesterday that I realized that it was something that Mother said on the day of my wedding that was directly linked to that piece of jewelry. Right before Robert and I left for our honeymoon, I asked her if she had any secrets for a successful marriage. Of course, I thought she would say something like 'Always support your husband' or 'Take an interest in his career.' After thinking about it for a few seconds, she smiled and said 'Always remember that only through love two can become one.' I am now certain that it must have been a gift from our father (since the engraving is in Spanish she must have acquired it in Cuba). Further, the inscription supports her previous comment to me concerning the endurance of love. Who would have thought that she was such a romantic!

The brooch depicting a gondolier—and what a beautiful piece of jewelry it is—really has me baffled. I do not believe that Mother ever visited Venice. Could it have been a present (just as I suspect the metal plaque was) from a close acquaintance? Since it is clearly an expensive piece, whoever gave it to her must have held her in the highest esteem.

I am very happy that Thomas is returning to his routine; you don't have to tell me how close he was to Mother. Give him a hug from me.

All my love to you and Aunt Silvia.
Your sister, Adriana

Pittsburgh, Pa
August 21, 2005

Dear Adriana,

How exciting that you and Robert had the opportunity to tour the Napa Valley and visit some of the wineries. I am sure the weather there was a lot cooler than what we have here; you know how oppressive summers can be in Pittsburgh.

As usual, you were most insightful concerning the photographs that I sent you. Although we may never know for sure, at least we are managing to draw a sketch (even if it is based on pure conjectures) of Mother's life. The comment you made about her being a romantic really hit home. Although she was not one to meddle in other people's affairs, from time to time she would tell me that 'There is nothing more tragic than going through life without love.' This reinforces what you said about the inscription on the medallion and that she must have received it as a gift from our father. I also believe the brooch was another one of his presents. Perhaps he found it in Havana and thought she would like it because it was a connection to Italy. Of one thing I am certain: only a man very much in love would give such an expensive and beautiful piece of jewelry to a woman. All this leads me to conclude (as aunt Silvia already pointed out) that the years she spent in Cuba were perhaps the happiest of her life.

The only remaining articles in Mother's box are a pair of coral earrings, a small oil painting of a winter scene, and a letter written in Italian. I will send you photographs and a copy of the letter the next time I write. I will also show these items to Aunt Silvia; maybe they will bring back some memories and she can give us some details about them. As you know, her memory comes and goes.

Thomas is working harder than ever, preparing for an exhibition of his work this coming fall. I know he wishes that Mother were here to share all of it with him.

All my love,
Francesca.

Taos, New Mexico
August 30, 2005

Dear Francesca,

What great news I have! You will recall I mentioned to Robert that I wanted to spend more time with the family, especially now that Mother is gone. Well, he asked to be assigned a project on the east coast and the architectural firm agreed to send him to Pittsburgh this fall. He did all this without telling me, to save me the disappointment just in case it did not work out. What a sweetheart he is. So, that means we will be spending lots of time together and we will be able to attend Thomas' upcoming exhibit. As far as my teaching duties with the university are concerned, I will ask for a sabbatical and do some research while I have the time.

The oil painting that you mentioned (I cannot be completely certain without looking at it) hung in Mother's bedroom for many years. I believe that Thomas gave it to her during one of her first visits to Pittsburgh, so it must have been done when he was quite young. If you show it to him, he will surely recognize it. I also remember Mother wearing the coral earrings that you mentioned, but it never occurred to me to ask her about them. Maybe Aunt Silvia can give us a clue.

As we examine Mother's life, the items that she left behind, and think about the comments that she made to you and me, the more I realize that she valued love (in all its manifestations) above all things. I am only sorry (and I repeat myself) that she did not leave us a journal with detailed descriptions of what was surely a most remarkable life.

Concerning the letter you mentioned, maybe if you have it translated it will give us further clues about her. Please write soon, and make sure to tell Aunt Silvia and Thomas the news of our return to Pittsburgh.

All my love,
Adriana

Pittsburgh, Pa.
September 10, 2005

Dear Adriana,

What wonderful news! I can hardly wait until your arrival; we have years of catching up to do. When I told Thomas he was ecstatic, especially since you will be here for the upcoming exhibit of his new paintings. By the way, you are indeed a lucky woman to have a man like Robert, who is always looking for ways to make you happy. I am sure it would make Mother smile.

I now remember the oil painting in Mother's bedroom. I showed it to Thomas and he was visibly moved; he also confirmed that it was a gift he made to our mother during her first visit to Pittsburgh. That same day, during dinner, I wore the coral earrings I mentioned, but did not make any comments. Aunt Silvia must have noticed, for during the meal she called me Anna. I asked her if she liked the earrings and she said that I had shown them to her before, right after Harold proposed. The greatest mystery, you will agree, is the letter in her box. I followed your advice and tried to have it translated. The only person I knew that was fluent in Italian was Father Alberti, the old priest that has been in our church for as long as I can remember. To tell you the truth, I was not sure if I would find him, since he has been retired for a while. At any rate, I drove to the Church of the Epiphany last week and he happened to be there, kneeling in the back with a rosary in his hand.

I am sure he did not recognize me, but as soon as I told him who I was his eyes became more alert and I could see that he was curious as to the purpose of my visit. When I explained that I needed something translated from Italian to English he smiled and said that he would be glad to do it, but after I handed him the letter things became rather strange. Even though the only light was that of the candles, as soon as he saw it his expression changed. At first, I detected a fleeting smile, but suddenly it was replaced by a subdued sobbing and a stream of tears that fell on the pages that he was holding. Needless to say, I was completely taken aback by his reaction. When I asked him if he was all right, he clutched the letter close to his heart, but did not answer. I sat with him in the silence and solitude of the empty church, hoping that he would eventually gain his composure. 'I cannot translate this letter,' he finally said. I thought that maybe it was written in a dialect of Italian with which he was not familiar, but I was wrong. 'I cannot translate this letter,' he repeated, 'Because I am the one who wrote it.' I told him that I did not understand how Mother could have in her possession such a letter. He simply said, without going into details, that they had known each other in Italy, before the war, and that the contents of the letter were personal. I thought of taking the letter to someone else for a translation, but before I could ask for it back, the old priest pleaded with me to let him keep it. He argued that the content was information he wanted to take with him to the grave. Adriana, if you had seen the anguish on his face you would have acquiesced, just as I did. I knew then that the letter would remain a mystery. Before leaving the church, I asked him if there was any information he could give me about Mother. Here he smiled again and his eyes for an instant became young. 'All I can tell you,' he said softly, as if confessing a secret that had burdened him his entire life, 'Is that Anna is the only woman I have ever loved, and that I would like to think that she loved me too.' After that, he would say no more. I suppose he wanted to keep all those memories private; they were all he had left.

You can draw your own conclusions from this account, but we surely will discuss it further once you arrive. One thing is certain: Mother's life was a lot more complex than any of us realized while she was alive. It is not until now, when we are left with her absence and with these *forgotten objects* that we pause and take a look away from our own lives and try to assess the type of woman she really was.

I look forward to seeing you soon.

All my love,
Francesca

Table of Contents